Born as Dumas Davy de la Pailleterie on 24 July 1802, in Villers-Cotterêts, Picardy, France, ALEXANDRE DUMAS was one of the most prolific authors of his time. The last name 'Dumas' was adopted from his grandmother, a former enslaved Haitian woman. His father, Thomas-Alexandre, assumed the name Dumas when he enlisted in Napoleon's army. Here, he was given the dubious nickname 'Black Devil.'

Popular for his historical adventure novels like *The Count of Monte Cristo* and *The Three Musketeers* (initially published as serials), Dumas immersed himself in literature after he moved to Paris in 1822. During the 1830 revolution, he worked as a scribe for the Duc d'Orléans (later named King Louis Philippe), and began writing dramas and comedies. Dumas had a penchant for writing volumes of essays on some of the most infamous cases in history. It is believed that his published works totalled 100,000 pages and his works have been translated into more than 100 languages.

A household name and a celebrity in France and across Europe, Dumas founded the Théâtre Historique in Paris in the 1840s.

Dumas died on 5 December 1870, in Puys, France. He was buried at his birthplace of Villers-Cotterêts in the department of Aisne.

In 1970, as a mark of honour, the Alexandre Dumas Paris Métro station was named after the author. His country home outside Paris, the Château de Monte-Cristo, has been restored as a museum.

AF730277

ESTD 1936
AMRIT BOOK CO.
Books on History, Politics, Philosophy, Religion, Yoga, Ayurveda, Travel, Music, Dance, Astrology, Palmistry, Children Books, Computer, Law Management, Medical, Civil Engineering & Hindi Books
21, Connaught Circus, Opp. Scindia House, New Delhi-110001
Mob.: 9810778775, 9811113613

The Three Musketeers

Alexandre Dumas, Pere

Om Books International

This edition first published in 2019 by

Om Books International

Corporate & Editorial Office
A-12, Sector 64, Noida 201 301
Uttar Pradesh, India
Phone: +91 120 477 4100
Email: editorial@ombooks.com
Website: www.ombooksinternational.com

Sales Office
107, Ansari Road, Darya Ganj,
New Delhi 110 002, India
Phone: +91 11 4000 9000
Fax: +91 11 2327 8091
Email: sales@ombooks.com
Website: www.ombooks.com

This edition copyright © Om Books International 2019

ALL RIGHTS RESERVED. No part of this book may be reproduced or transmitted in any form by any means, electronic or mechanical, including photocopying and recording, or by any information storage and retrieval system, except as may be expressly permitted in writing by the publisher.

ISBN: 9789352766864

Printed in India

10 9 8 7 6 5 4 3 2 1

Contents

Author's Preface

In which it is proved that, notwithstanding their names' ending in OS and IS, the heroes of the story which we are about to have the honour to relate to our readers have nothing mythological about them.

A short time ago, while making researches in the Royal Library for my History of Louis XIV, I stumbled by chance upon the Memoirs of M. d'Artagnan, printed–as were most of the works of that period, in which authors could not tell the truth without the risk of a residence, more or less long, in the Bastille–at Amsterdam, by Pierre Rouge. The title attracted me; I took them home with me, with the permission of the guardian, and devoured them.

It is not my intention here to enter into an analysis of this curious work; and I shall satisfy myself with referring such of my readers as appreciate the pictures of the period to its pages. They will therein find portraits penciled by the hand of a master; and although these squibs may be, for the most part, traced upon the doors of barracks and the walls of cabarets, they will not find the likenesses of Louis XIII, Anne of Austria, Richelieu, Mazarin, and the courtiers of the period, less faithful than in the history of M. Anquetil.

But, it is well known, what strikes the capricious mind of the poet is not always what affects the mass of readers. Now, while admiring, as others doubtless will admire, the details we have to relate, our main preoccupation concerned a matter to which no one before ourselves had given a thought.

D'Artagnan relates that on his first visit to M. de Tréville, captain of the king's Musketeers, he met in the antechamber three young men, serving in the illustrious corps into which he was soliciting the honour of being received, bearing the names of Athos, Porthos, and Aramis.

We must confess these three strange names struck us; and it immediately occurred to us that they were but pseudonyms, under which d'Artagnan had disguised names perhaps illustrious, or else that the bearers of these borrowed names had themselves chosen them on the day in which, from caprice, discontent, or want of fortune, they had donned the simple Musketeer's uniform.

From that moment we had no rest till we could find some trace in contemporary works of these extraordinary names which had so strongly awakened our curiosity.

The catalogue alone of the books we read with this object would fill a whole chapter, which, although it might be very instructive, would certainly afford our readers but little amusement. It will suffice, then, to tell them that at the moment at which, discouraged by so many fruitless investigations, we were about to abandon our search, we at length found, guided by the counsels of our illustrious friend Paulin Paris, a manuscript in folio, endorsed 4772 or 4773, we do not recollect which, having for title, "Memoirs of the Comte de la Fere, Touching Some Events Which Passed in France Toward the End of the Reign of King Louis XIII and the Commencement of the Reign of King Louis XIV."

It may be easily imagined how great was our joy when, in turning over this manuscript, our last hope, we found at the twentieth page the name of Athos, at the twenty-seventh the name of Porthos, and at the thirty-first the name of Aramis.

The discovery of a completely unknown manuscript at a period in which historical science is carried to such a high degree appeared almost miraculous. We hastened, therefore, to obtain permission to print it, with the view of presenting ourselves someday with the pack of others at the doors of the Academie des Inscriptions et Belles Lettres, if we should not succeed–a very probable thing, by the by–in gaining admission to the Academie Francaise with our own proper pack. This permission, we feel bound to say, was graciously granted, which compels us here to give a public contradiction to the slanderers who pretend that we live under a government but moderately indulgent to men of letters.

Now, this is the first part of this precious manuscript which we offer to our readers, restoring it to the title which belongs to it, and entering into an engagement that if (of which we have no doubt) this first part should obtain the success it merits, we will publish the second immediately.

In the meanwhile, as the godfather is a second father, we beg the reader to lay to our account, and not to that of the Comte de la Fere, the pleasure or the ENNUI he may experience.

This being understood, let us proceed with our history.

Chapter 1

The Three Presents Of d'Artagnan The Elder

On the first Monday of the month of April, 1625, the market town of Meung, in which the author of *Romance Of The Rose* was born, appeared to be in as perfect a state of revolution as if the Huguenots had just made a second La Rochelle of it. Many citizens, seeing the women flying toward the High Street, leaving their children crying at the open doors, hastened to don the cuirass, and supporting their somewhat uncertain courage with a musket or a partisan, directed their steps toward the hostelry of the Jolly Miller, before which was gathered, increasing every minute, a compact group, vociferous and full of curiosity.

In those times panics were common, and few days passed without some city or other registering in its archives an event of this kind. There were nobles, who made war against each other; there was the king, who made war against the cardinal; there was Spain, which made war against the king. Then, in addition to these concealed or public, secret or open wars, there were robbers, mendicants, Huguenots, wolves, and scoundrels, who made war upon everybody. The citizens always took up arms readily against thieves, wolves or scoundrels, often against nobles or Huguenots, sometimes against the king, but never against the cardinal or Spain. It resulted, then, from this habit that on the said first Monday of April, 1625, the citizens, on hearing the clamor, and seeing neither the red-and-yellow standard nor the livery of the Duc de Richelieu, rushed toward the hostel of the Jolly Miller. When arrived there, the cause of the hubbub was apparent to all.

A young man–we can sketch his portrait at a dash. Imagine to yourself a Don Quixote of eighteen; a Don Quixote without his corselet, without his coat of mail, without his cuisses; a Don Quixote clothed in a woolen doublet, the blue colour of which had faded into a nameless shade between lees of wine and a heavenly azure; face long and brown; high cheek bones, a sign of sagacity; the maxillary muscles enormously developed, an infallible sign by which a Gascon may always be detected, even without his cap–and our young man wore a cap set off with a sort of feather; the eye open and intelligent; the nose hooked, but finely chiseled. Too big for a youth, too small for a grown man, an experienced eye might have taken him for a farmer's son upon a journey had it not been for the long sword which, dangling from a leather baldric, hit against the calves of its owner as he walked, and against the rough side of his steed when he was on horseback.

For our young man had a steed which was the observed of all observers. It was a Bearn pony, from twelve to fourteen years old, yellow in his hide, without a hair in his tail, but not without windgalls on his legs, which, though going with his head lower than his knees, rendering a martingale quite unnecessary, contrived nevertheless to perform his eight leagues a day. Unfortunately, the qualities of this horse were so well concealed under his strange-coloured hide and his unaccountable gait, that at a time when everybody was a connoisseur in horseflesh, the appearance of the aforesaid pony at Meung–which place he had entered about a quarter of an hour before, by the gate of Beaugency–produced an unfavourable feeling, which extended to his rider.

And this feeling had been more painfully perceived by young d'Artagnan–for so was the Don Quixote of this second Rosinante named–from his not being able to conceal from himself the ridiculous appearance that such a steed gave him, good horseman as he was. He had sighed deeply, therefore, when accepting the gift of the pony from M. d'Artagnan the elder. He was not ignorant that such a beast was worth at least twenty livres; and the words which had accompanied the present were above all price.

"My son," said the old Gascon gentleman, in that pure Bearn PATOIS of which Henry IV could never rid himself, "this horse was born in the house of your father about thirteen years ago, and has remained in it ever since, which ought to make you love it. Never sell it; allow it to die tranquilly and honourably of old age, and if you make a campaign with it, take as much care of it as you would of an old servant. At court, provided you have ever the honour to go there," continued M. d'Artagnan the elder, "–an honour to which, remember, your ancient nobility gives you the right–sustain worthily your name of gentleman, which has been worthily borne by your ancestors for five hundred years, both for your own sake and the sake of those who belong to you. By the latter I mean your relatives and friends. Endure nothing from anyone except Monsieur the Cardinal and the king. It is by his courage, please observe, by his courage alone, that a gentleman can make his way nowadays. Whoever hesitates for a second perhaps allows the bait to escape which during that exact second fortune held out to him. You are young. You ought to be brave for two reasons: the first is that you are a Gascon, and the second is that you are my son. Never fear quarrels, but seek adventures. I have taught you how to handle a sword; you have thews of iron, a wrist of steel. Fight on all occasions. Fight the more for duels being forbidden, since consequently there is twice as much courage in fighting. I have nothing to give you, my son, but fifteen crowns, my horse, and the counsels you have just heard. Your mother will add to them a recipe for a certain balsam, which she had from a Bohemian and which has the miraculous virtue of curing all wounds that do not reach the heart. Take advantage of all, and live happily and long. I have but one word to add, and that is to propose an example to you–not mine, for I myself have never appeared at court, and have only taken part in religious wars as a volunteer; I speak of Monsieur de Tréville, who was formerly my neighbour, and who had the honour to be, as a child, the play-fellow of our king, Louis XIII, whom God preserve! Sometimes their play degenerated into battles, and in these battles the king was not always the stronger. The blows which he received increased greatly his esteem and friendship for Monsieur de Tréville. Afterward, Monsieur de Tréville fought with others: in his first journey to Paris, five times; from the death of the late king till the young one came of age, without reckoning wars and sieges, seven times; and from that date up to the present day, a hundred times, perhaps! So that in spite of edicts, ordinances, and decrees, there he is, captain of the Musketeers; that is to say, chief of a legion of Caesars, whom the king holds in great esteem and whom the cardinal dreads–he who dreads nothing, as it is said. Still further, Monsieur de Tréville gains ten thousand crowns a year; he is therefore a great noble. He began as you begin. Go to him with this letter, and make him your model in order that you may do as he has done."

Upon which M. d'Artagnan the elder girded his own sword round his son, kissed him tenderly on both cheeks, and gave him his benediction.

On leaving the paternal chamber, the young man found his mother, who was waiting for him with the famous recipe of which the counsels we have just repeated would necessitate frequent employment. The adieux were on this side longer and more tender than they had been on the other–not that M. d'Artagnan did not love his son, who was his only offspring, but M. d'Artagnan was a man, and he would have considered it unworthy of a man to give way to his feelings; whereas Mme. d'Artagnan was a woman, and still more, a mother. She wept abundantly; and–let us speak it to the praise of M. d'Artagnan the younger–notwithstanding the efforts he made to remain firm, as a future Musketeer ought, nature prevailed, and he shed many tears, of which he succeeded with great difficulty in concealing the half.

The same day the young man set forward on his journey, furnished with the three paternal gifts, which consisted, as we have said, of fifteen crowns, the horse, and the letter for M. de Tréville–the counsels being thrown into the bargain.

With such a VADE MECUM d'Artagnan was morally and physically an exact copy of the hero of Cervantes, to whom we so happily compared him when our duty of an historian placed us under the necessity of sketching his portrait. Don Quixote took windmills for giants, and sheep for armies; d'Artagnan took every smile for an insult, and every look as a provocation–whence it resulted that from Tarbes to Meung his fist was constantly doubled, or his hand on the hilt of his sword; and yet the fist did not descend upon any jaw, nor did the sword issue from its scabbard. It was not that the sight of the wretched pony did not excite numerous smiles on the countenances of passers-by, but as against the side of this pony rattled a sword of respectable length, and as over this sword gleamed an eye rather ferocious than haughty, these passers-by repressed their hilarity, or if hilarity prevailed over prudence, they endeavoured to laugh only on one side, like the masks of the ancients. D'Artagnan, then, remained majestic and intact in his susceptibility, till he came to this unlucky city of Meung.

But there, as he was alighting from his horse at the gate of the Jolly Miller, without anyone–host, waiter, or hostler–coming to hold his stirrup or take his horse, d'Artagnan spied, though an open window on the ground floor, a gentleman, well-made and of good carriage, although of rather a stern countenance, talking with two persons who appeared to listen to him with respect. D'Artagnan fancied quite naturally, according to his custom, that he must be the object of their conversation, and listened. This time d'Artagnan was only in part mistaken; he himself was not in question, but his horse was. The gentleman appeared to be enumerating all his qualities to his auditors; and, as I have said, the auditors seeming to have great deference for the narrator, they every moment burst into fits of laughter. Now, as a half-smile was sufficient to awaken the irascibility of the young man, the effect produced upon him by this vociferous mirth may be easily imagined.

Nevertheless, d'Artagnan was desirous of examining the appearance of this impertinent personage who ridiculed him. He fixed his haughty eye upon the stranger, and perceived a man of from forty to forty-five years of age, with black and piercing eyes, pale complexion, a strongly marked nose, and a black and well-shaped moustache. He was dressed in a doublet and hose of a violet colour, with aiguillettes of the same colour, without any other ornaments than the customary slashes, through which the shirt appeared. This doublet and hose, though new, were creased, like travelling clothes for a long time packed in a portmanteau. D'Artagnan made all these remarks with the rapidity of a most minute observer, and doubtless from an instinctive feeling that this stranger was destined to have a great influence over his future life.

Now, as at the moment in which d'Artagnan fixed his eyes upon the gentleman in the violet doublet, the gentleman made one of his most knowing and profound remarks respecting the Bearnese pony, his two auditors laughed even louder than before, and he himself, though contrary to his custom, allowed a pale smile (if I may be allowed to use such an expression) to stray over his countenance. This time there could be no doubt; d'Artagnan was really insulted. Full, then, of this conviction, he pulled his cap down over his eyes, and endeavouring to copy some of the court airs he had picked up in Gascony among young travelling nobles, he advanced with one hand on the hilt of his sword and the other resting on his hip. Unfortunately, as he advanced, his anger increased at every step; and instead of the proper and lofty speech he had prepared as a prelude to his challenge, he found nothing at the tip of his tongue but a gross personality, which he accompanied with a furious gesture.

"I say, Sir, you Sir, who are hiding yourself behind that shutter–yes, you, Sir, tell me what you are laughing at, and we will laugh together!"

The gentleman raised his eyes slowly from the nag to his cavalier, as if he required some time to ascertain whether it could be to him that such strange reproaches were addressed; then, when he could not possibly entertain any doubt of the matter, his eyebrows slightly bent, and with an accent of irony and insolence impossible to be described, he replied to d'Artagnan, "I was not speaking to you, Sir."

"But I am speaking to you!" replied the young man, additionally exasperated with this mixture of insolence and good manners, of politeness and scorn.

The stranger looked at him again with a slight smile, and retiring from the window, came out of the hostelry with a slow step, and placed himself before the horse, within two paces of d'Artagnan. His quiet manner and the ironical expression of his countenance redoubled the mirth of the persons with whom he had been talking, and who still remained at the window.

D'Artagnan, seeing him approach, drew his sword a foot out of the scabbard.

"This horse is decidedly, or rather has been in his youth, a buttercup," resumed the stranger, continuing the remarks he had begun, and addressing himself to his auditors at the window, without paying the least attention to the exasperation of d'Artagnan, who, however, placed himself between him and them. "It is a colour very well known in botany, but till the present time very rare among horses."

"There are people who laugh at the horse that would not dare to laugh at the master," cried the young emulator of the furious Tréville.

"I do not often laugh, Sir," replied the stranger, "as you may perceive by the expression of my countenance, but nevertheless I retain the privilege of laughing when I please."

"And I," cried d'Artagnan, "will allow no man to laugh when it displeases me!"

"Indeed, Sir," continued the stranger, more calm than ever, "well, that is perfectly right!" and turning on his heel, was about to re-enter the hostelry by the front gate, beneath which d'Artagnan on arriving had observed a saddled horse.

But, d'Artagnan was not of a character to allow a man to escape him thus who had the insolence to ridicule him. He drew his sword entirely from the scabbard, and followed him, crying, "Turn, turn, Master Joker, lest I strike you behind!"

"Strike me!" said the other, turning on his heels, and surveying the young man with as much astonishment as contempt. "Why, my good fellow, you must be mad!" Then, in a suppressed tone, as if speaking to himself, "This is annoying," continued he. "What a godsend this would be for his Majesty, who is seeking everywhere for brave fellows to recruit for his Musketeers!"

He had scarcely finished, when d'Artagnan made such a furious lunge at him that if he had not sprung nimbly backward, it is probable he would have jested for the last time. The stranger, then perceiving that the matter went beyond raillery, drew his sword, saluted his adversary, and seriously placed himself on guard. But at the same moment, his two auditors, accompanied by the host, fell upon d'Artagnan with sticks, shovels and tongs. This caused so rapid and complete a diversion from the attack that d'Artagnan's adversary, while the latter turned round to face this shower of blows, sheathed his sword with the same precision, and instead of an actor, which he had nearly been, became a spectator of the fight–a part in which he acquitted himself with his usual impassiveness, muttering, nevertheless, "A plague upon these Gascons! Replace him on his orange horse, and let him begone!"

"Not before I have killed you, poltroon!" cried d'Artagnan, making the best face possible, and never retreating one step before his three assailants, who continued to shower blows upon him.

"Another gasconade!" murmured the gentleman. "By my honour, these Gascons are incorrigible! Keep up the dance, then, since he will have it so. When he is tired, he will perhaps tell us that he has had enough of it."

But the stranger knew not the headstrong personage he had to do with; d'Artagnan was not the man ever to cry for quarter. The fight was therefore prolonged for some seconds, but at length d'Artagnan dropped his sword, which was broken in two pieces by the blow of a stick. Another blow full upon his forehead at the same moment brought him to the ground, covered with blood and almost fainting.

It was at this moment that people came flocking to the scene of action from all sides. The host, fearful of consequences, with the help of his servants carried the wounded man into the kitchen, where some trifling attentions were bestowed upon him.

As to the gentleman, he resumed his place at the window, and surveyed the crowd with a certain impatience, evidently annoyed by their remaining undispersed.

"Well, how is it with this madman?" exclaimed he, turning round as the noise of the door announced the entrance of the host, who came in to inquire if he was unhurt.

"Your excellency is safe and sound?" asked the host.

"Oh, yes! Perfectly safe and sound, my good host; and I wish to know what has become of our young man."

"He is better," said the host, "he fainted quite away."

"Indeed!" said the gentleman.

"But before he fainted, he collected all his strength to challenge you, and to defy you while challenging you."

"Why, this fellow must be the devil in person!" cried the stranger.

"Oh, no, your Excellency, he is not the devil," replied the host, with a grin of contempt, "for during his fainting we rummaged his valise and found nothing but a clean shirt and eleven crowns– which however, did not prevent his saying, as he was fainting, that if such a thing had happened in Paris, you should have cause to repent of it at a later period."

"Then," said the stranger coolly, "he must be some prince in disguise."

"I have told you this, good sir," resumed the host, "in order that you may be on your guard."

"Did he name no one in his passion?"

"Yes; he struck his pocket and said, 'We shall see what Monsieur de Tréville will think of this insult offered to his protégé.'"

"Monsieur de Tréville?" said the stranger, becoming attentive, "he put his hand upon his pocket while pronouncing the name of Monsieur de Tréville? Now, my dear host, while your young man was insensible, you did not fail, I am quite sure, to ascertain what that pocket contained. What was there in it?"

"A letter addressed to Monsieur de Tréville, captain of the Musketeers."

"Indeed!"

"Exactly as I have the honour to tell your Excellency."

The host, who was not endowed with great perspicacity, did not observe the expression which his words had given to the physiognomy of the stranger. The latter rose from the front of the window, upon the sill of which he had leaned with his elbow, and knitted his brow like a man disquieted.

"The devil!" murmured he, between his teeth. "Can Tréville have set this Gascon upon me? He is very young, but a sword thrust is a sword thrust, whatever be the age of him who gives it, and a youth is less to be suspected than an older man," and the stranger fell into a reverie which lasted some minutes. "A weak obstacle is sometimes sufficient to overthrow a great design.

"Host," said he, "could you not contrive to get rid of this frantic boy for me? In conscience, I cannot kill him; and yet," added he, with a coldly menacing expression, "he annoys me. Where is he?"

"In my wife's chamber, on the first flight, where they are dressing his wounds."

"His things and his bag are with him? Has he taken off his doublet?"

"On the contrary, everything is in the kitchen. But if he annoys you, this young fool–"

"To be sure he does. He causes a disturbance in your hostelry, which respectable people cannot put up with. Go; make out my bill and notify my servant."

"What, Monsieur, will you leave us so soon?"

"You know that very well, as I gave my order to saddle my horse. Have they not obeyed me?"

"It is done; as your Excellency may have observed, your horse is in the great gateway, ready saddled for your departure."

"That is well; do as I have directed you, then."

"What the devil!" said the host to himself. "Can he be afraid of this boy?" But an imperious glance from the stranger stopped him short; he bowed humbly and retired.

"It is not necessary for Milady to be seen by this fellow," continued the stranger. "She will soon pass; she is already late. I had better get on horseback, and go and meet her. I should like, however, to know what this letter addressed to Tréville contains."

And the stranger, muttering to himself, directed his steps toward the kitchen.

In the meantime, the host, who entertained no doubt that it was the presence of the young man that drove the stranger from his hostelry, re-ascended to his wife's chamber, and found d'Artagnan just recovering his senses. Giving him to understand that the police would deal with him pretty severely for having sought a quarrel with a great lord–for in the opinion of the host the stranger could be nothing less than a great lord–he insisted that notwithstanding his weakness d'Artagnan should get up and depart as quickly as possible. D'Artagnan, half stupefied, without his doublet, and with his head bound up in a linen cloth, arose then, and urged by the host, began to descend the stairs, but on arriving at the kitchen, the first thing he saw was his antagonist talking calmly at the step of a heavy carriage, drawn by two large Norman horses.

His interlocutor, whose head appeared through the carriage window, was a woman of from twenty to two-and-twenty years. We have already observed with what rapidity d'Artagnan seized the expression of a countenance. He perceived then, at a glance, that this woman was young and beautiful; and her style of beauty struck him more forcibly from its being totally different from that of the southern countries in which d'Artagnan had hitherto resided. She was pale and fair, with long curls falling in profusion over her shoulders, had large, blue, languishing eyes, rosy lips, and hands of alabaster. She was talking with great animation with the stranger.

"His Eminence, then, orders me–" said the lady.

"To return instantly to England, and to inform him as soon as the duke leaves London."

"And as to my other instructions?" asked the fair traveller.

"They are contained in this box, which you will not open until you are on the other side of the Channel."

"Very well; and you–what will you do?"

"I–I return to Paris."

"What, without chastising this insolent boy?" asked the lady.

The stranger was about to reply, but at the moment he opened his mouth, d'Artagnan, who had heard all, precipitated himself over the threshold of the door.

"This insolent boy chastises others," cried he, "and I hope that this time he whom he ought to chastise will not escape him as before."

"Will not escape him?" replied the stranger, knitting his brow.

"No; before a woman you would dare not fly, I presume?"

"Remember," said Milady, seeing the stranger lay his hand on his sword, "the least delay may ruin everything."

"You are right," cried the gentleman, "begone then, on your part, and I will depart as quickly on mine." And bowing to the lady, he sprang into his saddle, while her coachman applied his whip vigorously to his horses. The two interlocutors thus separated, taking opposite directions, at full gallop.

"Pay him, booby!" cried the stranger to his servant, without checking the speed of his horse; and the man, after throwing two or three silver pieces at the foot of mine host, galloped after his master.

"Base coward! False gentleman!" cried d'Artagnan, springing forward, in his turn, after the servant. But his wound had rendered him too weak to support such an exertion. Scarcely had he gone ten steps when his ears began to tingle, a faintness seized him, a cloud of blood passed over his eyes, and he fell in the middle of the street, crying still, "Coward! Coward! Coward!"

"He is a coward, indeed," grumbled the host, drawing near to d'Artagnan, and endeavouring by this little flattery to make up matters with the young man, as the heron of the fable did with the snail he had despised the evening before.

"Yes, a base coward," murmured d'Artagnan, "but she–she was very beautiful."

"What she?" demanded the host.

"Milady," faltered d'Artagnan, and fainted a second time.

"Ah, it's all one," said the host, "I have lost two customers, but this one remains, of whom I am pretty certain for some days to come. There will be eleven crowns gained."

It is to be remembered that eleven crowns was just the sum that remained in d'Artagnan's purse.

The host had reckoned upon eleven days of confinement at a crown a day, but he had reckoned without his guest. On the following morning at five o'clock d'Artagnan arose, and descending to the kitchen without help, asked, among other ingredients the list of which has not come down to us, for some oil, some wine, and some rosemary, and with his mother's recipe in his hand composed a balsam, with which he anointed his numerous wounds, replacing his bandages himself, and positively refusing the assistance of any doctor, d'Artagnan walked about that same evening, and was almost cured by the morrow.

But when the time came to pay for his rosemary, this oil, and the wine, the only expense the master had incurred, as he had preserved a strict abstinence–while on the contrary, the yellow horse, by the account of the hostler at least, had eaten three times as much as a horse of his size could reasonably be supposed to have done–d'Artagnan found nothing in his pocket but his little old velvet purse with the eleven crowns it contained; for as to the letter addressed to M. de Tréville, it had disappeared.

The young man commenced his search for the letter with the greatest patience, turning out his pockets of all kinds over and over again, rummaging and rerummaging in his valise, and opening and reopening his purse, but when he found that he had come to the conviction that the letter was not to be found, he flew, for the third time, into such a rage as was near costing him a fresh consumption of wine, oil, and rosemary–for upon seeing this hot-headed youth become exasperated and threaten to destroy everything in the establishment if his letter were not found, the host seized a spit, his wife a broom handle, and the servants the same sticks they had used the day before.

"My letter of recommendation!" cried d'Artagnan, "my letter of recommendation! Or, the holy blood, I will spit you all like ortolans!"

Unfortunately, there was one circumstance which created a powerful obstacle to the accomplishment of this threat, which was, as we have related, that his sword had been in his first conflict broken in two, and which he had entirely forgotten. Hence, it resulted when d'Artagnan proceeded to draw his sword in earnest, he found himself purely and simply armed with a stump of a sword about eight or ten inches in length, which the host had carefully placed in the scabbard. As to the rest of the blade, the master had slyly put that on one side to make himself a larding pin.

But this deception would probably not have stopped our fiery young man if the host had not reflected that the reclamation which his guest made was perfectly just.

"But, after all," said he, lowering the point of his spit, "where is this letter?"

"Yes, where is this letter?" cried d'Artagnan. "In the first place, I warn you that that letter is for Monsieur de Tréville, and it must be found, or if it is not found, he will know how to find it."

His threat completed the intimidation of the host. After the king and the cardinal, M. de Tréville was the man whose name was perhaps most frequently repeated by the military, and even by citizens. There was, to be sure, Father Joseph, but his name was never pronounced but with a subdued voice, such was the terror inspired by his Gray Eminence, as the cardinal's familiar was called.

Throwing down his spit, and ordering his wife to do the same with her broom handle, and the servants with their sticks, he set the first example of commencing an earnest search for the lost letter.

"Does the letter contain anything valuable?" demanded the host, after a few minutes of useless investigation.

"Zounds! I think it does indeed!" cried the Gascon, who reckoned upon this letter for making his way at court. "It contained my fortune!"

"Bills upon Spain?" asked the disturbed host.

"Bills upon his Majesty's private treasury," answered d'Artagnan, who, reckoning upon entering into the king's service in consequence of this recommendation, believed he could make this somewhat hazardous reply without telling of a falsehood.

"The devil!" cried the host, at his wit's end.

"But it's of no importance," continued d'Artagnan, with natural assurance, "it's of no importance. The money is nothing; that letter was everything. I would rather have lost a thousand pistoles than have lost it." He would not have risked more if he had said twenty thousand, but a certain juvenile modesty restrained him.

A ray of light all at once broke upon the mind of the host as he was giving himself to the devil upon finding nothing.

"That letter is not lost!" cried he.

"What!" cried d'Artagnan.

"No, it has been stolen from you."

"Stolen? By whom?"

"By the gentleman who was here yesterday. He came down into the kitchen, where your doublet was. He remained there some time alone. I would lay a wager he has stolen it."

"Do you think so?" answered d'Artagnan, but little convinced, as he knew better than anyone else how entirely personal the value of this letter was, and saw nothing in it likely to tempt cupidity. The fact was that none of his servants, none of the travellers present, could have gained anything by being possessed of this paper.

"Do you say," resumed d'Artagnan, "that you suspect that impertinent gentleman?"

"I tell you I am sure of it," continued the host. "When I informed him that your lordship was the protégé of Monsieur de Tréville, and that you even had a letter for that illustrious gentleman, he appeared to be very much disturbed, and asked me where that letter was, and immediately came down into the kitchen, where he knew your doublet was."

"Then that's my thief," replied d'Artagnan. "I will complain to Monsieur de Tréville, and Monsieur de Tréville will complain to the king." He then drew two crowns majestically from his purse and gave them to the host, who accompanied him, cap in hand, to the gate, and remounted his yellow horse, which bore him without any further accident to the gate of St. Antoine at Paris, where his owner sold him for three crowns, which was a very good price, considering that d'Artagnan had ridden him hard during the last stage. Thus the dealer to whom d'Artagnan sold him for the nine livres did not conceal from the young man that he only gave that enormous sum for him on the account of the originality of his colour.

Thus d'Artagnan entered Paris on foot, carrying his little packet under his arm, and walked about till he found an apartment to be let on terms suited to the scantiness of his means. This chamber was a sort of garret, situated in the Rue des Fossoyeurs, near the Luxembourg.

As soon as the earnest money was paid, d'Artagnan took possession of his lodging, and passed the remainder of the day in sewing onto his doublet and hose some ornamental braiding which his mother had taken off an almost-new doublet of the elder M. d'Artagnan, and which she had given her son secretly. Next he went to the Quai de Feraille to have a new blade put to his sword, and then returned toward the Louvre, inquiring of the first Musketeer he met for the situation of the hotel of M. de Tréville, which proved to be in the Rue du Vieux-Colombier; that is to say, in the immediate vicinity of the chamber hired by d'Artagnan–a circumstance which appeared to furnish a happy augury for the success of his journey.

After this, satisfied with the way in which he had conducted himself at Meung, without remorse for the past, confident in the present, and full of hope for the future, he retired to bed and slept the sleep of the brave.

This sleep, provincial as it was, brought him to nine o'clock in the morning; at which hour he rose, in order to repair to the residence of M. de Tréville, the third personage in the kingdom, in the paternal estimation.

Chapter 2

The Antechamber Of M. De Tréville

M. de Troisville, as his family was still called in Gascony, or M. de Tréville, as he has ended by styling himself in Paris, had really commenced life as d'Artagnan now did; that is to say, without a sou in his pocket, but with a fund of audacity, shrewdness, and intelligence which makes the poorest Gascon gentleman often derive more in his hope from the paternal inheritance than the richest Perigordian or Berrichan gentleman derives in reality from his. His insolent bravery, his still more insolent success at a time when blows poured down like hail, had borne him to the top of that difficult ladder called Court Favour, which he had climbed four steps at a time.

He was the friend of the king, who honoured highly, as everyone knows, the memory of his father, Henry IV. The father of M. de Tréville had served him so faithfully in his wars against the league that in default of money–a thing to which the Bearnais was accustomed all his life, and who constantly paid his debts with that of which he never stood in need of borrowing, that is to say, with ready wit–in default of money, we repeat, he authorised him, after the reduction of Paris, to assume for his arms a golden lion passant upon gules, with the motto FIDELIS ET FORTIS. This was a great matter in the way of honour, but very little in the way of wealth; so that when the illustrious companion of the great Henry died, the only inheritance he was able to leave his son was his sword and his motto. Thanks to this double gift and the spotless name that accompanied it, M. de Tréville was admitted into the household of the young prince where he made such good use of his sword, and was so faithful to his motto, that Louis XIII, one of the good blades of his kingdom, was accustomed to say that if he had a friend who was about to fight, he would advise him to choose as a second, himself first, and Tréville next–or even, perhaps, before himself.

Thus Louis XIII had a real liking for Tréville–a royal liking, a self-interested liking, it is true, but still a liking. At that unhappy period it was an important consideration to be surrounded by such men as Tréville. Many might take for their device the epithet STRONG, which formed the second part of his motto, but very few gentlemen could lay claim to the FAITHFUL, which constituted the first. Tréville was one of these latter. His was one of those rare organisations, endowed with an obedient intelligence like that of the dog; with a blind valor, a quick eye, and a prompt hand; to whom sight appeared only to be given to see if the king were dissatisfied with anyone, and the hand to strike this displeasing personage, whether a Besme, a Maurevers, a Poltiot de Mere, or a Vitry. In short, up to this period nothing had been wanting to Tréville but opportunity, but he was ever on the watch for it, and he faithfully promised himself that he would not fail to seize it by its three hairs whenever it came within reach of his hand. At last Louis XIII made Tréville the captain of his Musketeers, who were to Louis XIII in devotedness, or rather in fanaticism, what his Ordinaries had been to Henry III, and his Scotch Guard to Louis XI.

On his part, the cardinal was not behind the king in this respect. When he saw the formidable and chosen body with which Louis

XIII had surrounded himself, this second, or rather this first king of France, became desirous that he, too, should have his guard. He had his Musketeers therefore, as Louis XIII had his, and these two powerful rivals vied with each other in procuring, not only from all the provinces of France, but even from all foreign states, the most celebrated swordsmen. It was not uncommon for Richelieu and Louis XIII to dispute over their evening game of chess upon the merits of their servants. Each boasted the bearing and the courage of his own people. While exclaiming loudly against duels and brawls, they excited them secretly to quarrel, deriving an immoderate satisfaction or genuine regret from the success or defeat of their own combatants. We learn this from the memoirs of a man who was concerned in some few of these defeats and in many of these victories.

Tréville had grasped the weak side of his master; and it was to this address that he owed the long and constant favour of a king who has not left the reputation behind him of being very faithful in his friendships. He paraded his Musketeers before the Cardinal Armand Duplessis with an insolent air which made the gray moustache of his Eminence curl with ire. Tréville understood admirably the war method of that period, in which he who could not live at the expense of the enemy must live at the expense of his compatriots. His soldiers formed a legion of devil-may-care fellows, perfectly undisciplined toward all but himself.

Loose, half-drunk, imposing, the king's Musketeers, or rather M. de Tréville's, spread themselves about in the cabarets, in the public walks, and the public sports, shouting, twisting their moustaches, clanking their swords, and taking great pleasure in annoying the Guards of the cardinal whenever they could fall in with them; then drawing in the open streets, as if it were the best of all possible sports; sometimes killed, but sure in that case to be both wept and avenged; often killing others, but then certain of not rotting in prison, M. de Tréville being there to claim them. Thus M. de Tréville was praised to the highest note by these men, who adored him, and who, ruffians as they were, trembled before him like scholars before their master, obedient to his least word, and ready to sacrifice themselves to wash out the smallest insult.

M. de Tréville employed this powerful weapon for the king, in the first place, and the friends of the king–and then for himself and his own friends. For the rest, in the memoirs of this period, which has left so many memoirs, one does not find this worthy gentleman blamed even by his enemies; and he had many such among men of the pen as well as among men of the sword. In no instance, let us say, was this worthy gentleman accused of deriving personal advantage from the cooperation of his minions. Endowed with a rare genius for intrigue which rendered him the equal of the ablest intriguers, he remained an honest man. Still further, in spite of sword thrusts which weaken, and painful exercises which fatigue, he had become one of the most gallant frequenters of revels, one of the most insinuating lady's men, one of the softest whisperers of interesting nothings of his day; the BONNES FORTUNES of de Tréville were talked of as those of M. de Bassompierre had been talked of twenty years before, and that was not saying a little. The captain of the Musketeers was therefore admired, feared, and loved; and this constitutes the zenith of human fortune.

Louis XIV absorbed all the smaller stars of his court in his own vast radiance, but his father, a sun PLURIBUS IMPAR, left his personal splendor to each of his favourites, his individual value to each of his courtiers. In addition to the leeves of the king and the cardinal, there might be reckoned in Paris at that time more than two hundred smaller but still noteworthy leeves. Among these two hundred leeves, that of Tréville was one of the most sought.

The court of his hotel, situated in the Rue du Vieux-Colombier, resembled a camp from by six o'clock in the morning in summer and eight o'clock in winter. From fifty to sixty Musketeers, who appeared to replace one another in order always to present an imposing number, paraded constantly, armed to the teeth and ready for anything. On one of those immense staircases, upon whose space modern civilisation would build a whole house, ascended and descended the office seekers of Paris, who ran after any sort of favour–gentlemen from the provinces anxious to be enrolled, and servants in all sorts of liveries, bringing and carrying messages between their masters and M. de Tréville. In the antechamber, upon long circular benches, reposed the elect; that is to say, those who were called. In this apartment a continued buzzing prevailed from morning till night, while M. de Tréville, in his office contiguous to this antechamber, received visits, listened to complaints, gave his orders, and like the king in his balcony at the Louvre, had only to place himself at the window to review both his men and arms.

The day on which d'Artagnan presented himself the assemblage was imposing, particularly for a provincial just arriving from his province. It is true that this provincial was a Gascon; and that, particularly at this period, the compatriots of d'Artagnan had the reputation of not being easily intimidated. When he had once passed the massive door covered with long square-headed nails, he fell into the midst of a troop of swordsmen, who crossed one another in their passage, calling out, quarrelling, and playing tricks one with another. In order to make one's way amid these turbulent and conflicting waves, it was necessary to be an officer, a great noble, or a pretty woman.

It was, then, into the midst of this tumult and disorder that our young man advanced with a beating heart, ranging his long rapier up his lanky leg, and keeping one hand on the edge of his cap, with that half-smile of the embarrassed provincial who wishes to put on a good face. When he had passed one group he began to breathe more freely, but he could not help observing that they turned round to look at him, and for the first time in his life d'Artagnan, who had till that day entertained a very good opinion of himself, felt ridiculous.

Arrived at the staircase, it was still worse. There were four Musketeers on the bottom steps, amusing themselves with the following exercise, while ten or twelve of their comrades waited upon the landing place to take their turn in the sport.

One of them, stationed upon the top stair, naked sword in hand, prevented, or at least endeavoured to prevent, the three others from ascending.

These three others fenced against him with their agile swords.

D'Artagnan at first took these weapons for foils, and believed them to be buttoned, but he soon perceived by certain scratches that every weapon was pointed and sharpened, and that at each of these scratches not only the spectators, but even the actors themselves, laughed like so many madmen.

He who at the moment occupied the upper step kept his adversaries marvellously in check. A circle was formed around them. The conditions required that at every hit the man touched should quit the game, yielding his turn for the benefit of the adversary who had hit him. In five minutes three were slightly wounded, one on the hand, another on the ear, by the defender of the stair, who himself remained intact–a piece of skill which was worth to him, according to the rules agreed upon, three turns of favour.

However difficult it might be, or rather as he pretended it was, to astonish our young traveller, this pastime really astonished him. He had seen in his province–that land in which heads become so easily heated–a few of the preliminaries of duels, but the daring of these four fencers appeared to him the strongest he had ever heard of even in Gascony. He believed himself transported into that famous country of giants into which Gulliver afterward went and was so frightened; and yet he had not gained the goal, for there were still the landing place and the antechamber.

On the landing they were no longer fighting, but amused themselves with stories about women, and in the antechamber, with stories about the court. On the landing d'Artagnan blushed; in the antechamber he trembled. His warm and fickle imagination, which in Gascony had rendered him formidable to young chambermaids, and even sometimes their mistresses, had never dreamed, even in moments of delirium, of half the amorous wonders or a quarter of the feats of gallantry which were here set forth in connection with names the best known and with details the least concealed. But if his morals were shocked on the landing, his respect for the cardinal was scandalised in the antechamber. There, to his great astonishment, d'Artagnan heard the policy which made all Europe tremble criticised aloud and openly, as well as the private life of the cardinal, which so many great nobles had been punished for trying to pry into. That great man who was so revered by d'Artagnan the elder served as an object of ridicule to the Musketeers of Tréville, who cracked their jokes upon his bandy legs and his crooked back. Some sang ballads about Mme. d'Aguillon, his mistress, and Mme. Cambalet, his niece; while others formed parties and plans to annoy the pages and guards of the cardinal duke–all things which appeared to d'Artagnan monstrous impossibilities.

Nevertheless, when the name of the king was now and then uttered unthinkingly amid all these cardinal jests, a sort of gag seemed to close for a moment on all these jeering mouths. They looked hesitatingly around them, and appeared to doubt the thickness of the partition between them and the office of M. de Tréville, but a fresh allusion soon brought back the conversation to his Eminence, and then the laughter recovered its loudness and the light was not withheld from any of his actions.

"Certes, these fellows will all either be imprisoned or hanged," thought the terrified d'Artagnan, "and I, no doubt, with them; for from the moment I have either listened to or heard them, I shall be held as an accomplice. What would my good father say, who so strongly pointed out to me the respect due to the cardinal, if he knew I was in the society of such pagans?"

We have no need, therefore, to say that d'Artagnan dared not join in the conversation, only he looked with all his eyes and listened with all his ears, stretching his five senses so as to lose nothing; and despite his confidence on the paternal admonitions, he felt himself carried by his tastes and led by his instincts to praise rather than to blame the unheard-of things which were taking place.

Although he was a perfect stranger in the court of M. de Tréville's courtiers, and this his first appearance in that place, he was at length noticed, and somebody came and asked him what he wanted. At this demand d'Artagnan gave his name very modestly, emphasised the title of compatriot, and begged the servant who had put the question to him to request a moment's audience of M. de Tréville–a request which the other, with an air of protection, promised to transmit in due season.

D'Artagnan, a little recovered from his first surprise, had now leisure to study costumes and physiognomy.

The centre of the most animated group was a Musketeer of great height and haughty countenance, dressed in a costume so peculiar as to attract general attention. He did not wear the uniform cloak–which was not obligatory at that epoch of less liberty but more independence–but a cerulean-blue doublet, a little faded and worn, and over this a magnificent baldric, worked in gold, which shone like water ripples in the sun. A long cloak of crimson velvet fell in graceful folds from his shoulders, disclosing in front the splendid baldric, from which was suspended a gigantic rapier. This Musketeer had just come off guard, complained of having a cold, and coughed from time to time affectedly. It was for this reason, as he said to those around him, that he had put on his cloak; and while he spoke with a lofty air and twisted his moustache disdainfully, all admired his embroidered baldric, and d'Artagnan more than anyone.

"What would you have?" said the Musketeer. "This fashion is coming in. It is a folly, I admit, but still it is the fashion. Besides, one must lay out one's inheritance somehow."

"Ah, Porthos!" cried one of his companions, "don't try to make us believe you obtained that baldric by paternal generosity. It was given to you by that veiled lady I met you with the other Sunday, near the gate St. honour."

"No, upon honour and by the faith of a gentleman, I bought it with the contents of my own purse," answered he whom they designated by the name Porthos.

"Yes; about in the same manner," said another Musketeer, "that I bought this new purse with what my mistress put into the old one."

"It's true, though," said Porthos, "and the proof is that I paid twelve pistoles for it."

The wonder was increased, though the doubt continued to exist.

"Is it not true, Aramis?" said Porthos, turning toward another Musketeer.

This other Musketeer formed a perfect contrast to his interrogator, who had just designated him by the name of Aramis. He was a stout man, of about two- or three-and-twenty, with an open, ingenuous countenance, a black, mild eye, and cheeks rosy and downy as an autumn peach. His delicate moustache marked a perfectly straight line upon his upper lip; he appeared to dread to lower his hands lest their veins should swell, and he pinched the tips of his ears from time to time to preserve their delicate pink transparency. Habitually he spoke little and slowly, bowed frequently, laughed without noise, showing his teeth, which were fine and of which, as the rest of his person, he appeared to take great care. He answered the appeal of his friend by an affirmative nod of the head.

This affirmation appeared to dispel all doubts with regard to the baldric. They continued to admire it, but said no more about it; and with a rapid change of thought, the conversation passed suddenly to another subject.

"What do you think of the story Chalais's esquire relates?" asked another Musketeer, without addressing anyone in particular, but on the contrary speaking to everybody.

"And what does he say?" asked Porthos, in a self-sufficient tone.

"He relates that he met at Brussels Rochefort, the ÂME DAMNÉE of the cardinal disguised as a Capuchin, and that this cursed Rochefort, thanks to his disguise, had tricked Monsieur de Laigues, like a ninny as he is."

"A ninny, indeed!" said Porthos, "but is the matter certain?"

"I had it from Aramis," replied the Musketeer.

"Indeed?"

"Why, you knew it, Porthos," said Aramis. "I told you of it yesterday. Let us say no more about it."

"Say no more about it? That's YOUR opinion!" replied Porthos.

"Say no more about it! PESTE! You come to your conclusions quickly. What! The cardinal sets a spy upon a gentleman, has his letters stolen from him by means of a traitor, a brigand, a rascal–has, with the help of this spy and thanks to this correspondence, Chalais's throat cut, under the stupid pretext that he wanted to kill the king and marry Monsieur to the queen! Nobody knew a word of this enigma. You unraveled it yesterday to the great satisfaction of all; and while we are still gaping with wonder at the news, you come and tell us today, 'Let us say no more about it.'"

"Well, then, let us talk about it, since you desire it," replied Aramis, patiently.

"This Rochefort," cried Porthos, "if I were the esquire of poor Chalais, should pass a minute or two very uncomfortably with me."

"And you–you would pass rather a sad quarter-hour with the Red Duke," replied Aramis.

"Oh, the Red Duke! Bravo! Bravo! The Red Duke!" cried Porthos, clapping his hands and nodding his head. "The Red Duke is capital. I'll circulate that saying, be assured, my dear fellow. Who says this Aramis is not a wit? What a misfortune it is you did not follow your first vocation; what a delicious abbé you would have made!"

"Oh, it's only a temporary postponement," replied Aramis, "I shall be one someday. You very well know, Porthos, that I continue to study theology for that purpose."

"He will be one, as he says," cried Porthos, "he will be one, sooner or later."

"Sooner," said Aramis.

"He only waits for one thing to determine him to resume his cassock, which hangs behind his uniform," said another Musketeer.

"What is he waiting for?" asked another.

"Only till the queen has given an heir to the crown of France."

"No jesting upon that subject, gentlemen," said Porthos, "thank God the queen is still of an age to give one!"

"They say that Monsieur de Buckingham is in France," replied Aramis, with a significant smile which gave to this sentence, apparently so simple, a tolerably scandalous meaning.

"Aramis, my good friend, this time you are wrong," interrupted Porthos. "Your wit is always leading you beyond bounds; if Monsieur de Tréville heard you, you would repent of speaking thus."

"Are you going to give me a lesson, Porthos?" cried Aramis, from whose usually mild eye a flash passed like lightning.

"My dear fellow, be a Musketeer or an abbé. Be one or the other, but not both," replied Porthos. "You know what Athos told you the other day; you eat at everybody's mess. Ah, don't be angry, I beg of you, that would be useless; you know what is agreed upon between you, Athos and me. You go to Madame d'Aguillon's, and you pay your court to her; you go to Madame de Bois-Tracy's, the cousin of Madame de Chevreuse, and you pass for being far advanced in the good graces of that lady. Oh, good Lord! Don't trouble yourself to reveal your good luck; no one asks for your secret-all the world knows your discretion. But since you possess that virtue, why the devil don't you make use of it with respect to her Majesty? Let whoever likes talk of the king and the cardinal, and how he likes, but the queen is sacred, and if anyone speaks of her, let it be respectfully."

"Porthos, you are as vain as Narcissus; I plainly tell you so," replied Aramis. "You know I hate moralising, except when it is done by Athos. As to you, good Sir, you wear too magnificent a baldric to be strong on that head. I will be an abbé if it suits me. In the meanwhile I am a Musketeer; in that quality I say what I please, and at this moment it pleases me to say that you weary me."

"Aramis!"

"Porthos!"

"Gentlemen! Gentlemen!" cried the surrounding group.

"Monsieur de Tréville awaits Monsieur d'Artagnan," cried a servant, throwing open the door of the cabinet.

At this announcement, during which the door remained open, everyone became mute, and amid the general silence the young man crossed part of the length of the antechamber, and entered the apartment of the captain of the Musketeers, congratulating himself with all his heart at having so narrowly escaped the end of this strange quarrel.

Chapter 3

The Audience

M. de Tréville was at the moment in rather ill-humor, nevertheless he saluted the young man politely, who bowed to the very ground; and he smiled on receiving d'Artagnan's response, the Bearnese accent of which recalled to him at the same time his youth and his country–a double remembrance which makes a man smile at all ages, but stepping toward the antechamber and making a sign to d'Artagnan with his hand, as if to ask his permission to finish with others before he began with him, he called three times, with a louder voice at each time, so that he ran through the intervening tones between the imperative accent and the angry accent.

"Athos! Porthos! Aramis!"

The two Musketeers with whom we have already made acquaintance, and who answered to the last of these three names, immediately quitted the group of which they had formed a part, and advanced toward the cabinet, the door of which closed after them as soon as they had entered. Their appearance, although it was not quite at ease, excited by its carelessness, at once full of dignity and submission, the admiration of d'Artagnan, who beheld in these two men demigods, and in their leader an Olympian Jupiter, armed with all his thunders.

When the two Musketeers had entered; when the door was closed behind them; when the buzzing murmur of the antechamber, to which the summons which had been made had doubtless furnished fresh food, had recommenced; when M. de Tréville had three or four times paced in silence, and with a frowning brow, the whole length of his cabinet, passing each time before Porthos and Aramis, who were as upright and silent as if on parade–he stopped all at once full in front of them, and covering them from head to foot with an angry look, "Do you know what the king said to me," cried he, "and that no longer ago than yesterday evening–do you know, gentlemen?"

"No," replied the two Musketeers, after a moment's silence, "no, Sir, we do not."

"But I hope that you will do us the honour to tell us," added Aramis, in his politest tone and with his most graceful bow.

"He told me that he should henceforth recruit his Musketeers from among the Guards of Monsieur the Cardinal."

"The Guards of the cardinal! And why so?" asked Porthos, warmly.

"Because he plainly perceives that his piquette stands in need of being enlivened by a mixture of good wine."

The two Musketeers reddened to the whites of their eyes. D'Artagnan did not know where he was, and wished himself a hundred feet underground.

"Yes, yes," continued M. de Tréville, growing warmer as he spoke, "and his majesty was right; for, upon my honour, it is true that the Musketeers make but a miserable figure at court. The cardinal related yesterday while playing with the king, with an air of condolence very displeasing to me, that the day before yesterday those DAMNED MUSKETEERS, those DAREDEVILS–he dwelt upon those words with an ironical tone still more displeasing to me–those BRAGGARTS, added he, glancing at me with his tiger-cat's eye, had made a riot in the Rue Ferou in a cabaret, and that a party of his Guards (I thought he was going to laugh in my face) had been forced to arrest the rioters! MORBLEU! You must know something about it. Arrest Musketeers! You were among them–you were! Don't deny it; you were recognised, and the cardinal named you. But it's all my fault; yes, it's all my fault, because it is myself who selects my men. You, Aramis, why the devil did you ask me for a uniform when you would have been so much better in a cassock? And you, Porthos, do you only wear such a fine golden baldric to suspend a sword of straw from it? And Athos–I don't see Athos. Where is he?"

"Ill–"

"Very ill, say you? And of what malady?"

"It is feared that it may be the smallpox, Sir," replied Porthos, desirous of taking his turn in the conversation, "and what is serious is that it will certainly spoil his face."

"The smallpox! That's a great story to tell me, Porthos! Sick of the smallpox at his age! No, no, but wounded without doubt, killed, perhaps. Ah, if I knew! S'blood! Messieurs Musketeers, I will not have this haunting of bad places, this quarreling in the streets, this swordplay at the crossways; and above all, I will not have occasion given for the cardinal's Guards, who are brave, quiet, skillful men who never put themselves in a position to be arrested, and who, besides, never allow themselves to be arrested, to laugh at you! I am sure of it–they would prefer dying on the spot to being arrested or taking back a step. To save yourselves, to scamper away, to flee–that is good for the king's Musketeers!"

Porthos and Aramis trembled with rage. They could willingly have strangled M. de Tréville, if, at the bottom of all this, they had not felt it was the great love he bore them which made him speak thus. They stamped upon the carpet with their feet; they bit their lips till the blood came, and grasped the hilts of their swords with all their might. All without had heard, as we have said, Athos, Porthos, and Aramis called, and had guessed, from M. de Tréville's tone of voice, that he was very angry about something. Ten curious heads were glued to the tapestry and became pale with fury; for their ears, closely applied to the door, did not lose a syllable of what he said, while their mouths repeated as he went on, the insulting expressions of the captain to all the people in the antechamber. In an instant, from the door of the cabinet to the street gate, the whole hotel was boiling.

"Ah! The king's Musketeers are arrested by the Guards of the cardinal, are they?" continued M. de Tréville, as furious at heart as his soldiers, but emphasising his words and plunging them, one by one, so to say, like so many blows of a stiletto, into the bosoms of his auditors. "What! Six of his Eminence's Guards arrest six of his Majesty's Musketeers! MORBLEU! My part is taken! I will go straight to the Louvre; I will give in my resignation as captain of the king's Musketeers to take a lieutenancy in the cardinal's Guards, and if he refuses me, MORBLEU! I will turn abbé."

At these words, the murmur without became an explosion; nothing was to be heard but oaths and blasphemies. The MORBLEUS, the SANG DIEUS, the MORTS TOUTS LES DIABLES, crossed one another in the air. D'Artagnan looked for some tapestry behind which he might hide himself, and felt an immense inclination to crawl under the table.

"Well, my Captain," said Porthos, quite beside himself, "the truth is that we were six against six. But we were not captured by fair means; and before we had time to draw our swords, two of our party were dead, and Athos, grievously wounded, was very little better. For you know Athos. Well, Captain, he endeavoured twice to get up, and fell again twice. And we did not surrender–no! They dragged us away by force. On the way we escaped. As for Athos, they believed him to be dead, and left him very quiet on the field of battle, not thinking it worth the trouble to carry him away. That's the whole story. What the devil, Captain, one cannot win all one's battles! The great Pompey lost that of Pharsalia; and Francis the First, who was, as I have heard say, as good as other folks, nevertheless lost the Battle of Pavia."

"And I have the honour of assuring you that I killed one of them with his own sword," said Aramis, "for mine was broken at the first parry. Killed him, or poniarded him, Sir, as is most agreeable to you."

"I did not know that," replied M. de Tréville, in a somewhat softened tone. "The cardinal exaggerated, as I perceive."

"But pray, Sir," continued Aramis, who, seeing his captain become appeased, ventured to risk a prayer, "do not say that Athos is wounded. He would be in despair if that should come to the ears of the king; and as the wound is very serious, seeing that after crossing the shoulder it penetrates into the chest, it is to be feared–"

At this instant the tapestry was raised and a noble and handsome head, but frightfully pale, appeared under the fringe.

"Athos!" cried the two Musketeers.

"Athos!" repeated M. de Tréville himself.

"You have sent for me, Sir," said Athos to M. de Tréville, in a feeble yet perfectly calm voice, "you have sent for me, as my comrades inform me, and I have hastened to receive your orders. I am here; what do you want with me?"

And at these words, the Musketeer, in irreproachable costume, belted as usual, with a tolerably firm step, entered the cabinet. M. de Tréville, moved to the bottom of his heart by this proof of courage, sprang toward him.

"I was about to say to these gentlemen," added he, "that I forbid my Musketeers to expose their lives needlessly; for brave men are very dear to the king, and the king knows that his Musketeers are the bravest on the earth. Your hand, Athos!"

And without waiting for the answer of the newcomer to this proof of affection, M. de Tréville seized his right hand and pressed it with all his might, without perceiving that Athos, whatever might be his self-command, allowed a slight murmur of pain to escape him, and if possible, grew paler than he was before.

The door had remained open, so strong was the excitement produced by the arrival of Athos, whose wound, though kept as a secret, was known to all. A burst of satisfaction hailed the last words of the captain; and two or three heads, carried away by the enthusiasm of the moment, appeared through the openings of the tapestry. M. de Tréville was about to reprehend this breach of the rules of etiquette, when he felt the hand of Athos, who had rallied all his energies to contend against pain, at length overcome by it, fell upon the floor as if he were dead.

"A surgeon!" cried M. de Tréville, "mine! The king's! The best! A surgeon! Or, s'blood, my brave Athos will die!"

At the cries of M. de Tréville, the whole assemblage rushed into the cabinet, he not thinking to shut the door against anyone, and all crowded round the wounded man. But all this eager attention might have been useless if the doctor so loudly called for had not chanced to be in the hotel. He pushed through the crowd, approached Athos, still insensible, and as all this noise and commotion inconvenienced him greatly, he required, as the first and most urgent thing, that the Musketeer should be carried into an adjoining chamber. Immediately M. de Tréville opened and pointed the way to Porthos and Aramis, who bore their comrade in their arms. Behind this group walked the surgeon; and behind the surgeon the door closed.

The cabinet of M. de Tréville, generally held so sacred, became in an instant the annex of the antechamber. Everyone spoke, harangued, and vociferated, swearing, cursing, and consigning the cardinal and his Guards to all the devils.

An instant after, Porthos and Aramis re-entered, the surgeon and M. de Tréville alone remaining with the wounded.

At length, M. de Tréville himself returned. The injured man had recovered his senses. The surgeon declared that the situation of the Musketeer had nothing in it to render his friends uneasy, his weakness having been purely and simply caused by loss of blood.

Then M. de Tréville made a sign with his hand, and all retired except d'Artagnan, who did not forget that he had an audience, and with the tenacity of a Gascon remained in his place.

When all had gone out and the door was closed, M. de Tréville, on turning round, found himself alone with the young man. The event which had occurred had in some degree broken the thread of his ideas. He inquired what was the will of his persevering visitor. D'Artagnan then repeated his name, and in an instant recovering all his remembrances of the present and the past, M. de Tréville grasped the situation.

"Pardon me," said he, smiling, "pardon me my dear compatriot, but I had wholly forgotten you. But what help is there for it! A captain is nothing but a father of a family, charged with even a greater responsibility than the father of an ordinary family. Soldiers are big children, but as I maintain that the orders of the king, and more particularly the orders of the cardinal, should be executed–"

D'Artagnan could not restrain a smile. By this smile M. de Tréville judged that he had not to deal with a fool, and changing the conversation, came straight to the point.

"I respected your father very much," said he. "What can I do for the son? Tell me quickly; my time is not my own."

"Monsieur," said d'Artagnan, "on quitting Tarbes and coming hither, it was my intention to request of you, in remembrance of the friendship which you have not forgotten, the uniform of a Musketeer, but after all that I have seen during the last two hours, I comprehend that such a favour is enormous, and tremble lest I should not merit it."

"It is indeed a favour, young man," replied M. de Tréville, "but it may not be so far beyond your hopes as you believe, or rather as you appear to believe. But his majesty's decision is always necessary; and I inform you with regret that no one becomes a Musketeer without the preliminary ordeal of several campaigns, certain brilliant actions, or a service of two years in some other regiment less favoured than ours."

D'Artagnan bowed without replying, feeling his desire to don the Musketeer's uniform vastly increased by the great difficulties which preceded the attainment of it.

"But," continued M. de Tréville, fixing upon his compatriot a look so piercing that it might be said he wished to read the thoughts of his heart, "on account of my old companion, your father, as I have said, I will do something for you, young man. Our recruits from Bearn are not generally very rich, and I have no reason to think matters have much changed in this respect since I left the province. I dare say you have not brought too large a stock of money with you?"

D'Artagnan drew himself up with a proud air which plainly said, "I ask alms of no man."

"Oh, that's very well, young man," continued M. de Tréville, "that's all very well. I know these airs; I myself came to Paris with four crowns in my purse, and would have fought with anyone who dared to tell me I was not in a condition to purchase the Louvre."

D'Artagnan's bearing became still more imposing. Thanks to the sale of his horse, he commenced his career with four more crowns than M. de Tréville possessed at the commencement of his.

"You ought, I say, then, to husband the means you have, however large the sum may be, but you ought also to endeavour to perfect yourself in the exercises becoming a gentleman. I will write a letter today to the Director of the Royal Academy, and tomorrow he will admit you without any expense to yourself. Do not refuse this little service. Our best-born and richest gentlemen sometimes solicit it without being able to obtain it. You will learn horsemanship, swordsmanship in all its branches, and dancing. You will make some desirable acquaintances; and from time to time you can call upon me, just to tell me how you are getting on, and to say whether I can be of further service to you."

D'Artagnan, stranger as he was to all the manners of a court, could not but perceive a little coldness in this reception.

"Alas, Sir," said he, "I cannot but perceive how sadly I miss the letter of introduction which my father gave me to present to you."

"I certainly am surprised," replied M. de Tréville, "that you should undertake so long a journey without that necessary passport, the sole resource of us poor Bearnese."

"I had one, Sir, and, thank God, such as I could wish," cried d'Artagnan, "but it was perfidiously stolen from me."

He then related the adventure of Meung, described the unknown gentleman with the greatest minuteness, and all with a warmth and truthfulness that delighted M. de Tréville.

"This is all very strange," said M. de Tréville, after meditating a minute, "you mentioned my name, then, aloud?"

"Yes, Sir, I certainly committed that imprudence, but why should I have done otherwise? A name like yours must be as a buckler to me on my way. Judge if I should not put myself under its protection."

Flattery was at that period very current, and M. de Tréville loved incense as well as a king, or even a cardinal. He could not refrain from a smile of visible satisfaction, but this smile soon disappeared, and returning to the adventure of Meung, "Tell me," continued he, "had not this gentlemen a slight scar on his cheek?"

"Yes, such a one as would be made by the grazing of a ball."

"Was he not a fine-looking man?"

"Yes."

"Of lofty stature."

"Yes."

"Of pale complexion and brown hair?"

"Yes, yes, that is he; how is it, Sir, that you are acquainted with this man? If I ever find him again–and I will find him, I swear, were it in hell!"

"He was waiting for a woman," continued Tréville.

"He departed immediately after having conversed for a minute with her whom he awaited."

"You know not the subject of their conversation?"

"He gave her a box, told her not to open it except in London."

"Was this woman English?"

"He called her Milady."

"It is he; it must be he!" murmured Tréville. "I believed him still at Brussels."

"Oh, Sir, if you know who this man is," cried d'Artagnan, "tell me who he is, and whence he is. I will then release you from all your promises–even that of procuring my admission into the Musketeers; for before everything, I wish to avenge myself."

"Beware, young man!" cried Tréville. "If you see him coming on one side of the street, pass by on the other. Do not cast yourself against such a rock; he would break you like glass."

"That will not prevent me," replied d'Artagnan, "if ever I find him."

"In the meantime," said Tréville, "seek him not–if I have a right to advise you."

All at once the captain stopped, as if struck by a sudden suspicion. This great hatred which the young traveller manifested so loudly for this man, who–a rather improbable thing–had stolen his father's letter from him–was there not some perfidy concealed under this hatred? Might not this young man be sent by his Eminence? Might he not have come for the purpose of laying a snare for him? This pretended d'Artagnan–was he not an emissary of the cardinal, whom the cardinal sought to introduce into Tréville's house, to place near him, to win his confidence, and afterward to ruin him as had been done in a thousand other instances? He fixed his eyes upon d'Artagnan even more earnestly than before. He was moderately reassured, however, by the aspect of that countenance, full of astute intelligence and affected humility. "I know he is a Gascon," reflected he, "but he may be one for the cardinal as well as for me. Let us try him."

"My friend," said he, slowly, "I wish, as the son of an ancient friend–for I consider this story of the lost letter perfectly true–I wish, I say, in order to repair the coldness you may have remarked in my reception of you, to discover to you the secrets of our policy. The king and the cardinal are the best of friends; their apparent bickerings are only feints to deceive fools. I am not willing that a compatriot, a handsome cavalier, a brave youth, quite fit to make his way, should become the dupe of all these artifices and fall into the snare after the example of so many others who have been ruined by it. Be assured that I am devoted to both these all-powerful masters, and that my earnest endeavours have no other aim than the service of the king, and also the cardinal–one of the most illustrious geniuses that France has ever produced.

"Now, young man, regulate your conduct accordingly; and if you entertain, whether from your family, your relations, or even from your instincts, any of these enmities which we see constantly breaking out against the cardinal, bid me adieu and let us separate. I will aid you in many ways, but without attaching you to my person. I hope that my frankness at least will make you my friend; for you are the only young man to whom I have hitherto spoken as I have done to you."

Tréville said to himself: "If the cardinal has set this young fox upon me, he will certainly not have failed–he, who knows how bitterly I execrate him–to tell his spy that the best means of making his court to me is to rail at him. Therefore, in spite of all my protestations, if it be as I suspect, my cunning gossip will assure me that he holds his Eminence in horror."

It, however, proved otherwise. D'Artagnan answered, with the greatest simplicity: "I came to Paris with exactly such intentions. My father advised me to stoop to nobody but the king, the cardinal, and yourself–whom he considered the first three personages in France."

D'Artagnan added M. de Tréville to the others, as may be perceived, but he thought this addition would do no harm.

"I have the greatest veneration for the cardinal," continued he, "and the most profound respect for his actions. So much the better for me, Sir, if you speak to me, as you say, with frankness–for then you will do me the honour to esteem the resemblance of our opinions, but if you have entertained any doubt, as naturally you may, I feel that I am ruining myself by speaking the truth. But I still trust you will not esteem me the less for it, and that is my object beyond all others."

M. de Tréville was surprised to the greatest degree. So much penetration, so much frankness, created admiration, but did not entirely remove his suspicions. The more this young man was superior to others, the more he was to be dreaded if he meant to deceive him. Nevertheless, he pressed d'Artagnan's hand, and said to him: "You are an honest youth, but at the present moment I can only do for you that which I just now offered. My hotel will be always open to you. Hereafter, being able to ask for me at all hours, and consequently to take advantage of all opportunities, you will probably obtain that which you desire."

"That is to say," replied d'Artagnan, "that you will wait until I have proved myself worthy of it. Well, be assured," added he, with the familiarity of a Gascon, "you shall not wait long." And he bowed in order to retire, and as if he considered the future in his own hands.

"But wait a minute," said M. de Tréville, stopping him. "I promised you a letter for the director of the Academy. Are you too proud to accept it, young gentleman?"

"No, Sir," said d'Artagnan, "and I will guard it so carefully that I will be sworn it shall arrive at its address, and woe be to him who shall attempt to take it from me!"

M. de Tréville smiled at this flourish; and leaving his young man compatriot in the embrasure of the window, where they had talked together, he seated himself at a table in order to write the promised letter of recommendation. While he was doing this, d'Artagnan, having no better employment, amused himself with beating a march upon the window and with looking at the Musketeers, who went away, one after another, following them with his eyes until they disappeared.

M. de Tréville, after having written the letter, sealed it, and rising, approached the young man in order to give it to him. But at the very moment when d'Artagnan stretched out his hand to receive it, M. de Tréville was highly astonished to see his protégé make a sudden spring, become crimson with passion, and rush from the cabinet crying, "S'blood, he shall not escape me this time!"

"And who?" asked M. de Tréville.

"He, my thief!" replied d'Artagnan. "Ah, the traitor!" and he disappeared.

"The devil take the madman!" murmured M. de Tréville, "unless," added he, "this is a cunning mode of escaping, seeing that he had failed in his purpose!"

Chapter 4

The Shoulder Of Athos, The Baldric Of Porthos And The Handkerchief Of Aramis

D'Artagnan, in a state of fury, crossed the antechamber at three bounds, and was darting toward the stairs, which he reckoned upon descending four at a time, when, in his heedless course, he ran head foremost against a Musketeer who was coming out of one of M. de Tréville's private rooms, and striking his shoulder violently, made him utter a cry, or rather a howl.

"Excuse me," said d'Artagnan, endeavouring to resume his course, "excuse me, but I am in a hurry."

Scarcely had he descended the first stair, when a hand of iron seized him by the belt and stopped him.

"You are in a hurry?" said the Musketeer, as pale as a sheet. "Under that pretense you run against me! You say, 'Excuse me,' and you believe that is sufficient? Not at all, my young man. Do you fancy because you have heard Monsieur de Tréville speak to us a little cavalierly today that other people are to treat us as he speaks to us? Undeceive yourself, comrade, you are not Monsieur de Tréville."

"My faith!" replied d'Artagnan, recognising Athos, who, after the dressing performed by the doctor, was returning to his own apartment. "I did not do it intentionally, and not doing it intentionally, I said 'Excuse me.' It appears to me that this is quite enough. I repeat to you, however, and this time on my word of honour–I think perhaps too often–that I am in haste, great haste. Leave your hold, then, I beg of you, and let me go where my business calls me."

"Monsieur," said Athos, letting him go, "you are not polite; it is easy to perceive that you come from a distance."

D'Artagnan had already strode down three or four stairs, but at Athos's last remark he stopped short.

"MORBLEU, Monsieur!" said he, "however far I may come, it is not you who can give me a lesson in good manners, I warn you."

"Perhaps," said Athos.

"Ah! If I were not in such haste, and if I were not running after someone," said d'Artagnan.

"Monsieur Man-in-a-hurry, you can find me without running–ME, you understand?"

"And where, I pray you?"

"Near the Carmes-Deschaux."

"At what hour?"

"About noon."

"About noon? That will do; I will be there."

"Endeavour not to make me wait; for at quarter past twelve I will cut off your ears as you run."

"Good!" cried d'Artagnan, "I will be there ten minutes before twelve." And he set off running as if the devil possessed him, hoping that he might yet find the stranger, whose slow pace could not have carried him far.

But at the street gate, Porthos was talking with the soldier on guard. Between the two talkers there was just enough room for a man to pass. D'Artagnan thought it would suffice for him, and he sprang forward like a dart between them. But d'Artagnan had reckoned without the wind. As he was about to pass, the wind blew out Porthos's long cloak, and d'Artagnan rushed straight into the middle of it. Without doubt, Porthos had reasons for not abandoning this part of his vestments, for instead of quitting his hold on the flap in his hand, he pulled it toward him, so that d'Artagnan rolled himself up in the velvet by a movement of rotation explained by the persistency of Porthos.

D'Artagnan, hearing the Musketeer swear, wished to escape from the cloak, which blinded him, and sought to find his way from under the folds of it. He was particularly anxious to avoid marring the freshness of the magnificent baldric we are acquainted with, but on timidly opening his eyes, he found himself with his nose fixed between the two shoulders of Porthos–that is to say, exactly upon the baldric.

Alas, like most things in this world which have nothing in their favour but appearances, the baldric was glittering with gold in the front, but was nothing but simple buff behind. Vainglorious as he was, Porthos could not afford to have a baldric wholly of gold, but had at least half. One could comprehend the necessity of the cold and the urgency of the cloak.

"Bless me!" cried Porthos, making strong efforts to disembarrass himself of d'Artagnan, who was wriggling about his back, "you must be mad to run against people in this manner."

"Excuse me," said d'Artagnan, reappearing under the shoulder of the giant, "but I am in such haste–I was running after someone and–"

"And do you always forget your eyes when you run?" asked Porthos.

"No," replied d'Artagnan, piqued, "and thanks to my eyes, I can see what other people cannot see."

Whether Porthos understood him or did not understand him, giving way to his anger, "Monsieur," said he, "you stand a chance of getting chastised if you rub Musketeers in this fashion."

"Chastised, Monsieur!" said d'Artagnan, "the expression is strong."

"It is one that becomes a man accustomed to look his enemies in the face."

"Ah, PARDIEU! I know full well that you don't turn your back to yours."

And the young man, delighted with his joke, went away laughing loudly.

Porthos foamed with rage, and made a movement to rush after d'Artagnan.

"Presently, presently," cried the latter, "when you haven't your cloak on."

"At one o'clock, then, behind the Luxembourg."

"Very well, at one o'clock, then," replied d'Artagnan, turning the angle of the street.

But neither in the street he had passed through, nor in the one which his eager glance pervaded, could he see anyone; however slowly the stranger had walked, he was gone on his way, or perhaps had entered some house. D'Artagnan inquired of everyone he met with, went down to the ferry, came up again by the Rue de Seine, and the Red Cross, but nothing, absolutely nothing! This chase was, however, advantageous to him in one sense, for in proportion as the perspiration broke from his forehead, his heart began to cool.

He began to reflect upon the events that had passed; they were numerous and inauspicious. It was scarcely eleven o'clock in the morning, and yet this morning had already brought him into disgrace with M. de Tréville, who could not fail to think the manner in which d'Artagnan had left him a little cavalier.

Besides this, he had drawn upon himself two good duels with two men, each capable of killing three d'Artagnans–with two Musketeers, in short, with two of those beings whom he esteemed so greatly that he placed them in his mind and heart above all other men.

The outlook was sad. Sure of being killed by Athos, it may easily be understood that the young man was not very uneasy about Porthos. As hope, however, is the last thing extinguished in the heart of man, he finished by hoping that he might survive, even though with terrible wounds, in both these duels; and in case of surviving, he made the following reprehensions upon his own conduct:

"What a madcap I was, and what a stupid fellow I am! That brave and unfortunate Athos was wounded on that very shoulder against which I must run head foremost, like a ram. The only thing that astonishes me is that he did not strike me dead at once. He had good cause to do so; the pain I gave him must have been atrocious. As to Porthos–oh, as to Porthos, faith, that's a droll affair!"

And in spite of himself, the young man began to laugh aloud, looking round carefully, however, to see that his solitary laugh, without a cause in the eyes of passers-by, offended no one.

"As to Porthos, that is certainly droll, but I am not the less a giddy fool. Are people to be run against without warning? No! And have I any right to go and peep under their cloaks to see what is not there? He would have pardoned me, he would certainly have pardoned me, if I had not said anything to him about that cursed baldric–in ambiguous words, it is true, but rather drolly ambiguous. Ah, cursed Gascon that I am, I get from one hobble into another. Friend d'Artagnan," continued he, speaking to himself with all the amenity that he thought due himself, "if you escape, of which there is not much chance, I would advise you to practice perfect politeness for the future. You must henceforth be admired and quoted as a model of it. To be obliging and polite does not necessarily make a man a coward. Look at Aramis, now; Aramis is mildness and grace personified. Well, did anybody ever dream of calling Aramis a coward? No, certainly not, and from this moment I will endeavour to model myself after him. Ah! That's strange! Here he is!"

D'Artagnan, walking and soliloquising, had arrived within a few steps of the Hotel d'Arguillon and in front of that hotel perceived Aramis, chatting gaily with three gentlemen, but as he had not forgotten that it was in presence of this young man that M. de Tréville had been so angry in the morning, and as a witness of the rebuke the Musketeers had received was not likely to be at all agreeable, he pretended not to see him. D'Artagnan, on the contrary, quite full of his plans of conciliation and courtesy, approached the young men with a profound bow, accompanied by a most gracious smile. All four, besides, immediately broke off their conversation.

D'Artagnan was not so dull as not to perceive that he was one too many, but he was not sufficiently broken into the fashions of the gay world to know how to extricate himself gallantly from a false position, like that of a man who begins to mingle with people he is scarcely acquainted with and in a conversation that does not concern him. He was seeking in his mind, then, for the least awkward means of retreat, when he remarked that Aramis had let his handkerchief fall, and by mistake, no doubt, had placed his foot upon it. This appeared to be a favourable opportunity to repair his intrusion. He stooped, and with the most gracious air he could assume, drew the handkerchief from under the foot of the Musketeer in spite of the efforts the latter made to detain it, and holding it out to him, said, "I believe, Monsieur, that this is a handkerchief you would be sorry to lose?"

The handkerchief was indeed richly embroidered, and had a coronet and arms at one of its corners. Aramis blushed excessively, and snatched rather than took the handkerchief from the hand of the Gascon.

"Ah, ah!" cried one of the Guards, "will you persist in saying, most discreet Aramis, that you are not on good terms with Madame de Bois-Tracy, when that gracious lady has the kindness to lend you one of her handkerchiefs?"

Aramis darted at d'Artagnan one of those looks which inform a man that he has acquired a mortal enemy. Then, resuming his mild air, "You are deceived, gentlemen," said he, "this handkerchief is not mine, and I cannot fancy why Monsieur has taken it into his head to offer it to me rather than to one of you; and as a proof of what I say, here is mine in my pocket."

So saying, he pulled out his own handkerchief, likewise a very elegant handkerchief, and of fine cambric–though cambric was dear at the period–but a handkerchief without embroidery and without arms, only ornamented with a single cipher, that of its proprietor.

This time d'Artagnan was not hasty. He perceived his mistake, but the friends of Aramis were not at all convinced by his denial, and one of them addressed the young Musketeer with affected seriousness. "If it were as you pretend it is," said he, "I should be forced, my dear Aramis, to reclaim it myself; for, as you very well know, Bois-Tracy is an intimate friend of mine, and I cannot allow the property of his wife to be sported as a trophy."

"You make the demand badly," replied Aramis, "and while acknowledging the justice of your reclamation, I refuse it on account of the form."

"The fact is," hazarded d'Artagnan, timidly, "I did not see the handkerchief fall from the pocket of Monsieur Aramis. He had his foot upon it, that is all; and I thought from having his foot upon it the handkerchief was his."

"And you were deceived, my dear Sir," replied Aramis, coldly, very little sensible to the reparation. Then turning toward that one of the guards who had declared himself the friend of Bois-Tracy, "Besides," continued he, "I have reflected, my dear intimate of Bois-Tracy, that I am not less tenderly his friend than you can possibly be; so that decidedly this handkerchief is as likely to have fallen from your pocket as mine."

"No, upon my honour!" cried his Majesty's Guardsman.

"You are about to swear upon your honour and I upon my word, and then it will be pretty evident that one of us will have lied. Now, here, Montaran, we will do better than that–let each take a half."

"Of the handkerchief?"

"Yes."

"Perfectly just," cried the other two Guardsmen, "the judgement of King Solomon! Aramis, you certainly are full of wisdom!"

The young men burst into a laugh, and as may be supposed, the affair had no other sequel. In a moment or two the conversation ceased, and the three Guardsmen and the Musketeer, after having cordially shaken hands, separated, the Guardsmen going one way and Aramis another.

"Now is my time to make peace with this gallant man," said d'Artagnan to himself, having stood on one side during the whole of the latter part of the conversation; and with this good feeling drawing near to Aramis, who was departing without paying any attention to him, "Monsieur," said he, "you will excuse me, I hope."

"Ah, Monsieur," interrupted Aramis, "permit me to observe to you that you have not acted in this affair as a gallant man ought."

"What, Monsieur!" cried d'Artagnan, "and do you suppose–"

"I suppose, Monsieur, that you are not a fool, and that you knew very well, although coming from Gascony, that people do not tread upon handkerchiefs without a reason. What the devil! Paris is not paved with cambric!"

"Monsieur, you act wrongly in endeavouring to mortify me," said d'Artagnan, in whom the natural quarrelsome spirit began to speak more loudly than his pacific resolutions. "I am from Gascony, it is true; and since you know it, there is no occasion to tell you that Gascons are not very patient, so that when they have begged to be excused once, were it even for a folly, they are convinced that they have done already at least as much again as they ought to have done."

"Monsieur, what I say to you about the matter," said Aramis, "is not for the sake of seeking a quarrel. Thank God, I am not a bravo! And being a Musketeer but for a time, I only fight when I am forced to do so, and always with great repugnance, but this time the affair is serious, for here is a lady compromised by you."

"By US, you mean!" cried d'Artagnan.

"Why did you so maladroitly restore me the handkerchief?"

"Why did you so awkwardly let it fall?"

"I have said, Monsieur, and I repeat, that the handkerchief did not fall from my pocket."

"And thereby you have lied twice, Monsieur, for I saw it fall."

"Ah, you take it with that tone, do you, Master Gascon? Well, I will teach you how to behave yourself."

"And I will send you back to your Mass book, Master Abbé. Draw, if you please, and instantly–"

"Not so, if you please, my good friend–not here, at least. Do you not perceive that we are opposite the Hotel d'Arguillon, which is full of the cardinal's creatures? How do I know that this is not his Eminence who has honoured you with the commission to procure my head? Now, I entertain a ridiculous partiality for my head, it seems to suit my shoulders so correctly. I wish to kill you, be at rest as to that, but to kill you quietly in a snug, remote place, where you will not be able to boast of your death to anybody."

"I agree, Monsieur, but do not be too confident. Take your handkerchief; whether it belongs to you or another, you may perhaps stand in need of it."

"Monsieur is a Gascon?" asked Aramis.

"Yes. Monsieur does not postpone an interview through prudence?"

"Prudence, Monsieur, is a virtue sufficiently useless to Musketeers, I know, but indispensable to churchmen; and as I am only a Musketeer provisionally, I hold it good to be prudent. At two o'clock I shall have the honour of expecting you at the hotel of Monsieur de Tréville. There I will indicate to you the best place and time."

The two young men bowed and separated, Aramis ascending the street which led to the Luxembourg, while d'Artagnan, perceiving the appointed hour was approaching, took the road to the Carmes-Deschaux, saying to himself, "Decidedly I can't draw back, but at least, if I am killed, I shall be killed by a Musketeer."

Chapter 5

The King's Musketeers And The Cardinal's Guards

D'Artagnan was acquainted with nobody in Paris. He went therefore to his appointment with Athos without a second, determined to be satisfied with those his adversary should choose. Besides, his intention was formed to make the brave Musketeer all suitable apologies, but without meanness or weakness, fearing that might result from this duel which generally results from an affair of this kind, when a young and vigorous man fights with an adversary who is wounded and weakened–if conquered, he doubles the triumph of his antagonist; if a conqueror, he is accused of foul play and want of courage.

Now, we must have badly painted the character of our adventure seeker, or our readers must have already perceived that d'Artagnan was not an ordinary man; therefore, while repeating to himself that his death was inevitable, he did not make up his mind to die quietly, as one less courageous and less restrained might have done in his place. He reflected upon the different characters of those with whom he was going to fight, and began to view his situation more clearly. He hoped, by means of loyal excuses, to make a friend of Athos, whose lordly air and austere bearing pleased him much. He flattered himself he should be able to frighten Porthos with the adventure of the baldric, which he might, if not killed upon the spot, relate to everybody a recital which, well managed, would cover Porthos with ridicule. As to the astute Aramis, he did not entertain much dread of him; and supposing he should be able to get so far, he determined to dispatch him in good style or at least, by hitting him in the face, as Caesar recommended his soldiers do to those of Pompey, to damage forever the beauty of which he was so proud.

In addition to this, d'Artagnan possessed that invincible stock of resolution which the counsels of his father had implanted in his heart: "Endure nothing from anyone but the king, the cardinal, and Monsieur de Tréville." He flew, then, rather than walked, toward the convent of the Carmes Dechausses, or rather Deschaux, as it was called at that period, a sort of building without a window, surrounded by barren fields–an accessory to the Preaux-Clercs, and which was generally employed as the place for the duels of men who had no time to lose.

When d'Artagnan arrived in sight of the bare spot of ground which extended along the foot of the monastery, Athos had been waiting about five minutes, and twelve o'clock was striking. He was, then, as punctual as the Samaritan woman, and the most rigorous casuist with regard to duels could have nothing to say.

Athos, who still suffered grievously from his wound, though it had been dressed anew by M. de Tréville's surgeon, was seated on a post and waiting for his adversary with hat in hand, his feather even touching the ground.

"Monsieur," said Athos, "I have engaged two of my friends as seconds, but these two friends are not yet come, at which I am astonished, as it is not at all their custom."

"I have no seconds on my part, Monsieur," said d'Artagnan, "for having only arrived yesterday in Paris, I as yet know no one but Monsieur de Tréville, to whom I was recommended by my father, who has the honour to be, in some degree, one of his friends."

Athos reflected for an instant. "You know no one but Monsieur de Tréville?" he asked.

"Yes, Monsieur, I know only him."

"Well, but then," continued Athos, speaking half to himself, "if I kill you, I shall have the air of a boy-slayer."

"Not too much so," replied d'Artagnan, with a bow that was not deficient in dignity, "since you do me the honour to draw a sword with me while suffering from a wound which is very inconvenient."

"Very inconvenient, upon my word; and you hurt me devilishly, I can tell you. But I will take the left hand–it is my custom in such circumstances. Do not fancy that I do you a favour; I use either hand easily. And it will be even a disadvantage to you; a left-handed man is very troublesome to people who are not prepared for it. I regret I did not inform you sooner of this circumstance."

"You have truly, Monsieur," said d'Artagnan, bowing again, "a courtesy, for which, I assure you, I am very grateful."

"You confuse me," replied Athos, with his gentlemanly air, "let us talk of something else, if you please. Ah, s'blood, how you have hurt me! My shoulder quite burns."

"If you would permit me–" said d'Artagnan, with timidity.

"What, Monsieur?"

"I have a miraculous balsam for wounds–a balsam given to me by my mother and of which I have made a trial upon myself."

"Well?"

"Well, I am sure that in less than three days this balsam would cure you; and at the end of three days, when you would be cured–well, Sir, it would still do me a great honour to be your man."

D'Artagnan spoke these words with a simplicity that did honour to his courtesy, without throwing the least doubt upon his courage.

"PARDIEU, Monsieur!" said Athos, "that's a proposition that pleases me; not that I can accept it, but a league off it savors of the gentleman. Thus spoke and acted the gallant knights of the time of Charlemagne, in whom every cavalier ought to seek his model. Unfortunately, we do not live in the times of the great emperor, we live in the times of the cardinal; and three days hence, however well the secret might be guarded, it would be known, I say, that we were to fight, and our combat would be prevented. I think these fellows will never come."

"If you are in haste, Monsieur," said d'Artagnan, with the same simplicity with which a moment before he had proposed to him to put off the duel for three days, "and if it be your will to dispatch me at once, do not inconvenience yourself, I pray you."

"There is another word which pleases me," cried Athos, with a gracious nod to d'Artagnan. "That did not come from a man without a heart. Monsieur, I love men of your kidney; and I foresee plainly that if we don't kill each other, I shall hereafter have much pleasure in your conversation. We will wait for these gentlemen, so please you; I have plenty of time, and it will be more correct. Ah, here is one of them, I believe."

In fact, at the end of the Rue Vaugirard the gigantic Porthos appeared.

"What!" cried d'Artagnan, "is your first witness Monsieur Porthos?"

"Yes, that disturbs you?"

"By no means."

"And here is the second."

D'Artagnan turned in the direction pointed to by Athos, and perceived Aramis.

"What!" cried he, in an accent of greater astonishment than before, "your second witness is Monsieur Aramis?"

"Doubtless! Are you not aware that we are never seen one without the others, and that we are called among the Musketeers and the Guards, at court and in the city, Athos, Porthos, and Aramis, or the Three Inseparables? And yet, as you come from Dax or Pau–"

"From Tarbes," said d'Artagnan.

"It is probable you are ignorant of this little fact," said Athos.

"My faith!" replied d'Artagnan, "you are well named, gentlemen; and my adventure, if it should make any noise, will prove at least that your union is not founded upon contrasts."

In the meantime, Porthos had come up, waved his hand to Athos, and then turning toward d'Artagnan, stood quite astonished.

Let us say in passing that he had changed his baldric and relinquished his cloak.

"Ah, ah!" said he, "what does this mean?"

"This is the gentleman I am going to fight with," said Athos, pointing to d'Artagnan with his hand and saluting him with the same gesture.

"Why, it is with him I am also going to fight," said Porthos.

"But not before one o'clock," replied d'Artagnan.

"And I also am to fight with this gentleman," said Aramis, coming in his turn onto the place.

"But not until two o'clock," said d'Artagnan, with the same calmness.

"But what are you going to fight about, Athos?" asked Aramis.

"Faith! I don't very well know. He hurt my shoulder. And you, Porthos?"

"Faith! I am going to fight–because I am going to fight," answered Porthos, reddening.

Athos, whose keen eye lost nothing, perceived a faintly sly smile pass over the lips of the young Gascon as he replied, "We had a short discussion upon dress."

"And you, Aramis?" asked Athos.

"Oh, ours is a theological quarrel," replied Aramis, making a sign to d'Artagnan to keep secret the cause of their duel.

Athos indeed saw a second smile on the lips of d'Artagnan.

"Indeed?" said Athos.

"Yes; a passage of St. Augustine, upon which we could not agree," said the Gascon.

"Decidedly, this is a clever fellow," murmured Athos.

"And now you are assembled, gentlemen," said d'Artagnan, "permit me to offer you my apologies."

At this word APOLOGIES, a cloud passed over the brow of Athos, a haughty smile curled the lip of Porthos, and a negative sign was the reply of Aramis.

"You do not understand me, gentlemen," said d'Artagnan, throwing up his head, the sharp and bold lines of which were at the moment gilded by a bright ray of the sun. "I asked to be excused in case I should not be able to discharge my debt to all three; for Monsieur Athos has the right to kill me first, which must much diminish the face-value of your bill, Monsieur Porthos, and render yours almost null, Monsieur Aramis. And now, gentlemen, I repeat, excuse me, but on that account only, and—on guard!"

At these words, with the most gallant air possible, d'Artagnan drew his sword.

The blood had mounted to the head of d'Artagnan, and at that moment he would have drawn his sword against all the Musketeers in the kingdom as willingly as he now did against Athos, Porthos, and Aramis.

It was a quarter past midday. The sun was in its zenith, and the spot chosen for the scene of the duel was exposed to its full ardor.

"It is very hot," said Athos, drawing his sword in its turn, "and yet I cannot take off my doublet; for I just now felt my wound begin to bleed again, and I should not like to annoy Monsieur with the sight of blood which he has not drawn from me himself."

"That is true, Monsieur," replied d'Artagnan, "and whether drawn by myself or another, I assure you I shall always view with regret the blood of so brave a gentleman. I will therefore fight in my doublet, like yourself."

"Come, come, enough of such compliments!" cried Porthos. "Remember, we are waiting for our turns."

"Speak for yourself when you are inclined to utter such incongruities," interrupted Aramis. "For my part, I think what they say is very well said, and quite worthy of two gentlemen."

"When you please, Monsieur," said Athos, putting himself on guard.

"I waited your orders," said d'Artagnan, crossing swords.

But scarcely had the two rapiers clashed, when a company of the Guards of his Eminence, commanded by M. de Jussac, turned the corner of the convent.

"The cardinal's Guards!" cried Aramis and Porthos at the same time. "Sheathe your swords, gentlemen, sheathe your swords!"

But it was too late. The two combatants had been seen in a position which left no doubt of their intentions.

"Halloo!" cried Jussac, advancing toward them and making a sign to his men to do so likewise, "halloo, Musketeers? Fighting here, are you? And the edicts? What is become of them?"

"You are very generous, gentlemen of the Guards," said Athos, full of rancor, for Jussac was one of the aggressors of the preceding day. "If we were to see you fighting, I can assure you that we would make no effort to prevent you. Leave us alone, then, and you will enjoy a little amusement without cost to yourselves."

"Gentlemen," said Jussac, "it is with great regret that I pronounce the thing impossible. Duty before everything. Sheathe, then, if you please, and follow us."

"Monsieur," said Aramis, parodying Jussac, "it would afford us great pleasure to obey your polite invitation if it depended upon ourselves, but unfortunately the thing is impossible–Monsieur de Tréville has forbidden it. Pass on your way, then; it is the best thing to do."

This raillery exasperated Jussac. "We will charge upon you, then," said he, "if you disobey."

"There are five of them," said Athos, half aloud, "and we are but three; we shall be beaten again, and must die on the spot, for, on my part, I declare I will never appear again before the captain as a conquered man."

Athos, Porthos, and Aramis instantly drew near one another, while Jussac drew up his soldiers.

This short interval was sufficient to determine d'Artagnan on the part he was to take. It was one of those events which decide the life of a man; it was a choice between the king and the cardinal–the choice made, it must be persisted in. To fight, that was to disobey the law, that was to risk his head, that was to make at one blow an enemy of a minister more powerful than the king himself. All this the young man perceived, and yet, to his praise we speak it, he did not hesitate a second. Turning towards Athos and his friends, "Gentlemen," said he, "allow me to correct your words, if you please. You said you were but three, but it appears to me we are four."

"But you are not one of us," said Porthos.

"That's true," replied d'Artagnan, "I have not the uniform, but I have the spirit. My heart is that of a Musketeer; I feel it, Monsieur, and that impels me on."

"Withdraw, young man," cried Jussac, who doubtless, by his gestures and the expression of his countenance, had guessed d'Artagnan's design. "You may retire; we consent to that. Save your skin; begone quickly."

D'Artagnan did not budge.

"Decidedly, you are a brave fellow," said Athos, pressing the young man's hand.

"Come, come, choose your part," replied Jussac.

"Well," said Porthos to Aramis, "we must do something."

"Monsieur is full of generosity," said Athos.

But all three reflected upon the youth of d'Artagnan, and dreaded his inexperience.

"We should only be three, one of whom is wounded, with the addition of a boy," resumed Athos, "and yet it will not be the less said we were four men."

"Yes, but to yield!" said Porthos.

"That IS difficult," replied Athos.

D'Artagnan comprehended their irresolution.

"Try me, gentlemen," said he, "and I swear to you by my honour that I will not go hence if we are conquered."

"What is your name, my brave fellow?" said Athos.

"D'Artagnan, Monsieur."

"Well, then, Athos, Porthos, Aramis, and d'Artagnan, forward!" cried Athos.

"Come, gentlemen, have you decided?" cried Jussac for the third time.

"It is done, gentlemen," said Athos.

"And what is your choice?" asked Jussac.

"We are about to have the honour of charging you," replied Aramis, lifting his hat with one hand and drawing his sword with the other.

"Ah! You resist, do you?" cried Jussac.

"S'blood; does that astonish you?"

And the nine combatants rushed upon each other with a fury which however did not exclude a certain degree of method.

Athos fixed upon a certain Cahusac, a favourite of the cardinal's. Porthos had Bicarat, and Aramis found himself opposed to two adversaries. As to d'Artagnan, he sprang toward Jussac himself.

The heart of the young Gascon beat as if it would burst through his side–not from fear, God be thanked, he had not the shade of it, but with emulation; he fought like a furious tiger, turning ten times round his adversary, and changing his ground and his guard twenty times. Jussac was, as was then said, a fine blade, and had had much practice; nevertheless it required all his skill to defend himself against an adversary who, active and energetic, departed every instant from received rules, attacking him on all sides at once, and yet parrying like a man who had the greatest respect for his own epidermis.

This contest at length exhausted Jussac's patience. Furious at being held in check by one whom he had considered a boy, he became warm and began to make mistakes. D'Artagnan, who though wanting in practice had a sound theory, redoubled his agility. Jussac, anxious to put an end to this, springing forward, aimed a terrible thrust at his adversary, but the latter parried it; and while Jussac was recovering himself, glided like a serpent beneath his blade, and passed his sword through his body. Jussac fell like a dead mass.

D'Artagnan then cast an anxious and rapid glance over the field of battle.

Aramis had killed one of his adversaries, but the other pressed him warmly. Nevertheless, Aramis was in a good situation, and able to defend himself.

Bicarat and Porthos had just made counterhits. Porthos had received a thrust through his arm, and Bicarat one through his thigh. But neither of these two wounds was serious, and they only fought more earnestly.

Athos, wounded anew by Cahusac, became evidently paler, but did not give way a foot. He only changed his sword hand, and fought with his left hand.

According to the laws of dueling at that period, d'Artagnan was at liberty to assist whom he pleased. While he was endeavouring to find out which of his companions stood in greatest need, he caught a glance from Athos. The glance was of sublime eloquence. Athos would have died rather than appeal for help, but he could look, and with that look ask assistance. D'Artagnan interpreted it; with a terrible bound he sprang to the side of Cahusac, crying, "To me, Monsieur Guardsman; I will slay you!"

Cahusac turned. It was time; for Athos, whose great courage alone supported him, sank upon his knee.

"S'blood!" cried he to d'Artagnan, "do not kill him, young man, I beg of you. I have an old affair to settle with him when I am cured and sound again. Disarm him only–make sure of his sword. That's it! Very well done!"

The exclamation was drawn from Athos by seeing the sword of Cahusac fly twenty paces from him. D'Artagnan and Cahusac sprang forward at the same instant, the one to recover, the other to obtain, the sword, but d'Artagnan, being the more active, reached it first and placed his foot upon it.

Cahusac immediately ran to the Guardsman whom Aramis had killed, seized his rapier, and returned toward d'Artagnan, but on his way he met Athos, who during his relief which d'Artagnan had procured him had recovered his breath, and who, for fear that d'Artagnan would kill his enemy, wished to resume the fight.

D'Artagnan perceived that it would be disobliging Athos not to leave him alone; and in a few minutes Cahusac fell, with a sword thrust through his throat.

At the same instant Aramis placed his sword point on the breast of his fallen enemy, and forced him to ask for mercy.

There only then remained Porthos and Bicarat. Porthos made a thousand flourishes, asking Bicarat what o'clock it could be, and offering him his compliments upon his brother's having just obtained a company in the regiment of Navarre; but, jest as he might, he gained nothing. Bicarat was one of those iron men who never fell dead.

Nevertheless, it was necessary to finish. The watch might come up and take all the combatants, wounded or not, royalists or cardinalists. Athos, Aramis, and d'Artagnan surrounded Bicarat, and required him to surrender. Though alone against all and with a wound in his thigh, Bicarat wished to hold out, but Jussac, who had risen upon his elbow, cried out to him to yield. Bicarat was a Gascon, as d'Artagnan was; he turned a deaf ear, and contented himself with laughing, and between two parries finding time to point to a spot of earth with his sword, "Here," cried he, parodying a verse of the Bible, "here will Bicarat die; for I only am left, and they seek my life."

"But there are four against you; leave off, I command you."

"Ah, if you command me, that's another thing," said Bicarat. "As you are my commander, it is my duty to obey." And springing backward, he broke his sword across his knee to avoid the necessity of surrendering it, threw the pieces over the convent wall, and crossed him arms, whistling a cardinalist air.

Bravery is always respected, even in an enemy. The Musketeers saluted Bicarat with their swords, and returned them to their sheaths. D'Artagnan did the same. Then, assisted by Bicarat, the only one left standing, they bore Jussac, Cahusac, and one of Aramis's adversaries who was only wounded, under the porch of the convent. The fourth, as we have said, was dead. They then rang the bell, and carrying away four swords out of five, they took their road, intoxicated with joy, toward the hotel of M. de Tréville.

They walked arm in arm, occupying the whole width of the street and taking in every Musketeer they met, so that in the end it became a triumphal march. The heart of d'Artagnan swam in delirium; he marched between Athos and Porthos, pressing them tenderly.

"If I am not yet a Musketeer," said he to his new friends, as he passed through the gateway of M. de Tréville's hotel, "at least I have entered upon my apprenticeship, haven't I?"

Chapter 6

His Majesty King Louis XIII

This affair made a great noise. M. de Tréville scolded his Musketeers in public, and congratulated them in private, but as no time was to be lost in gaining the king, M. de Tréville hastened to report himself at the Louvre. It was already too late. The king was closeted with the cardinal, and M. de Tréville was informed that the king was busy and could not receive him at that moment. In the evening M. de Tréville attended the king's gaming table. The king was winning; and as he was very avaricious, he was in an excellent humor. Perceiving M. de Tréville at a distance–

"Come here, Monsieur Captain," said he, "come here, that I may growl at you. Do you know that his Eminence has been making fresh complaints against your Musketeers, and that with so much emotion, that this evening his Eminence is indisposed? Ah, these Musketeers of yours are very devils–fellows to be hanged."

"No, Sire," replied Tréville, who saw at the first glance how things would go, "on the contrary, they are good creatures, as meek as lambs, and have but one desire, I'll be their warranty. And that is that their swords may never leave their scabbards but in your majesty's service. But what are they to do? The Guards of Monsieur the Cardinal are forever seeking quarrels with them, and for the honour of the corps even, the poor young men are obliged to defend themselves."

"Listen to Monsieur de Tréville," said the king, "listen to him! Would not one say he was speaking of a religious community? In truth, my dear Captain, I have a great mind to take away your commission and give it to Mademoiselle de Chemerault, to whom I promised an abbey. But don't fancy that I am going to take you on your bare word. I am called Louis the Just, Monsieur de Tréville, and by and by, by and by we will see."

"Ah, Sire; it is because I confide in that justice that I shall wait patiently and quietly the good pleasure of your Majesty."

"Wait, then, Monsieur, wait," said the king, "I will not detain you long."

In fact, fortune changed; and as the king began to lose what he had won, he was not sorry to find an excuse for playing Charlemagne–if we may use a gaming phrase of whose origin we confess our ignorance. The king therefore arose a minute after, and putting the money which lay before him into his pocket, the major part of which arose from his winnings, "La Vieuville," said he, "take my place; I must speak to Monsieur de Tréville on an affair of importance. Ah, I had eighty louis before me; put down the same sum, so that they who have lost may have nothing to complain of. Justice before everything."

Then turning toward M. de Tréville and walking with him toward the embrasure of a window, "Well, Monsieur," continued he, "you say it is his Eminence's Guards who have sought a quarrel with your Musketeers?"

"Yes, Sire, as they always do."

"And how did the thing happen? Let us see, for you know, my dear Captain, a judge must hear both sides."

"Good Lord! In the most simple and natural manner possible. Three of my best soldiers, whom your Majesty knows by name, and whose devotedness you have more than once appreciated, and who have, I dare affirm to the king, his service much at heart– three of my best soldiers, I say, Athos, Porthos, and Aramis, had made a party of pleasure with a young fellow from Gascony, whom I had introduced to them the same morning. The party was to take place at St. Germain, I believe, and they had appointed to meet at the Carmes-Deschaux, when they were disturbed by de Jussac, Cahusac, Bicarat, and two other Guardsmen, who certainly did not go there in such a numerous company without some ill intention against the edicts."

"Ah, ah! You incline me to think so," said the king. "There is no doubt they went thither to fight themselves."

"I do not accuse them, Sire, but I leave your Majesty to judge what five armed men could possibly be going to do in such a deserted place as the neighbourhood of the Convent des Carmes."

"Yes, you are right, Tréville, you are right!"

"Then, upon seeing my Musketeers they changed their minds, and forgot their private hatred for partisan hatred; for your Majesty cannot be ignorant that the Musketeers, who belong to the king and nobody but the king, are the natural enemies of the Guardsmen, who belong to the cardinal."

"Yes, Tréville, yes," said the king, in a melancholy tone, "and it is very sad, believe me, to see thus two parties in France, two heads to royalty. But all this will come to an end, Tréville, will come to an end. You say, then, that the Guardsmen sought a quarrel with the Musketeers?"

"I say that it is probable that things have fallen out so, but I will not swear to it, Sire. You know how difficult it is to discover the truth; and unless a man be endowed with that admirable instinct which causes Louis XIII to be named the Just–"

"You are right, Tréville, but they were not alone, your Musketeers. They had a youth with them?"

"Yes, Sire, and one wounded man; so that three of the king's Musketeers–one of whom was wounded–and a youth not only maintained their ground against five of the most terrible of the cardinal's Guardsmen, but absolutely brought four of them to earth."

"Why, this is a victory!" cried the king, all radiant, "a complete victory!"

"Yes, Sire; as complete as that of the Bridge of Ce."

"Four men, one of them wounded, and a youth, say you?"

"One hardly a young man, but who, however, behaved himself so admirably on this occasion that I will take the liberty of recommending him to your Majesty."

"How does he call himself?"

"D'Artagnan, Sire; he is the son of one of my oldest friends–the son of a man who served under the king your father, of glorious memory, in the civil war."

"And you say this young man behaved himself well? Tell me how, Tréville–you know how I delight in accounts of war and fighting."

And Louis XIII twisted his moustache proudly, placing his hand upon his hip.

"Sire," resumed Tréville, "as I told you, Monsieur d'Artagnan is little more than a boy; and as he has not the honour of being a Musketeer, he was dressed as a citizen. The Guards of the cardinal, perceiving his youth and that he did not belong to the corps, invited him to retire before they attacked."

"So you may plainly see, Tréville," interrupted the king, "it was they who attacked?"

"That is true, Sire; there can be no more doubt on that head. They called upon him then to retire, but he answered that he was a Musketeer at heart, entirely devoted to your Majesty, and that therefore he would remain with Messieurs the Musketeers."

"Brave young man!" murmured the king.

"Well, he did remain with them; and your Majesty has in him so firm a champion that it was he who gave Jussac the terrible sword thrust which has made the cardinal so angry."

"He who wounded Jussac!" cried the king, "he, a boy! Tréville, that's impossible!"

"It is as I have the honour to relate it to your Majesty."

"Jussac, one of the first swordsmen in the kingdom?"

"Well, Sire, for once he found his master."

"I will see this young man, Tréville–I will see him; and if anything can be done–well, we will make it our business."

"When will your Majesty deign to receive him?"

"Tomorrow, at midday, Tréville."

"Shall I bring him alone?"

"No, bring me all four together. I wish to thank them all at once. Devoted men are so rare, Tréville, by the back staircase. It is useless to let the cardinal know."

"Yes, Sire."

"You understand, Tréville–an edict is still an edict, it is forbidden to fight, after all."

"But this encounter, Sire, is quite out of the ordinary conditions of a duel. It is a brawl; and the proof is that there were five of the cardinal's Guardsmen against my three Musketeers and Monsieur d'Artagnan."

"That is true," said the king, "but never mind, Tréville, come still by the back staircase."

Tréville smiled, but as it was indeed something to have prevailed upon this child to rebel against his master, he saluted the king respectfully, and with this agreement, took leave of him.

That evening the three Musketeers were informed of the honour accorded them. As they had long been acquainted with the king, they were not much excited, but d'Artagnan, with his Gascon imagination, saw in it his future fortune, and passed the night in golden dreams. By eight o'clock in the morning he was at the apartment of Athos.

D'Artagnan found the Musketeer dressed and ready to go out. As the hour to wait upon the king was not till twelve, he had made a party with Porthos and Aramis to play a game at tennis in a tennis court situated near the stables of the Luxembourg. Athos invited d'Artagnan to follow them; and although ignorant of the game, which he had never played, he accepted, not knowing what to do with his time from nine o'clock in the morning, as it then scarcely was, till twelve.

The two Musketeers were already there, and were playing together. Athos, who was very expert in all bodily exercises, passed with d'Artagnan to the opposite side and challenged them, but at the first effort he made, although he played with his left hand, he found that his wound was yet too recent to allow of such exertion. D'Artagnan remained, therefore, alone; and as he declared he was too ignorant of the game to play it regularly they only continued giving balls to one another without counting. But one of these balls, launched by Porthos' herculean hand, passed so close to d'Artagnan's face that he thought that if, instead of passing near, it had hit him, his audience would have been probably lost, as it would have been impossible for him to present himself before the king. Now, as upon this audience, in his Gascon imagination, depended his future life, he saluted Aramis and Porthos politely, declaring that he would not resume the game until he should be prepared to play with them on more equal terms, and went and took his place near the cord and in the gallery.

Unfortunately for d'Artagnan, among the spectators was one of his Eminence's Guardsmen, who, still irritated by the defeat of his companions, which had happened only the day before, had promised himself to seize the first opportunity of avenging it. He believed this opportunity was now come and addressed his neighbour: "It is not astonishing that that young man should be afraid of a ball, for he is doubtless a Musketeer apprentice."

D'Artagnan turned round as if a serpent had stung him, and fixed his eyes intensely upon the Guardsman who had just made this insolent speech.

"PARDIEU," resumed the latter, twisting his moustache, "look at me as long as you like, my little gentleman! I have said what I have said."

"And as since that which you have said is too clear to require any explanation," replied d'Artagnan, in a low voice, "I beg you to follow me."

"And when?" asked the Guardsman, with the same jeering air.

"At once, if you please."

"And you know who I am, without doubt?"

"I? I am completely ignorant; nor does it much disquiet me."

"You're in the wrong there; for if you knew my name, perhaps you would not be so pressing."

"What is your name?"

"Bernajoux, at your service."

"Well, then, Monsieur Bernajoux," said d'Artagnan, tranquilly, "I will wait for you at the door."

"Go, Monsieur, I will follow you."

"Do not hurry yourself, Monsieur, lest it be observed that we go out together. You must be aware that for our undertaking, company would be in the way."

"That's true," said the Guardsman, astonished that his name had not produced more effect upon the young man.

Indeed, the name of Bernajoux was known to all the world, d'Artagnan alone excepted, perhaps; for it was one of those which figured most frequently in the daily brawls which all the edicts of the cardinal could not repress.

Porthos and Aramis were so engaged with their game, and Athos was watching them with so much attention, that they did not even perceive their young companion go out, who, as he had told the Guardsman of his Eminence, stopped outside the door. An instant after, the Guardsman descended in his turn. As d'Artagnan had no time to lose, on account of the audience of the king, which was fixed for midday, he cast his eyes around, and seeing that the street was empty, said to his adversary, "My faith! It is fortunate for you, although your name is Bernajoux, to have only to deal with an apprentice Musketeer. Never mind; be content, I will do my best. On guard!"

"But," said he whom d'Artagnan thus provoked, "it appears to me that this place is badly chosen, and that we should be better behind the Abbey St. Germain or in the Pre-aux-Clercs."

"What you say is full of sense," replied d'Artagnan, "but unfortunately I have very little time to spare, having an appointment at twelve precisely. On guard, then, Monsieur, on guard!"

Bernajoux was not a man to have such a compliment paid to him twice. In an instant his sword glittered in his hand, and he sprang upon his adversary, whom, thanks to his great youthfulness, he hoped to intimidate.

But d'Artagnan had on the preceding day served his apprenticeship. Fresh sharpened by his victory, full of hopes of future favour, he was resolved not to recoil a step. So the two swords were crossed close to the hilts, and as d'Artagnan stood firm, it was his adversary who made the retreating step, but d'Artagnan seized the moment at which, in this movement, the sword of Bernajoux deviated from the line. He freed his weapon, made a lunge, and touched his adversary on the shoulder. D'Artagnan immediately made a step backward and raised his sword, but Bernajoux cried out that it was nothing, and rushing blindly upon him, absolutely spitted himself upon d'Artagnan's sword. As, however, he did not fall, as he did not declare himself conquered, but only broke away toward the hotel of M. de la Trémouille, in whose service he had a relative, d'Artagnan was ignorant of the seriousness of the last wound his adversary had received, and pressing him warmly, without doubt would soon have completed his work with a third blow, when the noise which arose from the street being heard in the tennis court, two of the friends of the Guardsman, who had seen him go out after exchanging some words with d'Artagnan, rushed, sword in hand, from the court, and fell upon the conqueror. But Athos, Porthos, and Aramis quickly appeared in their turn, and the moment the two Guardsmen attacked their young companion, drove them back. Bernajoux now fell, and as the Guardsmen were only two against four, they began to cry, "To the rescue! The Hotel de la Trémouille!" At these cries, all who were in the hotel rushed out and fell upon the four companions, who on their side cried aloud, "To the rescue, Musketeers!"

This cry was generally heeded; for the Musketeers were known to be enemies of the cardinal, and were beloved on account of the hatred they bore to his Eminence. Thus the soldiers of other companies than those which belonged to the Red Duke, as Aramis had called him, often took part with the king's Musketeers in these quarrels. Of three Guardsmen of the company of M. Dessessart who were passing, two came to the assistance of the four companions, while the other ran toward the hotel of M. de Tréville, crying, "To the rescue, Musketeers! To the rescue!" As usual, this hotel was full of soldiers of this company, who hastened to the succor of their comrades. The MÊLÉE became general, but strength was on the side of the Musketeers. The cardinal's Guards and M. de la Trémouille's people retreated into the hotel, the doors of which they closed just in time to prevent their enemies from entering with them. As to the wounded man, he had been taken in at once, and, as we have said, in a very bad state.

Excitement was at its height among the Musketeers and their allies, and they even began to deliberate whether they should not set fire to the hotel to punish the insolence of M. de la Trémouille's domestics in daring to make a SORTIE upon the king's Musketeers. The proposition had been made, and received with enthusiasm, when fortunately eleven o'clock struck. D'Artagnan and his companions remembered their audience, and as they would very much have regretted that such an opportunity should be lost, they succeeded in calming their friends, who contented themselves with hurling some paving stones against the gates, but the gates were too strong. They soon tired of the sport. Besides, those who must be considered the leaders of the enterprise had quit the group and were making their way toward the hotel of M. de Tréville, who was waiting for them, already informed of this fresh disturbance.

"Quick to the Louvre," said he, "to the Louvre without losing an instant, and let us endeavour to see the king before he is prejudiced by the cardinal. We will describe the thing to him as a consequence of the affair of yesterday, and the two will pass off together."

M. de Tréville, accompanied by the four young fellows, directed his course toward the Louvre, but to the great astonishment of the captain of the Musketeers, he was informed that the king had gone stag hunting in the forest of St. Germain. M. de Tréville required this intelligence to be repeated to him twice, and each time his companions saw his brow become darker.

"Had his Majesty," asked he, "any intention of holding this hunting party yesterday?"

"No, your Excellency," replied the valet de chambre, "the Master of the Hounds came this morning to inform him that he had marked down a stag. At first the king answered that he would not go, but he could not resist his love of sport, and set out after dinner."

"And the king has seen the cardinal?" asked M. de Tréville.

"In all probability he has," replied the valet, "for I saw the horses harnessed to his Eminence's carriage this morning, and when I asked where he was going, they told me, 'To St. Germain.'"

"He is beforehand with us," said M. de Tréville. "Gentlemen, I will see the king this evening, but as to you, I do not advise you to risk doing so."

This advice was too reasonable, and moreover came from a man who knew the king too well, to allow the four young men to dispute it. M. de Tréville recommended everyone to return home and wait for news.

On entering his hotel, M. de Tréville thought it best to be first in making the complaint. He sent one of his servants to M. de la Trémouille with a letter in which he begged of him to eject the cardinal's Guardsmen from his house, and to reprimand his people for their audacity in making SORTIE against the king's Musketeers. But M. de la Trémouille–already prejudiced by his esquire, whose relative, as we already know, Bernajoux was–replied that it was neither for M. de Tréville nor the Musketeers to complain, but, on the contrary, for him, whose people the Musketeers had assaulted and whose hotel they had endeavoured to burn. Now, as the debate between these two nobles might last a long time, each becoming, naturally, more firm in his own opinion, M. de Tréville thought of an expedient which might terminate it quietly. This was to go himself to M. de la Trémouille.

He repaired, therefore, immediately to his hotel, and caused himself to be announced.

The two nobles saluted each other politely, for if no friendship existed between them, there was at least esteem. Both were men of courage and honour; and as M. de la Trémouille–a Protestant, and seeing the king seldom–was of no party, he did not, in general, carry any bias into his social relations. This time, however, his address, although polite, was cooler than usual.

"Monsieur," said M. de Tréville, "we fancy that we have each cause to complain of the other, and I am come to endeavour to clear up this affair."

"I have no objection," replied M. de la Trémouille, "but I warn you that I am well informed, and all the fault is with your Musketeers."

"You are too just and reasonable a man, Monsieur!" said Tréville, "not to accept the proposal I am about to make to you."

"Make it, Monsieur, I listen."

"How is Monsieur Bernajoux, your esquire's relative?"

"Why, Monsieur, very ill indeed! In addition to the sword thrust in his arm, which is not dangerous, he has received another right through his lungs, of which the doctor says bad things."

"But has the wounded man retained his senses?"

"Perfectly."

"Does he talk?"

"With difficulty, but he can speak."

"Well, Monsieur, let us go to him. Let us adjure him, in the name of the God before whom he must perhaps appear, to speak the truth. I will take him for judge in his own cause, Monsieur, and will believe what he will say."

M. de la Trémouille reflected for an instant; then as it was difficult to suggest a more reasonable proposal, he agreed to it.

Both descended to the chamber in which the wounded man lay. The latter, on seeing these two noble lords who came to visit him, endeavoured to raise himself up in his bed, but he was too weak, and exhausted by the effort, he fell back again almost senseless.

M. de la Trémouille approached him, and made him inhale some salts, which recalled him to life. Then M. de Tréville, unwilling that it should be thought that he had influenced the wounded man, requested M. de la Trémouille to interrogate him himself.

That happened which M. de Tréville had foreseen. Placed between life and death, as Bernajoux was, he had no idea for a moment of concealing the truth; and he described to the two nobles the affair exactly as it had passed.

This was all that M. de Tréville wanted. He wished Bernajoux a speedy convalescence, took leave of M. de la Trémouille, returned to his hotel, and immediately sent word to the four friends that he awaited their company at dinner.

M. de Tréville entertained good company, wholly anticardinalist, though. It may easily be understood, therefore, that the conversation during the whole of dinner turned upon the two checks that his Eminence's Guardsmen had received. Now, as d'Artagnan had been the hero of these two fights, it was upon him that all the felicitations fell, which Athos, Porthos, and Aramis abandoned to him, not only as good comrades, but as men who had so often had their turn that they could very well afford him his.

Toward six o'clock M. de Tréville announced that it was time to go to the Louvre, but as the hour of audience granted by his Majesty was past, instead of claiming the ENTRÉE by the back stairs, he placed himself with the four young men in the antechamber. The king had not yet returned from hunting. Our young men had been waiting about half an hour, amid a crowd of courtiers, when all the doors were thrown open, and his Majesty was announced.

At his announcement d'Artagnan felt himself tremble to the very marrow of his bones. The coming instant would in all probability decide the rest of his life. His eyes therefore were fixed in a sort of agony upon the door through which the king must enter.

Louis XIII appeared, walking fast. He was in hunting costume covered with dust, wearing large boots, and holding a whip in his hand. At the first glance, d'Artagnan judged that the mind of the king was stormy.

This disposition, visible as it was in his Majesty, did not prevent the courtiers from ranging themselves along his pathway. In royal antechambers it is worth more to be viewed with an angry eye than not to be seen at all. The three Musketeers therefore did not hesitate to make a step forward. D'Artagnan on the contrary remained concealed behind them, but although the king knew Athos, Porthos, and Aramis personally, he passed before them without speaking or looking–indeed, as if he had never seen them before. As for M. de Tréville, when the eyes of the king fell upon him, he sustained the look with so much firmness that it was the king who dropped his eyes; after which his Majesty, grumbling, entered his apartment.

"Matters go but badly," said Athos, smiling, "and we shall not be made Chevaliers of the Order this time."

"Wait here ten minutes," said M. de Tréville, "and if at the expiration of ten minutes you do not see me come out, return to my hotel, for it will be useless for you to wait for me longer."

The four young men waited ten minutes, a quarter of an hour, twenty minutes; and seeing that M. de Tréville did not return, went away very uneasy as to what was going to happen.

M. de Tréville entered the king's cabinet boldly, and found his Majesty in a very ill humor, seated on an armchair, beating his boot with the handle of his whip. This, however, did not prevent his asking, with the greatest coolness, after his Majesty's health.

"Bad, Monsieur, bad!" replied the king, "I am bored."

This was, in fact, the worst complaint of Louis XIII, who would sometimes take one of his courtiers to a window and say, "Monsieur So-and-so, let us weary ourselves together."

"How! Your Majesty is bored? Have you not enjoyed the pleasures of the chase today?"

"A fine pleasure, indeed, Monsieur! Upon my soul, everything degenerates; and I don't know whether it is the game which leaves no scent, or the dogs that have no noses. We started a stag of ten branches. We chased him for six hours, and when he was near being taken–when St.-Simon was already putting his horn to his mouth to sound the mort–crack, all the pack takes the wrong scent and sets off after a two-year-older. I shall be obliged to give up hunting, as I have given up hawking. Ah, I am an unfortunate king, Monsieur de Tréville! I had but one gerfalcon, and he died day before yesterday."

"Indeed, Sire, I wholly comprehend your disappointment. The misfortune is great, but I think you have still a good number of falcons, sparrow hawks, and tiercets."

"And not a man to instruct them. Falconers are declining. I know no one but myself who is acquainted with the noble art of venery. After me it will all be over, and people will hunt with gins, snares, and traps. If I had but the time to train pupils! But there is the cardinal always at hand, who does not leave me a moment's repose; who talks to me about Spain, who talks to me about Austria, who talks to me about England! Ah! À PROPOS of the cardinal, Monsieur de Tréville, I am vexed with you!"

This was the chance at which M. de Tréville waited for the king. He knew the king of old, and he knew that all these complaints were but a preface–a sort of excitation to encourage himself–and that he had now come to his point at last.

"And in what have I been so unfortunate as to displease your Majesty?" asked M. de Tréville, feigning the most profound astonishment.

"Is it thus you perform your charge, Monsieur?" continued the king, without directly replying to de Tréville's question. "Is it for this I name you captain of my Musketeers, that they should assassinate a man, disturb a whole quarter, and endeavour to set fire to Paris, without your saying a word? But yet," continued the king, "undoubtedly my haste accuses you wrongfully; without doubt the rioters are in prison, and you come to tell me justice is done."

"Sire," replied M. de Tréville, calmly, "on the contrary, I come to demand it of you."

"And against whom?" cried the king.

"Against calumniators," said M. de Tréville.

"Ah! This is something new," replied the king. "Will you tell me that your three damned Musketeers, Athos, Porthos, and Aramis, and your youngster from Bearn, have not fallen, like so many furies, upon poor Bernajoux, and have not maltreated him in such a fashion that probably by this time he is dead? Will you tell me that they did not lay siege to the hotel of the Duc de la Trémouille, and that they did not endeavour to burn it?–Which would not, perhaps, have been a great misfortune in time of war, seeing that it is nothing but a nest of Huguenots, but which is, in time of peace, a frightful example. Tell me, now, can you deny all this?"

"And who told you this fine story, Sire?" asked Tréville, quietly.

"Who has told me this fine story, Monsieur? Who should it be but he who watches while I sleep, who labors while I amuse myself, who conducts everything at home and abroad–in France as in Europe?"

"Your Majesty probably refers to God," said M. de Tréville, "for I know no one except God who can be so far above your Majesty."

"No, Monsieur; I speak of the prop of the state, of my only servant, of my only friend–of the cardinal."

"His Eminence is not his holiness, Sire."

"What do you mean by that, Monsieur?"

"That it is only the Pope who is infallible, and that this infallibility does not extend to cardinals."

"You mean to say that he deceives me; you mean to say that he betrays me? You accuse him, then? Come, speak; avow freely that you accuse him!"

"No, Sire, but I say that he deceives himself. I say that he is ill-informed. I say that he has hastily accused your Majesty's Musketeers, toward whom he is unjust, and that he has not obtained his information from good sources."

"The accusation comes from Monsieur de la Trémouille, from the duke himself. What do you say to that?"

"I might answer, Sire, that he is too deeply interested in the question to be a very impartial witness, but so far from that, Sire, I know the duke to be a royal gentleman, and I refer the matter to him–but upon one condition, Sire."

"What?"

"It is that your Majesty will make him come here, will interrogate him yourself, TÊTE-À-TÊTE, without witnesses, and that I shall see your Majesty as soon as you have seen the duke."

"What, then! You will bind yourself," cried the king, "by what Monsieur de la Trémouille shall say?"

"Yes, Sire."

"You will accept his judgement?"

"Undoubtedly."

"And you will submit to the reparation he may require?"

"Certainly."

"La Chesnaye," said the king. "La Chesnaye!"

Louis XIII's confidential valet, who never left the door, entered in reply to the call.

"La Chesnaye," said the king, "let someone go instantly and find Monsieur de la Trémouille; I wish to speak with him this evening."

"Your Majesty gives me your word that you will not see anyone between Monsieur de la Trémouille and myself?"

"Nobody, by the faith of a gentleman."

"Tomorrow, then, Sire?"

"Tomorrow, Monsieur."

"At what o'clock, please your Majesty?"

"At any hour you will."

"But in coming too early I should be afraid of awakening your Majesty."

"Awaken me! Do you think I ever sleep, then? I sleep no longer, Monsieur. I sometimes dream, that's all. Come, then, as early as you like–at seven o'clock, but beware, if you and your Musketeers are guilty."

"If my Musketeers are guilty, Sire, the guilty shall be placed in your Majesty's hands, who will dispose of them at your good pleasure. Does your Majesty require anything further? Speak, I am ready to obey."

"No, Monsieur, no; I am not called Louis the Just without reason. Tomorrow, then, Monsieur–tomorrow."

"Till then, God preserve your Majesty!"

However ill the king might sleep, M. de Tréville slept still worse. He had ordered his three Musketeers and their companion to be with him at half past six in the morning. He took them with him, without encouraging them or promising them anything, and without concealing from them that their luck, and even his own, depended upon the cast of the dice.

Arrived at the foot of the back stairs, he desired them to wait. If the king was still irritated against them, they would depart without being seen; if the king consented to see them, they would only have to be called.

On arriving at the king's private antechamber, M. de Tréville found La Chesnaye, who informed him that they had not been able to find M. de la Trémouille on the preceding evening at his hotel, that he returned too late to present himself at the Louvre, that he had only that moment arrived and that he was at that very hour with the king.

This circumstance pleased M. de Tréville much, as he thus became certain that no foreign suggestion could insinuate itself between M. de la Trémouille's testimony and himself.

In fact, ten minutes had scarcely passed away when the door of the king's closet opened, and M. de Tréville saw M. de la Trémouille come out. The duke came straight up to him, and said: "Monsieur de Tréville, his Majesty has just sent for me in order to inquire respecting the circumstances which took place yesterday at my hotel. I have told him the truth; that is to say, that the fault lay with my people, and that I was ready to offer you my excuses. Since I have the good fortune to meet you, I beg you to receive them, and to hold me always as one of your friends."

"Monsieur the Duke," said M. de Tréville, "I was so confident of your loyalty that I required no other defender before his Majesty than yourself. I find that I have not been mistaken, and I thank you that there is still one man in France of whom may be said, without disappointment, what I have said of you."

"That's well said," cried the king, who had heard all these compliments through the open door, "only tell him, Tréville, since he wishes to be considered your friend, that I also wish to be one of his, but he neglects me; that it is nearly three years since I have seen him, and that I never do see him unless I send for him. Tell him all this for me, for these are things which a king cannot say for himself."

"Thanks, Sire, thanks," said the duke, "but your Majesty may be assured that it is not those–I do not speak of Monsieur de Tréville–whom your Majesty sees at all hours of the day that are most devoted to you."

"Ah! You have heard what I said? So much the better, Duke, so much the better," said the king, advancing toward the door. "Ah! It is you, Tréville. Where are your Musketeers? I told you the day before yesterday to bring them with you; why have you not done so?"

"They are below, Sire, and with your permission La Chesnaye will bid them come up."

"Yes, yes, let them come up immediately. It is nearly eight o'clock, and at nine I expect a visit. Go, Monsieur Duke, and return often. Come in, Tréville."

The Duke saluted and retired. At the moment he opened the door, the three Musketeers and d'Artagnan, conducted by La Chesnaye, appeared at the top of the staircase.

"Come in, my braves," said the king, "come in; I am going to scold you."

The Musketeers advanced, bowing, d'Artagnan following closely behind them.

"What the devil!" continued the king. "Seven of his Eminence's Guards placed HORS DE COMBAT by you four in two days! That's too many, gentlemen, too many! If you go on so, his Eminence will be forced to renew his company in three weeks, and I to put the edicts in force in all their rigor. One now and then I don't say much about, but seven in two days, I repeat, it is too many, it is far too many!"

"Therefore, Sire, your Majesty sees that they are come, quite contrite and repentant, to offer you their excuses."

"Quite contrite and repentant! Hem!" said the king. "I place no confidence in their hypocritical faces. In particular, there is one yonder of a Gascon look. Come hither, Monsieur."

D'Artagnan, who understood that it was to him this compliment was addressed, approached, assuming a most deprecating air.

"Why, you told me he was a young man? This is a boy, Tréville, a mere boy! Do you mean to say that it was he who bestowed that severe thrust at Jussac?"

"And those two equally fine thrusts at Bernajoux."

"Truly!"

"Without reckoning," said Athos, "that if he had not rescued me from the hands of Cahusac, I should not now have the honour of making my very humble reverence to your Majesty."

"Why he is a very devil, this Bearnais! VENTRE-SAINT-GRIS, Monsieur de Tréville, as the king my father would have said. But at this sort of work, many doublets must be slashed and many swords broken. Now, Gascons are always poor, are they not?"

"Sire, I can assert that they have hitherto discovered no gold mines in their mountains; though the Lord owes them this miracle in recompense for the manner in which they supported the pretensions of the king your father."

"Which is to say that the Gascons made a king of me, myself, seeing that I am my father's son, is it not, Tréville? Well, happily,

I don't say nay to it. La Chesnaye, go and see if by rummaging all my pockets you can find forty pistoles; and if you can find them, bring them to me. And now let us see, young man, with your hand upon your conscience, how did all this come to pass?"

D'Artagnan related the adventure of the preceding day in all its details; how, not having been able to sleep for the joy he felt in the expectation of seeing his Majesty, he had gone to his three friends three hours before the hour of audience; how they had gone together to the tennis court, and how, upon the fear he had manifested lest he receive a ball in the face, he had been jeered at by Bernajoux, who had nearly paid for his jeer with his life, and M. de la Trémouille, who had nothing to do with the matter, with the loss of his hotel.

"This is all very well," murmured the king, "yes, this is just the account the duke gave me of the affair. Poor cardinal! Seven men in two days, and those of his very best! But that's quite enough, gentlemen; please to understand, that's enough. You have taken your revenge for the Rue Ferou, and even exceeded it; you ought to be satisfied."

"If your Majesty is so," said Tréville, "we are."

"Oh, yes; I am," added the king, taking a handful of gold from La Chesnaye, and putting it into the hand of d'Artagnan. "Here," said he, "is a proof of my satisfaction."

At this epoch, the ideas of pride which are in fashion in our days did not prevail. A gentleman received, from hand to hand, money from the king, and was not the least in the world humiliated. D'Artagnan put his forty pistoles into his pocket without any scruple–on the contrary, thanking his Majesty greatly.

"There," said the king, looking at a clock, "there, now, as it is half past eight, you may retire; for as I told you, I expect someone at nine. Thanks for your devotedness, gentlemen. I may continue to rely upon it, may I not?"

"Oh, Sire!" cried the four companions, with one voice, "we would allow ourselves to be cut to pieces in your Majesty's service."

"Well, well, but keep whole; that will be better, and you will be more useful to me. Tréville," added the king, in a low voice, as the others were retiring, "as you have no room in the Musketeers, and as we have besides decided that a novitiate is necessary before entering that corps, place this young man in the company of the Guards of Monsieur Dessessart, your brother-in-law. Ah, PARDIEU, Tréville! I enjoy beforehand the face the cardinal will make. He will be furious, but I don't care. I am doing what is right."

The king waved his hand to Tréville, who left him and rejoined the Musketeers, whom he found sharing the forty pistoles with d'Artagnan.

The cardinal, as his Majesty had said, was really furious, so furious that during eight days he absented himself from the king's gaming table. This did not prevent the king from being as complacent to him as possible whenever he met him, or from asking in the kindest tone, "Well, Monsieur Cardinal, how fares it with that poor Jussac and that poor Bernajoux of yours?"

Chapter 7

The Interior Of The Musketeers

When d'Artagnan was out of the Louvre, and consulted his friends upon the use he had best make of his share of the forty pistoles, Athos advised him to order a good repast at the Pomme-de-Pin, Porthos to engage a lackey, and Aramis to provide himself with a suitable mistress.

The repast was carried into effect that very day, and the lackey waited at table. The repast had been ordered by Athos, and the lackey furnished by Porthos. He was a Picard, whom the glorious Musketeer had picked up on the Bridge Tournelle, making rings and plashing in the water.

Porthos pretended that this occupation was proof of a reflective and contemplative organisation, and he had brought him away without any other recommendation. The noble carriage of this gentleman, for whom he believed himself to be engaged, had won Planchet–that was the name of the Picard. He felt a slight disappointment, however, when he saw that this place was already taken by a compeer named Mousqueton, and when Porthos signified to him that the state of his household, though great, would not support two servants, and that he must enter into the service of d'Artagnan. Nevertheless, when he waited at the dinner given by his master, and saw him take out a handful of gold to pay for it, he believed his fortune made, and returned thanks to heaven for having thrown him into the service of such a Croesus. He preserved this opinion even after the feast, with the remnants of which he repaired his own long abstinence, but when in the evening he made his master's bed, the chimeras of Planchet faded away. The bed was the only one in the apartment, which consisted of an antechamber and a bedroom. Planchet slept in the antechamber upon a coverlet taken from the bed of d'Artagnan, and which d'Artagnan from that time made shift to do without.

Athos, on his part, had a valet whom he had trained in his service in a thoroughly peculiar fashion, and who was named Grimaud. He was very taciturn, this worthy signor. Be it understood we are speaking of Athos. During the five or six years that he had lived in the strictest intimacy with his companions, Porthos and Aramis, they could remember having often seen him smile, but had never heard him laugh. His words were brief and expressive, conveying all that was meant, and no more; no embellishments, no embroidery, no arabesques. His conversation was a matter of fact, without a single romance.

Although Athos was scarcely thirty years old, and was of great personal beauty and intelligence of mind, no one knew whether he had ever had a mistress. He never spoke of women. He certainly did not prevent others from speaking of them before him, although it was easy to perceive that this kind of conversation, in which he only mingled by bitter words and misanthropic remarks, was very disagreeable to him. His reserve, his roughness, and his silence made almost an old man of him. He had, then, in order not to disturb his habits, accustomed Grimaud to obey him upon a simple gesture or upon a simple movement of his lips. He never spoke to him, except under the most extraordinary occasions.

Sometimes, Grimaud, who feared his master as he did fire, while entertaining a strong attachment to his person and a great veneration for his talents, believed he perfectly understood what he wanted, flew to execute the order received, and did precisely the contrary. Athos then shrugged his shoulders, and, without putting himself in a passion, thrashed Grimaud. On these days he spoke a little.

Porthos, as we have seen, had a character exactly opposite to that of Athos. He not only talked much, but he talked loudly, little caring, we must render him that justice, whether anybody listened to him or not. He talked for the pleasure of talking and for the pleasure of hearing himself talk. He spoke upon all subjects except the sciences, alleging in this respect the inveterate hatred he had borne to scholars from his childhood. He had not so noble an air as Athos, and the commencement of their intimacy often rendered him unjust toward that gentleman, whom he endeavoured to eclipse by his splendid dress. But with his simple Musketeer's uniform and nothing but the manner in which he threw back his head and advanced his foot, Athos instantly took the place which was his due and consigned the ostentatious Porthos to the second rank. Porthos consoled himself by filling the antechamber of M. de Tréville and the guardroom of the Louvre with the accounts of his love scrapes, after having passed from professional ladies to military ladies, from the lawyer's dame to the baroness, there was question of nothing less with Porthos than a foreign princess, who was enormously fond of him.

An old proverb says, "Like master, like man." Let us pass, then, from the valet of Athos to the valet of Porthos, from Grimaud to Mousqueton.

Mousqueton was a Norman, whose pacific name of Boniface his master had changed into the infinitely more sonorous name of Mousqueton. He had entered the service of Porthos upon condition that he should only be clothed and lodged, though in a handsome manner, but he claimed two hours a day to himself, consecrated to an employment which would provide for his other wants. Porthos agreed to the bargain; the thing suited him wonderfully well. He had doublets cut out of his old clothes and cast-off cloaks for Mousqueton, and thanks to a very intelligent tailor, who made his clothes look as good as new by turning them, and whose wife was suspected of wishing to make Porthos descend from his aristocratic habits, Mousqueton made a very good figure when attending on his master.

As for Aramis, of whom we believe we have sufficiently explained the character–a character which, like that of his companions, we shall be able to follow in its development–his lackey was called Bazin. Thanks to the hopes which his master entertained of someday entering into orders, he was always clothed in black, as became the servant of a churchman. He was a Berrichon, thirty-five or forty years old, mild, peaceable, sleek, employing the leisure his master left him in the perusal of pious works, providing rigorously for two a dinner of few dishes, but excellent. For the rest, he was dumb, blind, and deaf, and of unimpeachable fidelity.

And now that we are acquainted, superficially at least, with the masters and the valets, let us pass on to the dwellings occupied by each of them.

Athos dwelt in the Rue Ferou, within two steps of the Luxembourg. His apartment consisted of two small chambers, very nicely fitted up, in a furnished house, the hostess of which, still young and still really handsome, cast tender glances uselessly at him. Some fragments of past splendor appeared here and there upon the walls of this modest lodging; a sword, for example, richly embossed, which belonged by its make to the times of Francis I, the hilt of which alone, encrusted with precious stones, might be worth two hundred pistoles, and which, nevertheless, in his moments of greatest distress Athos had never pledged or offered for sale. It had long been an object of ambition for Porthos. Porthos would have given ten years of his life to possess this sword.

One day, when he had an appointment with a duchess, he endeavoured even to borrow it of Athos. Athos, without saying anything, emptied his pockets, got together all his jewels, purses, aiguillettes, and gold chains, and offered them all to Porthos, but as to the sword, he said it was sealed to its place and should never quit it until its master should himself quit his lodgings. In addition to the sword, there was a portrait representing a nobleman of the time of Henry III, dressed with the greatest elegance, and who wore the Order of the Holy Ghost; and this portrait had certain resemblances of lines with Athos, certain family likenesses which indicated that this great noble, a knight of the Order of the King, was his ancestor.

Besides these, a casket of magnificent goldwork, with the same arms as the sword and the portrait, formed a middle ornament to the mantelpiece, and assorted badly with the rest of the furniture. Athos always carried the key of this coffer about him, but he one day opened it before Porthos, and Porthos was convinced that this coffer contained nothing but letters and papers–love letters and family papers, no doubt.

Porthos lived in an apartment, large in size and of very sumptuous appearance, in the Rue du Vieux-Colombier. Every time he passed with a friend before his windows, at one of which Mousqueton was sure to be placed in full livery, Porthos raised his head and his hand, and said, "That is my abode!" But he was never to be found at home; he never invited anybody to go up with him, and no one could form an idea of what his sumptuous apartment contained in the shape of real riches.

As to Aramis, he dwelt in a little lodging composed of a boudoir, an eating room, and a bedroom, which room, situated, as the others were, on the ground floor, looked out upon a little fresh green garden, shady and impenetrable to the eyes of his neighbours.

With regard to d'Artagnan, we know how he was lodged, and we have already made acquaintance with his lackey, Master Planchet.

D'Artagnan, who was by nature very curious–as people generally are who possess the genius of intrigue–did all he could to make out who Athos, Porthos, and Aramis really were (for under these pseudonyms each of these young men concealed his family name)–Athos in particular, who, a league away, savored of nobility. He addressed himself then to Porthos to gain information respecting Athos and Aramis, and to Aramis in order to learn something of Porthos.

Unfortunately Porthos knew nothing of the life of his silent companion but what revealed itself. It was said Athos had met with great crosses in love, and that a frightful treachery had forever poisoned the life of this gallant man. What could this treachery be? All the world was ignorant of it.

As to Porthos, except his real name (as was the case with those of his two comrades), his life was very easily known. Vain and indiscreet, it was as easy to see through him as through a crystal. The only thing to mislead the investigator would have been belief in all the good things he said of himself.

With respect to Aramis, though having the air of having nothing secret about him, he was a young fellow made up of mysteries, answering little to questions put to him about others, and having learned from him the report which prevailed concerning the success of the Musketeer with a princess, wished to gain a little insight into the amorous adventures of his interlocutor. "And you, my dear companion," said he, "you speak of the baronesses, countesses, and princesses of others?"

"PARDIEU! I spoke of them because Porthos talked of them himself, because he had paraded all these fine things before me. But be assured, my dear Monsieur d'Artagnan, that if I had obtained them from any other source, or if they had been confided to me, there exists no confessor more discreet than myself."

"Oh, I don't doubt that," replied d'Artagnan, "but it seems to me that you are tolerably familiar with coats of arms–a certain embroidered handkerchief, for instance, to which I owe the honour of your acquaintance?"

This time Aramis was not angry, but assumed the most modest air and replied in a friendly tone, "My dear friend, do not forget that I wish to belong to the Church, and that I avoid all mundane opportunities. The handkerchief you saw had not been given to me, but it had been forgotten and left at my house by one of my friends. I was obliged to pick it up in order not to compromise him and the lady he loves. As for myself, I neither have, nor desire to have, a mistress, following in that respect the very judicious example of Athos, who has none any more than I have."

"But what the devil! You are not a priest, you are a Musketeer!"

"A Musketeer for a time, my friend, as the cardinal says, a Musketeer against my will, but a churchman at heart, believe me. Athos and Porthos dragged me into this to occupy me. I had, at the moment of being ordained, a little difficulty with–But that would not interest you, and I am taking up your valuable time."

"Not at all; it interests me very much," cried d'Artagnan, "and at this moment I have absolutely nothing to do."

"Yes, but I have my breviary to repeat," answered Aramis, "then some verses to compose, which Madame d'Aiguillon begged of me. Then I must go to the Rue St. Honoré in order to purchase some rouge for Madame de Chevreuse. So you see, my dear friend, that if you are not in a hurry, I am very much in a hurry."

Aramis held out his hand in a cordial manner to his young companion, and took leave of him.

Notwithstanding all the pains he took, d'Artagnan was unable to learn any more concerning his three new-made friends. He formed, therefore, the resolution of believing for the present all that was said of their past, hoping for more certain and extended revelations in the future. In the meanwhile, he looked upon Athos as an Achilles, Porthos as an Ajax, and Aramis as a Joseph.

As to the rest, the life of the four young friends was joyous enough. Athos played, and that as a rule unfortunately. Nevertheless, he never borrowed a sou of his companions, although his purse was ever at their service; and when he had played upon honour, he always awakened his creditor by six o'clock the next morning to pay the debt of the preceding evening.

Porthos had his fits. On the days when he won he was insolent and ostentatious; if he lost, he disappeared completely for several days, after which he reappeared with a pale face and thinner person, but with money in his purse.

As to Aramis, he never played. He was the worst Musketeer and the most unconvivial companion imaginable. He had always something or other to do. Sometimes in the midst of dinner, when everyone, under the attraction of wine and in the warmth of conversation, believed they had two or three hours longer to enjoy themselves at table, Aramis looked at his watch, arose with a bland smile, and took leave of the company, to go, as he said, to consult a casuist with whom he had an appointment. At other times he would return home to write a treatise, and requested his friends not to disturb him.

At this Athos would smile, with his charming, melancholy smile, which so became his noble countenance, and Porthos would drink, swearing that Aramis would never be anything but a village CURE.

Planchet, d'Artagnan's valet, supported his good fortune nobly. He received thirty sous per day, and for a month he returned to his lodgings gay as a chaffinch, and affable toward his master. When the wind of adversity began to blow upon the housekeeping of the Rue des Fossoyeurs–that is to say, when the forty pistoles of King Louis XIII were consumed or nearly so–he commenced complaints which Athos thought nauseous, Porthos indecent, and Aramis ridiculous. Athos counseled d'Artagnan to dismiss the fellow; Porthos was of the opinion that he should give him a good thrashing first; and Aramis contended that a master should never attend to anything but the civilities paid to him.

"This is all very easy for you to say," replied d'Artagnan, "for you, Athos, who live like a dumb man with Grimaud, who forbid him to speak, and consequently never exchange ill words with him; for you, Porthos, who carry matters in such a magnificent style, and are a god to your valet, Mousqueton; and for you, Aramis, who, always abstracted by your theological studies, inspire your servant, Bazin, a mild, religious man, with a profound respect, but for me, who am without any settled means and without resources–for me, who am neither a Musketeer nor even a Guardsman, what am I to do to inspire either the affection, the terror, or the respect in Planchet?"

"This is serious," answered the three friends, "it is a family affair. It is with valets as with wives, they must be placed at once upon the footing in which you wish them to remain. Reflect upon it."

D'Artagnan did reflect, and resolved to thrash Planchet provisionally, which he did with the conscientiousness that d'Artagnan carried into everything. After having well beaten him, he forbade him to leave his service without his permission. "For," added he, "the future cannot fail to mend; I inevitably look for better times. Your fortune is therefore made if you remain with me, and I am too good a master to allow you to miss such a chance by granting you the dismissal you require."

This manner of acting roused much respect for d'Artagnan's policy among the Musketeers. Planchet was equally seized with admiration, and said no more about going away.

The life of the four young men had become fraternal. D'Artagnan, who had no settled habits of his own, as he came from his province into the midst of a world quite new to him, fell easily into the habits of his friends.

They rose about eight o'clock in the winter, about six in summer, and went to take the countersign and see how things went on at M. de Tréville's. D'Artagnan, although he was not a Musketeer, performed the duty of one with remarkable punctuality. He went on guard because he always kept company with whoever of his friends was on duty. He was well known at the Hotel of the Musketeers, where everyone considered him a good comrade. M. de Tréville, who had appreciated him at the first glance and who bore him a real affection, never ceased recommending him to the king.

On their side, the three Musketeers were much attached to their young comrade. The friendship which united these four men, and the need they felt of seeing another three or four times a day, whether for dueling, business, or pleasure, caused them to be continually running after one another like shadows; and the Inseparables were constantly to be met with seeking one another, from the Luxembourg to the Place St. Sulpice, or from the Rue du Vieux-Colombier to the Luxembourg.

In the meanwhile the promises of M. de Tréville went on prosperously. One fine morning the king commanded M. de Chevalier Dessessart to admit d'Artagnan as a cadet in his company of Guards. D'Artagnan, with a sigh, donned his uniform, which he would have exchanged for that of a Musketeer at the expense of ten years of his existence. But M. de Tréville promised this favour after a novitiate of two years–a novitiate which might besides be abridged if an opportunity should present itself for d'Artagnan to render the king any signal service, or to distinguish himself by some brilliant action. Upon this promise d'Artagnan withdrew, and the next day he began service.

Then it became the turn of Athos, Porthos, and Aramis to mount guard with d'Artagnan when he was on duty. The company of M. le Chevalier Dessessart thus received four instead of one when it admitted d'Artagnan.

Chapter 8

Concerning A Court Intrigue

In the meantime, the forty pistoles of King Louis XIII, like all other things of this world, after having had a beginning had an end, and after this end our four companions began to be somewhat embarrassed. At first, Athos supported the association for a time with his own means.

Porthos succeeded him; and thanks to one of those disappearances to which he was accustomed, he was able to provide for the wants of all for a fortnight. At last it became Aramis's turn, who performed it with a good grace and who succeeded–as he said, by selling some theological books–in procuring a few pistoles.

Then, as they had been accustomed to do, they had recourse to M. de Tréville, who made some advances on their pay, but these advances could not go far with three Musketeers who were already much in arrears and a Guardsman who as yet had no pay at all.

At length when they found they were likely to be really in want, they got together, as a last effort, eight or ten pistoles, with which Porthos went to the gaming table. Unfortunately he was in a bad vein; he lost all, together with twenty-five pistoles for which he had given his word.

Then the inconvenience became distress. The hungry friends, followed by their lackeys, were seen haunting the quays and Guard rooms, picking up among their friends abroad all the dinners they could meet with; for according to the advice of Aramis, it was prudent to sow repasts right and left in prosperity, in order to reap a few in time of need.

Athos was invited four times, and each time took his friends and their lackeys with him. Porthos had six occasions, and contrived in the same manner that his friends should partake of them; Aramis had eight of them. He was a man, as must have been already perceived, who made but little noise, and yet was much sought after.

As to d'Artagnan, who as yet knew nobody in the capital, he only found one chocolate breakfast at the house of a priest of his own province, and one dinner at the house of a cornet of the Guards. He took his army to the priest's, where they devoured as much provision as would have lasted him for two months, and to the cornet's, who performed wonders, but as Planchet said, "People do not eat at once for all time, even when they eat a good deal."

D'Artagnan thus felt himself humiliated in having only procured one meal and a half for his companions–as the breakfast at the priest's could only be counted as half a repast–in return for the feasts which Athos, Porthos, and Aramis had procured him. He fancied himself a burden to the society, forgetting in his perfectly juvenile good faith that he had fed this society for a month; and he set his mind actively to work. He reflected that this coalition of four young, brave, enterprising, and active men ought to have some other object than swaggering walks, fencing lessons, and practical jokes, more or less witty.

In fact, four men such as they were–four men devoted to one another, from their purses to their lives; four men always supporting one another, never yielding, executing singly or together the resolutions formed in common; four arms threatening the four cardinal points, or turning toward a single point–must inevitably, either subterraneously, in open day, by mining, in the trench, by cunning, or by force, open themselves a way toward the object they wished to attain, however well it might be defended, or however distant it may seem. The only thing that astonished d'Artagnan was that his friends had never thought of this.

He was thinking by himself, and even seriously racking his brain to find a direction for this single force four times multiplied, with which he did not doubt, as with the lever for which Archimedes sought, they should succeed in moving the world, when someone tapped gently at his door. D'Artagnan awakened Planchet and ordered him to open it.

From this phrase, "d'Artagnan awakened Planchet," the reader must not suppose it was night, or that day was hardly come. No, it had just struck four. Planchet, two hours before, had asked his master for some dinner, and he had answered him with the proverb, "He who sleeps, dines." And Planchet dined by sleeping.

A man was introduced of simple mien, who had the appearance of a tradesman. Planchet, by way of dessert, would have liked to hear the conversation, but the citizen declared to d'Artagnan that, what he had to say being important and confidential, he desired to be left alone with him.

D'Artagnan dismissed Planchet, and requested his visitor to be seated. There was a moment of silence, during which the two men looked at each other, as if to make a preliminary acquaintance, after which d'Artagnan bowed, as a sign that he listened.

"I have heard Monsieur d'Artagnan spoken of as a very brave young man," said the citizen, "and this reputation which he justly enjoys had decided me to confide a secret to him."

"Speak, Monsieur, speak," said d'Artagnan, who instinctively scented something advantageous.

The citizen made a fresh pause and continued, "I have a wife who is seamstress to the queen, Monsieur, and who is not deficient in either virtue or beauty. I was induced to marry her about three years ago, although she had but very little dowry, because

Monsieur Laporte, the queen's cloak bearer, is her godfather, and befriends her."

"Well, Monsieur?" asked d'Artagnan.

"Well!" resumed the citizen, "well, Monsieur, my wife was abducted yesterday morning, as she was coming out of her workroom."

"And by whom was your wife abducted?"

"I know nothing surely, Monsieur, but I suspect someone."

"And who is the person whom you suspect?"

"A man who has pursued her a long time."

"The devil!"

"But allow me to tell you, Monsieur," continued the citizen, "that I am convinced that there is less love than politics in all this."

"Less love than politics," replied d'Artagnan, with a reflective air, "and what do you suspect?"

"I do not know whether I ought to tell you what I suspect."

"Monsieur, I beg you to observe that I ask you absolutely nothing. It is you who have come to me. It is you who have told me that you had a secret to confide in me. Act, then, as you think proper; there is still time to withdraw."

"No, Monsieur, no; you appear to be an honest young man, and I will have confidence in you. I believe, then, that it is not on account of any intrigues of her own that my wife has been arrested, but because of those of a lady much greater than herself."

"Ah, ah! Can it be on account of the amours of Madame de Bois-Tracy?" said d'Artagnan, wishing to have the air, in the eyes of the citizen, of being posted as to court affairs.

"Higher, Monsieur, higher."

"Of Madame d'Aiguillon?"

"Still higher."

"Of Madame de Chevreuse?"

"Of the–" d'Artagnan checked himself.

"Yes, Monsieur," replied the terrified citizen, in a tone so low that he was scarcely audible.

"And with whom?"

"With whom can it be, if not the Duke of–"

"The Duke of–"

"Yes, Monsieur," replied the citizen, giving a still fainter intonation to his voice.

"But how do you know all this?"

"How do I know it?"

"Yes, how do you know it? No half-confidence, or–you understand!"

"I know it from my wife, Monsieur–from my wife herself."

"Who learns it from whom?"

"From Monsieur Laporte. Did I not tell you that she was the goddaughter of Monsieur Laporte, the confidential man of the queen? Well, Monsieur Laporte placed her near her Majesty in order that our poor queen might at least have someone in whom she could place confidence, abandoned as she is by the king, watched as she is by the cardinal, betrayed as she is by everybody."

"Ah, ah! It begins to develop itself," said d'Artagnan.

"Now, my wife came home four days ago, Monsieur. One of her conditions was that she should come and see me twice a week; for, as I had the honour to tell you, my wife loves me dearly–my wife, then, came and confided to me that the queen at that very moment entertained great fears."

"Truly!"

"Yes. The cardinal, as it appears, pursues her and persecutes her more than ever. He cannot pardon her the history of the Saraband. You know the history of the Saraband?"

"PARDIEU! Know it!" replied d'Artagnan, who knew nothing about it, but who wished to appear to know everything that was going on.

"So that now it is no longer hatred, but vengeance."

"Indeed!"

"And the queen believes–"

"Well, what does the queen believe?"

"She believes that someone has written to the Duke of Buckingham in her name."

"In the queen's name?"

"Yes, to make him come to Paris; and when once come to Paris, to draw him into some snare."

"The devil! But your wife, Monsieur, what has she to do with all this?"

"Her devotion to the queen is known; and they wish either to remove her from her mistress, or to intimidate her, in order to obtain her Majesty's secrets, or to seduce her and make use of her as a spy."

"That is likely," said d'Artagnan, "but the man who has abducted her–do you know him?"

"I have told you that I believe I know him."

"His name?"

"I do not know that; what I do know is that he is a creature of the cardinal, his evil genius."

"But you have seen him?"

"Yes, my wife pointed him out to me one day."

"Has he anything remarkable about him by which one may recognise him?"

"Oh, certainly; he is a noble of very lofty carriage, black hair, swarthy complexion, piercing eye, white teeth, and has a scar on his temple."

"A scar on his temple!" cried d'Artagnan, "and with that, white teeth, a piercing eye, dark complexion, black hair, and haughty carriage–why, that's my man of Meung."

"He is your man, do you say?"

"Yes, yes, but that has nothing to do with it. No, I am wrong. On the contrary, that simplifies the matter greatly. If your man is mine, with one blow I shall obtain two revenges, that's all, but where to find this man?"

"I know not."

"Have you no information as to his abiding place?"

"None. One day, as I was conveying my wife back to the Louvre, he was coming out as she was going in, and she showed him to me."

"The devil! The devil!" murmured d'Artagnan, "all this is vague enough. From whom have you learned of the abduction of your wife?"

"From Monsieur Laporte."

"Did he give you any details?"

"He knew none himself."

"And you have learned nothing from any other quarter?"

"Yes, I have received–"

"What?"

"I fear I am committing a great imprudence."

"You always come back to that, but I must make you see this time that it is too late to retreat."

"I do not retreat, MORDIEU!" cried the citizen, swearing in order to rouse his courage. "Besides, by the faith of Bonacieux–"

"You call yourself Bonacieux?" interrupted d'Artagnan.

"Yes, that is my name."

"You said, then, by the word of Bonacieux. Pardon me for interrupting you, but it appears to me that that name is familiar to me."

"Possibly, Monsieur. I am your landlord."

"Ah, ah!" said d'Artagnan, half rising and bowing, "you are my landlord?"

"Yes, Monsieur, yes. And as it is three months since you have been here, and though, distracted as you must be in your important occupations, you have forgotten to pay me my rent–as, I say, I have not tormented you a single instant, I thought you would appreciate my delicacy."

"How can it be otherwise, my dear Bonacieux?" replied d'Artagnan, "trust me, I am fully grateful for such unparalleled conduct, and if, as I told you, I can be of any service to you–"

"I believe you, Monsieur, I believe you; and as I was about to say, by the word of Bonacieux, I have confidence in you."

"Finish, then, what you were about to say."

The citizen took a paper from his pocket, and presented it to d'Artagnan.

"A letter?" said the young man.

"Which I received this morning."

D'Artagnan opened it, and as the day was beginning to decline, he approached the window to read it. The citizen followed him.

"'Do not seek your wife,'" read d'Artagnan, "'she will be restored to you when there is no longer occasion for her. If you make a single step to find her you are lost.'

"That's pretty positive," continued d'Artagnan, "but after all, it is but a menace."

"Yes, but that menace terrifies me. I am not a fighting man at all, Monsieur, and I am afraid of the Bastille."

"Hum!" said d'Artagnan. "I have no greater regard for the Bastille than you. If it were nothing but a sword thrust, why then–"

"I have counted upon you on this occasion, Monsieur."

"Yes?"

"Seeing you constantly surrounded by Musketeers of a very superb appearance, and knowing that these Musketeers belong to Monsieur de Tréville, and were consequently enemies of the cardinal, I thought that you and your friends, while rendering justice to your poor queen, would be pleased to play his Eminence an ill turn."

"Without doubt."

"And then I have thought that considering three months' lodging, about which I have said nothing–"

"Yes, yes; you have already given me that reason, and I find it excellent."

"Reckoning still further, that as long as you do me the honour to remain in my house I shall never speak to you about rent–"

"Very kind!"

"And adding to this, if there be need of it, meaning to offer you fifty pistoles, if, against all probability, you should be short at the present moment."

"Admirable! You are rich then, my dear Monsieur Bonacieux?"

"I am comfortably off, Monsieur, that's all; I have scraped together some such things as an income of two or three thousand crowns in the haberdashery business, but more particularly in venturing some funds in the last voyage of the celebrated navigator Jean Moquet; so that you understand, Monsieur–But!–" cried the citizen.

"What!" demanded d'Artagnan.

"Whom do I see yonder?"

"Where?"

"In the street, facing your window, in the embrasure of that door–a man wrapped in a cloak."

"It is he!" cried d'Artagnan and the citizen at the same time, each having recognised his man.

"Ah, this time," cried d'Artagnan, springing to his sword, "this time he will not escape me!"

Drawing his sword from its scabbard, he rushed out of the apartment. On the staircase he met Athos and Porthos, who were coming to see him. They separated, and d'Artagnan rushed between them like a dart.

"Pah! Where are you going?" cried the two Musketeers in a breath.

"The man of Meung!" replied d'Artagnan, and disappeared.

D'Artagnan had more than once related to his friends his adventure with the stranger, as well as the apparition of the beautiful foreigner, to whom this man had confided some important missive.

The opinion of Athos was that d'Artagnan had lost his letter in the skirmish. A gentleman, in his opinion–and according to d'Artagnan's portrait of him, the stranger must be a gentleman–would be incapable of the baseness of stealing a letter.

Porthos saw nothing in all this but a love meeting, given by a lady to a cavalier, or by a cavalier to a lady, which had been disturbed by the presence of d'Artagnan and his yellow horse.

Aramis said that as these sorts of affairs were mysterious, it was better not to fathom them.

They understood, then, from the few words which escaped from d'Artagnan, what affair was in hand, and as they thought that overtaking his man, or losing sight of him, d'Artagnan would return to his rooms, they kept on their way.

When they entered d'Artagnan's chamber, it was empty; the landlord, dreading the consequences of the encounter which was doubtless about to take place between the young man and the stranger, had, consistent with the character he had given himself, judged it prudent to decamp.

Chapter 9

D'Artagnan Shows Himself

As Athos and Porthos had foreseen, at the expiration of a half hour, d'Artagnan returned. He had again missed his man, who had disappeared as if by enchantment. D'Artagnan had run, sword in hand, through all the neighbouring streets, but had found nobody resembling the man he sought for. Then he came back to the point where, perhaps, he ought to have begun, and that was to knock at the door against which the stranger had leaned, but this proved useless–for though he knocked ten or twelve times in succession, no one answered, and some of the neighbours, who put their noses out of their windows or were brought to their doors by the noise, had assured him that that house, all the openings of which were tightly closed, had not been inhabited for six months.

While d'Artagnan was running through the streets and knocking at doors, Aramis had joined his companions; so that on returning home d'Artagnan found the reunion complete.

"Well!" cried the three Musketeers all together, on seeing d'Artagnan enter with his brow covered with perspiration and his countenance upset with anger.

"Well!" cried he, throwing his sword upon the bed, "this man must be the devil in person; he has disappeared like a phantom, like a shade, like a specter."

"Do you believe in apparitions?" asked Athos of Porthos.

"I never believe in anything I have not seen, and as I never have seen apparitions, I don't believe in them."

"The Bible," said Aramis, "makes our belief in them a law; the ghost of Samuel appeared to Saul, and it is an article of faith that I should be very sorry to see any doubt thrown upon, Porthos."

"At all events, man or devil, body or shadow, illusion or reality, this man is born for my damnation; for his flight has caused us to miss a glorious affair, gentlemen–an affair by which there were a hundred pistoles, and perhaps more, to be gained."

"How is that?" cried Porthos and Aramis in a breath.

As to Athos, faithful to his system of reticence, he contented himself with interrogating d'Artagnan by a look.

"Planchet," said d'Artagnan to his domestic, who just then insinuated his head through the half-open door in order to catch some fragments of the conversation, "go down to my landlord, Monsieur Bonacieux, and ask him to send me half a dozen bottles of Beaugency wine; I prefer that."

"Ah, ah! You have credit with your landlord, then?" asked Porthos.

"Yes," replied d'Artagnan, "from this very day; and mind, if the wine is bad, we will send him to find better."

"We must use, and not abuse," said Aramis, sententiously.

"I always said that d'Artagnan had the longest head of the four," said Athos, who, having uttered his opinion, to which d'Artagnan replied with a bow, immediately resumed his accustomed silence.

"But come, what is this about?" asked Porthos.

"Yes," said Aramis, "impart it to us, my dear friend, unless the honour of any lady be hazarded by this confidence; in that case you would do better to keep it to yourself."

"Be satisfied," replied d'Artagnan, "the honour of no one will have cause to complain of what I have to tell."

He then related to his friends, word for word, all that had passed between him and his host, and how the man who had abducted the wife of his worthy landlord was the same with whom he had had the difference at the hostelry of the Jolly Miller.

"Your affair is not bad," said Athos, after having tasted like a connoisseur and indicated by a nod of his head that he thought the wine good, "and one may draw fifty or sixty pistoles from this good man. Then there only remains to ascertain whether these fifty or sixty pistoles are worth the risk of four heads."

"But observe," cried d'Artagnan, "that there is a woman in the affair–a woman carried off, a woman who is doubtless threatened, tortured perhaps, and all because she is faithful to her mistress."

"Beware, d'Artagnan, beware," said Aramis. "You grow a little too warm, in my opinion, about the fate of Madame Bonacieux. Woman was created for our destruction, and it is from her we inherit all our miseries."

At this speech of Aramis, the brow of Athos became clouded and he bit his lips.

"It is not Madame Bonacieux about whom I am anxious," cried d'Artagnan, "but the queen, whom the king abandons, whom the cardinal persecutes, and who sees the heads of all her friends fall, one after the other."

"Why does she love what we hate most in the world, the Spaniards and the English?"

"Spain is her country," replied d'Artagnan, "and it is very natural that she should love the Spanish, who are the children of the same soil as herself. As to the second reproach, I have heard it said that she does not love the English, but an Englishman."

"Well, and by my faith," said Athos, "it must be acknowledged that this Englishman is worthy of being loved. I never saw a man with a nobler air than his."

"Without reckoning that he dresses as nobody else can," said Porthos. "I was at the Louvre on the day when he scattered his pearls; and, PARDIEU, I picked up two that I sold for ten pistoles each. Do you know him, Aramis?"

"As well as you do, gentlemen; for I was among those who seized him in the garden at Amiens, into which Monsieur Putange, the queen's equerry, introduced me. I was at school at the time, and the adventure appeared to me to be cruel for the king."

"Which would not prevent me," said d'Artagnan, "if I knew where the Duke of Buckingham was, from taking him by the hand and conducting him to the queen, were it only to enrage the cardinal, and if we could find means to play him a sharp turn, I vow that I would voluntarily risk my head in doing it."

"And did the mercer," rejoined Athos, "tell you, d'Artagnan, that the queen thought that Buckingham had been brought over by a forged letter?"

"She is afraid so."

"Wait a minute, then," said Aramis.

"What for?" demanded Porthos.

"Go on, while I endeavour to recall circumstances."

"And now I am convinced," said d'Artagnan, "that this abduction of the queen's woman is connected with the events of which we are speaking, and perhaps with the presence of Buckingham in Paris."

"The Gascon is full of ideas," said Porthos, with admiration.

"I like to hear him talk," said Athos, "his dialect amuses me."

"Gentlemen," cried Aramis, "listen to this."

"Listen to Aramis," said his three friends.

"Yesterday I was at the house of a doctor of theology, whom I sometimes consult about my studies."

Athos smiled.

"He resides in a quiet quarter," continued Aramis, "his tastes and his profession require it. Now, at the moment when I left his house–"

Here Aramis paused.

"Well," cried his auditors, "at the moment you left his house?"

Aramis appeared to make a strong inward effort, like a man who, in the full relation of a falsehood, finds himself stopped by some unforeseen obstacle, but the eyes of his three companions were fixed upon him, their ears were wide open, and there were no means of retreat.

"This doctor has a niece," continued Aramis.

"Ah, he has a niece!" interrupted Porthos.

"A very respectable lady," said Aramis.

The three friends burst into laughter.

"Ah, if you laugh, if you doubt me," replied Aramis, "you shall know nothing."

"We believe like Mohammedans, and are as mute as tombstones," said Athos.

"I will continue, then," resumed Aramis. "This niece comes sometimes to see her uncle; and by chance was there yesterday at the same time that I was, and it was my duty to offer to conduct her to her carriage."

"Ah! She has a carriage, then, this niece of the doctor?" interrupted Porthos, one of whose faults was a great looseness of tongue. "A nice acquaintance, my friend!"

"Porthos," replied Aramis, "I have had the occasion to observe to you more than once that you are very indiscreet; and that is injurious to you among the women."

"Gentlemen, gentlemen," cried d'Artagnan, who began to get a glimpse of the result of the adventure, "the thing is serious. Let us try not to jest, if we can. Go on Aramis, go on."

"All at once, a tall, dark gentleman–just like yours, d'Artagnan."

"The same, perhaps," said he.

"Possibly," continued Aramis, "came toward me, accompanied by five or six men who followed about ten paces behind him; and in the politest tone, 'Monsieur Duke,' said he to me, 'and you madame,' continued he, addressing the lady on my arm–"

"The doctor's niece?"

"Hold your tongue, Porthos," said Athos, "you are insupportable."

"'–will you enter this carriage, and that without offering the least resistance, without making the least noise?'"

"He took you for Buckingham!" cried d'Artagnan.

"I believe so," replied Aramis.

"But the lady?" asked Porthos.

"He took her for the queen!" said d'Artagnan.

"Just so," replied Aramis.

"The Gascon is the devil!" cried Athos, "nothing escapes him."

"The fact is," said Porthos, "Aramis is of the same height, and something of the shape of the duke, but it nevertheless appears to me that the dress of a Musketeer–"

"I wore an enormous cloak," said Aramis.

"In the month of July? The devil!" said Porthos. "Is the doctor afraid that you may be recognised?"

"I can comprehend that the spy may have been deceived by the person, but the face–"

"I had a large hat," said Aramis.

"Oh, good lord," cried Porthos, "what precautions for the study of theology!"

"Gentlemen, gentlemen," said d'Artagnan, "do not let us lose our time in jesting. Let us separate, and let us seek the mercer's wife–that is the key of the intrigue."

"A woman of such inferior condition! Can you believe so?" said Porthos, protruding his lips with contempt.

"She is goddaughter to Laporte, the confidential valet of the queen. Have I not told you so, gentlemen? Besides, it has perhaps been her Majesty's calculation to seek on this occasion for support so lowly. High heads expose themselves from afar, and the cardinal is longsighted."

"Well," said Porthos, "in the first place make a bargain with the mercer, and a good bargain."

"That's useless," said d'Artagnan, "for I believe if he does not pay us, we shall be well enough paid by another party."

At this moment a sudden noise of footsteps was heard upon the stairs; the door was thrown violently open, and the unfortunate mercer rushed into the chamber in which the council was held.

"Save me, gentlemen, for the love of heaven, save me!" cried he. "There are four men come to arrest me. Save me! Save me!"

Porthos and Aramis arose.

"A moment," cried d'Artagnan, making them a sign to replace in the scabbard their half-drawn swords. "It is not courage that is needed; it is prudence."

"And yet," cried Porthos, "we will not leave–"

"You will leave d'Artagnan to act as he thinks proper," said Athos. "He has, I repeat, the longest head of the four, and for my part I declare that I will obey him. Do as you think best, d'Artagnan."

At this moment the four Guards appeared at the door of the antechamber, but seeing four Musketeers standing, and their swords by their sides, they hesitated about going farther.

"Come in, gentlemen, come in," called d'Artagnan, "you are here in my apartment, and we are all faithful servants of the king and cardinal."

"Then, gentlemen, you will not oppose our executing the orders we have received?" asked one who appeared to be the leader of the party.

"On the contrary, gentlemen, we would assist you if it were necessary."

"What does he say?" grumbled Porthos.

"You are a simpleton," said Athos. "Silence!"

"But you promised me–" whispered the poor mercer.

"We can only save you by being free ourselves," replied d'Artagnan, in a rapid, low tone, "and if we appear inclined to defend you, they will arrest us with you."

"It seems, nevertheless–"

"Come, gentlemen, come!" said d'Artagnan, aloud, "I have no motive for defending Monsieur. I saw him today for the first time, and he can tell you on what occasion; he came to demand the rent of my lodging. Is that not true, Monsieur Bonacieux? Answer!"

"That is the very truth," cried the mercer, "but Monsieur does not tell you–"

"Silence, with respect to me, silence, with respect to my friends; silence about the queen, above all, or you will ruin everybody without saving yourself! Come, come, gentlemen, remove the fellow." And d'Artagnan pushed the half-stupefied mercer among the Guards, saying to him, "You are a shabby old fellow, my dear. You come to demand money of me–of a Musketeer! To prison with him! Gentlemen, once more, take him to prison, and keep him under key as long as possible; that will give me time to pay him."

The officers were full of thanks, and took away their prey. As they were going down d'Artagnan laid his hand on the shoulder of their leader.

"May I not drink to your health, and you to mine?" said d'Artagnan, filling two glasses with the Beaugency wine which he had obtained from the liberality of M. Bonacieux.

"That will do me great honour," said the leader of the posse, "and I accept thankfully."

"Then to yours, Monsieur–what is your name?"

"Boisrenard."

"Monsieur Boisrenard."

"To yours, my gentlemen! What is your name, in your turn, if you please?"

"D'Artagnan."

"To yours, Monsieur."

"And above all others," cried d'Artagnan, as if carried away by his enthusiasm, "to that of the king and the cardinal."

The leader of the posse would perhaps have doubted the sincerity of d'Artagnan if the wine had been bad, but the wine was good, and he was convinced.

"What diabolical villainy you have performed here," said Porthos, when the officer had rejoined his companions and the four friends found themselves alone. "Shame, shame, for four Musketeers to allow an unfortunate fellow who cried for help to be arrested in their midst! And a gentleman to hobnob with a bailiff!"

"Porthos," said Aramis, "Athos has already told you that you are a simpleton, and I am quite of his opinion. D'Artagnan, you are a great man; and when you occupy Monsieur de Tréville's place, I will come and ask your influence to secure me an abbey."

"Well, I am in a maze," said Porthos, "do YOU approve of what d'Artagnan has done?"

"PARBLEU! Indeed I do," said Athos, "I not only approve of what he has done, but I congratulate him upon it."

"And now, gentlemen," said d'Artagnan, without stopping to explain his conduct to Porthos, "All for one, one for all–that is our motto, is it not?"

"And yet–" said Porthos.

"Hold out your hand and swear!" cried Athos and Aramis at once.

Overcome by example, grumbling to himself, nevertheless, Porthos stretched out his hand, and the four friends repeated with one voice the formula dictated by d'Artagnan:

"All for one, one for all."

"That's well! Now let us everyone retire to his own home," said d'Artagnan, as if he had done nothing but command all his life, "and attention! For from this moment we are at feud with the cardinal."

Chapter 10

A Mousetrap In The Seventeenth Century

The invention of the mousetrap does not date from our days; as soon as societies, in forming, had invented any kind of police, that police invented mousetraps.

As perhaps our readers are not familiar with the slang of the Rue de Jerusalem, and as it is fifteen years since we applied this word for the first time to this thing, allow us to explain to them what is a mousetrap.

When in a house, of whatever kind it may be, an individual suspected of any crime is arrested, the arrest is held secret. Four or five men are placed in ambuscade in the first room. The door is opened to all who knock. It is closed after them, and they are arrested; so that at the end of two or three days they have in their power almost all the HABITUÉS of the establishment. And that is a mousetrap.

The apartment of M. Bonacieux, then, became a mousetrap; and whoever appeared there was taken and interrogated by the cardinal's people. It must be observed that as a separate passage led to the first floor, in which d'Artagnan lodged, those who called on him were exempted from this detention.

Besides, nobody came thither but the three Musketeers; they had all been engaged in earnest search and inquiries, but had discovered nothing. Athos had even gone so far as to question M. de Tréville–a thing which, considering the habitual reticence of the worthy Musketeer, had very much astonished his captain. But M. de Tréville knew nothing, except that the last time he had seen the cardinal, the king, and the queen, the cardinal looked very thoughtful, the king uneasy, and the redness of the queen's eyes donated that she had been sleepless or tearful. But this last circumstance was not striking, as the queen since her marriage had slept badly and wept much.

M. de Tréville requested Athos, whatever might happen, to be observant of his duty to the king, but particularly to the queen, begging him to convey his desires to his comrades.

As to d'Artagnan, he did not budge from his apartment. He converted his chamber into an observatory. From his windows he saw all the visitors who were caught. Then, having removed a plank from his floor, and nothing remaining but a simple ceiling between him and the room beneath, in which the interrogatories were made, he heard all that passed between the inquisitors and the accused.

The interrogatories, preceded by a minute search operated upon the persons arrested, were almost always framed thus: "Has Madame Bonacieux sent anything to you for her husband, or any other person? Has Monsieur Bonacieux sent anything to you for his wife, or for any other person? Has either of them confided anything to you by word of mouth?"

"If they knew anything, they would not question people in this manner," said d'Artagnan to himself. "Now, what is it they want to know? Why, they want to know if the Duke of Buckingham is in Paris, and if he has had, or is likely to have, an interview with the queen."

D'Artagnan held onto this idea, which, from what he had heard, was not wanting in probability.

In the meantime, the mousetrap continued in operation, and likewise d'Artagnan's vigilance.

On the evening of the day after the arrest of poor Bonacieux, as Athos had just left d'Artagnan to report at M. de Tréville's, as nine o'clock had just struck, and as Planchet, who had not yet made the bed, was beginning his task, a knocking was heard at the street door. The door was instantly opened and shut; someone was taken in the mousetrap.

D'Artagnan flew to his hole, laid himself down on the floor at full length, and listened.

Cries were soon heard, and then moans, which someone appeared to be endeavouring to stifle. There were no questions.

"The devil!" said d'Artagnan to himself. "It seems like a woman! They search her; she resists; they use force–the scoundrels!"

In spite of his prudence, d'Artagnan restrained himself with great difficulty from taking a part in the scene that was going on below.

"But I tell you that I am the mistress of the house, gentlemen! I tell you I am Madame Bonacieux; I tell you I belong to the queen!" cried the unfortunate woman.

"Madame Bonacieux!" murmured d'Artagnan. "Can I be so lucky as to find what everybody is seeking for?"

The voice became more and more indistinct; a tumultuous movement shook the partition. The victim resisted as much as a woman could resist four men.

"Pardon, gentlemen–par–" murmured the voice, which could now only be heard in inarticulate sounds.

"They are binding her; they are going to drag her away," cried d'Artagnan to himself, springing up from the floor. "My sword! Good, it is by my side! Planchet!"

"Monsieur."

"Run and seek Athos, Porthos and Aramis. One of the three will certainly be at home, perhaps all three. Tell them to take arms, to come here, and to run! Ah, I remember, Athos is at Monsieur de Tréville's."

"But where are you going, Monsieur, where are you going?"

"I am going down by the window, in order to be there the sooner," cried d'Artagnan. "You put back the boards, sweep the floor, go out at the door, and run as I told you."

"Oh, Monsieur! Monsieur! You will kill yourself," cried Planchet.

"Hold your tongue, stupid fellow," said d'Artagnan; and laying hold of the casement, he let himself gently down from the first story, which fortunately was not very elevated, without doing himself the slightest injury.

He then went straight to the door and knocked, murmuring, "I will go myself and be caught in the mousetrap, but woe be to the cats that shall pounce upon such a mouse!"

The knocker had scarcely sounded under the hand of the young man before the tumult ceased, steps approached, the door was opened, and d'Artagnan, sword in hand, rushed into the rooms of M. Bonacieux, the door of which, doubtless acted upon by a spring, closed after him.

Then those who dwelt in Bonacieux's unfortunate house, together with the nearest neighbours, heard loud cries, stamping of feet, clashing of swords, and breaking of furniture. A moment after, those who, surprised by this tumult, had gone to their windows to learn the cause of it, saw the door open, and four men, clothed in black, not COME out of it, but FLY, like so many frightened crows, leaving on the ground and on the corners of the furniture, feathers from their wings; that is to say, patches of their clothes and fragments of their cloaks.

D'Artagnan was conqueror–without much effort, it must be confessed, for only one of the officers was armed, and even he defended himself for form's sake. It is true that the three others had endeavoured to knock the young man down with chairs, stools, and crockery, but two or three scratches made by the Gascon's blade terrified them. Ten minutes sufficed for their defeat, and d'Artagnan remained master of the field of battle.

The neighbours who had opened their windows, with the coolness peculiar to the inhabitants of Paris in these times of perpetual riots and disturbances, closed them again as soon as they saw the four men in black flee–their instinct telling them that for the time all was over. Besides, it began to grow late, and then, as today, people went to bed early in the quarter of the Luxembourg.

On being left alone with Mme. Bonacieux, d'Artagnan turned toward her; the poor woman reclined where she had been left, half-fainting upon an armchair. D'Artagnan examined her with a rapid glance.

She was a charming woman of twenty-five or twenty-six years, with dark hair, blue eyes, and a nose slightly turned up, admirable teeth, and a complexion marbled with rose and opal. There, however, ended the signs which might have confounded her with a lady of rank. The hands were white, but without delicacy; the feet did not bespeak the woman of quality. Happily, d'Artagnan was not yet acquainted with such niceties.

While d'Artagnan was examining Mme. Bonacieux, and was, as we have said, close to her, he saw on the ground a fine cambric handkerchief, which he picked up, as was his habit, and at the corner of which he recognised the same cipher he had seen on the handkerchief which had nearly caused him and Aramis to cut each other's throat.

From that time, d'Artagnan had been cautious with respect to handkerchiefs with arms on them, and he therefore placed in the pocket of Mme. Bonacieux the one he had just picked up.

At that moment Mme. Bonacieux recovered her senses. She opened her eyes, looked around her with terror, saw that the apartment was empty and that she was alone with her liberator. She extended her hands to him with a smile. Mme. Bonacieux had the sweetest smile in the world.

"Ah, Monsieur!" said she, "you have saved me; permit me to thank you."

"Madame," said d'Artagnan, "I have only done what every gentleman would have done in my place; you owe me no thanks."

"Oh, yes, Monsieur, oh, yes; and I hope to prove to you that you have not served an ingrate. But what could these men, whom I at first took for robbers, want with me, and why is Monsieur Bonacieux not here?"

"Madame, those men were more dangerous than any robbers could have been, for they are the agents of the cardinal; and as to your husband, Monsieur Bonacieux, he is not here because he was yesterday evening conducted to the Bastille."

"My husband in the Bastille!" cried Mme. Bonacieux. "Oh, my God! What has he done? Poor dear man, he is innocence itself!"

And something like a faint smile lighted the still-terrified features of the young woman.

"What has he done, Madame?" said d'Artagnan. "I believe that his only crime is to have at the same time the good fortune and the misfortune to be your husband."

"But, Monsieur, you know then–"

"I know that you have been abducted, Madame."

"And by whom? Do you know him? Oh, if you know him, tell me!"

"By a man of from forty to forty-five years, with black hair, a dark complexion, and a scar on his left temple."

"That is he, that is he, but his name?"

"Ah, his name? I do not know that."

"And did my husband know I had been carried off?"

"He was informed of it by a letter, written to him by the abductor himself."

"And does he suspect," said Mme. Bonacieux, with some embarrassment, "the cause of this event?"

"He attributed it, I believe, to a political cause."

"I doubted from the first; and now I think entirely as he does. Then my dear Monsieur Bonacieux has not suspected me a single instant?"

"So far from it, Madame, he was too proud of your prudence, and above all, of your love."

A second smile, almost imperceptible, stole over the rosy lips of the pretty young woman.

"But," continued d'Artagnan, "how did you escape?"

"I took advantage of a moment when they left me alone; and as I had known since morning the reason of my abduction, with the help of the sheets I let myself down from the window. Then, as I believed my husband would be at home, I hastened hither."

"To place yourself under his protection?"

"Oh, no, poor dear man! I knew very well that he was incapable of defending me, but as he could serve us in other ways, I wished to inform him."

"Of what?"

"Oh, that is not my secret; I must not, therefore, tell you."

"Besides," said d'Artagnan, "pardon me, Madame, if, guardsman as I am, I remind you of prudence–besides, I believe we are not here in a very proper place for imparting confidences. The men I have put to flight will return reinforced; if they find us here, we are lost. I have sent for three of my friends, but who knows whether they were at home?"

"Yes, yes! You are right," cried the affrighted Mme. Bonacieux, "let us fly! Let us save ourselves."

At these words she passed her arm under that of d'Artagnan, and urged him forward eagerly.

"But whither shall we fly–whither escape?"

"Let us first withdraw from this house; afterward we shall see."

The young woman and the young man, without taking the trouble to shut the door after them, descended the Rue des Fossoyeurs rapidly, turned into the Rue des Fosses-Monsieur-le-Prince, and did not stop till they came to the Place St. Sulpice.

"And now what are we to do, and where do you wish me to conduct you?" asked d'Artagnan.

"I am at quite a loss how to answer you, I admit," said Mme. Bonacieux. "My intention was to inform Monsieur Laporte, through my husband, in order that Monsieur Laporte might tell us precisely what had taken place at the Louvre in the last three days, and whether there is any danger in presenting myself there."

"But I," said d'Artagnan, "can go and inform Monsieur Laporte."

"No doubt you could, only there is one misfortune, and that is that Monsieur Bonacieux is known at the Louvre, and would be allowed to pass; whereas you are not known there, and the gate would be closed against you."

"Ah, bah!" said d'Artagnan, "you have at some wicket of the Louvre a CONCIERGE who is devoted to you, and who, thanks to a password, would–"

Mme. Bonacieux looked earnestly at the young man.

"And if I give you this password," said she, "would you forget it as soon as you used it?"

"By my honour, by the faith of a gentleman!" said d'Artagnan, with an accent so truthful that no one could mistake it.

"Then I believe you. You appear to be a brave young man; besides, your fortune may perhaps be the result of your devotedness."

"I will do, without a promise and voluntarily, all that I can do to serve the king and be agreeable to the queen. Dispose of me, then, as a friend."

"But I–where shall I go meanwhile?"

"Is there nobody from whose house Monsieur Laporte can come and fetch you?"

"No, I can trust nobody."

"Stop," said d'Artagnan, "we are near Athos's door. Yes, here it is."

"Who is this Athos?"

"One of my friends."

"But if he should be at home and see me?"

"He is not at home, and I will carry away the key, after having placed you in his apartment."

"But if he should return?"

"Oh, he won't return; and if he should, he will be told that I have brought a woman with me, and that woman is in his apartment."

"But that will compromise me sadly, you know."

"Of what consequence? Nobody knows you. Besides, we are in a situation to overlook ceremony."

"Come, then, let us go to your friend's house. Where does he live?"

"Rue Ferou, two steps from here."

"Let us go!"

Both resumed their way. As d'Artagnan had foreseen, Athos was not within. He took the key, which was customarily given him as one of the family, ascended the stairs, and introduced Mme. Bonacieux into the little apartment of which we have given a description.

"You are at home," said he. "Remain here, fasten the door inside, and open it to nobody unless you hear three taps like this;" and he tapped thrice–two taps close together and pretty hard, the other after an interval, and lighter.

"That is well," said Mme. Bonacieux. "Now, in my turn, let me give you my instructions."

"I am all attention."

"Present yourself at the wicket of the Louvre, on the side of the Rue de l'Echelle, and ask for Germain."

"Well, and then?"

"He will ask you what you want, and you will answer by these two words, 'Tours' and 'Bruxelles.' He will at once put himself at your orders."

"And what shall I command him?"

"To go and fetch Monsieur Laporte, the queen's VALET DE CHAMBRE."

"And when he shall have informed him, and Monsieur Laporte is come?"

"You will send him to me."

"That is well, but where and how shall I see you again?"

"Do you wish to see me again?"

"Certainly."

"Well, let that care be mine, and be at ease."

"I depend upon your word."

"You may."

D'Artagnan bowed to Mme. Bonacieux, darting at her the most loving glance that he could possibly concentrate upon her charming little person; and while he descended the stairs, he heard the door closed and double-locked. In two bounds he was at the Louvre; as he entered the wicket of L'Echelle, ten o'clock struck. All the events we have described had taken place within a half hour.

Everything fell out as Mme. Bonacieux prophesied. On hearing the password, Germain bowed. In a few minutes, Laporte was at the lodge; in two words d'Artagnan informed him where Mme. Bonacieux was. Laporte assured himself, by having it twice repeated, of the accurate address, and set off at a run. Hardly, however, had he taken ten steps before he returned.

"Young man," said he to d'Artagnan, "a suggestion."

"What?"

"You may get into trouble by what has taken place."

"You believe so?"

"Yes. Have you any friend whose clock is too slow?"

"Well?"

"Go and call upon him, in order that he may give evidence of your having been with him at half past nine. In a court of justice that is called an alibi."

D'Artagnan found his advice prudent. He took to his heels, and was soon at M. de Tréville's, but instead of going into the saloon with the rest of the crowd, he asked to be introduced to M. de Tréville's office. As d'Artagnan so constantly frequented the hotel, no difficulty was made in complying with his request, and a servant went to inform M. de Tréville that his young compatriot, having something important to communicate, solicited a private audience. Five minutes after, M. de Tréville was asking d'Artagnan what he could do to serve him, and what caused his visit at so late an hour.

"Pardon me, Monsieur," said d'Artagnan, who had profited by the moment he had been left alone to put back M. de Tréville's clock three-quarters of an hour, "but I thought, as it was yet only twenty-five minutes past nine, it was not too late to wait upon you."

"Twenty-five minutes past nine!" cried M. de Tréville, looking at the clock, "why, that's impossible!"

"Look, rather, Monsieur," said d'Artagnan, "the clock shows it."

"That's true," said M. de Tréville, "I believed it later. But what can I do for you?"

Then d'Artagnan told M. de Tréville a long history about the queen. He expressed to him the fears he entertained with respect to her Majesty; he related to him what he had heard of the projects of the cardinal with regard to Buckingham, and all with a tranquillity and candor of which M. de Tréville was the more the dupe, from having himself, as we have said, observed something fresh between the cardinal, the king, and the queen.

As ten o'clock was striking, d'Artagnan left M. de Tréville, who thanked him for his information, recommended him to have the service of the king and queen always at heart, and returned to the saloon, but at the foot of the stairs, d'Artagnan remembered he had forgotten his cane. He consequently sprang up again, re-entered the office, with a turn of his finger set the clock right again, that it might not be perceived the next day that it had been put wrong, and certain from that time that he had a witness to prove his alibi, he ran downstairs and soon found himself in the street.

Chapter 11

In Which The Plot Thickens

His visit to M. de Tréville being paid, the pensive d'Artagnan took the longest way homeward.

On what was d'Artagnan thinking, that he strayed thus from his path, gazing at the stars of heaven, and sometimes sighing, sometimes smiling?

He was thinking of Mme. Bonacieux. For an apprentice Musketeer the young woman was almost an ideal of love. Pretty, mysterious, initiated in almost all the secrets of the court, which reflected such a charming gravity over her pleasing features, it might be surmised that she was not wholly unmoved; and this is an irresistible charm to novices in love. Moreover, d'Artagnan had delivered her from the hands of the demons who wished to search and ill treat her; and this important service had established between them one of those sentiments of gratitude which so easily assume a more tender character.

D'Artagnan already fancied himself, so rapid is the flight of our dreams upon the wings of imagination, accosted by a messenger from the young woman, who brought him some billet appointing a meeting, a gold chain, or a diamond. We have observed that young cavaliers received presents from their king without shame. Let us add that in these times of lax morality they had no more delicacy with respect to the mistresses; and that the latter almost always left them valuable and durable remembrances, as if they essayed to conquer the fragility of their sentiments by the solidity of their gifts.

Without a blush, men made their way in the world by the means of women blushing. Such as were only beautiful gave their beauty, whence, without doubt, comes the proverb, "The most beautiful girl in the world can only give what she has." Such as were rich gave in addition a part of their money; and a vast number of heroes of that gallant period may be cited who would neither have won their spurs in the first place, nor their battles afterward, without the purse, more or less furnished, which their mistress fastened to the saddle bow.

D'Artagnan owned nothing. Provincial diffidence, that slight varnish, the ephemeral flower, that down of the peach, had evaporated to the winds through the little orthodox counsels which the three Musketeers gave their friend. D'Artagnan, following the strange custom of the times, considered himself at Paris as on a campaign, neither more nor less than if he had been in Flanders–Spain yonder, woman here. In each there was an enemy to contend with, and contributions to be levied.

But, we must say, at the present moment d'Artagnan was ruled by a feeling much more noble and disinterested. The mercer had said that he was rich; the young man might easily guess that with so weak a man as M. Bonacieux; and interest was almost foreign to this commencement of love, which had been the consequence of it. We say ALMOST, for the idea that a young, handsome, kind, and witty woman is at the same time rich takes nothing from the beginning of love, but on the contrary strengthens it.

There are in affluence a crowd of aristocratic cares and caprices which are highly becoming to beauty. A fine and white stocking, a silken robe, a lace kerchief, a pretty slipper on the foot, a tasty ribbon on the head do not make an ugly woman pretty, but they make a pretty woman beautiful, without reckoning the hands, which gain by all this; the hands, among women particularly, to be beautiful must be idle.

Then d'Artagnan, as the reader, from whom we have not concealed the state of his fortune, very well knows–d'Artagnan was not a millionaire; he hoped to become one someday, but the time which in his own mind he fixed upon for this happy change was still far distant. In the meanwhile, how disheartening to see the woman one loves long for those thousands of nothings which constitute a woman's happiness, and be unable to give her those thousands of nothings. At least, when the woman is rich and the lover is not, that which he cannot offer she offers to herself; and although it is generally with her husband's money that she procures herself this indulgence, the gratitude for it seldom reverts to him.

Then d'Artagnan, disposed to become the most tender of lovers, was at the same time a very devoted friend. In the midst of his amorous projects for the mercer's wife, he did not forget his friends. The pretty Mme. Bonacieux was just the woman to walk with in the Plain St. Denis or in the fair of St. Germain, in company with Athos, Porthos, and Aramis, to whom d'Artagnan had often remarked this. Then one could enjoy charming little dinners, where one touches on one side the hand of a friend, and on the other the foot of a mistress. Besides, on pressing occasions, in extreme difficulties, d'Artagnan would become the preserver of his friends.

And M. Bonacieux, whom d'Artagnan had pushed into the hands of the officers, denying him aloud although he had promised in a whisper to save him? We are compelled to admit to our readers that d'Artagnan thought nothing about him in any way; or that if he did think of him, it was only to say to himself that he was very well where he was, wherever it might be. Love is the most selfish of all the passions.

Let our readers reassure themselves. If d'Artagnan forgets his host, or appears to forget him, under the pretense of not knowing where he has been carried, we will not forget him, and we know where he is. But for the moment, let us do as did the amorous Gascon; we will see after the worthy mercer later.

D'Artagnan, reflecting on his future amours, addressing himself to the beautiful night, and smiling at the stars, ascended the Rue Cherish-Midi, or Chase-Midi, as it was then called. As he found himself in the quarter in which Aramis lived, he took it into his head to pay his friend a visit in order to explain the motives which had led him to send Planchet with a request that he would come instantly to the mousetrap. Now, if Aramis had been at home when Planchet came to his abode, he had doubtless hastened to the Rue des Fossoyeurs, and finding nobody there but his other two companions perhaps, they would not be able to conceive what all this meant. This mystery required an explanation; at least, so d'Artagnan declared to himself.

He likewise thought this was an opportunity for talking about pretty little Mme. Bonacieux, of whom his head, if not his heart, was already full. We must never look for discretion in first love. First love is accompanied by such excessive joy that unless the joy be allowed to overflow, it will stifle you.

Paris for two hours past had been dark, and seemed a desert. Eleven o'clock sounded from all the clocks of the Faubourg St. Germain. It was delightful weather. D'Artagnan was passing along a lane on the spot where the Rue d'Assas is now situated, breathing the balmy emanations which were borne upon the wind from the Rue de Vaugirard, and which arose from the gardens refreshed by the dews of evening and the breeze of night. From a distance resounded, deadened, however, by good shutters, the songs of the tipplers, enjoying themselves in the cabarets scattered along the plain. Arrived at the end of the lane, d'Artagnan turned to the left. The house in which Aramis dwelt was situated between the Rue Cassette and the Rue Servandoni.

D'Artagnan had just passed the Rue Cassette, and already perceived the door of his friend's house, shaded by a mass of sycamores and clematis which formed a vast arch opposite the front of it, when he perceived something like a shadow issuing from the Rue Servandoni. This something was enveloped in a cloak, and d'Artagnan at first believed it was a man, but by the smallness of the form, the hesitation of the walk, and the indecision of the step, he soon discovered that it was a woman. Further, this woman, as if not certain of the house she was seeking, lifted up her eyes to look around her, stopped, went backward, and then returned again. D'Artagnan was perplexed.

"Shall I go and offer her my services?" thought he. "By her step she must be young; perhaps she is pretty. Oh, yes! But a woman who wanders in the streets at this hour only ventures out to meet her lover. If I should disturb a rendezvous, that would not be the best means of commencing an acquaintance."

Meantime the young woman continued to advance, counting the houses and windows. This was neither long nor difficult. There were but three hotels in this part of the street; and only two windows looking toward the road, one of which was in a pavilion parallel to that which Aramis occupied, the other belonging to Aramis himself.

"PARDIEU!" said d'Artagnan to himself, to whose mind the niece of the theologian reverted, "PARDIEU, it would be droll if this belated dove should be in search of our friend's house. But on my soul, it looks so. Ah, my dear Aramis, this time I shall find you out." And d'Artagnan, making himself as small as he could, concealed himself in the darkest side of the street near a stone bench placed at the back of a niche.

The young woman continued to advance; and in addition to the lightness of her step, which had betrayed her, she emitted a little cough which denoted a sweet voice. D'Artagnan believed this cough to be a signal.

Nevertheless, whether the cough had been answered by a similar signal which had fixed the irresolution of the nocturnal seeker, or whether without this aid she saw that she had arrived at the end of her journey, she resolutely drew near to Aramis's shutter, and tapped, at three equal intervals, with her bent finger.

"This is all very fine, dear Aramis," murmured d'Artagnan. "Ah, Monsieur Hypocrite, I understand how you study theology."

The three blows were scarcely struck, when the inside blind was opened and a light appeared through the panes of the outside shutter.

"Ah, ah!" said the listener, "not through doors, but through windows! Ah, this visit was expected. We shall see the windows open, and the lady enter by escalade. Very pretty!"

But to the great astonishment of d'Artagnan, the shutter remained closed. Still more, the light which had shone for an instant disappeared, and all was again in obscurity.

D'Artagnan thought this could not last long, and continued to look with all his eyes and listen with all his ears.

He was right; at the end of some seconds two sharp taps were heard inside. The young woman in the street replied by a single tap, and the shutter was opened a little way.

It may be judged whether d'Artagnan looked or listened with avidity. Unfortunately the light had been removed into another chamber, but the eyes of the young man were accustomed to the night. Besides, the eyes of the Gascons have, as it is asserted, like those of cats, the faculty of seeing in the dark.

D'Artagnan then saw that the young woman took from her pocket a white object, which she unfolded quickly, and which took the form of a handkerchief. She made her interlocutor observe the corner of this unfolded object.

This immediately recalled to d'Artagnan's mind the handkerchief which he had found at the feet of Mme. Bonacieux, which had reminded him of that which he had dragged from under the feet of Aramis.

"What the devil could that handkerchief signify?"

Placed where he was, d'Artagnan could not perceive the face of Aramis. We say Aramis, because the young man entertained no doubt that it was his friend who held this dialogue from the interior with the lady of the exterior. Curiosity prevailed over prudence; and profiting by the preoccupation into which the sight of the handkerchief appeared to have plunged the two personages now on the scene, he stole from his hiding place, and quick as lightning, but stepping with utmost caution, he ran and placed himself close to the angle of the wall, from which his eye could pierce the interior of Aramis's room.

Upon gaining this advantage d'Artagnan was near uttering a cry of surprise; it was not Aramis who was conversing with the nocturnal visitor, it was a woman! D'Artagnan, however, could only see enough to recognise the form of her vestments, not enough to distinguish her features.

At the same instant the woman inside drew a second handkerchief from her pocket, and exchanged it for that which had just been shown to her. Then some words were spoken by the two women. At length the shutter closed. The woman who was outside the window turned round, and passed within four steps of d'Artagnan, pulling down the hood of her mantle, but the precaution was too late, d'Artagnan had already recognised Mme. Bonacieux.

Mme. Bonacieux! The suspicion that it was she had crossed the mind of d'Artagnan when she drew the handkerchief from her pocket, but what probability was there that Mme. Bonacieux, who had sent for M. Laporte in order to be reconducted to the Louvre, should be running about the streets of Paris at half past eleven at night, at the risk of being abducted a second time?

This must be, then, an affair of importance; and what is the most important affair to a woman of twenty-five! Love.

But was it on her own account, or on account of another, that she exposed herself to such hazards? This was a question the young man asked himself, whom the demon of jealousy already gnawed, being in heart neither more nor less than an accepted lover.

There was a very simple means of satisfying himself whither Mme. Bonacieux was going; that was to follow her. This method was so simple that d'Artagnan employed it quite naturally and instinctively.

But at the sight of the young man, who detached himself from the wall like a statue walking from its niche, and at the noise of the steps which she heard resound behind her, Mme. Bonacieux uttered a little cry and fled.

D'Artagnan ran after her. It was not difficult for him to overtake a woman embarrassed with her cloak. He came up with her before she had traversed a third of the street. The unfortunate woman was exhausted, not by fatigue, but by terror, and when d'Artagnan placed his hand upon her shoulder, she sank upon one knee, crying in a choking voice, "Kill me, if you please, you shall know nothing!"

D'Artagnan raised her by passing his arm round her waist, but as he felt by her weight she was on the point of fainting, he made haste to reassure her by protestations of devotedness. These protestations were nothing for Mme. Bonacieux, for such protestations may be made with the worst intentions in the world, but the voice was all. Mme. Bonacieux thought she recognised the sound of that voice; she reopened her eyes, cast a quick glance upon the man who had terrified her so, and at once perceiving it was d'Artagnan, she uttered a cry of joy, "Oh, it is you, it is you! Thank God, thank God!"

"Yes, it is I," said d'Artagnan, "it is I, whom God has sent to watch over you."

"Was it with that intention you followed me?" asked the young woman, with a coquettish smile, whose somewhat bantering character resumed its influence, and with whom all fear had disappeared from the moment in which she recognised a friend in one she had taken for an enemy.

"No," said d'Artagnan, "no, I confess it. It was chance that threw me in your way; I saw a woman knocking at the window of one of my friends."

"One of your friends?" interrupted Mme. Bonacieux.

"Without doubt; Aramis is one of my best friends."

"Aramis! Who is he?"

"Come, come, you won't tell me you don't know Aramis?"

"This is the first time I ever heard his name pronounced."

"It is the first time, then, that you ever went to that house?"

"Undoubtedly."

"And you did not know that it was inhabited by a young man?"

"No."

"By a Musketeer?"

"No, indeed!"

"It was not he, then, you came to seek?"

"Not the least in the world. Besides, you must have seen that the person to whom I spoke was a woman."

"That is true, but this woman is a friend of Aramis–"

"I know nothing of that."

"–since she lodges with him."

"That does not concern me."

"But who is she?"

"Oh, that is not my secret."

"My dear Madame Bonacieux, you are charming, but at the same time you are one of the most mysterious women."

"Do I lose by that?"

"No; you are, on the contrary, adorable."

"Give me your arm, then."

"Most willingly. And now?"

"Now escort me."

"Where?"

"Where I am going."

"But where are you going?"

"You will see, because you will leave me at the door."

"Shall I wait for you?"

"That will be useless."

"You will return alone, then?"

"Perhaps yes, perhaps no."

"But will the person who shall accompany you afterward be a man or a woman?"

"I don't know yet."

"But I will know it!"

"How so?"

"I will wait until you come out."

"In that case, adieu."

"Why so?"

"I do not want you."

"But you have claimed–"

"The aid of a gentleman, not the watchfulness of a spy."

"The word is rather hard."

"How are they called who follow others in spite of them?"

"They are indiscreet."

"The word is too mild."

"Well, Madame, I perceive I must do as you wish."

"Why did you deprive yourself of the merit of doing so at once?"

"Is there no merit in repentance?"

"And do you really repent?"

"I know nothing about it myself. But what I know is that I promise to do all you wish if you allow me to accompany you where you are going."

"And you will leave me then?"

"Yes."

"Without waiting for my coming out again?"

"Yes."

"Word of honour?"

"By the faith of a gentleman. Take my arm, and let us go."

D'Artagnan offered his arm to Mme. Bonacieux, who willingly took it, half laughing, half trembling, and both gained the top of Rue de la Harpe. Arriving there, the young woman seemed to hesitate, as she had before done in the Rue Vaugirard. She seemed, however, by certain signs, to recognise a door, and approaching that door, "And now, Monsieur," said she, "it is here I have business; a thousand thanks for your honourable company, which has saved me from all the dangers to which, alone, I was exposed.

But the moment is come to keep your word; I have reached my destination."

"And you will have nothing to fear on your return?"

"I shall have nothing to fear but robbers."

"And that is nothing?"

"What could they take from me? I have not a penny about me."

"You forget that beautiful handkerchief with the coat of arms."

"Which?"

"That which I found at your feet, and replaced in your pocket."

"Hold your tongue, imprudent man! Do you wish to destroy me?"

"You see very plainly that there is still danger for you, since a single word makes you tremble; and you confess that if that word were heard you would be ruined. Come, come, Madame!" cried d'Artagnan, seizing her hands, and surveying her with an ardent glance, "come, be more generous. Confide in me. Have you not read in my eyes that there is nothing but devotion and sympathy in my heart?"

"Yes," replied Mme. Bonacieux, "therefore, ask my own secrets, and I will reveal them to you, but those of others–that is quite another thing."

"Very well," said d'Artagnan, "I shall discover them; as these secrets may have an influence over your life, these secrets must become mine."

"Beware of what you do!" cried the young woman, in a manner so serious as to make d'Artagnan start in spite of himself. "Oh, meddle in nothing which concerns me. Do not seek to assist me in that which I am accomplishing. This I ask of you in the name of the interest with which I inspire you, in the name of the service you have rendered me and which I never shall forget while I have life. Rather, place faith in what I tell you. Have no more concern about me; I exist no longer for you, any more than if you had never seen me."

"Must Aramis do as much as I, Madame?" said d'Artagnan, deeply piqued.

"This is the second or third time, Monsieur, that you have repeated that name, and yet I have told you that I do not know him."

"You do not know the man at whose shutter you have just knocked? Indeed, Madame, you believe me too credulous!"

"Confess that it is for the sake of making me talk that you invent this story and create this personage."

"I invent nothing, Madame; I create nothing. I only speak that exact truth."

"And you say that one of your friends lives in that house?"

"I say so, and I repeat it for the third time; that house is one inhabited by my friend, and that friend is Aramis."

"All this will be cleared up at a later period," murmured the young woman, "no, Monsieur, be silent."

"If you could see my heart," said d'Artagnan, "you would there read so much curiosity that you would pity me and so much love that you would instantly satisfy my curiosity. We have nothing to fear from those who love us."

"You speak very suddenly of love, Monsieur," said the young woman, shaking her head.

"That is because love has come suddenly upon me, and for the first time; and because I am only twenty."

The young woman looked at him furtively.

"Listen; I am already upon the scent," resumed d'Artagnan. "About three months ago I was near having a duel with Aramis concerning a handkerchief resembling the one you showed to the woman in his house–for a handkerchief marked in the same manner, I am sure."

"Monsieur," said the young woman, "you weary me very much, I assure you, with your questions."

"But you, Madame, prudent as you are, think, if you were to be arrested with that handkerchief, and that handkerchief were to be seized, would you not be compromised?"

"In what way? The initials are only mine–C. B., Constance Bonacieux."

"Or Camille de Bois-Tracy."

"Silence, Monsieur! Once again, silence! Ah, since the dangers I incur on my own account cannot stop you, think of those you may yourself run!"

"Me?"

"Yes; there is peril of imprisonment, risk of life in knowing me."

"Then I will not leave you."

"Monsieur!" said the young woman, supplicating him and clasping her hands together, "monsieur, in the name of heaven, by the honour of a soldier, by the courtesy of a gentleman, depart! There, there midnight sounds! That is the hour when I am expected."

"Madame," said the young man, bowing, "I can refuse nothing asked of me thus. Be content; I will depart."

"But you will not follow me; you will not watch me?"

"I will return home instantly."

"Ah, I was quite sure you were a good and brave young man," said Mme. Bonacieux, holding out her hand to him, and placing the other upon the knocker of a little door almost hidden in the wall.

D'Artagnan seized the hand held out to him, and kissed it ardently.

"Ah! I wish I had never seen you!" cried d'Artagnan, with that ingenuous roughness which women often prefer to the affectations of politeness, because it betrays the depths of the thought and proves that feeling prevails over reason.

"Well!" resumed Mme. Bonacieux, in a voice almost caressing, and pressing the hand of d'Artagnan, who had not relinquished hers, "well: I will not say as much as you do; what is lost for today may not be lost forever. Who knows, when I shall be at liberty, that I may not satisfy your curiosity?"

"And will you make the same promise to my love?" cried d'Artagnan, beside himself with joy.

"Oh, as to that, I do not engage myself. That depends upon the sentiments with which you may inspire me."

"Then today, Madame–"

"Oh, today, I am no further than gratitude."

"Ah! You are too charming," said d'Artagnan, sorrowfully, "and you abuse my love."

"No, I use your generosity, that's all. But be of good cheer; with certain people, everything comes round."

"Oh, you render me the happiest of men! Do not forget this evening–do not forget that promise."

"Be satisfied. In the proper time and place I will remember everything. Now then, go, go, in the name of heaven! I was expected at sharp midnight, and I am late."

"By five minutes."

"Yes, but in certain circumstances five minutes are five ages."

"When one loves."

"Well! And who told you I had no affair with a lover?"

"It is a man, then, who expects you?" cried d'Artagnan. "A man!"

"The discussion is going to begin again!" said Mme. Bonacieux, with a half-smile which was not exempt from a tinge of impatience.

"No, no; I go, I depart! I believe in you, and I would have all the merit of my devotion, even if that devotion were stupidity. Adieu, Madame, adieu!"

And as if he only felt strength to detach himself by a violent effort from the hand he held, he sprang away, running, while Mme. Bonacieux knocked, as at the shutter, three light and regular taps. When he had gained the angle of the street, he turned. The door had been opened, and shut again; the mercer's pretty wife had disappeared.

D'Artagnan pursued his way. He had given his word not to watch Mme. Bonacieux, and if his life had depended upon the spot to which she was going or upon the person who should accompany her, d'Artagnan would have returned home, since he had so promised. Five minutes later he was in the Rue des Fossoyeurs.

"Poor Athos!" said he, "he will never guess what all this means. He will have fallen asleep waiting for me, or else he will have returned home, where he will have learned that a woman had been there. A woman with Athos! After all," continued d'Artagnan, "there was certainly one with Aramis. All this is very strange; and I am curious to know how it will end."

"Badly, Monsieur, badly!" replied a voice which the young man recognised as that of Planchet; for, soliloquising aloud, as very preoccupied people do, he had entered the alley, at the end of which were the stairs which led to his chamber.

"How, badly? What do you mean by that, you idiot?" asked d'Artagnan. "What has happened?"

"All sorts of misfortunes."

"What?"

"In the first place, Monsieur Athos is arrested."

"Arrested! Athos arrested! What for?"

"He was found in your lodging; they took him for you."

"And by whom was he arrested?"

"By Guards brought by the men in black whom you put to flight."

"Why did he not tell them his name? Why did he not tell them he knew nothing about this affair?"

"He took care not to do so, Monsieur; on the contrary, he came up to me and said, 'It is your master that needs his liberty at this moment and not I, since he knows everything and I know nothing. They will believe he is arrested, and that will give him time; in three days I will tell them who I am, and they cannot fail to let me go.'"

"Bravo, Athos! Noble heart!" murmured d'Artagnan. "I know him well there! And what did the officers do?"

"Four conveyed him away, I don't know where–to the Bastille or Fort l'Eveque. Two remained with the men in black, who rummaged every place and took all the papers. The last two mounted guard at the door during this examination; then, when all was over, they went away, leaving the house empty and exposed."

"And Porthos and Aramis?"

"I could not find them; they did not come."

"But they may come any moment, for you left word that I awaited them?"

"Yes, Monsieur."

"Well, don't budge, then; if they come, tell them what has happened. Let them wait for me at the Pomme-de-Pin. Here it would be dangerous; the house may be watched. I will run to Monsieur de Tréville to tell them all this, and will meet them there."

"Very well, Monsieur," said Planchet.

"But you will remain; you are not afraid?" said d'Artagnan, coming back to recommend courage to his lackey.

"Be easy, Monsieur," said Planchet, "you do not know me yet. I am brave when I set about it. It is all in beginning. Besides, I am a Picard."

"Then it is understood," said d'Artagnan, "you would rather be killed than desert your post?"

"Yes, Monsieur; and there is nothing I would not do to prove to Monsieur that I am attached to him."

"Good!" said d'Artagnan to himself. "It appears that the method I have adopted with this boy is decidedly the best. I shall use it again upon occasion."

And with all the swiftness of his legs, already a little fatigued, however, with the perambulations of the day, d'Artagnan directed his course toward M. de Tréville's.

M. de Tréville was not at his hotel. His company was on guard at the Louvre; he was at the Louvre with his company.

It was necessary to reach M. de Tréville; it was important that he should be informed of what was passing. D'Artagnan resolved to try and enter the Louvre. His costume of Guardsman in the company of M. Dessessart ought to be his passport.

He therefore went down the Rue des Petits Augustins, and came up to the quay, in order to take the New Bridge. He had at first an idea of crossing by the ferry, but on gaining the riverside, he had mechanically put his hand into his pocket, and perceived that he had not wherewithal to pay his passage.

As he gained the top of the Rue Guenegaud, he saw two persons coming out of the Rue Dauphine whose appearance very much struck him. Of the two persons who composed this group, one was a man and the other a woman. The woman had the outline of Mme. Bonacieux; the man resembled Aramis so much as to be mistaken for him.

Besides, the woman wore that black mantle which d'Artagnan could still see outlined on the shutter of the Rue de Vaugirard and on the door of the Rue de la Harpe; still further, the man wore the uniform of a Musketeer.

The woman's hood was pulled down, and the man held a handkerchief to his face. Both, as this double precaution indicated, had an interest in not being recognised.

They took the bridge. That was d'Artagnan's road, as he was going to the Louvre. D'Artagnan followed them.

He had not gone twenty steps before he became convinced that the woman was really Mme. Bonacieux and that the man was Aramis.

He felt at that instant all the suspicions of jealousy agitating his heart. He felt himself doubly betrayed, by his friend and by her whom he already loved like a mistress. Mme. Bonacieux had declared to him, by all the gods, that she did not know Aramis; and a quarter of an hour after having made this assertion, he found her hanging on the arm of Aramis.

D'Artagnan did not reflect that he had only known the mercer's pretty wife for three hours; that she owed him nothing but a little gratitude for having delivered her from the men in black, who wished to carry her off, and that she had promised him nothing.

He considered himself an outraged, betrayed, and ridiculed lover. Blood and anger mounted to his face; he was resolved to unravel the mystery.

The young man and young woman perceived they were watched, and redoubled their speed. D'Artagnan determined upon his course. He passed them, then returned so as to meet them exactly before the Samaritaine, which was illuminated by a lamp which threw its light over all that part of the bridge.

D'Artagnan stopped before them, and they stopped before him.

"What do you want, Monsieur?" demanded the Musketeer, recoiling a step, and with a foreign accent, which proved to d'Artagnan that he was deceived in one of his conjectures.

"It is not Aramis!" cried he.

"No, Monsieur, it is not Aramis; and by your exclamation I perceive you have mistaken me for another, and pardon you."

"You pardon me?" cried d'Artagnan.

"Yes," replied the stranger. "Allow me, then, to pass on, since it is not with me you have anything to do."

"You are right, Monsieur, it is not with you that I have anything to do; it is with Madame."

"With Madame! You do not know her," replied the stranger.

"You are deceived, Monsieur; I know her very well."

"Ah," said Mme. Bonacieux; in a tone of reproach, "ah, Monsieur, I had your promise as a soldier and your word as a gentleman. I hoped to be able to rely upon that."

"And I, Madame!" said d'Artagnan, embarrassed, "you promised me–"

"Take my arm, Madame," said the stranger, "and let us continue our way."

D'Artagnan, however, stupefied, cast down, annihilated by all that happened, stood, with crossed arms, before the Musketeer and Mme. Bonacieux.

The Musketeer advanced two steps, and pushed d'Artagnan aside with his hand. D'Artagnan made a spring backward and drew his sword. At the same time, and with the rapidity of lightning, the stranger drew his.

"In the name of heaven, my Lord!" cried Mme. Bonacieux, throwing herself between the combatants and seizing the swords with her hands.

"My Lord!" cried d'Artagnan, enlightened by a sudden idea, "my Lord! Pardon me, Monsieur, but you are not–"

"My Lord the Duke of Buckingham," said Mme. Bonacieux, in an undertone, "and now you may ruin us all."

"My Lord, Madame, I ask a hundred pardons! But I love her, my Lord, and was jealous. You know what it is to love, my Lord. Pardon me, and then tell me how I can risk my life to serve your Grace?"

"You are a brave young man," said Buckingham, holding out his hand to d'Artagnan, who pressed it respectfully. "You offer me your services; with the same frankness I accept them. Follow us at a distance of twenty paces, as far as the Louvre, and if anyone watches us, slay him!"

D'Artagnan placed his naked sword under his arm, allowed the duke and Mme. Bonacieux to take twenty steps ahead, and then followed them, ready to execute the instructions of the noble and elegant minister of Charles I.

Fortunately, he had no opportunity to give the duke this proof of his devotion, and the young woman and the handsome Musketeer entered the Louvre by the wicket of the Echelle without any interference.

As for d'Artagnan, he immediately repaired to the cabaret of the Pomme-de-Pin, where he found Porthos and Aramis awaiting him. Without giving them any explanation of the alarm and inconvenience he had caused them, he told them that he had terminated the affair alone in which he had for a moment believed he should need their assistance.

Meanwhile, carried away as we are by our narrative, we must leave our three friends to themselves, and follow the Duke of Buckingham and his guide through the labyrinths of the Louvre.

Chapter 12

George Villiers, Duke Of Buckingham

Mme. Bonacieux and the duke entered the Louvre without difficulty. Mme. Bonacieux was known to belong to the queen; the duke wore the uniform of the Musketeers of M. de Tréville, who, as we have said, were that evening on guard. Besides, Germain was in the interests of the queen; and if anything should happen, Mme. Bonacieux would be accused of having introduced her lover into the Louvre, that was all. She took the risk upon herself. Her reputation would be lost, it is true, but of what value in the world was the reputation of the little wife of a mercer?

Once within the interior of the court, the duke and the young woman followed the wall for the space of about twenty-five steps. This space passed, Mme. Bonacieux pushed a little servants' door, open by day but generally closed at night. The door yielded. Both entered, and found themselves in darkness, but Mme. Bonacieux was acquainted with all the turnings and windings of this part of the Louvre, appropriated for the people of the household. She closed the door after her, took the duke by the hand, and after a few experimental steps, grasped a balustrade, put her foot upon the bottom step, and began to ascend the staircase. The duke counted two stories. She then turned to the right, followed the course of a long corridor, descended a flight, went a few steps farther, introduced a key into a lock, opened a door, and pushed the duke into an apartment lighted only by a lamp, saying, "Remain here, my Lord Duke; someone will come." She then went out by the same door, which she locked, so that the duke found himself literally a prisoner.

Nevertheless, isolated as he was, we must say that the Duke of Buckingham did not experience an instant of fear. One of the salient points of his character was the search for adventures and a love of romance. Brave, rash, and enterprising, this was not the first time he had risked his life in such attempts. He had learned that the pretended message from Anne of Austria, upon the faith of which he had come to Paris, was a snare, but instead of regaining England, he had, abusing the position in which he had been placed, declared to the queen that he would not depart without seeing her. The queen had at first positively refused, but at length became afraid that the duke, if exasperated, would commit some folly. She had already decided upon seeing him and urging his immediate departure, when, on the very evening of coming to this decision, Mme. Bonacieux, who was charged with going to fetch the duke and conducting him to the Louvre, was abducted. For two days no one knew what had become of her, and everything remained in suspense, but once free, and placed in communication with Laporte, matters resumed their course, and she accomplished the perilous enterprise which, but for her arrest, would have been executed three days earlier.

Buckingham, left alone, walked toward a mirror. His Musketeer's uniform became him marvellously.

At thirty-five, which was then his age, he passed, with just title, for the handsomest gentleman and the most elegant cavalier of France or England.

The favourite of two kings, immensely rich, all-powerful in a kingdom which he disordered at his fancy and calmed again at his caprice, George Villiers, Duke of Buckingham, had lived one of those fabulous existences which survive, in the course of centuries, to astonish posterity.

Sure of himself, convinced of his own power, certain that the laws which rule other men could not reach him, he went straight to the object he aimed at, even were this object were so elevated and so dazzling that it would have been madness for any other even to have contemplated it. It was thus he had succeeded in approaching several times the beautiful and proud Anne of Austria, and in making himself loved by dazzling her.

George Villiers placed himself before the glass, as we have said, restored the undulations to his beautiful hair, which the weight of his hat had disordered, twisted his moustache, and, his heart swelling with joy, happy and proud at being near the moment he had so long sighed for, he smiled upon himself with pride and hope.

At this moment a door concealed in the tapestry opened, and a woman appeared. Buckingham saw this apparition in the glass; he uttered a cry. It was the queen!

Anne of Austria was then twenty-six or twenty-seven years of age; that is to say, she was in the full splendor of her beauty.

Her carriage was that of a queen or a goddess; her eyes, which cast the brilliancy of emeralds, were perfectly beautiful, and yet were at the same time full of sweetness and majesty.

Her mouth was small and rosy; and although her underlip, like that of all princes of the House of Austria, protruded slightly beyond the other, it was eminently lovely in its smile, but as profoundly disdainful in its contempt.

Her skin was admired for its velvety softness; her hands and arms were of surpassing beauty, all the poets of the time singing them as incomparable.

Lastly, her hair, which, from being light in her youth, had become chestnut, and which she wore curled very plainly, and with much powder, admirably set off her face, in which the most rigid critic could only have desired a little less rouge, and the most fastidious sculptor a little more fineness in the nose.

Buckingham remained for a moment dazzled. Never had Anne of Austria appeared to him so beautiful, amid balls, fêtes, or carousals, as she appeared to him at this moment, dressed in a simple robe of white satin, and accompanied by Donna Estafania–the only one of her Spanish women who had not been driven from her by the jealousy of the king or by the persecutions of Richelieu.

Anne of Austria took two steps forward. Buckingham threw himself at her feet, and before the queen could prevent him, kissed the hem of her robe.

"Duke, you already know that it is not I who caused you to be written to."

"Yes, yes, Madame! Yes, your Majesty!" cried the duke. "I know that I must have been mad, senseless, to believe that snow would become animated or marble warm, but what then! They who love believe easily in love. Besides, I have lost nothing by this journey because I see you."

"Yes," replied Anne, "but you know why and how I see you; because, insensible to all my sufferings, you persist in remaining in a city where, by remaining, you run the risk of your life, and make me run the risk of my honour. I see you to tell you that everything separates us–the depths of the sea, the enmity of kingdoms, the sanctity of vows. It is sacrilege to struggle against so many things, my Lord. In short, I see you to tell you that we must never see each other again."

"Speak on, Madame, speak on, Queen," said Buckingham, "the sweetness of your voice covers the harshness of your words. You talk of sacrilege! Why, the sacrilege is the separation of two hearts formed by God for each other."

"My Lord," cried the queen, "you forget that I have never said that I love you."

"But you have never told me that you did not love me; and truly, to speak such words to me would be, on the part of your Majesty, too great an ingratitude. For tell me, where can you find a love like mine–a love which neither time, nor absence, nor despair can extinguish, a love which contents itself with a lost ribbon, a stray look, or a chance word? It is now three years, Madame, since I saw you for the first time, and during those three years I have loved you thus. Shall I tell you each ornament of your toilet? Mark! I see you now. You were seated upon cushions in the Spanish fashion; you wore a robe of green satin embroidered with gold and silver, hanging sleeves knotted upon your beautiful arms–those lovely arms–with large diamonds. You wore a close ruff, a small cap upon your head of the same colour as your robe, and in that cap a heron's feather. Hold! Hold! I shut my eyes, and I can see you as you then were; I open them again, and I see what you are now–a hundred times more beautiful!"

"What folly," murmured Anne of Austria, who had not the courage to find fault with the duke for having so well preserved her portrait in his heart, "what folly to feed a useless passion with such remembrances!"

"And upon what then must I live? I have nothing but memory. It is my happiness, my treasure, my hope. Every time I see you is a fresh diamond which I enclose in the casket of my heart. This is the fourth which you have let fall and I have picked up; for in three years, Madame, I have only seen you four times–the first, which I have described to you; the second, at the mansion of Madame de Chevreuse; the third, in the gardens of Amiens."

"Duke," said the queen, blushing, "never speak of that evening."

"Oh, let us speak of it; on the contrary, let us speak of it! That is the most happy and brilliant evening of my life! You remember what a beautiful night it was? How soft and perfumed was the air; how lovely the blue heavens and star-enameled sky! Ah, then, Madame, I was able for one instant to be alone with you. Then you were about to tell me all–the isolation of your life, the griefs of your heart. You leaned upon my arm–upon this, Madame! I felt, in bending my head toward you, your beautiful hair touch my cheek; and every time that it touched me I trembled from head to foot. Oh, Queen! Queen! You do not know what felicity from heaven, what joys from paradise, are comprised in a moment like that. Take my wealth, my fortune, my glory, all the days I have to live, for such an instant, for a night like that. For that night, Madame, that night you loved me, I will swear it."

"My Lord, yes; it is possible that the influence of the place, the charm of the beautiful evening, the fascination of your look–the thousand circumstances, in short, which sometimes unite to destroy a woman–were grouped around me on that fatal evening; but, my Lord, you saw the queen come to the aid of the woman who faltered. At the first word you dared to utter, at the first freedom to which I had to reply, I called for help."

"Yes, yes, that is true. And any other love but mine would have sunk beneath this ordeal, but my love came out from it more ardent and more eternal. You believed that you would fly from me by returning to Paris; you believed that I would not dare to quit the treasure over which my master had charged me to watch. What to me were all the treasures in the world, or all the kings of the earth! Eight days after, I was back again, Madame. That time you had nothing to say to me; I had risked my life and favour to see you but for a second. I did not even touch your hand, and you pardoned me on seeing me so submissive and so repentant."

"Yes, but calumny seized upon all those follies in which I took no part, as you well know, my Lord. The king, excited by the cardinal, made a terrible clamor. Madame de Vernet was driven from me, Putange was exiled, Madame de Chevreuse fell into disgrace, and when you wished to come back as ambassador to France, the king himself–remember, my lord–the king himself opposed it."

"Yes, and France is about to pay for her king's refusal with a war. I am not allowed to see you, Madame, but you shall every day hear of me. What object, think you, have this expedition to Re and this league with the Protestants of La Rochelle which I am projecting? The pleasure of seeing you. I have no hope of penetrating, sword in hand, to Paris, I know that well. But this war may bring round a peace; this peace will require a negotiator; that negotiator will be me. They will not dare to refuse me then; and I will return to Paris, and will see you again, and will be happy for an instant. Thousands of men, it is true, will have to pay for my happiness with their lives, but what is that to me, provided I see you again! All this is perhaps folly–perhaps insanity, but tell me what woman has a lover more truly in love; what queen a servant more ardent?"

"My Lord, my Lord, you invoke in your defense things which accuse you more strongly. All these proofs of love which you would give me are almost crimes."

"Because you do not love me, Madame! If you loved me, you would view all this otherwise. If you loved me, oh, if you loved me, that would be too great happiness, and I should run mad. Ah, Madame de Chevreuse was less cruel than you. Holland loved her, and she responded to his love."

"Madame de Chevreuse was not queen," murmured Anne of Austria, overcome, in spite of herself, by the expression of so profound a passion.

"You would love me, then, if you were not queen! Madame, say that you would love me then! I can believe that it is the dignity of your rank alone which makes you cruel to me; I can believe that, had you been Madame de Chevreuse, poor Buckingham might have hoped. Thanks for those sweet words! Oh, my beautiful sovereign, a hundred times, thanks!"

"Oh, my Lord! You have ill understood, wrongly interpreted; I did not mean to say–"

"Silence, silence!" cried the duke. "If I am happy in an error, do not have the cruelty to lift me from it. You have told me yourself, Madame, that I have been drawn into a snare; I, perhaps, may leave my life in it–for, although it may be strange, I have for some time had a presentiment that I should shortly die." And the duke smiled, with a smile at once sad and charming.

"Oh, my God!" cried Anne of Austria, with an accent of terror which proved how much greater an interest she took in the duke than she ventured to tell.

"I do not tell you this, Madame, to terrify you; no, it is even ridiculous for me to name it to you, and, believe me, I take no heed of such dreams. But the words you have just spoken, the hope you have almost given me, will have richly paid all–were it my life."

"Oh, but I," said Anne, "I also, duke, have had presentiments; I also have had dreams. I dreamed that I saw you lying bleeding, wounded."

"In the left side, was it not, and with a knife?" interrupted Buckingham.

"Yes, it was so, my Lord, it was so–in the left side, and with a knife. Who can possibly have told you I had had that dream? I have imparted it to no one but my God, and that in my prayers."

"I ask for no more. You love me, Madame; it is enough."

"I love you, I?"

"Yes, yes. Would God send the same dreams to you as to me if you did not love me? Should we have the same presentiments if our existences did not touch at the heart? You love me, my beautiful queen, and you will weep for me?"

"Oh, my God, my God!" cried Anne of Austria, "this is more than I can bear. In the name of heaven, Duke, leave me, go! I do not know whether I love you or love you not, but what I know is that I will not be perjured. Take pity on me, then, and go! Oh, if you are struck in France, if you die in France, if I could imagine that your love for me was the cause of your death, I could not console myself; I should run mad. Depart then, depart, I implore you!"

"Oh, how beautiful you are thus! Oh, how I love you!" said Buckingham.

"Go, go, I implore you, and return hereafter! Come back as ambassador, come back as minister, come back surrounded with guards who will defend you, with servants who will watch over you, and then I shall no longer fear for your days, and I shall be happy in seeing you."

"Oh, is this true what you say?"

"Yes."

"Oh, then, some pledge of your indulgence, some object which came from you, and may remind me that I have not been dreaming; something you have worn, and that I may wear in my turn–a ring, a necklace, a chain."

"Will you depart–will you depart, if I give you that you demand?"

"Yes."

"This very instant?"

"Yes."

"You will leave France, you will return to England?"

"I will, I swear to you."

"Wait, then, wait."

Anne of Austria re-entered her apartment, and came out again almost immediately, holding a rosewood casket in her hand, with her cipher encrusted with gold.

"Here, my Lord, here," said she, "keep this in memory of me."

Buckingham took the casket, and fell a second time on his knees.

"You have promised me to go," said the queen.

"And I keep my word. Your hand, Madame, your hand, and I depart!"

Anne of Austria stretched forth her hand, closing her eyes, and leaning with the other upon Estafania, for she felt that her strength was about to fail her.

Buckingham pressed his lips passionately to that beautiful hand, and then rising, said, "Within six months, if I am not dead, I shall have seen you again, Madame–even if I have to overturn the world." And faithful to the promise he had made, he rushed out of the apartment.

In the corridor he met Mme. Bonacieux, who waited for him, and who, with the same precautions and the same good luck, conducted him out of the Louvre.

Chapter 13

Monsieur Bonacieux

There was in all this, as may have been observed, one personage concerned, of whom, notwithstanding his precarious position, we have appeared to take but very little notice. This personage was M. Bonacieux, the respectable martyr of the political and amorous intrigues which entangled themselves so nicely together at this gallant and chivalric period.

Fortunately, the reader may remember, or may not remember—fortunately we have promised not to lose sight of him.

The officers who arrested him conducted him straight to the Bastille, where he passed trembling before a party of soldiers who were loading their muskets. Thence, introduced into a half-subterranean gallery, he became, on the part of those who had brought him, the object of the grossest insults and the harshest treatment. The officers perceived that they had not to deal with a gentleman, and they treated him like a very peasant.

At the end of half an hour or thereabouts, a clerk came to put an end to his tortures, but not to his anxiety, by giving the order to conduct M. Bonacieux to the Chamber of Examination. Ordinarily, prisoners were interrogated in their cells, but they did not do so with M. Bonacieux.

Two guards attended the mercer who made him traverse a court and enter a corridor in which were three sentinels, opened a door and pushed him unceremoniously into a low room, where the only furniture was a table, a chair, and a commissary. The commissary was seated in the chair, and was writing at the table.

The two guards led the prisoner toward the table, and upon a sign from the commissary drew back so far as to be unable to hear anything.

The commissary, who had till this time held his head down over his papers, looked up to see what sort of person he had to do with. This commissary was a man of very repulsive mien, with a pointed nose, with yellow and salient cheek bones, with eyes small but keen and penetrating, and an expression of countenance resembling at once the polecat and the fox. His head, supported by a long and flexible neck, issued from his large black robe, balancing itself with a motion very much like that of the tortoise thrusting his head out of his shell. He began by asking M. Bonacieux his name, age, condition, and abode.

The accused replied that his name was Jacques Michel Bonacieux, that he was fifty-one years old, a retired mercer, and lived Rue des Fossoyeurs, No. 14.

The commissary then, instead of continuing to interrogate him, made him a long speech upon the danger there is for an obscure citizen to meddle with public matters. He complicated this exordium by an exposition in which he painted the power and the deeds of the cardinal, that incomparable minister, that conqueror of past ministers, that example for ministers to come–deeds and power which none could thwart with impunity.

After this second part of his discourse, fixing his hawk's eye upon poor Bonacieux, he bade him reflect upon the gravity of his situation.

The reflections of the mercer were already made; he cursed the instant when M. Laporte formed the idea of marrying him to his goddaughter, and particularly the moment when that goddaughter had been received as Lady of the Linen to her Majesty.

At bottom the character of M. Bonacieux was one of profound selfishness mixed with sordid avarice, the whole seasoned with extreme cowardice. The love with which his young wife had inspired him was a secondary sentiment, and was not strong enough to contend with the primitive feelings we have just enumerated. Bonacieux indeed reflected on what had just been said to him.

"But, Monsieur Commissary," said he, calmly, "believe that I know and appreciate, more than anybody, the merit of the incomparable eminence by whom we have the honour to be governed."

"Indeed?" asked the commissary, with an air of doubt. "If that is really so, how came you in the Bastille?"

"How I came there, or rather why I am there," replied Bonacieux, "that is entirely impossible for me to tell you, because I don't know myself, but to a certainty it is not for having, knowingly at least, disobliged Monsieur the Cardinal."

"You must, nevertheless, have committed a crime, since you are here and are accused of high treason."

"Of high treason!" cried Bonacieux, terrified, "of high treason! How is it possible for a poor mercer, who detests Huguenots and who abhors Spaniards, to be accused of high treason? Consider, Monsieur, the thing is absolutely impossible."

"Monsieur Bonacieux," said the commissary, looking at the accused as if his little eyes had the faculty of reading to the very depths of hearts, "you have a wife?"

"Yes, Monsieur," replied the mercer, in a tremble, feeling that it was at this point affairs were likely to become perplexing, "that is to say, I HAD one."

"What, you 'had one'? What have you done with her, then, if you have her no longer?"

"They have abducted her, Monsieur."

"They have abducted her? Ah!"

Bonacieux inferred from this "Ah" that the affair grew more and more intricate.

"They have abducted her," added the commissary, "and do you know the man who has committed this deed?"

"I think I know him."

"Who is he?"

"Remember that I affirm nothing, Monsieur the Commissary, and that I only suspect."

"Whom do you suspect? Come, answer freely."

M Bonacieux was in the greatest perplexity possible. Had he better deny everything or tell everything? By denying all, it might be suspected that he must know too much to avow; by confessing all he might prove his good will. He decided, then, to tell all.

"I suspect," said he, "a tall, dark man, of lofty carriage, who has the air of a great lord. He has followed us several times, as I think, when I have waited for my wife at the wicket of the Louvre to escort her home."

The commissary now appeared to experience a little uneasiness.

"And his name?" said he.

"Oh, as to his name, I know nothing about it, but if I were ever to meet him, I should recognise him in an instant, I will answer for it, were he among a thousand persons."

The face of the commissary grew still darker.

"You should recognise him among a thousand, say you?" continued he.

"That is to say," cried Bonacieux, who saw he had taken a false step, "that is to say–"

"You have answered that you should recognise him," said the commissary. "That is all very well, and enough for today; before we proceed further, someone must be informed that you know the ravisher of your wife."

"But I have not told you that I know him!" cried Bonacieux, in despair. "I told you, on the contrary–"

"Take away the prisoner," said the commissary to the two guards.

"Where must we place him?" demanded the chief.

"In a dungeon."

"Which?"

"Good Lord! In the first one handy, provided it is safe," said the commissary, with an indifference which penetrated poor Bonacieux with horror.

"Alas, alas!" said he to himself, "misfortune is over my head; my wife must have committed some frightful crime. They believe me her accomplice, and will punish me with her. She must have spoken; she must have confessed everything–a woman is so weak! A dungeon! The first he comes to! That's it! A night is soon passed; and tomorrow to the wheel, to the gallows! Oh, my God, my God, have pity on me!"

Without listening the least in the world to the lamentations of M. Bonacieux–lamentations to which, besides, they must have been pretty well accustomed–the two guards took the prisoner each by an arm, and led him away, while the commissary wrote a letter in haste and dispatched it by an officer in waiting.

Bonacieux could not close his eyes; not because his dungeon was so very disagreeable, but because his uneasiness was so great. He sat all night on his stool, starting at the least noise; and when the first rays of the sun penetrated into his chamber, the dawn itself appeared to him to have taken funereal tints.

All at once he heard his bolts drawn, and made a terrified bound. He believed they were come to conduct him to the scaffold; so that when he saw merely and simply, instead of the executioner he expected, only his commissary of the preceding evening, attended by his clerk, he was ready to embrace them both.

"Your affair has become more complicated since yesterday evening, my good man, and I advise you to tell the whole truth; for your repentance alone can remove the anger of the cardinal."

"Why, I am ready to tell everything," cried Bonacieux, "at least, all that I know. Interrogate me, I entreat you!"

"Where is your wife, in the first place?"

"Why, did not I tell you she had been stolen from me?"

"Yes, but yesterday at five o'clock in the afternoon, thanks to you, she escaped."

"My wife escaped!" cried Bonacieux. "Oh, unfortunate creature! Monsieur, if she has escaped, it is not my fault, I swear."

"What business had you, then, to go into the chamber of Monsieur d'Artagnan, your neighbour, with whom you had a long conference during the day?"

"Ah, yes, Monsieur Commissary; yes, that is true, and I confess that I was in the wrong. I did go to Monsieur d'Artagnan's."

"What was the aim of that visit?"

"To beg him to assist me in finding my wife. I believed I had a right to endeavour to find her. I was deceived, as it appears, and I ask your pardon."

"And what did Monsieur d'Artagnan reply?"

"Monsieur d'Artagnan promised me his assistance, but I soon found out that he was betraying me."

"You impose upon justice. Monsieur d'Artagnan made a compact with you; and in virtue of that compact put to flight the police who had arrested your wife, and has placed her beyond reach."

"M. d'Artagnan has abducted my wife! Come now, what are you telling me?"

"Fortunately, Monsieur d'Artagnan is in our hands, and you shall be confronted with him."

"By my faith, I ask no better," cried Bonacieux, "I shall not be sorry to see the face of an acquaintance."

"Bring in the Monsieur d'Artagnan," said the commissary to the guards. The two guards led in Athos.

"Monsieur d'Artagnan," said the commissary, addressing Athos, "declare all that passed yesterday between you and Monsieur."

"But," cried Bonacieux, "this is not Monsieur d'Artagnan whom you show me."

"What! Not Monsieur d'Artagnan?" exclaimed the commissary.

"Not the least in the world," replied Bonacieux.

"What is this gentleman's name?" asked the commissary.

"I cannot tell you; I don't know him."

"How! You don't know him?"

"No."

"Did you never see him?"

"Yes, I have seen him, but I don't know what he calls himself."

"Your name?" replied the commissary.

"Athos," replied the Musketeer.

"But that is not a man's name; that is the name of a mountain," cried the poor questioner, who began to lose his head.

"That is my name," said Athos, quietly.

"But you said that your name was d'Artagnan."

"Who, I?"

"Yes, you."

"Somebody said to me, 'You are Monsieur d'Artagnan?' I answered, 'You think so?' My guards exclaimed that they were sure of it. I did not wish to contradict them; besides, I might be deceived."

"Monsieur, you insult the majesty of justice."

"Not at all," said Athos, calmly.

"You are Monsieur d'Artagnan."

"You see, Monsieur, that you say it again."

"But I tell you, Monsieur Commissary," cried Bonacieux, in his turn, "there is not the least doubt about the matter. Monsieur d'Artagnan is my tenant, although he does not pay me my rent–and even better on that account ought I to know him. Monsieur d'Artagnan is a young man, scarcely nineteen or twenty, and this gentleman must be thirty at least. Monsieur d'Artagnan is in Monsieur Dessessart's Guards, and this gentleman is in the company of Monsieur de Tréville's Musketeers. Look at his uniform, Monsieur Commissary, look at his uniform!"

"That's true," murmured the commissary, "PARDIEU, that's true."

At this moment the door was opened quickly, and a messenger, introduced by one of the gatekeepers of the Bastille, gave a letter to the commissary.

"Oh, unhappy woman!" cried the commissary.

"How? What do you say? Of whom do you speak? It is not of my wife, I hope!"

"On the contrary, it is of her. Yours is a pretty business."

"But," said the agitated mercer, "do me the pleasure, Monsieur, to tell me how my own proper affair can become worse by anything my wife does while I am in prison?"

"Because that which she does is part of a plan concerted between you–of an infernal plan."

"I swear to you, Monsieur Commissary, that you are in the profoundest error, that I know nothing in the world about what my wife had to do, that I am entirely a stranger to what she has done; and that if she has committed any follies, I renounce her, I abjure her, I curse her!"

"Bah!" said Athos to the commissary, "if you have no more need of me, send me somewhere. Your Monsieur Bonacieux is very tiresome."

The commissary designated by the same gesture Athos and Bonacieux, "Let them be guarded more closely than ever."

"And yet," said Athos, with his habitual calmness, "if it be Monsieur d'Artagnan who is concerned in this matter, I do not perceive how I can take his place."

"Do as I bade you," cried the commissary, "and preserve absolute secrecy. You understand!"

Athos shrugged his shoulders, and followed his guards silently, while M. Bonacieux uttered lamentations enough to break the heart of a tiger.

They locked the mercer in the same dungeon where he had passed the night, and left him to himself during the day. Bonacieux wept all day, like a true mercer, not being at all a military man, as he himself informed us. In the evening, about nine o'clock, at the moment he had made up his mind to go to bed, he heard steps in his corridor. These steps drew near to his dungeon, the door was thrown open, and the guards appeared.

"Follow me," said an officer, who came up behind the guards.

"Follow you!" cried Bonacieux, "follow you at this hour! Where, my God?"

"Where we have orders to lead you."

"But that is not an answer."

"It is, nevertheless, the only one we can give."

"Ah, my God, my God!" murmured the poor mercer, "now, indeed, I am lost!" And he followed the guards who came for him, mechanically and without resistance.

He passed along the same corridor as before, crossed one court, then a second side of a building; at length, at the gate of the entrance court he found a carriage surrounded by four guards on horseback. They made him enter this carriage, the officer placed himself by his side, the door was locked, and they were left in a rolling prison. The carriage was put in motion as slowly as a funeral car. Through the closely fastened windows the prisoner could perceive the houses and the pavement, that was all; but, true Parisian as he was, Bonacieux could recognise every street by the milestones, the signs, and the lamps. At the moment of arriving at St. Paul–the spot where such as were condemned at the Bastille were executed–he was near fainting and crossed himself twice. He thought the carriage was about to stop there. The carriage, however, passed on.

Farther on, a still greater terror seized him on passing by the cemetery of St. Jean, where state criminals were buried. One thing, however, reassured him; he remembered that before they were buried their heads were generally cut off, and he felt that his head was still on his shoulders. But when he saw the carriage take the way to La Greve, when he perceived the pointed roof of the Hotel de Ville, and the carriage passed under the arcade, he believed it was over with him. He wished to confess to the officer, and upon his refusal, uttered such pitiable cries that the officer told him that if he continued to deafen him thus, he should put a gag in his mouth.

This measure somewhat reassured Bonacieux. If they meant to execute him at La Greve, it could scarcely be worth while to gag him, as they had nearly reached the place of execution. Indeed, the carriage crossed the fatal spot without stopping. There remained, then, no other place to fear but the Traitor's Cross; the carriage was taking the direct road to it.

This time there was no longer any doubt; it was at the Traitor's Cross that lesser criminals were executed. Bonacieux had flattered himself in believing himself worthy of St. Paul or of the Place de Greve; it was at the Traitor's Cross that his journey and his destiny were about to end! He could not yet see that dreadful cross, but he felt somehow as if it were coming to meet him. When he was within twenty paces of it, he heard a noise of people and the carriage stopped. This was more than poor Bonacieux could endure, depressed as he was by the successive emotions which he had experienced; he uttered a feeble groan which night have been taken for the last sigh of a dying man, and fainted.

Chapter 14

The Man Of Meung

The crowd was caused, not by the expectation of a man to be hanged, but by the contemplation of a man who was hanged.

The carriage, which had been stopped for a minute, resumed its way, passed through the crowd, threaded the Rue St. Honoré, turned into the Rue des Bons Enfants, and stopped before a low door.

The door opened; two guards received Bonacieux in their arms from the officer who supported him. They carried him through an alley, up a flight of stairs, and deposited him in an antechamber.

All these movements had been effected mechanically, as far as he was concerned. He had walked as one walks in a dream; he had a glimpse of objects as through a fog. His ears had perceived sounds without comprehending them; he might have been executed at that moment without his making a single gesture in his own defense or uttering a cry to implore mercy.

He remained on the bench, with his back leaning against the wall and his hands hanging down, exactly on the spot where the guards placed him.

On looking around him, however, as he could perceive no threatening object, as nothing indicated that he ran any real danger, as the bench was comfortably covered with a well-stuffed cushion, as the wall was ornamented with a beautiful Cordova leather, and as large red damask curtains, fastened back by gold clasps, floated before the window, he perceived by degrees that his fear was exaggerated, and he began to turn his head to the right and the left, upward and downward.

At this movement, which nobody opposed, he resumed a little courage, and ventured to draw up one leg and then the other. At length, with the help of his two hands he lifted himself from the bench, and found himself on his feet.

At this moment an officer with a pleasant face opened a door, continued to exchange some words with a person in the next chamber and then came up to the prisoner. "Is your name Bonacieux?" said he.

"Yes, Monsieur Officer," stammered the mercer, more dead than alive, "at your service."

"Come in," said the officer.

And he moved out of the way to let the mercer pass. The latter obeyed without reply, and entered the chamber, where he appeared to be expected.

It was a large cabinet, close and stifling, with the walls furnished with arms offensive and defensive, and in which there was already a fire, although it was scarcely the end of the month of September. A square table, covered with books and papers, upon which was unrolled an immense plan of the city of La Rochelle, occupied the centre of the room.

Standing before the chimney was a man of middle height, of a haughty, proud mien; with piercing eyes, a large brow, and a thin face, which was made still longer by a ROYAL (or IMPERIAL, as it is now called), surmounted by a pair of moustaches. Although this man was scarcely thirty-six or thirty-seven years of age, hair, moustaches, and royal, all began to be gray. This man, except a sword, had all the appearance of a soldier; and his buff boots, still slightly covered with dust, indicated that he had been on horseback in the course of the day.

This man was Armand Jean Duplessis, Cardinal de Richelieu; not such as he is now represented–broken down like an old man, suffering like a martyr, his body bent, his voice failing, buried in a large armchair as in an anticipated tomb; no longer living but by the strength of his genius, and no longer maintaining the struggle with Europe but by the eternal application of his thoughts–but such as he really was at this period; that is to say, an active and gallant cavalier, already weak of body, but sustained by that moral power which made of him one of the most extraordinary men that ever lived, preparing, after having supported the Duc de Nevers in his duchy of Mantua, after having taken Nimes, Castres, and Uzes, to drive the English from the Isle of Re and lay siege to La Rochelle.

At first sight, nothing denoted the cardinal; and it was impossible for those who did not know his face to guess in whose presence they were.

The poor mercer remained standing at the door, while the eyes of the personage we have just described were fixed upon him, and appeared to wish to penetrate even into the depths of the past.

"Is this that Bonacieux?" asked he, after a moment of silence.

"Yes, Monseigneur," replied the officer.

"That's well. Give me those papers, and leave us."

The officer took from the table the papers pointed out, gave them to him who asked for them, bowed to the ground, and retired.

Bonacieux recognised in these papers his interrogatories of the Bastille. From time to time the man by the chimney raised his eyes from the writings, and plunged them like poniards into the heart of the poor mercer.

At the end of ten minutes of reading and ten seconds of examination, the cardinal was satisfied.

"That head has never conspired," murmured he, "but it matters not; we will see."

"You are accused of high treason," said the cardinal, slowly.

"So I have been told already, Monseigneur," cried Bonacieux, giving his interrogator the title he had heard the officer give him, "but I swear to you that I know nothing about it."

The cardinal repressed a smile.

"You have conspired with your wife, with Madame de Chevreuse, and with my Lord Duke of Buckingham."

"Indeed, Monseigneur," responded the mercer, "I have heard her pronounce all those names."

"And on what occasion?"

"She said that the Cardinal de Richelieu had drawn the Duke of Buckingham to Paris to ruin him and to ruin the queen."

"She said that?" cried the cardinal, with violence.

"Yes, Monseigneur, but I told her she was wrong to talk about such things; and that his Eminence was incapable–"

"Hold your tongue! You are stupid," replied the cardinal.

"That's exactly what my wife said, Monseigneur."

"Do you know who carried off your wife?"

"No, Monseigneur."

"You have suspicions, nevertheless?"

"Yes, Monseigneur, but these suspicions appeared to be disagreeable to Monsieur the Commissary, and I no longer have them."

"Your wife has escaped. Did you know that?"

"No, Monseigneur. I learned it since I have been in prison, and that from the conversation of Monsieur the Commissary–an amiable man."

The cardinal repressed another smile.

"Then you are ignorant of what has become of your wife since her flight."

"Absolutely, Monseigneur, but she has most likely returned to the Louvre."

"At one o'clock this morning she had not returned."

"My God! What can have become of her, then?"

"We shall know, be assured. Nothing is concealed from the cardinal; the cardinal knows everything."

"In that case, Monseigneur, do you believe the cardinal will be so kind as to tell me what has become of my wife?"

"Perhaps he may, but you must, in the first place, reveal to the cardinal all you know of your wife's relations with Madame de Chevreuse."

"But, Monseigneur, I know nothing about them; I have never seen her."

"When you went to fetch your wife from the Louvre, did you always return directly home?"

"Scarcely ever; she had business to transact with linen drapers, to whose houses I conducted her."

"And how many were there of these linen drapers?"

"Two, Monseigneur."

"And where did they live?"

"One in Rue de Vaugirard, the other Rue de la Harpe."

"Did you go into these houses with her?"

"Never, Monseigneur; I waited at the door."

"And what excuse did she give you for entering all alone?"

"She gave me none; she told me to wait, and I waited."

"You are a very complacent husband, my dear Monsieur Bonacieux," said the cardinal.

"He calls me his dear Monsieur," said the mercer to himself. "PESTE! Matters are going all right."

"Should you know those doors again?"

"Yes."

"Do you know the numbers?"

"Yes."

"What are they?"

"No. 25 in the Rue de Vaugirard; 75 in the Rue de la Harpe."

"That's well," said the cardinal.

At these words he took up a silver bell, and rang it; the officer entered.

"Go," said he, in a subdued voice, "and find Rochefort. Tell him to come to me immediately, if he has returned."

"The count is here," said the officer, "and requests to speak with your Eminence instantly."

"Let him come in, then!" said the cardinal, quickly.

The officer sprang out of the apartment with that alacrity which all the servants of the cardinal displayed in obeying him.

"To your Eminence!" murmured Bonacieux, rolling his eyes round in astonishment.

Five seconds has scarcely elapsed after the disappearance of the officer, when the door opened, and a new personage entered.

"It is he!" cried Bonacieux.

"He! What he?" asked the cardinal.

"The man who abducted my wife."

The cardinal rang a second time. The officer reappeared.

"Place this man in the care of his guards again, and let him wait till I send for him."

"No, Monseigneur, no, it is not he!" cried Bonacieux, "no, I was deceived. This is quite another man, and does not resemble him at all. Monsieur is, I am sure, an honest man."

"Take away that fool!" said the cardinal.

The officer took Bonacieux by the arm, and led him into the antechamber, where he found his two guards.

The newly introduced personage followed Bonacieux impatiently with his eyes till he had gone out; and the moment the door closed, "They have seen each other;" said he, approaching the cardinal eagerly.

"Who?" asked his Eminence.

"He and she."

"The queen and the duke?" cried Richelieu.

"Yes."

"Where?"

"At the Louvre."

"Are you sure of it?"

"Perfectly sure."

"Who told you of it?"

"Madame de Lannoy, who is devoted to your Eminence, as you know."

"Why did she not let me know sooner?"

"Whether by chance or mistrust, the queen made Madame de Surgis sleep in her chamber, and detained her all day."

"Well, we are beaten! Now let us try to take our revenge."

"I will assist you with all my heart, Monseigneur; be assured of that."

"How did it come about?"

"At half past twelve the queen was with her women–"

"Where?"

"In her bedchamber–"

"Go on."

"When someone came and brought her a handkerchief from her laundress."

"And then?"

"The queen immediately exhibited strong emotion; and despite the rouge with which her face was covered evidently turned pale–"

"And then, and then?"

"She then arose, and with altered voice, 'Ladies,' said she, 'wait for me ten minutes, I shall soon return.' She then opened the door of her alcove, and went out."

"Why did not Madame de Lannoy come and inform you instantly?"

"Nothing was certain; besides, her Majesty had said, 'Ladies, wait for me,' and she did not dare to disobey the queen."

"How long did the queen remain out of the chamber?"

"Three-quarters of an hour."

"None of her women accompanied her?"

"Only Donna Estafania."

"Did she afterward return?"

"Yes, but only to take a little rosewood casket, with her cipher upon it, and went out again immediately."

"And when she finally returned, did she bring that casket with her?"

"No."

"Does Madame de Lannoy know what was in that casket?"

"Yes; the diamond studs which his Majesty gave the queen."

"And she came back without this casket?"

"Yes."

"Madame de Lannoy, then, is of opinion that she gave them to Buckingham?"

"She is sure of it."

"How can she be so?"

"In the course of the day Madame de Lannoy, in her quality of tire-woman of the queen, looked for this casket, appeared uneasy at not finding it, and at length asked information of the queen."

"And then the queen?"

"The queen became exceedingly red, and replied that having in the evening broken one of those studs, she had sent it to her goldsmith to be repaired."

"He must be called upon, and so ascertain if the thing be true or not."

"I have just been with him."

"And the goldsmith?"

"The goldsmith has heard nothing of it."

"Well, well! Rochefort, all is not lost; and perhaps–perhaps everything is for the best."

"The fact is that I do not doubt your Eminence's genius–"

"Will repair the blunders of his agent–is that it?"

"That is exactly what I was going to say, if your Eminence had let me finish my sentence."

"Meanwhile, do you know where the Duchesse de Chevreuse and the Duke of Buckingham are now concealed?"

"No, Monseigneur; my people could tell me nothing on that head."

"But I know."

"You, Monseigneur?"

"Yes; or at least I guess. They were, one in the Rue de Vaugirard, No. 25; the other in the Rue de la Harpe, No. 75."

"Does your Eminence command that they both be instantly arrested?"

"It will be too late; they will be gone."

"But still, we can make sure that they are so."

"Take ten men of my Guardsmen, and search the two houses thoroughly."

"Instantly, Monseigneur." And Rochefort went hastily out of the apartment.

The cardinal, being left alone, reflected for an instant and then rang the bell a third time. The same officer appeared.

"Bring the prisoner in again," said the cardinal.

M Bonacieux was introduced afresh, and upon a sign from the cardinal, the officer retired.

"You have deceived me!" said the cardinal, sternly.

"I," cried Bonacieux, "I deceive your Eminence!"

"Your wife, in going to Rue de Vaugirard and Rue de la Harpe, did not go to find linen drapers."

"Then why did she go, just God?"

"She went to meet the Duchesse de Chevreuse and the Duke of Buckingham."

"Yes," cried Bonacieux, recalling all his remembrances of the circumstances, "yes, that's it. Your Eminence is right. I told my wife several times that it was surprising that linen drapers should live in such houses as those, in houses that had no signs, but she always laughed at me. Ah, Monseigneur!" continued Bonacieux, throwing himself at his Eminence's feet, "ah, how truly you are the cardinal, the great cardinal, the man of genius whom all the world reveres!"

The cardinal, however contemptible might be the triumph gained over so vulgar a being as Bonacieux, did not the less enjoy it for an instant; then, almost immediately, as if a fresh thought has occurred, a smile played upon his lips, and he said, offering his hand to the mercer, "Rise, my friend, you are a worthy man."

"The cardinal has touched me with his hand! I have touched the hand of the great man!" cried Bonacieux. "The great man has called me his friend!"

"Yes, my friend, yes," said the cardinal, with that paternal tone which he sometimes knew how to assume, but which deceived none who knew him, "and as you have been unjustly suspected, well, you must be indemnified. Here, take this purse of a hundred pistoles, and pardon me."

"I pardon you, Monseigneur!" said Bonacieux, hesitating to take the purse, fearing, doubtless, that this pretended gift was but a pleasantry. "But you are able to have me arrested, you are able to have me tortured, you are able to have me hanged; you are the master, and I could not have the least word to say. Pardon you, Monseigneur! You cannot mean that!"

"Ah, my dear Monsieur Bonacieux, you are generous in this matter. I see it and I thank you for it. Thus, then, you will take this bag, and you will go away without being too malcontent."

"I go away enchanted."

"Farewell, then, or rather, AU REVOIR!"

"Whenever Monseigneur wishes, I shall be firmly at the orders of his Eminence."

"That will be often, be assured, for I have found your conversation quite charming."

"Oh! Monseigneur!"

"AU REVOIR, Monsieur Bonacieux, AU REVOIR."

And the cardinal made him a sign with his hand, to which Bonacieux replied by bowing to the ground. He then went out backward, and when he was in the antechamber the cardinal heard him, in his enthusiasm, crying aloud, "Long life to the Monseigneur! Long life to his Eminence! Long life to the great cardinal!" The cardinal listened with a smile to this vociferous manifestation of the feelings of M. Bonacieux; and then, when Bonacieux's cries were no longer audible, "Good!" said he, "that man would henceforward lay down his life for me." And the cardinal began to examine with the greatest attention the map of La Rochelle, which, as we have said, lay open on the desk, tracing with a pencil the line in which the famous dyke was to pass which, eighteen months later, shut up the port of the besieged city. As he was in the deepest of his strategic meditations, the door opened, and Rochefort returned.

"Well?" said the cardinal, eagerly, rising with a promptitude which proved the degree of importance he attached to the commission with which he had charged the count.

"Well," said the latter, "a young woman of about twenty-six or twenty-eight years of age, and a man of from thirty-five to forty, have indeed lodged at the two houses pointed out by your Eminence, but the woman left last night, and the man this morning."

"It was they!" cried the cardinal, looking at the clock, "and now it is too late to have them pursued. The duchess is at Tours, and the duke at Boulogne. It is in London they must be found."

"What are your Eminence's orders?"

"Not a word of what has passed. Let the queen remain in perfect security; let her be ignorant that we know her secret. Let her believe that we are in search of some conspiracy or other. Send me the keeper of the seals, Seguier."

"And that man, what has your Eminence done with him?"

"What man?" asked the cardinal.

"That Bonacieux."

"I have done with him all that could be done. I have made him a spy upon his wife."

The Comte de Rochefort bowed like a man who acknowledges the superiority of the master as great, and retired.

Left alone, the cardinal seated himself again and wrote a letter, which he secured with his special seal. Then he rang. The officer entered for the fourth time.

"Tell Vitray to come to me," said he, "and tell him to get ready for a journey."

An instant after, the man he asked for was before him, booted and spurred.

"Vitray," said he, "you will go with all speed to London. You must not stop an instant on the way. You will deliver this letter to Milady. Here is an order for two hundred pistoles; call upon my treasurer and get the money. You shall have as much again if you are back within six days, and have executed your commission well."

The messenger, without replying a single word, bowed, took the letter, with the order for the two hundred pistoles, and retired.

Here is what the letter contained:

MILADY, Be at the first ball at which the Duke of Buckingham shall be present. He will wear on his doublet twelve diamond studs; get as near to him as you can, and cut off two.

As soon as these studs shall be in your possession, inform me.

Chapter 15

Men Of The Robe And Men Of The Sword

On the day after these events had taken place, Athos not having reappeared, M. de Tréville was informed by d'Artagnan and Porthos of the circumstance. As to Aramis, he had asked for leave of absence for five days, and was gone, it was said, to Rouen on family business.

M. de Tréville was the father of his soldiers. The lowest or the least known of them, as soon as he assumed the uniform of the company, was as sure of his aid and support as if he had been his own brother.

He repaired, then, instantly to the office of the LIEUTENANT-CRIMINEL. The officer who commanded the post of the Red Cross was sent for, and by successive inquiries they learned that Athos was then lodged in Fort l'Eveque.

Athos had passed through all the examinations we have seen Bonacieux undergo.

We were present at the scene in which the two captives were confronted with each other. Athos, who had till that time said nothing for fear that d'Artagnan, interrupted in his turn, should not have the time necessary, from this moment declared that his name was Athos, and not d'Artagnan. He added that he did not know either M. or Mme. Bonacieux; that he had never spoken to the one or the other; that he had come, at about ten o'clock in the evening, to pay a visit to his friend M. d'Artagnan, but that till that hour he had been at M. de Tréville's, where he had dined. "Twenty witnesses," added he, "could attest the fact"; and he named several distinguished gentlemen, and among them was M. le Duc de la Trémouille.

The second commissary was as much bewildered as the first had been by the simple and firm declaration of the Musketeer, upon whom he was anxious to take the revenge which men of the robe like at all times to gain over men of the sword, but the name of M. de Tréville, and that of M. de la Trémouille, commanded a little reflection.

Athos was then sent to the cardinal, but unfortunately the cardinal was at the Louvre with the king.

It was precisely at this moment that M. de Tréville, on leaving the residence of the LIEUTENANT-CRIMINEL and the governor of Fort l'Eveque without being able to find Athos, arrived at the palace.

As captain of the Musketeers, M. de Tréville had the right of entry at all times.

It is well known how violent the king's prejudices were against the queen, and how carefully these prejudices were kept up by the cardinal, who in affairs of intrigue mistrusted women infinitely more than men. One of the grand causes of this prejudice was the friendship of Anne of Austria for Mme. de Chevreuse. These two women gave him more uneasiness than the war with Spain, the quarrel with England, or the embarrassment of the finances. In his eyes and to his conviction, Mme. de Chevreuse not only served the queen in her political intrigues, but, what tormented him still more, in her amorous intrigues.

At the first word the cardinal spoke of Mme. de Chevreuse–who, though exiled to Tours and believed to be in that city, had come to Paris, remained there five days, and outwitted the police–the king flew into a furious passion. Capricious and unfaithful, the king wished to be called Louis the Just and Louis the Chaste. Posterity will find a difficulty in understanding this character, which history explains only by facts and never by reason.

But when the cardinal added that not only Mme. de Chevreuse had been in Paris, but still further, that the queen had renewed with her one of those mysterious correspondences which at that time was named a CABAL; when he affirmed that he, the cardinal, was about to unravel the most closely twisted thread of this intrigue; that at the moment of arresting in the very act, with all the proofs about her, the queen's emissary to the exiled duchess, a Musketeer had dared to interrupt the course of justice violently, by falling sword in hand upon the honest men of the law, charged with investigating impartially the whole affair in order to place it before the eyes of the king–Louis XIII could not contain himself, and he made a step toward the queen's apartment with that pale and mute indignation which, when it broke out, led this prince to the commission of the most pitiless cruelty. And yet, in all this, the cardinal had not yet said a word about the Duke of Buckingham.

At this instant M. de Tréville entered, cool, polite, and in irreproachable costume.

Informed of what had passed by the presence of the cardinal and the alteration in the king's countenance, M. de Tréville felt himself something like Samson before the Philistines.

Louis XIII had already placed his hand on the knob of the door; at the noise of M. de Tréville's entrance he turned round. "You arrive in good time, Monsieur," said the king, who, when his passions were raised to a certain point, could not dissemble, "I have learned some fine things concerning your Musketeers."

"And I," said Tréville, coldly, "I have some pretty things to tell your Majesty concerning these gownsmen."

"What?" said the king, with hauteur.

"I have the honour to inform your Majesty," continued M. de Tréville, in the same tone, "that a party of PROCUREURS, commissaries, and men of the police–very estimable people, but very inveterate, as it appears, against the uniform–have taken upon themselves to arrest in a house, to lead away through the open street, and throw into Fort l'Eveque, all upon an order which they have refused to show me, one of my, or rather your Musketeers, Sire, of irreproachable conduct, of an almost illustrious reputation, and whom your Majesty knows favourably, Monsieur Athos."

"Athos," said the king, mechanically, "yes, certainly I know that name."

"Let your Majesty remember," said Tréville, "that Monsieur Athos is the Musketeer who, in the annoying duel which you are acquainted with, had the misfortune to wound Monsieur de Cahusac so seriously. À PROPOS, Monseigneur," continued Tréville, addressing the cardinal, "Monsieur de Cahusac is quite recovered, is he not?"

"Thank you," said the cardinal, biting his lips with anger.

"Athos, then, went to pay a visit to one of his friends absent at the time," continued Tréville, "to a young Bearnais, a cadet in his Majesty's Guards, the company of Monsieur Dessessart, but scarcely had he arrived at his friend's and taken up a book, while waiting his return, when a mixed crowd of bailiffs and soldiers came and laid siege to the house, broke open several doors–"

The cardinal made the king a sign, which signified, "That was on account of the affair about which I spoke to you."

"We all know that," interrupted the king, "for all that was done for our service."

"Then," said Tréville, "it was also for your Majesty's service that one of my Musketeers, who was innocent, has been seized, that he has been placed between two guards like a malefactor, and that this gallant man, who has ten times shed his blood in your Majesty's service and is ready to shed it again, has been paraded through the midst of an insolent populace?"

"Bah!" said the king, who began to be shaken, "was it so managed?"

"Monsieur de Tréville," said the cardinal, with the greatest phlegm, "does not tell your Majesty that this innocent Musketeer, this gallant man, had only an hour before attacked, sword in hand, four commissaries of inquiry, who were delegated by myself to examine into an affair of the highest importance."

"I defy your Eminence to prove it," cried Tréville, with his Gascon freedom and military frankness, "for one hour before, Monsieur Athos, who, I will confide it to your Majesty, is really a man of the highest quality, did me the honour after having dined with me to be conversing in the saloon of my hotel, with the Duc de la Trémouille and the Comte de Chalus, who happened to be there."

The king looked at the cardinal.

"A written examination attests it," said the cardinal, replying aloud to the mute interrogation of his Majesty, "and the ill-treated people have drawn up the following, which I have the honour to present to your Majesty."

"And is the written report of the gownsmen to be placed in comparison with the word of honour of a swordsman?" replied Tréville haughtily.

"Come, come, Tréville, hold your tongue," said the king.

"If his Eminence entertains any suspicion against one of my Musketeers," said Tréville, "the justice of Monsieur the Cardinal is so well known that I demand an inquiry."

"In the house in which the judicial inquiry was made," continued the impassive cardinal, "there lodges, I believe, a young Bearnais, a friend of the Musketeer."

"Your Eminence means Monsieur d'Artagnan."

"I mean a young man whom you patronise, Monsieur de Tréville."

"Yes, your Eminence, it is the same."

"Do you not suspect this young man of having given bad counsel?"

"To Athos, to a man double his age?" interrupted Tréville. "No, Monseigneur. Besides, d'Artagnan passed the evening with me."

"Well," said the cardinal, "everybody seems to have passed the evening with you."

"Does your Eminence doubt my word?" said Tréville, with a brow flushed with anger.

"No, God forbid," said the cardinal, "only, at what hour was he with you?"

"Oh, as to that I can speak positively, your Eminence; for as he came in I remarked that it was but half past nine by the clock, although I had believed it to be later."

"At what hour did he leave your hotel?"

"At half past ten–an hour after the event."

"Well," replied the cardinal, who could not for an instant suspect the loyalty of Tréville, and who felt that the victory was escaping him, "well, but Athos WAS taken in the house in the Rue des Fossoyeurs."

"Is one friend forbidden to visit another, or a Musketeer of my company to fraternise with a Guard of Dessessart's company?"

"Yes, when the house where he fraternises is suspected."

"That house is suspected, Tréville," said the king, "perhaps you did not know it?"

"Indeed, Sire, I did not. The house may be suspected, but I deny that it is so in the part of it inhabited by Monsieur d'Artagnan, for I can affirm, Sire, if I can believe what he says, that there does not exist a more devoted servant of your Majesty, or a more profound admirer of Monsieur the Cardinal."

"Was it not this d'Artagnan who wounded Jussac one day, in that unfortunate encounter which took place near the Convent of the Carmes-Dechausses?" asked the king, looking at the cardinal, who coloured with vexation.

"And the next day, Bernajoux. Yes, Sire, yes, it is the same; and your Majesty has a good memory."

"Come, how shall we decide?" said the king.

"That concerns your Majesty more than me," said the cardinal. "I should affirm the culpability."

"And I deny it," said Tréville. "But his Majesty has judges, and these judges will decide."

"That is best," said the king. "Send the case before the judges; it is their business to judge, and they shall judge."

"Only," replied Tréville, "it is a sad thing that in the unfortunate times in which we live, the purest life, the most incontestable virtue, cannot exempt a man from infamy and persecution. The army, I will answer for it, will be but little pleased at being exposed to rigorous treatment on account of police affairs."

The expression was imprudent, but M. de Tréville launched it with knowledge of his cause. He was desirous of an explosion, because in that case the mine throws forth fire, and fire enlightens.

"Police affairs!" cried the king, taking up Tréville's words, "police affairs! And what do you know about them, Monsieur? Meddle with your Musketeers, and do not annoy me in this way. It appears, according to your account, that if by mischance a Musketeer is arrested, France is in danger. What a noise about a Musketeer! I would arrest ten of them, VENTREBLEU, a hundred, even, all the company, and I would not allow a whisper."

"From the moment they are suspected by your Majesty," said Tréville, "the Musketeers are guilty; therefore, you see me prepared to surrender my sword–for after having accused my soldiers, there can be no doubt that Monsieur the Cardinal will end by accusing me. It is best to constitute myself at once a prisoner with Athos, who is already arrested, and with d'Artagnan, who most probably will be."

"Gascon-headed man, will you have done?" said the king.

"Sire," replied Tréville, without lowering his voice in the least, "either order my Musketeer to be restored to me, or let him be tried."

"He shall be tried," said the cardinal.

"Well, so much the better; for in that case I shall demand of his Majesty permission to plead for him."

The king feared an outbreak.

"If his Eminence," said he, "did not have personal motives–"

The cardinal saw what the king was about to say and interrupted him:

"Pardon me," said he, "but the instant your Majesty considers me a prejudiced judge, I withdraw."

"Come," said the king, "will you swear, by my father, that Athos was at your residence during the event and that he took no part in it?"

"By your glorious father, and by yourself, whom I love and venerate above all the world, I swear it."

"Be so kind as to reflect, Sire," said the cardinal. "If we release the prisoner thus, we shall never know the truth."

"Athos may always be found," replied Tréville, "ready to answer, when it shall please the gownsmen to interrogate him. He will not desert, Monsieur the Cardinal, be assured of that; I will answer for him."

"No, he will not desert," said the king, "he can always be found, as Tréville says. Besides," added he, lowering his voice and looking with a suppliant air at the cardinal, "let us give them apparent security; that is policy."

This policy of Louis XIII made Richelieu smile.

"Order it as you please, Sire; you possess the right of pardon."

"The right of pardoning only applies to the guilty," said Tréville, who was determined to have the last word, "and my Musketeer is innocent. It is not mercy, then, that you are about to accord, Sire, it is justice."

"And he is in the Fort l'Eveque?" said the king.

"Yes, Sire, in solitary confinement, in a dungeon, like the lowest criminal."

"The devil!" murmured the king, "what must be done?"

"Sign an order for his release, and all will be said," replied the cardinal. "I believe with your Majesty that Monsieur de Tréville's guarantee is more than sufficient."

Tréville bowed very respectfully, with a joy that was not unmixed with fear; he would have preferred an obstinate resistance on the part of the cardinal to this sudden yielding.

The king signed the order for release, and Tréville carried it away without delay. As he was about to leave the presence, the cardinal gave him a friendly smile, and said, "A perfect harmony reigns, Sire, between the leaders and the soldiers of your Musketeers, which must be profitable for the service and honourable to all."

"He will play me some dog's trick or other, and that immediately," said Tréville. "One has never the last word with such a man. But let us be quick–the king may change his mind in an hour; and at all events it is more difficult to replace a man in the Fort l'Eveque or the Bastille who has got out, than to keep a prisoner there who is in."

M. de Tréville made his entrance triumphantly into the Fort l'Eveque, whence he delivered the Musketeer, whose peaceful indifference had not for a moment abandoned him.

The first time he saw d'Artagnan, "You have come off well," said he to him, "there is your Jussac thrust paid for. There still remains that of Bernajoux, but you must not be too confident."

As to the rest, M. de Tréville had good reason to mistrust the cardinal and to think that all was not over, for scarcely had the captain of the Musketeers closed the door after him, than his Eminence said to the king, "Now that we are at length by ourselves, we will, if your Majesty pleases, converse seriously. Sire, Buckingham has been in Paris five days, and only left this morning."

Chapter 16

In Which M. Seguier, Keeper Of The Seals, Looks More Than Once For The Bell

It is impossible to form an idea of the impression these few words made upon Louis XIII. He grew pale and red alternately; and the cardinal saw at once that he had recovered by a single blow all the ground he had lost.

"Buckingham in Paris!" cried he, "and why does he come?"

"To conspire, no doubt, with your enemies, the Huguenots and the Spaniards."

"No, PARDIEU, no! To conspire against my honour with Madame de Chevreuse, Madame de Longueville, and the Condes."

"Oh, Sire, what an idea! The queen is too virtuous; and besides, loves your Majesty too well."

"Woman is weak, Monsieur Cardinal," said the king, "and as to loving me much, I have my own opinion as to that love."

"I not the less maintain," said the cardinal, "that the Duke of Buckingham came to Paris for a project wholly political."

"And I am sure that he came for quite another purpose, Monsieur Cardinal, but if the queen be guilty, let her tremble!"

"Indeed," said the cardinal, "whatever repugnance I may have to directing my mind to such a treason, your Majesty compels me to think of it. Madame de Lannoy, whom, according to your Majesty's command, I have frequently interrogated, told me this morning that the night before last her Majesty sat up very late, that this morning she wept much, and that she was writing all day."

"That's it!" cried the king, "to him, no doubt. Cardinal, I must have the queen's papers."

"But how to take them, Sire? It seems to me that it is neither your Majesty nor myself who can charge himself with such a mission."

"How did they act with regard to the Marechale d'Ancre?" cried the king, in the highest state of choler, "first her closets were thoroughly searched, and then she herself."

"The Marechale d'Ancre was no more than the Marechale d'Ancre. A Florentine adventurer, Sire, and that was all; while the august spouse of your Majesty is Anne of Austria, Queen of France–that is to say, one of the greatest princesses in the world."

"She is not the less guilty, Monsieur Duke! The more she has forgotten the high position in which she was placed, the more degrading is her fall. Besides, I long ago determined to put an end to all these petty intrigues of policy and love. She has near her a certain Laporte."

"Who, I believe, is the mainspring of all this, I confess," said the cardinal.

"You think then, as I do, that she deceives me?" said the king.

"I believe, and I repeat it to your Majesty, that the queen conspires against the power of the king, but I have not said against his honour."

"And I–I tell you against both. I tell you the queen does not love me; I tell you she loves another; I tell you she loves that infamous Buckingham! Why did you not have him arrested while in Paris?"

"Arrest the Duke! Arrest the prime minister of King Charles I! Think of it, Sire! What a scandal! And if the suspicions of your Majesty, which I still continue to doubt, should prove to have any foundation, what a terrible disclosure, what a fearful scandal!"

"But as he exposed himself like a vagabond or a thief, he should have been–"

Louis XIII stopped, terrified at what he was about to say, while Richelieu, stretching out his neck, waited uselessly for the word which had died on the lips of the king.

"He should have been–?"

"Nothing," said the king, "nothing. But all the time he was in Paris, you, of course, did not lose sight of him?"

"No, Sire."

"Where did he lodge?"

"Rue de la Harpe. No. 75."

"Where is that?"

"By the side of the Luxembourg."

"And you are certain that the queen and he did not see each other?"

"I believe the queen to have too high a sense of her duty, Sire."

"But they have corresponded; it is to him that the queen has been writing all the day. Monsieur Duke, I must have those letters!"

"Sire, notwithstanding–"

"Monsieur Duke, at whatever price it may be, I will have them."

"I would, however, beg your Majesty to observe–"

"Do you, then, also join in betraying me, Monsieur Cardinal, by thus always opposing my will? Are you also in accord with Spain and England, with Madame de Chevreuse and the queen?"

"Sire," replied the cardinal, sighing, "I believed myself secure from such a suspicion."

"Monsieur Cardinal, you have heard me; I will have those letters."

"There is but one way."

"What is that?"

"That would be to charge Monsieur de Seguier, the keeper of the seals, with this mission. The matter enters completely into the duties of the post."

"Let him be sent for instantly."

"He is most likely at my hotel. I requested him to call, and when I came to the Louvre I left orders if he came, to desire him to wait."

"Let him be sent for instantly."

"Your Majesty's orders shall be executed; but–"

"But what?"

"But the queen will perhaps refuse to obey."

"My orders?"

"Yes, if she is ignorant that these orders come from the king."

"Well, that she may have no doubt on that head, I will go and inform her myself."

"Your Majesty will not forget that I have done everything in my power to prevent a rupture."

"Yes, Duke, yes, I know you are very indulgent toward the queen, too indulgent, perhaps; we shall have occasion, I warn you, at some future period to speak of that."

"Whenever it shall please your Majesty, but I shall be always happy and proud, Sire, to sacrifice myself to the harmony which I desire to see reign between you and the Queen of France."

"Very well, Cardinal, very well; but, meantime, send for Monsieur the Keeper of the Seals. I will go to the queen."

And Louis XIII, opening the door of communication, passed into the corridor which led from his apartments to those of Anne of Austria.

The queen was in the midst of her women–Mme. de Guitaut, Mme. de Sable, Mme. de Montbazon, and Mme. de Guemene. In a corner was the Spanish companion, Donna Estafania, who had followed her from Madrid. Mme. Guemene was reading aloud, and everybody was listening to her with attention with the exception of the queen, who had, on the contrary, desired this reading in order that she might be able, while feigning to listen, to pursue the thread of her own thoughts.

These thoughts, gilded as they were by a last reflection of love, were not the less sad. Anne of Austria, deprived of the confidence of her husband, pursued by the hatred of the cardinal, who could not pardon her for having repulsed a more tender feeling, having before her eyes the example of the queen-mother whom that hatred had tormented all her life–though Marie de Medicis, if the memoirs of the time are to be believed, had begun by according to the cardinal that sentiment which Anne of Austria always refused him–Anne of Austria had seen her most devoted servants fall around her, her most intimate confidants, her dearest favourites. Like those unfortunate persons endowed with a fatal gift, she brought misfortune upon everything she touched. Her friendship was a fatal sign which called down persecution. Mme. de Chevreuse and Mme. de Bernet were exiled, and Laporte did not conceal from his mistress that he expected to be arrested every instant.

It was at the moment when she was plunged in the deepest and darkest of these reflections that the door of the chamber opened, and the king entered.

The reader hushed herself instantly. All the ladies rose, and there was a profound silence. As to the king, he made no demonstration of politeness, only stopping before the queen. "Madame," said he, "you are about to receive a visit from the chancellor, who will communicate certain matters to you with which I have charged him."

The unfortunate queen, who was constantly threatened with divorce, exile, and trial even, turned pale under her rouge, and could not refrain from saying, "But why this visit, Sire? What can the chancellor have to say to me that your Majesty could not say yourself?"

The king turned upon his heel without reply, and almost at the same instant the captain of the Guards, M. de Guitant, announced the visit of the chancellor.

When the chancellor appeared, the king had already gone out by another door.

The chancellor entered, half smiling, half blushing. As we shall probably meet with him again in the course of our history, it may be well for our readers to be made at once acquainted with him.

This chancellor was a pleasant man. He was Des Roches le Masle, canon of Notre Dame, who had formerly been valet of a bishop, who introduced him to his Eminence as a perfectly devout man. The cardinal trusted him, and therein found his advantage.

There are many stories related of him, and among them this. After a wild youth, he had retired into a convent, there to expiate, at least for some time, the follies of adolescence. On entering this holy place, the poor penitent was unable to shut the door so close as to prevent the passions he fled from entering with him. He was incessantly attacked by them, and the superior, to whom he had confided this misfortune, wishing as much as in him lay to free him from them, had advised him, in order to conjure away the tempting demon, to have recourse to the bell rope, and ring with all his might. At the denunciating sound, the monks would be rendered aware that temptation was besieging a brother, and all the community would go to prayers.

This advice appeared good to the future chancellor. He conjured the evil spirit with abundance of prayers offered up by the monks. But the devil does not suffer himself to be easily dispossessed from a place in which he has fixed his garrison. In proportion as they redoubled the exorcisms he redoubled the temptations; so that day and night the bell was ringing full swing, announcing the extreme desire for mortification which the penitent experienced.

The monks had no longer an instant of repose. By day they did nothing but ascend and descend the steps which led to the chapel; at night, in addition to complines and matins, they were further obliged to leap twenty times out of their beds and prostrate themselves on the floor of their cells.

It is not known whether it was the devil who gave way, or the monks who grew tired, but within three months the penitent reappeared in the world with the reputation of being the most terrible POSSESSED that ever existed.

On leaving the convent he entered into the magistracy, became president on the place of his uncle, embraced the cardinal's party, which did not prove want of sagacity, became chancellor, served his Eminence with zeal in his hatred against the queen-mother and his vengeance against Anne of Austria, stimulated the judges in the affair of Calais, encouraged the attempts of M. de Laffemas, chief gamekeeper of France; then, at length, invested with the entire confidence of the cardinal–a confidence which he had so well earned–he received the singular commission for the execution of which he presented himself in the queen's apartments.

The queen was still standing when he entered, but scarcely had she perceived him then she reseated herself in her armchair, and made a sign to her women to resume their cushions and stools, and with an air of supreme hauteur, said, "What do you desire, Monsieur, and with what object do you present yourself here?"

"To make, Madame, in the name of the king, and without prejudice to the respect which I have the honour to owe to your Majesty a close examination into all your papers."

"How, Monsieur, an investigation of my papers–mine! Truly, this is an indignity!"

"Be kind enough to pardon me, Madame, but in this circumstance I am but the instrument which the king employs. Has not his Majesty just left you, and has he not himself asked you to prepare for this visit?"

"Search, then, Monsieur! I am a criminal, as it appears. Estafania, give up the keys of my drawers and my desks."

For form's sake the chancellor paid a visit to the pieces of furniture named, but he well knew that it was not in a piece of furniture that the queen would place the important letter she had written that day.

When the chancellor had opened and shut twenty times the drawers of the secretaries, it became necessary, whatever hesitation he might experience–it became necessary, I say, to come to the conclusion of the affair; that is to say, to search the queen herself. The chancellor advanced, therefore, toward Anne of Austria, and said with a very perplexed and embarrassed air, "And now it remains for me to make the principal examination."

"What is that?" asked the queen, who did not understand, or rather was not willing to understand.

"His majesty is certain that a letter has been written by you during the day; he knows that it has not yet been sent to its address. This letter is not in your table nor in your secretary; and yet this letter must be somewhere."

"Would you dare to lift your hand to your queen?" said Anne of Austria, drawing herself up to her full height, and fixing her eyes upon the chancellor with an expression almost threatening.

"I am a faithful subject of the king, Madame, and all that his Majesty commands I shall do."

"Well, it is true!" said Anne of Austria, "and the spies of the cardinal have served him faithfully. I have written a letter today; that letter is not yet gone. The letter is here." And the queen laid her beautiful hand on her bosom.

"Then give me that letter, Madame," said the chancellor.

"I will give it to none but the king, Monsieur," said Anne.

"If the king had desired that the letter should be given to him, Madame, he would have demanded it of you himself. But I repeat to you, I am charged with reclaiming it; and if you do not give it up–"

"Well?"

"He has, then, charged me to take it from you."

"How! What do you say?"

"That my orders go far, Madame; and that I am authorised to seek for the suspected paper, even on the person of your Majesty."

"What horror!" cried the queen.

"Be kind enough, then, Madame, to act more compliantly."

"The conduct is infamously violent! Do you know that, Monsieur?"

"The king commands it, Madame; excuse me."

"I will not suffer it! No, no, I would rather die!" cried the queen, in whom the imperious blood of Spain and Austria began to rise.

The chancellor made a profound reverence. Then, with the intention quite patent of not drawing back a foot from the accomplishment of the commission with which he was charged, and as the attendant of an executioner might have done in the chamber of torture, he approached Anne of Austria, from whose eyes at the same instant sprang tears of rage.

The queen was, as we have said, of great beauty. The commission might well be called delicate; and the king had reached, in his jealousy of Buckingham, the point of not being jealous of anyone else.

Without doubt the chancellor Seguier looked about at that moment for the rope of the famous bell, but not finding it he summoned his resolution, and stretched forth his hands toward the place where the queen had acknowledged the paper was to be found.

Anne of Austria took one step backward, became so pale that it might be said she was dying, and leaning with her left hand upon a table behind her to keep herself from falling, she with her right hand drew the paper from her bosom and held it out to the keeper of the seals.

"There, Monsieur, there is that letter!" cried the queen, with a broken and trembling voice, "take it, and deliver me from your odious presence."

The chancellor, who, on his part, trembled with an emotion easily to be conceived, took the letter, bowed to the ground, and retired. The door was scarcely closed upon him, when the queen sank, half fainting, into the arms of her women.

The chancellor carried the letter to the king without having read a single word of it. The king took it with a trembling hand, looked for the address, which was wanting, became very pale, opened it slowly, then seeing by the first words that it was addressed to the King of Spain, he read it rapidly.

It was nothing but a plan of attack against the cardinal. The queen pressed her brother and the Emperor of Austria to appear to be wounded, as they really were, by the policy of Richelieu–the eternal object of which was the abasement of the house of Austria–to declare war against France, and as a condition of peace, to insist upon the dismissal of the cardinal, but as to love, there was not a single word about it in all the letter.

The king, quite delighted, inquired if the cardinal was still at the Louvre; he was told that his Eminence awaited the orders of his Majesty in the business cabinet.

The king went straight to him.

"There, Duke," said he, "you were right and I was wrong. The whole intrigue is political, and there is not the least question of love in this letter; but, on the other hand, there is abundant question of you."

The cardinal took the letter, and read it with the greatest attention; then, when he had arrived at the end of it, he read it a second time. "Well, your Majesty," said he, "you see how far my enemies go; they menace you with two wars if you do not dismiss me. In your place, in truth, Sire, I should yield to such powerful instance; and on my part, it would be a real happiness to withdraw from public affairs."

"What say you, Duke?"

"I say, Sire, that my health is sinking under these excessive struggles and these never-ending labors. I say that according to all probability I shall not be able to undergo the fatigues of the siege of La Rochelle, and that it would be far better that you should appoint there either Monsieur de Conde, Monsieur de Bassopierre, or some valiant gentleman whose business is war, and not me, who am a churchman, and who am constantly turned aside for my real vocation to look after matters for which I have no aptitude. You would be the happier for it at home, Sire, and I do not doubt you would be the greater for it abroad."

"Monsieur Duke," said the king, "I understand you. Be satisfied, all who are named in that letter shall be punished as they deserve, even the queen herself."

"What do you say, Sire? God forbid that the queen should suffer the least inconvenience or uneasiness on my account! She has always believed me, Sire, to be her enemy; although your Majesty can bear witness that I have always taken her part warmly, even against you. Oh, if she betrayed your Majesty on the side of your honour, it would be quite another thing, and I should be the first to say, 'No grace, Sire–no grace for the guilty!' Happily, there is nothing of the kind, and your Majesty has just acquired a new proof of it."

"That is true, Monsieur Cardinal," said the king, "and you were right, as you always are, but the queen, not the less, deserves all my anger."

"It is you, Sire, who have now incurred hers. And even if she were to be seriously offended, I could well understand it; your Majesty has treated her with a severity–"

"It is thus I will always treat my enemies and yours, Duke, however high they may be placed, and whatever peril I may incur in acting severely toward them."

"The queen is my enemy, but is not yours, Sire; on the contrary, she is a devoted, submissive, and irreproachable wife. Allow me, then, Sire, to intercede for her with your Majesty."

"Let her humble herself, then, and come to me first."

"On the contrary, Sire, set the example. You have committed the first wrong, since it was you who suspected the queen."

"What! I make the first advances?" said the king. "Never!"

"Sire, I entreat you to do so."

"Besides, in what manner can I make advances first?"

"By doing a thing which you know will be agreeable to her."

"What is that?"

"Give a ball; you know how much the queen loves dancing. I will answer for it, her resentment will not hold out against such an attention."

"Monsieur Cardinal, you know that I do not like worldly pleasures."

"The queen will only be the more grateful to you, as she knows your antipathy for that amusement; besides, it will be an opportunity for her to wear those beautiful diamonds which you gave her recently on her birthday and with which she has since had no occasion to adorn herself."

"We shall see, Monsieur Cardinal, we shall see," said the king, who, in his joy at finding the queen guilty of a crime which he cared little about, and innocent of a fault of which he had great dread, was ready to make up all differences with her, "we shall see, but upon my honour, you are too indulgent toward her."

"Sire," said the cardinal, "leave severity to your ministers. Clemency is a royal virtue; employ it, and you will find that you derive advantage therein."

Thereupon the cardinal, hearing the clock strike eleven, bowed low, asking permission of the king to retire, and supplicating him to come to a good understanding with the queen.

Anne of Austria, who, in consequence of the seizure of her letter, expected reproaches, was much astonished the next day to see the king make some attempts at reconciliation with her. Her first movement was repellent. Her womanly pride and her queenly dignity had both been so cruelly offended that she could not come round at the first advance; but, overpersuaded by the advice of her women, she at last had the appearance of beginning to forget. The king took advantage of this favourable moment to tell her that he had the intention of shortly giving a fête.

A fête was so rare a thing for poor Anne of Austria that at this announcement, as the cardinal had predicted, the last trace of her resentment disappeared, if not from her heart, at least from her countenance. She asked upon what day this fête would take place, but the king replied that he must consult the cardinal upon that head.

Indeed, every day the king asked the cardinal when this fête should take place; and every day the cardinal, under some pretext, deferred fixing it. Ten days passed away thus.

On the eighth day after the scene we have described, the cardinal received a letter with the London stamp which only contained these lines: "I have them, but I am unable to leave London for want of money. Send me five hundred pistoles, and four or five days after I have received them I shall be in Paris."

On the same day the cardinal received this letter the king put his customary question to him.

Richelieu counted on his fingers, and said to himself, "She will arrive, she says, four or five days after having received the money. It will require four or five days for the transmission of the money, four or five days for her to return; that makes ten days. Now, allowing for contrary winds, accidents, and a woman's weakness, there are twelve days."

"Well, Monsieur Duke," said the king, "have you made your calculations?"

"Yes, Sire. Today is the twentieth of September. The aldermen of the city give a fête on the third of October. That will fall in wonderfully well; you will not appear to have gone out of your way to please the queen."

Then the cardinal added, "À PROPOS, Sire, do not forget to tell her Majesty the evening before the fête that you should like to see how her diamond studs become her."

Chapter 17

Bonacieux At Home

It was the second time the cardinal had mentioned these diamond studs to the king. Louis XIII was struck with this insistence, and began to fancy that this recommendation concealed some mystery.

More than once the king had been humiliated by the cardinal, whose police, without having yet attained the perfection of the modern police, were excellent, being better informed than himself, even upon what was going on in his own household. He hoped, then, in a conversation with Anne of Austria, to obtain some information from that conversation, and afterward to come upon his Eminence with some secret which the cardinal either knew or did not know, but which, in either case, would raise him infinitely in the eyes of his minister.

He went then to the queen, and according to custom accosted her with fresh menaces against those who surrounded her. Anne of Austria lowered her head, allowed the torrent to flow on without replying, hoping that it would cease of itself, but this was not what Louis XIII meant. Louis XIII wanted a discussion from which some light or other might break, convinced as he was that the cardinal had some afterthought and was preparing for him one of those terrible surprises which his Eminence was so skillful in getting up. He arrived at this end by his persistence in accusation.

"But," cried Anne of Austria, tired of these vague attacks, "but, Sire, you do not tell me all that you have in your heart. What have I done, then? Let me know what crime I have committed. It is impossible that your Majesty can make all this ado about a letter written to my brother."

The king, attacked in a manner so direct, did not know what to answer; and he thought that this was the moment for expressing the desire which he was not going to have made until the evening before the fête.

"Madame," said he, with dignity, "there will shortly be a ball at the Hotel de Ville. I wish, in order to honour our worthy aldermen, you should appear in ceremonial costume, and above all, ornamented with the diamond studs which I gave you on your birthday. That is my answer."

The answer was terrible. Anne of Austria believed that Louis XIII knew all, and that the cardinal had persuaded him to employ this long dissimulation of seven or eight days, which, likewise, was characteristic. She became excessively pale, leaned her beautiful hand upon a CONSOLE, which hand appeared then like one of wax, and looking at the king with terror in her eyes, she was unable to reply by a single syllable.

"You hear, Madame," said the king, who enjoyed the embarrassment to its full extent, but without guessing the cause. "You hear, Madame?"

"Yes, Sire, I hear," stammered the queen.

"You will appear at this ball?"

"Yes."

"With those studs?"

"Yes."

The queen's paleness, if possible, increased; the king perceived it, and enjoyed it with that cold cruelty which was one of the worst sides of his character.

"Then that is agreed," said the king, "and that is all I had to say to you."

"But on what day will this ball take place?" asked Anne of Austria.

Louis XIII felt instinctively that he ought not to reply to this question, the queen having put it in an almost dying voice.

"Oh, very shortly, Madame," said he, "but I do not precisely recollect the date of the day. I will ask the cardinal."

"It was the cardinal, then, who informed you of this fête?"

"Yes, Madame," replied the astonished king, "but why do you ask that?"

"It was he who told you to invite me to appear with these studs?"

"That is to say, Madame–"

"It was he, Sire, it was he!"

"Well, and what does it signify whether it was he or I? Is there any crime in this request?"

"No, Sire."

"Then you will appear?"

"Yes, Sire."

"That is well," said the king, retiring, "that is well; I count upon it."

The queen made a curtsy, less from etiquette than because her knees were sinking under her. The king went away enchanted.

"I am lost," murmured the queen, "lost!–For the cardinal knows all, and it is he who urges on the king, who as yet knows nothing but will soon know everything. I am lost! My God, my God, my God!"

She knelt upon a cushion and prayed, with her head buried between her palpitating arms.

In fact, her position was terrible. Buckingham had returned to London; Mme. de Chevreuse was at Tours. More closely watched than ever, the queen felt certain, without knowing how to tell which, that one of her women had betrayed her. Laporte could not leave the Louvre; she had not a soul in the world in whom she could confide. Thus, while contemplating the misfortune which threatened her and the abandonment in which she was left, she broke out into sobs and tears.

"Can I be of service to your Majesty?" said all at once a voice full of sweetness and pity.

The queen turned sharply round, for there could be no deception in the expression of that voice; it was a friend who spoke thus.

In fact, at one of the doors which opened into the queen's apartment appeared the pretty Mme. Bonacieux. She had been engaged in arranging the dresses and linen in a closet when the king entered; she could not get out and had heard all.

The queen uttered a piercing cry at finding herself surprised—for in her trouble she did not at first recognise the young woman who had been given to her by Laporte.

"Oh, fear nothing, Madame!" said the young woman, clasping her hands and weeping herself at the queen's sorrows, "I am your Majesty's, body and soul, and however far I may be from you, however inferior may be my position, I believe I have discovered a means of extricating your Majesty from your trouble."

"You, oh, heaven, you!" cried the queen, "but look me in the face. I am betrayed on all sides. Can I trust in you?"

"Oh, Madame!" cried the young woman, falling on her knees, "upon my soul, I am ready to die for your Majesty!"

This expression sprang from the very bottom of the heart, and, like the first, there was no mistaking it.

"Yes," continued Mme. Bonacieux, "yes, there are traitors here, but by the holy name of the Virgin, I swear that no one is more devoted to your Majesty than I am. Those studs which the king speaks of, you gave them to the Duke of Buckingham, did you not? Those studs were enclosed in a little rosewood box which he held under his arm? Am I deceived? Is it not so, Madame?"

"Oh, my God, my God!" murmured the queen, whose teeth chattered with fright.

"Well, those studs," continued Mme. Bonacieux, "we must have them back again."

"Yes, without doubt, it is necessary," cried the queen, "but how am I to act? How can it be effected?"

"Someone must be sent to the duke."

"But who, who? In whom can I trust?"

"Place confidence in me, Madame; do me that honour, my queen, and I will find a messenger."

"But I must write."

"Oh, yes; that is indispensable. Two words from the hand of your Majesty and your private seal."

"But these two words would bring about my condemnation, divorce, exile!"

"Yes, if they fell into infamous hands. But I will answer for these two words being delivered to their address."

"Oh, my God! I must then place my life, my honour, my reputation, in your hands?"

"Yes, yes, Madame, you must; and I will save them all."

"But how? Tell me at least the means."

"My husband had been at liberty these two or three days. I have not yet had time to see him again. He is a worthy, honest man who entertains neither love nor hatred for anybody. He will do anything I wish. He will set out upon receiving an order from me, without knowing what he carries, and he will carry your Majesty's letter, without even knowing it is from your Majesty, to the address which is on it."

The queen took the two hands of the young woman with a burst of emotion, gazed at her as if to read her very heart, and, seeing nothing but sincerity in her beautiful eyes, embraced her tenderly.

"Do that," cried she, "and you will have saved my life, you will have saved my honour!"

"Do not exaggerate the service I have the happiness to render your Majesty. I have nothing to save for your Majesty; you are only the victim of perfidious plots."

"That is true, that is true, my child," said the queen, "you are right."

"Give me then, that letter, Madame; time presses."

The queen ran to a little table, on which were ink, paper, and pens. She wrote two lines, sealed the letter with her private seal, and gave it to Mme. Bonacieux.

"And now," said the queen, "we are forgetting one very necessary thing."

"What is that, Madame?"

"Money."

Mme. Bonacieux blushed.

"Yes, that is true," said she, "and I will confess to your Majesty that my husband–"

"Your husband has none. Is that what you would say?"

"He has some, but he is very avaricious; that is his fault. Nevertheless, let not your Majesty be uneasy, we will find means."

"And I have none, either," said the queen. Those who have read the MEMOIRS of Mme. de Motteville will not be astonished at this reply. "But wait a minute."

Anne of Austria ran to her jewel case.

"Here," said she, "here is a ring of great value, as I have been assured. It came from my brother, the King of Spain. It is mine, and I am at liberty to dispose of it. Take this ring; raise money with it, and let your husband set out."

"In an hour you shall be obeyed."

"You see the address," said the queen, speaking so low that Mme. Bonacieux could hardly hear what she said, "To my Lord Duke of Buckingham, London."

"The letter shall be given to himself."

"Generous girl!" cried Anne of Austria.

Mme. Bonacieux kissed the hands of the queen, concealed the paper in the bosom of her dress, and disappeared with the lightness of a bird.

Ten minutes afterward she was at home. As she told the queen, she had not seen her husband since his liberation; she was ignorant of the change that had taken place in him with respect to the cardinal–a change which had since been strengthened by two or three visits from the Comte de Rochefort, who had become the best friend of Bonacieux, and had persuaded him, without much trouble, that no culpable sentiments had prompted the abduction of his wife, but that it was only a political precaution.

She found M. Bonacieux alone; the poor man was recovering with difficulty the order in his house, in which he had found most of the furniture broken and the closets nearly emptied–justice not being one of the three things which King Solomon names as leaving no traces of their passage. As to the servant, she had run away at the moment of her master's arrest. Terror had had such an effect upon the poor girl that she had never ceased walking from Paris till she reached Burgundy, her native place.

The worthy mercer had, immediately upon re-entering his house, informed his wife of his happy return, and his wife had replied by congratulating him, and telling him that the first moment she could steal from her duties should be devoted to paying him a visit.

This first moment had been delayed five days, which, under any other circumstances, might have appeared rather long to M. Bonacieux, but he had, in the visit he had made to the cardinal and in the visits Rochefort had made him, ample subjects for reflection, and as everybody knows, nothing makes time pass more quickly than reflection.

This was the more so because Bonacieux's reflections were all rose-coloured. Rochefort called him his friend, his dear Bonacieux, and never ceased telling him that the cardinal had a great respect for him. The mercer fancied himself already on the high road to honours and fortune.

On her side Mme. Bonacieux had also reflected; but, it must be admitted, upon something widely different from ambition. In spite of herself her thoughts constantly reverted to that handsome young man who was so brave and appeared to be so much in love. Married at eighteen to M. Bonacieux, having always lived among her husband's friends–people little capable of inspiring any sentiment whatever in a young woman whose heart was above her position–Mme. Bonacieux had remained insensible to vulgar seductions, but at this period the title of gentleman had great influence with the citizen class, and d'Artagnan was a gentleman. Besides, he wore the uniform of the Guards, which, next to that of the Musketeers, was most admired by the ladies. He was, we repeat, handsome, young, and bold; he spoke of love like a man who did love and was anxious to be loved in return. There was certainly enough in all this to turn a head only twenty-three years old, and Mme. Bonacieux had just attained that happy period of life.

The couple, then, although they had not seen each other for eight days, and during that time serious events had taken place in which both were concerned, accosted each other with a degree of preoccupation. Nevertheless, Bonacieux manifested real joy, and advanced toward his wife with open arms. Madame Bonacieux presented her cheek to him.

"Let us talk a little," said she.

"How!" said Bonacieux, astonished.

"Yes, I have something of the highest importance to tell you."

"True," said he, "and I have some questions sufficiently serious to put to you. Describe to me your abduction, I pray you."

"Oh, that's of no consequence just now," said Mme. Bonacieux.

"And what does it concern, then–my captivity?"

"I heard of it the day it happened, but as you were not guilty of any crime, as you were not guilty of any intrigue, as you, in short, knew nothing that could compromise yourself or anybody else, I attached no more importance to that event than it merited."

"You speak very much at your ease, Madame," said Bonacieux, hurt at the little interest his wife showed in him. "Do you know that I was plunged during a day and night in a dungeon of the Bastille?"

"Oh, a day and night soon pass away. Let us return to the object that brings me here."

"What, that which brings you home to me? Is it not the desire of seeing a husband again from whom you have been separated for a week?" asked the mercer, piqued to the quick.

"Yes, that first, and other things afterward."

"Speak."

"It is a thing of the highest interest, and upon which our future fortune perhaps depends."

"The complexion of our fortune has changed very much since I saw you, Madame Bonacieux, and I should not be astonished if in the course of a few months it were to excite the envy of many folks."

"Yes, particularly if you follow the instructions I am about to give you."

"Me?"

"Yes, you. There is good and holy action to be performed, Monsieur, and much money to be gained at the same time."

Mme. Bonacieux knew that in talking of money to her husband, she took him on his weak side. But a man, were he even a mercer, when he had talked for ten minutes with Cardinal Richelieu, is no longer the same man.

"Much money to be gained?" said Bonacieux, protruding his lip.

"Yes, much."

"About how much?"

"A thousand pistoles, perhaps."

"What you demand of me is serious, then?"

"It is indeed."

"What must be done?"

"You must go away immediately. I will give you a paper which you must not part with on any account, and which you will deliver into the proper hands."

"And whither am I to go?"

"To London."

"I go to London? Go to! You jest! I have no business in London."

"But others wish that you should go there."

"But who are those others? I warn you that I will never again work in the dark, and that I will know not only to what I expose myself, but for whom I expose myself."

"An illustrious person sends you; an illustrious person awaits you. The recompense will exceed your expectations; that is all I promise you."

"More intrigues! Nothing but intrigues! Thank you, Madame, I am aware of them now; Monsieur Cardinal has enlightened me on that head."

"The cardinal?" cried Mme. Bonacieux. "Have you seen the cardinal?"

"He sent for me," answered the mercer, proudly.

"And you responded to his bidding, you imprudent man?"

"Well, I can't say I had much choice of going or not going, for I was taken to him between two guards. It is true also, that as I did not then know his Eminence, if I had been able to dispense with the visit, I should have been enchanted."

"He ill-treated you, then; he threatened you?"

"He gave me his hand, and called me his friend. His friend! Do you hear that, Madame? I am the friend of the great cardinal!"

"Of the great cardinal!"

"Perhaps you would contest his right to that title, Madame?"

"I would contest nothing, but I tell you that the favour of a minister is ephemeral, and that a man must be mad to attach himself to a minister. There are powers above his which do not depend upon a man or the issue of an event; it is to these powers we should rally."

"I am sorry for it, Madame, but I acknowledge no other power but that of the great man whom I have the honour to serve."

"You serve the cardinal?"

"Yes, Madame; and as his servant, I will not allow you to be concerned in plots against the safety of the state, or to serve the intrigues of a woman who is not French and who has a Spanish heart. Fortunately we have the great cardinal; his vigilant eye watches over and penetrates to the bottom of the heart."

Bonacieux was repeating, word for word, a sentence which he had heard from the Comte de Rochefort, but the poor wife, who had reckoned on her husband, and who, in that hope, had answered for him to the queen, did not tremble the less, both at the danger into which she had nearly cast herself and at the helpless state to which she was reduced. Nevertheless, knowing the weakness of her husband, and more particularly his cupidity, she did not despair of bringing him round to her purpose.

"Ah, you are a cardinalist, then, Monsieur, are you?" cried she, "and you serve the party of those who maltreat your wife and insult your queen?"

"Private interests are as nothing before the interests of all. I am for those who save the state," said Bonacieux, emphatically.

"And what do you know about the state you talk of?" said Mme. Bonacieux, shrugging her shoulders. "Be satisfied with being a plain, straightforward citizen, and turn to that side which offers the most advantages."

"Eh, eh!" said Bonacieux, slapping a plump, round bag, which returned a sound a money, "what do you think of this, Madame Preacher?"

"Whence comes that money?"

"You do not guess?"

"From the cardinal?"

"From him, and from my friend the Comte de Rochefort."

"The Comte de Rochefort! Why, it was he who carried me off!"

"That may be, Madame!"

"And you receive silver from that man?"

"Have you not said that that abduction was entirely political?"

"Yes, but that abduction had for its object the betrayal of my mistress, to draw from me by torture confessions that might compromise the honour, and perhaps the life, of my august mistress."

"Madame," replied Bonacieux, "your august mistress is a perfidious Spaniard, and what the cardinal does is well done."

"Monsieur," said the young woman, "I know you to be cowardly, avaricious, and foolish, but I never till now believed you infamous!"

"Madame," said Bonacieux, who had never seen his wife in a passion, and who recoiled before this conjugal anger, "Madame, what do you say?"

"I say you are a miserable creature!" continued Mme. Bonacieux, who saw she was regaining some little influence over her husband. "You meddle with politics, do you–and still more, with cardinalist politics? Why, you sell yourself, body and soul, to the demon, the devil, for money!"

"No, to the cardinal."

"It's the same thing," cried the young woman. "Who calls Richelieu calls Satan."

"Hold your tongue, hold your tongue, Madame! You may be overheard."

"Yes, you are right; I should be ashamed for anyone to know your baseness."

"But what do you require of me, then? Let us see."

"I have told you. You must depart instantly, Monsieur. You must accomplish loyally the commission with which I deign to charge you, and on that condition I pardon everything, I forget everything; and what is more," and she held out her hand to him, "I restore my love."

Bonacieux was cowardly and avaricious, but he loved his wife. He was softened. A man of fifty cannot long bear malice with a wife of twenty-three. Mme. Bonacieux saw that he hesitated.

"Come! Have you decided?" said she.

"But, my dear love, reflect a little upon what you require of me. London is far from Paris, very far, and perhaps the commission with which you charge me is not without dangers?"

"What matters it, if you avoid them?"

"Hold, Madame Bonacieux," said the mercer, "hold! I positively refuse; intrigues terrify me. I have seen the Bastille. My! Whew! That's a frightful place, that Bastille! Only to think of it makes my flesh crawl. They threatened me with torture. Do you know what torture is? Wooden points that they stick in between your legs till your bones stick out! No, positively I will not go. And, MORBLEU, why do you not go yourself? For in truth, I think I have hitherto been deceived in you. I really believe you are a man, and a violent one, too."

"And you, you are a woman–a miserable woman, stupid and brutal. You are afraid, are you? Well, if you do not go this very instant, I will have you arrested by the queen's orders, and I will have you placed in the Bastille which you dread so much."

Bonacieux fell into a profound reflection. He weighed the two angers in his brain–that of the cardinal and that of the queen; that of the cardinal predominated enormously.

"Have me arrested on the part of the queen," said he, "and I–I will appeal to his Eminence."

At once Mme. Bonacieux saw that she had gone too far, and she was terrified at having communicated so much. She for a moment contemplated with fright that stupid countenance, impressed with the invincible resolution of a fool that is overcome by fear.

"Well, be it so!" said she. "Perhaps, when all is considered, you are right. In the long run, a man knows more about politics than a woman, particularly such as, like you, Monsieur Bonacieux, have conversed with the cardinal. And yet it is very hard," added she, "that a man upon whose affection I thought I might depend, treats me thus unkindly and will not comply with any of my fancies."

"That is because your fancies go too far," replied the triumphant Bonacieux, "and I mistrust them."

"Well, I will give it up, then," said the young woman, sighing. "It is well as it is; say no more about it."

"At least you should tell me what I should have to do in London," replied Bonacieux, who remembered a little too late that Rochefort had desired him to endeavour to obtain his wife's secrets.

"It is of no use for you to know anything about it," said the young woman, whom an instinctive mistrust now impelled to draw back. "It was about one of those purchases that interest women–a purchase by which much might have been gained."

But the more the young woman excused herself, the more important Bonacieux thought the secret which she declined to confide to him. He resolved then to hasten immediately to the residence of the Comte de Rochefort, and tell him that the queen was seeking for a messenger to send to London.

"Pardon me for quitting you, my dear Madame Bonacieux," said he, "but, not knowing you would come to see me, I had made an engagement with a friend. I shall soon return; and if you will wait only a few minutes for me, as soon as I have concluded my business with that friend, as it is growing late, I will come back and reconduct you to the Louvre."

"Thank you, Monsieur, you are not brave enough to be of any use to me whatever," replied Mme. Bonacieux. "I shall return very safely to the Louvre all alone."

"As you please, Madame Bonacieux," said the ex-mercer. "Shall I see you again soon?"

"Next week I hope my duties will afford me a little liberty, and I will take advantage of it to come and put things in order here, as they must necessarily be much deranged."

"Very well; I shall expect you. You are not angry with me?"

"Not the least in the world."

"Till then, then?"

"Till then."

Bonacieux kissed his wife's hand, and set off at a quick pace.

"Well," said Mme. Bonacieux, when her husband had shut the street door and she found herself alone, "that imbecile lacked but one thing: to become a cardinalist. And I, who have answered for him to the queen–I, who have promised my poor mistress–ah, my God, my God! She will take me for one of those wretches with whom the palace swarms and who are placed about her as spies! Ah, Monsieur Bonacieux, I never did love you much, but now it is worse than ever. I hate you, and on my word you shall pay for this!"

At the moment she spoke these words a rap on the ceiling made her raise her head, and a voice which reached her through the ceiling cried, "Dear Madame Bonacieux, open for me the little door on the alley, and I will come down to you."

Chapter 18

Lover And Husband

"Ah, Madame," said d'Artagnan, entering by the door which the young woman opened for him, "allow me to tell you that you have a bad sort of a husband."

"You have, then, overheard our conversation?" asked Mme. Bonacieux, eagerly, and looking at d'Artagnan with disquiet.

"The whole."

"But how, my God?"

"By a mode of proceeding known to myself, and by which I likewise overheard the more animated conversation which he had with the cardinal's police."

"And what did you understand by what we said?"

"A thousand things. In the first place, that, unfortunately, your husband is a simpleton and a fool; in the next place, you are in trouble, of which I am very glad, as it gives me an opportunity of placing myself at your service, and God knows I am ready to throw myself into the fire for you; finally, that the queen wants a brave, intelligent, devoted man to make a journey to London for her. I have at least two of the three qualities you stand in need of, and here I am."

Mme. Bonacieux made no reply, but her heart beat with joy and secret hope shone in her eyes.

"And what guarantee will you give me," asked she, "if I consent to confide this message to you?"

"My love for you. Speak! Command! What is to be done?"

"My God, my God!" murmured the young woman, "ought I to confide such a secret to you, Monsieur? You are almost a boy."

"I see that you require someone to answer for me?"

"I admit that would reassure me greatly."

"Do you know Athos?"

"No."

"Porthos?"

"No."

"Aramis?"

"No. Who are these gentleman?"

"Three of the king's Musketeers. Do you know Monsieur de Tréville, their captain?"

"Oh, yes, him! I know him; not personally, but from having heard the queen speak of him more than once as a brave and loyal gentleman."

"You do not fear lest he should betray you to the cardinal?"

"Oh, no, certainly not!"

"Well, reveal your secret to him, and ask him whether, however important, however valuable, however terrible it may be, you may not confide it to me."

"But this secret is not mine, and I cannot reveal it in this manner."

"You were about to confide it to Monsieur Bonacieux," said d'Artagnan, with chagrin.

"As one confides a letter to the hollow of a tree, to the wing of a pigeon, to the collar of a dog."

"And yet, me–you see plainly that I love you."

"You say so."

"I am an honourable man."

"You say so."

"I am a gallant fellow."

"I believe it."

"I am brave."

"Oh, I am sure of that!"

"Then, put me to the proof."

Mme. Bonacieux looked at the young man, restrained for a minute by a last hesitation, but there was such an ardor in his eyes, such persuasion in his voice, that she felt herself constrained to confide in him. Besides, she found herself in circumstances where everything must be risked for the sake of everything. The queen might be as much injured by too much reticence as by too much confidence; and–let us admit it–the involuntary sentiment which she felt for her young protector decided her to speak.

"Listen," said she, "I yield to your protestations, I yield to your assurances. But I swear to you, before God who hears us, that if you betray me, and my enemies pardon me, I will kill myself, while accusing you of my death."

"And I–I swear to you before God, Madame," said d'Artagnan, "that if I am taken while accomplishing the orders you give me, I will die sooner than do anything that may compromise anyone."

Then the young woman confided in him the terrible secret of which chance had already communicated to him a part in front of the Samaritaine. This was their mutual declaration of love.

D'Artagnan was radiant with joy and pride. This secret which he possessed, this woman whom he loved! Confidence and love made him a giant.

"I go," said he, "I go at once."

"How, you will go!" said Mme. Bonacieux, "and your regiment, your captain?"

"By my soul, you had made me forget all that, dear Constance! Yes, you are right; a furlough is needful."

"Still another obstacle," murmured Mme. Bonacieux, sorrowfully.

"As to that," cried d'Artagnan, after a moment of reflection, "I shall surmount it, be assured."

"How so?"

"I will go this very evening to Tréville, whom I will request to ask this favour for me of his brother-in-law, Monsieur Dessessart."

"But another thing."

"What?" asked d'Artagnan, seeing that Mme. Bonacieux hesitated to continue.

"You have, perhaps, no money?"

"PERHAPS is too much," said d'Artagnan, smiling.

"Then," replied Mme. Bonacieux, opening a cupboard and taking from it the very bag which a half hour before her husband had caressed so affectionately, "take this bag."

"The cardinal's?" cried d'Artagnan, breaking into a loud laugh, he having heard, as may be remembered, thanks to the broken boards, every syllable of the conversation between the mercer and his wife.

"The cardinal's," replied Mme. Bonacieux. "You see it makes a very respectable appearance."

"PARDIEU," cried d'Artagnan, "it will be a double amusing affair to save the queen with the cardinal's money!"

"You are an amiable and charming young man," said Mme. Bonacieux. "Be assured you will not find her Majesty ungrateful."

"Oh, I am already grandly recompensed!" cried d'Artagnan. "I love you; you permit me to tell you that I do–that is already more happiness than I dared to hope."

"Silence!" said Mme. Bonacieux, starting.

"What!"

"Someone is talking in the street."

"It is the voice of–"

"Of my husband! Yes, I recognise it!"

D'Artagnan ran to the door and pushed the bolt.

"He shall not come in before I am gone," said he, "and when I am gone, you can open to him."

"But I ought to be gone, too. And the disappearance of his money; how am I to justify it if I am here?"

"You are right; we must go out."

"Go out? How? He will see us if we go out."

"Then you must come up into my room."

"Ah," said Mme. Bonacieux, "you speak that in a tone that frightens me!"

Mme. Bonacieux pronounced these words with tears in her eyes. D'Artagnan saw those tears, and much disturbed, softened, he threw himself at her feet.

"With me you will be as safe as in a temple; I give you my word of a gentleman."

"Let us go," said she, "I place full confidence in you, my friend!"

D'Artagnan drew back the bolt with precaution, and both, light as shadows, glided through the interior door into the passage, ascended the stairs as quietly as possible, and entered d'Artagnan's chambers.

Once there, for greater security, the young man barricaded the door. They both approached the window, and through a slit in the shutter they saw Bonacieux talking with a man in a cloak.

At sight of this man, d'Artagnan started, and half drawing his sword, sprang toward the door.

It was the man of Meung.

"What are you going to do?" cried Mme. Bonacieux, "you will ruin us all!"

"But I have sworn to kill that man!" said d'Artagnan.

"Your life is devoted from this moment, and does not belong to you. In the name of the queen I forbid you to throw yourself into any peril which is foreign to that of your journey."

"And do you command nothing in your own name?"

"In my name," said Mme. Bonacieux, with great emotion, "in my name I beg you! But listen; they appear to be speaking of me."

D'Artagnan drew near the window, and lent his ear.

M Bonacieux had opened his door, and seeing the apartment, had returned to the man in the cloak, whom he had left alone for an instant.

"She is gone," said he, "she must have returned to the Louvre."

"You are sure," replied the stranger, "that she did not suspect the intentions with which you went out?"

"No," replied Bonacieux, with a self-sufficient air, "she is too superficial a woman."

"Is the young Guardsman at home?"

"I do not think he is; as you see, his shutter is closed, and you can see no light shine through the chinks of the shutters."

"All the same, it is well to be certain."

"How so?"

"By knocking at his door. Go."

"I will ask his servant."

Bonacieux re-entered the house, passed through the same door that had afforded a passage for the two fugitives, went up to d'Artagnan's door, and knocked.

No one answered. Porthos, in order to make a greater display, had that evening borrowed Planchet. As to d'Artagnan, he took care not to give the least sign of existence.

The moment the hand of Bonacieux sounded on the door, the two young people felt their hearts bound within them.

"There is nobody within," said Bonacieux.

"Never mind. Let us return to your apartment. We shall be safer there than in the doorway."

"Ah, my God!" whispered Mme. Bonacieux, "we shall hear no more."

"On the contrary," said d'Artagnan, "we shall hear better."

D'Artagnan raised the three or four boards which made his chamber another ear of Dionysius, spread a carpet on the floor, went upon his knees, and made a sign to Mme. Bonacieux to stoop as he did toward the opening.

"You are sure there is nobody there?" said the stranger.

"I will answer for it," said Bonacieux.

"And you think that your wife–"

"Has returned to the Louvre."

"Without speaking to anyone but yourself?"

"I am sure of it."

"That is an important point, do you understand?"

"Then the news I brought you is of value?"

"The greatest, my dear Bonacieux; I don't conceal this from you."

"Then the cardinal will be pleased with me?"

"I have no doubt of it."

"The great cardinal!"

"Are you sure, in her conversation with you, that your wife mentioned no names?"

"I think not."

"She did not name Madame de Chevreuse, the Duke of Buckingham, or Madame de Vernet?"

"No; she only told me she wished to send me to London to serve the interests of an illustrious personage."

"The traitor!" murmured Mme. Bonacieux.

"Silence!" said d'Artagnan, taking her hand, which, without thinking of it, she abandoned to him.

"Never mind," continued the man in the cloak, "you were a fool not to have pretended to accept the mission. You would then be in present possession of the letter. The state, which is now threatened, would be safe, and you–"

"And I?"

"Well you–the cardinal would have given you letters of nobility."

"Did he tell you so?"

"Yes, I know that he meant to afford you that agreeable surprise."

"Be satisfied," replied Bonacieux, "my wife adores me, and there is yet time."

"The ninny!" murmured Mme. Bonacieux.

"Silence!" said d'Artagnan, pressing her hand more closely.

"How is there still time?" asked the man in the cloak.

"I go to the Louvre; I ask for Mme. Bonacieux; I say that I have reflected; I renew the affair; I obtain the letter, and I run directly to the cardinal."

"Well, go quickly! I will return soon to learn the result of your trip."

The stranger went out.

"Infamous!" said Mme. Bonacieux, addressing this epithet to her husband.

"Silence!" said d'Artagnan, pressing her hand still more warmly.

A terrible howling interrupted these reflections of d'Artagnan and Mme. Bonacieux. It was her husband, who had discovered the disappearance of the moneybag, and was crying "Thieves!"

"Oh, my God!" cried Mme. Bonacieux, "he will rouse the whole quarter."

Bonacieux called a long time, but as such cries, on account of their frequency, brought nobody in the Rue des Fossoyeurs, and as lately the mercer's house had a bad name, finding that nobody came, he went out continuing to call, his voice being heard fainter and fainter as he went in the direction of the Rue du Bac.

"Now he is gone, it is your turn to get out," said Mme. Bonacieux. "Courage, my friend, but above all, prudence, and think what you owe to the queen."

"To her and to you!" cried d'Artagnan. "Be satisfied, beautiful Constance. I shall become worthy of her gratitude, but shall I likewise return worthy of your love?"

The young woman only replied by the beautiful glow which mounted to her cheeks. A few seconds afterward d'Artagnan also went out enveloped in a large cloak, which ill-concealed the sheath of a long sword.

Mme. Bonacieux followed him with her eyes, with that long, fond look with which he had turned the angle of the street, she fell on her knees, and clasping her hands, "Oh, my God," cried she, "protect the queen, protect me!"

Chapter 19

Plan Of Campaign

D'Artagnan went straight to M. de Tréville's. He had reflected that in a few minutes the cardinal would be warned by this cursed stranger, who appeared to be his agent, and he judged, with reason, he had not a moment to lose.

The heart of the young man overflowed with joy. An opportunity presented itself to him in which there would be at the same time glory to be acquired, and money to be gained; and as a far higher encouragement, it brought him into close intimacy with a woman he adored. This chance did, then, for him at once more than he would have dared to ask of Providence.

M. de Tréville was in his saloon with his habitual court of gentlemen. D'Artagnan, who was known as a familiar of the house, went straight to his office, and sent word that he wished to see him on something of importance.

D'Artagnan had been there scarcely five minutes when M. de Tréville entered. At the first glance, and by the joy which was painted on his countenance, the worthy captain plainly perceived that something new was on foot.

All the way along d'Artagnan had been consulting with himself whether he should place confidence in M. de Tréville, or whether he should only ask him to give him CARTE BLANCHE for some secret affair. But M. de Tréville had always been so thoroughly his friend, had always been so devoted to the king and queen, and hated the cardinal so cordially, that the young man resolved to tell him everything.

"Did you ask for me, my good friend?" said M. de Tréville.

"Yes, Monsieur," said d'Artagnan, lowering his voice, "and you will pardon me, I hope, for having disturbed you when you know the importance of my business."

"Speak, then, I am all attention."

"It concerns nothing less," said d'Artagnan, "than the honour, perhaps the life of the queen."

"What did you say?" asked M. de Tréville, glancing round to see if they were surely alone, and then fixing his questioning look upon d'Artagnan.

"I say, Monsieur, that chance has rendered me master of a secret–"

"Which you will guard, I hope, young man, as your life."

"But which I must impart to you, Monsieur, for you alone can assist me in the mission I have just received from her Majesty."

"Is this secret your own?"

"No, Monsieur; it is her Majesty's."

"Are you authorised by her Majesty to communicate it to me?"

"No, Monsieur, for, on the contrary, I am desired to preserve the profoundest mystery."

"Why, then, are you about to betray it to me?"

"Because, as I said, without you I can do nothing; and I am afraid you will refuse me the favour I come to ask if you do not know to what end I ask it."

"Keep your secret, young man, and tell me what you wish."

"I wish you to obtain for me, from Monsieur Dessessart, leave of absence for fifteen days."

"When?"

"This very night."

"You leave Paris?"

"I am going on a mission."

"May you tell me whither?"

"To London."

"Has anyone an interest in preventing your arrival there?"

"The cardinal, I believe, would give the world to prevent my success."

"And you are going alone?"

"I am going alone."

"In that case you will not get beyond Bondy. I tell you so, by the faith of de Tréville."

"How so?"

"You will be assassinated."

"And I shall die in the performance of my duty."

"But your mission will not be accomplished."

"That is true," replied d'Artagnan.

"Believe me," continued Tréville, "in enterprises of this kind, in order that one may arrive, four must set out."

"Ah, you are right, Monsieur," said d'Artagnan, "but you know Athos, Porthos, and Aramis, and you know if I can dispose of them."

"Without confiding to them the secret which I am not willing to know?"

"We are sworn, once for all, to implicit confidence and devotedness against all proof. Besides, you can tell them that you have full confidence in me, and they will not be more incredulous than you."

"I can send to each of them leave of absence for fifteen days, that is all–to Athos, whose wound still makes him suffer, to go to the waters of Forges; to Porthos and Aramis to accompany their friend, whom they are not willing to abandon in such a painful condition. Sending their leave of absence will be proof enough that I authorise their journey."

"Thanks, Monsieur. You are a hundred times too good."

"Begone, then, find them instantly, and let all be done tonight! Ha! But first write your request to Dessessart. Perhaps you had a spy at your heels; and your visit, if it should ever be known to the cardinal, will thus seem legitimate."

D'Artagnan drew up his request, and M. de Tréville, on receiving it, assured him that by two o'clock in the morning the four leaves of absence should be at the respective domiciles of the travellers.

"Have the goodness to send mine to Athos's residence. I should dread some disagreeable encounter if I were to go home."

"Be easy. Adieu, and a prosperous voyage. À PROPOS," said M. de Tréville, calling him back.

D'Artagnan returned.

"Have you any money?"

D'Artagnan tapped the bag he had in his pocket.

"Enough?" asked M. de Tréville.

"Three hundred pistoles."

"Oh, plenty! That would carry you to the end of the world. Begone, then!"

D'Artagnan saluted M. de Tréville, who held out his hand to him; d'Artagnan pressed it with a respect mixed with gratitude. Since his first arrival at Paris, he had had constant occasion to honour this excellent man, whom he had always found worthy, loyal, and great.

His first visit was to Aramis, at whose residence he had not been since the famous evening on which he had followed Mme. Bonacieux. Still further, he had seldom seen the young Musketeer, but every time he had seen him, he had remarked a deep sadness imprinted on his countenance.

This evening, especially, Aramis was melancholy and thoughtful. D'Artagnan asked some questions about this prolonged melancholy. Aramis pleaded as his excuse a commentary upon the eighteenth chapter of St. Augustine, which he was forced to write in Latin for the following week, and which preoccupied him a good deal.

After the two friends had been chatting a few moments, a servant from M. de Tréville entered, bringing a sealed packet.

"What is that?" asked Aramis.

"The leave of absence Monsieur has asked for," replied the lackey.

"For me! I have asked for no leave of absence."

"Hold your tongue and take it!" said d'Artagnan. "And you, my friend, there is a demipistole for your trouble; you will tell Monsieur de Tréville that Monsieur Aramis is very much obliged to him. Go."

The lackey bowed to the ground and departed.

"What does all this mean?" asked Aramis.

"Pack up all you want for a journey of a fortnight, and follow me."

"But I cannot leave Paris just now without knowing–"

Aramis stopped.

"What is become of her? I suppose you mean–" continued d'Artagnan.

"Become of whom?" replied Aramis.

"The woman who was here–the woman with the embroidered handkerchief."

"Who told you there was a woman here?" replied Aramis, becoming as pale as death.

"I saw her."

"And you know who she is?"

"I believe I can guess, at least."

"Listen!" said Aramis. "Since you appear to know so many things, can you tell me what is become of that woman?"

"I presume that she has returned to Tours."

"To Tours? Yes, that may be. You evidently know her. But why did she return to Tours without telling me anything?"

"Because she was in fear of being arrested."

"Why has she not written to me, then?"

"Because she was afraid of compromising you."

"D'Artagnan, you restore me to life!" cried Aramis. "I fancied myself despised, betrayed. I was so delighted to see her again! I could not have believed she would risk her liberty for me, and yet for what other cause could she have returned to Paris?"

"For the cause which today takes us to England."

"And what is this cause?" demanded Aramis.

"Oh, you'll know it someday, Aramis, but at present I must imitate the discretion of 'the doctor's niece.'"

Aramis smiled, as he remembered the tale he had told his friends on a certain evening. "Well, then, since she has left Paris, and you are sure of it, d'Artagnan, nothing prevents me, and I am ready to follow you. You say we are going–"

"To see Athos now, and if you will come thither, I beg you to make haste, for we have lost much time already. À PROPOS, inform Bazin."

"Will Bazin go with us?" asked Aramis.

"Perhaps so. At all events, it is best that he should follow us to Athos's."

Aramis called Bazin, and, after having ordered him to join them at Athos's residence, said "Let us go then," at the same time taking his cloak, sword, and three pistols, opening uselessly two or three drawers to see if he could not find stray coin. When well assured this search was superfluous, he followed d'Artagnan, wondering to himself how this young Guardsman should know so well who the lady was to whom he had given hospitality, and that he should know better than himself what had become of her.

Only as they went out Aramis placed his hand upon the arm of d'Artagnan, and looking at him earnestly, "You have not spoken of this lady?" said he.

"To nobody in the world."

"Not even to Athos or Porthos?"

"I have not breathed a syllable to them."

"Good enough!"

Tranquil on this important point, Aramis continued his way with d'Artagnan, and both soon arrived at Athos's dwelling. They found him holding his leave of absence in one hand, and M. de Tréville's note in the other.

"Can you explain to me what signify this leave of absence and this letter, which I have just received?" said the astonished Athos.

My dear Athos,

I wish, as your health absolutely requires it, that you should rest for a fortnight. Go, then, and take the waters of Forges, or any that may be more agreeable to you, and recuperate yourself as quickly as possible.

Yours affectionate,

de Tréville

"Well, this leave of absence and that letter mean that you must follow me, Athos."

"To the waters of Forges?"

"There or elsewhere."

"In the king's service?"

"Either the king's or the queen's. Are we not their Majesties' servants?"

At that moment Porthos entered. "PARDIEU!" said he, "here is a strange thing! Since when, I wonder, in the Musketeers, did they grant men leave of absence without their asking for it?"

"Since," said d'Artagnan, "they have friends who ask it for them."

"Ah, ah!" said Porthos, "it appears there's something fresh here."

"Yes, we are going–" said Aramis.

"To what country?" demanded Porthos.

"My faith! I don't know much about it," said Athos. "Ask d'Artagnan."

"To London, gentlemen," said d'Artagnan.

"To London!" cried Porthos, "and what the devil are we going to do in London?"

"That is what I am not at liberty to tell you, gentlemen; you must trust to me."

"But in order to go to London," added Porthos, "money is needed, and I have none."

"Nor I," said Aramis.

"Nor I," said Athos.

"I have," replied d'Artagnan, pulling out his treasure from his pocket, and placing it on the table. "There are in this bag three hundred pistoles. Let each take seventy-five; that is enough to take us to London and back. Besides, make yourselves easy; we shall not all arrive at London."

"Why so?"

"Because, in all probability, some one of us will be left on the road."

"Is this, then, a campaign upon which we are now entering?"

"One of a most dangerous kind, I give you notice."

"Ah! But if we do risk being killed," said Porthos, "at least I should like to know what for."

"You would be all the wiser," said Athos.

"And yet," said Aramis, "I am somewhat of Porthos's opinion."

"Is the king accustomed to give you such reasons? No. He says to you jauntily, 'Gentlemen, there is fighting going on in Gascony or in Flanders; go and fight,' and you go there. Why? You need give yourselves no more uneasiness about this."

"d'Artagnan is right," said Athos, "here are our three leaves of absence which came from Monsieur de Tréville, and here are three hundred pistoles which came from I don't know where. So let us go and get killed where we are told to go. Is life worth the trouble of so many questions? D'Artagnan, I am ready to follow you."

"And I also," said Porthos.

"And I also," said Aramis. "And, indeed, I am not sorry to quit Paris; I had need of distraction."

"Well, you will have distractions enough, gentlemen, be assured," said d'Artagnan.

"And, now, when are we to go?" asked Athos.

"Immediately," replied d'Artagnan, "we have not a minute to lose."

"Hello, Grimaud! Planchet! Mousqueton! Bazin!" cried the four young men, calling their lackeys, "clean my boots, and fetch the horses from the hotel."

Each Musketeer was accustomed to leave at the general hotel, as at a barrack, his own horse and that of his lackey. Planchet, Grimaud, Mousqueton, and Bazin set off at full speed.

"Now let us lay down the plan of campaign," said Porthos. "Where do we go first?"

"To Calais," said d'Artagnan, "that is the most direct line to London."

"Well," said Porthos, "this is my advice–"

"Speak!"

"Four men travelling together would be suspected. D'Artagnan will give each of us his instructions. I will go by the way of Boulogne to clear the way; Athos will set out two hours after, by that of Amiens; Aramis will follow us by that of Noyon; as to d'Artagnan, he will go by what route he thinks is best, in Planchet's clothes, while Planchet will follow us like d'Artagnan, in the uniform of the Guards."

"Gentlemen," said Athos, "my opinion is that it is not proper to allow lackeys to have anything to do in such an affair. A secret may, by chance, be betrayed by gentlemen, but it is almost always sold by lackeys."

"Porthos's plan appears to me to be impracticable," said d'Artagnan, "inasmuch as I am myself ignorant of what instructions I can give you. I am the bearer of a letter, that is all. I have not, and I cannot make three copies of that letter, because it is sealed. We must, then, as it appears to me, travel in company. This letter is here, in this pocket," and he pointed to the pocket which contained the letter. "If I should be killed, one of you must take it, and continue the route; if he be killed, it will be another's turn, and so on–provided a single one arrives, that is all that is required."

"Bravo, d'Artagnan, your opinion is mine," cried Athos, "Besides, we must be consistent; I am going to take the waters, you will accompany me. Instead of taking the waters of Forges, I go and take sea waters; I am free to do so. If anyone wishes to stop us, I will show Monsieur de Tréville's letter, and you will show your leaves of absence. If we are attacked, we will defend ourselves; if we are tried, we will stoutly maintain that we were only anxious to dip ourselves a certain number of times in the sea. They would have an easy bargain of four isolated men; whereas four men together make a troop. We will arm our four lackeys with pistols and musketoons; if they send an army out against us, we will give battle, and the survivor, as d'Artagnan says, will carry the letter."

"Well said," cried Aramis, "you don't often speak, Athos, but when you do speak, it is like St. John of the Golden Mouth. I agree to Athos's plan. And you, Porthos?"

"I agree to it, too," said Porthos, "if d'Artagnan approves of it. D'Artagnan, being the bearer of the letter, is naturally the head of the enterprise; let him decide, and we will execute."

"Well," said d'Artagnan, "I decide that we should adopt Athos's plan, and that we set off in half an hour."

"Agreed!" shouted the three Musketeers in chorus.

Each one, stretching out his hand to the bag, took his seventy-five pistoles, and made his preparations to set out at the time appointed.

Chapter 20

The Journey

At two o'clock in the morning, our four adventurers left Paris by the Barrière St. Denis. As long as it was dark they remained silent; in spite of themselves they submitted to the influence of the obscurity, and apprehended ambushes on every side.

With the first rays of day their tongues were loosened; with the sun gaiety revived. It was like the eve of a battle; the heart beat, the eyes laughed, and they felt that the life they were perhaps going to lose, was, after all, a good thing.

Besides, the appearance of the caravan was formidable. The black horses of the Musketeers, their martial carriage, with the regimental step of these noble companions of the soldier, would have betrayed the most strict incognito. The lackeys followed, armed to the teeth.

All went well till they arrived at Chantilly, which they reached about eight o'clock in the morning. They needed breakfast, and alighted at the door of an AUBERGE, recommended by a sign representing St. Martin giving half his cloak to a poor man. They ordered the lackeys not to unsaddle the horses, and to hold themselves in readiness to set off again immediately.

They entered the common hall, and placed themselves at table. A gentleman, who had just arrived by the route of Dammartin, was seated at the same table, and was breakfasting. He opened the conversation about rain and fine weather; the travellers replied. He drank to their good health, and the travellers returned his politeness.

But at the moment Mousqueton came to announce that the horses were ready, and they were arising from table, the stranger proposed to Porthos to drink the health of the cardinal. Porthos replied that he asked no better if the stranger, in his turn, would drink the health of the king. The stranger cried that he acknowledged no other king but his Eminence. Porthos called him drunk, and the stranger drew his sword.

"You have committed a piece of folly," said Athos, "but it can't be helped; there is no drawing back. Kill the fellow, and rejoin us as soon as you can."

All three remounted their horses, and set out at a good pace, while Porthos was promising his adversary to perforate him with all the thrusts known in the fencing schools.

"There goes one!" cried Athos, at the end of five hundred paces.

"But why did that man attack Porthos rather than any other one of us?" asked Aramis.

"Because, as Porthos was talking louder than the rest of us, he took him for the chief," said d'Artagnan.

"I always said that this cadet from Gascony was a well of wisdom," murmured Athos; and the travellers continued their route.

At Beauvais they stopped two hours, as well to breathe their horses a little as to wait for Porthos. At the end of two hours, as Porthos did not come, not any news of him, they resumed their journey.

At a league from Beauvais, where the road was confined between two high banks, they fell in with eight or ten men who, taking advantage of the road being unpaved in this spot, appeared to be employed in digging holes and filling up the ruts with mud.

Aramis, not liking to soil his boots with this artificial mortar, apostrophised them rather sharply. Athos wished to restrain him, but it was too late. The laborers began to jeer the travellers and by their insolence disturbed the equanimity even of the cool Athos, who urged on his horse against one of them.

Then each of these men retreated as far as the ditch, from which each took a concealed musket; the result was that our seven travellers were outnumbered in weapons. Aramis received a ball which passed through his shoulder, and Mousqueton another ball which lodged in the fleshy part which prolongs the lower portion of the loins. Therefore Mousqueton alone fell from his horse, not because he was severely wounded, but not being able to see the wound, he judged it to be more serious than it really was.

"It was an ambuscade!" shouted d'Artagnan. "Don't waste a charge! Forward!"

Aramis, wounded as he was, seized the mane of his horse, which carried him on with the others. Mousqueton's horse rejoined them, and galloped by the side of his companions.

"That will serve us for a relay," said Athos.

"I would rather have had a hat," said d'Artagnan. "Mine was carried away by a ball. By my faith, it is very fortunate that the letter was not in it."

"They'll kill poor Porthos when he comes up," said Aramis.

"If Porthos were on his legs, he would have rejoined us by this time," said Athos. "My opinion is that on the ground the drunken man was not intoxicated."

They continued at their best speed for two hours, although the horses were so fatigued that it was to be feared they would soon refuse service.

The travellers had chosen crossroads in the hope that they might meet with less interruption, but at Crèvecoeur, Aramis declared he could proceed no farther. In fact, it required all the courage which he concealed beneath his elegant form and polished manners to bear him so far. He grew more pale every minute, and they were obliged to support him on his horse. They lifted him off at the door of a cabaret, left Bazin with him, who, besides, in a skirmish was more embarrassing than useful, and set forward again in the hope of sleeping at Amiens.

"MORBLEU," said Athos, as soon as they were again in motion, "reduced to two masters and Grimaud and Planchet! MORBLEU! I won't be their dupe, I will answer for it. I will neither open my mouth nor draw my sword between this and Calais. I swear by–"

"Don't waste time in swearing," said d'Artagnan, "let us gallop, if our horses will consent."

And the travellers buried their rowels in their horses' flanks, who thus vigorously stimulated recovered their energies. They arrived at Amiens at midnight, and alighted at the AUBERGE of the Golden Lily.

The host had the appearance of as honest a man as any on earth. He received the travellers with his candlestick in one hand and his cotton nightcap in the other. He wished to lodge the two travellers each in a charming chamber, but unfortunately these charming chambers were at the opposite extremities of the hotel. D'Artagnan and Athos refused them. The host replied that he had no other worthy of their Excellencies, but the travellers declared they would sleep in the common chamber, each on a mattress which might be thrown upon the ground. The host insisted, but the travellers were firm, and he was obliged to do as they wished.

They had just prepared their beds and barricaded their door within, when someone knocked at the yard shutter; they demanded who was there, and recognising the voices of their lackeys, opened the shutter. It was indeed Planchet and Grimaud.

"Grimaud can take care of the horses," said Planchet. "If you are willing, gentlemen, I will sleep across your doorway, and you will then be certain that nobody can reach you."

"And on what will you sleep?" said d'Artagnan.

"Here is my bed," replied Planchet, producing a bundle of straw.

"Come, then," said d'Artagnan, "you are right. Mine host's face does not please me at all; it is too gracious."

"Nor me either," said Athos.

Planchet mounted by the window and installed himself across the doorway, while Grimaud went and shut himself up in the stable, undertaking that by five o'clock in the morning he and the four horses should be ready.

The night was quiet enough. Toward two o'clock in the morning somebody endeavoured to open the door, but as Planchet awoke in an instant and cried, "Who goes there?" somebody replied that he was mistaken, and went away.

At four o'clock in the morning they heard a terrible riot in the stables. Grimaud had tried to waken the stable boys, and the stable boys had beaten him. When they opened the window, they saw the poor lad lying senseless, with his head split by a blow with a pitchfork.

Planchet went down into the yard, and wished to saddle the horses, but the horses were all used up. Mousqueton's horse which had traveled for five or six hours without a rider the day before, might have been able to pursue the journey, but by an inconceivable error the veterinary surgeon, who had been sent for, as it appeared, to bleed one of the host's horses, had bled Mousqueton's.

This began to be annoying. All these successive accidents were perhaps the result of chance, but they might be the fruits of a plot. Athos and d'Artagnan went out, while Planchet was sent to inquire if there were not three horses for sale in the neighbourhood. At the door stood two horses, fresh, strong, and fully equipped. These would just have suited them. He asked where their masters were, and was informed that they had passed the night in the inn, and were then settling their bill with the host.

Athos went down to pay the reckoning, while d'Artagnan and Planchet stood at the street door. The host was in a lower and back room, to which Athos was requested to go.

Athos entered without the least mistrust, and took out two pistoles to pay the bill. The host was alone, seated before his desk, one of the drawers of which was partly open. He took the money which Athos offered to him, and after turning and turning it over and over in his hands, suddenly cried out that it was bad, and that he would have him and his companions arrested as forgers.

"You blackguard!" cried Athos, going toward him, "I'll cut your ears off!"

At the same instant, four men, armed to the teeth, entered by side doors, and rushed upon Athos.

"I am taken!" shouted Athos, with all the power of his lungs. "Go on, d'Artagnan! Spur, spur!" and he fired two pistols.

D'Artagnan and Planchet did not require twice bidding; they unfastened the two horses that were waiting at the door, leaped upon them, buried their spurs in their sides, and set off at full gallop.

"Do you know what has become of Athos?" asked d'Artagnan of Planchet, as they galloped on.

"Ah, Monsieur," said Planchet, "I saw one fall at each of his two shots, and he appeared to me, through the glass door, to be fighting with his sword with the others."

"Brave Athos!" murmured d'Artagnan, "and to think that we are compelled to leave him; maybe the same fate awaits us two paces hence. Forward, Planchet, forward! You are a brave fellow."

"As I told you, Monsieur," replied Planchet, "Picards are found out by being used. Besides, I am here in my own country, and that excites me."

And both, with free use of the spur, arrived at St. Omer without drawing bit. At St. Omer they breathed their horses with the bridles passed under their arms for fear of accident, and ate a morsel from their hands on the stones of the street, after they departed again.

At a hundred paces from the gates of Calais, d'Artagnan's horse gave out, and could not by any means be made to get up again, the blood flowing from his eyes and his nose. There still remained Planchet's horse, but he stopped short, and could not be made to move a step.

Fortunately, as we have said, they were within a hundred paces of the city; they left their two nags upon the high road, and ran toward the quay. Planchet called his master's attention to a gentleman who had just arrived with his lackey, and only preceded them by about fifty paces. They made all speed to come up to this gentleman, who appeared to be in great haste. His boots were covered with dust, and he inquired if he could not instantly cross over to England.

"Nothing would be more easy," said the captain of a vessel ready to set sail, "but this morning came an order to let no one leave without express permission from the cardinal."

"I have that permission," said the gentleman, drawing the paper from his pocket, "here it is."

"Have it examined by the governor of the port," said the shipmaster, "and give me the preference."

"Where shall I find the governor?"

"At his country house."

"And that is situated?"

"At a quarter of a league from the city. Look, you may see it from here–at the foot of that little hill, that slated roof."

"Very well," said the gentleman. And, with his lackey, he took the road to the governor's country house.

D'Artagnan and Planchet followed the gentleman at a distance of five hundred paces. Once outside the city, d'Artagnan overtook the gentleman as he was entering a little wood.

"Monsieur, you appear to be in great haste?"

"No one can be more so, Monsieur."

"I am sorry for that," said d'Artagnan, "for as I am in great haste likewise, I wish to beg you to render me a service."

"What?"

"To let me sail first."

"That's impossible," said the gentleman, "I have traveled sixty leagues in forty hours, and by tomorrow at midday I must be in London."

"I have performed that same distance in forty hours, and by ten o'clock in the morning I must be in London."

"Very sorry, Monsieur, but I was here first, and will not sail second."

"I am sorry, too, Monsieur, but I arrived second, and must sail first."

"The king's service!" said the gentleman.

"My own service!" said d'Artagnan.

"But this is a needless quarrel you seek with me, as it seems to me."

"PARBLEU! What do you desire it to be?"

"What do you want?"

"Would you like to know?"

"Certainly."

"Well, then, I wish that order of which you are bearer, seeing that I have not one of my own and must have one."

"You jest, I presume."

"I never jest."

"Let me pass!"

"You shall not pass."

"My brave young man, I will blow out your brains. HOLA, Lubin, my pistols!"

"Planchet," called out d'Artagnan, "take care of the lackey; I will manage the master."

Planchet, emboldened by the first exploit, sprang upon Lubin; and being strong and vigorous, he soon got him on the broad of his back, and placed his knee upon his breast.

"Go on with your affair, Monsieur," cried Planchet, "I have finished mine."

Seeing this, the gentleman drew his sword, and sprang upon d'Artagnan, but he had too strong an adversary. In three seconds d'Artagnan had wounded him three times, exclaiming at each thrust, "One for Athos, one for Porthos; and one for Aramis!"

At the third hit the gentleman fell like a log. D'Artagnan believed him to be dead, or at least insensible, and went toward him for the purpose of taking the order, but the moment he extended his hand to search for it, the wounded man, who had not dropped his sword, plunged the point into d'Artagnan's breast, crying, "One for you!"

"And one for me–the best for last!" cried d'Artagnan, furious, nailing him to the earth with a fourth thrust through his body.

This time the gentleman closed his eyes and fainted. D'Artagnan searched his pockets, and took from one of them the order for the passage. It was in the name of Comte de Wardes.

Then, casting a glance on the handsome young man, who was scarcely twenty-five years of age, and whom he was leaving in his gore, deprived of sense and perhaps dead, he gave a sigh for that unaccountable destiny which leads men to destroy each other for the interests of people who are strangers to them and who often do not even know that they exist. But he was soon aroused from these reflections by Lubin, who uttered loud cries and screamed for help with all his might.

Planchet grasped him by the throat, and pressed as hard as he could. "Monsieur," said he, "as long as I hold him in this manner, he can't cry, I'll be bound, but as soon as I let go he will howl again. I know him for a Norman, and Normans are obstinate."

In fact, tightly held as he was, Lubin endeavoured still to cry out.

"Stay!" said d'Artagnan; and taking out his handkerchief, he gagged him.

"Now," said Planchet, "let us bind him to a tree."

This being properly done, they drew the Comte de Wardes close to his servant; and as night was approaching, and as the wounded man and the bound man were at some little distance within the wood, it was evident they were likely to remain there till the next day.

"And now," said d'Artagnan, "to the Governor's."

"But you are wounded, it seems," said Planchet.

"Oh, that's nothing! Let us attend to what is more pressing first, and then we will attend to my wound; besides, it does not seem very dangerous."

And they both set forward as fast as they could toward the country house of the worthy functionary.

The Comte de Wardes was announced, and d'Artagnan was introduced.

"You have an order signed by the cardinal?" said the governor.

"Yes, Monsieur," replied d'Artagnan, "here it is."

"Ah, ah! It is quite regular and explicit," said the governor.

"Most likely," said d'Artagnan, "I am one of his most faithful servants."

"It appears that his Eminence is anxious to prevent someone from crossing to England?"

"Yes; a certain d'Artagnan, a Bearnese gentleman who left Paris in company with three of his friends, with the intention of going to London."

"Do you know him personally?" asked the governor.

"Whom?"

"This d'Artagnan."

"Perfectly well."

"Describe him to me, then."

"Nothing more easy."

And d'Artagnan gave, feature for feature, a description of the Comte de Wardes.

"Is he accompanied?"

"Yes; by a lackey named Lubin."

"We will keep a sharp lookout for them; and if we lay hands on them his Eminence may be assured they will be reconducted to Paris under a good escort."

"And by doing so, Monsieur the Governor," said d'Artagnan, "you will deserve well of the cardinal."

"Shall you see him on your return, Monsieur Count?"

"Without a doubt."

"Tell him, I beg you, that I am his humble servant."

"I will not fail."

Delighted with this assurance the governor countersigned the passport and delivered it to d'Artagnan. D'Artagnan lost no time in useless compliments. He thanked the governor, bowed, and departed. Once outside, he and Planchet set off as fast as they could; and by making a long detour avoided the wood and reentered the city by another gate.

The vessel was quite ready to sail, and the captain was waiting on the wharf. "Well?" said he, on perceiving d'Artagnan.

"Here is my pass countersigned," said the latter.

"And that other gentleman?

"He will not go today," said d'Artagnan, "but here, I'll pay you for us two."

"In that case let us go," said the shipmaster.

"Let us go," repeated d'Artagnan.

He leaped with Planchet into the boat, and five minutes after they were on board. It was time; for they had scarcely sailed half a league, when d'Artagnan saw a flash and heard a detonation. It was the cannon which announced the closing of the port.

He had now leisure to look to his wound. Fortunately, as d'Artagnan had thought, it was not dangerous. The point of the sword had touched a rib, and glanced along the bone. Still further, his shirt had stuck to the wound, and he had lost only a few drops of blood.

D'Artagnan was worn out with fatigue. A mattress was laid upon the deck for him. He threw himself upon it, and fell asleep.

On the morrow, at break of day, they were still three or four leagues from the coast of England. The breeze had been so light all night, they had made but little progress. At ten o'clock the vessel cast anchor in the harbor of Dover, and at half past ten d'Artagnan placed his foot on English land, crying, "Here I am at last!"

But that was not all; they must get to London. In England the post was well served. D'Artagnan and Planchet took each a post horse, and a postillion rode before them. In a few hours they were in the capital.

D'Artagnan did not know London; he did not know a word of English, but he wrote the name of Buckingham on a piece of paper, and everyone pointed out to him the way to the duke's hotel.

The duke was at Windsor hunting with the king. D'Artagnan inquired for the confidential valet of the duke, who, having accompanied him in all his voyages, spoke French perfectly well; he told him that he came from Paris on an affair of life and death, and that he must speak with his master instantly.

The confidence with which d'Artagnan spoke convinced Patrick, which was the name of this minister of the minister. He ordered two horses to be saddled, and himself went as guide to the young Guardsman. As for Planchet, he had been lifted from his horse as stiff as a rush; the poor lad's strength was almost exhausted. D'Artagnan seemed iron.

On their arrival at the castle they learned that Buckingham and the king were hawking in the marshes two or three leagues away. In twenty minutes they were on the spot named. Patrick soon caught the sound of his master's voice calling his falcon.

"Whom must I announce to my Lord Duke?" asked Patrick.

"The young man who one evening sought a quarrel with him on the Pont Neuf, opposite the Samaritaine."

"A singular introduction!"

"You will find that it is as good as another."

Patrick galloped off, reached the duke, and announced to him in the terms directed that a messenger awaited him.

Buckingham at once remembered the circumstance, and suspecting that something was going on in France of which it was necessary he should be informed, he only took the time to inquire where the messenger was, and recognising from afar the uniform of the Guards, he put his horse into a gallop, and rode straight up to d'Artagnan. Patrick discreetly kept in the background.

"No misfortune has happened to the queen?" cried Buckingham, the instant he came up, throwing all his fear and love into the question.

"I believe not; nevertheless I believe she runs some great peril from which your Grace alone can extricate her."

"I!" cried Buckingham. "What is it? I should be too happy to be of any service to her. Speak, speak!"

"Take this letter," said d'Artagnan.

"This letter! From whom comes this letter?"

"From her Majesty, as I think."

"From her Majesty!" said Buckingham, becoming so pale that d'Artagnan feared he would faint as he broke the seal.

"What is this rent?" said he, showing d'Artagnan a place where it had been pierced through.

"Ah," said d'Artagnan, "I did not see that; it was the sword of the Comte de Wardes which made that hole, when he gave me a good thrust in the breast."

"You are wounded?" asked Buckingham, as he opened the letter.

"Oh, nothing but a scratch," said d'Artagnan.

"Just heaven, what have I read?" cried the duke. "Patrick, remain here, or rather join the king, wherever he may be, and tell his Majesty that I humbly beg him to excuse me, but an affair of the greatest importance recalls me to London. Come, Monsieur, come!" and both set off towards the capital at full gallop.

Chapter 21

The Countess De Winter

As they rode along, the duke endeavoured to draw from d'Artagnan, not all that had happened, but what d'Artagnan himself knew. By adding all that he heard from the mouth of the young man to his own remembrances, he was enabled to form a pretty exact idea of a position of the seriousness of which, for the rest, the queen's letter, short but explicit, gave him the clue. But that which astonished him most was that the cardinal, so deeply interested in preventing this young man from setting his foot in England, had not succeeded in arresting him on the road. It was then, upon the manifestation of this astonishment, that d'Artagnan related to him the precaution taken, and how, thanks to the devotion of his three friends, whom he had left scattered and bleeding on the road, he had succeeded in coming off with a single sword thrust, which had pierced the queen's letter and for which he had repaid M. de Wardes with such terrible coin. While he was listening to this recital, delivered with the greatest simplicity, the duke looked from time to time at the young man with astonishment, as if he could not comprehend how so much prudence, courage, and devotedness could be allied with a countenance which indicated not more than twenty years.

The horses went like the wind, and in a few minutes they were at the gates of London. D'Artagnan imagined that on arriving in town the duke would slacken his pace, but it was not so. He kept on his way at the same rate, heedless about upsetting those whom he met on the road. In fact, in crossing the city two or three accidents of this kind happened, but Buckingham did not even turn his head to see what became of those he had knocked down. D'Artagnan followed him amid cries which strongly resembled curses.

On entering the court of his hotel, Buckingham sprang from his horse, and without thinking what became of the animal, threw the bridle on his neck, and sprang toward the vestibule. D'Artagnan did the same, with a little more concern, however, for the noble creatures, whose merits he fully appreciated, but he had the satisfaction of seeing three or four grooms run from the kitchens and the stables, and busy themselves with the steeds.

The duke walked so fast that d'Artagnan had some trouble in keeping up with him. He passed through several apartments, of an elegance of which even the greatest nobles of France had not even an idea, and arrived at length in a bedchamber which was at once a miracle of taste and of richness. In the alcove of this chamber was a door concealed in the tapestry which the duke opened with a little gold key which he wore suspended from his neck by a chain of the same metal. With discretion d'Artagnan remained behind, but at the moment when Buckingham crossed the threshold, he turned round, and seeing the hesitation of the young man, "Come in!" cried he, "and if you have the good fortune to be admitted to her Majesty's presence, tell her what you have seen."

Encouraged by this invitation, d'Artagnan followed the duke, who closed the door after them. The two found themselves in a small chapel covered with a tapestry of Persian silk worked with gold, and brilliantly lighted with a vast number of candles. Over a species of altar, and beneath a canopy of blue velvet, surmounted by white and red plumes, was a full-length portrait of Anne of Austria, so perfect in its resemblance that d'Artagnan uttered a cry of surprise on beholding it. One might believe the queen was about to speak. On the altar, and beneath the portrait, was the casket containing the diamond studs.

The duke approached the altar, knelt as a priest might have done before a crucifix, and opened the casket. "There," said he, drawing from the casket a large bow of blue ribbon all sparkling with diamonds, "there are the precious studs which I have taken an oath should be buried with me. The queen gave them to me, the queen requires them again. Her will be done, like that of God, in all things."

Then, he began to kiss, one after the other, those dear studs with which he was about to part. All at once he uttered a terrible cry.

"What is the matter?" exclaimed d'Artagnan, anxiously, "what has happened to you, my Lord?"

"All is lost!" cried Buckingham, becoming as pale as a corpse, "two of the studs are wanting, there are only ten."

"Can you have lost them, my Lord, or do you think they have been stolen?"

"They have been stolen," replied the duke, "and it is the cardinal who has dealt this blow. Hold; see! The ribbons which held them have been cut with scissors."

"If my Lord suspects they have been stolen, perhaps the person who stole them still has them in his hands."

"Wait, wait!" said the duke. "The only time I have worn these studs was at a ball given by the king eight days ago at Windsor. The Comtesse de Winter, with whom I had quarreled, became reconciled to me at that ball. That reconciliation was nothing but the vengeance of a jealous woman. I have never seen her from that day. The woman is an agent of the cardinal."

"He has agents, then, throughout the world?" cried d'Artagnan.

"Oh, yes," said Buckingham, grating his teeth with rage. "Yes, he is a terrible antagonist. But when is this ball to take place?"

"Monday next."

"Monday next! Still five days before us. That's more time than we want. Patrick!" cried the duke, opening the door of the chapel, "Patrick!" His confidential valet appeared.

"My jeweler and my secretary."

The valet went out with a mute promptitude which showed him accustomed to obey blindly and without reply.

But although the jeweler had been mentioned first, it was the secretary who first made his appearance. This was simply because he lived in the hotel. He found Buckingham seated at a table in his bedchamber, writing orders with his own hand.

"Mr. Jackson," said he, "go instantly to the Lord Chancellor, and tell him that I charge him with the execution of these orders. I wish them to be promulgated immediately."

"But, my Lord, if the Lord Chancellor interrogates me upon the motives which may have led your Grace to adopt such an extraordinary measure, what shall I reply?"

"That such is my pleasure, and that I answer for my will to no man."

"Will that be the answer," replied the secretary, smiling, "which he must transmit to his Majesty if, by chance, his Majesty should have the curiosity to know why no vessel is to leave any of the ports of Great Britain?"

"You are right, Mr. Jackson," replied Buckingham. "He will say, in that case, to the king that I am determined on war, and that this measure is my first act of hostility against France."

The secretary bowed and retired.

"We are safe on that side," said Buckingham, turning toward d'Artagnan. "If the studs are not yet gone to Paris, they will not arrive till after you."

"How so?"

"I have just placed an embargo on all vessels at present in his Majesty's ports, and without particular permission, not one dare lift an anchor."

D'Artagnan looked with stupefaction at a man who thus employed the unlimited power with which he was clothed by the confidence of a king in the prosecution of his intrigues. Buckingham saw by the expression of the young man's face what was passing in his mind, and he smiled.

"Yes," said he, "yes, Anne of Austria is my true queen. Upon a word from her, I would betray my country, I would betray my king, I would betray my God. She asked me not to send the Protestants of La Rochelle the assistance I promised them; I have not done so. I broke my word, it is true, but what signifies that? I obeyed my love; and have I not been richly paid for that obedience? It was to that obedience I owe her portrait."

D'Artagnan was amazed to note by what fragile and unknown threads the destinies of nations and the lives of men are suspended. He was lost in these reflections when the goldsmith entered. He was an Irishman–one of the most skillful of his craft, and who himself confessed that he gained a hundred thousand livres a year by the Duke of Buckingham.

"Mr. O'Reilly," said the duke, leading him into the chapel, "look at these diamond studs, and tell me what they are worth apiece."

The goldsmith cast a glance at the elegant manner in which they were set, calculated, one with another, what the diamonds were worth, and without hesitation said, "Fifteen hundred pistoles each, my Lord."

"How many days would it require to make two studs exactly like them? You see there are two wanting."

"Eight days, my Lord."

"I will give you three thousand pistoles apiece if I can have them by the day after tomorrow."

"My Lord, they shall be yours."

"You are a jewel of a man, Mr. O'Reilly, but that is not all. These studs cannot be trusted to anybody; it must be done in the palace."

"Impossible, my Lord! There is no one but myself can so execute them that one cannot tell the new from the old."

"Therefore, my dear Mr. O'Reilly, you are my prisoner. And if you wish ever to leave my palace, you cannot; so make the best of it. Name to me such of your workmen as you need, and point out the tools they must bring."

The goldsmith knew the duke. He knew all objection would be useless, and instantly determined how to act.

"May I be permitted to inform my wife?" said he.

"Oh, you may even see her if you like, my dear Mr. O'Reilly. Your captivity shall be mild, be assured; and as every inconvenience deserves its indemnification, here is, in addition to the price of the studs, an order for a thousand pistoles, to make you forget the annoyance I cause you."

D'Artagnan could not get over the surprise created in him by this minister, who thus open-handed, sported with men and millions.

As to the goldsmith, he wrote to his wife, sending her the order for the thousand pistoles, and charging her to send him, in exchange, his most skillful apprentice, an assortment of diamonds, of which he gave the names and the weight, and the necessary tools.

Buckingham conducted the goldsmith to the chamber destined for him, and which, at the end of half an hour, was transformed into a workshop. Then he placed a sentinel at each door, with an order to admit nobody upon any pretense but his VALET DE CHAMBRE, Patrick. We need not add that the goldsmith, O'Reilly, and his assistant, were prohibited from going out under any pretext. This point, settled, the duke turned to d'Artagnan. "Now, my young friend," said he, "England is all our own. What do you wish for? What do you desire?"

"A bed, my Lord," replied d'Artagnan. "At present, I confess, that is the thing I stand most in need of."

Buckingham gave d'Artagnan a chamber adjoining his own. He wished to have the young man at hand–not that he at all mistrusted him, but for the sake of having someone to whom he could constantly talk of the queen.

In one hour after, the ordinance was published in London that no vessel bound for France should leave port, not even the packet boat with letters. In the eyes of everybody this was a declaration of war between the two kingdoms.

On the day after the morrow, by eleven o'clock, the two diamond studs were finished, and they were so completely imitated, so perfectly alike, that Buckingham could not tell the new ones from the old ones, and experts in such matters would have been deceived as he was. He immediately called d'Artagnan. "Here," said he to him, "are the diamond studs that you came to bring; and be my witness that I have done all that human power could do."

"Be satisfied, my Lord, I will tell all that I have seen. But does your Grace mean to give me the studs without the casket?"

"The casket would encumber you. Besides, the casket is the more precious from being all that is left to me. You will say that I keep it."

"I will perform your commission, word for word, my Lord."

"And now," resumed Buckingham, looking earnestly at the young man, "how shall I ever acquit myself of the debt I owe you?"

D'Artagnan blushed up to the whites of his eyes. He saw that the duke was searching for a means of making him accept something and the idea that the blood of his friends and himself was about to be paid for with English gold was strangely repugnant to him.

"Let us understand each other, my Lord," replied d'Artagnan, "and let us make things clear beforehand in order that there may be no mistake. I am in the service of the King and Queen of France, and form part of the company of Monsieur Dessessart, who, as well as his brother-in-law, Monsieur de Tréville, is particularly attached to their Majesties. What I have done, then, has been for the queen, and not at all for your Grace. And still further, it is very probable I should not have done anything of this, if it had not been to make myself agreeable to someone who is my lady, as the queen is yours."

"Yes," said the duke, smiling, "and I even believe that I know that other person; it is–"

"My Lord, I have not named her!" interrupted the young man, warmly.

"That is true," said the duke, "and it is to this person I am bound to discharge my debt of gratitude."

"You have said, my Lord; for truly, at this moment when there is question of war, I confess to you that I see nothing in your Grace but an Englishman, and consequently an enemy whom I should have much greater pleasure in meeting on the field of battle than in the park at Windsor or the corridors of the Louvre–all which, however, will not prevent me from executing to the very point my commission or from laying down my life, if there be need of it, to accomplish it, but I repeat it to your Grace, without your having personally on that account more to thank me for in this second interview than for what I did for you in the first."

"We say, 'Proud as a Scotsman,'" murmured the Duke of Buckingham.

"And we say, 'Proud as a Gascon,'" replied d'Artagnan. "The Gascons are the Scots of France."

D'Artagnan bowed to the duke, and was retiring.

"Well, are you going away in that manner? Where, and how?"

"That's true!"

"Fore Gad, these Frenchmen have no consideration!"

"I had forgotten that England was an island, and that you were the king of it."

"Go to the riverside, ask for the brig SUND, and give this letter to the captain; he will convey you to a little port, where certainly you are not expected, and which is ordinarily only frequented by fishermen."

"The name of that port?"

"St. Valery, but listen. When you have arrived there you will go to a mean tavern, without a name and without a sign–a mere fisherman's hut. You cannot be mistaken; there is but one."

"Afterward?"

"You will ask for the host, and will repeat to him the word 'Forward!'"

"Which means?"

"In French, EN AVANT. It is the password. He will give you a horse all saddled, and will point out to you the road you ought to take. You will find, in the same way, four relays on your route. If you will give at each of these relays your address in Paris, the four horses will follow you thither. You already know two of them, and you appeared to appreciate them like a judge. They were those we rode on; and you may rely upon me for the others not being inferior to them. These horses are equipped for the field. However proud you may be, you will not refuse to accept one of them, and to request your three companions to accept the others–that is, in order to make war against us. Besides, the end justified the means, as you Frenchmen say, does it not?"

"Yes, my Lord, I accept them," said d'Artagnan, "and if it please God, we will make a good use of your presents."

"Well, now, your hand, young man. Perhaps we shall soon meet on the field of battle, but in the meantime we shall part good friends, I hope."

"Yes, my Lord, but with the hope of soon becoming enemies."

"Be satisfied; I promise you that."

"I depend upon your word, my Lord."

D'Artagnan bowed to the duke, and made his way as quickly as possible to the riverside. Opposite the Tower of London he found the vessel that had been named to him, delivered his letter to the captain, who after having it examined by the governor of the port made immediate preparations to sail.

Fifty vessels were waiting to set out. Passing alongside one of them, d'Artagnan fancied he perceived on board it the woman of Meung–the same whom the unknown gentleman had called Milady, and whom d'Artagnan had thought so handsome, but thanks to the current of the stream and a fair wind, his vessel passed so quickly that he had little more than a glimpse of her.

The next day about nine o'clock in the morning, he landed at St. Valery. D'Artagnan went instantly in search of the inn, and easily discovered it by the riotous noise which resounded from it. War between England and France was talked of as near and certain, and the jolly sailors were having a carousal.

D'Artagnan made his way through the crowd, advanced toward the host, and pronounced the word "Forward!" The host instantly made him a sign to follow, went out with him by a door which opened into a yard, led him to the stable, where a saddled horse awaited him, and asked him if he stood in need of anything else.

"I want to know the route I am to follow," said d'Artagnan.

"Go from hence to Blangy, and from Blangy to Neufchatel. At Neufchatel, go to the tavern of the Golden Harrow, give the password to the landlord, and you will find, as you have here, a horse ready saddled."

"Have I anything to pay?" demanded d'Artagnan.

"Everything is paid," replied the host, "and liberally. Begone, and may God guide you!"

"Amen!" cried the young man, and set off at full gallop.

Four hours later he was in Neufchatel. He strictly followed the instructions he had received. At Neufchatel, as at St. Valery, he found a horse quite ready and awaiting him. He was about to remove the pistols from the saddle he had quit to the one he was about to fill, but he found the holsters furnished with similar pistols.

"Your address at Paris?"

"Hotel of the Guards, company of Dessessart."

"Enough," replied the questioner.

"Which route must I take?" demanded d'Artagnan, in his turn.

"That of Rouen, but you will leave the city on your right. You must stop at the little village of Eccuis, in which there is but one tavern–the Shield of France. Don't condemn it from appearances; you will find a horse in the stables quite as good as this."

"The same password?"

"Exactly."

"Adieu, master!"

"A good journey, gentlemen! Do you want anything?"

D'Artagnan shook his head, and set off at full speed. At Eccuis, the same scene was repeated. He found as provident a host and a fresh horse. He left his address as he had done before, and set off again at the same pace for Pontoise. At Pontoise he changed his horse for the last time, and at nine o'clock galloped into the yard of Tréville's hotel. He had made nearly sixty leagues in little more than twelve hours.

M. de Tréville received him as if he had seen him that same morning; only, when pressing his hand a little more warmly than usual, he informed him that the company of Dessessart was on duty at the Louvre, and that he might repair at once to his post.

Chapter 22

The Ballet Of La Merlaison

On the morrow, nothing was talked of in Paris but the ball which the aldermen of the city were to give to the king and queen, and in which their Majesties were to dance the famous La Merlaison–the favourite ballet of the king.

Eight days had been occupied in preparations at the Hotel de Ville for this important evening. The city carpenters had erected scaffolds upon which the invited ladies were to be placed; the city grocer had ornamented the chambers with two hundred FLAMBEAUX of white wax, a piece of luxury unheard of at that period; and twenty violins were ordered, and the price for them fixed at double the usual rate, upon condition, said the report, that they should be played all night.

At ten o'clock in the morning the Sieur de la Coste, ensign in the king's Guards, followed by two officers and several archers of that body, came to the city registrar, named Clement, and demanded of him all the keys of the rooms and offices of the hotel. These keys were given up to him instantly. Each of them had ticket attached to it, by which it might be recognised; and from that moment the Sieur de la Coste was charged with the care of all the doors and all the avenues.

At eleven o'clock came in his turn Duhallier, captain of the Guards, bringing with him fifty archers, who were distributed immediately through the Hotel de Ville, at the doors assigned them.

At three o'clock came two companies of the Guards, one French, the other Swiss. The company of French guards was composed of half of M. Duhallier's men and half of M. Dessessart's men.

At six in the evening the guests began to come. As fast as they entered, they were placed in the grand saloon, on the platforms prepared for them.

At nine o'clock Madame la Premiere Presidente arrived. As next to the queen, she was the most considerable personage of the fête, she was received by the city officials, and placed in a box opposite to that which the queen was to occupy.

At ten o'clock, the king's collation, consisting of preserves and other delicacies, was prepared in the little room on the side of the church of St. Jean, in front of the silver buffet of the city, which was guarded by four archers.

At midnight great cries and loud acclamations were heard. It was the king, who was passing through the streets which led from the Louvre to the Hotel de Ville, and which were all illuminated with coloured lanterns.

Immediately the aldermen, clothed in their cloth robes and preceded by six sergeants, each holding a FLAMBEAU in his hand, went to attend upon the king, whom they met on the steps, where the provost of the merchants made him the speech of welcome–a compliment to which his Majesty replied with an apology for coming so late, laying the blame upon the cardinal, who had detained him till eleven o'clock, talking of affairs of state.

His Majesty, in full dress, was accompanied by his royal Highness, M. le Comte de Soissons, by the Grand Prior, by the Duc de Longueville, by the Duc d'Euboeuf, by the Comte d'Harcourt, by the Comte de la Roche-Guyon, by M. de Liancourt, by M. de Baradas, by the Comte de Cramail, and by the Chevalier de Souveray. Everybody noticed that the king looked dull and preoccupied.

A private room had been prepared for the king and another for Monsieur. In each of these closets were placed masquerade dresses. The same had been done for the queen and Madame the President. The nobles and ladies of their Majesties' suites were to dress, two by two, in chambers prepared for the purpose. Before entering his closet the king desired to be informed the moment the cardinal arrived.

Half an hour after the entrance of the king, fresh acclamations were heard; these announced the arrival of the queen. The aldermen did as they had done before, and preceded by their sergeants, advanced to receive their illustrious guest. The queen entered the great hall; and it was remarked that, like the king, she looked dull and even weary.

At the moment she entered, the curtain of a small gallery which to that time had been closed, was drawn, and the pale face of the cardinal appeared, he being dressed as a Spanish cavalier. His eyes were fixed upon those of the queen, and a smile of terrible joy passed over his lips; the queen did not wear her diamond studs.

The queen remained for a short time to receive the compliments of the city dignitaries and to reply to the salutations of the ladies. All at once the king appeared with the cardinal at one of the doors of the hall. The cardinal was speaking to him in a low voice, and the king was very pale.

The king made his way through the crowd without a mask, and the ribbons of his doublet scarcely tied. He went straight to the queen, and in an altered voice said, "Why, Madame, have you not thought proper to wear your diamond studs, when you know it would give me so much gratification?"

The queen cast a glance around her, and saw the cardinal behind, with a diabolical smile on his countenance.

"Sire," replied the queen, with a faltering voice, "because, in the midst of such a crowd as this, I feared some accident might happen to them."

"And you were wrong, Madame. If I made you that present it was that you might adorn yourself therewith. I tell you that you were wrong."

The voice of the king was tremulous with anger. Everybody looked and listened with astonishment, comprehending nothing of what passed.

"Sire," said the queen, "I can send for them to the Louvre, where they are, and thus your Majesty's wishes will be complied with."

"Do so, Madame, do so, and that at once; for within an hour the ballet will commence."

The queen bent in token of submission, and followed the ladies who were to conduct her to her room. On his part the king returned to his apartment.

There was a moment of trouble and confusion in the assembly. Everybody had remarked that something had passed between the king and queen, but both of them had spoken so low that everybody, out of respect, withdrew several steps, so that nobody had heard anything. The violins began to sound with all their might, but nobody listened to them.

The king came out first from his room. He was in a most elegant hunting costume; and Monsieur and the other nobles were dressed like him. This was the costume that best became the king. So dressed, he really appeared the first gentleman of his kingdom.

The cardinal drew near to the king, and placed in his hand a small casket. The king opened it, and found in it two diamond studs.

"What does this mean?" demanded he of the cardinal.

"Nothing," replied the latter, "only, if the queen has the studs, which I very much doubt, count them, Sire, and if you only find ten, ask her Majesty who can have stolen from her the two studs that are here."

The king looked at the cardinal as if to interrogate him, but he had not time to address any question to him–a cry of admiration burst from every mouth. If the king appeared to be the first gentleman of his kingdom, the queen was without doubt the most beautiful woman in France.

It is true that the habit of a huntress became her admirably. She wore a beaver hat with blue feathers, a surtout of gray-pearl velvet, fastened with diamond clasps, and a petticoat of blue satin, embroidered with silver. On her left shoulder sparkled the diamond studs, on a bow of the same colour as the plumes and the petticoat.

The king trembled with joy and the cardinal with vexation; although, distant as they were from the queen, they could not count the studs. The queen had them. The only question was, had she ten or twelve?

At that moment the violins sounded the signal for the ballet. The king advanced toward Madame the President, with whom he was to dance, and his Highness Monsieur with the queen. They took their places, and the ballet began.

The king danced facing the queen, and every time he passed by her, he devoured with his eyes those studs of which he could not ascertain the number. A cold sweat covered the brow of the cardinal.

The ballet lasted an hour, and had sixteen ENTRÉES. The ballet ended amid the applause of the whole assemblage, and everyone reconducted his lady to her place, but the king took advantage of the privilege he had of leaving his lady, to advance eagerly toward the queen.

"I thank you, Madame," said he, "for the deference you have shown to my wishes, but I think you want two of the studs, and I bring them back to you."

With these words he held out to the queen the two studs the cardinal had given him.

"How, Sire?" cried the young queen, affecting surprise, "you are giving me, then, two more: I shall have fourteen."

In fact the king counted them, and the twelve studs were all on her Majesty's shoulder.

The king called the cardinal.

"What does this mean, Monsieur Cardinal?" asked the king in a severe tone.

"This means, Sire," replied the cardinal, "that I was desirous of presenting her Majesty with these two studs, and that not daring to offer them myself, I adopted this means of inducing her to accept them."

"And I am the more grateful to your Eminence," replied Anne of Austria, with a smile that proved she was not the dupe of this ingenious gallantry, "from being certain that these two studs alone have cost you as much as all the others cost his Majesty."

Then saluting the king and the cardinal, the queen resumed her way to the chamber in which she had dressed, and where she was to take off her costume.

The attention which we have been obliged to give, during the commencement of the chapter, to the illustrious personages we have introduced into it, has diverted us for an instant from him to whom Anne of Austria owed the extraordinary triumph she had obtained over the cardinal; and who, confounded, unknown, lost in the crowd gathered at one of the doors, looked on at this scene, comprehensible only to four persons–the king, the queen, his Eminence, and himself.

The queen had just regained her chamber, and d'Artagnan was about to retire, when he felt his shoulder lightly touched. He turned and saw a young woman, who made him a sign to follow her. The face of this young woman was covered with a black velvet mask, but notwithstanding this precaution, which was in fact taken rather against others than against him, he at once recognised his usual guide, the light and intelligent Mme. Bonacieux.

On the evening before, they had scarcely seen each other for a moment at the apartment of the Swiss guard, Germain, whither d'Artagnan had sent for her. The haste which the young woman was in to convey to the queen the excellent news of the happy return of her messenger prevented the two lovers from exchanging more than a few words. D'Artagnan therefore followed Mme. Bonacieux moved by a double sentiment–love and curiosity. All the way, and in proportion as the corridors became more deserted, d'Artagnan wished to stop the young woman, seize her and gaze upon her, were it only for a minute, but quick as a bird she glided between his hands, and when he wished to speak to her, her finger placed upon her mouth, with a little imperative gesture full of grace, reminded him that he was under the command of a power which he must blindly obey, and which forbade him even to make the slightest complaint. At length, after winding about for a minute or two, Mme. Bonacieux opened the door of a closet, which was entirely dark, and led d'Artagnan into it. There she made a fresh sign of silence, and opened a second door concealed by tapestry. The opening of this door disclosed a brilliant light, and she disappeared.

D'Artagnan remained for a moment motionless, asking himself where he could be, but soon a ray of light which penetrated through the chamber, together with the warm and perfumed air which reached him from the same aperture, the conversation of two of three ladies in language at once respectful and refined, and the word "Majesty" several times repeated, indicated clearly that he was in a closet attached to the queen's apartment. The young man waited in comparative darkness and listened.

The queen appeared cheerful and happy, which seemed to astonish the persons who surrounded her and who were accustomed to see her almost always sad and full of care. The queen attributed this joyous feeling to the beauty of the fête, to the pleasure she had experienced in the ballet; and as it is not permissible to contradict a queen, whether she smile or weep, everybody expatiated on the gallantry of the aldermen of the city of Paris.

Although d'Artagnan did not at all know the queen, he soon distinguished her voice from the others, at first by a slightly foreign accent, and next by that tone of domination naturally impressed upon all royal words. He heard her approach and withdraw from the partially open door; and twice or three times he even saw the shadow of a person intercept the light.

At length a hand and an arm, surpassingly beautiful in their form and whiteness, glided through the tapestry. D'Artagnan at once comprehended that this was his recompense. He cast himself on his knees, seized the hand, and touched it respectfully with his lips. Then the hand was withdrawn, leaving in his an object which he perceived to be a ring. The door immediately closed, and d'Artagnan found himself again in complete obscurity.

D'Artagnan placed the ring on his finger, and again waited; it was evident that all was not yet over. After the reward of his devotion, that of his love was to come. Besides, although the ballet was danced, the evening had scarcely begun. Supper was to be served at three, and the clock of St. Jean had struck three quarters past two.

The sound of voices diminished by degrees in the adjoining chamber. The company was then heard departing; then the door of the closet in which d'Artagnan was, was opened, and Mme. Bonacieux entered.

"You at last?" cried d'Artagnan.

"Silence!" said the young woman, placing her hand upon his lips, "silence, and go the same way you came!"

"But where and when shall I see you again?" cried d'Artagnan.

"A note which you will find at home will tell you. Begone, begone!"

At these words she opened the door of the corridor, and pushed d'Artagnan out of the room. D'Artagnan obeyed like a child, without the least resistance or objection, which proved that he was really in love.

Chapter 23

The Rendezvous

D'Artagnan ran home immediately, and although it was three o'clock in the morning and he had some of the worst quarters of Paris to traverse, he met with no misadventure. Everyone knows that drunkards and lovers have a protecting deity.

He found the door of his passage open, sprang up the stairs and knocked softly in a manner agreed upon between him and his lackey. Planchet, whom he had sent home two hours before from the Hotel de Ville, telling him to sit up for him, opened the door for him.

"Has anyone brought a letter for me?" asked d'Artagnan, eagerly.

"No one has BROUGHT a letter, Monsieur," replied Planchet, "but one has come of itself."

"What do you mean, blockhead?"

"I mean to say that when I came in, although I had the key of your apartment in my pocket, and that key had never quit me, I found a letter on the green table cover in your bedroom."

"And where is that letter?"

"I left it where I found it, Monsieur. It is not natural for letters to enter people's houses in this manner. If the window had been open or even ajar, I should think nothing of it; but, no–all was hermetically sealed. Beware, Monsieur; there is certainly some magic underneath."

Meanwhile, the young man had darted in to his chamber, and opened the letter. It was from Mme. Bonacieux, and was expressed in these terms:

"There are many thanks to be offered to you, and to be transmitted to you. Be this evening about ten o'clock at St. Cloud, in front of the pavilion which stands at the corner of the house of M. d'Estrees.–C.B."

While reading this letter, d'Artagnan felt his heart dilated and compressed by that delicious spasm which tortures and caresses the hearts of lovers.

It was the first billet he had received; it was the first rendezvous that had been granted him. His heart, swelled by the intoxication of joy, felt ready to dissolve away at the very gate of that terrestrial paradise called Love!

"Well, Monsieur," said Planchet, who had observed his master grow red and pale successively, "did I not guess truly? Is it not some bad affair?"

"You are mistaken, Planchet," replied d'Artagnan, "and as a proof, there is a crown to drink my health."

"I am much obliged to Monsieur for the crown he had given me, and I promise him to follow his instructions exactly, but it is not the less true that letters which come in this way into shut-up houses–"

"Fall from heaven, my friend, fall from heaven."

"Then Monsieur is satisfied?" asked Planchet.

"My dear Planchet, I am the happiest of men!"

"And I may profit by Monsieur's happiness, and go to bed?"

"Yes, go."

"May the blessings of heaven fall upon Monsieur! But it is not the less true that that letter–"

And Planchet retired, shaking his head with an air of doubt, which the liberality of d'Artagnan had not entirely effaced.

Left alone, d'Artagnan read and reread his billet. Then he kissed and rekissed twenty times the lines traced by the hand of his beautiful mistress. At length he went to bed, fell asleep, and had golden dreams.

At seven o'clock in the morning he arose and called Planchet, who at the second summons opened the door, his countenance not yet quite freed from the anxiety of the preceding night.

"Planchet," said d'Artagnan, "I am going out for all day, perhaps. You are, therefore, your own master till seven o'clock in the evening, but at seven o'clock you must hold yourself in readiness with two horses."

"There!" said Planchet. "We are going again, it appears, to have our hides pierced in all sorts of ways."

"You will take your musketoon and your pistols."

"There, now! Didn't I say so?" cried Planchet. "I was sure of it–the cursed letter!"

"Don't be afraid, you idiot; there is nothing in hand but a party of pleasure."

"Ah, like the charming journey the other day, when it rained bullets and produced a crop of steel traps!"

"Well, if you are really afraid, Monsieur Planchet," resumed d'Artagnan, "I will go without you. I prefer travelling alone to having a companion who entertains the least fear."

"Monsieur does me wrong," said Planchet, "I thought he had seen me at work."

"Yes, but I thought perhaps you had worn out all your courage the first time."

"Monsieur shall see that upon occasion I have some left; only I beg Monsieur not to be too prodigal of it if he wishes it to last long."

"Do you believe you have still a certain amount of it to expend this evening?"

"I hope so, Monsieur."

"Well, then, I count on you."

"At the appointed hour I shall be ready; only I believed that Monsieur had but one horse in the Guard stables."

"Perhaps there is but one at this moment, but by this evening there will be four."

"It appears that our journey was a remounting journey, then?"

"Exactly so," said d'Artagnan; and nodding to Planchet, he went out.

M Bonacieux was at his door. D'Artagnan's intention was to go out without speaking to the worthy mercer, but the latter made so polite and friendly a salutation that his tenant felt obliged, not only to stop, but to enter into conversation with him.

Besides, how is it possible to avoid a little condescension toward a husband whose pretty wife has appointed a meeting with you that same evening at St. Cloud, opposite D'Estrees's pavilion? D'Artagnan approached him with the most amiable air he could assume.

The conversation naturally fell upon the incarceration of the poor man. M. Bonacieux, who was ignorant that d'Artagnan had overheard his conversation with the stranger of Meung, related to his young tenant the persecutions of that monster, M. de Laffemas, whom he never ceased to designate, during his account, by the title of the "cardinal's executioner," and expatiated at great length upon the Bastille, the bolts, the wickets, the dungeons, the gratings, the instruments of torture.

D'Artagnan listened to him with exemplary complaisance, and when he had finished said, "And Madame Bonacieux, do you know who carried her off?–For I do not forget that I owe to that unpleasant circumstance the good fortune of having made your acquaintance."

"Ah!" said Bonacieux, "they took good care not to tell me that; and my wife, on her part, has sworn to me by all that's sacred that she does not know. But you," continued M. Bonacieux, in a tine of perfect good fellowship, "what has become of you all these days? I have not seen you nor your friends, and I don't think you could gather all that dust that I saw Planchet brush off your boots yesterday from the pavement of Paris."

"You are right, my dear Monsieur Bonacieux, my friends and I have been on a little journey."

"Far from here?"

"Oh, Lord, no! About forty leagues only. We went to take Monsieur Athos to the waters of Forges, where my friends still remain."

"And you have returned, have you not?" replied M. Bonacieux, giving to his countenance a most sly air. "A handsome young fellow like you does not obtain long leaves of absence from his mistress; and we were impatiently waited for at Paris, were we not?"

"My faith!" said the young man, laughing, "I confess it, and so much more the readily, my dear Bonacieux, as I see there is no concealing anything from you. Yes, I was expected, and very impatiently, I acknowledge."

A slight shade passed over the brow of Bonacieux, but so slight that d'Artagnan did not perceive it.

"And we are going to be recompensed for our diligence?" continued the mercer, with a trifling alteration in his voice–so trifling, indeed, that d'Artagnan did not perceive it any more than he had the momentary shade which, an instant before, had darkened the countenance of the worthy man.

"Ah, may you be a true prophet!" said d'Artagnan, laughing.

"No; what I say," replied Bonacieux, "is only that I may know whether I am delaying you."

"Why that question, my dear host?" asked d'Artagnan. "Do you intend to sit up for me?"

"No, but since my arrest and the robbery that was committed in my house, I am alarmed every time I hear a door open, particularly in the night. What the deuce can you expect? I am no swordsman."

"Well, don't be alarmed if I return at one, two or three o'clock in the morning; indeed, do not be alarmed if I do not come at all."

This time Bonacieux became so pale that d'Artagnan could not help perceiving it, and asked him what was the matter.

"Nothing," replied Bonacieux, "nothing. Since my misfortunes I have been subject to faintnesses, which seize me all at once, and I have just felt a cold shiver. Pay no attention to it; you have nothing to occupy yourself with but being happy."

"Then I have full occupation, for I am so."

"Not yet; wait a little! This evening, you said."

"Well, this evening will come, thank God! And perhaps you look for it with as much impatience as I do; perhaps this evening Madame Bonacieux will visit the conjugal domicile."

"Madame Bonacieux is not at liberty this evening," replied the husband, seriously, "she is detained at the Louvre this evening by her duties."

"So much the worse for you, my dear host, so much the worse! When I am happy, I wish all the world to be so, but it appears that is not possible."

The young man departed, laughing at the joke, which he thought he alone could comprehend.

"Amuse yourself well!" replied Bonacieux, in a sepulchral tone.

But d'Artagnan was too far off to hear him; and if he had heard him in the disposition of mind he then enjoyed, he certainly would not have remarked it.

He took his way toward the hotel of M. de Tréville; his visit of the day before, it is to be remembered, had been very short and very little explicative.

He found Tréville in a joyful mood. He had thought the king and queen charming at the ball. It is true the cardinal had been particularly ill-tempered. He had retired at one o'clock under the pretense of being indisposed. As to their Majesties, they did not return to the Louvre till six o'clock in the morning.

"Now," said Tréville, lowering his voice, and looking into every corner of the apartment to see if they were alone, "now let us talk about yourself, my young friend; for it is evident that your happy return has something to do with the joy of the king, the triumph of the queen, and the humiliation of his Eminence. You must look out for yourself."

"What have I to fear," replied d'Artagnan, "as long as I shall have the luck to enjoy the favour of their Majesties?"

"Everything, believe me. The cardinal is not the man to forget a mystification until he has settled account with the mystifier; and the mystifier appears to me to have the air of being a certain young Gascon of my acquaintance."

"Do you believe that the cardinal is as well posted as yourself, and knows that I have been to London?"

"The devil! You have been to London! Was it from London you brought that beautiful diamond that glitters on your finger? Beware, my dear d'Artagnan! A present from an enemy is not a good thing. Are there not some Latin verses upon that subject? Stop!"

"Yes, doubtless," replied d'Artagnan, who had never been able to cram the first rudiments of that language into his head, and who had by his ignorance driven his master to despair, "yes, doubtless there is one."

"There certainly is one," said M. de Tréville, who had a tincture of literature, "and Monsieur de Benserade was quoting it to me the other day. Stop a minute–ah, this is it: 'Timeo Danaos et dona ferentes,' which means, 'Beware of the enemy who makes you presents."

"This diamond does not come from an enemy, Monsieur," replied d'Artagnan, "it comes from the queen."

"From the queen! Oh, oh!" said M. de Tréville. "Why, it is indeed a true royal jewel, which is worth a thousand pistoles if it is worth a denier. By whom did the queen send you this jewel?"

"She gave it to me herself."

"Where?"

"In the room adjoining the chamber in which she changed her toilet."

"How?"

"Giving me her hand to kiss."

"You have kissed the queen's hand?" said M. de Tréville, looking earnestly at d'Artagnan.

"Her Majesty did me the honour to grant me that favour."

"And that in the presence of witnesses! Imprudent, thrice imprudent!"

"No, Monsieur, be satisfied; nobody saw her," replied d'Artagnan, and he related to M. de Tréville how the affair came to pass.

"Oh, the women, the women!" cried the old soldier. "I know them by their romantic imagination. Everything that savors of mystery charms them. So you have seen the arm, that was all. You would meet the queen, and she would not know who you are?"

"No, but thanks to this diamond," replied the young man.

"Listen," said M. de Tréville, "shall I give you counsel, good counsel, the counsel of a friend?"

"You will do me honour, Monsieur," said d'Artagnan.

"Well, then, off to the nearest goldsmith's, and sell that diamond for the highest price you can get from him. However much of a Jew he may be, he will give you at least eight hundred pistoles. Pistoles have no name, young man, and that ring has a terrible one, which may betray him who wears it."

"Sell this ring, a ring which comes from my sovereign? Never!" said d'Artagnan.

"Then, at least turn the gem inside, you silly fellow; for everybody must be aware that a cadet from Gascony does not find such stones in his mother's jewel case."

"You think, then, I have something to dread?" asked d'Artagnan.

"I mean to say, young man, that he who sleeps over a mine the match of which is already lighted, may consider himself in safety in comparison with you."

"The devil!" said d'Artagnan, whom the positive tone of M. de Tréville began to disquiet, "the devil! What must I do?"

"Above all things be always on your guard. The cardinal has a tenacious memory and a long arm; you may depend upon it, he will repay you by some ill turn."

"But of what sort?"

"Eh! How can I tell? Has he not all the tricks of a demon at his command? The least that can be expected is that you will be arrested."

"What! Will they dare to arrest a man in his Majesty's service?"

"PARDIEU! They did not scruple much in the case of Athos. At all events, young man, rely upon one who has been thirty years at court. Do not lull yourself in security, or you will be lost; but, on the contrary–and it is I who say it–see enemies in all directions. If anyone seeks a quarrel with you, shun it, were it with a child of ten years old. If you are attacked by day or by night, fight, but retreat, without shame; if you cross a bridge, feel every plank of it with your foot, lest one should give way beneath you; if you pass before a house which is being built, look up, for fear a stone should fall upon your head; if you stay out late, be always followed by your lackey, and let your lackey be armed–if, by the by, you can be sure of your lackey. Mistrust everybody, your friend, your brother, your mistress–your mistress above all."

D'Artagnan blushed.

"My mistress above all," repeated he, mechanically, "and why her rather than another?"

"Because a mistress is one of the cardinal's favourite means; he has not one that is more expeditious. A woman will sell you for ten pistoles, witness Delilah. You are acquainted with the Scriptures?"

D'Artagnan thought of the appointment Mme. Bonacieux had made with him for that very evening, but we are bound to say, to the credit of our hero, that the bad opinion entertained by M. de Tréville of women in general, did not inspire him with the least suspicion of his pretty hostess.

"But, À PROPOS," resumed M. de Tréville, "what has become of your three companions?"

"I was about to ask you if you had heard any news of them?"

"None, Monsieur."

"Well, I left them on my road–Porthos at Chantilly, with a duel on his hands; Aramis at Crèvecoeur, with a ball in his shoulder; and Athos at Amiens, detained by an accusation of coining."

"See there, now!" said M. de Tréville, "and how the devil did you escape?"

"By a miracle, Monsieur, I must acknowledge, with a sword thrust in my breast, and by nailing the Comte de Wardes on the byroad to Calais, like a butterfly on a tapestry."

"There again! De Wardes, one of the cardinal's men, a cousin of Rochefort! Stop, my friend, I have an idea."

"Speak, Monsieur."

"In your place, I would do one thing."

"What?"

"While his Eminence was seeking for me in Paris, I would take, without sound of drum or trumpet, the road to Picardy, and would go and make some inquiries concerning my three companions. What the devil! They merit richly that piece of attention on your part."

"The advice is good, Monsieur, and tomorrow I will set out."

"Tomorrow! Any why not this evening?"

"This evening, Monsieur, I am detained in Paris by indispensable business."

"Ah, young man, young man, some flirtation or other. Take care, I repeat to you, take care. It is woman who has ruined us, still ruins us, and will ruin us, as long as the world stands. Take my advice and set out this evening."

"Impossible, Monsieur."

"You have given your word, then?"

"Yes, Monsieur."

"Ah, that's quite another thing, but promise me, if you should not be killed tonight, that you will go tomorrow."

"I promise it."

"Do you need money?"

"I have still fifty pistoles. That, I think, is as much as I shall want."

"But your companions?"

"I don't think they can be in need of any. We left Paris, each with seventy-five pistoles in his pocket."

"Shall I see you again before your departure?"

"I think not, Monsieur, unless something new should happen."

"Well, a pleasant journey."

"Thanks, Monsieur."

D'Artagnan left M. de Tréville, touched more than ever by his paternal solicitude for his Musketeers.

He called successively at the abodes of Athos, Porthos, and Aramis. Neither of them had returned. Their lackeys likewise were absent, and nothing had been heard of either the one or the other. He would have inquired after them of their mistresses, but he was neither acquainted with Porthos's nor Aramis's, and as to Athos, he had none.

As he passed the Hotel des Gardes, he took a glance in to the stables. Three of the four horses had already arrived. Planchet, all astonishment, was busy grooming them, and had already finished two.

"Ah, Monsieur," said Planchet, on perceiving d'Artagnan, "how glad I am to see you."

"Why so, Planchet?" asked the young man.

"Do you place confidence in our landlord–Monsieur Bonacieux?"

"I? Not the least in the world."

"Oh, you do quite right, Monsieur."

"But why this question?"

"Because, while you were talking with him, I watched you without listening to you; and, Monsieur, his countenance changed colour two or three times!"

"Bah!"

"Preoccupied as Monsieur was with the letter he had received, he did not observe that, but I, whom the strange fashion in which that letter came into the house had placed on my guard–I did not lose a movement of his features."

"And you found it?"

"Traitorous, Monsieur."

"Indeed!"

"Still more; as soon as Monsieur had left and disappeared round the corner of the street, Monsieur Bonacieux took his hat, shut his door, and set off at a quick pace in an opposite direction."

"It seems you are right, Planchet; all this appears to be a little mysterious; and be assured that we will not pay him our rent until the matter shall be categorically explained to us."

"Monsieur jests, but Monsieur will see."

"What would you have, Planchet? What must come is written."

"Monsieur does not then renounce his excursion for this evening?"

"Quite the contrary, Planchet; the more ill will I have toward Monsieur Bonacieux, the more punctual I shall be in keeping the appointment made by that letter which makes you so uneasy."

"Then that is Monsieur's determination?"

"Undeniably, my friend. At nine o'clock, then, be ready here at the hotel, I will come and take you."

Planchet seeing there was no longer any hope of making his master renounce his project, heaved a profound sigh and set to work to groom the third horse.

As to d'Artagnan, being at bottom a prudent youth, instead of returning home, went and dined with the Gascon priest, who, at the time of the distress of the four friends, had given them a breakfast of chocolate.

Chapter 24

The Pavilion

At nine o'clock d'Artagnan was at the Hotel des Gardes; he found Planchet all ready. The fourth horse had arrived.

Planchet was armed with his musketoon and a pistol. D'Artagnan had his sword and placed two pistols in his belt; then both mounted and departed quietly. It was quite dark, and no one saw them go out. Planchet took place behind his master, and kept at a distance of ten paces from him.

D'Artagnan crossed the quays, went out by the gate of La Conference and followed the road, much more beautiful then than it is now, which leads to St. Cloud.

As long as he was in the city, Planchet kept at the respectful distance he had imposed upon himself, but as soon as the road began to be more lonely and dark, he drew softly nearer, so that when they entered the Bois de Boulogne he found himself riding quite naturally side by side with his master. In fact, we must not dissemble that the oscillation of the tall trees and the reflection of the moon in the dark underwood gave him serious uneasiness. D'Artagnan could not help perceiving that something more than usual was passing in the mind of his lackey and said, "Well, Monsieur Planchet, what is the matter with us now?"

"Don't you think, Monsieur, that woods are like churches?"

"How so, Planchet?"

"Because we dare not speak aloud in one or the other."

"But why did you not dare to speak aloud, Planchet–because you are afraid?"

"Afraid of being heard? Yes, Monsieur."

"Afraid of being heard! Why, there is nothing improper in our conversation, my dear Planchet, and no one could find fault with it."

"Ah, Monsieur!" replied Planchet, recurring to his besetting idea, "that Monsieur Bonacieux has something vicious in his eyebrows, and something very unpleasant in the play of his lips."

"What the devil makes you think of Bonacieux?"

"Monsieur, we think of what we can, and not of what we will."

"Because you are a coward, Planchet."

"Monsieur, we must not confound prudence with cowardice; prudence is a virtue."

"And you are very virtuous, are you not, Planchet?"

"Monsieur, is not that the barrel of a musket which glitters yonder? Had we not better lower our heads?"

"In truth," murmured d'Artagnan, to whom M. de Tréville's recommendation recurred, "this animal will end by making me afraid." And he put his horse into a trot.

Planchet followed the movements of his master as if he had been his shadow, and was soon trotting by his side.

"Are we going to continue this pace all night?" asked Planchet.

"No; you are at your journey's end."

"How, Monsieur! And you?"

"I am going a few steps farther."

"And Monsieur leaves me here alone?"

"You are afraid, Planchet?"

"No; I only beg leave to observe to Monsieur that the night will be very cold, that chills bring on rheumatism, and that a lackey who has the rheumatism makes but a poor servant, particularly to a master as active as Monsieur."

"Well, if you are cold, Planchet, you can go into one of those cabarets that you see yonder, and be in waiting for me at the door by six o'clock in the morning."

"Monsieur, I have eaten and drunk respectfully the crown you gave me this morning, so that I have not a sou left in case I should be cold."

"Here's half a pistole. Tomorrow morning."

D'Artagnan sprang from his horse, threw the bridle to Planchet, and departed at a quick pace, folding his cloak around him.

"Good Lord, how cold I am!" cried Planchet, as soon as he had lost sight of his master; and in such haste was he to warm himself that he went straight to a house set out with all the attributes of a suburban tavern, and knocked at the door.

In the meantime d'Artagnan, who had plunged into a bypath, continued his route and reached St. Cloud, but instead of following the main street he turned behind the château, reached a sort of retired lane, and found himself soon in front of the pavilion named. It was situated in a very private spot. A high wall, at the angle of which was the pavilion, ran along one side of this lane, and on the other was a little garden connected with a poor cottage which was protected by a hedge from passers-by.

He gained the place appointed, and as no signal had been given him by which to announce his presence, he waited.

Not the least noise was to be heard; it might be imagined that he was a hundred miles from the capital. D'Artagnan leaned against the hedge, after having cast a glance behind it. Beyond that hedge, that garden, and that cottage, a dark mist enveloped with its folds that immensity where Paris slept–a vast void from which glittered a few luminous points, the funeral stars of that hell!

But for d'Artagnan all aspects were clothed happily, all ideas wore a smile, all shades were diaphanous. The appointed hour was about to strike. In fact, at the end of a few minutes the belfry of St. Cloud let fall slowly ten strokes from its sonorous jaws. There was something melancholy in this brazen voice pouring out its lamentations in the middle of the night, but each of those strokes, which made up the expected hour, vibrated harmoniously to the heart of the young man.

His eyes were fixed upon the little pavilion situated at the angle of the wall, of which all the windows were closed with shutters, except one on the first story. Through this window shone a mild light which silvered the foliage of two or three linden trees which formed a group outside the park. There could be no doubt that behind this little window, which threw forth such friendly beams, the pretty Mme. Bonacieux expected him.

Wrapped in this sweet idea, d'Artagnan waited half an hour without the least impatience, his eyes fixed upon that charming little abode of which he could perceive a part of the ceiling with its gilded moldings, attesting the elegance of the rest of the apartment.

The belfry of St. Cloud sounded half past ten.

This time, without knowing why, d'Artagnan felt a cold shiver run through his veins. Perhaps the cold began to affect him, and he took a perfectly physical sensation for a moral impression.

Then the idea seized him that he had read incorrectly, and that the appointment was for eleven o'clock. He drew near to the window, and placing himself so that a ray of light should fall upon the letter as he held it, he drew it from his pocket and read it again, but he had not been mistaken, the appointment was for ten o'clock. He went and resumed his post, beginning to be rather uneasy at this silence and this solitude.

Eleven o'clock sounded.

D'Artagnan began now really to fear that something had happened to Mme. Bonacieux. He clapped his hands three times–the ordinary signal of lovers, but nobody replied to him, not even an echo.

He then thought, with a touch of vexation, that perhaps the young woman had fallen asleep while waiting for him. He approached the wall, and tried to climb it, but the wall had been recently pointed, and d'Artagnan could get no hold.

At that moment he thought of the trees, upon whose leaves the light still shone; and as one of them drooped over the road, he thought that from its branches he might get a glimpse of the interior of the pavilion.

The tree was easy to climb. Besides, d'Artagnan was but twenty years old, and consequently had not yet forgotten his schoolboy habits. In an instant he was among the branches, and his keen eyes plunged through the transparent panes into the interior of the pavilion.

It was a strange thing, and one which made d'Artagnan tremble from the sole of his foot to the roots of his hair, to find that this soft light, this calm lamp, enlightened a scene of fearful disorder. One of the windows was broken, the door of the chamber had been beaten in and hung, split in two, on its hinges. A table, which had been covered with an elegant supper, was overturned. The decanters broken in pieces, and the fruits crushed, strewed the floor. Everything in the apartment gave evidence of a violent and desperate struggle. D'Artagnan even fancied he could recognise amid this strange disorder, fragments of garments, and some bloody spots staining the cloth and the curtains. He hastened to descend into the street, with a frightful beating at his heart; he wished to see if he could find other traces of violence.

The little soft light shone on in the calmness of the night. D'Artagnan then perceived a thing that he had not before remarked–for nothing had led him to the examination–that the ground, trampled here and hoofmarked there, presented confused traces of men and horses. Besides, the wheels of a carriage, which appeared to have come from Paris, had made a deep impression in the soft earth, which did not extend beyond the pavilion, but turned again toward Paris.

At length d'Artagnan, in pursuing his researches, found near the wall a woman's torn glove. This glove, wherever it had not touched the muddy ground, was of irreproachable odor. It was one of those perfumed gloves that lovers like to snatch from a pretty hand.

As d'Artagnan pursued his investigations, a more abundant and more icy sweat rolled in large drops from his forehead; his heart was oppressed by a horrible anguish; his respiration was broken and short. And yet he said, to reassure himself, that this pavilion perhaps had nothing in common with Mme. Bonacieux; that the young woman had made an appointment with him before the pavilion, and not in the pavilion; that she might have been detained in Paris by her duties, or perhaps by the jealousy of her husband.

But all these reasons were combated, destroyed, overthrown, by that feeling of intimate pain which, on certain occasions, takes possession of our being, and cries to us so as to be understood unmistakably that some great misfortune is hanging over us.

Then d'Artagnan became almost wild. He ran along the high road, took the path he had before taken, and reaching the ferry, interrogated the boatman.

About seven o'clock in the evening, the boatman had taken over a young woman, wrapped in a black mantle, who appeared to be very anxious not to be recognised, but entirely on account of her precautions, the boatman had paid more attention to her and discovered that she was young and pretty.

There were then, as now, a crowd of young and pretty women who came to St. Cloud, and who had reasons for not being seen, and yet d'Artagnan did not for an instant doubt that it was Mme. Bonacieux whom the boatman had noticed.

D'Artagnan took advantage of the lamp which burned in the cabin of the ferryman to read the billet of Mme. Bonacieux once again, and satisfy himself that he had not been mistaken, that the appointment was at St. Cloud and not elsewhere, before the D'Estrees's pavilion and not in another street. Everything conspired to prove to d'Artagnan that his presentiments had not deceived him, and that a great misfortune had happened.

He again ran back to the château. It appeared to him that something might have happened at the pavilion in his absence, and that fresh information awaited him. The lane was still deserted, and the same calm soft light shone through the window.

D'Artagnan then thought of that cottage, silent and obscure, which had no doubt seen all, and could tell its tale. The gate of the enclosure was shut, but he leaped over the hedge, and in spite of the barking of a chained-up dog, went up to the cabin.

No one answered to his first knocking. A silence of death reigned in the cabin as in the pavilion, but as the cabin was his last resource, he knocked again.

It soon appeared to him that he heard a slight noise within–a timid noise which seemed to tremble lest it should be heard.

Then d'Artagnan ceased knocking, and prayed with an accent so full of anxiety and promises, terror and cajolery, that his voice was of a nature to reassure the most fearful. At length an old, worm-eaten shutter was opened, or rather pushed ajar, but closed again as soon as the light from a miserable lamp which burned in the corner had shone upon the baldric, sword belt, and pistol pommels of d'Artagnan. Nevertheless, rapid as the movement had been, d'Artagnan had had time to get a glimpse of the head of an old man.

"In the name of heaven!" cried he, "listen to me; I have been waiting for someone who has not come. I am dying with anxiety. Has anything particular happened in the neighbourhood? Speak!"

The window was again opened slowly, and the same face appeared, only it was now still more pale than before.

D'Artagnan related his story simply, with the omission of names. He told how he had a rendezvous with a young woman before that pavilion, and how, not seeing her come, he had climbed the linden tree, and by the light of the lamp had seen the disorder of the chamber.

The old man listened attentively, making a sign only that it was all so; and then, when d'Artagnan had ended, he shook his head with an air that announced nothing good.

"What do you mean?" cried d'Artagnan. "In the name of heaven, explain yourself!"

"Oh! Monsieur," said the old man, "ask me nothing; for if I dared tell you what I have seen, certainly no good would befall me."

"You have, then, seen something?" replied d'Artagnan. "In that case, in the name of heaven," continued he, throwing him a pistole, "tell me what you have seen, and I will pledge you the word of a gentleman that not one of your words shall escape from my heart."

The old man read so much truth and so much grief in the face of the young man that he made him a sign to listen, and repeated in a low voice: "It was scarcely nine o'clock when I heard a noise in the street, and was wondering what it could be, when on coming to my door, I found that somebody was endeavouring to open it. As I am very poor and am not afraid of being robbed, I went and opened the gate and saw three men at a few paces from it. In the shadow was a carriage with two horses, and some saddlehorses. These horses evidently belonged to the three men, who were dressed as cavaliers. 'Ah, my worthy gentlemen,' cried I, 'what do you want?' 'You must have a ladder?' said he who appeared to be the leader of the party. 'Yes, Monsieur, the one with which I gather my fruit.' 'Lend it to us, and go into your house again; there is a crown for the annoyance we have caused you. Only remember this–if you speak a word of what you may see or what you may hear (for you will look and you will listen, I am quite sure, however we may threaten you), you are lost.' At these words he threw me a crown, which I picked up, and he took the ladder. After shutting the gate behind them, I pretended to return to the house, but I immediately went out a back door, and stealing along in the shade of the hedge, I gained yonder clump of elder, from which I could hear and see everything. The three men brought the carriage up quietly, and took out of it a little man, stout, short, elderly, and commonly dressed in clothes of a dark colour, who ascended the ladder very carefully, looked suspiciously in at the window of the pavilion, came down as quietly as he had gone up, and whispered, 'It is she!' Immediately, he who had spoken to me approached the door of the pavilion, opened it with a key he had in his hand, closed the door and disappeared, while at the same time the other two men ascended the ladder. The little old man remained at the coach door; the coachman took care of his horses, the lackey held the saddlehorses. All at once great cries resounded in the pavilion, and a woman came to the window, and opened it, as if to throw herself out of it, but as soon as she perceived the other two men, she fell back and they went into the chamber. Then I saw no more, but I heard the noise of breaking furniture. The woman screamed, and cried for help, but her cries were soon stifled. Two of the men appeared, bearing the woman in their arms, and carried her to the carriage, into which the little old man got after her. The leader closed the window, came out an instant after by the door, and satisfied himself that the woman was in the carriage. His two companions were already on horseback. He sprang into his saddle; the lackey took his place by the coachman; the carriage went off at a quick pace, escorted by the three horsemen, and all was over. From that moment I have neither seen nor heard anything."

D'Artagnan, entirely overcome by this terrible story, remained motionless and mute, while all the demons of anger and jealousy were howling in his heart.

"But, my good gentleman," resumed the old man, upon whom this mute despair certainly produced a greater effect than cries and tears would have done, "do not take on so; they did not kill her, and that's a comfort."

"Can you guess," said d'Artagnan, "who was the man who headed this infernal expedition?"

"I don't know him."

"But as you spoke to him you must have seen him."

"Oh, it's a description you want?"

"Exactly so."

"A tall, dark man, with black moustaches, dark eyes, and the air of a gentleman."

"That's the man!" cried d'Artagnan, "again he, forever he! He is my demon, apparently. And the other?"

"Which?"

"The short one."

"Oh, he was not a gentleman, I'll answer for it; besides, he did not wear a sword, and the others treated him with small consideration."

"Some lackey," murmured d'Artagnan. "Poor woman, poor woman, what have they done with you?"

"You have promised to be secret, my good monsieur?" said the old man.

"And I renew my promise. Be easy, I am a gentleman. A gentleman has but his word, and I have given you mine."

With a heavy heart, d'Artagnan again bent his way toward the ferry. Sometimes he hoped it could not be Mme. Bonacieux, and that he should find her next day at the Louvre; sometimes he feared she had had an intrigue with another, who, in a jealous fit, had surprised her and carried her off. His mind was torn by doubt, grief, and despair.

"Oh, if I had my three friends here," cried he, "I should have, at least, some hopes of finding her, but who knows what has become of them?"

It was past midnight; the next thing was to find Planchet. D'Artagnan went successively into all the cabarets in which there was a light, but could not find Planchet in any of them.

At the sixth he began to reflect that the search was rather dubious. D'Artagnan had appointed six o'clock in the morning for his lackey, and wherever he might be, he was right.

Besides, it came into the young man's mind that by remaining in the environs of the spot on which this sad event had passed, he would, perhaps, have some light thrown upon the mysterious affair. At the sixth cabaret, then, as we said, d'Artagnan stopped, asked for a bottle of wine of the best quality, and placing himself in the darkest corner of the room, determined thus to wait till daylight, but this time again his hopes were disappointed, and although he listened with all his ears, he heard nothing, amid the oaths, coarse jokes, and abuse which passed between the laborers, servants, and carters who comprised the honourable society of which he formed a part, which could put him upon the least track of her who had been stolen from him. He was compelled, then, after having swallowed the contents of his bottle, to pass the time as well as to evade suspicion, to fall into the easiest position in his corner and to sleep, whether well or ill. D'Artagnan, be it remembered, was only twenty years old, and at that age sleep has its imprescriptible rights which it imperiously insists upon, even with the saddest hearts.

Toward six o'clock d'Artagnan awoke with that uncomfortable feeling which generally accompanies the break of day after a bad night. He was not long in making his toilet. He examined himself to see if advantage had been taken of his sleep, and having found his diamond ring on his finger, his purse in his pocket, and his pistols in his belt, he rose, paid for his bottle, and went out to try if he could have any better luck in his search after his lackey than he had had the night before. The first thing he perceived through the damp gray mist was honest Planchet, who, with the two horses in hand, awaited him at the door of a little blind cabaret, before which d'Artagnan had passed without even a suspicion of its existence.

Chapter 25

Porthos

Instead of returning directly home, d'Artagnan alighted at the door of M. de Tréville, and ran quickly up the stairs. This time he had decided to relate all that had passed. M. de Tréville would doubtless give him good advice as to the whole affair. Besides, as M. de Tréville saw the queen almost daily, he might be able to draw from her Majesty some intelligence of the poor young woman, whom they were doubtless making pay very dearly for her devotedness to her mistress.

M. de Tréville listened to the young man's account with a seriousness which proved that he saw something else in this adventure besides a love affair. When d'Artagnan had finished, he said, "Hum! All this savors of his Eminence, a league off."

"But what is to be done?" said d'Artagnan.

"Nothing, absolutely nothing, at present, but quitting Paris, as I told you, as soon as possible. I will see the queen; I will relate to her the details of the disappearance of this poor woman, of which she is no doubt ignorant. These details will guide her on her part, and on your return, I shall perhaps have some good news to tell you. Rely on me."

D'Artagnan knew that, although a Gascon, M. de Tréville was not in the habit of making promises, and that when by chance he did promise, he more than kept his word. He bowed to him, then, full of gratitude for the past and for the future; and the worthy captain, who on his side felt a lively interest in this young man, so brave and so resolute, pressed his hand kindly, wishing him a pleasant journey.

Determined to put the advice of M. de Tréville in practice instantly, d'Artagnan directed his course toward the Rue des Fossoyeurs, in order to superintend the packing of his valise. On approaching the house, he perceived M. Bonacieux in morning costume, standing at his threshold. All that the prudent Planchet had said to him the preceding evening about the sinister character of the old man recurred to the mind of d'Artagnan, who looked at him with more attention than he had done before. In fact, in addition to that yellow, sickly paleness which indicates the insinuation of the bile in the blood, and which might, besides, be accidental, d'Artagnan remarked something perfidiously significant in the play of the wrinkled features of his countenance. A rogue does not laugh in the same way that an honest man does; a hypocrite does not shed the tears of a man of good faith. All falsehood is a mask; and however well made the mask may be, with a little attention we may always succeed in distinguishing it from the true face.

It appeared, then, to d'Artagnan that M. Bonacieux wore a mask, and likewise that that mask was most disagreeable to look upon. In consequence of this feeling of repugnance, he was about to pass without speaking to him, but, as he had done the day before, M. Bonacieux accosted him.

"Well, young man," said he, "we appear to pass rather gay nights! Seven o'clock in the morning! PESTE! You seem to reverse ordinary customs, and come home at the hour when other people are going out."

"No one can reproach you for anything of the kind, Monsieur Bonacieux," said the young man, "you are a model for regular people. It is true that when a man possesses a young and pretty wife, he has no need to seek happiness elsewhere. Happiness comes to meet him, does it not, Monsieur Bonacieux?"

Bonacieux became as pale as death, and grinned a ghastly smile.

"Ah, ah!" said Bonacieux, "you are a jocular companion! But where the devil were you gadding last night, my young master? It does not appear to be very clean in the crossroads."

D'Artagnan glanced down at his boots, all covered with mud, but that same glance fell upon the shoes and stockings of the mercer, and it might have been said they had been dipped in the same mud heap. Both were stained with splashes of mud of the same appearance.

Then a sudden idea crossed the mind of d'Artagnan. That little stout man, short and elderly, that sort of lackey, dressed in dark clothes, treated without ceremony by the men wearing swords who composed the escort, was Bonacieux himself. The husband had presided at the abduction of his wife.

A terrible inclination seized d'Artagnan to grasp the mercer by the throat and strangle him; but, as we have said, he was a very prudent youth, and he restrained himself. However, the revolution which appeared upon his countenance was so visible that Bonacieux was terrified at it, and he endeavoured to draw back a step or two, but as he was standing before the half of the door which was shut, the obstacle compelled him to keep his place.

"Ah, but you are joking, my worthy man!" said d'Artagnan. "It appears to me that if my boots need a sponge, your stockings and shoes stand in equal need of a brush. May you not have been philandering a little also, Monsieur Bonacieux? Oh, the devil! That's unpardonable in a man of your age, and who besides, has such a pretty wife as yours."

"Oh, Lord! No," said Bonacieux, "but yesterday I went to St. Mande to make some inquiries after a servant, as I cannot possibly do without one; and the roads were so bad that I brought back all this mud, which I have not yet had time to remove."

The place named by Bonacieux as that which had been the object of his journey was a fresh proof in support of the suspicions d'Artagnan had conceived. Bonacieux had named Mande because Mande was in an exactly opposite direction from St. Cloud. This probability afforded him his first consolation. If Bonacieux knew where his wife was, one might, by extreme means, force the mercer to open his teeth and let his secret escape. The question, then, was how to change this probability into a certainty.

"Pardon, my dear Monsieur Bonacieux, if I don't stand upon ceremony," said d'Artagnan, "but nothing makes one so thirsty as want of sleep. I am parched with thirst. Allow me to take a glass of water in your apartment; you know that is never refused among neighbours."

Without waiting for the permission of his host, d'Artagnan went quickly into the house, and cast a rapid glance at the bed. It had not been used. Bonacieux had not been abed. He had only been back an hour or two; he had accompanied his wife to the place of her confinement, or else at least to the first relay.

"Thanks, Monsieur Bonacieux," said d'Artagnan, emptying his glass, "that is all I wanted of you. I will now go up into my apartment. I will make Planchet brush my boots; and when he has done, I will, if you like, send him to you to brush your shoes."

He left the mercer quite astonished at his singular farewell, and asking himself if he had not been a little inconsiderate.

At the top of the stairs he found Planchet in a great fright.

"Ah, Monsieur!" cried Planchet, as soon as he perceived his master, "here is more trouble. I thought you would never come in."

"What's the matter now, Planchet?" demanded d'Artagnan.

"Oh! I give you a hundred, I give you a thousand times to guess, Monsieur, the visit I received in your absence."

"When?"

"About half an hour ago, while you were at Monsieur de Tréville's."

"Who has been here? Come, speak."

"Monsieur de Cavois."

"Monsieur de Cavois?"

"In person."

"The captain of the cardinal's Guards?"

"Himself."

"Did he come to arrest me?"

"I have no doubt that he did, Monsieur, for all his wheedling manner."

"Was he so sweet, then?"

"Indeed, he was all honey, Monsieur."

"Indeed!"

"He came, he said, on the part of his Eminence, who wished you well, and to beg you to follow him to the Palais-Royal."

"What did you answer him?"

"That the thing was impossible, seeing that you were not at home, as he could see."

"Well, what did he say then?"

"That you must not fail to call upon him in the course of the day; and then he added in a low voice, 'Tell your master that his Eminence is very well disposed toward him, and that his fortune perhaps depends upon this interview.'"

"The snare is rather MALADROIT for the cardinal," replied the young man, smiling.

"Oh, I saw the snare, and I answered you would be quite in despair on your return.

"'Where has he gone?' asked Monsieur de Cavois.

"'To Troyes, in Champagne,' I answered.

"'And when did he set out?'

"'Yesterday evening.'"

"Planchet, my friend," interrupted d'Artagnan, "you are really a precious fellow."

"You will understand, Monsieur, I thought there would be still time, if you wish, to see Monsieur de Cavois to contradict me by saying you were not yet gone. The falsehood would then lie at my door, and as I am not a gentleman, I may be allowed to lie."

"Be of good heart, Planchet, you shall preserve your reputation as a veracious man. In a quarter of an hour we set off."

"That's the advice I was about to give Monsieur; and where are we going, may I ask, without being too curious?"

"PARDIEU! In the opposite direction to that which you said I was gone. Besides, are you not as anxious to learn news of Grimaud, Mousqueton, and Bazin as I am to know what has become of Athos, Porthos, and Aramis?"

"Yes, Monsieur," said Planchet, "and I will go as soon as you please. Indeed, I think provincial air will suit us much better just now than the air of Paris. So then–"

"So then, pack up our luggage, Planchet, and let us be off. On my part, I will go out with my hands in my pockets, that nothing may be suspected. You may join me at the Hotel des Gardes. By the way, Planchet, I think you are right with respect to our host, and that he is decidedly a frightfully low wretch."

"Ah, Monsieur, you may take my word when I tell you anything. I am a physiognomist, I assure you."

D'Artagnan went out first, as had been agreed upon. Then, in order that he might have nothing to reproach himself with, he directed his steps, for the last time, toward the residences of his three friends. No news had been received of them; only a letter, all perfumed and of an elegant writing in small characters, had come for Aramis. D'Artagnan took charge of it. Ten minutes afterward Planchet joined him at the stables of the Hotel des Gardes. D'Artagnan, in order that there might be no time lost, had saddled his horse himself.

"That's well," said he to Planchet, when the latter added the portmanteau to the equipment. "Now saddle the other three horses."

"Do you think, then, Monsieur, that we shall travel faster with two horses apiece?" said Planchet, with his shrewd air.

"No, Monsieur Jester," replied d'Artagnan, "but with our four horses we may bring back our three friends, if we should have the good fortune to find them living."

"Which is a great chance," replied Planchet, "but we must not despair of the mercy of God."

"Amen!" said d'Artagnan, getting into his saddle.

As they went from the Hotel des Gardes, they separated, leaving the street at opposite ends, one having to quit Paris by the Barrière de la Villette and the other by the Barrière Montmartre, to meet again beyond St. Denis–a strategic maneuver which, having been executed with equal punctuality, was crowned with the most fortunate results. D'Artagnan and Planchet entered Pierrefitte together.

Planchet was more courageous, it must be admitted, by day than by night. His natural prudence, however, never forsook him for a single instant. He had forgotten not one of the incidents of the first journey, and he looked upon everybody he met on the road as an enemy. It followed that his hat was forever in his hand, which procured him some severe reprimands from d'Artagnan, who feared that his excess of politeness would lead people to think he was the lackey of a man of no consequence.

Nevertheless, whether the passengers were really touched by the urbanity of Planchet or whether this time nobody was posted on the young man's road, our two travellers arrived at Chantilly without any accident, and alighted at the tavern of Great St. Martin, the same at which they had stopped on their first journey.

The host, on seeing a young man followed by a lackey with two extra horses, advanced respectfully to the door. Now, as they had already traveled eleven leagues, d'Artagnan thought it time to stop, whether Porthos were or were not in the inn. Perhaps it would not be prudent to ask at once what had become of the Musketeer. The result of these reflections was that d'Artagnan, without asking information of any kind, alighted, commended the horses to the care of his lackey, entered a small room destined to receive those who wished to be alone, and desired the host to bring him a bottle of his best wine and as good a breakfast as possible–a desire which further corroborated the high opinion the innkeeper had formed of the traveller at first sight.

D'Artagnan was therefore served with miraculous celerity. The regiment of the Guards was recruited among the first gentlemen of the kingdom; and d'Artagnan, followed by a lackey, and travelling with four magnificent horses, despite the simplicity of his uniform, could not fail to make a sensation. The host desired himself to serve him, which d'Artagnan perceiving, ordered two glasses to be brought, and commenced the following conversation.

"My faith, my good host," said d'Artagnan, filling the two glasses, "I asked for a bottle of your best wine, and if you have deceived me, you will be punished in what you have sinned; for seeing that I hate drinking by myself, you shall drink with me. Take your glass, then, and let us drink. But what shall we drink to, so as to avoid wounding any susceptibility? Let us drink to the prosperity of your establishment."

"Your Lordship does me much honour," said the host, "and I thank you sincerely for your kind wish."

"But don't mistake," said d'Artagnan, "there is more selfishness in my toast than perhaps you may think–for it is only in prosperous establishments that one is well received. In hotels that do not flourish, everything is in confusion, and the traveller is a victim to the embarrassments of his host. Now, I travel a great deal, particularly on this road, and I wish to see all innkeepers making a fortune."

"It seems to me," said the host, "that this is not the first time I have had the honour of seeing Monsieur."

"Bah, I have passed perhaps ten times through Chantilly, and out of the ten times I have stopped three or four times at your house at least. Why I was here only ten or twelve days ago. I was conducting some friends, Musketeers, one of whom, by the by, had a dispute with a stranger–a man who sought a quarrel with him, for I don't know what."

"Exactly so," said the host, "I remember it perfectly. It is not Monsieur Porthos that your Lordship means?"

"Yes, that is my companion's name. My God, my dear host, tell me if anything has happened to him?"

"Your Lordship must have observed that he could not continue his journey."

"Why, to be sure, he promised to rejoin us, and we have seen nothing of him."

"He has done us the honour to remain here."

"What, he had done you the honour to remain here?"

"Yes, Monsieur, in this house; and we are even a little uneasy–"

"On what account?"

"Of certain expenses he has contracted."

"Well, but whatever expenses he may have incurred, I am sure he is in a condition to pay them."

"Ah, Monsieur, you infuse genuine balm into my blood. We have made considerable advances; and this very morning the surgeon declared that if Monsieur Porthos did not pay him, he should look to me, as it was I who had sent for him."

"Porthos is wounded, then?"

"I cannot tell you, Monsieur."

"What! You cannot tell me? Surely you ought to be able to tell me better than any other person."

"Yes, but in our situation we must not say all we know–particularly as we have been warned that our ears should answer for our tongues."

"Well, can I see Porthos?"

"Certainly, Monsieur. Take the stairs on your right; go up the first flight and knock at Number One. Only warn him that it is you."

"Why should I do that?"

"Because, Monsieur, some mischief might happen to you."

"Of what kind, in the name of wonder?"

"Monsieur Porthos may imagine you belong to the house, and in a fit of passion might run his sword through you or blow out your brains."

"What have you done to him, then?"

"We have asked him for money."

"The devil! Ah, I can understand that. It is a demand that Porthos takes very ill when he is not in funds, but I know he must be so at present."

"We thought so, too, Monsieur. As our house is carried on very regularly, and we make out our bills every week, at the end of eight days we presented our account, but it appeared we had chosen an unlucky moment, for at the first word on the subject, he sent us to all the devils. It is true he had been playing the day before."

"Playing the day before! And with whom?"

"Lord, who can say, Monsieur? With some gentleman who was travelling this way, to whom he proposed a game of LANSQUENET."

"That's it, then, and the foolish fellow lost all he had?"

"Even to his horse, Monsieur; for when the gentleman was about to set out, we perceived that his lackey was saddling Monsieur Porthos's horse, as well as his master's. When we observed this to him, he told us all to trouble ourselves about our own business, as this horse belonged to him. We also informed Monsieur Porthos of what was going on, but he told us we were scoundrels to doubt a gentleman's word, and that as he had said the horse was his, it must be so."

"That's Porthos all over," murmured d'Artagnan.

"Then," continued the host, "I replied that as from the moment we seemed not likely to come to a good understanding with respect to payment, I hoped that he would have at least the kindness to grant the favour of his custom to my brother host of the Golden Eagle, but Monsieur Porthos replied that, my house being the best, he should remain where he was. This reply was too flattering to allow me to insist on his departure. I confined myself then to begging him to give up his chamber, which is the handsomest in the hotel, and to be satisfied with a pretty little room on the third floor, but to this Monsieur Porthos replied that as he every moment expected his mistress, who was one of the greatest ladies in the court, I might easily comprehend that the chamber he did me the honour to occupy in my house was itself very mean for the visit of such a personage. Nevertheless, while acknowledging the truth of what he said, I thought proper to insist, but without even giving himself the trouble to enter into any discussion with me, he took one of his pistols, laid it on his table, day and night, and said that at the first word that should be spoken to him about removing, either within the house or out of it, he would blow out the brains of the person who should be so imprudent as to meddle with a matter which only concerned himself. Since that time, Monsieur, nobody entered his chamber but his servant."

"What! Mousqueton is here, then?"

"Oh, yes, Monsieur. Five days after your departure, he came back, and in a very bad condition, too. It appears that he had met with disagreeableness, likewise, on his journey. Unfortunately, he is more nimble than his master; so that for the sake of his master, he puts us all under his feet, and as he thinks we might refuse what he asked for, he takes all he wants without asking at all."

"The fact is," said d'Artagnan, "I have always observed a great degree of intelligence and devotedness in Mousqueton."

"That is possible, Monsieur, but suppose I should happen to be brought in contact, even four times a year, with such intelligence and devotedness–why, I should be a ruined man!"

"No, for Porthos will pay you."

"Hum!" said the host, in a doubtful tone.

"The favourite of a great lady will not be allowed to be inconvenienced for such a paltry sum as he owes you."

"If I durst say what I believe on that head–"

"What you believe?"

"I ought rather to say, what I know."

"What you know?"

"And even what I am sure of."

"And of what are you so sure?"

"I would say that I know this great lady."

"You?"

"Yes; I."

"And how do you know her?"

"Oh, Monsieur, if I could believe I might trust in your discretion."

"Speak! By the word of a gentleman, you shall have no cause to repent of your confidence."

"Well, Monsieur, you understand that uneasiness makes us do many things."

"What have you done?"

"Oh, nothing which was not right in the character of a creditor."

"Well?"

"Monsieur Porthos gave us a note for his duchess, ordering us to put it in the post. This was before his servant came. As he could not leave his chamber, it was necessary to charge us with this commission."

"And then?"

"Instead of putting the letter in the post, which is never safe, I took advantage of the journey of one of my lads to Paris, and ordered him to convey the letter to this duchess himself. This was fulfilling the intentions of Monsieur Porthos, who had desired us to be so careful of this letter, was it not?"

"Nearly so."

"Well, Monsieur, do you know who this great lady is?"

"No; I have heard Porthos speak of her, that's all."

"Do you know who this pretended duchess is?

"I repeat to you, I don't know her."

"Why, she is the old wife of a procurator of the Chatelet, Monsieur, named Madame Coquenard, who, although she is at least fifty, still gives herself jealous airs. It struck me as very odd that a princess should live in the Rue aux Ours."

"But how do you know all this?"

"Because she flew into a great passion on receiving the letter, saying that Monsieur Porthos was a weathercock, and that she was sure it was for some woman he had received this wound."

"Has he been wounded, then?"

"Oh, good Lord! What have I said?"

"You said that Porthos had received a sword cut."

"Yes, but he has forbidden me so strictly to say so."

"And why so."

"Zounds, Monsieur! Because he had boasted that he would perforate the stranger with whom you left him in dispute; whereas the stranger, on the contrary, in spite of all his rodomontades quickly threw him on his back. As Monsieur Porthos is a very boastful man, he insists that nobody shall know he has received this wound except the duchess, whom he endeavoured to interest by an account of his adventure."

"It is a wound that confines him to his bed?"

"Ah, and a master stroke, too, I assure you. Your friend's soul must stick tight to his body."

"Were you there, then?"

"Monsieur, I followed them from curiosity, so that I saw the combat without the combatants seeing me."

"And what took place?"

"Oh! The affair was not long, I assure you. They placed themselves on guard; the stranger made a feint and a lunge, and that so rapidly that when Monsieur Porthos came to the PARADE, he had already three inches of steel in his breast. He immediately fell backward. The stranger placed the point of his sword at his throat; and Monsieur Porthos, finding himself at the mercy of his adversary, acknowledged himself conquered. Upon which the stranger asked his name, and learning that it was Porthos, and not d'Artagnan, he assisted him to rise, brought him back to the hotel, mounted his horse, and disappeared."

"So it was with Monsieur d'Artagnan this stranger meant to quarrel?"

"It appears so."

"And do you know what has become of him?"

"No, I never saw him until that moment, and have not seen him since."

"Very well; I know all that I wish to know. Porthos's chamber is, you say, on the first story, Number One?"

"Yes, Monsieur, the handsomest in the inn–a chamber that I could have let ten times over."

"Bah! Be satisfied," said d'Artagnan, laughing, "Porthos will pay you with the money of the Duchess Coquenard."

"Oh, Monsieur, procurator's wife or duchess, if she will but loosen her purse strings, it will be all the same, but she positively answered that she was tired of the exigencies and infidelities of Monsieur Porthos, and that she would not send him a denier."

"And did you convey this answer to your guest?"

"We took good care not to do that; he would have found in what fashion we had executed his commission."

"So that he still expects his money?"

"Oh, Lord, yes, Monsieur! Yesterday he wrote again, but it was his servant who this time put the letter in the post."

"Do you say the procurator's wife is old and ugly?"

"Fifty at least, Monsieur, and not at all handsome, according to Pathaud's account."

"In that case, you may be quite at ease; she will soon be softened. Besides, Porthos cannot owe you much."

"How, not much! Twenty good pistoles, already, without reckoning the doctor. He denies himself nothing; it may easily be seen he has been accustomed to live well."

"Never mind; if his mistress abandons him, he will find friends, I will answer for it. So, my dear host, be not uneasy, and continue to take all the care of him that his situation requires."

"Monsieur has promised me not to open his mouth about the procurator's wife, and not to say a word of the wound?"

"That's agreed; you have my word."

"Oh, he would kill me!"

"Don't be afraid; he is not so much of a devil as he appears."

Saying these words, d'Artagnan went upstairs, leaving his host a little better satisfied with respect to two things in which he appeared to be very much interested–his debt and his life.

At the top of the stairs, upon the most conspicuous door of the corridor, was traced in black ink a gigantic number "1." d'Artagnan knocked, and upon the bidding to come in which came from inside, he entered the chamber.

Porthos was in bed, and was playing a game at LANSQUENET with Mousqueton, to keep his hand in; while a spit loaded with partridges was turning before the fire, and on each side of a large chimney piece, over two chafing dishes, were boiling two stewpans, from which exhaled a double odor of rabbit and fish stews, rejoicing to the smell. In addition to this he perceived that the top of a wardrobe and the marble of a commode were covered with empty bottles.

At the sight of his friend, Porthos uttered a loud cry of joy; and Mousqueton, rising respectfully, yielded his place to him, and went to give an eye to the two stew pans, of which he appeared to have the particular inspection.

"Ah, PARDIEU! Is that you?" said Porthos to d'Artagnan. "You are right welcome. Excuse my not coming to meet you; but," added he, looking at d'Artagnan with a certain degree of uneasiness, "you know what has happened to me?"

"No."

"Has the host told you nothing, then?"

"I asked after you, and came up as soon as I could."

Porthos seemed to breathe more freely.

"And what has happened to you, my dear Porthos?" continued d'Artagnan.

"Why, on making a thrust at my adversary, whom I had already hit three times, and whom I meant to finish with the fourth, I put my foot on a stone, slipped, and strained my knee."

"Truly?"

"Honor! Luckily for the rascal, for I should have left him dead on the spot, I assure you."

"And what has became of him?"

"Oh, I don't know; he had enough, and set off without waiting for the rest. But you, my dear d'Artagnan, what has happened to you?"

"So that this strain of the knee," continued d'Artagnan, "my dear Porthos, keeps you in bed?"

"My God, that's all. I shall be about again in a few days."

"Why did you not have yourself conveyed to Paris? You must be cruelly bored here."

"That was my intention; but, my dear friend, I have one thing to confess to you."

"What's that?"

"It is that as I was cruelly bored, as you say, and as I had the seventy-five pistoles in my pocket which you had distributed to me, in order to amuse myself I invited a gentleman who was travelling this way to walk up, and proposed a cast of dice. He accepted my challenge, and, my faith, my seventy-five pistoles passed from my pocket to his, without reckoning my horse, which he won into the bargain. But you, my dear d'Artagnan?"

"What can you expect, my dear Porthos; a man is not privileged in all ways," said d'Artagnan. "You know the proverb 'Unlucky at play, lucky in love.' You are too fortunate in your love for play not to take its revenge. What consequence can the reverses of fortune be to you? Have you not, happy rogue that you are–have you not your duchess, who cannot fail to come to your aid?"

"Well, you see, my dear d'Artagnan, with what ill luck I play," replied Porthos, with the most careless air in the world. "I wrote to her to send me fifty louis or so, of which I stood absolutely in need on account of my accident."

"Well?"

"Well, she must be at her country seat, for she has not answered me."

"Truly?"

"No; so I yesterday addressed another epistle to her, still more pressing than the first. But you are here, my dear fellow, let us speak of you. I confess I began to be very uneasy on your account."

"But your host behaves very well toward you, as it appears, my dear Porthos," said d'Artagnan, directing the sick man's attention to the full stewpans and the empty bottles.

"So, so," replied Porthos. "Only three or four days ago the impertinent jackanapes gave me his bill, and I was forced to turn both him and his bill out of the door; so that I am here something in the fashion of a conqueror, holding my position, as it were, my conquest. So you see, being in constant fear of being forced from that position, I am armed to the teeth."

"And yet," said d'Artagnan, laughing, "it appears to me that from time to time you must make SORTIES." And he again pointed to the bottles and the stew pans.

"Not I, unfortunately!" said Porthos. "This miserable strain confines me to my bed, but Mousqueton forages, and brings in provisions. Friend Mousqueton, you see that we have a reinforcement, and we must have an increase of supplies."

"Mousqueton," said d'Artagnan, "you must render me a service."

"What, Monsieur?"

"You must give your recipe to Planchet. I may be besieged in my turn, and I shall not be sorry for him to be able to let me enjoy the same advantages with which you gratify your master."

"Lord, Monsieur! There is nothing more easy," said Mousqueton, with a modest air. "One only needs to be sharp, that's all. I was brought up in the country, and my father in his leisure time was something of a poacher."

"And what did he do the rest of his time?"

"Monsieur, he carried on a trade which I have always thought satisfactory."

"Which?"

"As it was a time of war between the Catholics and the Huguenots, and as he saw the Catholics exterminate the Huguenots and the Huguenots exterminate the Catholics–all in the name of religion–he adopted a mixed belief which permitted him to be sometimes Catholic, sometimes a Huguenot. Now, he was accustomed to walk with his fowling piece on his shoulder, behind the hedges which border the roads, and when he saw a Catholic coming alone, the Protestant religion immediately prevailed in his mind. He lowered his gun in the direction of the traveller; then, when he was within ten paces of him, he commenced a conversation which almost always ended by the traveller's abandoning his purse to save his life. It goes without saying that when he saw a Huguenot coming, he felt himself filled with such ardent Catholic zeal that he could not understand how, a quarter of an hour before, he had been able to have any doubts upon the superiority of our holy religion. For my part, Monsieur, I am Catholic–my father, faithful to his principles, having made my elder brother a Huguenot."

"And what was the end of this worthy man?" asked d'Artagnan.

"Oh, of the most unfortunate kind, Monsieur. One day he was surprised in a lonely road between a Huguenot and a Catholic, with both of whom he had before had business, and who both knew him again; so they united against him and hanged him on a tree. Then they came and boasted of their fine exploit in the cabaret of the next village, where my brother and I were drinking."

"And what did you do?" said d'Artagnan.

"We let them tell their story out," replied Mousqueton. "Then, as in leaving the cabaret they took different directions, my brother went and hid himself on the road of the Catholic, and I on that of the Huguenot. Two hours after, all was over; we had done the business of both, admiring the foresight of our poor father, who had taken the precaution to bring each of us up in a different religion."

"Well, I must allow, as you say, your father was a very intelligent fellow. And you say in his leisure moments the worthy man was a poacher?"

"Yes, Monsieur, and it was he who taught me to lay a snare and ground a line. The consequence is that when I saw our laborers, which did not at all suit two such delicate stomachs as ours, I had recourse to a little of my old trade. While walking near the wood of Monsieur le Prince, I laid a few snare in the runs; and while reclining on the banks of his Highness's pieces of water, I slipped a few lines into his fish ponds. So that now, thanks be to God, we do not want, as Monsieur can testify, for partridges, rabbits, carp or eels–all light, wholesome food, suitable for the sick."

"But the wine," said d'Artagnan, "who furnishes the wine? Your host?"

"That is to say, yes and no."

"How yes and no?"

"He furnishes it, it is true, but he does not know that he has that honour."

"Explain yourself, Mousqueton; your conversation is full of instructive things."

"That is it, Monsieur. It has so chanced that I met with a Spaniard in my peregrinations who had seen many countries, and among them the New World."

"What connection can the New World have with the bottles which are on the commode and the wardrobe?"

"Patience, Monsieur, everything will come in its turn."

"This Spaniard had in his service a lackey who had accompanied him in his voyage to Mexico. This lackey was my compatriot; and we became the more intimate from there being many resemblances of character between us. We loved sporting of all kinds better than anything; so that he related to me how in the plains of the Pampas the natives hunt the tiger and the wild bull with simple running nooses which they throw to a distance of twenty or thirty paces the end of a cord with such nicety, but in face of the proof I was obliged to acknowledge the truth of the recital. My friend placed a bottle at the distance of thirty paces, and at each cast he caught the neck of the bottle in his running noose. I practiced this exercise, and as nature has endowed me with some faculties, at this day I can throw the lasso with any man in the world. Well, do you understand, Monsieur? Our host has a well-furnished cellar the key of which never leaves him; only this cellar has a ventilating hole. Now through this ventilating hole I throw my lasso, and as I now know in which part of the cellar is the best wine, that's my point for sport. You see, Monsieur, what the New World has to do with the bottles which are on the commode and the wardrobe. Now, will you taste our wine, and without prejudice say what you think of it?"

"Thank you, my friend, thank you; unfortunately, I have just breakfasted."

"Well," said Porthos, "arrange the table, Mousqueton, and while we breakfast, d'Artagnan will relate to us what has happened to him during the ten days since he left us."

"Willingly," said d'Artagnan.

While Porthos and Mousqueton were breakfasting, with the appetites of convalescents and with that brotherly cordiality which unites men in misfortune, d'Artagnan related how Aramis, being wounded, was obliged to stop at Crèvecoeur, how he had left Athos fighting at Amiens with four men who accused him of being a coiner, and how he, d'Artagnan, had been forced to run the Comtes de Wardes through the body in order to reach England.

But there the confidence of d'Artagnan stopped. He only added that on his return from Great Britain he had brought back four magnificent horses–one for himself, and one for each of his companions; then he informed Porthos that the one intended for him was already installed in the stable of the tavern.

At this moment Planchet entered, to inform his master that the horses were sufficiently refreshed and that it would be possible to sleep at Clermont.

As d'Artagnan was tolerably reassured with regard to Porthos, and as he was anxious to obtain news of his two other friends, he held out his hand to the wounded man, and told him he was about to resume his route in order to continue his researches. For the rest, as he reckoned upon returning by the same route in seven or eight days, if Porthos were still at the Great St. Martin, he would call for him on his way.

Porthos replied that in all probability his sprain would not permit him to depart yet awhile. Besides, it was necessary he should stay at Chantilly to wait for the answer from his duchess.

D'Artagnan wished that answer might be prompt and favourable; and having again recommended Porthos to the care of Mousqueton, and paid his bill to the host, he resumed his route with Planchet, already relieved of one of his led horses.

Chapter 26

Aramis And His Thesis

D'Artagnan had said nothing to Porthos of his wound or of his procurator's wife. Our Bearnais was a prudent lad, however young he might be. Consequently he had appeared to believe all that the vainglorious Musketeer had told him, convinced that no friendship will hold out against a surprised secret. Besides, we feel always a sort of mental superiority over those whose lives we know better than they suppose. In his projects of intrigue for the future, and determined as he was to make his three friends the instruments of his fortune, d'Artagnan was not sorry at getting into his grasp beforehand the invisible strings by which he reckoned upon moving them.

And yet, as he journeyed along, a profound sadness weighed upon his heart. He thought of that young and pretty Mme. Bonacieux who was to have paid him the price of his devotedness, but let us hasten to say that this sadness possessed the young man less from the regret of the happiness he had missed, than from the fear he entertained that some serious misfortune had befallen the poor woman. For himself, he had no doubt she was a victim of the cardinal's vengeance; and, as was well known, the vengeance of his Eminence was terrible. How he had found grace in the eyes of the minister, he did not know, but without doubt M. de Cavois would have revealed this to him if the captain of the Guards had found him at home.

Nothing makes time pass more quickly or more shortens a journey than a thought which absorbs in itself all the faculties of the organization of him who thinks. External existence then resembles a sleep of which this thought is the dream. By its influence, time has no longer measure, space has no longer distance. We depart from one place, and arrive at another, that is all. Of the interval passed, nothing remains in the memory but a vague mist in which a thousand confused images of trees, mountains, and landscapes are lost. It was as a prey to this hallucination that d'Artagnan traveled, at whatever pace his horse pleased, the six or eight leagues that separated Chantilly from Crèvecoeur, without his being able to remember on his arrival in the village any of the things he had passed or met with on the road.

There only his memory returned to him. He shook his head, perceived the cabaret at which he had left Aramis, and putting his horse to the trot, he shortly pulled up at the door.

This time it was not a host but a hostess who received him. D'Artagnan was a physiognomist. His eye took in at a glance the plump, cheerful countenance of the mistress of the place, and he at once perceived there was no occasion for dissembling with her, or of fearing anything from one blessed with such a joyous physiognomy.

"My good dame," asked d'Artagnan, "can you tell me what has become of one of my friends, whom we were obliged to leave here about a dozen days ago?"

"A handsome young man, three- or four-and-twenty years old, mild, amiable, and well made?"

"That is he–wounded in the shoulder."

"Just so. Well, Monsieur, he is still here."

"Ah, PARDIEU! My dear dame," said d'Artagnan, springing from his horse, and throwing the bridle to Planchet, "you restore me to life; where is this dear Aramis? Let me embrace him, I am in a hurry to see him again."

"Pardon, Monsieur, but I doubt whether he can see you at this moment."

"Why so? Has he a lady with him?"

"Jesus! What do you mean by that? Poor lad! No, Monsieur, he has not a lady with him."

"With whom is he, then?"

"With the curate of Montdidier and the superior of the Jesuits of Amiens."

"Good heavens!" cried d'Artagnan, "is the poor fellow worse, then?"

"No, Monsieur, quite the contrary, but after his illness grace touched him, and he determined to take orders."

"That's it!" said d'Artagnan, "I had forgotten that he was only a Musketeer for a time."

"Monsieur still insists upon seeing him?"

"More than ever."

"Well, Monsieur has only to take the right-hand staircase in the courtyard, and knock at Number Five on the second floor."

D'Artagnan walked quickly in the direction indicated, and found one of those exterior staircases that are still to be seen in the yards of our old-fashioned taverns. But there was no getting at the place of sojourn of the future abbé; the defiles of the chamber of Aramis were as well guarded as the gardens of Armida. Bazin was stationed in the corridor, and barred his passage with the more intrepidity that, after many years of trial, Bazin found himself near a result of which he had ever been ambitious.

In fact, the dream of poor Bazin had always been to serve a churchman; and he awaited with impatience the moment, always in the future, when Aramis would throw aside the uniform and assume the cassock. The daily-renewed promise of the young man that the moment would not long be delayed, had alone kept him in the service of a Musketeer–a service in which, he said, his soul was in constant jeopardy.

Bazin was then at the height of joy. In all probability, this time his master would not retract. The union of physical pain with moral uneasiness had produced the effect so long desired. Aramis, suffering at once in body and mind, had at length fixed his eyes and his thoughts upon religion, and he had considered as a warning from heaven the double accident which had happened to him; that is to say, the sudden disappearance of his mistress and the wound in his shoulder.

It may be easily understood that in the present disposition of his master nothing could be more disagreeable to Bazin than the arrival of d'Artagnan, which might cast his master back again into that vortex of mundane affairs which had so long carried him away. He resolved, then, to defend the door bravely; and as, betrayed by the mistress of the inn, he could not say that Aramis was absent, he endeavoured to prove to the newcomer that it would be the height of indiscretion to disturb his master in his pious conference, which had commenced with the morning and would not, as Bazin said, terminate before night.

But d'Artagnan took very little heed of the eloquent discourse of M. Bazin; and as he had no desire to support a polemic discussion with his friend's valet, he simply moved him out of the way with one hand, and with the other turned the handle of the door of Number Five. The door opened, and d'Artagnan went into the chamber.

Aramis, in a black gown, his head enveloped in a sort of round flat cap, not much unlike a CALOTTE, was seated before an oblong table, covered with rolls of paper and enormous volumes in folio. At his right hand was placed the superior of the Jesuits, and on his left the curate of Montdidier. The curtains were half drawn, and only admitted the mysterious light calculated for beatific reveries. All the mundane objects that generally strike the eye on entering the room of a young man, particularly when that young man is a Musketeer, had disappeared as if by enchantment; and for fear, no doubt, that the sight of them might bring his master back to ideas of this world, Bazin had laid his hands upon sword, pistols, plumed hat, and embroideries and laces of all kinds and sorts. In their stead d'Artagnan thought he perceived in an obscure corner a discipline cord suspended from a nail in the wall.

At the noise made by d'Artagnan in entering, Aramis lifted up his head, and beheld his friend, but to the great astonishment of the young man, the sight of him did not produce much effect upon the Musketeer, so completely was his mind detached from the things of this world.

"Good day, dear d'Artagnan," said Aramis, "believe me, I am glad to see you."

"So am I delighted to see you," said d'Artagnan, "although I am not yet sure that it is Aramis I am speaking to."

"To himself, my friend, to himself! But what makes you doubt it?"

"I was afraid I had made a mistake in the chamber, and that I had found my way into the apartment of some churchman. Then another error seized me on seeing you in company with these gentlemen–I was afraid you were dangerously ill."

The two men in black, who guessed d'Artagnan's meaning, darted at him a glance which might have been thought threatening, but d'Artagnan took no heed of it.

"I disturb you, perhaps, my dear Aramis," continued d'Artagnan, "for by what I see, I am led to believe that you are confessing to these gentlemen."

Aramis coloured imperceptibly. "You disturb me? Oh, quite the contrary, dear friend, I swear; and as a proof of what I say, permit me to declare I am rejoiced to see you safe and sound."

"Ah, he'll come round," thought d'Artagnan, "that's not bad!"

"This gentleman, who is my friend, has just escaped from a serious danger," continued Aramis, with unction, pointing to d'Artagnan with his hand, and addressing the two ecclesiastics.

"Praise God, Monsieur," replied they, bowing together.

"I have not failed to do so, your Reverences," replied the young man, returning their salutation.

"You arrive in good time, dear d'Artagnan," said Aramis, "and by taking part in our discussion may assist us with your intelligence. Monsieur the Principal of Amiens, Monsieur the Curate of Montdidier, and I are arguing certain theological questions in which we have been much interested; I shall be delighted to have your opinion."

"The opinion of a swordsman can have very little weight," replied d'Artagnan, who began to be uneasy at the turn things were taking, "and you had better be satisfied, believe me, with the knowledge of these gentlemen."

The two men in black bowed in their turn.

"On the contrary," replied Aramis, "your opinion will be very valuable. The question is this: Monsieur the Principal thinks that my thesis ought to be dogmatic and didactic."

"Your thesis! Are you then making a thesis?"

"Without doubt," replied the Jesuit. "In the examination which precedes ordination, a thesis is always a requisite."

"Ordination!" cried d'Artagnan, who could not believe what the hostess and Bazin had successively told him; and he gazed, half stupefied, upon the three persons before him.

"Now," continued Aramis, taking the same graceful position in his easy chair that he would have assumed in bed, and complacently examining his hand, which was as white and plump as that of a woman, and which he held in the air to cause the blood to descend, "now, as you have heard, d'Artagnan, Monsieur the Principal is desirous that my thesis should be dogmatic, while I, for my part, would rather it should be ideal. This is the reason why Monsieur the Principal has proposed to me the following subject, which has not yet been treated upon, and in which I perceive there is matter for magnificent elaboration–'UTRAQUE MANUS IN BENEDICENDO CLERICIS INFERIORIBUS NECESSARIA EST.'"

D'Artagnan, whose erudition we are well acquainted with, evinced no more interest on hearing this quotation than he had at that of M. de Tréville in allusion to the gifts he pretended that d'Artagnan had received from the Duke of Buckingham.

"Which means," resumed Aramis, that he might perfectly understand, "'The two hands are indispensable for priests of the inferior orders, when they bestow the benediction.'"

"An admirable subject!" cried the Jesuit.

"Admirable and dogmatic!" repeated the curate, who, about as strong as d'Artagnan with respect to Latin, carefully watched the Jesuit in order to keep step with him, and repeated his words like an echo.

As to d'Artagnan, he remained perfectly insensible to the enthusiasm of the two men in black.

"Yes, admirable! PRORSUS ADMIRABILE!" continued Aramis, "but which requires a profound study of both the Scriptures and the Fathers. Now, I have confessed to these learned ecclesiastics, and that in all humility, that the duties of mounting guard and the service of the king have caused me to neglect study a little. I should find myself, therefore, more at my ease, FACILUS NATANS, in a subject of my own choice, which would be to these hard theological questions what morals are to metaphysics in philosophy."

D'Artagnan began to be tired, and so did the curate.

"See what an exordium!" cried the Jesuit.

"Exordium," repeated the curate, for the sake of saying something. "QUEMADMODUM INTER COELORUM IMMNSITATEM."

Aramis cast a glance upon d'Artagnan to see what effect all this produced, and found his friend gaping enough to split his jaws.

"Let us speak French, my father," said he to the Jesuit, "Monsieur d'Artagnan will enjoy our conversation better."

"Yes," replied d'Artagnan, "I am fatigued with reading, and all this Latin confuses me."

"Certainly," replied the Jesuit, a little put out, while the curate, greatly delighted, turned upon d'Artagnan a look full of gratitude. "Well, let us see what is to be derived from this gloss. Moses, the servant of God-he was but a servant, please to understand-Moses blessed with the hands; he held out both his arms while the Hebrews beat their enemies, and then he blessed them with his two hands. Besides, what does the Gospel say? IMPONITE MANUS, and not MANUM–place the HANDS, not the HAND."

"Place the HANDS," repeated the curate, with a gesture.

"St. Peter, on the contrary, of whom the Popes are the successors," continued the Jesuit, "PORRIGE DIGITOS–present the fingers. Are you there, now?"

"CERTES," replied Aramis, in a pleased tone, "but the thing is subtle."

"The FINGERS," resumed the Jesuit, "St. Peter blessed with the FINGERS. The Pope, therefore blesses with the fingers. And with how many fingers does he bless? With THREE fingers, to be sure-one for the Father, one for the Son, and one for the Holy Ghost."

All crossed themselves. D'Artagnan thought it was proper to follow this example.

"The Pope is the successor of St. Peter, and represents the three divine powers; the rest–ORDINES INFERIORES–of the ecclesiastical hierarchy bless in the name of the holy archangels and angels. The most humble clerks such as our deacons and sacristans, bless with holy water sprinklers, which resemble an infinite number of blessing fingers. There is the subject simplified. ARGUMENTUM OMNI DENUDATUM ORNAMENTO. I could make of that subject two volumes the size of this," continued the Jesuit; and in his enthusiasm he struck a St. Chrysostom in folio, which made the table bend beneath its weight.

D'Artagnan trembled.

"CERTES," said Aramis, "I do justice to the beauties of this thesis, but at the same time I perceive it would be overwhelming for me. I had chosen this text-tell me, dear d'Artagnan, if it is not to your taste–'NON INUTILE EST DESIDERIUM IN OBLATIONE'; that is, 'A little regret is not unsuitable in an offering to the Lord.'"

"Stop there!" cried the Jesuit, "for that thesis touches closely upon heresy. There is a proposition almost like it in the

AUGUSTINUS of the heresiarch Jansenius, whose book will sooner or later be burned by the hands of the executioner. Take care, my young friend. You are inclining toward false doctrines, my young friend; you will be lost."

"You will be lost," said the curate, shaking his head sorrowfully.

"You approach that famous point of free will which is a mortal rock. You face the insinuations of the Pelagians and the semi-Pelagians."

"But, my Reverend–" replied Aramis, a little amazed by the shower of arguments that poured upon his head.

"How will you prove," continued the Jesuit, without allowing him time to speak, "that we ought to regret the world when we offer ourselves to God? Listen to this dilemma: God is God, and the world is the devil. To regret the world is to regret the devil; that is my conclusion."

"And that is mine also," said the curate.

"But, for heaven's sake-" resumed Aramis.

"DESIDERAS DIABOLUM, unhappy man!" cried the Jesuit.

"He regrets the devil! Ah, my young friend," added the curate, groaning, "do not regret the devil, I implore you!"

D'Artagnan felt himself bewildered. It seemed to him as though he were in a madhouse, and was becoming as mad as those he saw. He was, however, forced to hold his tongue from not comprehending half the language they employed.

"But listen to me, then," resumed Aramis with politeness mingled with a little impatience. "I do not say I regret; no, I will never pronounce that sentence, which would not be orthodox."

The Jesuit raised his hands toward heaven, and the curate did the same.

"No, but pray grant me that it is acting with an ill grace to offer to the Lord only that with which we are perfectly disgusted! Don't you think so, d'Artagnan?"

"I think so, indeed," cried he.

The Jesuit and the curate quite started from their chairs.

"This is the point of departure; it is a syllogism. The world is not wanting in attractions. I quit the world; then I make a sacrifice. Now, the Scripture says positively, 'Make a sacrifice unto the Lord.'"

"That is true," said his antagonists.

"And then," said Aramis, pinching his ear to make it red, as he rubbed his hands to make them white, "and then I made a certain RONDEAU upon it last year, which I showed to Monsieur Voiture, and that great man paid me a thousand compliments."

"A RONDEAU!" said the Jesuit, disdainfully.

"A RONDEAU!" said the curate, mechanically.

"Repeat it! Repeat it!" cried d'Artagnan, "it will make a little change."

"Not so, for it is religious," replied Aramis, "it is theology in verse."

"The devil!" said d'Artagnan.

"Here it is," said Aramis, with a little look of diffidence, which, however, was not exempt from a shade of hypocrisy:

"Vous qui pleurez un passe plein de charmes, Et qui trainez des jours infortunes, Tous vos malheurs se verront terminés, Quand a Dieu seul vous offrirez vos larmes, Vous qui pleurez!"

"You who weep for pleasures fled, While dragging on a life of care, All your woes will melt in air, If to God your tears are shed, You who weep!"

D'Artagnan and the curate appeared pleased. The Jesuit persisted in his opinion. "Beware of a profane taste in your theological style. What says Augustine on this subject: 'SEVERUS SIT CLERICORUM VERBO.'"

"Yes, let the sermon be clear," said the curate.

"Now," hastily interrupted the Jesuit, on seeing that his acolyte was going astray, "now your thesis would please the ladies; it would have the success of one of Monsieur Patru's pleadings."

"Please God!" cried Aramis, transported.

"There it is," cried the Jesuit, "the world still speaks within you in a loud voice, ALTISIMM VOCE. You follow the world, my young friend, and I tremble lest grace prove not efficacious."

"Be satisfied, my reverend father, I can answer for myself."

"Mundane presumption!"

"I know myself, Father; my resolution is irrevocable."

"Then you persist in continuing that thesis?"

"I feel myself called upon to treat that, and no other. I will see about the continuation of it, and tomorrow I hope you will be satisfied with the corrections I shall have made in consequence of your advice."

"Work slowly," said the curate, "we leave you in an excellent tone of mind."

"Yes, the ground is all sown," said the Jesuit, "and we have not to fear that one portion of the seed may have fallen upon stone, another upon the highway, or that the birds of heaven have eaten the rest, AVES COELI COMEDERUNT ILLAM."

"Plague stifle you and your Latin!" said d'Artagnan, who began to feel all his patience exhausted.

"Farewell, my son," said the curate, "till tomorrow."

"Till tomorrow, rash youth," said the Jesuit. "You promise to become one of the lights of the Church. Heaven grant that this light prove not a devouring fire!"

D'Artagnan, who for an hour past had been gnawing his nails with impatience, was beginning to attack the quick.

The two men in black rose, bowed to Aramis and d'Artagnan, and advanced toward the door. Bazin, who had been standing listening to all this controversy with a pious jubilation, sprang toward them, took the breviary of the curate and the missal of the Jesuit, and walked respectfully before them to clear their way.

Aramis conducted them to the foot of the stairs, and then immediately came up again to d'Artagnan, whose senses were still in a state of confusion.

When left alone, the two friends at first kept an embarrassed silence. It however became necessary for one of them to break it first, and as d'Artagnan appeared determined to leave that honour to his companion, Aramis said, "you see that I am returned to my fundamental ideas."

"Yes, efficacious grace has touched you, as that gentleman said just now."

"Oh, these plans of retreat have been formed for a long time. You have often heard me speak of them, have you not, my friend?"

"Yes, but I confess I always thought you jested."

"With such things! Oh, d'Artagnan!"

"The devil! Why, people jest with death."

"And people are wrong, d'Artagnan; for death is the door which leads to perdition or to salvation."

"Granted, but if you please, let us not theologise, Aramis. You must have had enough for today. As for me, I have almost forgotten the little Latin I have ever known. Then I confess to you that I have eaten nothing since ten o'clock this morning, and I am devilish hungry."

"We will dine directly, my friend; only you must please to remember that this is Friday. Now, on such a day I can neither eat flesh nor see it eaten. If you can be satisfied with my dinner-it consists of cooked tetragones and fruits."

"What do you mean by tetragones?" asked d'Artagnan, uneasily.

"I mean spinach," replied Aramis, "but on your account I will add some eggs, and that is a serious infraction of the rule-for eggs are meat, since they engender chickens."

"This feast is not very succulent, but never mind, I will put up with it for the sake of remaining with you."

"I am grateful to you for the sacrifice," said Aramis, "but if your body be not greatly benefited by it, be assured your soul will."

"And so, Aramis, you are decidedly going into the Church? What will our two friends say? What will Monsieur de Tréville say? They will treat you as a deserter, I warn you."

"I do not enter the Church; I re-enter it. I deserted the Church for the world, for you know that I forced myself when I became a Musketeer."

"I? I know nothing about it."

"You don't know I quit the seminary?"

"Not at all."

"This is my story, then. Besides, the Scriptures say, 'Confess yourselves to one another,' and I confess to you, d'Artagnan."

"And I give you absolution beforehand. You see I am a good sort of a man."

"Do not jest about holy things, my friend."

"Go on, then, I listen."

"I had been at the seminary from nine years old; in three days I should have been twenty. I was about to become an abbé, and all was arranged. One evening I went, according to custom, to a house which I frequented with much pleasure: when one is young, what can be expected?–one is weak. An officer who saw me, with a jealous eye, reading the *LIVES OF THE SAINTS* to the mistress of the house, entered suddenly and without being announced. That evening I had translated an episode of Judith, and had just communicated my verses to the lady, who gave me all sorts of compliments, and leaning on my shoulder, was reading them a second time with me. Her pose, which I must admit was rather free, wounded this officer. He said nothing, but when I went out he followed, and quickly came up with me. 'Monsieur the Abbé,' said he, 'do you like blows with a cane?' 'I cannot say, Monsieur,' answered I; 'no one has ever dared to give me any.' 'Well, listen to me, then, Monsieur the Abbé! If you venture again into the house in which I have met you this evening, I will dare it myself.' I really think I must have been frightened. I became very pale; I felt my legs fail me; I sought for a reply, but could find none-I was silent. The officer waited for his reply, and seeing it so long coming, he burst into a laugh, turned upon his heel, and re-entered the house. I returned to the seminary.

"I am a gentleman born, and my blood is warm, as you may have remarked, my dear d'Artagnan. The insult was terrible, and although unknown to the rest of the world, I felt it live and fester at the bottom of my heart. I informed my superiors that I did not feel myself sufficiently prepared for ordination, and at my request the ceremony was postponed for a year. I sought out the best fencing master in Paris, I made an agreement with him to take a lesson every day, and every day for a year I took that lesson. Then, on the anniversary of the day on which I had been insulted, I hung my cassock on a peg, assumed the costume of a cavalier, and went to a ball given by a lady friend of mine and to which I knew my man was invited. It was in the Rue des France-Bourgeois, close to La Force. As I expected, my officer was there. I went up to him as he was singing a love ditty and looking tenderly at a lady, and interrupted him exactly in the middle of the second couplet. 'Monsieur,' said I, 'does it still displease you that I should frequent a certain house of La Rue Payenne? And would you still cane me if I took it into my head to disobey you? The officer looked at me with astonishment, and then said, 'What is your business with me, Monsieur? I do not know you.' 'I am,' said I, 'the little abbé who reads *LIVES OF THE SAINTS*, and translates Judith into verse.' 'Ah, ah! I recollect now,' said the officer, in a jeering tone; 'well, what do you want with me?' 'I want you to spare time to take a walk with me.' 'Tomorrow morning, if you like, with the greatest pleasure.' 'No, not tomorrow morning, if you please, but immediately.' 'If you absolutely insist.' 'I do insist upon it.' 'Come, then. Ladies,' said the officer, 'do not disturb yourselves;

allow me time just to kill this gentleman, and I will return and finish the last couplet.'

"We went out. I took him to the Rue Payenne, to exactly the same spot where, a year before, at the very same hour, he had paid me the compliment I have related to you. It was a superb moonlight night. We immediately drew, and at the first pass I laid him stark dead."

"The devil!" cried d'Artagnan.

"Now," continued Aramis, "as the ladies did not see the singer come back, and as he was found in the Rue Payenne with a great sword wound through his body, it was supposed that I had accommodated him thus; and the matter created some scandal which obliged me to renounce the cassock for a time. Athos, whose acquaintance I made about that period, and Porthos, who had in addition to my lessons taught me some effective tricks of fence, prevailed upon me to solicit the uniform of a Musketeer. The king entertained great regard for my father, who had fallen at the siege of Arras, and the uniform was granted. You may understand that the moment has come for me to re-enter the bosom of the Church."

"And why today, rather than yesterday or tomorrow? What has happened to you today, to raise all these melancholy ideas?"

"This wound, my dear d'Artagnan, has been a warning to me from heaven."

"This wound? Bah, it is now nearly healed, and I am sure it is not that which gives you the most pain."

"What, then?" said Aramis, blushing.

"You have one at heart, Aramis, one deeper and more painful–a wound made by a woman."

The eye of Aramis kindled in spite of himself.

"Ah," said he, dissembling his emotion under a feigned carelessness, "do not talk of such things, and suffer love pains? VANITAS VANITATUM! According to your idea, then, my brain is turned. And for whom–for some GRISETTE, some chambermaid with whom I have trifled in some garrison? Fie!"

"Pardon, my dear Aramis, but I thought you carried your eyes higher."

"Higher? And who am I, to nourish such ambition? A poor Musketeer, a beggar, an unknown–who hates slavery, and finds himself ill-placed in the world."

"Aramis, Aramis!" cried d'Artagnan, looking at his friend with an air of doubt.

"Dust I am, and to dust I return. Life is full of humiliations and sorrows," continued he, becoming still more melancholy, "all the ties which attach him to life break in the hand of man, particularly the golden ties. Oh, my dear d'Artagnan," resumed Aramis, giving to his voice a slight tone of bitterness, "trust me! Conceal your wounds when you have any; silence is the last joy of the unhappy. Beware of giving anyone the clue to your griefs; the curious suck our tears as flies suck the blood of a wounded hart."

"Alas, my dear Aramis," said d'Artagnan, in his turn heaving a profound sigh, "that is my story you are relating!"

"How?"

"Yes; a woman whom I love, whom I adore, has just been torn from me by force. I do not know where she is or whither they have conducted her. She is perhaps a prisoner; she is perhaps dead!"

"Yes, but you have at least this consolation, that you can say to yourself she has not quit you voluntarily, that if you learn no news of her, it is because all communication with you is interdicted; while I–"

"Well?"

"Nothing," replied Aramis, "nothing."

"So you renounce the world, then, forever; that is a settled thing–a resolution registered!"

"Forever! You are my friend today; tomorrow you will be no more to me than a shadow, or rather, even, you will no longer exist. As for the world, it is a sepulcher and nothing else."

"The devil! All this is very sad which you tell me."

"What will you? My vocation commands me; it carries me away."

D'Artagnan smiled, but made no answer.

Aramis continued, "And yet, while I do belong to the earth, I wish to speak of you–of our friends."

"And on my part," said d'Artagnan, "I wished to speak of you, but I find you so completely detached from everything! To love you cry, 'Fie! Friends are shadows! The world is a sepulcher!'"

"Alas, you will find it so yourself," said Aramis, with a sigh.

"Well, then, let us say no more about it," said d'Artagnan, "and let us burn this letter, which, no doubt, announces to you some fresh infidelity of your GRISETTE or your chambermaid."

"What letter?" cried Aramis, eagerly.

"A letter which was sent to your abode in your absence, and which was given to me for you."

"But from whom is that letter?"

"Oh, from some heartbroken waiting woman, some desponding GRISETTE; from Madame de Chevreuse's chambermaid, perhaps, who was obliged to return to Tours with her mistress, and who, in order to appear smart and attractive, stole some perfumed paper, and sealed her letter with a duchess's coronet."

"What do you say?"

"Hold! I must have lost it," said the young man maliciously, pretending to search for it. "But fortunately the world is a sepulcher; the men, and consequently the women, are but shadows, and love is a sentiment to which you cry, 'Fie! Fie!'"

"D'Artagnan, d'Artagnan," cried Aramis, "you are killing me!"

"Well, here it is at last!" said d'Artagnan, as he drew the letter from his pocket.

Aramis made a bound, seized the letter, read it, or rather devoured it, his countenance radiant.

"This same waiting maid seems to have an agreeable style," said the messenger, carelessly.

"Thanks, d'Artagnan, thanks!" cried Aramis, almost in a state of delirium. "She was forced to return to Tours; she is not faithless; she still loves me! Come, my friend, come, let me embrace you. Happiness almost stifles me!"

The two friends began to dance around the venerable St. Chrysostom, kicking about famously the sheets of the thesis, which had fallen on the floor.

At that moment Bazin entered with the spinach and the omelette.

"Be off, you wretch!" cried Aramis, throwing his skullcap in his face. "Return whence you came; take back those horrible vegetables, and that poor kickshaw! Order a larded hare, a fat capon, mutton leg dressed with garlic, and four bottles of old Burgundy."

Bazin, who looked at his master, without comprehending the cause of this change, in a melancholy manner, allowed the omelette to slip into the spinach, and the spinach onto the floor.

"Now this is the moment to consecrate your existence to the King of kings," said d'Artagnan, "if you persist in offering him a civility. NON INUTILE DESIDERIUM OBLATIONE."

"Go to the devil with your Latin. Let us drink, my dear d'Artagnan, MORBLEU! Let us drink while the wine is fresh! Let us drink heartily, and while we do so, tell me a little of what is going on in the world yonder."

Chapter 27

The Wife Of Athos

"We have now to search for Athos," said d'Artagnan to the vivacious Aramis, when he had informed him of all that had passed since their departure from the capital, and an excellent dinner had made one of them forget his thesis and the other his fatigue.

"Do you think, then, that any harm can have happened to him?" asked Aramis. "Athos is so cool, so brave, and handles his sword so skillfully."

"No doubt. Nobody has a higher opinion of the courage and skill of Athos than I have, but I like better to hear my sword clang against lances than against staves. I fear lest Athos should have been beaten down by serving men. Those fellows strike hard, and don't leave off in a hurry. This is why I wish to set out again as soon as possible."

"I will try to accompany you," said Aramis, "though I scarcely feel in a condition to mount on horseback. Yesterday I undertook to employ that cord which you see hanging against the wall, but pain prevented my continuing the pious exercise."

"That's the first time I ever heard of anybody trying to cure gunshot wounds with cat-o'-nine-tails, but you were ill, and illness renders the head weak, therefore you may be excused."

"When do you mean to set out?"

"Tomorrow at daybreak. Sleep as soundly as you can tonight, and tomorrow, if you can, we will take our departure together."

"Till tomorrow, then," said Aramis, "for iron-nerved as you are, you must need repose."

The next morning, when d'Artagnan entered Aramis's chamber, he found him at the window.

"What are you looking at?" asked d'Artagnan.

"My faith! I am admiring three magnificent horses which the stable boys are leading about. It would be a pleasure worthy of a prince to travel upon such horses."

"Well, my dear Aramis, you may enjoy that pleasure, for one of those three horses is yours."

"Ah, bah! Which?"

"Whichever of the three you like, I have no preference."

"And the rich caparison, is that mine, too?"

"Without doubt."

"You laugh, d'Artagnan."

"No, I have left off laughing, now that you speak French."

"What, those rich holsters, that velvet housing, that saddle studded with silver-are they all for me?"

"For you and nobody else, as the horse which paws the ground is mine, and the other horse, which is caracoling, belongs to Athos."

"PESTE! They are three superb animals!"

"I am glad they please you."

"Why, it must have been the king who made you such a present."

"Certainly it was not the cardinal, but don't trouble yourself whence they come, think only that one of the three is your property."

"I choose that which the red-headed boy is leading."

"It is yours!"

"Good heaven! That is enough to drive away all my pains; I could mount him with thirty balls in my body. On my soul, handsome stirrups! HOLA, Bazin, come here this minute."

Bazin appeared on the threshold, dull and spiritless.

"That last order is useless," interrupted d'Artagnan, "there are loaded pistols in your holsters."

Bazin sighed.

"Come, Monsieur Bazin, make yourself easy," said d'Artagnan, "people of all conditions gain the kingdom of heaven."

"Monsieur was already such a good theologian," said Bazin, almost weeping, "he might have become a bishop, and perhaps a cardinal."

"Well, but my poor Bazin, reflect a little. Of what use is it to be a churchman, pray? You do not avoid going to war by that means; you see, the cardinal is about to make the next campaign, helm on head and partisan in hand. And Monsieur de Nogaret de la Valette, what do you say of him? He is a cardinal likewise. Ask his lackey how often he has had to prepare lint of him."

"Alas!" sighed Bazin. "I know it, Monsieur; everything is turned topsy-turvy in the world nowadays."

While this dialogue was going on, the two young men and the poor lackey descended.

"Hold my stirrup, Bazin," cried Aramis; and Aramis sprang into the saddle with his usual grace and agility, but after a few vaults and curvets of the noble animal his rider felt his pains come on so insupportably that he turned pale and became unsteady in his seat. D'Artagnan, who, foreseeing such an event, had kept his eye on him, sprang toward him, caught him in his arms, and assisted him to his chamber.

"That's all right, my dear Aramis, take care of yourself," said he, "I will go alone in search of Athos."

"You are a man of brass," replied Aramis.

"No, I have good luck, that is all. But how do you mean to pass your time till I come back? No more theses, no more glosses upon the fingers or upon benedictions, hey?"

Aramis smiled. "I will make verses," said he.

"Yes, I dare say; verses perfumed with the odor of the billet from the attendant of Madame de Chevreuse. Teach Bazin prosody; that will console him. As to the horse, ride him a little every day, and that will accustom you to his maneuvers."

"Oh, make yourself easy on that head," replied Aramis. "You will find me ready to follow you."

They took leave of each other, and in ten minutes, after having commended his friend to the cares of the hostess and Bazin, d'Artagnan was trotting along in the direction of Amiens.

How was he going to find Athos? Should he find him at all? The position in which he had left him was critical. He probably had succumbed. This idea, while darkening his brow, drew several sighs from him, and caused him to formulate to himself a few vows of vengeance. Of all his friends, Athos was the eldest, and the least resembling him in appearance, in his tastes and sympathies.

Yet he entertained a marked preference for this gentleman. The noble and distinguished air of Athos, those flashes of greatness which from time to time broke out from the shade in which he voluntarily kept himself, that unalterable equality of temper which made him the most pleasant companion in the world, that forced and cynical gaiety, that bravery which might have been termed blind if it had not been the result of the rarest coolness–such qualities attracted more than the esteem, more than the friendship of d'Artagnan; they attracted his admiration.

Indeed, when placed beside M. de Tréville, the elegant and noble courtier, Athos in his most cheerful days might advantageously sustain a comparison. He was of middle height, but his person was so admirably shaped and so well proportioned that more than once in his struggles with Porthos he had overcome the giant whose physical strength was proverbial among the Musketeers. His head, with piercing eyes, a straight nose, a chin cut like that of Brutus, had altogether an indefinable character of grandeur and grace. His hands, of which he took little care, were the despair of Aramis, who cultivated his with almond paste and perfumed oil. The sound of his voice was at once penetrating and melodious; and then, that which was inconceivable in Athos, who was always retiring, was that delicate knowledge of the world and of the usages of the most brilliant society–those manners of a high degree which appeared, as if unconsciously to himself, in his least actions.

If a repast were on foot, Athos presided over it better than any other, placing every guest exactly in the rank which his ancestors had earned for him or that he had made for himself. If a question in heraldry were started, Athos knew all the noble families of the kingdom, their genealogy, their alliances, their coats of arms, and the origin of them. Etiquette had no minutiae unknown to him. He knew what were the rights of the great land owners. He was profoundly versed in hunting and falconry, and had one day when conversing on this great art astonished even Louis XIII himself, who took a pride in being considered a past master therein.

Like all the great nobles of that period, Athos rode and fenced to perfection. But still further, his education had been so little neglected, even with respect to scholastic studies, so rare at this time among gentlemen, that he smiled at the scraps of Latin which Aramis sported and which Porthos pretended to understand. Two or three times, even, to the great astonishment of his friends, he had, when Aramis allowed some rudimental error to escape him, replaced a verb in its right tense and a noun in its case. Besides, his probity was irreproachable, in an age in which soldiers compromised so easily with their religion and their consciences, lovers with the rigorous delicacy of our era, and the poor with God's Seventh Commandment. This Athos, then, was a very extraordinary man.

And yet this nature so distinguished, this creature so beautiful, this essence so fine, was seen to turn insensibly toward material life, as old men turn toward physical and moral imbecility. Athos, in his hours of gloom–and these hours were frequent–was extinguished as to the whole of the luminous portion of him, and his brilliant side disappeared as into profound darkness.

Then the demigod vanished; he remained scarcely a man. His head hanging down, his eye dull, his speech slow and painful, Athos would look for hours together at his bottle, his glass, or at Grimaud, who, accustomed to obey him by signs, read in the faint glance of his master his least desire, and satisfied it immediately. If the four friends were assembled at one of these moments, a word, thrown forth occasionally with a violent effort, was the share Athos furnished to the conversation. In exchange for his silence Athos drank enough for four, and without appearing to be otherwise affected by wine than by a more marked constriction of the brow and by a deeper sadness.

D'Artagnan, whose inquiring disposition we are acquainted with, had not–whatever interest he had in satisfying his curiosity on this subject–been able to assign any cause for these fits, or for the periods of their recurrence. Athos never received any letters; Athos never had concerns which all his friends did not know.

It could not be said that it was wine which produced this sadness; for in truth he only drank to combat this sadness, which wine however, as we have said, rendered still darker. This excess of bilious humor could not be attributed to play; for unlike Porthos, who accompanied the variations of chance with songs or oaths, Athos when he won remained as unmoved as when he lost. He had been known, in the circle of the Musketeers, to win in one night three thousand pistoles; to lose them even to the gold-embroidered belt for gala days, win all this again with the addition of a hundred louis, without his beautiful eyebrow being heightened or lowered half a line, without his hands losing their pearly hue, without his conversation, which was cheerful that evening, ceasing to be calm and agreeable.

Neither was it, as with our neighbours, the English, an atmospheric influence which darkened his countenance; for the sadness generally became more intense toward the fine season of the year. June and July were the terrible months with Athos.

For the present he had no anxiety. He shrugged his shoulders when people spoke of the future. His secret, then, was in the past, as had often been vaguely said to d'Artagnan.

This mysterious shade, spread over his whole person, rendered still more interesting the man whose eyes or mouth, even in the most complete intoxication, had never revealed anything, however skillfully questions had been put to him.

"Well," thought d'Artagnan, "poor Athos is perhaps at this moment dead, and dead by my fault–for it was I who dragged him into this affair, of which he did not know the origin, of which he is ignorant of the result, and from which he can derive no advantage."

"Without reckoning, Monsieur," added Planchet to his master's audibly expressed reflections, "that we perhaps owe our lives to him. Do you remember how he cried, 'On, d'Artagnan, on, I am taken'? And when he had discharged his two pistols, what a terrible noise he made with his sword! One might have said that twenty men, or rather twenty mad devils, were fighting."

These words redoubled the eagerness of d'Artagnan, who urged his horse, though he stood in need of no incitement, and they proceeded at a rapid pace. About eleven o'clock in the morning they perceived Amiens, and at half past eleven they were at the door of the cursed inn.

D'Artagnan had often meditated against the perfidious host one of those hearty vengeances which offer consolation while they are hoped for. He entered the hostelry with his hat pulled over his eyes, his left hand on the pommel of the sword, and cracking his whip with his right hand.

"Do you remember me?" said he to the host, who advanced to greet him.

"I have not that honour, Monseigneur," replied the latter, his eyes dazzled by the brilliant style in which d'Artagnan traveled.

"What, you don't know me?"

"No, Monseigneur."

"Well, two words will refresh your memory. What have you done with that gentleman against whom you had the audacity, about twelve days ago, to make an accusation of passing false money?"

The host became as pale as death; for d'Artagnan had assumed a threatening attitude, and Planchet modeled himself after his master.

"Ah, Monseigneur, do not mention it!" cried the host, in the most pitiable voice imaginable. "Ah, Monseigneur, how dearly have I paid for that fault, unhappy wretch as I am!"

"That gentleman, I say, what has become of him?"

"Deign to listen to me, Monseigneur, and be merciful! Sit down, in mercy!"

D'Artagnan, mute with anger and anxiety, took a seat in the threatening attitude of a judge. Planchet glared fiercely over the back of his armchair.

"Here is the story, Monseigneur," resumed the trembling host, "for I now recollect you. It was you who rode off at the moment I had that unfortunate difference with the gentleman you speak of."

"Yes, it was I; so you may plainly perceive that you have no mercy to expect if you do not tell me the whole truth."

"Condescend to listen to me, and you shall know all."

"I listen."

"I had been warned by the authorities that a celebrated coiner of bad money would arrive at my inn, with several of his companions, all disguised as Guards or Musketeers. Monseigneur, I was furnished with a description of your horses, your lackeys, your countenances–nothing was omitted."

"Go on, go on!" said d'Artagnan, who quickly understood whence such an exact description had come.

"I took then, in conformity with the orders of the authorities, who sent me a reinforcement of six men, such measures as I thought necessary to get possession of the persons of the pretended coiners."

"Again!" said d'Artagnan, whose ears chafed terribly under the repetition of this word COINERS.

"Pardon me, Monseigneur, for saying such things, but they form my excuse. The authorities had terrified me, and you know that an innkeeper must keep on good terms with the authorities."

"But once again, that gentleman–where is he? What has become of him? Is he dead? Is he living?"

"Patience, Monseigneur, we are coming to it. There happened then that which you know, and of which your precipitate departure," added the host, with an acuteness that did not escape d'Artagnan, "appeared to authorise the issue. That gentleman, your friend, defended himself desperately. His lackey, who, by an unforeseen piece of ill luck, had quarreled with the officers, disguised as stable lads–"

"Miserable scoundrel!" cried d'Artagnan, "you were all in the plot, then! And I really don't know what prevents me from exterminating you all."

"Alas, Monseigneur, we were not in the plot, as you will soon see. Monsieur your friend (pardon for not calling him by the honourable name which no doubt he bears, but we do not know that name), Monsieur your friend, having disabled two men with his pistols, retreated fighting with his sword, with which he disabled one of my men, and stunned me with a blow of the flat side of it."

"You villain, will you finish?" cried d'Artagnan, "Athos–what has become of Athos?"

"While fighting and retreating, as I have told Monseigneur, he found the door of the cellar stairs behind him, and as the door was open, he took out the key, and barricaded himself inside. As we were sure of finding him there, we left him alone."

"Yes," said d'Artagnan, "you did not really wish to kill; you only wished to imprison him."

"Good God! To imprison him, Monseigneur? Why, he imprisoned himself, I swear to you he did. In the first place he had made rough work of it; one man was killed on the spot, and two others were severely wounded. The dead man and the two wounded were carried off by their comrades, and I have heard nothing of either of them since. As for myself, as soon as I recovered my senses I went to Monsieur the Governor, to whom I related all that had passed, and asked, what I should do with my prisoner. Monsieur the Governor was all astonishment. He told me he knew nothing about the matter, that the orders I had received did not come from him, and that if I had the audacity to mention his name as being concerned in this disturbance he would have me hanged. It appears that I had made a mistake, Monsieur, that I had arrested the wrong person, and that he whom I ought to have arrested had escaped."

"But Athos!" cried d'Artagnan, whose impatience was increased by the disregard of the authorities, "Athos, where is he?"

"As I was anxious to repair the wrongs I had done the prisoner," resumed the innkeeper, "I took my way straight to the cellar in order to set him at liberty. Ah, Monsieur, he was no longer a man, he was a devil! To my offer of liberty, he replied that it was nothing but a snare, and that before he came out he intended to impose his own conditions. I told him very humbly–for I could not conceal from myself the scrape I had got into by laying hands on one of his Majesty's Musketeers–I told him I was quite ready to submit to his conditions.

"'In the first place,' said he, 'I wish my lackey placed with me, fully armed.' We hastened to obey this order; for you will please to understand, Monsieur, we were disposed to do everything your friend could desire. Monsieur Grimaud (he told us his name, although he does not talk much)–Monsieur Grimaud, then, went down to the cellar, wounded as he was; then his master, having admitted him, barricaded the door afresh, and ordered us to remain quietly in our own bar."

"But where is Athos now?" cried d'Artagnan. "Where is Athos?"

"In the cellar, Monsieur."

"What, you scoundrel! Have you kept him in the cellar all this time?"

"Merciful heaven! No, Monsieur! We keep him in the cellar! You do not know what he is about in the cellar. Ah! If you could but persuade him to come out, Monsieur, I should owe you the gratitude of my whole life; I should adore you as my patron saint!"

"Then he is there? I shall find him there?"

"Without doubt you will, Monsieur; he persists in remaining there. We every day pass through the air hole some bread at the end of a fork, and some meat when he asks for it, but alas! It is not of bread and meat of which he makes the greatest consumption. I once endeavoured to go down with two of my servants, but he flew into terrible rage. I heard the noise he made in loading his pistols, and his servant in loading his musketoon. Then, when we asked them what were their intentions, the master replied that he had forty charges to fire, and that he and his lackey would fire to the last one before he would allow a single soul of us to set foot in the cellar. Upon this I went and complained to the governor, who replied that I only had what I deserved, and that it would teach me to insult honourable gentlemen who took up their abode in my house."

"So that since that time–" replied d'Artagnan, totally unable to refrain from laughing at the pitiable face of the host.

"So from that time, Monsieur," continued the latter, "we have led the most miserable life imaginable; for you must know, Monsieur, that all our provisions are in the cellar. There is our wine in bottles, and our wine in casks; the beer, the oil, and the spices, the bacon, and sausages. And as we are prevented from going down there, we are forced to refuse food and drink to the travellers who come to the house; so that our hostelry is daily going to ruin. If your friend remains another week in my cellar I shall be a ruined man."

"And not more than justice, either, you ass! Could you not perceive by our appearance that we were people of quality, and not coiners–say?"

"Yes, Monsieur, you are right," said the host. "But, hark, hark! There he is!"

"Somebody has disturbed him, without doubt," said d'Artagnan.

"But he must be disturbed," cried the host, "Here are two English gentlemen just arrived."

"Well?"

"Well, the English like good wine, as you may know, Monsieur; these have asked for the best. My wife has perhaps requested permission of Monsieur Athos to go into the cellar to satisfy these gentlemen; and he, as usual, has refused. Ah, good heaven! There is the hullabaloo louder than ever!"

D'Artagnan, in fact, heard a great noise on the side next the cellar. He rose, and preceded by the host wringing his hands, and followed by Planchet with his musketoon ready for use, he approached the scene of action.

The two gentlemen were exasperated; they had had a long ride, and were dying with hunger and thirst.

"But this is tyranny!" cried one of them, in very good French, though with a foreign accent, "that this madman will not allow these good people access to their own wine! Nonsense, let us break open the door, and if he is too far gone in his madness, well, we will kill him!"

"Softly, gentlemen!" said d'Artagnan, drawing his pistols from his belt, "you will kill nobody, if you please!"

"Good, good!" cried the calm voice of Athos, from the other side of the door, "let them just come in, these devourers of little children, and we shall see!"

Brave as they appeared to be, the two English gentlemen looked at each other hesitatingly. One might have thought there was in that cellar one of those famished ogres–the gigantic heroes of popular legends, into whose cavern nobody could force their way with impunity.

There was a moment of silence, but at length the two Englishmen felt ashamed to draw back, and the angrier one descended the five or six steps which led to the cellar, and gave a kick against the door enough to split a wall.

"Planchet," said d'Artagnan, cocking his pistols, "I will take charge of the one at the top; you look to the one below. Ah, gentlemen, you want battle; and you shall have it."

"Good God!" cried the hollow voice of Athos, "I can hear d'Artagnan, I think."

"Yes," cried d'Artagnan, raising his voice in turn, "I am here, my friend."

"Ah, good, then," replied Athos, "we will teach them, these door breakers!"

The gentlemen had drawn their swords, but they found themselves taken between two fires. They still hesitated an instant; but, as before, pride prevailed, and a second kick split the door from bottom to top.

"Stand on one side, d'Artagnan, stand on one side," cried Athos. "I am going to fire!"

"Gentlemen," exclaimed d'Artagnan, whom reflection never abandoned, "gentlemen, think of what you are about. Patience, Athos! You are running your heads into a very silly affair; you will be riddled. My lackey and I will have three shots at you, and you will get as many from the cellar. You will then have our swords, with which, I can assure you, my friend and I can play tolerably well. Let me conduct your business and my own. You shall soon have something to drink; I give you my word."

"If there is any left," grumbled the jeering voice of Athos.

The host felt a cold sweat creep down his back.

"How! 'If there is any left!'" murmured he.

"What the devil! There must be plenty left," replied d'Artagnan. "Be satisfied of that; these two cannot have drunk all the cellar. Gentlemen, return your swords to their scabbards."

"Well, provided you replace your pistols in your belt."

"Willingly."

And d'Artagnan set the example. Then, turning toward Planchet, he made him a sign to uncock his musketoon.

The Englishmen, convinced of these peaceful proceedings, sheathed their swords grumblingly. The history of Athos's imprisonment was then related to them; and as they were really gentlemen, they pronounced the host in the wrong.

"Now, gentlemen," said d'Artagnan, "go up to your room again; and in ten minutes, I will answer for it, you shall have all you desire."

The Englishmen bowed and went upstairs.

"Now I am alone, my dear Athos," said d'Artagnan, "open the door, I beg of you."

"Instantly," said Athos.

Then was heard a great noise of fagots being removed and of the groaning of posts; these were the counterscarps and bastions of Athos, which the besieged himself demolished.

An instant after, the broken door was removed, and the pale face of Athos appeared, who with a rapid glance took a survey of the surroundings.

D'Artagnan threw himself on his neck and embraced him tenderly. He then tried to draw him from his moist abode, but to his surprise he perceived that Athos staggered.

"You are wounded," said he.

"I! Not at all. I am dead drunk, that's all, and never did a man more strongly set about getting so. By the Lord, my good host! I must at least have drunk for my part a hundred and fifty bottles."

"Mercy!" cried the host, "if the lackey has drunk only half as much as the master, I am a ruined man."

"Grimaud is a well-bred lackey. He would never think of faring in the same manner as his master; he only drank from the cask. Hark! I don't think he put the faucet in again. Do you hear it? It is running now."

D'Artagnan burst into a laugh which changed the shiver of the host into a burning fever.

In the meantime, Grimaud appeared in his turn behind his master, with the musketoon on his shoulder, and his head shaking. Like one of those drunken satyrs in the pictures of Rubens. He was moistened before and behind with a greasy liquid which the host recognised as his best olive oil.

The four crossed the public room and proceeded to take possession of the best apartment in the house, which d'Artagnan occupied with authority.

In the meantime the host and his wife hurried down with lamps into the cellar, which had so long been interdicted to them and where a frightful spectacle awaited them.

Beyond the fortifications through which Athos had made a breach in order to get out, and which were composed of fagots, planks, and empty casks, heaped up according to all the rules of the strategic art, they found, swimming in puddles of oil and wine, the bones and fragments of all the hams they had eaten; while a heap of broken bottles filled the whole left-hand corner of the cellar, and a tun, the cock of which was left running, was yielding, by this means, the last drop of its blood. "The image of devastation and death," as the ancient poet says, "reigned as over a field of battle."

Of fifty large sausages, suspended from the joists, scarcely ten remained.

Then the lamentations of the host and hostess pierced the vault of the cellar. D'Artagnan himself was moved by them. Athos did not even turn his head.

To grief succeeded rage. The host armed himself with a spit, and rushed into the chamber occupied by the two friends.

"Some wine!" said Athos, on perceiving the host.

"Some wine!" cried the stupefied host, "some wine? Why you have drunk more than a hundred pistoles' worth! I am a ruined man, lost, destroyed!"

"Bah," said Athos, "we were always dry."

"If you had been contented with drinking, well and good, but you have broken all the bottles."

"You pushed me upon a heap which rolled down. That was your fault."

"All my oil is lost!"

"Oil is a sovereign balm for wounds; and my poor Grimaud here was obliged to dress those you had inflicted on him."

"All my sausages are gnawed!"

"There is an enormous quantity of rats in that cellar."

"You shall pay me for all this," cried the exasperated host.

"Triple ass!" said Athos, rising, but he sank down again immediately. He had tried his strength to the utmost. D'Artagnan came to his relief with his whip in his hand.

The host drew back and burst into tears.

"This will teach you," said d'Artagnan, "to treat the guests God sends you in a more courteous fashion."

"God? Say the devil!"

"My dear friend," said d'Artagnan, "if you annoy us in this manner we will all four go and shut ourselves up in your cellar, and we will see if the mischief is as great as you say."

"Oh, gentlemen," said the host, "I have been wrong. I confess it, but pardon to every sin! You are gentlemen, and I am a poor innkeeper. You will have pity on me."

"Ah, if you speak in that way," said Athos, "you will break my heart, and the tears will flow from my eyes as the wine flowed from the cask. We are not such devils as we appear to be. Come hither, and let us talk."

The host approached with hesitation.

"Come hither, I say, and don't be afraid," continued Athos. "At the very moment when I was about to pay you, I had placed my purse on the table."

"Yes, Monsieur."

"That purse contained sixty pistoles; where is it?"

"Deposited with the justice; they said it was bad money."

"Very well; get me my purse back and keep the sixty pistoles."

"But Monseigneur knows very well that justice never lets go that which it once lays hold of. If it were bad money, there might be some hopes, but unfortunately, those were all good pieces."

"Manage the matter as well as you can, my good man; it does not concern me, the more so as I have not a livre left."

"Come," said d'Artagnan, "let us inquire further. Athos's horse, where is that?"

"In the stable."

"How much is it worth?"

"Fifty pistoles at most."

"It's worth eighty. Take it, and there ends the matter."

"What," cried Athos, "are you selling my horse–my Bajazet? And pray upon what shall I make my campaign; upon Grimaud?"

"I have brought you another," said d'Artagnan.

"Another?"

"And a magnificent one!" cried the host.

"Well, since there is another finer and younger, why, you may take the old one; and let us drink."

"What?" asked the host, quite cheerful again.

"Some of that at the bottom, near the laths. There are twenty-five bottles of it left; all the rest were broken by my fall. Bring six of them."

"Why, this man is a cask!" said the host, aside. "If he only remains here a fortnight, and pays for what he drinks, I shall soon re-establish my business."

"And don't forget," said d'Artagnan, "to bring up four bottles of the same sort for the two English gentlemen."

"And now," said Athos, "while they bring the wine, tell me, d'Artagnan, what has become of the others, come!"

D'Artagnan related how he had found Porthos in bed with a strained knee, and Aramis at a table between two theologians. As he finished, the host entered with the wine ordered and a ham which, fortunately for him, had been left out of the cellar.

"That's well!" said Athos, filling his glass and that of his friend, "here's to Porthos and Aramis! But you, d'Artagnan, what is the matter with you, and what has happened to you personally? You have a sad air."

"Alas," said d'Artagnan, "it is because I am the most unfortunate."

"Tell me."

"Presently," said d'Artagnan.

"Presently! And why presently? Because you think I am drunk? D'Artagnan, remember this! My ideas are never so clear as when I have had plenty of wine. Speak, then, I am all ears."

D'Artagnan related his adventure with Mme. Bonacieux. Athos listened to him without a frown; and when he had finished, said, "Trifles, only trifles!" That was his favourite word.

"You always say TRIFLES, my dear Athos!" said d'Artagnan, "and that come very ill from you, who have never loved."

The drink-deadened eye of Athos flashed out, but only for a moment; it became as dull and vacant as before.

"That's true," said he, quietly, "for my part I have never loved."

"Acknowledge, then, you stony heart," said d'Artagnan, "that you are wrong to be so hard upon us tender hearts."

"Tender hearts! Pierced hearts!" said Athos.

"What do you say?"

"I say that love is a lottery in which he who wins, wins death! You are very fortunate to have lost, believe me, my dear d'Artagnan. And if I have any counsel to give, it is, always lose!"

"She seemed to love me so!"

"She SEEMED, did she?"

"Oh, she DID love me!"

"You child, why, there is not a man who has not believed, as you do, that his mistress loved him, and there lives not a man who has not been deceived by his mistress."

"Except you, Athos, who never had one."

"That's true," said Athos, after a moment's silence, "that's true! I never had one! Let us drink!"

"But then, philosopher that you are," said d'Artagnan, "instruct me, support me. I stand in need of being taught and consoled."

"Consoled for what?"

"For my misfortune."

"Your misfortune is laughable," said Athos, shrugging his shoulders, "I should like to know what you would say if I were to relate to you a real tale of love!"

"Which has happened to you?"

"Or one of my friends, what matters?"

"Tell it, Athos, tell it."

"Better if I drink."

"Drink and relate, then."

"Not a bad idea!" said Athos, emptying and refilling his glass. "The two things agree marvellously well."

"I am all attention," said d'Artagnan.

Athos collected himself, and in proportion as he did so, d'Artagnan saw that he became pale. He was at that period of intoxication in which vulgar drinkers fall on the floor and go to sleep. He kept himself upright and dreamed, without sleeping. This somnambulism of drunkenness had something frightful in it.

"You particularly wish it?" asked he.

"I pray for it," said d'Artagnan.

"Be it then as you desire. One of my friends–one of my friends, please to observe, not myself," said Athos, interrupting himself with a melancholy smile, "one of the counts of my province–that is to say, of Berry–noble as a Dandolo or a Montmorency, at twenty-five years of age fell in love with a girl of sixteen, beautiful as fancy can paint. Through the ingenuousness of her age beamed an ardent mind, not of the woman, but of the poet. She did not please; she intoxicated. She lived in a small town with her brother, who was a curate. Both had recently come into the country. They came nobody knew whence, but when seeing her so lovely and her brother so pious, nobody thought of asking whence they came. They were said, however, to be of good extraction. My friend, who was seigneur of the country, might have seduced her, or taken her by force, at his will–for he was master. Who would have come to the assistance of two strangers, two unknown persons? Unfortunately he was an honourable man; he married her. The fool! The ass! The idiot!"

"How so, if he love her?" asked d'Artagnan.

"Wait," said Athos. "He took her to his château, and made her the first lady in the province; and in justice it must be allowed that she supported her rank becomingly."

"Well?" asked d'Artagnan.

"Well, one day when she was hunting with her husband," continued Athos, in a low voice, and speaking very quickly, "she fell from her horse and fainted. The count flew to her to help, and as she appeared to be oppressed by her clothes, he ripped them open with his poniard, and in so doing laid bare her shoulder. D'Artagnan," said Athos, with a maniacal burst of laughter, "guess what she had on her shoulder."

"How can I tell?" said d'Artagnan.

"A FLEUR-DE-LIS," said Athos. "She was branded."

Athos emptied at a single draught the glass he held in his hand.

"Horror!" cried d'Artagnan. "What do you tell me?"

"Truth, my friend. The angel was a demon; the poor young girl had stolen the sacred vessels from a church."

"And what did the count do?"

"The count was of the highest nobility. He had on his estates the rights of high and low tribunals. He tore the dress of the countess to pieces; he tied her hands behind her, and hanged her on a tree."

"Heavens, Athos, a murder?" cried d'Artagnan.

"No less," said Athos, as pale as a corpse. "But methinks I need wine!" and he seized by the neck the last bottle that was left, put it to his mouth, and emptied it at a single draught, as he would have emptied an ordinary glass.

Then he let his head sink upon his two hands, while d'Artagnan stood before him, stupefied.

"That has cured me of beautiful, poetical, and loving women," said Athos, after a considerable pause, raising his head, and forgetting to continue the fiction of the count. "God grant you as much! Let us drink."

"Then she is dead?" stammered d'Artagnan.

"PARBLEU!" said Athos. "But hold out your glass. Some ham, my boy, or we can't drink."

"And her brother?" added d'Artagnan, timidly.

"Her brother?" replied Athos.

"Yes, the priest."

"Oh, I inquired after him for the purpose of hanging him likewise, but he was beforehand with me, he had quit the curacy the night before."

"Was it ever known who this miserable fellow was?"

"He was doubtless the first lover and accomplice of the fair lady. A worthy man, who had pretended to be a curate for the purpose of getting his mistress married, and securing her a position. He has been hanged and quartered, I hope."

"My God, my God!" cried d'Artagnan, quite stunned by the relation of this horrible adventure.

"Taste some of this ham, d'Artagnan; it is exquisite," said Athos, cutting a slice, which he placed on the young man's plate.

"What a pity it is there were only four like this in the cellar. I could have drunk fifty bottles more."

D'Artagnan could no longer endure this conversation, which had made him bewildered. Allowing his head to sink upon his two hands, he pretended to sleep.

"These young fellows can none of them drink," said Athos, looking at him with pity, "and yet this is one of the best!"

Chapter 28

The Return

D'Artagnan was astounded by the terrible confidence of Athos; yet many things appeared very obscure to him in this half revelation. In the first place it had been made by a man quite drunk to one who was half drunk; and yet, in spite of the uncertainty which the vapor of three or four bottles of Burgundy carries with it to the brain, d'Artagnan, when awaking on the following morning, had all the words of Athos as present to his memory as if they then fell from his mouth–they had been so impressed upon his mind. All this doubt only gave rise to a more lively desire of arriving at a certainty, and he went into his friend's chamber with a fixed determination of renewing the conversation of the preceding evening, but he found Athos quite himself again–that is to say, the most shrewd and impenetrable of men. Besides which, the Musketeer, after having exchanged a hearty shake of the hand with him, broached the matter first.

"I was pretty drunk yesterday, d'Artagnan," said he, "I can tell that by my tongue, which was swollen and hot this morning, and by my pulse, which was very tremulous. I wager that I uttered a thousand extravagances."

While saying this he looked at his friend with an earnestness that embarrassed him.

"No," replied d'Artagnan, "if I recollect well what you said, it was nothing out of the common way."

"Ah, you surprise me. I thought I had told you a most lamentable story." And he looked at the young man as if he would read the bottom of his heart.

"My faith," said d'Artagnan, "it appears that I was more drunk than you, since I remember nothing of the kind."

Athos did not trust this reply, and he resumed, "you cannot have failed to remark, my dear friend, that everyone has his particular kind of drunkenness, sad or gay. My drunkenness is always sad, and when I am thoroughly drunk my mania is to relate all the lugubrious stories which my foolish nurse inculcated into my brain. That is my failing–a capital failing, I admit, but with that exception, I am a good drinker."

Athos spoke this in so natural a manner that d'Artagnan was shaken in his conviction.

"It is that, then," replied the young man, anxious to find out the truth, "it is that, then, I remember as we remember a dream. We were speaking of hanging."

"Ah, you see how it is," said Athos, becoming still paler, but yet attempting to laugh, "I was sure it was so–the hanging of people is my nightmare."

"Yes, yes," replied d'Artagnan. "I remember now; yes, it was about–stop a minute–yes, it was about a woman."

"That's it," replied Athos, becoming almost livid, "that is my grand story of the fair lady, and when I relate that, I must be very drunk."

"Yes, that was it," said d'Artagnan, "the story of a tall, fair lady, with blue eyes."

"Yes, who was hanged."

"By her husband, who was a nobleman of your acquaintance," continued d'Artagnan, looking intently at Athos.

"Well, you see how a man may compromise himself when he does not know what he says," replied Athos, shrugging his shoulders as if he thought himself an object of pity. "I certainly never will get drunk again, d'Artagnan; it is too bad a habit."

D'Artagnan remained silent; and then changing the conversation all at once, Athos said:

"By the by, I thank you for the horse you have brought me."

"Is it to your mind?" asked d'Artagnan.

"Yes, but it is not a horse for hard work."

"You are mistaken; I rode him nearly ten leagues in less than an hour and a half, and he appeared no more distressed than if he had only made the tour of the Place St. Sulpice."

"Ah, you begin to awaken my regret."

"Regret?"

"Yes; I have parted with him."

"How?"

"Why, here is the simple fact. This morning I awoke at six o'clock. You were still fast asleep, and I did not know what to do with myself; I was still stupid from our yesterday's debauch. As I came into the public room, I saw one of our Englishman bargaining with a dealer for a horse, his own having died yesterday from bleeding. I drew near, and found he was bidding a hundred pistoles for a chestnut nag. 'PARDIEU,' said I, 'my good gentleman, I have a horse to sell, too.' 'Ay, and a very fine one! I saw him yesterday; your friend's lackey was leading him.' 'Do you think he is worth a hundred pistoles?' 'Yes! Will you sell him to me for that sum?' 'No, but I will play for him.' 'What?' 'At dice.' No sooner said than done, and I lost the horse. Ah, ah! But please to observe I won back the equipage," cried Athos.

D'Artagnan looked much disconcerted.

"This vexes you?" said Athos.

"Well, I must confess it does," replied d'Artagnan. "That horse was to have identified us in the day of battle. It was a pledge, a remembrance. Athos, you have done wrong."

"But, my dear friend, put yourself in my place," replied the Musketeer. "I was hipped to death; and still further, upon my honour, I don't like English horses. If it is only to be recognised, why the saddle will suffice for that; it is quite remarkable enough. As to the horse, we can easily find some excuse for its disappearance. Why the devil! A horse is mortal; suppose mine had had the glanders or the farcy?"

D'Artagnan did not smile.

"It vexes me greatly," continued Athos, "that you attach so much importance to these animals, for I am not yet at the end of my story."

"What else have you done."

"After having lost my own horse, nine against ten–see how near–I formed an idea of staking yours."

"Yes, but you stopped at the idea, I hope?"

"No; for I put it in execution that very minute."

"And the consequence?" said d'Artagnan, in great anxiety.

"I threw, and I lost."

"What, my horse?"

"Your horse, seven against eight; a point short–you know the proverb."

"Athos, you are not in your right senses, I swear."

"My dear lad, that was yesterday, when I was telling you silly stories, it was proper to tell me that, and not this morning. I lost him then, with all his appointments and furniture."

"Really, this is frightful."

"Stop a minute; you don't know all yet. I should make an excellent gambler if I were not too hot-headed, but I was hot-headed, just as if I had been drinking. Well, I was not hot-headed then–"

"Well, but what else could you play for? You had nothing left?"

"Oh, yes, my friend; there was still that diamond left which sparkles on your finger, and which I had observed yesterday."

"This diamond!" said d'Artagnan, placing his hand eagerly on his ring.

"And as I am a connoisseur in such things, having had a few of my own once, I estimated it at a thousand pistoles."

"I hope," said d'Artagnan, half dead with fright, "you made no mention of my diamond?"

"On the contrary, my dear friend, this diamond became our only resource; with it I might regain our horses and their harnesses, and even money to pay our expenses on the road."

"Athos, you make me tremble!" cried d'Artagnan.

"I mentioned your diamond then to my adversary, who had likewise remarked it. What the devil, my dear, do you think you can wear a star from heaven on your finger, and nobody observe it? Impossible!"

"Go on, go on, my dear fellow!" said d'Artagnan, "for upon my honour, you will kill me with your indifference."

"We divided, then, this diamond into ten parts of a hundred pistoles each."

"You are laughing at me, and want to try me!" said d'Artagnan, whom anger began to take by the hair, as Minerva takes Achilles, in the *ILLIAD*.

"No, I do not jest, MORDIEU! I should like to have seen you in my place! I had been fifteen days without seeing a human face, and had been left to brutalise myself in the company of bottles."

"That was no reason for staking my diamond!" replied d'Artagnan, closing his hand with a nervous spasm.

"Hear the end. Ten parts of a hundred pistoles each, in ten throws, without revenge; in thirteen throws I had lost all–in thirteen throws. The number thirteen was always fatal to me; it was on the thirteenth of July that–"

"VENTREBLEU!" cried d'Artagnan, rising from the table, the story of the present day making him forget that of the preceding one.

"Patience!" said Athos, "I had a plan. The Englishman was an original; I had seen him conversing that morning with Grimaud, and Grimaud had told me that he had made him proposals to enter into his service. I staked Grimaud, the silent Grimaud, divided into ten portions."

"Well, what next?" said d'Artagnan, laughing in spite of himself.

"Grimaud himself, understand; and with the ten parts of Grimaud, which are not worth a ducatoon, I regained the diamond. Tell me, now, if persistence is not a virtue?"

"My faith! But this is droll," cried d'Artagnan, consoled, and holding his sides with laughter.

"You may guess, finding the luck turned, that I again staked the diamond."

"The devil!" said d'Artagnan, becoming angry again.

"I won back your harness, then your horse, then my harness, then my horse, and then I lost again. In brief, I regained your harness and then mine. That's where we are. That was a superb throw, so I left off there."

D'Artagnan breathed as if the whole hostelry had been removed from his breast.

"Then the diamond is safe?" said he, timidly.

"Intact, my dear friend; besides the harness of your Bucephalus and mine."

"But what is the use of harnesses without horses?"

"I have an idea about them."

"Athos, you make me shudder."

"Listen to me. You have not played for a long time, d'Artagnan."

"And I have no inclination to play."

"Swear to nothing. You have not played for a long time, I said; you ought, then, to have a good hand."

"Well, what then?"

"Well; the Englishman and his companion are still here. I remarked that he regretted the horse furniture very much. You appear to think much of your horse. In your place I would stake the furniture against the horse."

"But he will not wish for only one harness."

"Stake both, PARDIEU! I am not selfish, as you are."

"You would do so?" said d'Artagnan, undecided, so strongly did the confidence of Athos begin to prevail, in spite of himself.

"On my honour, in one single throw."

"But having lost the horses, I am particularly anxious to preserve the harnesses."

"Stake your diamond, then."

"This? That's another matter. Never, never!"

"The devil!" said Athos. "I would propose to you to stake Planchet, but as that has already been done, the Englishman would not, perhaps, be willing."

"Decidedly, my dear Athos," said d'Artagnan, "I should like better not to risk anything."

"That's a pity," said Athos, coolly. "The Englishman is overflowing with pistoles. Good Lord, try one throw! One throw is soon made!"

"And if I lose?"

"You will win."

"But if I lose?"

"Well, you will surrender the harnesses."

"Have with you for one throw!" said d'Artagnan.

Athos went in quest of the Englishman, whom he found in the stable, examining the harnesses with a greedy eye. The opportunity was good. He proposed the conditions–the two harnesses, either against one horse or a hundred pistoles. The Englishman calculated fast; the two harnesses were worth three hundred pistoles. He consented.

D'Artagnan threw the dice with a trembling hand, and turned up the number three; his paleness terrified Athos, who, however, consented himself with saying, "That's a sad throw, comrade; you will have the horses fully equipped, Monsieur."

The Englishman, quite triumphant, did not even give himself the trouble to shake the dice. He threw them on the table without looking at them, so sure was he of victory; d'Artagnan turned aside to conceal his ill humor.

"Hold, hold, hold!" said Athos, wit his quiet tone, "that throw of the dice is extraordinary. I have not seen such a one four times in my life. Two aces!"

The Englishman looked, and was seized with astonishment. D'Artagnan looked, and was seized with pleasure.

"Yes," continued Athos, "four times only; once at the house of Monsieur Crequy; another time at my own house in the country, in my château at–when I had a château; a third time at Monsieur de Tréville's where it surprised us all; and the fourth time at a cabaret, where it fell to my lot, and where I lost a hundred louis and a supper on it."

"Then Monsieur takes his horse back again," said the Englishman.

"Certainly," said d'Artagnan.

"Then there is no revenge?"

"Our conditions said, 'No revenge,' you will please to recollect."

"That is true; the horse shall be restored to your lackey, Monsieur."

"A moment," said Athos, "with your permission, Monsieur, I wish to speak a word with my friend."

"Say on."

Athos drew d'Artagnan aside.

"Well, Tempter, what more do you want with me?" said d'Artagnan. "You want me to throw again, do you not?"

"No, I would wish you to reflect."

"On what?"

"You mean to take your horse?"

"Without doubt."

"You are wrong, then. I would take the hundred pistoles. You know you have staked the harnesses against the horse or a hundred pistoles, at your choice."

"Yes."

"Well, then, I repeat, you are wrong. What is the use of one horse for us two? I could not ride behind. We should look like the two sons of Anmon, who had lost their brother. You cannot think of humiliating me by prancing along by my side on that magnificent charger. For my part, I should not hesitate a moment; I should take the hundred pistoles. We want money for our return to Paris."

"I am much attached to that horse, Athos."

"And there again you are wrong. A horse slips and injures a joint; a horse stumbles and breaks his knees to the bone; a horse eats out of a manger in which a glandered horse has eaten. There is a horse, while on the contrary, the hundred pistoles feed their master."

"But how shall we get back?"

"Upon our lackey's horses, PARDIEU. Anybody may see by our bearing that we are people of condition."

"Pretty figures we shall cut on ponies while Aramis and Porthos caracole on their steeds."

"Aramis! Porthos!" cried Athos, and laughed aloud.

"What is it?" asked d'Artagnan, who did not at all comprehend the hilarity of his friend.

"Nothing, nothing! Go on!"

"Your advice, then?"

"To take the hundred pistoles, d'Artagnan. With the hundred pistoles we can live well to the end of the month. We have undergone a great deal of fatigue, remember, and a little rest will do no harm."

"I rest? Oh, no, Athos. Once in Paris, I shall prosecute my search for that unfortunate woman!"

"Well, you may be assured that your horse will not be half so serviceable to you for that purpose as good golden louis. Take the hundred pistoles, my friend; take the hundred pistoles!"

D'Artagnan only required one reason to be satisfied. This last reason appeared convincing. Besides, he feared that by resisting longer he should appear selfish in the eyes of Athos. He acquiesced, therefore, and chose the hundred pistoles, which the Englishman paid down on the spot.

They then determined to depart. Peace with the landlord, in addition to Athos's old horse, cost six pistoles. D'Artagnan and Athos took the nags of Planchet and Grimaud, and the two lackeys started on foot, carrying the saddles on their heads.

However ill our two friends were mounted, they were soon far in advance of their servants, and arrived at Creveccoeur. From a distance they perceived Aramis, seated in a melancholy manner at his window, looking out, like Sister Anne, at the dust in the horizon.

"HOLA, Aramis! What the devil are you doing there?" cried the two friends.

"Ah, is that you, d'Artagnan, and you, Athos?" said the young man. "I was reflecting upon the rapidity with which the blessings of this world leave us. My English horse, which has just disappeared amid a cloud of dust, has furnished me with a living image of the fragility of the things of the earth. Life itself may be resolved into three words: ERAT, EST, FUIT."

"Which means–" said d'Artagnan, who began to suspect the truth.

"Which means that I have just been duped-sixty louis for a horse which by the manner of his gait can do at least five leagues an hour."

D'Artagnan and Athos laughed aloud.

"My dear d'Artagnan," said Aramis, "don't be too angry with me, I beg. Necessity has no law; besides, I am the person punished, as that rascally horse-dealer has robbed me of fifty louis, at least. Ah, you fellows are good managers! You ride on our lackey's horses, and have your own gallant steeds led along carefully by hand, at short stages."

At the same instant a market cart, which some minutes before had appeared upon the Amiens road, pulled up at the inn, and Planchet and Grimaud came out of it with the saddles on their heads. The cart was returning empty to Paris, and the two lackeys had agreed, for their transport, to slake the wagoner's thirst along the route.

"What is this?" said Aramis, on seeing them arrive. "Nothing but saddles?"

"Now do you understand?" said Athos.

"My friends, that's exactly like me! I retained my harness by instinct. HOLA, Bazin! Bring my new saddle and carry it along with those of these gentlemen."

"And what have you done with your ecclesiastics?" asked d'Artagnan.

"My dear fellow, I invited them to a dinner the next day," replied Aramis. "They have some capital wine here–please to observe that in passing. I did my best to make them drunk. Then the curate forbade me to quit my uniform, and the Jesuit entreated me to get him made a Musketeer."

"Without a thesis?" cried d'Artagnan, "without a thesis? I demand the suppression of the thesis."

"Since then," continued Aramis, "I have lived very agreeably. I have begun a poem in verses of one syllable. That is rather difficult, but the merit in all things consists in the difficulty. The matter is gallant. I will read you the first canto. It has four hundred lines, and lasts a minute."

"My faith, my dear Aramis," said d'Artagnan, who detested verses almost as much as he did Latin, "add to the merit of the difficulty that of the brevity, and you are sure that your poem will at least have two merits."

"You will see," continued Aramis, "that it breathes irreproachable passion. And so, my friends, we return to Paris? Bravo! I am ready. We are going to rejoin that good fellow, Porthos. So much the better. You can't think how I have missed him, the great simpleton. To see him so self-satisfied reconciles me with myself. He would not sell his horse; not for a kingdom! I think I can see him now, mounted upon his superb animal and seated in his handsome saddle. I am sure he will look like the Great Mogul!"

They made a halt for an hour to refresh their horses. Aramis discharged his bill, placed Bazin in the cart with his comrades, and they set forward to join Porthos.

They found him up, less pale than when d'Artagnan left him after his first visit, and seated at a table on which, though he was alone, was spread enough for four persons. This dinner consisted of meats nicely dressed, choice wines, and superb fruit.

"Ah, PARDIEU!" said he, rising, "you come in the nick of time, gentlemen. I was just beginning the soup, and you will dine with me."

"Oh, oh!" said d'Artagnan, "Mousqueton has not caught these bottles with his lasso. Besides, here is a piquant FRICANDEAU and a fillet of beef."

"I am recruiting myself," said Porthos, "I am recruiting myself. Nothing weakens a man more than these devilish strains. Did you ever suffer from a strain, Athos?"

"Never! Though I remember, in our affair of the Rue Ferou, I received a sword wound which at the end of fifteen or eighteen days produced the same effect."

"But this dinner was not intended for you alone, Porthos?" said Aramis.

"No," said Porthos, "I expected some gentlemen of the neighbourhood, who have just sent me word they could not come. You will take their places and I shall not lose by the exchange. HOLA, Mousqueton, seats, and order double the bottles!"

"Do you know what we are eating here?" said Athos, at the end of ten minutes.

"PARDIEU!" replied d'Artagnan, "for my part, I am eating veal garnished with shrimps and vegetables."

"And I some lamb chops," said Porthos.

"And I a plain chicken," said Aramis.

"You are all mistaken, gentlemen," answered Athos, gravely, "you are eating horse."

"Eating what?" said d'Artagnan.

"Horse!" said Aramis, with a grimace of disgust.

Porthos alone made no reply.

"Yes, horse. Are we not eating a horse, Porthos? And perhaps his saddle, therewith."

"No, gentlemen, I have kept the harness," said Porthos.

"My faith," said Aramis, "we are all alike. One would think we had tipped the wink."

"What could I do?" said Porthos. "This horse made my visitors ashamed of theirs, and I don't like to humiliate people."

"Then your duchess is still at the waters?" asked d'Artagnan.

"Still," replied Porthos. "And, my faith, the governor of the province–one of the gentlemen I expected today–seemed to have such a wish for him, that I gave him to him."

"Gave him?" cried d'Artagnan.

"My God, yes, GAVE, that is the word," said Porthos, "for the animal was worth at least a hundred and fifty louis, and the stingy fellow would only give me eighty."

"Without the saddle?" said Aramis.

"Yes, without the saddle."

"You will observe, gentlemen," said Athos, "that Porthos has made the best bargain of any of us."

And then commenced a roar of laughter in which they all joined, to the astonishment of poor Porthos, but when he was informed of the cause of their hilarity, he shared it vociferously according to his custom.

"There is one comfort, we are all in cash," said d'Artagnan.

"Well, for my part," said Athos, "I found Aramis's Spanish wine so good that I sent on a hamper of sixty bottles of it in the wagon with the lackeys. That has weakened my purse."

"And I," said Aramis, "imagined that I had given almost my last sou to the church of Montdidier and the Jesuits of Amiens, with whom I had made engagements which I ought to have kept. I have ordered Masses for myself, and for you, gentlemen, which will be said, gentlemen, for which I have not the least doubt you will be marvellously benefited."

"And I," said Porthos, "do you think my strain cost me nothing?–Without reckoning Mousqueton's wound, for which I had to have the surgeon twice a day, and who charged me double on account of that foolish Mousqueton having allowed himself a ball in a part which people generally only show to an apothecary; so I advised him to try never to get wounded there any more."

"Ay, ay!" said Athos, exchanging a smile with d'Artagnan and Aramis, "it is very clear you acted nobly with regard to the poor lad; that is like a good master."

"In short," said Porthos, "when all my expenses are paid, I shall have, at most, thirty crowns left."

"And I about ten pistoles," said Aramis.

"Well, then it appears that we are the Croesuses of the society. How much have you left of your hundred pistoles, d'Artagnan?"

"Of my hundred pistoles? Why, in the first place I gave you fifty."

"You think so?"

"PARDIEU!"

"Ah, that is true. I recollect."

"Then I paid the host six."

"What a brute of a host! Why did you give him six pistoles?"

"You told me to give them to him."

"It is true; I am too good-natured. In brief, how much remains?"

"Twenty-five pistoles," said d'Artagnan.

"And I," said Athos, taking some small change from his pocket, "I–"

"You? Nothing!"

"My faith! So little that it is not worth reckoning with the general stock."

"Now, then, let us calculate how much we posses in all."

"Porthos?"

"Thirty crowns."

"Aramis?"

"Ten pistoles."

"And you, d'Artagnan?"

"Twenty-five."

"That makes in all?" said Athos.

"Four hundred and seventy-five livres," said d'Artagnan, who reckoned like Archimedes.

"On our arrival in Paris, we shall still have four hundred, besides the harnesses," said Porthos.

"But our troop horses?" said Aramis.

"Well, of the four horses of our lackeys we will make two for the masters, for which we will draw lots. With the four hundred livres we will make the half of one for one of the unmounted, and then we will give the turnings out of our pockets to d'Artagnan, who has a steady hand, and will go and play in the first gaming house we come to. There!"

"Let us dine, then," said Porthos, "it is getting cold."

The friends, at ease with regard to the future, did honour to the repast, the remains of which were abandoned to Mousqueton, Bazin, Planchet, and Grimaud.

On arriving in Paris, d'Artagnan found a letter from M. de Tréville, which informed him that, at his request, the king had promised that he should enter the company of the Musketeers.

As this was the height of d'Artagnan's worldly ambition–apart, be it well understood, from his desire of finding Mme. Bonacieux–he ran, full of joy, to seek his comrades, whom he had left only half an hour before, but whom he found very sad and deeply preoccupied. They were assembled in council at the residence of Athos, which always indicated an event of some gravity. M. de Tréville had intimated to them his Majesty's fixed intention to open the campaign on the first of May, and they must immediately prepare their outfits.

The four philosophers looked at one another in a state of bewilderment. M. de Tréville never jested in matters relating to discipline.

"And what do you reckon your outfit will cost?" said d'Artagnan.

"Oh, we can scarcely say. We have made our calculations with Spartan economy, and we each require fifteen hundred livres."

"Four times fifteen makes sixty–six thousand livres," said Athos.

"It seems to me," said d'Artagnan, "with a thousand livres each–I do not speak as a Spartan, but as a procurator–"

This word PROCURATOR roused Porthos. "Stop," said he, "I have an idea."

"Well, that's something, for I have not the shadow of one," said Athos coolly, "but as to d'Artagnan, gentlemen, the idea of belonging to OURS has driven him out of his senses. A thousand livres! For my part, I declare I want two thousand."

"Four times two makes eight," then said Aramis, "it is eight thousand that we want to complete our outfits, toward which, it is true, we have already the saddles."

"Besides," said Athos, waiting till d'Artagnan, who went to thank Monsieur de Tréville, had shut the door, "besides, there is that beautiful ring which beams from the finger of our friend. What the devil! D'Artagnan is too good a comrade to leave his brothers in embarrassment while he wears the ransom of a king on his finger."

Chapter 29

Hunting For The Equipments

The most preoccupied of the four friends was certainly d'Artagnan, although he, in his quality of Guardsman, would be much more easily equipped than Messieurs the Musketeers, who were all of high rank, but our Gascon cadet was, as may have been observed, of a provident and almost avaricious character, and with that (explain the contradiction) so vain as almost to rival Porthos. To this preoccupation of his vanity, d'Artagnan at this moment joined an uneasiness much less selfish. Notwithstanding all his inquiries respecting Mme. Bonacieux, he could obtain no intelligence of her. M. de Tréville had spoken of her to the queen. The queen was ignorant where the mercer's young wife was, but had promised to have her sought for, but this promise was very vague and did not at all reassure d'Artagnan.

Athos did not leave his chamber; he made up his mind not to take a single step to equip himself.

"We have still fifteen days before us," said he to his friends, "well, if at the end of a fortnight I have found nothing, or rather if nothing has come to find me, as I, too good a Catholic to kill myself with a pistol bullet, I will seek a good quarrel with four of his Eminence's Guards or with eight Englishmen, and I will fight until one of them has killed me, which, considering the number, cannot fail to happen. It will then be said of me that I died for the king; so that I shall have performed my duty without the expense of an outfit."

Porthos continued to walk about with his hands behind him, tossing his head and repeating, "I shall follow up on my idea."

Aramis, anxious and negligently dressed, said nothing.

It may be seen by these disastrous details that desolation reigned in the community.

The lackeys on their part, like the coursers of Hippolytus, shared the sadness of their masters. Mousqueton collected a store of crusts; Bazin, who had always been inclined to devotion, never quit the churches; Planchet watched the flight of flies; and Grimaud, whom the general distress could not induce to break the silence imposed by his master, heaved sighs enough to soften the stones.

The three friends–for, as we have said, Athos had sworn not to stir a foot to equip himself–went out early in the morning, and returned late at night. They wandered about the streets, looking at the pavement as if to see whether the passengers had not left a purse behind them. They might have been supposed to be following tracks, so observant were they wherever they went. When they met they looked desolately at one another, as much as to say, "Have you found anything?"

However, as Porthos had first found an idea, and had thought of it earnestly afterward, he was the first to act. He was a man of execution, this worthy Porthos. D'Artagnan perceived him one day walking toward the church of St. Leu, and followed him instinctively. He entered, after having twisted his moustache and elongated his imperial, which always announced on his part the most triumphant resolutions. As d'Artagnan took some precautions to conceal himself, Porthos believed he had not been seen. D'Artagnan entered behind him. Porthos went and leaned against the side of a pillar. D'Artagnan, still unperceived, supported himself against the other side.

There happened to be a sermon, which made the church very full of people. Porthos took advantage of this circumstance to ogle the women. Thanks to the cares of Mousqueton, the exterior was far from announcing the distress of the interior. His hat was a little napless, his feather was a little faded, his gold lace was a little tarnished, his laces were a trifle frayed, but in the obscurity of the church these things were not seen, and Porthos was still the handsome Porthos.

D'Artagnan observed, on the bench nearest to the pillar against which Porthos leaned, a sort of ripe beauty, rather yellow and rather dry, but erect and haughty under her black hood. The eyes of Porthos were furtively cast upon this lady, and then roved about at large over the nave.

On her side the lady, who from time to time blushed, darted with the rapidity of lightning a glance toward the inconstant Porthos; and then immediately the eyes of Porthos wandered anxiously. It was plain that this mode of proceeding piqued the lady in the black hood, for she bit her lips till they bled, scratched the end of her nose, and could not sit still in her seat.

Porthos, seeing this, retwisted his moustache, elongated his imperial a second time, and began to make signals to a beautiful lady who was near the choir, and who not only was a beautiful lady, but still further, no doubt, a great lady–for she had behind her a Negro boy who had brought the cushion on which she knelt, and a female servant who held the emblazoned bag in which was placed the book from which she read the Mass.

The lady with the black hood followed through all their wanderings the looks of Porthos, and perceived that they rested upon the lady with the velvet cushion, the little Negro, and the maid-servant.

During this time Porthos played close. It was almost imperceptible motions of his eyes, fingers placed upon the lips, little assassinating smiles, which really did assassinate the disdained beauty.

Then she cried, "Ahem!" under cover of the MEA CULPA, striking her breast so vigorously that everybody, even the lady with the red cushion, turned round toward her. Porthos paid no attention. Nevertheless, he understood it all, but was deaf.

The lady with the red cushion produced a great effect–for she was very handsome–upon the lady with the black hood, who saw in her a rival really to be dreaded; a great effect upon Porthos, who thought her much prettier than the lady with the black hood; a great effect upon d'Artagnan, who recognised in her the lady of Meung, of Calais, and of Dover, whom his persecutor, the man with the scar, had saluted by the name of Milady.

D'Artagnan, without losing sight of the lady of the red cushion, continued to watch the proceedings of Porthos, which amused him greatly. He guessed that the lady of the black hood was the procurator's wife of the Rue aux Ours, which was the more probable from the church of St. Leu being not far from that locality.

He guessed, likewise, by induction, that Porthos was taking his revenge for the defeat of Chantilly, when the procurator's wife had proved so refractory with respect to her purse.

Amid all this, d'Artagnan remarked also that not one countenance responded to the gallantries of Porthos. There were only chimeras and illusions, but for real love, for true jealousy, is there any reality except illusions and chimeras?

The sermon over, the procurator's wife advanced toward the holy font. Porthos went before her, and instead of a finger, dipped his whole hand in. The procurator's wife smiled, thinking that it was for her Porthos had put himself to this trouble, but she was cruelly and promptly undeceived. When she was only about three steps from him, he turned his head round, fixing his eyes steadfastly upon the lady with the red cushion, who had risen and was approaching, followed by her black boy and her woman.

When the lady of the red cushion came close to Porthos, Porthos drew his dripping hand from the font. The fair worshipper touched the great hand of Porthos with her delicate fingers, smiled, made the sign of the cross, and left the church.

This was too much for the procurator's wife; she doubted not there was an intrigue between this lady and Porthos. If she had been a great lady she would have fainted, but as she was only a procurator's wife, she contented herself saying to the Musketeer with concentrated fury, "Eh, Monsieur Porthos, you don't offer me any holy water?"

Porthos, at the sound of that voice, started like a man awakened from a sleep of a hundred years.

"Ma-madame!" cried he, "is that you? How is your husband, our dear Monsieur Coquenard? Is he still as stingy as ever? Where can my eyes have been not to have seen you during the two hours of the sermon?"

"I was within two paces of you, Monsieur," replied the procurator's wife, "but you did not perceive me because you had no eyes but for the pretty lady to whom you just now gave the holy water."

Porthos pretended to be confused. "Ah," said he, "you have remarked–"

"I must have been blind not to have seen."

"Yes," said Porthos, "that is a duchess of my acquaintance whom I have great trouble to meet on account of the jealousy of her husband, and who sent me word that she should come today to this poor church, buried in this vile quarter, solely for the sake of seeing me."

"Monsieur Porthos," said the procurator's wife, "will you have the kindness to offer me your arm for five minutes? I have something to say to you."

"Certainly, Madame," said Porthos, winking to himself, as a gambler does who laughs at the dupe he is about to pluck.

At that moment d'Artagnan passed in pursuit of Milady; he cast a passing glance at Porthos, and beheld this triumphant look.

"Eh, eh!" said he, reasoning to himself according to the strangely easy morality of that gallant period, "there is one who will be equipped in good time!"

Porthos, yielding to the pressure of the arm of the procurator's wife, as a bark yields to the rudder, arrived at the cloister St. Magloire–a little-frequented passage, enclosed with a turnstile at each end. In the daytime nobody was seen there but mendicants devouring their crusts, and children at play.

"Ah, Monsieur Porthos," cried the procurator's wife, when she was assured that no one who was a stranger to the population of the locality could either see or hear her, "ah, Monsieur Porthos, you are a great conqueror, as it appears!"

"I, Madame?" said Porthos, drawing himself up proudly, "how so?"

"The signs just now, and the holy water! But that must be a princess, at least–that lady with her Negro boy and her maid!"

"My God! Madame, you are deceived," said Porthos, "she is simply a duchess."

"And that running footman who waited at the door, and that carriage with a coachman in grand livery who sat waiting on his seat?"

Porthos had seen neither the footman nor the carriage, but with the eye of a jealous woman, Mme. Coquenard had seen everything.

Porthos regretted that he had not at once made the lady of the red cushion a princess.

"Ah, you are quite the pet of the ladies, Monsieur Porthos!" resumed the procurator's wife, with a sigh.

"Well," responded Porthos, "you may imagine, with the physique with which nature has endowed me, I am not in want of good luck."

"Good Lord, how quickly men forget!" cried the procurator's wife, raising her eyes toward heaven.

"Less quickly than the women, it seems to me," replied Porthos, "for I, Madame, I may say I was your victim, when wounded, dying, I was abandoned by the surgeons. I, the offspring of a noble family, who placed reliance upon your friendship–I was near dying of my wounds at first, and of hunger afterward, in a beggarly inn at Chantilly, without you ever deigning once to reply to the burning letters I addressed to you."

"But, Monsieur Porthos," murmured the procurator's wife, who began to feel that, to judge by the conduct of the great ladies of the time, she was wrong.

"I, who had sacrificed for you the Baronne de–"

"I know it well."

"The Comtesse de–"

"Monsieur Porthos, be generous!"

"You are right, Madame, and I will not finish."

"But it was my husband who would not hear of lending."

"Madame Coquenard," said Porthos, "remember the first letter you wrote me, and which I preserve engraved in my memory."

The procurator's wife uttered a groan.

"Besides," said she, "the sum you required me to borrow was rather large."

"Madame Coquenard, I gave you the preference. I had but to write to the Duchesse–but I won't repeat her name, for I am incapable of compromising a woman, but this I know, that I had but to write to her and she would have sent me fifteen hundred."

The procurator's wife shed a tear.

"Monsieur Porthos," said she, "I can assure you that you have severely punished me; and if in the time to come you should find yourself in a similar situation, you have but to apply to me."

"Fie, Madame, fie!" said Porthos, as if disgusted. "Let us not talk about money, if you please; it is humiliating."

"Then you no longer love me!" said the procurator's wife, slowly and sadly.

Porthos maintained a majestic silence.

"And that is the only reply you make? Alas, I understand."

"Think of the offense you have committed toward me, Madame! It remains HERE!" said Porthos, placing his hand on his heart, and pressing it strongly.

"I will repair it, indeed I will, my dear Porthos."

"Besides, what did I ask of you?" resumed Porthos, with a movement of the shoulders full of good fellowship. "A loan, nothing more! After all, I am not an unreasonable man. I know you are not rich, Madame Coquenard, and that your husband is obliged to bleed his poor clients to squeeze a few paltry crowns from them. Oh! If you were a duchess, a marchioness, or a countess, it would be quite a different thing; it would be unpardonable."

The procurator's wife was piqued.

"Please to know, Monsieur Porthos," said she, "that my strongbox, the strongbox of a procurator's wife though it may be, is better filled than those of your affected minxes."

"That doubles the offense," said Porthos, disengaging his arm from that of the procurator's wife, "for if you are rich, Madame Coquenard, then there is no excuse for your refusal."

"When I said rich," replied the procurator's wife, who saw that she had gone too far, "you must not take the word literally. I am not precisely rich, though I am pretty well off."

"Hold, Madame," said Porthos, "let us say no more upon the subject, I beg of you. You have misunderstood me, all sympathy is extinct between us."

"Ingrate that you are!"

"Ah! I advise you to complain!" said Porthos.

"Begone, then, to your beautiful duchess; I will detain you no longer."

"And she is not to be despised, in my opinion."

"Now, Monsieur Porthos, once more, and this is the last! Do you love me still?"

"Ah, Madame," said Porthos, in the most melancholy tone he could assume, "when we are about to enter upon a campaign–a campaign, in which my presentiments tell me I shall be killed–"

"Oh, don't talk of such things!" cried the procurator's wife, bursting into tears.

"Something whispers me so," continued Porthos, becoming more and more melancholy.

"Rather say that you have a new love."

"Not so; I speak frankly to you. No object affects me; and I even feel here, at the bottom of my heart, something which speaks for you. But in fifteen days, as you know, or as you do not know, this fatal campaign is to open. I shall be fearfully preoccupied with my outfit. Then I must make a journey to see my family, in the lower part of Brittany, to obtain the sum necessary for my departure."

Porthos observed a last struggle between love and avarice.

"And as," continued he, "the duchess whom you saw at the church has estates near to those of my family, we mean to make the journey together. Journeys, you know, appear much shorter when we travel two in company."

"Have you no friends in Paris, then, Monsieur Porthos?" said the procurator's wife.

"I thought I had," said Porthos, resuming his melancholy air, "but I have been taught my mistake."

"You have some!" cried the procurator's wife, in a transport that surprised even herself. "Come to our house tomorrow. You are the son of my aunt, consequently my cousin; you come from Noyon, in Picardy; you have several lawsuits and no attorney. Can you recollect all that?"

"Perfectly, Madame."

"Come at dinnertime."

"Very well."

"And be upon your guard before my husband, who is rather shrewd, notwithstanding his seventy-six years."

"Seventy-six years! PESTE! That's a fine age!" replied Porthos.

"A great age, you mean, Monsieur Porthos. Yes, the poor man may be expected to leave me a widow, any hour," continued she, throwing a significant glance at Porthos. "Fortunately, by our marriage contract, the survivor takes everything."

"All?"

"Yes, all."

"You are a woman of precaution, I see, my dear Madame Coquenard," said Porthos, squeezing the hand of the procurator's wife tenderly.

"We are then reconciled, dear Monsieur Porthos?" said she, simpering.

"For life," replied Porthos, in the same manner.

"Till we meet again, then, dear traitor!"

"Till we meet again, my forgetful charmer!"

"Tomorrow, my angel!"

"Tomorrow, flame of my life!"

Chapter 30

D'Artagnan And The Englishman

D'Artagnan followed Milady without being perceived by her. He saw her get into her carriage, and heard her order the coachman to drive to St. Germain.

It was useless to try to keep pace on foot with a carriage drawn by two powerful horses. D'Artagnan therefore returned to the Rue Ferou.

In the Rue de Seine he met Planchet, who had stopped before the house of a pastry cook, and was contemplating with ecstasy a cake of the most appetising appearance.

He ordered him to go and saddle two horses in M. de Tréville's stables–one for himself, d'Artagnan, and one for Planchet–and bring them to Athos's place. Once for all, Tréville had placed his stable at d'Artagnan's service.

Planchet proceeded toward the Rue du Colombier, and d'Artagnan toward the Rue Ferou. Athos was at home, emptying sadly a bottle of the famous Spanish wine he had brought back with him from his journey into Picardy. He made a sign for Grimaud to bring a glass for d'Artagnan, and Grimaud obeyed as usual.

D'Artagnan related to Athos all that had passed at the church between Porthos and the procurator's wife, and how their comrade was probably by that time in a fair way to be equipped.

"As for me," replied Athos to this recital, "I am quite at my ease; it will not be women that will defray the expense of my outfit."

"Handsome, well-bred, noble lord as you are, my dear Athos, neither princesses nor queens would be secure from your amorous solicitations."

"How young this d'Artagnan is!" said Athos, shrugging his shoulders; and he made a sign to Grimaud to bring another bottle.

At that moment Planchet put his head modestly in at the half-open door, and told his master that the horses were ready.

"What horses?" asked Athos.

"Two horses that Monsieur de Tréville lends me at my pleasure, and with which I am now going to take a ride to St. Germain."

"Well, and what are you going to do at St. Germain?" then demanded Athos.

Then d'Artagnan described the meeting which he had at the church, and how he had found that lady who, with the seigneur in the black cloak and with the scar near his temple, filled his mind constantly.

"That is to say, you are in love with this lady as you were with Madame Bonacieux," said Athos, shrugging his shoulders contemptuously, as if he pitied human weakness.

"I? Not at all!" said d'Artagnan. "I am only curious to unravel the mystery to which she is attached. I do not know why, but I imagine that this woman, wholly unknown to me as she is, and wholly unknown to her as I am, has an influence over my life."

"Well, perhaps you are right," said Athos. "I do not know a woman that is worth the trouble of being sought for when she is once lost. Madame Bonacieux is lost; so much the worse for her if she is found."

"No, Athos, no, you are mistaken," said d'Artagnan, "I love my poor Constance more than ever, and if I knew the place in which she is, were it at the end of the world, I would go to free her from the hands of her enemies, but I am ignorant. All my researches have been useless. What is to be said? I must divert my attention!"

"Amuse yourself with Milady, my dear d'Artagnan; I wish you may with all my heart, if that will amuse you."

"Hear me, Athos," said d'Artagnan. "Instead of shutting yourself up here as if you were under arrest, get on horseback and come and take a ride with me to St. Germain."

"My dear fellow," said Athos, "I ride horses when I have any; when I have none, I go afoot."

"Well," said d'Artagnan, smiling at the misanthropy of Athos, which from any other person would have offended him, "I ride what I can get; I am not so proud as you. So AU REVOIR, dear Athos."

"AU REVOIR," said the Musketeer, making a sign to Grimaud to uncork the bottle he had just brought.

D'Artagnan and Planchet mounted, and took the road to St. Germain.

All along the road, what Athos had said respecting Mme. Bonacieux recurred to the mind of the young man. Although d'Artagnan was not of a very sentimental character, the mercer's pretty wife had made a real impression upon his heart. As he said, he was ready to go to the end of the world to seek her, but the world, being round, has many ends, so that he did not know which way to turn. Meantime, he was going to try to find out Milady. Milady had spoken to the man in the black cloak; therefore she knew him. Now, in the opinion of d'Artagnan, it was certainly the man in the black cloak who had carried off Mme. Bonacieux the second time, as he had carried her off the first. D'Artagnan then only half-lied, which is lying but little, when he said that by going in search of Milady he at the same time went in search of Constance.

Thinking of all this, and from time to time giving a touch of the spur to his horse, d'Artagnan completed his short journey, and arrived at St. Germain. He had just passed by the pavilion in which ten years later Louis XIV was born. He rode up a very quiet street, looking to the right and the left to see if he could catch any vestige of his beautiful Englishwoman, when from the ground floor of a pretty house, which, according to the fashion of the time, had no window toward the street, he saw a face peep out with which he thought he was acquainted. This person walked along the terrace, which was ornamented with flowers. Planchet recognised him first.

"Eh, Monsieur!" said he, addressing d'Artagnan, "don't you remember that face which is blinking yonder?"

"No," said d'Artagnan, "and yet I am certain it is not the first time I have seen that visage."

"PARBLEU, I believe it is not," said Planchet. "Why, it is poor Lubin, the lackey of the Comte de Wardes–he whom you took such good care of a month ago at Calais, on the road to the governor's country house!"

"So it is!" said d'Artagnan, "I know him now. Do you think he would recollect you?"

"My faith, Monsieur, he was in such trouble that I doubt if he can have retained a very clear recollection of me."

"Well, go and talk with the boy," said d'Artagnan, "and make out if you can from his conversation whether his master is dead."

Planchet dismounted and went straight up to Lubin, who did not at all remember him, and the two lackeys began to chat with the best understanding possible; while d'Artagnan turned the two horses into a lane, went round the house, and came back to watch the conference from behind a hedge of filberts.

At the end of an instant's observation he heard the noise of a vehicle, and saw Milady's carriage stop opposite to him. He could not be mistaken; Milady was in it. D'Artagnan leaned upon the neck of his horse, in order that he might see without being seen.

Milady put her charming blond head out at the window, and gave her orders to her maid.

The latter–a pretty girl of about twenty or twenty-two years, active and lively, the true SOUBRETTE of a great lady–jumped from the step upon which, according to the custom of the time, she was seated, and took her way toward the terrace upon which d'Artagnan had perceived Lubin.

D'Artagnan followed the SOUBRETTE with his eyes, and saw her go toward the terrace, but it happened that someone in the house called Lubin, so that Planchet remained alone, looking in all directions for the road where d'Artagnan had disappeared.

The maid approached Planchet, whom she took for Lubin, and holding out a little billet to him said, "For your master."

"For my master?" replied Planchet, astonished.

"Yes, and important. Take it quickly."

Thereupon she ran toward the carriage, which had turned round toward the way it came, jumped upon the step, and the carriage drove off.

Planchet turned and returned the billet. Then, accustomed to passive obedience, he jumped down from the terrace, ran toward the lane, and at the end of twenty paces met d'Artagnan, who, having seen all, was coming to him.

"For you, Monsieur," said Planchet, presenting the billet to the young man.

"For me?" said d'Artagnan, "are you sure of that?"

"PARDIEU, Monsieur, I can't be more sure. The SOUBRETTE said, 'For your master.' I have no other master but you; so–a pretty little lass, my faith, is that SOUBRETTE!"

D'Artagnan opened the letter, and read these words:

"A person who takes more interest in you than she is willing to confess wishes to know on what day it will suit you to walk in the forest? Tomorrow, at the Hotel Field of the Cloth of Gold, a lackey in black and red will wait for your reply."

"Oh!" said d'Artagnan, "this is rather warm; it appears that Milady and I are anxious about the health of the same person. Well, Planchet, how is the good Monsieur de Wardes? He is not dead, then?"

"No, Monsieur, he is as well as a man can be with four sword wounds in his body; for you, without question, inflicted four upon the dear gentleman, and he is still very weak, having lost almost all his blood. As I said, Monsieur, Lubin did not know me, and told me our adventure from one end to the other."

"Well done, Planchet! you are the king of lackeys. Now jump onto your horse, and let us overtake the carriage."

This did not take long. At the end of five minutes they perceived the carriage drawn up by the roadside; a cavalier, richly dressed, was close to the door.

The conversation between Milady and the cavalier was so animated that d'Artagnan stopped on the other side of the carriage without anyone but the pretty SOUBRETTE perceiving his presence.

The conversation took place in English–a language which d'Artagnan could not understand, but by the accent the young man plainly saw that the beautiful Englishwoman was in a great rage. She terminated it by an action which left no doubt as to the nature of this conversation; this was a blow with her fan, applied with such force that the little feminine weapon flew into a thousand pieces.

The cavalier laughed aloud, which appeared to exasperate Milady still more.

D'Artagnan thought this was the moment to interfere. He approached the other door, and taking off his hat respectfully, said, "Madame, will you permit me to offer you my services? It appears to me that this cavalier has made you very angry. Speak one word, Madame, and I take upon myself to punish him for his want of courtesy."

At the first word Milady turned, looking at the young man with astonishment; and when he had finished, she said in very good French, "Monsieur, I should with great confidence place myself under your protection if the person with whom I quarrel were not my brother."

"Ah, excuse me, then," said d'Artagnan. "You must be aware that I was ignorant of that, Madame."

"What is that stupid fellow troubling himself about?" cried the cavalier whom Milady had designated as her brother, stooping down to the height of the coach window. "Why does not he go about his business?"

"Stupid fellow yourself!" said d'Artagnan, stooping in his turn on the neck of his horse, and answering on his side through the carriage window. "I do not go on because it pleases me to stop here."

The cavalier addressed some words in English to his sister.

"I speak to you in French," said d'Artagnan, "be kind enough, then, to reply to me in the same language. You are Madame's brother, I learn–be it so, but fortunately you are not mine."

It might be thought that Milady, timid as women are in general, would have interposed in this commencement of mutual provocations in order to prevent the quarrel from going too far, but on the contrary, she threw herself back in her carriage, and called out coolly to the coachman, "Go on–home!"

The pretty SOUBRETTE cast an anxious glance at d'Artagnan, whose good looks seemed to have made an impression on her.

The carriage went on, and left the two men facing each other; no material obstacle separated them.

The cavalier made a movement as if to follow the carriage, but d'Artagnan, whose anger, already excited, was much increased by recognising in him the Englishman of Amiens who had won his horse and had been very near winning his diamond of Athos, caught at his bridle and stopped him.

"Well, Monsieur," said he, "you appear to be more stupid than I am, for you forget there is a little quarrel to arrange between us two."

"Ah," said the Englishman, "is it you, my master? It seems you must always be playing some game or other."

"Yes; and that reminds me that I have a revenge to take. We will see, my dear monsieur, if you can handle a sword as skillfully as you can a dice box."

"You see plainly that I have no sword," said the Englishman. "Do you wish to play the braggart with an unarmed man?"

"I hope you have a sword at home, but at all events, I have two, and if you like, I will throw with you for one of them."

"Needless," said the Englishman, "I am well furnished with such playthings."

"Very well, my worthy gentleman," replied d'Artagnan, "pick out the longest, and come and show it to me this evening."

"Where, if you please?"

"Behind the Luxembourg; that's a charming spot for such amusements as the one I propose to you."

"That will do; I will be there."

"Your hour?"

"Six o'clock."

"À PROPOS, you have probably one or two friends?"

"I have three, who would be honoured by joining in the sport with me."

"Three? Marvellous! That falls out oddly! Three is just my number!"

"Now, then, who are you?" asked the Englishman.

"I am Monsieur d'Artagnan, a Gascon gentleman, serving in the king's Musketeers. And you?"

"I am Lord de Winter, Baron Sheffield."

"Well, then, I am your servant, Monsieur Baron," said d'Artagnan, "though you have names rather difficult to recollect."

And touching his horse with the spur, he cantered back to Paris. As he was accustomed to do in all cases of any consequence, d'Artagnan went straight to the residence of Athos.

He found Athos reclining upon a large sofa, where he was waiting, as he said, for his outfit to come and find him. He related to Athos all that had passed, except the letter to M. de Wardes.

Athos was delighted to find he was going to fight an Englishman. We might say that was his dream.

They immediately sent their lackeys for Porthos and Aramis, and on their arrival made them acquainted with the situation.

Porthos drew his sword from the scabbard, and made passes at the wall, springing back from time to time, and making contortions like a dancer.

Aramis, who was constantly at work at his poem, shut himself up in Athos's closet, and begged not to be disturbed before the moment of drawing swords.

Athos, by signs, desired Grimaud to bring another bottle of wine.

D'Artagnan employed himself in arranging a little plan, of which we shall hereafter see the execution, and which promised him some agreeable adventure, as might be seen by the smiles which from time to time passed over his countenance, whose thoughtfulness they animated.

Chapter 31

English And French

The hour having come, they went with their four lackeys to a spot behind the Luxembourg given up to the feeding of goats. Athos threw a piece of money to the goat keeper to withdraw. The lackeys were ordered to act as sentinels.

A silent party soon drew near to the same enclosure, entered, and joined the Musketeers. Then, according to foreign custom, the presentations took place.

The Englishmen were all men of rank; consequently the odd names of their adversaries were for them not only a matter of surprise, but of annoyance.

"But after all," said Lord de Winter, when the three friends had been named, "we do not know who you are. We cannot fight with such names; they are names of shepherds."

"Therefore your lordship may suppose they are only assumed names," said Athos.

"Which only gives us a greater desire to know the real ones," replied the Englishman.

"You played very willingly with us without knowing our names," said Athos, "by the same token that you won our horses."

"That is true, but we then only risked our pistoles; this time we risk our blood. One plays with anybody, but one fights only with equals."

"And that is but just," said Athos, and he took aside the one of the four Englishmen with whom he was to fight, and communicated his name in a low voice.

Porthos and Aramis did the same.

"Does that satisfy you?" said Athos to his adversary. "Do you find me of sufficient rank to do me the honour of crossing swords with me?"

"Yes, Monsieur," said the Englishman, bowing.

"Well! Now shall I tell you something?" added Athos, coolly.

"What?" replied the Englishman.

"Why, that is that you would have acted much more wisely if you had not required me to make myself known."

"Why so?"

"Because I am believed to be dead, and have reasons for wishing nobody to know I am living; so that I shall be obliged to kill you to prevent my secret from roaming over the fields."

The Englishman looked at Athos, believing that he jested, but Athos did not jest the least in the world.

"Gentlemen," said Athos, addressing at the same time his companions and their adversaries, "are we ready?"

"Yes!" answered the Englishmen and the Frenchmen, as with one voice.

"On guard, then!" cried Athos.

Immediately eight swords glittered in the rays of the setting sun, and the combat began with an animosity very natural between men twice enemies.

Athos fenced with as much calmness and method as if he had been practicing in a fencing school.

Porthos, abated, no doubt, of his too-great confidence by his adventure of Chantilly, played with skill and prudence. Aramis, who had the third canto of his poem to finish, behaved like a man in haste.

Athos killed his adversary first. He hit him but once, but as he had foretold, that hit was a mortal one; the sword pierced his heart.

Second, Porthos stretched his upon the grass with a wound through his thigh, As the Englishman, without making any further resistance, then surrendered his sword, Porthos took him up in his arms and bore him to his carriage.

Aramis pushed his so vigorously that after going back fifty paces, the man ended by fairly taking to his heels, and disappeared amid the hooting of the lackeys.

As to d'Artagnan, he fought purely and simply on the defensive; and when he saw his adversary pretty well fatigued, with a vigorous side thrust sent his sword flying. The baron, finding himself disarmed, took two or three steps back, but in this movement his foot slipped and he fell backward.

D'Artagnan was over him at a bound, and said to the Englishman, pointing his sword to his throat, "I could kill you, my Lord, you are completely in my hands, but I spare your life for the sake of your sister."

D'Artagnan was at the height of joy; he had realised the plan he had imagined beforehand, whose picturing had produced the smiles we noted upon his face.

The Englishman, delighted at having to do with a gentleman of such a kind disposition, pressed d'Artagnan in his arms, and paid a thousand compliments to the three Musketeers, and as Porthos's adversary was already installed in the carriage, and as Aramis's had taken to his heels, they had nothing to think about but the dead.

As Porthos and Aramis were undressing him, in the hope of finding his wound not mortal, a large purse dropped from his clothes. D'Artagnan picked it up and offered it to Lord de Winter.

"What the devil would you have me do with that?" said the Englishman.

"You can restore it to his family," said d'Artagnan.

"His family will care much about such a trifle as that! His family will inherit fifteen thousand louis a year from him. Keep the purse for your lackeys."

D'Artagnan put the purse into his pocket.

"And now, my young friend, for you will permit me, I hope, to give you that name," said Lord de Winter, "on this very evening, if agreeable to you, I will present you to my sister, Milady Clarik, for I am desirous that she should take you into her good graces; and as she is not in bad odor at court, she may perhaps on some future day speak a word that will not prove useless to you."

D'Artagnan blushed with pleasure, and bowed a sign of assent.

At this time Athos came up to d'Artagnan.

"What do you mean to do with that purse?" whispered he.

"Why, I meant to pass it over to you, my dear Athos."

"Me! Why to me?"

"Why, you killed him! They are the spoils of victory."

"I, the heir of an enemy!" said Athos, "for whom, then, do you take me?"

"It is the custom in war," said d'Artagnan, "why should it not be the custom in a duel?"

"Even on the field of battle, I have never done that."

Porthos shrugged his shoulders; Aramis by a movement of his lips endorsed Athos.

"Then," said d'Artagnan, "let us give the money to the lackeys, as Lord de Winter desired us to do."

"Yes," said Athos, "let us give the money to the lackeys–not to our lackeys, but to the lackeys of the Englishmen."

Athos took the purse, and threw it into the hand of the coachman. "For you and your comrades."

This greatness of spirit in a man who was quite destitute struck even Porthos; and this French generosity, repeated by Lord de Winter and his friend, was highly applauded, except by MM Grimaud, Bazin, Mousqueton and Planchet.

Lord de Winter, on quitting d'Artagnan, gave him his sister's address. She lived in the Place Royale–then the fashionable quarter–at Number 6, and he undertook to call and take d'Artagnan with him in order to introduce him. D'Artagnan appointed eight o'clock at Athos's residence.

This introduction to Milady Clarik occupied the head of our Gascon greatly. He remembered in what a strange manner this woman had hitherto been mixed up in his destiny. According to his conviction, she was some creature of the cardinal, and yet he felt himself invincibly drawn toward her by one of those sentiments for which we cannot account. His only fear was that Milady would recognise in him the man of Meung and of Dover. Then she knew that he was one of the friends of M. de Tréville, and consequently, that he belonged body and soul to the king, which would make him lose a part of his advantage, since when known to Milady as he knew her, he played only an equal game with her. As to the commencement of an intrigue between her and M. de Wardes, our presumptuous hero gave but little heed to that, although the marquis was young, handsome, rich, and high in the cardinal's favour. It is not for nothing we are but twenty years old, above all if we were born at Tarbes.

D'Artagnan began by making his most splendid toilet, then returned to Athos's, and according to custom, related everything to him. Athos listened to his projects, then shook his head, and recommended prudence to him with a shade of bitterness.

"What!" said he, "you have just lost one woman, whom you call good, charming, perfect; and here you are, running headlong after another."

D'Artagnan felt the truth of this reproach.

"I loved Madame Bonacieux with my heart, while I only love Milady with my head," said he. "In getting introduced to her, my principal object is to ascertain what part she plays at court."

"The part she plays, PARDIEU! It is not difficult to divine that, after all you have told me. She is some emissary of the cardinal; a woman who will draw you into a snare in which you will leave your head."

"The devil! My dear Athos, you view things on the dark side, methinks."

"My dear fellow, I mistrust women. Can it be otherwise? I bought my experience dearly–particularly fair women. Milady is fair, you say?"

"She has the most beautiful light hair imaginable!"

"Ah, my poor d'Artagnan!" said Athos.

"Listen to me! I want to be enlightened on a subject; then, when I shall have learned what I desire to know, I will withdraw."

"Be enlightened!" said Athos, phlegmatically.

Lord de Winter arrived at the appointed time, but Athos, being warned of his coming, went into the other chamber. He therefore found d'Artagnan alone, and as it was nearly eight o'clock he took the young man with him.

An elegant carriage waited below, and as it was drawn by two excellent horses, they were soon at the Place Royale.

Milady Clarik received d'Artagnan ceremoniously. Her hotel was remarkably sumptuous, and while the most part of the English had quit, or were about to quit, France on account of the war, Milady had just been laying out much money upon her residence, which proved that the general measure which drove the English from France did not affect her.

"You see," said Lord de Winter, presenting d'Artagnan to his sister, "a young gentleman who has held my life in his hands, and who has not abused his advantage, although we have been twice enemies, although it was I who insulted him, and although I am an Englishman. Thank him, then, Madame, if you have any affection for me."

Milady frowned slightly; a scarcely visible cloud passed over her brow, and so peculiar a smile appeared upon her lips that the young man, who saw and observed this triple shade, almost shuddered at it.

The brother did not perceive this; he had turned round to play with Milady's favourite monkey, which had pulled him by the doublet.

"You are welcome, Monsieur," said Milady, in a voice whose singular sweetness contrasted with the symptoms of ill-humor which d'Artagnan had just remarked, "you have today acquired eternal rights to my gratitude."

The Englishman then turned round and described the combat without omitting a single detail. Milady listened with the greatest attention, and yet it was easily to be perceived, whatever effort she made to conceal her impressions, that this recital was not agreeable to her. The blood rose to her head, and her little foot worked with impatience beneath her robe.

Lord de Winter perceived nothing of this. When he had finished, he went to a table upon which was a salver with Spanish wine and glasses. He filled two glasses, and by a sign invited d'Artagnan to drink.

D'Artagnan knew it was considered disobliging by an Englishman to refuse to pledge him. He therefore drew near to the table and took the second glass. He did not, however, lose sight of Milady, and in a mirror he perceived the change that came over her face. Now that she believed herself to be no longer observed, a sentiment resembling ferocity animated her countenance. She bit her handkerchief with her beautiful teeth.

That pretty little SOUBRETTE whom d'Artagnan had already observed then came in. She spoke some words to Lord de Winter in English, who thereupon requested d'Artagnan's permission to retire, excusing himself on account of the urgency of the business that had called him away, and charging his sister to obtain his pardon.

D'Artagnan exchanged a shake of the hand with Lord de Winter, and then returned to Milady. Her countenance, with surprising mobility, had recovered its gracious expression, but some little red spots on her handkerchief indicated that she had bitten her lips till the blood came. Those lips were magnificent; they might be said to be of coral.

The conversation took a cheerful turn. Milady appeared to have entirely recovered. She told d'Artagnan that Lord de Winter was her brother-in-law, and not her brother. She had married a younger brother of the family, who had left her a widow with one child. This child was the only heir to Lord de Winter, if Lord de Winter did not marry. All this showed d'Artagnan that there was a veil which concealed something, but he could not yet see under this veil.

In addition to this, after a half hour's conversation d'Artagnan was convinced that Milady was his compatriot; she spoke French with an elegance and a purity that left no doubt on that head.

D'Artagnan was profuse in gallant speeches and protestations of devotion. To all the simple things which escaped our Gascon, Milady replied with a smile of kindness. The hour came for him to retire. D'Artagnan took leave of Milady, and left the saloon the happiest of men.

On the staircase he met the pretty SOUBRETTE, who brushed gently against him as she passed, and then, blushing to the eyes, asked his pardon for having touched him in a voice so sweet that the pardon was granted instantly.

D'Artagnan came again on the morrow, and was still better received than on the evening before. Lord de Winter was not at home; and it was Milady who this time did all the honours of the evening. She appeared to take a great interest in him, asked him whence he came, who were his friends, and whether he had not sometimes thought of attaching himself to the cardinal.

D'Artagnan, who, as we have said, was exceedingly prudent for a young man of twenty, then remembered his suspicions regarding Milady. He launched into a eulogy of his Eminence, and said that he should not have failed to enter into the Guards of the cardinal instead of the king's Guards if he had happened to know M. de Cavois instead of M. de Tréville.

Milady changed the conversation without any appearance of affectation, and asked d'Artagnan in the most careless manner possible if he had ever been in England.

D'Artagnan replied that he had been sent thither by M. de Tréville to treat for a supply of horses, and that he had brought back four as specimens.

Milady in the course of the conversation twice or thrice bit her lips; she had to deal with a Gascon who played close.

At the same hour as on the preceding evening, d'Artagnan retired. In the corridor he again met the pretty Kitty; that was the name of the SOUBRETTE. She looked at him with an expression of kindness which it was impossible to mistake, but d'Artagnan was so preoccupied by the mistress that he noticed absolutely nothing but her.

D'Artagnan came again on the morrow and the day after that, and each day Milady gave him a more gracious reception.

Every evening, either in the antechamber, the corridor, or on the stairs, he met the pretty SOUBRETTE. But, as we have said, d'Artagnan paid no attention to this persistence of poor Kitty.

Chapter 32

A Procurator's Dinner

However brilliant had been the part played by Porthos in the duel, it had not made him forget the dinner of the procurator's wife.

On the morrow he received the last touches of Mousqueton's brush for an hour, and took his way toward the Rue aux Ours with the steps of a man who was doubly in favour with fortune.

His heart beat, but not like d'Artagnan's with a young and impatient love. No; a more material interest stirred his blood. He was about at last to pass that mysterious threshold, to climb those unknown stairs by which, one by one, the old crowns of M. Coquenard had ascended. He was about to see in reality a certain coffer of which he had twenty times beheld the image in his dreams–a coffer long and deep, locked, bolted, fastened in the wall; a coffer of which he had so often heard, and which the hands–a little wrinkled, it is true, but still not without elegance–of the procurator's wife were about to open to his admiring looks.

And then he–a wanderer on the earth, a man without fortune, a man without family, a soldier accustomed to inns, cabarets, taverns, and restaurants, a lover of wine forced to depend upon chance treats–was about to partake of family meals, to enjoy the pleasures of a comfortable establishment, and to give himself up to those little attentions which "the harder one is, the more they please," as old soldiers say.

To come in the capacity of a cousin, and seat himself every day at a good table; to smooth the yellow, wrinkled brow of the old procurator; to pluck the clerks a little by teaching them BASSETTE, PASSE-DIX, and LANSQUENET, in their utmost nicety, and winning from them, by way of fee for the lesson he would give them in an hour, their savings of a month–all this was enormously delightful to Porthos.

The Musketeer could not forget the evil reports which then prevailed, and which indeed have survived them, of the procurators of the period–meanness, stinginess, fasts, but as, after all, excepting some few acts of economy which Porthos had always found very unseasonable, the procurator's wife had been tolerably liberal–that is, be it understood, for a procurator's wife–he hoped to see a household of a highly comfortable kind.

And yet, at the very door the Musketeer began to entertain some doubts. The approach was not such as to prepossess people–an ill-smelling, dark passage, a staircase half-lighted by bars through which stole a glimmer from a neighbouring yard; on the first floor a low door studded with enormous nails, like the principal gate of the Grand Chatelet.

Porthos knocked with his hand. A tall, pale clerk, his face shaded by a forest of virgin hair, opened the door, and bowed with the air of a man forced at once to respect in another lofty stature, which indicated strength, the military dress, which indicated rank, and a ruddy countenance, which indicated familiarity with good living.

A shorter clerk came behind the first, a taller clerk behind the second, a stripling of a dozen years rising behind the third. In all, three clerks and a half, which, for the time, argued a very extensive clientage.

Although the Musketeer was not expected before one o'clock, the procurator's wife had been on the watch ever since midday, reckoning that the heart, or perhaps the stomach, of her lover would bring him before his time.

Mme. Coquenard therefore entered the office from the house at the same moment her guest entered from the stairs, and the appearance of the worthy lady relieved him from an awkward embarrassment. The clerks surveyed him with great curiosity, and he, not knowing well what to say to this ascending and descending scale, remained tongue-tied.

"It is my cousin!" cried the procurator's wife. "Come in, come in, Monsieur Porthos!"

The name of Porthos produced its effect upon the clerks, who began to laugh, but Porthos turned sharply round, and every countenance quickly recovered its gravity.

They reached the office of the procurator after having passed through the antechamber in which the clerks were, and the study in which they ought to have been. This last apartment was a sort of dark room, littered with papers. On quitting the study they left the kitchen on the right, and entered the reception room.

All these rooms, which communicated with one another, did not inspire Porthos favourably. Words might be heard at a distance through all these open doors. Then, while passing, he had cast a rapid, investigating glance into the kitchen; and he was obliged to confess to himself, to the shame of the procurator's wife and his own regret, that he did not see that fire, that animation, that bustle, which when a good repast is on foot prevails generally in that sanctuary of good living.

The procurator had without doubt been warned of his visit, as he expressed no surprise at the sight of Porthos, who advanced toward him with a sufficiently easy air, and saluted him courteously.

"We are cousins, it appears, Monsieur Porthos?" said the procurator, rising, yet supporting his weight upon the arms of his cane chair.

The old man, wrapped in a large black doublet, in which the whole of his slender body was concealed, was brisk and dry. His little gray eyes shone like carbuncles, and appeared, with his grinning mouth, to be the only part of his face in which life survived. Unfortunately the legs began to refuse their service to this bony machine. During the last five or six months that this weakness had been felt, the worthy procurator had nearly become the slave of his wife.

The cousin was received with resignation, that was all. M. Coquenard, firm upon his legs, would have declined all relationship with M. Porthos.

"Yes, Monsieur, we are cousins," said Porthos, without being disconcerted, as he had never reckoned upon being received enthusiastically by the husband.

"By the female side, I believe?" said the procurator, maliciously.

Porthos did not feel the ridicule of this, and took it for a piece of simplicity, at which he laughed in his large moustache. Mme. Coquenard, who knew that a simple-minded procurator was a very rare variety in the species, smiled a little, and coloured a great deal.

M Coquenard had, since the arrival of Porthos, frequently cast his eyes with great uneasiness upon a large chest placed in front of his oak desk. Porthos comprehended that this chest, although it did not correspond in shape with that which he had seen in his dreams, must be the blessed coffer, and he congratulated himself that the reality was several feet higher than the dream.

M Coquenard did not carry his genealogical investigations any further, but withdrawing his anxious look from the chest and fixing it upon Porthos, he contented himself with saying, "Monsieur our cousin will do us the favour of dining with us once before his departure for the campaign, will he not, Madame Coquenard?"

This time Porthos received the blow right in his stomach, and felt it. It appeared likewise that Mme. Coquenard was not less affected by it on her part, for she added, "My cousin will not return if he finds that we do not treat him kindly, but otherwise he has so little time to pass in Paris, and consequently to spare to us, that we must entreat him to give us every instant he can call his own previous to his departure."

"Oh, my legs, my poor legs! Where are you?" murmured Coquenard, and he tried to smile.

This succor, which came to Porthos at the moment in which he was attacked in his gastronomic hopes, inspired much gratitude in the Musketeer toward the procurator's wife.

The hour of dinner soon arrived. They passed into the eating room–a large dark room situated opposite the kitchen.

The clerks, who, as it appeared, had smelled unusual perfumes in the house, were of military punctuality, and held their stools in hand quite ready to sit down. Their jaws moved preliminarily with fearful threatenings.

"Indeed!" thought Porthos, casting a glance at the three hungry clerks–for the errand boy, as might be expected, was not admitted to the honours of the magisterial table, "in my cousin's place, I would not keep such gourmands! They look like shipwrecked sailors who have not eaten for six weeks."

M Coquenard entered, pushed along upon his armchair with casters by Mme. Coquenard, whom Porthos assisted in rolling her husband up to the table. He had scarcely entered when he began to agitate his nose and his jaws after the example of his clerks.

"Oh, oh!" said he, "here is a soup which is rather inviting."

"What the devil can they smell so extraordinary in this soup?" said Porthos, at the sight of a pale liquid, abundant but entirely free from meat, on the surface of which a few crusts swam about as rare as the islands of an archipelago.

Mme. Coquenard smiled, and upon a sign from her everyone eagerly took his seat.

M Coquenard was served first, then Porthos. Afterward Mme. Coquenard filled her own plate, and distributed the crusts without soup to the impatient clerks. At this moment the door of the dining room unclosed with a creak, and Porthos perceived through the half-open flap the little clerk who, not being allowed to take part in the feast, ate his dry bread in the passage with the double odor of the dining room and kitchen.

After the soup the maid brought a boiled fowl–a piece of magnificence which caused the eyes of the diners to dilate in such a manner that they seemed ready to burst.

"One may see that you love your family, Madame Coquenard," said the procurator, with a smile that was almost tragic. "You are certainly treating your cousin very handsomely!"

The poor fowl was thin, and covered with one of those thick, bristly skins through which the teeth cannot penetrate with all their efforts. The fowl must have been sought for a long time on the perch, to which it had retired to die of old age.

"The devil!" thought Porthos, "this is poor work. I respect old age, but I don't much like it boiled or roasted."

And he looked round to see if anybody partook of his opinion, but on the contrary, he saw nothing but eager eyes which were devouring, in anticipation, that sublime fowl which was the object of his contempt.

Mme. Coquenard drew the dish toward her, skillfully detached the two great black feet, which she placed upon her husband's plate, cut off the neck, which with the head she put on one side for herself, raised the wing for Porthos, and then returned the bird otherwise intact to the servant who had brought it in, who disappeared with it before the Musketeer had time to examine the variations which disappointment produces upon faces, according to the characters and temperaments of those who experience it.

In the place of the fowl a dish of haricot beans made its appearance–an enormous dish in which some bones of mutton that at first sight one might have believed to have some meat on them pretended to show themselves.

But the clerks were not the dupes of this deceit, and their lugubrious looks settled down into resigned countenances.

Mme. Coquenard distributed this dish to the young men with the moderation of a good housewife.

The time for wine came. M. Coquenard poured from a very small stone bottle the third of a glass for each of the young men, served himself in about the same proportion, and passed the bottle to Porthos and Mme. Coquenard.

The young men filled up their third of a glass with water; then, when they had drunk half the glass, they filled it up again, and continued to do so. This brought them, by the end of the repast, to swallowing a drink which from the colour of the ruby had passed to that of a pale topaz.

Porthos ate his wing of the fowl timidly, and shuddered when he felt the knee of the procurator's wife under the table, as it came in search of his. He also drank half a glass of this sparingly served wine, and found it to be nothing but that horrible Montreuil–the terror of all expert palates.

M Coquenard saw him swallowing this wine undiluted, and sighed deeply.

"Will you eat any of these beans, Cousin Porthos?" said Mme. Coquenard, in that tone which says, "Take my advice, don't touch them."

"Devil take me if I taste one of them!" murmured Porthos to himself, and then said aloud, "Thank you, my cousin, I am no longer hungry."

There was silence. Porthos could hardly keep his countenance.

The procurator repeated several times, "Ah, Madame Coquenard! Accept my compliments; your dinner has been a real feast. Lord, how I have eaten!"

M Coquenard had eaten his soup, the black feet of the fowl, and the only mutton bone on which there was the least appearance of meat.

Porthos fancied they were mystifying him, and began to curl his moustache and knit his eyebrows, but the knee of Mme. Coquenard gently advised him to be patient.

This silence and this interruption in serving, which were unintelligible to Porthos, had, on the contrary, a terrible meaning for the clerks. Upon a look from the procurator, accompanied by a smile from Mme. Coquenard, they arose slowly from the table, folded their napkins more slowly still, bowed, and retired.

"Go, young men! Go and promote digestion by working," said the procurator, gravely.

The clerks gone, Mme. Coquenard rose and took from a buffet a piece of cheese, some preserved quinces, and a cake which she had herself made of almonds and honey.

M Coquenard knit his eyebrows because there were too many good things. Porthos bit his lips because he saw not the wherewithal to dine. He looked to see if the dish of beans was still there; the dish of beans had disappeared.

"A positive feast!" cried M. Coquenard, turning about in his chair, "a real feast, EPULCE EPULORUM. Lucullus dines with Lucullus."

Porthos looked at the bottle, which was near him, and hoped that with wine, bread, and cheese, he might make a dinner, but wine was wanting, the bottle was empty. M. and Mme. Coquenard did not seem to observe it.

"This is fine!" said Porthos to himself, "I am prettily caught!"

He passed his tongue over a spoonful of preserves, and stuck his teeth into the sticky pastry of Mme. Coquenard.

"Now," said he, "the sacrifice is consummated! Ah! if I had not the hope of peeping with Madame Coquenard into her husband's chest!"

M Coquenard, after the luxuries of such a repast, which he called an excess, felt the want of a siesta. Porthos began to hope that the thing would take place at the present sitting, and in that same locality, but the procurator would listen to nothing, he would be taken to his room, and was not satisfied till he was close to his chest, upon the edge of which, for still greater precaution, he placed his feet.

The procurator's wife took Porthos into an adjoining room, and they began to lay the basis of a reconciliation.

"You can come and dine three times a week," said Mme. Coquenard.

"Thanks, Madame!" said Porthos, "but I don't like to abuse your kindness; besides, I must think of my outfit!"

"That's true," said the procurator's wife, groaning, "that unfortunate outfit!"

"Alas, yes," said Porthos, "it is so."

"But of what, then, does the equipment of your company consist, Monsieur Porthos?"

"Oh, of many things!" said Porthos. "The Musketeers are, as you know, picked soldiers, and they require many things useless to the Guardsmen or the Swiss."

"But yet, detail them to me."

"Why, they may amount to–," said Porthos, who preferred discussing the total to taking them one by one.

The procurator's wife waited tremblingly.

"To how much?" said she. "I hope it does not exceed–" She stopped; speech failed her.

"Oh, no," said Porthos, "it does not exceed two thousand five hundred livres! I even think that with economy I could manage it with two thousand livres."

"Good God!" cried she, "two thousand livres! Why, that is a fortune!"

Porthos made a most significant grimace; Mme. Coquenard understood it.

"I wished to know the detail," said she, "because, having many relatives in business, I was almost sure of obtaining things at a hundred per cent less than you would pay yourself."

"Ah, ah!" said Porthos, "that is what you meant to say!"

"Yes, dear Monsieur Porthos. Thus, for instance, don't you in the first place want a horse?"

"Yes, a horse."

"Well, then! I can just suit you."

"Ah!" said Porthos, brightening, "that's well as regards my horse, but I must have the appointments complete, as they include objects which a Musketeer alone can purchase, and which will not amount, besides, to more than three hundred livres."

"Three hundred livres? Then put down three hundred livres," said the procurator's wife, with a sigh.

Porthos smiled. It may be remembered that he had the saddle which came from Buckingham. These three hundred livres he reckoned upon putting snugly into his pocket.

"Then," continued he, "there is a horse for my lackey, and my valise. As to my arms, it is useless to trouble you about them; I have them."

"A horse for your lackey?" resumed the procurator's wife, hesitatingly, "but that is doing things in lordly style, my friend."

"Ah, Madame!" said Porthos, haughtily, "do you take me for a beggar?"

"No; I only thought that a pretty mule makes sometimes as good an appearance as a horse, and it seemed to me that by getting a pretty mule for Mousqueton–"

"Well, agreed for a pretty mule," said Porthos, "you are right, I have seen very great Spanish nobles whose whole suite were mounted on mules. But then you understand, Madame Coquenard, a mule with feathers and bells."

"Be satisfied," said the procurator's wife.

"There remains the valise," added Porthos.

"Oh, don't let that disturb you," cried Mme. Coquenard. "My husband has five or six valises; you shall choose the best. There is one in particular which he prefers in his journeys, large enough to hold all the world."

"Your valise is then empty?" asked Porthos, with simplicity.

"Certainly it is empty," replied the procurator's wife, in real innocence.

"Ah, but the valise I want," cried Porthos, "is a well-filled one, my dear."

Madame uttered fresh sighs. Moliere had not written his scene in "L'Avare" then. Mme. Coquenard was in the dilemma of Harpagan.

Finally, the rest of the equipment was successively debated in the same manner; and the result of the sitting was that the procurator's wife should give eight hundred livres in money, and should furnish the horse and the mule which should have the honour of carrying Porthos and Mousqueton to glory.

These conditions being agreed to, Porthos took leave of Mme. Coquenard. The latter wished to detain him by darting certain tender glances, but Porthos urged the commands of duty, and the procurator's wife was obliged to give place to the king.

The Musketeer returned home hungry and in bad humor.

Chapter 33

SOUBRETTE And Mistress

Meantime, as we have said, despite the cries of his conscience and the wise counsels of Athos, d'Artagnan became hourly more in love with Milady. Thus he never failed to pay his diurnal court to her; and the self-satisfied Gascon was convinced that sooner or later she could not fail to respond.

One day, when he arrived with his head in the air, and as light at heart as a man who awaits a shower of gold, he found the SOUBRETTE under the gateway of the hotel, but this time the pretty Kitty was not contented with touching him as he passed, she took him gently by the hand.

"Good!" thought d'Artagnan, "She is charged with some message for me from her mistress; she is about to appoint some rendezvous of which she had not courage to speak." And he looked down at the pretty girl with the most triumphant air imaginable.

"I wish to say three words to you, Monsieur Chevalier," stammered the SOUBRETTE.

"Speak, my child, speak," said d'Artagnan, "I listen."

"Here? Impossible! That which I have to say is too long, and above all, too secret."

"Well, what is to be done?"

"If Monsieur Chevalier would follow me?" said Kitty, timidly.

"Where you please, my dear child."

"Come, then."

And Kitty, who had not let go the hand of d'Artagnan, led him up a little dark, winding staircase, and after ascending about fifteen steps, opened a door.

"Come in here, Monsieur Chevalier," said she, "here we shall be alone, and can talk."

"And whose room is this, my dear child?"

"It is mine, Monsieur Chevalier; it communicates with my mistress's by that door. But you need not fear. She will not hear what we say; she never goes to bed before midnight."

D'Artagnan cast a glance around him. The little apartment was charming for its taste and neatness, but in spite of himself, his eyes were directed to that door which Kitty said led to Milady's chamber.

Kitty guessed what was passing in the mind of the young man, and heaved a deep sigh.

"You love my mistress, then, very dearly, Monsieur Chevalier?" said she.

"Oh, more than I can say, Kitty! I am mad for her!"

Kitty breathed a second sigh.

"Alas, Monsieur," said she, "that is too bad."

"What the devil do you see so bad in it?" said d'Artagnan.

"Because, Monsieur," replied Kitty, "my mistress loves you not at all."

"HEIN!" said d'Artagnan, "can she have charged you to tell me so?"

"Oh, no, Monsieur, but out of the regard I have for you, I have taken the resolution to tell you so."

"Much obliged, my dear Kitty, but for the intention only–for the information, you must agree, is not likely to be at all agreeable."

"That is to say, you don't believe what I have told you; is it not so?"

"We have always some difficulty in believing such things, my pretty dear, were it only from self-love."

"Then you don't believe me?"

"I confess that unless you deign to give me some proof of what you advance–"

"What do you think of this?"

Kitty drew a little note from her bosom.

"For me?" said d'Artagnan, seizing the letter.

"No; for another."

"For another?"

"Yes."

"His name; his name!" cried d'Artagnan.

"Read the address."

"Monsieur El Comte de Wardes."

The remembrance of the scene at St. Germain presented itself to the mind of the presumptuous Gascon. As quick as thought, he tore open the letter, in spite of the cry which Kitty uttered on seeing what he was going to do, or rather, what he was doing.

"Oh, good Lord, Monsieur Chevalier," said she, "what are you doing?"

"I?" said d'Artagnan, "nothing," and he read,

"You have not answered my first note. Are you indisposed, or have you forgotten the glances you favoured me with at the ball of Mme. de Guise? You have an opportunity now, Count; do not allow it to escape."

D'Artagnan became very pale; he was wounded in his SELF-LOVE: he thought that it was in his LOVE.

"Poor dear Monsieur d'Artagnan," said Kitty, in a voice full of compassion, and pressing anew the young man's hand.

"You pity me, little one?" said d'Artagnan.

"Oh, yes, and with all my heart; for I know what it is to be in love."

"You know what it is to be in love?" said d'Artagnan, looking at her for the first time with much attention.

"Alas, yes."

"Well, then, instead of pitying me, you would do much better to assist me in avenging myself on your mistress."

"And what sort of revenge would you take?"

"I would triumph over her, and supplant my rival."

"I will never help you in that, Monsieur Chevalier," said Kitty, warmly.

"And why not?" demanded d'Artagnan.

"For two reasons."

"What ones?"

"The first is that my mistress will never love you."

"How do you know that?"

"You have cut her to the heart."

"I? In what can I have offended her–I who ever since I have known her have lived at her feet like a slave? Speak, I beg you!"

"I will never confess that but to the man–who should read to the bottom of my soul!"

D'Artagnan looked at Kitty for the second time. The young girl had freshness and beauty which many duchesses would have purchased with their coronets.

"Kitty," said he, "I will read to the bottom of your soul whenever you like; don't let that disturb you." And he gave her a kiss at which the poor girl became as red as a cherry.

"Oh, no," said Kitty, "it is not me you love! It is my mistress you love; you told me so just now."

"And does that hinder you from letting me know the second reason?"

"The second reason, Monsieur the Chevalier," replied Kitty, emboldened by the kiss in the first place, and still further by the expression of the eyes of the young man, "is that in love, everyone for herself!"

Then only d'Artagnan remembered the languishing glances of Kitty, her constantly meeting him in the antechamber, the corridor, or on the stairs, those touches of the hand every time she met him, and her deep sighs, but absorbed by his desire to please the great lady, he had disdained the SOUBRETTE. He whose game is the eagle takes no heed of the sparrow.

But this time our Gascon saw at a glance all the advantage to be derived from the love which Kitty had just confessed so innocently, or so boldly: the interception of letters addressed to the Comte de Wardes, news on the spot, entrance at all hours into Kitty's chamber, which was contiguous to her mistress's. The perfidious deceiver was, as may plainly be perceived, already sacrificing, in intention, the poor girl in order to obtain Milady, willy-nilly.

"Well," said he to the young girl, "are you willing, my dear Kitty, that I should give you a proof of that love which you doubt?"

"What love?" asked the young girl.

"Of that which I am ready to feel toward you."

"And what is that proof?"

"Are you willing that I should this evening pass with you the time I generally spend with your mistress?"

"Oh, yes," said Kitty, clapping her hands, "very willing."

"Well, then, come here, my dear," said d'Artagnan, establishing himself in an easy chair, "come, and let me tell you that you are the prettiest SOUBRETTE I ever saw!"

And he did tell her so much, and so well, that the poor girl, who asked nothing better than to believe him, did believe him. Nevertheless, to d'Artagnan's great astonishment, the pretty Kitty defended herself resolutely.

Time passes quickly when it is passed in attacks and defenses. Midnight sounded, and almost at the same time the bell was rung in Milady's chamber.

"Good God," cried Kitty, "there is my mistress calling me! Go; go directly!"

D'Artagnan rose, took his hat, as if it had been his intention to obey, then, opening quickly the door of a large closet instead of that leading to the staircase, he buried himself amid the robes and dressing gowns of Milady.

"What are you doing?" cried Kitty.

D'Artagnan, who had secured the key, shut himself up in the closet without reply.

"Well," cried Milady, in a sharp voice. "Are you asleep, that you don't answer when I ring?"

And d'Artagnan heard the door of communication opened violently.

"Here am I, Milady, here am I!" cried Kitty, springing forward to meet her mistress.

Both went into the bedroom, and as the door of communication remained open, d'Artagnan could hear Milady for some time scolding her maid. She was at length appeased, and the conversation turned upon him while Kitty was assisting her mistress.

"Well," said Milady, "I have not seen our Gascon this evening."

"What, Milady! has he not come?" said Kitty. "Can he be inconstant before being happy?"

"Oh, no; he must have been prevented by Monsieur de Tréville or Monsieur Dessessart. I understand my game, Kitty; I have this one safe."

"What will you do with him, Madame?"

"What will I do with him? Be easy, Kitty, there is something between that man and me that he is quite ignorant of: he nearly made me lose my credit with his Eminence. Oh, I will be revenged!"

"I believed that Madame loved him."

"I love him? I detest him! An idiot, who held the life of Lord de Winter in his hands and did not kill him, by which I missed three hundred thousand livres' income."

"That's true," said Kitty, "your son was the only heir of his uncle, and until his majority you would have had the enjoyment of his fortune."

D'Artagnan shuddered to the marrow at hearing this suave creature reproach him, with that sharp voice which she took such pains to conceal in conversation, for not having killed a man whom he had seen load her with kindnesses.

"For all this," continued Milady, "I should long ago have revenged myself on him if, and I don't know why, the cardinal had not requested me to conciliate him."

"Oh, yes, but Madame has not conciliated that little woman he was so fond of."

"What, the mercer's wife of the Rue des Fossoyeurs? Has he not already forgotten she ever existed? Fine vengeance that, on my faith!"

A cold sweat broke from d'Artagnan's brow. Why, this woman was a monster! He resumed his listening, but unfortunately the toilet was finished.

"That will do," said Milady, "go into your own room, and tomorrow endeavour again to get me an answer to the letter I gave you."

"For Monsieur de Wardes?" said Kitty.

"To be sure; for Monsieur de Wardes."

"Now, there is one," said Kitty, "who appears to me quite a different sort of a man from that poor Monsieur d'Artagnan."

"Go to bed, mademoiselle," said Milady, "I don't like comments."

D'Artagnan heard the door close; then the noise of two bolts by which Milady fastened herself in. On her side, but as softly as possible, Kitty turned the key of the lock, and then d'Artagnan opened the closet door.

"Oh, good Lord!" said Kitty, in a low voice, "what is the matter with you? How pale you are!"

"The abominable creature," murmured d'Artagnan.

"Silence, silence, begone!" said Kitty. "There is nothing but a wainscot between my chamber and Milady's; every word that is uttered in one can be heard in the other."

"That's exactly the reason I won't go," said d'Artagnan.

"What!" said Kitty, blushing.

"Or, at least, I will go–later."

He drew Kitty to him. She had the less motive to resist, resistance would make so much noise. Therefore Kitty surrendered.

It was a movement of vengeance upon Milady. D'Artagnan believed it right to say that vengeance is the pleasure of the gods.

With a little more heart, he might have been contented with this new conquest, but the principal features of his character were ambition and pride. It must, however, be confessed in his justification that the first use he made of his influence over Kitty was to try and find out what had become of Mme. Bonacieux, but the poor girl swore upon the crucifix to d'Artagnan that she was entirely ignorant on that head, her mistress never admitting her into half her secrets–only she believed she could say she was not dead.

As to the cause which was near making Milady lose her credit with the cardinal, Kitty knew nothing about it, but this time d'Artagnan was better informed than she was. As he had seen Milady on board a vessel at the moment he was leaving England, he suspected that it was, almost without a doubt, on account of the diamond studs.

But what was clearest in all this was that the true hatred, the profound hatred, the inveterate hatred of Milady, was increased by his not having killed her brother-in-law.

D'Artagnan came the next day to Milady's, and finding her in a very ill-humor, had no doubt that it was lack of an answer from M. de Wardes that provoked her thus. Kitty came in, but Milady was very cross with her. The poor girl ventured a glance at d'Artagnan which said, "See how I suffer on your account!"

Toward the end of the evening, however, the beautiful lioness became milder; she smilingly listened to the soft speeches of d'Artagnan, and even gave him her hand to kiss.

D'Artagnan departed, scarcely knowing what to think, but as he was a youth who did not easily lose his head, while continuing to pay his court to Milady, he had framed a little plan in his mind.

He found Kitty at the gate, and, as on the preceding evening, went up to her chamber. Kitty had been accused of negligence and severely scolded. Milady could not at all comprehend the silence of the Comte de Wardes, and she ordered Kitty to come at nine o'clock in the morning to take a third letter.

D'Artagnan made Kitty promise to bring him that letter on the following morning. The poor girl promised all her lover desired; she was mad.

Things passed as on the night before. D'Artagnan concealed himself in his closet; Milady called, undressed, sent away Kitty, and shut the door. As the night before, d'Artagnan did not return home till five o'clock in the morning.

At eleven o'clock Kitty came to him. She held in her hand a fresh billet from Milady. This time the poor girl did not even argue with d'Artagnan; she gave it to him at once. She belonged body and soul to her handsome soldier.

D'Artagnan opened the letter and read as follows:

This is the third time I have written to you to tell you that I love you. Beware that I do not write to you a fourth time to tell you that I detest you.

If you repent of the manner in which you have acted toward me, the young girl who brings you this will tell you how a man of spirit may obtain his pardon.

D'Artagnan coloured and grew pale several times in reading this billet.

"Oh, you love her still," said Kitty, who had not taken her eyes off the young man's countenance for an instant.

"No, Kitty, you are mistaken. I do not love her, but I will avenge myself for her contempt."

"Oh, yes, I know what sort of vengeance! You told me that!"

"What matters it to you, Kitty? You know it is you alone whom I love."

"How can I know that?"

"By the scorn I will throw upon her."

D'Artagnan took a pen and wrote:

Madame, Until the present moment I could not believe that it was to me your first two letters were addressed, so unworthy did I feel myself of such an honour; besides, I was so seriously indisposed that I could not in any case have replied to them.

But now I am forced to believe in the excess of your kindness, since not only your letter but your servant assures me that I have the good fortune to be beloved by you.

She has no occasion to teach me the way in which a man of spirit may obtain his pardon. I will come and ask mine at eleven o'clock this evening.

To delay it a single day would be in my eyes now to commit a fresh offense.

From him whom you have rendered the happiest of men, Comte de Wardes

This note was in the first place a forgery; it was likewise an indelicacy. It was even, according to our present manners, something like an infamous action, but at that period people did not manage affairs as they do today. Besides, d'Artagnan from her own admission knew Milady culpable of treachery in matters more important, and could entertain no respect for her. And yet, notwithstanding this want of respect, he felt an uncontrollable passion for this woman boiling in his veins–passion drunk with contempt, but passion or thirst, as the reader pleases.

D'Artagnan's plan was very simple. By Kitty's chamber he could gain that of her mistress. He would take advantage of the first moment of surprise, shame, and terror, to triumph over her. He might fail, but something must be left to chance. In eight days the campaign would open, and he would be compelled to leave Paris; d'Artagnan had no time for a prolonged love siege.

"There," said the young man, handing Kitty the letter sealed, "give that to Milady. It is the count's reply."

Poor Kitty became as pale as death; she suspected what the letter contained.

"Listen, my dear girl," said d'Artagnan, "you cannot but perceive that all this must end, some way or other. Milady may discover that you gave the first billet to my lackey instead of to the count's; that it is I who have opened the others which ought to have been opened by de Wardes. Milady will then turn you out of doors, and you know she is not the woman to limit her vengeance."

"Alas!" said Kitty, "for whom have I exposed myself to all that?"

"For me, I well know, my sweet girl," said d'Artagnan. "But I am grateful, I swear to you."

"But what does this note contain?"

"Milady will tell you."

"Ah, you do not love me!" cried Kitty, "and I am very wretched."

To this reproach there is always one response which deludes women. D'Artagnan replied in such a manner that Kitty remained in her great delusion. Although she cried freely before deciding to transmit the letter to her mistress, she did at last so decide, which was all d'Artagnan wished. Finally he promised that he would leave her mistress's presence at an early hour that evening, and that when he left the mistress he would ascend with the maid. This promise completed poor Kitty's consolation.

Chapter 34

In Which The Equipment Of Aramis And Porthos Is Treated Of

Since the four friends had been each in search of his equipments, there had been no fixed meeting between them. They dined apart from one another, wherever they might happen to be, or rather where they could. Duty likewise on its part took a portion of that precious time which was gliding away so rapidly–only they had agreed to meet once a week, about one o'clock, at the residence of Athos, seeing that he, in agreement with the vow he had formed, did not pass over the threshold of his door.

This day of reunion was the same day as that on which Kitty came to find d'Artagnan. Soon as Kitty left him, d'Artagnan directed his steps toward the Rue Ferou.

He found Athos and Aramis philosophising. Aramis had some slight inclination to resume the cassock. Athos, according to his system, neither encouraged nor dissuaded him. Athos believed that everyone should be left to his own free will. He never gave advice but when it was asked, and even then he required to be asked twice.

"People, in general," he said, "only ask advice not to follow it; or if they do follow it, it is for the sake of having someone to blame for having given it."

Porthos arrived a minute after d'Artagnan. The four friends were reunited.

The four countenances expressed four different feelings: that of Porthos, tranquillity; that of d'Artagnan, hope; that of Aramis, uneasiness; that of Athos, carelessness.

At the end of a moment's conversation, in which Porthos hinted that a lady of elevated rank had condescended to relieve him from his embarrassment, Mousqueton entered. He came to request his master to return to his lodgings, where his presence was urgent, as he piteously said.

"Is it my equipment?"

"Yes and no," replied Mousqueton.

"Well, but can't you speak?"

"Come, Monsieur."

Porthos rose, saluted his friends, and followed Mousqueton. An instant after, Bazin made his appearance at the door.

"What do you want with me, my friend?" said Aramis, with that mildness of language which was observable in him every time that his ideas were directed toward the Church.

"A man wishes to see Monsieur at home," replied Bazin.

"A man! What man?"

"A mendicant."

"Give him alms, Bazin, and bid him pray for a poor sinner."

"This mendicant insists upon speaking to you, and pretends that you will be very glad to see him."

"Has he sent no particular message for me?"

"Yes. If Monsieur Aramis hesitates to come," he said, "tell him I am from Tours."

"From Tours!" cried Aramis. "A thousand pardons, gentlemen, but no doubt this man brings me the news I expected." And rising also, he went off at a quick pace. There remained Athos and d'Artagnan.

"I believe these fellows have managed their business. What do you think, d'Artagnan?" said Athos.

"I know that Porthos was in a fair way," replied d'Artagnan, "and as to Aramis to tell you the truth, I have never been seriously uneasy on his account. But you, my dear Athos–you, who so generously distributed the Englishman's pistoles, which were our legitimate property–what do you mean to do?"

"I am satisfied with having killed that fellow, my boy, seeing that it is blessed bread to kill an Englishman, but if I had pocketed his pistoles, they would have weighed me down like a remorse."

"Go to, my dear Athos; you have truly inconceivable ideas."

"Let it pass. What do you think of Monsieur de Tréville telling me, when he did me the honour to call upon me yesterday, that you associated with the suspected English, whom the cardinal protects?"

"That is to say, I visit an Englishwoman–the one I named."

"Oh, ay! The fair woman on whose account I gave you advice, which naturally you took care not to adopt."

"I gave you my reasons."

"Yes; you look there for your outfit, I think you said."

"Not at all. I have acquired certain knowledge that that woman was concerned in the abduction of Madame Bonacieux."

"Yes, I understand now: to find one woman, you court another. It is the longest road, but certainly the most amusing."

D'Artagnan was on the point of telling Athos all, but one consideration restrained him. Athos was a gentleman, punctilious in points of honour; and there were in the plan which our lover had devised for Milady, he was sure, certain things that would not obtain the assent of this Puritan. He was therefore silent; and as Athos was the least inquisitive of any man on earth, d'Artagnan's confidence stopped there. We will therefore leave the two friends, who had nothing important to say to each other, and follow Aramis.

Upon being informed that the person who wanted to speak to him came from Tours, we have seen with what rapidity the young man followed, or rather went before, Bazin; he ran without stopping from the Rue Ferou to the Rue de Vaugirard. On entering he found a man of short stature and intelligent eyes, but covered with rags.

"You have asked for me?" said the Musketeer.

"I wish to speak with Monsieur Aramis. Is that your name, Monsieur?"

"My very own. You have brought me something?"

"Yes, if you show me a certain embroidered handkerchief."

"Here it is," said Aramis, taking a small key from his breast and opening a little ebony box inlaid with mother of pearl, "here it is. Look."

"That is right," replied the mendicant, "dismiss your lackey."

In fact, Bazin, curious to know what the mendicant could want with his master, kept pace with him as well as he could, and arrived almost at the same time he did, but his quickness was not of much use to him. At the hint from the mendicant his master made him a sign to retire, and he was obliged to obey.

Bazin gone, the mendicant cast a rapid glance around him in order to be sure that nobody could either see or hear him, and opening his ragged vest, badly held together by a leather strap, he began to rip the upper part of his doublet, from which he drew a letter.

Aramis uttered a cry of joy at the sight of the seal, kissed the superscription with an almost religious respect, and opened the epistle, which contained what follows:

"My Friend, it is the will of fate that we should be still for some time separated, but the delightful days of youth are not lost beyond return. Perform your duty in camp; I will do mine elsewhere. Accept that which the bearer brings you; make the campaign like a handsome true gentleman, and think of me, who kisses tenderly your black eyes.

"Adieu; or rather, AU REVOIR."

The mendicant continued to rip his garments; and drew from amid his rags a hundred and fifty Spanish double pistoles, which he laid down on the table; then he opened the door, bowed, and went out before the young man, stupefied by his letter, had ventured to address a word to him.

Aramis then reperused the letter, and perceived a postscript:

PS. You may behave politely to the bearer, who is a count and a grandee of Spain!

"Golden dreams!" cried Aramis. "Oh, beautiful life! Yes, we are young; yes, we shall yet have happy days! My love, my blood, my life! all, all, all, are thine, my adored mistress!"

And he kissed the letter with passion, without even vouchsafing a look at the gold which sparkled on the table.

Bazin scratched at the door, and as Aramis had no longer any reason to exclude him, he bade him come in.

Bazin was stupefied at the sight of the gold, and forgot that he came to announce d'Artagnan, who, curious to know who the mendicant could be, came to Aramis on leaving Athos.

Now, as d'Artagnan used no ceremony with Aramis, seeing that Bazin forgot to announce him, he announced himself.

"The devil! My dear Aramis," said d'Artagnan, "if these are the prunes that are sent to you from Tours, I beg you will make my compliments to the gardener who gathers them."

"You are mistaken, friend d'Artagnan," said Aramis, always on his guard, "this is from my publisher, who has just sent me the price of that poem in one-syllable verse which I began yonder."

"Ah, indeed," said d'Artagnan. "Well, your publisher is very generous, my dear Aramis, that's all I can say."

"How, Monsieur?" cried Bazin, "a poem sell so dear as that! It is incredible! Oh, Monsieur, you can write as much as you like; you may become equal to Monsieur de Voiture and Monsieur de Benserade. I like that. A poet is as good as an abbé. Ah! Monsieur Aramis, become a poet, I beg of you."

"Bazin, my friend," said Aramis, "I believe you meddle with my conversation."

Bazin perceived he was wrong; he bowed and went out.

"Ah!" said d'Artagnan with a smile, "you sell your productions at their weight in gold. You are very fortunate, my friend, but take care or you will lose that letter which is peeping from your doublet, and which also comes, no doubt, from your publisher."

Aramis blushed to the eyes, crammed in the letter, and rebuttoned his doublet.

"My dear d'Artagnan," said he, "if you please, we will join our friends; as I am rich, we will today begin to dine together again, expecting that you will be rich in your turn."

"My faith!" said d'Artagnan, with great pleasure. "It is long since we have had a good dinner; and I, for my part, have a somewhat hazardous expedition for this evening, and shall not be sorry, I confess, to fortify myself with a few glasses of good old Burgundy."

"Agreed, as to the old Burgundy; I have no objection to that," said Aramis, from whom the letter and the gold had removed, as by magic, his ideas of conversion.

And having put three or four double pistoles into his pocket to answer the needs of the moment, he placed the others in the ebony box, inlaid with mother of pearl, in which was the famous handkerchief which served him as a talisman.

The two friends repaired to Athos's, and he, faithful to his vow of not going out, took upon him to order dinner to be brought to them. As he was perfectly acquainted with the details of gastronomy, d'Artagnan and Aramis made no objection to abandoning this important care to him.

They went to find Porthos, and at the corner of the Rue Bac met Mousqueton, who, with a most pitiable air, was driving before him a mule and a horse.

D'Artagnan uttered a cry of surprise, which was not quite free from joy.

"Ah, my yellow horse," cried he. "Aramis, look at that horse!"

"Oh, the frightful brute!" said Aramis.

"Ah, my dear," replied d'Artagnan, "upon that very horse I came to Paris."

"What, does Monsieur know this horse?" said Mousqueton.

"It is of an original colour," said Aramis, "I never saw one with such a hide in my life."

"I can well believe it," replied d'Artagnan, "and that was why I got three crowns for him. It must have been for his hide, for, CERTES, the carcass is not worth eighteen livres. But how did this horse come into your hands, Mousqueton?"

"Pray," said the lackey, "say nothing about it, Monsieur; it is a frightful trick of the husband of our duchess!"

"How is that, Mousqueton?"

"Why, we are looked upon with a rather favourable eye by a lady of quality, the Duchesse de–but, your pardon; my master has commanded me to be discreet. She had forced us to accept a little souvenir, a magnificent Spanish GENET and an Andalusian mule, which were beautiful to look upon. The husband heard of the affair; on their way he confiscated the two magnificent beasts which were being sent to us, and substituted these horrible animals."

"Which you are taking back to him?" said d'Artagnan.

"Exactly!" replied Mousqueton. "You may well believe that we will not accept such steeds as these in exchange for those which had been promised to us."

"No, PARDIEU; though I should like to have seen Porthos on my yellow horse. That would give me an idea of how I looked when I arrived in Paris. But don't let us hinder you, Mousqueton; go and perform your master's orders. Is he at home?"

"Yes, Monsieur," said Mousqueton, "but in a very ill humor. Get up!"

He continued his way toward the Quai des Grands Augustins, while the two friends went to ring at the bell of the unfortunate Porthos. He, having seen them crossing the yard, took care not to answer, and they rang in vain.

Meanwhile Mousqueton continued on his way, and crossing the Pont Neuf, still driving the two sorry animals before him, he reached the Rue aux Ours. Arrived there, he fastened, according to the orders of his master, both horse and mule to the knocker of the procurator's door; then, without taking any thought for their future, he returned to Porthos, and told him that his commission was completed.

In a short time the two unfortunate beasts, who had not eaten anything since the morning, made such a noise in raising and letting fall the knocker that the procurator ordered his errand boy to go and inquire in the neighbourhood to whom this horse and mule belonged.

Mme. Coquenard recognised her present, and could not at first comprehend this restitution, but the visit of Porthos soon enlightened her. The anger which fired the eyes of the Musketeer, in spite of his efforts to suppress it, terrified his sensitive inamorata. In fact, Mousqueton had not concealed from his master that he had met d'Artagnan and Aramis, and that d'Artagnan in the yellow horse had recognised the Bearnese pony upon which he had come to Paris, and which he had sold for three crowns.

Porthos went away after having appointed a meeting with the procurator's wife in the cloister of St. Magloire. The procurator, seeing he was going, invited him to dinner–an invitation which the Musketeer refused with a majestic air.

Mme. Coquenard repaired trembling to the cloister of St. Magloire, for she guessed the reproaches that awaited her there, but she was fascinated by the lofty airs of Porthos.

All that which a man wounded in his self-love could let fall in the shape of imprecations and reproaches upon the head of a woman Porthos let fall upon the bowed head of the procurator's wife.

"Alas," said she, "I did all for the best! One of our clients is a horsedealer; he owes money to the office, and is backward in his pay. I took the mule and the horse for what he owed us; he assured me that they were two noble steeds."

"Well, Madame," said Porthos, "if he owed you more than five crowns, your horsedealer is a thief."

"There is no harm in trying to buy things cheap, Monsieur Porthos," said the procurator's wife, seeking to excuse herself.

"No, Madame, but they who so assiduously try to buy things cheap ought to permit others to seek more generous friends." And Porthos, turning on his heel, made a step to retire.

"Monsieur Porthos! Monsieur Porthos!" cried the procurator's wife. "I have been wrong; I see it. I ought not to have driven a bargain when it was to equip a cavalier like you."

Porthos, without reply, retreated a second step. The procurator's wife fancied she saw him in a brilliant cloud, all surrounded by duchesses and marchionesses, who cast bags of money at his feet.

"Stop, in the name of heaven, Monsieur Porthos!" cried she. "Stop, and let us talk."

"Talking with you brings me misfortune," said Porthos.

"But, tell me, what do you ask?"

"Nothing; for that amounts to the same thing as if I asked you for something."

The procurator's wife hung upon the arm of Porthos, and in the violence of her grief she cried out, "Monsieur Porthos, I am ignorant of all such matters! How should I know what a horse is? How should I know what horse furniture is?"

"You should have left it to me, then, Madame, who know what they are, but you wished to be frugal, and consequently to lend at usury."

"It was wrong, Monsieur Porthos, but I will repair that wrong, upon my word of honour."

"How so?" asked the Musketeer.

"Listen. This evening M. Coquenard is going to the house of the Due de Chaulnes, who has sent for him. It is for a consultation, which will last three hours at least. Come! We shall be alone, and can make up our accounts."

"In good time. Now you talk, my dear."

"You pardon me?"

"We shall see," said Porthos, majestically; and the two separated saying, "Till this evening."

"The devil!" thought Porthos, as he walked away, "it appears I am getting nearer to Monsieur Coquenard's strongbox at last."

Chapter 35

A Gascon A Match For Cupid

The evening so impatiently waited for by Porthos and by d'Artagnan at last arrived.

As was his custom, d'Artagnan presented himself at Milady's at about nine o'clock. He found her in a charming humor. Never had he been so well received. Our Gascon knew, by the first glance of his eye, that his billet had been delivered, and that this billet had had its effect.

Kitty entered to bring some sherbet. Her mistress put on a charming face, and smiled on her graciously, but alas! the poor girl was so sad that she did not even notice Milady's condescension.

D'Artagnan looked at the two women, one after the other, and was forced to acknowledge that in his opinion Dame Nature had made a mistake in their formation. To the great lady she had given a heart vile and venal; to the SOUBRETTE she had given the heart of a duchess.

At ten o'clock Milady began to appear restless. D'Artagnan knew what she wanted. She looked at the clock, rose, reseated herself, smiled at d'Artagnan with an air which said, "You are very amiable, no doubt, but you would be charming if you would only depart."

D'Artagnan rose and took his hat; Milady gave him her hand to kiss. The young man felt her press his hand, and comprehended that this was a sentiment, not of coquetry, but of gratitude because of his departure.

"She loves him devilishly," he murmured. Then he went out.

This time Kitty was nowhere waiting for him; neither in the antechamber, nor in the corridor, nor beneath the great door. It was necessary that d'Artagnan should find alone the staircase and the little chamber. She heard him enter, but she did not raise her head. The young man went to her and took her hands; then she sobbed aloud.

As d'Artagnan had presumed, on receiving his letter, Milady in a delirium of joy had told her servant everything; and by way of recompense for the manner in which she had this time executed the commission, she had given Kitty a purse.

Returning to her own room, Kitty had thrown the purse into a corner, where it lay open, disgorging three or four gold pieces on the carpet. The poor girl, under the caresses of d'Artagnan, lifted her head. D'Artagnan himself was frightened by the change in her countenance. She joined her hands with a suppliant air, but without venturing to speak a word. As little sensitive as was the heart of d'Artagnan, he was touched by this mute sorrow, but he held too tenaciously to his projects, above all to this one, to change the program which he had laid out in advance. He did not therefore allow her any hope that he would flinch; only he represented his action as one of simple vengeance.

For the rest this vengeance was very easy; for Milady, doubtless to conceal her blushes from her lover, had ordered Kitty to extinguish all the lights in the apartment, and even in the little chamber itself. Before daybreak M. de Wardes must take his departure, still in obscurity.

Presently they heard Milady retire to her room. D'Artagnan slipped into the wardrobe. Hardly was he concealed when the little bell sounded. Kitty went to her mistress, and did not leave the door open, but the partition was so thin that one could hear nearly all that passed between the two women.

Milady seemed overcome with joy, and made Kitty repeat the smallest details of the pretended interview of the SOUBRETTE with de Wardes when he received the letter; how he had responded; what was the expression of his face; if he seemed very amorous. And to all these questions poor Kitty, forced to put on a pleasant face, responded in a stifled voice whose dolorous accent her mistress did not however remark, solely because happiness is egotistical.

Finally, as the hour for her interview with the count approached, Milady had everything about her darkened, and ordered Kitty to return to her own chamber, and introduce de Wardes whenever he presented himself.

Kitty's detention was not long. Hardly had d'Artagnan seen, through a crevice in his closet, that the whole apartment was in obscurity, than he slipped out of his concealment, at the very moment when Kitty reclosed the door of communication.

"What is that noise?" demanded Milady.

"It is I," said d'Artagnan in a subdued voice, "I, the Comte de Wardes."

"Oh, my God, my God!" murmured Kitty, "he has not even waited for the hour he himself named!"

"Well," said Milady, in a trembling voice, "why do you not enter? Count, Count," added she, "you know that I wait for you."

At this appeal d'Artagnan drew Kitty quietly away, and slipped into the chamber.

If rage or sorrow ever torture the heart, it is when a lover receives under a name which is not his own protestations of love addressed to his happy rival. D'Artagnan was in a dolorous situation which he had not foreseen. Jealousy gnawed his heart; and he suffered almost as much as poor Kitty, who at that very moment was crying in the next chamber.

"Yes, Count," said Milady, in her softest voice, and pressing his hand in her own, "I am happy in the love which your looks and your words have expressed to me every time we have met. I also–I love you. Oh, tomorrow, tomorrow, I must have some pledge from you which will prove that you think of me; and that you may not forget me, take this!" and she slipped a ring from her finger onto d'Artagnan's. D'Artagnan remembered having seen this ring on the finger of Milady; it was a magnificent sapphire, encircled with brilliants.

The first movement of d'Artagnan was to return it, but Milady added, "No, no! Keep that ring for love of me. Besides, in accepting it," she added, in a voice full of emotion, "you render me a much greater service than you imagine."

"This woman is full of mysteries," murmured d'Artagnan to himself. At that instant he felt himself ready to reveal all. He even opened his mouth to tell Milady who he was, and with what a revengeful purpose he had come, but she added, "Poor angel, whom that monster of a Gascon barely failed to kill."

The monster was himself.

"Oh," continued Milady, "do your wounds still make you suffer?"

"Yes, much," said d'Artagnan, who did not well know how to answer.

"Be tranquil," murmured Milady, "I will avenge you–and cruelly!"

"PESTE!" said d'Artagnan to himself, "the moment for confidences has not yet come."

It took some time for d'Artagnan to resume this little dialogue, but then all the ideas of vengeance which he had brought with him had completely vanished. This woman exercised over him an unaccountable power; he hated and adored her at the same time. He would not have believed that two sentiments so opposite could dwell in the same heart, and by their union constitute a passion so strange, and as it were, diabolical.

Presently it sounded one o'clock. It was necessary to separate. D'Artagnan at the moment of quitting Milady felt only the liveliest regret at the parting; and as they addressed each other in a reciprocally passionate adieu, another interview was arranged for the following week.

Poor Kitty hoped to speak a few words to d'Artagnan when he passed through her chamber, but Milady herself reconducted him through the darkness, and only quit him at the staircase.

The next morning d'Artagnan ran to find Athos. He was engaged in an adventure so singular that he wished for counsel. He therefore told him all.

"Your Milady," said he, "appears to be an infamous creature, but not the less you have done wrong to deceive her. In one fashion or another you have a terrible enemy on your hands."

While thus speaking Athos regarded with attention the sapphire set with diamonds which had taken, on d'Artagnan's finger, the place of the queen's ring, carefully kept in a casket.

"You notice my ring?" said the Gascon, proud to display so rich a gift in the eyes of his friends.

"Yes," said Athos, "it reminds me of a family jewel."

"It is beautiful, is it not?" said d'Artagnan.

"Yes," said Athos, "magnificent. I did not think two sapphires of such a fine water existed. Have you traded it for your diamond?"

"No. It is a gift from my beautiful Englishwoman, or rather Frenchwoman–for I am convinced she was born in France, though I have not questioned her."

"That ring comes from Milady?" cried Athos, with a voice in which it was easy to detect strong emotion.

"Her very self; she gave it me last night. Here it is," replied d'Artagnan, taking it from his finger.

Athos examined it and became very pale. He tried it on his left hand; it fit his finger as if made for it.

A shade of anger and vengeance passed across the usually calm brow of this gentleman.

"It is impossible it can be she," said he. "How could this ring come into the hands of Milady Clarik? And yet it is difficult to suppose such a resemblance should exist between two jewels."

"Do you know this ring?" said d'Artagnan.

"I thought I did," replied Athos, "but no doubt I was mistaken." And he returned d'Artagnan the ring without, however, ceasing to look at it.

"Pray, d'Artagnan," said Athos, after a minute, "either take off that ring or turn the mounting inside; it recalls such cruel recollections that I shall have no head to converse with you. Don't ask me for counsel; don't tell me you are perplexed what to do. But stop! let me look at that sapphire again; the one I mentioned to you had one of its faces scratched by accident."

D'Artagnan took off the ring, giving it again to Athos.

Athos started. "Look," said he, "is it not strange?" and he pointed out to d'Artagnan the scratch he had remembered.

"But from whom did this ring come to you, Athos?"

"From my mother, who inherited it from her mother. As I told you, it is an old family jewel."

"And you–sold it?" asked d'Artagnan, hesitatingly.

"No," replied Athos, with a singular smile. "I gave it away in a night of love, as it has been given to you."

D'Artagnan became pensive in his turn; it appeared as if there were abysses in Milady's soul whose depths were dark and unknown. He took back the ring, but put it in his pocket and not on his finger.

"D'Artagnan," said Athos, taking his hand, "you know I love you; if I had a son I could not love him better. Take my advice, renounce this woman. I do not know her, but a sort of intuition tells me she is a lost creature, and that there is something fatal about her."

"You are right," said d'Artagnan, "I will have done with her. I own that this woman terrifies me."

"Shall you have the courage?" said Athos.

"I shall," replied d'Artagnan, "and instantly."

"In truth, my young friend, you will act rightly," said the gentleman, pressing the Gascon's hand with an affection almost paternal, "and God grant that this woman, who has scarcely entered into your life, may not leave a terrible trace in it!" And Athos bowed to d'Artagnan like a man who wishes it understood that he would not be sorry to be left alone with his thoughts.

On reaching home d'Artagnan found Kitty waiting for him. A month of fever could not have changed her more than this one night of sleeplessness and sorrow.

She was sent by her mistress to the false de Wardes. Her mistress was mad with love, intoxicated with joy. She wished to know when her lover would meet her a second night; and poor Kitty, pale and trembling, awaited d'Artagnan's reply. The counsels of his friend, joined to the cries of his own heart, made him determine, now his pride was saved and his vengeance satisfied, not to see Milady again. As a reply, he wrote the following letter:

Do not depend upon me, Madame, for the next meeting. Since my convalescence I have so many affairs of this kind on my hands that I am forced to regulate them a little. When your turn comes, I shall have the honour to inform you of it. I kiss your hands.

Comte de Wardes

Not a word about the sapphire. Was the Gascon determined to keep it as a weapon against Milady, or else, let us be frank, did he not reserve the sapphire as a last resource for his outfit? It would be wrong to judge the actions of one period from the point of view of another. That which would now be considered as disgraceful to a gentleman was at that time quite a simple and natural affair, and the younger sons of the best families were frequently supported by their mistresses. D'Artagnan gave the open letter to Kitty, who at first was unable to comprehend it, but who became almost wild with joy on reading it a second time. She could scarcely believe in her happiness; and d'Artagnan was forced to renew with the living voice the assurances which he had written. And whatever might be–considering the violent character of Milady–the danger which the poor girl incurred in giving this billet to her mistress, she ran back to the Place Royale as fast as her legs could carry her.

The heart of the best woman is pitiless toward the sorrows of a rival.

Milady opened the letter with eagerness equal to Kitty's in bringing it, but at the first words she read she became livid. She crushed the paper in her hand, and turning with flashing eyes upon Kitty, she cried, "What is this letter?"

"The answer to Madame's," replied Kitty, all in a tremble.

"Impossible!" cried Milady. "It is impossible a gentleman could have written such a letter to a woman." Then all at once, starting, she cried, "My God! Can he have–" and she stopped. She ground her teeth; she was of the colour of ashes. She tried to go toward the window for air, but she could only stretch forth her arms; her legs failed her, and she sank into an armchair. Kitty, fearing she was ill, hastened toward her and was beginning to open her dress, but Milady started up, pushing her away. "What do you want with me?" said she, "and why do you place your hand on me?"

"I thought that Madame was ill, and I wished to bring her help," responded the maid, frightened at the terrible expression which had come over her mistress's face.

"I faint? I? I? Do you take me for half a woman? When I am insulted I do not faint; I avenge myself!"

And she made a sign for Kitty to leave the room.

Chapter 36

Dream Of Vengeance

That evening Milady gave orders that when M. d'Artagnan came as usual, he should be immediately admitted, but he did not come.

The next day Kitty went to see the young man again, and related to him all that had passed on the preceding evening. D'Artagnan smiled; this jealous anger of Milady was his revenge.

That evening Milady was still more impatient than on the preceding evening. She renewed the order relative to the Gascon, but as before she expected him in vain.

The next morning, when Kitty presented herself at d'Artagnan's, she was no longer joyous and alert as on the two preceding days, but on the contrary sad as death.

D'Artagnan asked the poor girl what was the matter with her, but she, as her only reply, drew a letter from her pocket and gave it to him.

This letter was in Milady's handwriting; only this time it was addressed to M. d'Artagnan, and not to M. de Wardes.

He opened it and read as follows:

Dear M. d'Artagnan, It is wrong thus to neglect your friends, particularly at the moment you are about to leave them for so long a time. My brother-in-law and myself expected you yesterday and the day before, but in vain. Will it be the same this evening?

Your very grateful, Milady Clarik

"That's all very simple," said d'Artagnan, "I expected this letter. My credit rises by the fall of that of the Comte de Wardes."

"And will you go?" asked Kitty.

"Listen to me, my dear girl," said the Gascon, who sought for an excuse in his own eyes for breaking the promise he had made Athos, "you must understand it would be impolitic not to accept such a positive invitation. Milady, not seeing me come again, would not be able to understand what could cause the interruption of my visits, and might suspect something; who could say how far the vengeance of such a woman would go?"

"Oh, my God!" said Kitty, "you know how to represent things in such a way that you are always in the right. You are going now to pay your court to her again, and if this time you succeed in pleasing her in your own name and with your own face, it will be much worse than before."

Instinct made poor Kitty guess a part of what was to happen. D'Artagnan reassured her as well as he could, and promised to remain insensible to the seductions of Milady.

He desired Kitty to tell her mistress that he could not be more grateful for her kindnesses than he was, and that he would be obedient to her orders. He did not dare to write for fear of not being able–to such experienced eyes as those of Milady–to disguise his writing sufficiently.

As nine o'clock sounded, d'Artagnan was at the Place Royale. It was evident that the servants who waited in the antechamber were warned, for as soon as d'Artagnan appeared, before even he had asked if Milady were visible, one of them ran to announce him.

"Show him in," said Milady, in a quick tone, but so piercing that d'Artagnan heard her in the antechamber.

He was introduced.

"I am at home to nobody," said Milady, "observe, to nobody." The servant went out.

D'Artagnan cast an inquiring glance at Milady. She was pale, and looked fatigued, either from tears or want of sleep. The number of lights had been intentionally diminished, but the young woman could not conceal the traces of the fever which had devoured her for two days.

D'Artagnan approached her with his usual gallantry. She then made an extraordinary effort to receive him, but never did a more distressed countenance give the lie to a more amiable smile.

To the questions which d'Artagnan put concerning her health, she replied, "Bad, very bad."

"Then," replied he, "my visit is ill-timed; you, no doubt, stand in need of repose, and I will withdraw."

"No, no!" said Milady. "On the contrary, stay, Monsieur d'Artagnan; your agreeable company will divert me."

"Oh, oh!" thought d'Artagnan. "She has never been so kind before. On guard!"

Milady assumed the most agreeable air possible, and conversed with more than her usual brilliancy. At the same time the fever, which for an instant abandoned her, returned to give luster to her eyes, colour to her cheeks, and vermilion to her lips. D'Artagnan was again in the presence of the Circe who had before surrounded him with her enchantments. His love, which he believed to be extinct but which was only asleep, awoke again in his heart. Milady smiled, and d'Artagnan felt that he could damn himself for that smile. There was a moment at which he felt something like remorse.

By degrees, Milady became more communicative. She asked d'Artagnan if he had a mistress.

"Alas!" said d'Artagnan, with the most sentimental air he could assume, "can you be cruel enough to put such a question to me–to me, who, from the moment I saw you, have only breathed and sighed through you and for you?"

Milady smiled with a strange smile.

"Then you love me?" said she.

"Have I any need to tell you so? Have you not perceived it?"

"It may be, but you know the more hearts are worth the capture, the more difficult they are to be won."

"Oh, difficulties do not affright me," said d'Artagnan. "I shrink before nothing but impossibilities."

"Nothing is impossible," replied Milady, "to true love."

"Nothing, Madame?"

"Nothing," replied Milady.

"The devil!" thought d'Artagnan. "The note is changed. Is she going to fall in love with me, by chance, this fair inconstant; and will she be disposed to give me myself another sapphire like that which she gave me for de Wardes?"

D'Artagnan rapidly drew his seat nearer to Milady's.

"Well, now," she said, "let us see what you would do to prove this love of which you speak."

"All that could be required of me. Order; I am ready."

"For everything?"

"For everything," cried d'Artagnan, who knew beforehand that he had not much to risk in engaging himself thus.

"Well, now let us talk a little seriously," said Milady, in her turn drawing her armchair nearer to d'Artagnan's chair.

"I am all attention, Madame," said he.

Milady remained thoughtful and undecided for a moment; then, as if appearing to have formed a resolution, she said, "I have an enemy."

"You, Madame!" said d'Artagnan, affecting surprise, "is that possible, my God?–Good and beautiful as you are!"

"A mortal enemy."

"Indeed!"

"An enemy who has insulted me so cruelly that between him and me it is war to the death. May I reckon on you as an auxiliary?"

D'Artagnan at once perceived the ground which the vindictive creature wished to reach.

"You may, Madame," said he, with emphasis. "My arm and my life belong to you, like my love."

"Then," said Milady, "since you are as generous as you are loving–"

She stopped.

"Well?" demanded d'Artagnan.

"Well," replied Milady, after a moment of silence, "from the present time, cease to talk of impossibilities."

"Do not overwhelm me with happiness," cried d'Artagnan, throwing himself on his knees, and covering with kisses the hands abandoned to him.

"Avenge me of that infamous de Wardes," said Milady, between her teeth, "and I shall soon know how to get rid of you–you double idiot, you animated sword blade!"

"Fall voluntarily into my arms, hypocritical and dangerous woman," said d'Artagnan, likewise to himself, "after having abused me with such effrontery, and afterward I will laugh at you with him whom you wish me to kill."

D'Artagnan lifted up his head.

"I am ready," said he.

"You have understood me, then, dear Monsieur d'Artagnan," said Milady.

"I could interpret one of your looks."

"Then you would employ for me your arm which has already acquired so much renown?"

"Instantly!"

"But on my part," said Milady, "how should I repay such a service? I know these lovers. They are men who do nothing for nothing."

"You know the only reply that I desire," said d'Artagnan, "the only one worthy of you and of me!"

And he drew nearer to her.

She scarcely resisted.

"Interested man!" cried she, smiling.

"Ah," cried d'Artagnan, really carried away by the passion this woman had the power to kindle in his heart, "ah, that is because my happiness appears so impossible to me; and I have such fear that it should fly away from me like a dream that I pant to make a reality of it."

"Well, merit this pretended happiness, then!"

"I am at your orders," said d'Artagnan.

"Quite certain?" said Milady, with a last doubt.

"Only name to me the base man that has brought tears into your beautiful eyes!"

"Who told you that I had been weeping?" said she.

"It appeared to me–"

"Such women as I never weep," said Milady.

"So much the better! Come, tell me his name!"

"Remember that his name is all my secret."

"Yet I must know his name."

"Yes, you must; see what confidence I have in you!"

"You overwhelm me with joy. What is his name?"

"You know him."

"Indeed."

"Yes."

"It is surely not one of my friends?" replied d'Artagnan, affecting hesitation in order to make her believe him ignorant.

"If it were one of your friends you would hesitate, then?" cried Milady; and a threatening glance darted from her eyes.

"Not if it were my own brother!" cried d'Artagnan, as if carried away by his enthusiasm.

Our Gascon promised this without risk, for he knew all that was meant.

"I love your devotedness," said Milady.

"Alas, do you love nothing else in me?" asked d'Artagnan.

"I love you also, YOU!" said she, taking his hand.

The warm pressure made d'Artagnan tremble, as if by the touch that fever which consumed Milady attacked himself.

"You love me, you!" cried he. "Oh, if that were so, I should lose my reason!"

And he folded her in his arms. She made no effort to remove her lips from his kisses; only she did not respond to them. Her lips were cold; it appeared to d'Artagnan that he had embraced a statue.

He was not the less intoxicated with joy, electrified by love. He almost believed in the tenderness of Milady; he almost believed in the crime of de Wardes. If de Wardes had at that moment been under his hand, he would have killed him.

Milady seized the occasion.

"His name is–" said she, in her turn.

"De Wardes; I know it," cried d'Artagnan.

"And how do you know it?" asked Milady, seizing both his hands, and endeavouring to read with her eyes to the bottom of his heart.

D'Artagnan felt he had allowed himself to be carried away, and that he had committed an error.

"Tell me, tell me, tell me, I say," repeated Milady, "how do you know it?"

"How do I know it?" said d'Artagnan.

"Yes."

"I know it because yesterday Monsieur de Wardes, in a saloon where I was, showed a ring which he said he had received from you."

"Wretch!" cried Milady.

The epithet, as may be easily understood, resounded to the very bottom of d'Artagnan's heart.

"Well?" continued she.

"Well, I will avenge you of this wretch," replied d'Artagnan, giving himself the airs of Don Japhet of Armenia.

"Thanks, my brave friend!" cried Milady, "and when shall I be avenged?"

"Tomorrow–immediately–when you please!"

Milady was about to cry out, "Immediately," but she reflected that such precipitation would not be very gracious toward d'Artagnan.

Besides, she had a thousand precautions to take, a thousand counsels to give to her defender, in order that he might avoid explanations with the count before witnesses. All this was answered by an expression of d'Artagnan's. "Tomorrow," said he, "you will be avenged, or I shall be dead."

"No," said she, "you will avenge me, but you will not be dead. He is a coward."

"With women, perhaps, but not with men. I know something of him."

"But it seems you had not much reason to complain of your fortune in your contest with him."

"Fortune is a courtesan; favourable yesterday, she may turn her back tomorrow."

"Which means that you now hesitate?"

"No, I do not hesitate; God forbid! But would it be just to allow me to go to a possible death without having given me at least something more than hope?"

Milady answered by a glance which said, "Is that all?–Speak, then." And then accompanying the glance with explanatory words, "That is but too just," said she, tenderly.

"Oh, you are an angel!" exclaimed the young man.

"Then all is agreed?" said she.

"Except that which I ask of you, dear love."

"But when I assure you that you may rely on my tenderness?"

"I cannot wait till tomorrow."

"Silence! I hear my brother. It will be useless for him to find you here."

She rang the bell and Kitty appeared.

"Go out this way," said she, opening a small private door, "and come back at eleven o'clock; we will then terminate this conversation. Kitty will conduct you to my chamber."

The poor girl almost fainted at hearing these words.

"Well, mademoiselle, what are you thinking about, standing there like a statue? Do as I bid you: show the chevalier out; and this evening at eleven o'clock–you have heard what I said."

"It appears that these appointments are all made for eleven o'clock," thought d'Artagnan, "that's a settled custom."

Milady held out her hand to him, which he kissed tenderly.

"But," said he, as he retired as quickly as possible from the reproaches of Kitty, "I must not play the fool. This woman is certainly a great liar. I must take care."

Chapter 37

Milady's Secret

D'Artagnan left the hotel instead of going up at once to Kitty's chamber, as she endeavoured to persuade him to do–and that for two reasons: the first, because by this means he should escape reproaches, recriminations, and prayers; the second, because he was not sorry to have an opportunity of reading his own thoughts and endeavouring, if possible, to fathom those of this woman.

What was most clear in the matter was that d'Artagnan loved Milady like a madman, and that she did not love him at all. In an instant d'Artagnan perceived that the best way in which he could act would be to go home and write Milady a long letter, in which he would confess to her that he and de Wardes were, up to the present moment absolutely the same, and that consequently he could not undertake, without committing suicide, to kill the Comte de Wardes. But he also was spurred on by a ferocious desire of vengeance. He wished to subdue this woman in his own name; and as this vengeance appeared to him to have a certain sweetness in it, he could not make up his mind to renounce it.

He walked six or seven times round the Place Royale, turning at every ten steps to look at the light in Milady's apartment, which was to be seen through the blinds. It was evident that this time the young woman was not in such haste to retire to her apartment as she had been the first.

At length the light disappeared. With this light was extinguished the last irresolution in the heart of d'Artagnan. He recalled to his mind the details of the first night, and with a beating heart and a brain on fire he re-entered the hotel and flew toward Kitty's chamber.

The poor girl, pale as death and trembling in all her limbs, wished to delay her lover, but Milady, with her ear on the watch, had heard the noise d'Artagnan had made, and opening the door, said, "Come in."

All this was of such incredible immodesty, of such monstrous effrontery, that d'Artagnan could scarcely believe what he saw or what he heard. He imagined himself to be drawn into one of those fantastic intrigues one meets in dreams. He, however, darted not the less quickly toward Milady, yielding to that magnetic attraction which the loadstone exercises over iron.

As the door closed after them Kitty rushed toward it. Jealousy, fury, offended pride, all the passions in short that dispute the heart of an outraged woman in love, urged her to make a revelation, but she reflected that she would be totally lost if she confessed having assisted in such a machination, and above all, that d'Artagnan would also be lost to her forever. This last thought of love counseled her to make this last sacrifice.

D'Artagnan, on his part, had gained the summit of all his wishes. It was no longer a rival who was beloved; it was himself who was apparently beloved. A secret voice whispered to him, at the bottom of his heart, that he was but an instrument of vengeance, that he was only caressed till he had given death, but pride, but self-love, but madness silenced this voice and stifled its murmurs.

And then our Gascon, with that large quantity of conceit which we know he possessed, compared himself with de Wardes, and asked himself why, after all, he should not be beloved for himself?

He was absorbed entirely by the sensations of the moment. Milady was no longer for him that woman of fatal intentions who had for a moment terrified him; she was an ardent, passionate mistress, abandoning herself to love which she also seemed to feel. Two hours thus glided away. When the transports of the two lovers were calmer, Milady, who had not the same motives for forgetfulness that d'Artagnan had, was the first to return to reality, and asked the young man if the means which were on the morrow to bring on the encounter between him and de Wardes were already arranged in his mind.

But d'Artagnan, whose ideas had taken quite another course, forgot himself like a fool, and answered gallantly that it was too late to think about duels and sword thrusts.

This coldness toward the only interests that occupied her mind terrified Milady, whose questions became more pressing.

Then d'Artagnan, who had never seriously thought of this impossible duel, endeavoured to turn the conversation, but he could not succeed. Milady kept him within the limits she had traced beforehand with her irresistible spirit and her iron will.

D'Artagnan fancied himself very cunning when advising Milady to renounce, by pardoning de Wardes, the furious projects she had formed.

But at the first word the young woman started, and exclaimed in a sharp, bantering tone, which sounded strangely in the darkness, "Are you afraid, dear Monsieur d'Artagnan?"

"You cannot think so, dear love!" replied d'Artagnan, "but now, suppose this poor Comte de Wardes were less guilty than you think him?"

"At all events," said Milady, seriously, "he has deceived me, and from the moment he deceived me, he merited death."

"He shall die, then, since you condemn him!" said d'Artagnan, in so firm a tone that it appeared to Milady an undoubted proof of devotion. This reassured her.

We cannot say how long the night seemed to Milady, but d'Artagnan believed it to be hardly two hours before the daylight peeped through the window blinds, and invaded the chamber with its paleness. Seeing d'Artagnan about to leave her, Milady recalled his promise to avenge her on the Comte de Wardes.

"I am quite ready," said d'Artagnan, "but in the first place I should like to be certain of one thing."

"And what is that?" asked Milady.

"That is, whether you really love me?"

"I have given you proof of that, it seems to me."

"And I am yours, body and soul!"

"Thanks, my brave lover, but as you are satisfied of my love, you must, in your turn, satisfy me of yours. Is it not so?"

"Certainly, but if you love me as much as you say," replied d'Artagnan, "do you not entertain a little fear on my account?"

"What have I to fear?"

"Why, that I may be dangerously wounded–killed even."

"Impossible!" cried Milady, "you are such a valiant man, and such an expert swordsman."

"You would not, then, prefer a method," resumed d'Artagnan, "which would equally avenge you while rendering the combat useless?"

Milady looked at her lover in silence. The pale light of the first rays of day gave to her clear eyes a strangely frightful expression.

"Really," said she, "I believe you now begin to hesitate."

"No, I do not hesitate, but I really pity this poor Comte de Wardes, since you have ceased to love him. I think that a man must be so severely punished by the loss of your love that he stands in need of no other chastisement."

"Who told you that I loved him?" asked Milady, sharply.

"At least, I am now at liberty to believe, without too much fatuity, that you love another," said the young man, in a caressing tone, "and I repeat that I am really interested for the count."

"You?" asked Milady.

"Yes, I."

"And why YOU?"

"Because I alone know–"

"What?"

"That he is far from being, or rather having been, so guilty toward you as he appears."

"Indeed!" said Milady, in an anxious tone, "explain yourself, for I really cannot tell what you mean."

And she looked at d'Artagnan, who embraced her tenderly, with eyes which seemed to burn themselves away.

"Yes; I am a man of honour," said d'Artagnan, determined to come to an end, "and since your love is mine, and I am satisfied I possess it–for I do possess it, do I not?"

"Entirely; go on."

"Well, I feel as if transformed–a confession weighs on my mind."

"A confession!"

"If I had the least doubt of your love I would not make it, but you love me, my beautiful mistress, do you not?"

"Without doubt."

"Then if through excess of love I have rendered myself culpable toward you, you will pardon me?"

"Perhaps."

D'Artagnan tried with his sweetest smile to touch his lips to Milady's, but she evaded him.

"This confession," said she, growing paler, "what is this confession?"

"You gave de Wardes a meeting on Thursday last in this very room, did you not?"

"No, no! It is not true," said Milady, in a tone of voice so firm, and with a countenance so unchanged, that if d'Artagnan had not been in such perfect possession of the fact, he would have doubted.

"Do not lie, my angel," said d'Artagnan, smiling, "that would be useless."

"What do you mean? Speak! you kill me."

"Be satisfied; you are not guilty toward me, and I have already pardoned you."

"What next? what next?"

"De Wardes cannot boast of anything."

"How is that? You told me yourself that that ring–"

"That ring I have! The Comte de Wardes of Thursday and the d'Artagnan of today are the same person."

The imprudent young man expected a surprise, mixed with shame–a slight storm which would resolve itself into tears, but he was strangely deceived, and his error was not of long duration.

Pale and trembling, Milady repulsed d'Artagnan's attempted embrace by a violent blow on the chest, as she sprang out of bed.

It was almost broad daylight.

D'Artagnan detained her by her night dress of fine India linen, to implore her pardon, but she, with a strong movement, tried to escape. Then the cambric was torn from her beautiful shoulders; and on one of those lovely shoulders, round and white, d'Artagnan recognised, with inexpressible astonishment, the FLEUR-DE-LIS–that indelible mark which the hand of the infamous executioner had imprinted.

"Great God!" cried d'Artagnan, loosing his hold of her dress, and remaining mute, motionless, and frozen.

But Milady felt herself denounced even by his terror. He had doubtless seen all. The young man now knew her secret, her terrible secret–the secret she concealed even from her maid with such care, the secret of which all the world was ignorant, except himself.

She turned upon him, no longer like a furious woman, but like a wounded panther.

"Ah, wretch!" cried she, "you have basely betrayed me, and still more, you have my secret! You shall die."

And she flew to a little inlaid casket which stood upon the dressing table, opened it with a feverish and trembling hand, drew from it a small poniard, with a golden haft and a sharp thin blade, and then threw herself with a bound upon d'Artagnan.

Although the young man was brave, as we know, he was terrified at that wild countenance, those terribly dilated pupils, those pale cheeks, and those bleeding lips. He recoiled to the other side of the room as he would have done from a serpent which was crawling toward him, and his sword coming in contact with his nervous hand, he drew it almost unconsciously from the scabbard. But without taking any heed of the sword, Milady endeavoured to get near enough to him to stab him, and did not stop till she felt the sharp point at her throat.

She then tried to seize the sword with her hands, but d'Artagnan kept it free from her grasp, and presenting the point, sometimes at her eyes, sometimes at her breast, compelled her to glide behind the bedstead, while he aimed at making his retreat by the door which led to Kitty's apartment.

Milady during this time continued to strike at him with horrible fury, screaming in a formidable way.

As all this, however, bore some resemblance to a duel, d'Artagnan began to recover himself little by little.

"Well, beautiful lady, very well," said he, "but, PARDIEU, if you don't calm yourself, I will design a second FLEUR-DE-LIS upon one of those pretty cheeks!"

"Scoundrel, infamous scoundrel!" howled Milady.

But d'Artagnan, still keeping on the defensive, drew near to Kitty's door. At the noise they made, she in overturning the furniture in her efforts to get at him, he in screening himself behind the furniture to keep out of her reach, Kitty opened the door. D'Artagnan, who had unceasingly maneuvered to gain this point, was not at more than three paces from it. With one spring he flew from the chamber of Milady into that of the maid, and quick as lightning, he slammed to the door, and placed all his weight against it, while Kitty pushed the bolts.

Then Milady attempted to tear down the doorcase, with a strength apparently above that of a woman, but finding she could not accomplish this, she in her fury stabbed at the door with her poniard, the point of which repeatedly glittered through the wood. Every blow was accompanied with terrible imprecations.

"Quick, Kitty, quick!" said d'Artagnan, in a low voice, as soon as the bolts were fast, "let me get out of the hotel; for if we leave her time to turn round, she will have me killed by the servants."

"But you can't go out so," said Kitty, "you are naked."

"That's true," said d'Artagnan, then first thinking of the costume he found himself in, "that's true. But dress me as well as you are able, only make haste; think, my dear girl, it's life and death!"

Kitty was but too well aware of that. In a turn of the hand she muffled him up in a flowered robe, a large hood, and a cloak. She gave him some slippers, in which he placed his naked feet, and then conducted him down the stairs. It was time. Milady had already rung her bell, and roused the whole hotel. The porter was drawing the cord at the moment Milady cried from her window, "Don't open!"

The young man fled while she was still threatening him with an impotent gesture. The moment she lost sight of him, Milady tumbled fainting into her chamber.

Chapter 38

How, Without Incommoding Himself, Athos Procures His Equipment

D'Artagnan was so completely bewildered that without taking any heed of what might become of Kitty he ran at full speed across half Paris, and did not stop till he came to Athos's door. The confusion of his mind, the terror which spurred him on, the cries of some of the patrol who started in pursuit of him, and the hooting of the people who, notwithstanding the early hour, were going to their work, only made him precipitate his course.

He crossed the court, ran up the two flights to Athos's apartment, and knocked at the door enough to break it down.

Grimaud came, rubbing his half-open eyes, to answer this noisy summons, and d'Artagnan sprang with such violence into the room as nearly to overturn the astonished lackey.

In spite of his habitual silence, the poor lad this time found his speech.

"Holloa, there!" cried he, "what do you want, you strumpet? What's your business here, you hussy?"

D'Artagnan threw off his hood, and disengaged his hands from the folds of the cloak. At sight of the moustaches and the naked sword, the poor devil perceived he had to deal with a man. He then concluded it must be an assassin.

"Help! Murder! Help!" cried he.

"Hold your tongue, you stupid fellow!" said the young man, "I am d'Artagnan; don't you know me? Where is your master?"

"You, Monsieur d'Artagnan!" cried Grimaud, "impossible."

"Grimaud," said Athos, coming out of his apartment in a dressing gown, "Grimaud, I thought I heard you permitting yourself to speak?"

"Ah, Monsieur, it is–"

"Silence!"

Grimaud contented himself with pointing d'Artagnan out to his master with his finger.

Athos recognised his comrade, and phlegmatic as he was, he burst into a laugh which was quite excused by the strange masquerade before his eyes–petticoats falling over his shoes, sleeves tucked up, and moustaches stiff with agitation.

"Don't laugh, my friend!" cried d'Artagnan, "For heaven's sake, don't laugh, for upon my soul, it's no laughing matter!"

And he pronounced these words with such a solemn air and with such a real appearance of terror, that Athos eagerly seized his hand, crying, "Are you wounded, my friend? How pale you are!"

"No, but I have just met with a terrible adventure! Are you alone, Athos?"

"PARBLEU! Whom do you expect to find with me at this hour?"

"Well, well!" and d'Artagnan rushed into Athos's chamber.

"Come, speak!" said the latter, closing the door and bolting it, that they might not be disturbed. "Is the king dead? Have you killed the cardinal? You are quite upset! Come, come, tell me; I am dying with curiosity and uneasiness!"

"Athos," said d'Artagnan, getting rid of his female garments, and appearing in his shirt, "prepare yourself to hear an incredible, an unheard-of story."

"Well, but put on this dressing gown first," said the Musketeer to his friend.

D'Artagnan donned the robe as quickly as he could, mistaking one sleeve for the other, so greatly was he still agitated.

"Well?" said Athos.

"Well," replied d'Artagnan, bending his mouth to Athos's ear, and lowering his voice, "Milady is marked with a FLEUR-DE-LIS upon her shoulder!"

"Ah!" cried the Musketeer, as if he had received a ball in his heart.

"Let us see," said d'Artagnan. "Are you SURE that the OTHER is dead?"

"THE OTHER?" said Athos, in so stifled a voice that d'Artagnan scarcely heard him.

"Yes, she of whom you told me one day at Amiens."

Athos uttered a groan, and let his head sink on his hands.

"This is a woman of twenty-six or twenty-eight years."

"Fair," said Athos, "is she not?"

"Very."

"Blue and clear eyes, of a strange brilliancy, with black eyelids and eyebrows?"

"Yes."

"Tall, well-made? She has lost a tooth, next to the eyetooth on the left?"

"Yes."

"The FLEUR-DE-LIS is small, rosy in colour, and looks as if efforts had been made to efface it by the application of poultices?"

"Yes."

"But you say she is English?"

"She is called Milady, but she may be French. Lord de Winter is only her brother-in-law."

"I will see her, d'Artagnan!"

"Beware, Athos, beware. You tried to kill her; she is a woman to return you the like, and not to fail."

"She will not dare to say anything; that would be to denounce herself."

"She is capable of anything or everything. Did you ever see her furious?"

"No," said Athos.

"A tigress, a panther! Ah, my dear Athos, I am greatly afraid I have drawn a terrible vengeance on both of us!"

D'Artagnan then related all–the mad passion of Milady and her menaces of death.

"You are right; and upon my soul, I would give my life for a hair," said Athos. "Fortunately, the day after tomorrow we leave Paris. We are going according to all probability to La Rochelle, and once gone–"

"She will follow you to the end of the world, Athos, if she recognises you. Let her, then, exhaust her vengeance on me alone!"

"My dear friend, of what consequence is it if she kills me?" said Athos. "Do you, perchance, think I set any great store by life?"

"There is something horribly mysterious under all this, Athos; this woman is one of the cardinal's spies, I am sure of that."

"In that case, take care! If the cardinal does not hold you in high admiration for the affair of London, he entertains a great hatred for you, but as, considering everything, he cannot accuse you openly, and as hatred must be satisfied, particularly when it's a cardinal's hatred, take care of yourself. If you go out, do not go out alone; when you eat, use every precaution. Mistrust everything, in short, even your own shadow."

"Fortunately," said d'Artagnan, "all this will be only necessary till after tomorrow evening, for when once with the army, we shall have, I hope, only men to dread."

"In the meantime," said Athos, "I renounce my plan of seclusion, and wherever you go, I will go with you. You must return to the Rue des Fossoyeurs; I will accompany you."

"But however near it may be," replied d'Artagnan, "I cannot go thither in this guise."

"That's true," said Athos, and he rang the bell.

Grimaud entered.

Athos made him a sign to go to d'Artagnan's residence, and bring back some clothes. Grimaud replied by another sign that he understood perfectly, and set off.

"All this will not advance your outfit," said Athos, "for if I am not mistaken, you have left the best of your apparel with Milady, and she will certainly not have the politeness to return it to you. Fortunately, you have the sapphire."

"The jewel is yours, my dear Athos! Did you not tell me it was a family jewel?"

"Yes, my grandfather gave two thousand crowns for it, as he once told me. It formed part of the nuptial present he made his wife, and it is magnificent. My mother gave it to me, and I, fool as I was, instead of keeping the ring as a holy relic, gave it to this wretch."

"Then, my friend, take back this ring, to which I see you attach much value."

"I take back the ring, after it has passed through the hands of that infamous creature? Never; that ring is defiled, d'Artagnan."

"Sell it, then."

"Sell a jewel which came from my mother! I vow I should consider it a profanation."

"Pledge it, then; you can borrow at least a thousand crowns on it. With that sum you can extricate yourself from your present difficulties; and when you are full of money again, you can redeem it, and take it back cleansed from its ancient stains, as it will have passed through the hands of usurers."

Athos smiled.

"You are a capital companion, d'Artagnan," said be, "your never-failing cheerfulness raises poor souls in affliction. Well, let us pledge the ring, but upon one condition."

"What?"

"That there shall be five hundred crowns for you, and five hundred crowns for me."

"Don't dream it, Athos. I don't need the quarter of such a sum–I who am still only in the Guards–and by selling my saddles, I shall procure it. What do I want? A horse for Planchet, that's all. Besides, you forget that I have a ring likewise."

"To which you attach more value, it seems, than I do to mine; at least, I have thought so."

"Yes, for in any extreme circumstance it might not only extricate us from some great embarrassment, but even a great danger. It is not only a valuable diamond, but it is an enchanted talisman."

"I don't at all understand you, but I believe all you say to be true. Let us return to my ring, or rather to yours. You shall take half the sum that will be advanced upon it, or I will throw it into the Seine; and I doubt, as was the case with Polycrates, whether any fish will be sufficiently complaisant to bring it back to us."

"Well, I will take it, then," said d'Artagnan.

At this moment Grimaud returned, accompanied by Planchet; the latter, anxious about his master and curious to know what had happened to him, had taken advantage of the opportunity and brought the garments himself.

D'Artagnan dressed himself, and Athos did the same. When the two were ready to go out, the latter made Grimaud the sign of a man taking aim, and the lackey immediately took down his musketoon, and prepared to follow his master.

They arrived without accident at the Rue des Fossoyeurs. Bonacieux was standing at the door, and looked at d'Artagnan hatefully.

"Make haste, dear lodger," said he, "there is a very pretty girl waiting for you upstairs; and you know women don't like to be kept waiting."

"That's Kitty!" said d'Artagnan to himself, and darted into the passage.

Sure enough! Upon the landing leading to the chamber, and crouching against the door, he found the poor girl, all in a tremble. As soon as she perceived him, she cried, "You have promised your protection; you have promised to save me from her anger. Remember, it is you who have ruined me!"

"Yes, yes, to be sure, Kitty," said d'Artagnan, "be at ease, my girl. But what happened after my departure?"

"How can I tell!" said Kitty. "The lackeys were brought by the cries she made. She was mad with passion. There exist no imprecations she did not pour out against you. Then I thought she would remember it was through my chamber you had penetrated hers, and that then she would suppose I was your accomplice; so I took what little money I had and the best of my things, and I got away.

"Poor dear girl! But what can I do with you? I am going away the day after tomorrow."

"Do what you please, Monsieur Chevalier. Help me out of Paris; help me out of France!"

"I cannot take you, however, to the siege of La Rochelle," aid d'Artagnan.

"No, but you can place me in one of the provinces with some lady of your acquaintance–in your own country, for instance."

"My dear little love! In my country the ladies do without chambermaids. But stop! I can manage your business for you. Planchet, go and find Aramis. Request him to come here directly. We have something very important to say to him."

"I understand," said Athos, "but why not Porthos? I should have thought that his duchess–"

"Oh, Porthos's duchess is dressed by her husband's clerks," said d'Artagnan, laughing. "Besides, Kitty would not like to live in the Rue aux Ours. Isn't it so, Kitty?"

"I do not care where I live," said Kitty, "provided I am well concealed, and nobody knows where I am."

"Meanwhile, Kitty, when we are about to separate, and you are no longer jealous of me–"

"Monsieur Chevalier, far off or near," said Kitty, "I shall always love you."

"Where the devil will constancy niche itself next?" murmured Athos.

"And I, also," said d'Artagnan, "I also. I shall always love you; be sure of that. But now answer me. I attach great importance to the question I am about to put to you. Did you never hear talk of a young woman who was carried off one night?"

"There, now! Oh, Monsieur Chevalier, do you love that woman still?"

"No, no; it is one of my friends who loves her–Monsieur Athos, this gentleman here."

"I?" cried Athos, with an accent like that of a man who perceives he is about to tread upon an adder.

"You, to be sure!" said d'Artagnan, pressing Athos's hand. "You know the interest we both take in this poor little Madame Bonacieux. Besides, Kitty will tell nothing; will you, Kitty? You understand, my dear girl," continued d'Artagnan, "she is the wife of that frightful baboon you saw at the door as you came in."

"Oh, my God! You remind me of my fright! If he should have known me again!"

"How? know you again? Did you ever see that man before?"

"He came twice to Milady's."

"That's it. About what time?"

"Why, about fifteen or eighteen days ago."

"Exactly so."

"And yesterday evening he came again."

"Yesterday evening?"

"Yes, just before you came."

"My dear Athos, we are enveloped in a network of spies. And do you believe he knew you again, Kitty?"

"I pulled down my hood as soon as I saw him, but perhaps it was too late."

"Go down, Athos–he mistrusts you less than me–and see if he be still at his door."

Athos went down and returned immediately.

"He has gone," said he, "and the house door is shut."

"He has gone to make his report, and to say that all the pigeons are at this moment in the dovecot."

"Well, then, let us all fly," said Athos, "and leave nobody here but Planchet to bring us news."

"A minute. Aramis, whom we have sent for!"

"That's true," said Athos, "we must wait for Aramis."

At that moment Aramis entered.

The matter was all explained to him, and the friends gave him to understand that among all his high connections he must find a place for Kitty.

Aramis reflected for a minute, and then said, colouring, "Will it be really rendering you a service, d'Artagnan?"

"I shall be grateful to you all my life."

"Very well. Madame de Bois-Tracy asked me, for one of her friends who resides in the provinces, I believe, for a trustworthy maid. If you can, my dear d'Artagnan, answer for Mademoiselle-"

"Oh, Monsieur, be assured that I shall be entirely devoted to the person who will give me the means of quitting Paris."

"Then," said Aramis, "this falls out very well."

He placed himself at the table and wrote a little note which he sealed with a ring, and gave the billet to Kitty.

"And now, my dear girl," said d'Artagnan, "you know that it is not good for any of us to be here. Therefore let us separate. We shall meet again in better days."

"And whenever we find each other, in whatever place it may be," said Kitty, "you will find me loving you as I love you today."

"Dicers' oaths!" said Athos, while d'Artagnan went to conduct Kitty downstairs.

An instant afterward the three young men separated, agreeing to meet again at four o'clock with Athos, and leaving Planchet to guard the house.

Aramis returned home, and Athos and d'Artagnan busied themselves about pledging the sapphire.

As the Gascon had foreseen, they easily obtained three hundred pistoles on the ring. Still further, the Jew told them that if they would sell it to him, as it would make a magnificent pendant for earrings, he would give five hundred pistoles for it.

Athos and d'Artagnan, with the activity of two soldiers and the knowledge of two connoisseurs, hardly required three hours to purchase the entire equipment of the Musketeer. Besides, Athos was very easy, and a noble to his fingers' ends. When a thing suited him he paid the price demanded, without thinking to ask for any abatement. D'Artagnan would have remonstrated at this, but Athos put his hand upon his shoulder, with a smile, and d'Artagnan understood that it was all very well for such a little Gascon gentleman as himself to drive a bargain, but not for a man who had the bearing of a prince. The Musketeer met with a superb Andalusian horse, black as jet, nostrils of fire, legs clean and elegant, rising six years. He examined him, and found him sound and without blemish. They asked a thousand livres for him.

He might perhaps have been bought for less, but while d'Artagnan was discussing the price with the dealer, Athos was counting out the money on the table.

Grimaud had a stout, short Picard cob, which cost three hundred livres.

But when the saddle and arms for Grimaud were purchased, Athos had not a sou left of his hundred and fifty pistoles. D'Artagnan offered his friend a part of his share which he should return when convenient.

But Athos only replied to this proposal by shrugging his shoulders.

"How much did the Jew say he would give for the sapphire if he purchased it?" said Athos.

"Five hundred pistoles."

"That is to say, two hundred more–a hundred pistoles for you and a hundred pistoles for me. Well, now, that would be a real fortune to us, my friend; let us go back to the Jew's again."

"What! Will you–"

"This ring would certainly only recall very bitter remembrances; then we shall never be masters of three hundred pistoles to redeem it, so that we really should lose two hundred pistoles by the bargain. Go and tell him the ring is his, d'Artagnan, and bring back the two hundred pistoles with you."

"Reflect, Athos!"

"Ready money is needful for the present time, and we must learn how to make sacrifices. Go, d'Artagnan, go; Grimaud will accompany you with his musketoon."

A half hour afterward, d'Artagnan returned with the two thousand livres, and without having met with any accident.

It was thus Athos found at home resources which he did not expect.

Chapter 39

A Vision

At four o'clock the four friends were all assembled with Athos. Their anxiety about their outfits had all disappeared, and each countenance only preserved the expression of its own secret disquiet–for behind all present happiness is concealed a fear for the future.

Suddenly Planchet entered, bringing two letters for d'Artagnan.

The one was a little billet, genteelly folded, with a pretty seal in green wax on which was impressed a dove bearing a green branch.

The other was a large square epistle, resplendent with the terrible arms of his Eminence the cardinal duke.

At the sight of the little letter the heart of d'Artagnan bounded, for he believed he recognised the handwriting, and although he had seen that writing but once, the memory of it remained at the bottom of his heart.

He therefore seized the little epistle, and opened it eagerly.

"Be," said the letter, "on Thursday next, at from six to seven o'clock in the evening, on the road to Chaillot, and look carefully into the carriages that pass, but if you have any consideration for your own life or that of those who love you, do not speak a single word, do not make a movement which may lead anyone to believe you have recognised her who exposes herself to everything for the sake of seeing you but for an instant."

No signature.

"That's a snare," said Athos, "don't go, d'Artagnan."

"And yet," replied d'Artagnan, "I think I recognise the writing."

"It may be counterfeit," said Athos. "Between six and seven o'clock the road of Chaillot is quite deserted; you might as well go and ride in the forest of Bondy."

"But suppose we all go," said d'Artagnan, "what the devil! They won't devour us all four, four lackeys, horses, arms, and all!"

"And besides, it will be a chance for displaying our new equipments," said Porthos.

"But if it is a woman who writes," said Aramis, "and that woman desires not to be seen, remember, you compromise her, d'Artagnan, which is not the part of a gentleman."

"We will remain in the background," said Porthos, "and he will advance alone."

"Yes, but a pistol shot is easily fired from a carriage which goes at a gallop."

"Bah!" said d'Artagnan, "they will miss me; if they fire we will ride after the carriage, and exterminate those who may be in it. They must be enemies."

"He is right," said Porthos, "battle. Besides, we must try our own arms."

"Bah, let us enjoy that pleasure," said Aramis, with his mild and careless manner.

"As you please," said Athos.

"Gentlemen," said d'Artagnan, "it is half past four, and we have scarcely time to be on the road of Chaillot by six."

"Besides, if we go out too late, nobody will see us," said Porthos, "and that will be a pity. Let us get ready, gentlemen."

"But this second letter," said Athos, "you forget that; it appears to me, however, that the seal denotes that it deserves to be opened. For my part, I declare, d'Artagnan, I think it of much more consequence than the little piece of waste paper you have so cunningly slipped into your bosom."

D'Artagnan blushed.

"Well," said he, "let us see, gentlemen, what are his Eminence's commands," and d'Artagnan unsealed the letter and read,

"M. d'Artagnan, of the king's Guards, company Dessessart, is expected at the Palais-Cardinal this evening, at eight o'clock.

"La Houdinière, CAPTAIN OF THE GUARDS"

"The devil!" said Athos, "here's a rendezvous much more serious than the other."

"I will go to the second after attending the first," said d'Artagnan. "One is for seven o'clock, and the other for eight; there will be time for both."

"Hum! I would not go at all," said Aramis. "A gallant knight cannot decline a rendezvous with a lady, but a prudent gentleman may excuse himself from not waiting on his Eminence, particularly when he has reason to believe he is not invited to make his compliments."

"I am of Aramis's opinion," said Porthos.

"Gentlemen," replied d'Artagnan, "I have already received by Monsieur de Cavois a similar invitation from his Eminence. I neglected it, and on the morrow a serious misfortune happened to me–Constance disappeared. Whatever may ensue, I will go."

"If you are determined," said Athos, "do so."

"But the Bastille?" said Aramis.

"Bah! You will get me out if they put me there," said d'Artagnan.

"To be sure we will," replied Aramis and Porthos, with admirable promptness and decision, as if that were the simplest thing in the world, "to be sure we will get you out, but meantime, as we are to set off the day after tomorrow, you would do much better not to risk this Bastille."

"Let us do better than that," said Athos, "do not let us leave him during the whole evening. Let each of us wait at a gate of the palace with three Musketeers behind him; if we see a close carriage, at all suspicious in appearance, come out, let us fall upon it. It is a long time since we have had a skirmish with the Guards of Monsieur the Cardinal; Monsieur de Tréville must think us dead."

"To a certainty, Athos," said Aramis, "you were meant to be a general of the army! What do you think of the plan, gentlemen?"

"Admirable!" replied the young men in chorus.

"Well," said Porthos, "I will run to the hotel, and engage our comrades to hold themselves in readiness by eight o'clock; the rendezvous, the Place du Palais-Cardinal. Meantime, you see that the lackeys saddle the horses."

"I have no horse," said d'Artagnan, "but that is of no consequence, I can take one of Monsieur de Tréville's."

"That is not worth while," said Aramis, "you can have one of mine."

"One of yours! How many have you, then?" asked d'Artagnan.

"Three," replied Aramis, smiling.

"Certes," cried Athos, "you are the best-mounted poet of France or Navarre."

"Well, my dear Aramis, you don't want three horses? I cannot comprehend what induced you to buy three!"

"Therefore I only purchased two," said Aramis.

"The third, then, fell from the clouds, I suppose?"

"No, the third was brought to me this very morning by a groom out of livery, who would not tell me in whose service he was, and who said he had received orders from his master."

"Or his mistress," interrupted d'Artagnan.

"That makes no difference," said Aramis, colouring, "and who affirmed, as I said, that he had received orders from his master or mistress to place the horse in my stable, without informing me whence it came."

"It is only to poets that such things happen," said Athos, gravely.

"Well, in that case, we can manage famously," said d'Artagnan, "which of the two horses will you ride–that which you bought or the one that was given to you?"

"That which was given to me, assuredly. You cannot for a moment imagine, d'Artagnan, that I would commit such an offense toward–"

"The unknown giver," interrupted d'Artagnan.

"Or the mysterious benefactress," said Athos.

"The one you bought will then become useless to you?"

"Nearly so."

"And you selected it yourself?"

"With the greatest care. The safety of the horseman, you know, depends almost always upon the goodness of his horse."

"Well, transfer it to me at the price it cost you?"

"I was going to make you the offer, my dear d'Artagnan, giving you all the time necessary for repaying me such a trifle."

"How much did it cost you?"

"Eight hundred livres."

"Here are forty double pistoles, my dear friend," said d'Artagnan, taking the sum from his pocket, "I know that is the coin in which you were paid for your poems."

"You are rich, then?" said Aramis.

"Rich? Richest, my dear fellow!"

And d'Artagnan chinked the remainder of his pistoles in his pocket.

"Send your saddle, then, to the hotel of the Musketeers, and your horse can be brought back with ours."

"Very well, but it is already five o'clock, so make haste."

A quarter of an hour afterward Porthos appeared at the end of the Rue Ferou on a very handsome genet. Mousqueton followed him upon an Auvergne horse, small but very handsome. Porthos was resplendent with joy and pride.

At the same time, Aramis made his appearance at the other end of the street upon a superb English charger. Bazin followed him upon a roan, holding by the halter a vigorous Mecklenburg horse; this was d'Artagnan's mount.

The two Musketeers met at the gate. Athos and d'Artagnan watched their approach from the window.

"The devil!" cried Aramis, "you have a magnificent horse there, Porthos."

"Yes," replied Porthos, "it is the one that ought to have been sent to me at first. A bad joke of the husband's substituted the other, but the husband has been punished since, and I have obtained full satisfaction."

Planchet and Grimaud appeared in their turn, leading their masters' steeds. D'Artagnan and Athos put themselves into saddle with their companions, and all four set forward; Athos upon a horse he owed to a woman, Aramis on a horse he owed to his mistress, Porthos on a horse he owed to his procurator's wife, and d'Artagnan on a horse he owed to his good fortune–the best mistress possible.

The lackeys followed.

As Porthos had foreseen, the cavalcade produced a good effect; and if Mme. Coquenard had met Porthos and seen what a superb appearance he made upon his handsome Spanish genet, she would not have regretted the bleeding she had inflicted upon the strongbox of her husband.

Near the Louvre the four friends met with M. de Tréville, who was returning from St. Germain; he stopped them to offer his compliments upon their appointments, which in an instant drew round them a hundred gapers.

D'Artagnan profited by the circumstance to speak to M. de Tréville of the letter with the great red seal and the cardinal's arms. It is well understood that he did not breathe a word about the other.

M. de Tréville approved of the resolution he had adopted, and assured him that if on the morrow he did not appear, he himself would undertake to find him, let him be where he might.

At this moment the clock of La Samaritaine struck six; the four friends pleaded an engagement, and took leave of M. de Tréville.

A short gallop brought them to the road of Chaillot; the day began to decline, carriages were passing and repassing. D'Artagnan, keeping at some distance from his friends, darted a scrutinising glance into every carriage that appeared, but saw no face with which he was acquainted.

At length, after waiting a quarter of an hour and just as twilight was beginning to thicken, a carriage appeared, coming at a quick pace on the road of Sevres. A presentiment instantly told d'Artagnan that this carriage contained the person who had appointed the rendezvous; the young man was himself astonished to find his heart beat so violently. Almost instantly a female head was put out at the window, with two fingers placed upon her mouth, either to enjoin silence or to send him a kiss. D'Artagnan uttered a slight cry of joy; this woman, or rather this apparition–for the carriage passed with the rapidity of a vision–was Mme. Bonacieux.

By an involuntary movement and in spite of the injunction given, d'Artagnan put his horse into a gallop, and in a few strides overtook the carriage, but the window was hermetically closed, the vision had disappeared.

D'Artagnan then remembered the injunction: "If you value your own life or that of those who love you, remain motionless, and as if you had seen nothing."

He stopped, therefore, trembling not for himself but for the poor woman who had evidently exposed herself to great danger by appointing this rendezvous.

The carriage pursued its way, still going at a great pace, till it dashed into Paris, and disappeared.

D'Artagnan remained fixed to the spot, astounded and not knowing what to think. If it was Mme. Bonacieux and if she was returning to Paris, why this fugitive rendezvous, why this simple exchange of a glance, why this lost kiss? If, on the other side, it was not she–which was still quite possible–for the little light that remained rendered a mistake easy–might it not be the commencement of some plot against him through the allurement of this woman, for whom his love was known?

His three companions joined him. All had plainly seen a woman's head appear at the window, but none of them, except

Athos, knew Mme. Bonacieux. The opinion of Athos was that it was indeed she, but less preoccupied by that pretty face than d'Artagnan, he had fancied he saw a second head, a man's head, inside the carriage.

"If that be the case," said d'Artagnan, "they are doubtless transporting her from one prison to another. But what can they intend to do with the poor creature, and how shall I ever meet her again?"

"Friend," said Athos, gravely, "remember that it is the dead alone with whom we are not likely to meet again on this earth. You know something of that, as well as I do, I think. Now, if your mistress is not dead, if it is she we have just seen, you will meet with her again some day or other. And perhaps, my God!" added he, with that misanthropic tone which was peculiar to him, "perhaps sooner than you wish."

Half past seven had sounded. The carriage had been twenty minutes behind the time appointed. D'Artagnan's friends reminded him that he had a visit to pay, but at the same time bade him observe that there was yet time to retract.

But d'Artagnan was at the same time impetuous and curious. He had made up his mind that he would go to the Palais-Cardinal, and that he would learn what his Eminence had to say to him. Nothing could turn him from his purpose.

They reached the Rue St. Honoré, and in the Place du Palais-Cardinal they found the twelve invited Musketeers, walking about in expectation of their comrades. There only they explained to them the matter in hand.

D'Artagnan was well known among the honourable corps of the king's Musketeers, in which it was known he would one day take his place; he was considered beforehand as a comrade. It resulted from these antecedents that everyone entered heartily into the purpose for which they met; besides, it would not be unlikely that they would have an opportunity of playing either the cardinal or his people an ill turn, and for such expeditions these worthy gentlemen were always ready.

Athos divided them into three groups, assumed the command of one, gave the second to Aramis, and the third to Porthos; and then each group went and took their watch near an entrance.

D'Artagnan, on his part, entered boldly at the principal gate.

Although he felt himself ably supported, the young man was not without a little uneasiness as he ascended the great staircase, step by step. His conduct toward Milady bore a strong resemblance to treachery, and he was very suspicious of the political relations which existed between that woman and the cardinal. Still further, de Wardes, whom he had treated so ill, was one of the tools of his Eminence; and d'Artagnan knew that while his Eminence was terrible to his enemies, he was strongly attached to his friends.

"If de Wardes has related all our affair to the cardinal, which is not to be doubted, and if he has recognised me, as is probable, I may consider myself almost as a condemned man," said d'Artagnan, shaking his head. "But why has he waited till now? That's all plain enough. Milady has laid her complaints against me with that hypocritical grief which renders her so interesting, and this last offense has made the cup overflow."

"Fortunately," added he, "my good friends are down yonder, and they will not allow me to be carried away without a struggle. Nevertheless, Monsieur de Tréville's company of Musketeers alone cannot maintain a war against the cardinal, who disposes of the forces of all France, and before whom the queen is without power and the king without will. D'Artagnan, my friend, you are brave, you are prudent, you have excellent qualities, but the women will ruin you!"

He came to this melancholy conclusion as he entered the antechamber. He placed his letter in the hands of the usher on duty, who led him into the waiting room and passed on into the interior of the palace.

In this waiting room were five or six of the cardinals Guards, who recognised d'Artagnan, and knowing that it was he who had wounded Jussac, they looked upon him with a smile of singular meaning.

This smile appeared to d'Artagnan to be of bad augury. Only, as our Gascon was not easily intimidated–or rather, thanks to a great pride natural to the men of his country, he did not allow one easily to see what was passing in his mind when that which was passing at all resembled fear–he placed himself haughtily in front of Messieurs the Guards, and waited with his hand on his hip, in an attitude by no means deficient in majesty.

The usher returned and made a sign to d'Artagnan to follow him. It appeared to the young man that the Guards, on seeing him depart, chuckled among themselves.

He traversed a corridor, crossed a grand saloon, entered a library, and found himself in the presence of a man seated at a desk and writing.

The usher introduced him, and retired without speaking a word. D'Artagnan remained standing and examined this man.

D'Artagnan at first believed that he had to do with some judge examining his papers, but he perceived that the man at the desk wrote, or rather corrected, lines of unequal length, scanning the words on his fingers. He saw then that he was with a poet. At the end of an instant the poet closed his manuscript, upon the cover of which was written *"Mirame, a Tragedy in Five Acts,"* and raised his head.

D'Artagnan recognised the cardinal.

Chapter 40

A Terrible Vision

The cardinal leaned his elbow on his manuscript, his cheek upon his hand, and looked intently at the young man for a moment. No one had a more searching eye than the Cardinal de Richelieu, and d'Artagnan felt this glance run through his veins like a fever.

He however kept a good countenance, holding his hat in his hand and awaiting the good pleasure of his Eminence, without too much assurance, but also without too much humility.

"Monsieur," said the cardinal, "are you a d'Artagnan from Bearn?"

"Yes, Monseigneur," replied the young man.

"There are several branches of the d'Artagnans at Tarbes and in its environs," said the cardinal, "to which do you belong?"

"I am the son of him who served in the Religious Wars under the great King Henry, the father of his gracious Majesty."

"That is well. It is you who set out seven or eight months ago from your country to seek your fortune in the capital?"

"Yes, Monseigneur."

"You came through Meung, where something befell you. I don't very well know what, but still something."

"Monseigneur," said d'Artagnan, "this was what happened to me–"

"Never mind, never mind!" resumed the cardinal, with a smile which indicated that he knew the story as well as he who wished to relate it. "You were recommended to Monsieur de Tréville, were you not?"

"Yes, Monseigneur, but in that unfortunate affair at Meung–"

"The letter was lost," replied his Eminence, "yes, I know that. But Monsieur de Tréville is a skilled physiognomist, who knows men at first sight; and he placed you in the company of his brother-in-law, Monsieur Dessessart, leaving you to hope that one day or other you should enter the Musketeers."

"Monseigneur is correctly informed," said d'Artagnan.

"Since that time many things have happened to you. You were walking one day behind the Chartreux, when it would have been better if you had been elsewhere. Then you took with your friends a journey to the waters of Forges; they stopped on the road, but you continued yours. That is all very simple: you had business in England."

"Monseigneur," said d'Artagnan, quite confused, "I went–"

"Hunting at Windsor, or elsewhere–that concerns nobody. I know, because it is my office to know everything. On your return you were received by an august personage, and I perceive with pleasure that you preserve the souvenir she gave you."

D'Artagnan placed his hand upon the queen's diamond, which he wore, and quickly turned the stone inward, but it was too late.

"The day after that, you received a visit from Cavois," resumed the cardinal. "He went to desire you to come to the palace. You have not returned that visit, and you were wrong."

"Monseigneur, I feared I had incurred disgrace with your Eminence."

"How could that be, Monsieur? Could you incur my displeasure by having followed the orders of your superiors with more intelligence and courage than another would have done? It is the people who do not obey that I punish, and not those who, like you, obey–but too well. As a proof, remember the date of the day on which I had you bidden to come to me, and seek in your memory for what happened to you that very night."

That was the very evening when the abduction of Mme. Bonacieux took place. D'Artagnan trembled; and he likewise recollected that during the past half hour the poor woman had passed close to him, without doubt carried away by the same power that had caused her disappearance.

"In short," continued the cardinal, "as I have heard nothing of you for some time past, I wished to know what you were doing. Besides, you owe me some thanks. You must yourself have remarked how much you have been considered in all the circumstances."

D'Artagnan bowed with respect.

"That," continued the cardinal, "arose not only from a feeling of natural equity, but likewise from a plan I have marked out with respect to you."

D'Artagnan became more and more astonished.

"I wished to explain this plan to you on the day you received my first invitation, but you did not come. Fortunately, nothing is lost by this delay, and you are now about to hear it. Sit down there, before me, d'Artagnan; you are gentleman enough not to listen standing." And the cardinal pointed with his finger to a chair for the young man, who was so astonished at what was passing that he awaited a second sign from his interlocutor before he obeyed.

"You are brave, Monsieur d'Artagnan," continued his Eminence, "you are prudent, which is still better. I like men of head and heart. Don't be afraid," said he, smiling. "By men of heart I mean men of courage. But young as you are, and scarcely entering into the world, you have powerful enemies; if you do not take great heed, they will destroy you."

"Alas, Monseigneur!" replied the young man, "very easily, no doubt, for they are strong and well supported, while I am alone."

"Yes, that's true, but alone as you are, you have done much already, and will do still more, I don't doubt. Yet you have need, I believe, to be guided in the adventurous career you have undertaken; for, if I mistake not, you came to Paris with the ambitious idea of making your fortune."

"I am at the age of extravagant hopes, Monseigneur," said d'Artagnan.

"There are no extravagant hopes but for fools, Monsieur, and you are a man of understanding. Now, what would you say to an ensign's commission in my Guards, and a company after the campaign?"

"Ah, Monseigneur."

"You accept it, do you not?"

"Monseigneur," replied d'Artagnan, with an embarrassed air.

"How? You refuse?" cried the cardinal, with astonishment.

"I am in his Majesty's Guards, Monseigneur, and I have no reason to be dissatisfied."

"But it appears to me that my Guards–mine–are also his Majesty's Guards; and whoever serves in a French corps serves the king."

"Monseigneur, your Eminence has ill understood my words."

"You want a pretext, do you not? I comprehend. Well, you have this excuse: advancement, the opening campaign, the opportunity which I offer you–so much for the world. As regards yourself, the need of protection; for it is fit you should know, Monsieur d'Artagnan, that I have received heavy and serious complaints against you. You do not consecrate your days and nights wholly to the king's service."

D'Artagnan coloured.

"In fact," said the cardinal, placing his hand upon a bundle of papers, "I have here a whole pile which concerns you. I know you to be a man of resolution; and your services, well directed, instead of leading you to ill, might be very advantageous to you. Come; reflect, and decide."

"Your goodness confounds me, Monseigneur," replied d'Artagnan, "and I am conscious of a greatness of soul in your Eminence that makes me mean as an earthworm, but since Monseigneur permits me to speak freely–"

D'Artagnan paused.

"Yes; speak."

"Then, I will presume to say that all my friends are in the king's Musketeers and Guards, and that by an inconceivable fatality my enemies are in the service of your Eminence; I should, therefore, be ill received here and ill regarded there if I accepted what Monseigneur offers me."

"Do you happen to entertain the haughty idea that I have not yet made you an offer equal to your value?" asked the cardinal, with a smile of disdain.

"Monseigneur, your Eminence is a hundred times too kind to me; and on the contrary, I think I have not proved myself worthy of your goodness. The siege of La Rochelle is about to be resumed, Monseigneur. I shall serve under the eye of your Eminence, and if I have the good fortune to conduct myself at the siege in such a manner as merits your attention, then I shall at least leave behind me some brilliant action to justify the protection with which you honour me. Everything is best in its time, Monseigneur. Hereafter, perhaps, I shall have the right of giving myself; at present I shall appear to sell myself."

"That is to say, you refuse to serve me, Monsieur," said the cardinal, with a tone of vexation, through which, however, might be seen a sort of esteem, "remain free, then, and guard your hatreds and your sympathies."

"Monseigneur–"

"Well, well," said the cardinal, "I don't wish you any ill, but you must be aware that it is quite trouble enough to defend and recompense our friends. We owe nothing to our enemies; and let me give you a piece of advice; take care of yourself, Monsieur d'Artagnan, for from the moment I withdraw my hand from behind you, I would not give an obolus for your life."

"I will try to do so, Monseigneur," replied the Gascon, with a noble confidence.

"Remember at a later period and at a certain moment, if any mischance should happen to you," said Richelieu, significantly, "that it was I who came to seek you, and that I did all in my power to prevent this misfortune befalling you."

"I shall entertain, whatever may happen," said d'Artagnan, placing his hand upon his breast and bowing, "an eternal gratitude toward your Eminence for that which you now do for me."

"Well, let it be, then, as you have said, Monsieur d'Artagnan; we shall see each other again after the campaign. I will have my eye upon you, for I shall be there," replied the cardinal, pointing with his finger to a magnificent suit of armor he was to wear, "and on our return, well–we will settle our account!"

"Young man," said Richelieu, "if I shall be able to say to you at another time what I have said to you today, I promise you to do so."

This last expression of Richelieu's conveyed a terrible doubt; it alarmed d'Artagnan more than a menace would have done, for it was a warning. The cardinal, then, was seeking to preserve him from some misfortune which threatened him. He opened his mouth to reply, but with a haughty gesture the cardinal dismissed him.

D'Artagnan went out, but at the door his heart almost failed him, and he felt inclined to return. Then the noble and severe countenance of Athos crossed his mind; if he made the compact with the cardinal which he required, Athos would no more give him his hand–Athos would renounce him.

It was this fear that restrained him, so powerful is the influence of a truly great character on all that surrounds it.

D'Artagnan descended by the staircase at which he had entered, and found Athos and the four Musketeers waiting his appearance, and beginning to grow uneasy. With a word, d'Artagnan reassured them; and Planchet ran to inform the other sentinels that it was useless to keep guard longer, as his master had come out safe from the Palais-Cardinal.

Returned home with Athos, Aramis and Porthos inquired eagerly the cause of the strange interview, but d'Artagnan confined himself to telling them that M. de Richelieu had sent for him to propose to him to enter into his guards with the rank of ensign, and that he had refused.

"And you were right," cried Aramis and Porthos, with one voice.

Athos fell into a profound reverie and answered nothing. But when they were alone he said, "You have done that which you ought to have done, d'Artagnan, but perhaps you have been wrong."

D'Artagnan sighed deeply, for this voice responded to a secret voice of his soul, which told him that great misfortunes awaited him.

The whole of the next day was spent in preparations for departure. D'Artagnan went to take leave of M. de Tréville. At that time it was believed that the separation of the Musketeers and the Guards would be but momentary, the king holding his Parliament that very day and proposing to set out the day after. M. de Tréville contented himself with asking d'Artagnan if he could do anything for him, but d'Artagnan answered that he was supplied with all he wanted.

That night brought together all those comrades of the Guards of M. Dessessart and the company of Musketeers of M. de Tréville who had been accustomed to associate together. They were parting to meet again when it pleased God, and if it pleased God. That night, then, was somewhat riotous, as may be imagined. In such cases extreme preoccupation is only to be combated by extreme carelessness.

At the first sound of the morning trumpet the friends separated; the Musketeers hastening to the hotel of M. de Tréville, the Guards to that of M. Dessessart. Each of the captains then led his company to the Louvre, where the king held his review.

The king was dull and appeared ill, which detracted a little from his usual lofty bearing. In fact, the evening before, a fever had seized him in the midst of the Parliament, while he was holding his Bed of Justice. He had, not the less, decided upon setting out that same evening; and in spite of the remonstrances that had been offered to him, he persisted in having the review, hoping by setting it at defiance to conquer the disease which began to lay hold upon him.

The review over, the Guards set forward alone on their march, the Musketeers waiting for the king, which allowed Porthos time to go and take a turn in his superb equipment in the Rue aux Ours.

The procurator's wife saw him pass in his new uniform and on his fine horse. She loved Porthos too dearly to allow him to part thus; she made him a sign to dismount and come to her. Porthos was magnificent; his spurs jingled, his cuirass glittered, his sword knocked proudly against his ample limbs. This time the clerks evinced no inclination to laugh, such a real ear clipper did Porthos appear.

The Musketeer was introduced to M. Coquenard, whose little gray eyes sparkled with anger at seeing his cousin all blazing new. Nevertheless, one thing afforded him inward consolation; it was expected by everybody that the campaign would be a severe one. He whispered a hope to himself that this beloved relative might be killed in the field.

Porthos paid his compliments to M. Coquenard and bade him farewell. M. Coquenard wished him all sorts of prosperities. As to Mme. Coquenard, she could not restrain her tears, but no evil impressions were taken from her grief as she was known to be very much attached to her relatives, about whom she was constantly having serious disputes with her husband.

But the real adieux were made in Mme. Coquenard's chamber; they were heartrending.

As long as the procurator's wife could follow him with her eyes, she waved her handkerchief to him, leaning so far out of the window as to lead people to believe she wished to precipitate herself. Porthos received all these attentions like a man accustomed to such demonstrations, only on turning the corner of the street he lifted his hat gracefully, and waved it to her as a sign of adieu.

On his part Aramis wrote a long letter. To whom? Nobody knew. Kitty, who was to set out that evening for Tours, was waiting in the next chamber.

Athos sipped the last bottle of his Spanish wine.

In the meantime d'Artagnan was defiling with his company. Arriving at the Faubourg St. Antoine, he turned round to look gaily at the Bastille, but as it was the Bastille alone he looked at, he did not observe Milady, who, mounted upon a light chestnut horse, designated him with her finger to two ill-looking men who came close up to the ranks to take notice of him. To a look of interrogation which they made, Milady replied by a sign that it was he. Then, certain that there could be no mistake in the execution of her orders, she started her horse and disappeared.

The two men followed the company, and on leaving the Faubourg St. Antoine, mounted two horses properly equipped, which a servant without livery had waiting for them.

Chapter 41

The Seige Of La Rochelle

The Siege of La Rochelle was one of the great political events of the reign of Louis XIII, and one of the great military enterprises of the cardinal. It is, then, interesting and even necessary that we should say a few words about it, particularly as many details of this siege are connected in too important a manner with the story we have undertaken to relate to allow us to pass it over in silence.

The political plans of the cardinal when he undertook this siege were extensive. Let us unfold them first, and then pass on to the private plans which perhaps had not less influence upon his Eminence than the others.

Of the important cities given up by Henry IV to the Huguenots as places of safety, there only remained La Rochelle. It became necessary, therefore, to destroy this last bulwark of Calvinism–a dangerous leaven with which the ferments of civil revolt and foreign war were constantly mingling.

Spaniards, Englishmen, and Italian malcontents, adventurers of all nations, and soldiers of fortune of every sect, flocked at the first summons under the standard of the Protestants, and organised themselves like a vast association, whose branches diverged freely over all parts of Europe.

La Rochelle, which had derived a new importance from the ruin of the other Calvinist cities, was, then, the focus of dissensions and ambition. Moreover, its port was the last in the kingdom of France open to the English, and by closing it against England, our eternal enemy, the cardinal completed the work of Joan of Arc and the Duc de Guise.

Thus Bassompierre, who was at once Protestant and Catholic–Protestant by conviction and Catholic as commander of the order of the Holy Ghost; Bassompierre, who was a German by birth and a Frenchman at heart–in short, Bassompierre, who had a distinguished command at the siege of La Rochelle, said, in charging at the head of several other Protestant nobles like himself, "You will see, gentlemen, that we shall be fools enough to take La Rochelle."

And Bassompierre was right. The cannonade of the Isle of Re presaged to him the dragonnades of the Cevennes; the taking of La Rochelle was the preface to the revocation of the Edict of Nantes.

We have hinted that by the side of these views of the leveling and simplifying minister, which belong to history, the chronicler is forced to recognise the lesser motives of the amorous man and jealous rival.

Richelieu, as everyone knows, had loved the queen. Was this love a simple political affair, or was it naturally one of those profound passions which Anne of Austria inspired in those who approached her? That we are not able to say, but at all events, we have seen, by the anterior developments of this story, that Buckingham had the advantage over him, and in two or three circumstances, particularly that of the diamond studs, had, thanks to the devotedness of the three Musketeers and the courage and conduct of d'Artagnan, cruelly mystified him.

It was, then, Richelieu's object, not only to get rid of an enemy of France, but to avenge himself on a rival, but this vengeance must be grand and striking and worthy in every way of a man who held in his hand, as his weapon for combat, the forces of a kingdom.

Richelieu knew that in combating England he combated Buckingham; that in triumphing over England he triumphed over Buckingham–in short, that in humiliating England in the eyes of Europe he humiliated Buckingham in the eyes of the queen.

On his side Buckingham, in pretending to maintain the honour of England, was moved by interests exactly like those of the cardinal. Buckingham also was pursuing a private vengeance. Buckingham could not under any pretense be admitted into France as an ambassador; he wished to enter it as a conqueror.

It resulted from this that the real stake in this game, which two most powerful kingdoms played for the good pleasure of two amorous men, was simply a kind look from Anne of Austria.

The first advantage had been gained by Buckingham. Arriving unexpectedly in sight of the Isle of Re with ninety vessels and nearly twenty thousand men, he had surprised the Comte de Toiras, who commanded for the king in the Isle, and he had, after a bloody conflict, effected his landing.

Allow us to observe in passing that in this fight perished the Baron de Chantal; that the Baron de Chantal left a little orphan girl eighteen months old, and that this little girl was afterward Mme. de Sevigne.

The Comte de Toiras retired into the citadel St. Martin with his garrison, and threw a hundred men into a little fort called the fort of La Prée.

This event had hastened the resolutions of the cardinal; and till the king and he could take the command of the siege of La Rochelle, which was determined, he had sent Monsieur to direct the first operations, and had ordered all the troops he could dispose of to march toward the theater of war. It was of this detachment, sent as a vanguard, that our friend d'Artagnan formed a part.

The king, as we have said, was to follow as soon as his Bed of Justice had been held, but on rising from his Bed of Justice on the twenty-eighth of June, he felt himself attacked by fever. He was, notwithstanding, anxious to set out, but his illness becoming more serious, he was forced to stop at Villeroy.

Now, whenever the king halted, the Musketeers halted. It followed that d'Artagnan, who was as yet purely and simply in the Guards, found himself, for the time at least, separated from his good friends–Athos, Porthos, and Aramis. This separation, which was no more than an unpleasant circumstance, would have certainly become a cause of serious uneasiness if he had been able to guess by what unknown dangers he was surrounded.

He, however, arrived without accident in the camp established before La Rochelle, on the tenth of the month of September of the year 1627.

Everything was in the same state. The Duke of Buckingham and his English, masters of the Isle of Re, continued to besiege, but without success, the citadel St. Martin and the fort of La Prée; and hostilities with La Rochelle had commenced, two or three days before, about a fort which the Duc d'Angoulême had caused to be constructed near the city.

The Guards, under the command of M. Dessessart, took up their quarters at the Minimes; but, as we know, d'Artagnan, possessed with ambition to enter the Musketeers, had formed but few friendships among his comrades, and he felt himself isolated and given up to his own reflections.

His reflections were not very cheerful. From the time of his arrival in Paris, he had been mixed up with public affairs, but his own private affairs had made no great progress, either in love or fortune. As to love, the only woman he could have loved was Mme. Bonacieux; and Mme. Bonacieux had disappeared, without his being able to discover what had become of her. As to fortune, he had made–he, humble as he was–an enemy of the cardinal; that is to say, of a man before whom trembled the greatest men of the kingdom, beginning with the king.

That man had the power to crush him, and yet he had not done so. For a mind so perspicuous as that of d'Artagnan, this indulgence was a light by which he caught a glimpse of a better future.

Then he had made himself another enemy, less to be feared, he thought, but nevertheless, he instinctively felt, not to be despised. This enemy was Milady.

In exchange for all this, he had acquired the protection and good will of the queen, but the favour of the queen was at the present time an additional cause of persecution, and her protection, as it was known, protected badly–as witness Chalais and Mme. Bonacieux.

What he had clearly gained in all this was the diamond, worth five or six thousand livres, which he wore on his finger; and even this diamond–supposing that d'Artagnan, in his projects of ambition, wished to keep it, to make it someday a pledge for the gratitude of the queen–had not in the meanwhile, since he could not part with it, more value than the gravel he trod under his feet.

We say the gravel he trod under his feet, for d'Artagnan made these reflections while walking solitarily along a pretty little road which led from the camp to the village of Angoutin. Now, these reflections had led him further than he intended, and the day was beginning to decline when, by the last ray of the setting sun, he thought he saw the barrel of a musket glitter from behind a hedge.

D'Artagnan had a quick eye and a prompt understanding. He comprehended that the musket had not come there of itself, and that he who bore it had not concealed himself behind a hedge with any friendly intentions. He determined, therefore, to direct his course as clear from it as he could when, on the opposite side of the road, from behind a rock, he perceived the extremity of another musket.

This was evidently an ambuscade.

The young man cast a glance at the first musket and saw, with a certain degree of inquietude, that it was leveled in his direction, but as soon as he perceived that the orifice of the barrel was motionless, he threw himself upon the ground. At the same instant the gun was fired, and he heard the whistling of a ball pass over his head.

No time was to be lost. D'Artagnan sprang up with a bound, and at the same instant the ball from the other musket tore up the gravel on the very spot on the road where he had thrown himself with his face to the ground.

D'Artagnan was not one of those foolhardy men who seek a ridiculous death in order that it may be said of them that they did not retreat a single step. Besides, courage was out of the question here; d'Artagnan had fallen into an ambush.

"If there is a third shot," said he to himself, "I am a lost man."

He immediately, therefore, took to his heels and ran toward the camp, with the swiftness of the young men of his country, so renowned for their agility, but whatever might be his speed, the first who fired, having had time to reload, fired a second shot, and this time so well aimed that it struck his hat, and carried it ten paces from him.

As he, however, had no other hat, he picked up this as he ran, and arrived at his quarters very pale and quite out of breath. He sat down without saying a word to anybody, and began to reflect.

This event might have three causes:

The first and the most natural was that it might be an ambuscade of the Rochellais, who might not be sorry to kill one of his Majesty's Guards, because it would be an enemy the less, and this enemy might have a well-furnished purse in his pocket.

D'Artagnan took his hat, examined the hole made by the ball, and shook his head. The ball was not a musket ball–it was an arquebus ball. The accuracy of the aim had first given him the idea that a special weapon had been employed. This could not, then, be a military ambuscade, as the ball was not of the regular caliber.

This might be a kind remembrance of Monsieur the Cardinal. It may be observed that at the very moment when, thanks to the ray of the sun, he perceived the gun barrel, he was thinking with astonishment on the forbearance of his Eminence with respect to him.

But d'Artagnan again shook his head. For people toward whom he had but to put forth his hand, his Eminence had rarely recourse to such means.

It might be a vengeance of Milady; that was most probable.

He tried in vain to remember the faces or dress of the assassins; he had escaped so rapidly that he had not had leisure to notice anything.

"Ah, my poor friends!" murmured d'Artagnan, "where are you? And that you should fail me!"

D'Artagnan passed a very bad night. Three or four times he started up, imagining that a man was approaching his bed for the purpose of stabbing him. Nevertheless, day dawned without darkness having brought any accident.

But d'Artagnan well suspected that that which was deferred was not relinquished.

D'Artagnan remained all day in his quarters, assigning as a reason to himself that the weather was bad.

At nine o'clock the next morning, the drums beat to arms. The Duc d'Orleans visited the posts. The guards were under arms, and d'Artagnan took his place in the midst of his comrades.

Monsieur passed along the front of the line; then all the superior officers approached him to pay their compliments, M. Dessessart, captain of the Guards, as well as the others.

At the expiration of a minute or two, it appeared to d'Artagnan that M. Dessessart made him a sign to approach. He waited for a fresh gesture on the part of his superior, for fear he might be mistaken, but this gesture being repeated, he left the ranks, and advanced to receive orders.

"Monsieur is about to ask for some men of good will for a dangerous mission, but one which will do honour to those who shall accomplish it; and I made you a sign in order that you might hold yourself in readiness."

"Thanks, my captain!" replied d'Artagnan, who wished for nothing better than an opportunity to distinguish himself under the eye of the lieutenant general.

In fact the Rochellais had made a sortie during the night, and had retaken a bastion of which the royal army had gained possession two days before. The matter was to ascertain, by reconnoitering, how the enemy guarded this bastion.

At the end of a few minutes Monsieur raised his voice, and said, "I want for this mission three or four volunteers, led by a man who can be depended upon."

"As to the man to be depended upon, I have him under my hand, Monsieur," said M. Dessessart, pointing to d'Artagnan, "and as to the four or five volunteers, Monsieur has but to make his intentions known, and the men will not be wanting."

"Four men of good will who will risk being killed with me!" said d'Artagnan, raising his sword.

Two of his comrades of the Guards immediately sprang forward, and two other soldiers having joined them, the number was deemed sufficient. D'Artagnan declined all others, being unwilling to take the first chance from those who had the priority.

It was not known whether, after the taking of the bastion, the Rochellais had evacuated it or left a garrison in it; the object then was to examine the place near enough to verify the reports.

D'Artagnan set out with his four companions, and followed the trench; the two Guards marched abreast with him, and the two soldiers followed behind.

They arrived thus, screened by the lining of the trench, till they came within a hundred paces of the bastion. There, on turning round, d'Artagnan perceived that the two soldiers had disappeared.

He thought that, beginning to be afraid, they had stayed behind, and he continued to advance.

At the turning of the counterscarp they found themselves within about sixty paces of the bastion. They saw no one, and the bastion seemed abandoned.

The three composing our forlorn hope were deliberating whether they should proceed any further, when all at once a circle of smoke enveloped the giant of stone, and a dozen balls came whistling around d'Artagnan and his companions.

They knew all they wished to know; the bastion was guarded. A longer stay in this dangerous spot would have been useless imprudence. D'Artagnan and his two companions turned their backs, and commenced a retreat which resembled a flight.

On arriving at the angle of the trench which was to serve them as a rampart, one of the Guardsmen fell. A ball had passed through his breast. The other, who was safe and sound, continued his way toward the camp.

D'Artagnan was not willing to abandon his companion thus, and stooped to raise him and assist him in regaining the lines, but at this moment two shots were fired. One ball struck the head of the already-wounded guard, and the other flattened itself against a rock, after having passed within two inches of d'Artagnan.

The young man turned quickly round, for this attack could not have come from the bastion, which was hidden by the angle of the trench. The idea of the two soldiers who had abandoned him occurred to his mind, and with them he remembered the assassins of two evenings before. He resolved this time to know with whom he had to deal, and fell upon the body of his comrade as if he were dead.

He quickly saw two heads appear above an abandoned work within thirty paces of him; they were the heads of the two soldiers. D'Artagnan had not been deceived; these two men had only followed for the purpose of assassinating him, hoping that the young man's death would be placed to the account of the enemy.

As he might be only wounded and might denounce their crime, they came up to him with the purpose of making sure. Fortunately, deceived by d'Artagnan's trick, they neglected to reload their guns.

When they were within ten paces of him, d'Artagnan, who in falling had taken care not to let go his sword, sprang up close to them.

The assassins comprehended that if they fled toward the camp without having killed their man, they should be accused by him; therefore their first idea was to join the enemy. One of them took his gun by the barrel, and used it as he would a club. He aimed a terrible blow at d'Artagnan, who avoided it by springing to one side, but by this movement he left a passage free to the bandit, who darted off toward the bastion. As the Rochellais who guarded the bastion were ignorant of the intentions of the man they saw coming toward them, they fired upon him, and he fell, struck by a ball which broke his shoulder.

Meantime d'Artagnan had thrown himself upon the other soldier, attacking him with his sword. The conflict was not long; the wretch had nothing to defend himself with but his discharged arquebus. The sword of the Guardsman slipped along the barrel of the now-useless weapon, and passed through the thigh of the assassin, who fell.

D'Artagnan immediately placed the point of his sword at his throat.

"Oh, do not kill me!" cried the bandit. "Pardon, pardon, my officer, and I will tell you all."

"Is your secret of enough importance to me to spare your life for it?" asked the young man, withholding his arm.

"Yes; if you think existence worth anything to a man of twenty, as you are, and who may hope for everything, being handsome and brave, as you are."

"Wretch," cried d'Artagnan, "speak quickly! Who employed you to assassinate me?"

"A woman whom I don't know, but who is called Milady."

"But if you don't know this woman, how do you know her name?"

"My comrade knows her, and called her so. It was with him she agreed, and not with me; he even has in his pocket a letter from that person, who attaches great importance to you, as I have heard him say."

"But how did you become concerned in this villainous affair?"

"He proposed to me to undertake it with him, and I agreed."

"And how much did she give you for this fine enterprise?"

"A hundred louis."

"Well, come!" said the young man, laughing, "she thinks I am worth something. A hundred louis? Well, that was a temptation for two wretches like you. I understand why you accepted it, and I grant you my pardon, but upon one condition."

"What is that?" said the soldier, uneasy at perceiving that all was not over.

"That you will go and fetch me the letter your comrade has in his pocket."

"But," cried the bandit, "that is only another way of killing me. How can I go and fetch that letter under the fire of the bastion?"

"You must nevertheless make up your mind to go and get it, or I swear you shall die by my hand."

"Pardon, Monsieur; pity! In the name of that young lady you love, and whom you perhaps believe dead but who is not!" cried the bandit, throwing himself upon his knees and leaning upon his hand–for he began to lose his strength with his blood.

"And how do you know there is a young woman whom I love, and that I believed that woman dead?" asked d'Artagnan.

"By that letter which my comrade has in his pocket."

"You see, then," said d'Artagnan, "that I must have that letter. So no more delay, no more hesitation; or else whatever may be my repugnance to soiling my sword a second time with the blood of a wretch like you, I swear by my faith as an honest man–" and at these words d'Artagnan made so fierce a gesture that the wounded man sprang up.

"Stop, stop!" cried he, regaining strength by force of terror. "I will go–I will go!"

D'Artagnan took the soldier's arquebus, made him go on before him, and urged him toward his companion by pricking him behind with his sword.

It was a frightful thing to see this wretch, leaving a long track of blood on the ground he passed over, pale with approaching death, trying to drag himself along without being seen to the body of his accomplice, which lay twenty paces from him.

Terror was so strongly painted on his face, covered with a cold sweat, that d'Artagnan took pity on him, and casting upon him a look of contempt, "Stop," said he, "I will show you the difference between a man of courage and such a coward as you. Stay where you are; I will go myself."

And with a light step, an eye on the watch, observing the movements of the enemy and taking advantage of the accidents of the ground, d'Artagnan succeeded in reaching the second soldier.

There were two means of gaining his object–to search him on the spot, or to carry him away, making a buckler of his body, and search him in the trench.

D'Artagnan preferred the second means, and lifted the assassin onto his shoulders at the moment the enemy fired.

A slight shock, the dull noise of three balls which penetrated the flesh, a last cry, a convulsion of agony, proved to d'Artagnan that the would-be assassin had saved his life.

D'Artagnan regained the trench, and threw the corpse beside the wounded man, who was as pale as death.

Then he began to search. A leather pocketbook, a purse, in which was evidently a part of the sum which the bandit had received, with a dice box and dice, completed the possessions of the dead man.

He left the box and dice where they fell, threw the purse to the wounded man, and eagerly opened the pocketbook.

Among some unimportant papers he found the following letter, that which he had sought at the risk of his life:

"Since you have lost sight of that woman and she is now in safety in the convent, which you should never have allowed her to reach, try, at least, not to miss the man. If you do, you know that my hand stretches far, and that you shall pay very dearly for the hundred louis you have from me."

No signature. Nevertheless it was plain the letter came from Milady. He consequently kept it as a piece of evidence, and being in safety behind the angle of the trench, he began to interrogate the wounded man. He confessed that he had undertaken with his comrade–the same who was killed–to carry off a young woman who was to leave Paris by the Barrière de La Villette, but having stopped to drink at a cabaret, they had missed the carriage by ten minutes.

"But what were you to do with that woman?" asked d'Artagnan, with anguish.

"We were to have conveyed her to a hotel in the Place Royale," said the wounded man.

"Yes, yes!" murmured d'Artagnan, "that's the place–Milady's own residence!"

Then the young man tremblingly comprehended what a terrible thirst for vengeance urged this woman on to destroy him, as well as all who loved him, and how well she must be acquainted with the affairs of the court, since she had discovered all. There could be no doubt she owed this information to the cardinal.

But amid all this he perceived, with a feeling of real joy, that the queen must have discovered the prison in which poor Mme. Bonacieux was explaining her devotion, and that she had freed her from that prison; and the letter he had received from the young woman, and her passage along the road of Chaillot like an apparition, were now explained.

Then also, as Athos had predicted, it became possible to find Mme. Bonacieux, and a convent was not impregnable.

This idea completely restored clemency to his heart. He turned toward the wounded man, who had watched with intense anxiety all the various expressions of his countenance, and holding out his arm to him, said, "Come, I will not abandon you thus. Lean upon me, and let us return to the camp."

"Yes," said the man, who could scarcely believe in such magnanimity, "but is it not to have me hanged?"

"You have my word," said he, "for the second time I give you your life."

The wounded man sank upon his knees, to again kiss the feet of his preserver, but d'Artagnan, who had no longer a motive for staying so near the enemy, abridged the testimonials of his gratitude.

The Guardsman who had returned at the first discharge announced the death of his four companions. They were therefore much astonished and delighted in the regiment when they saw the young man come back safe and sound.

D'Artagnan explained the sword wound of his companion by a sortie which he improvised. He described the death of the other soldier, and the perils they had encountered. This recital was for him the occasion of veritable triumph. The whole army talked of this expedition for a day, and Monsieur paid him his compliments upon it. Besides this, as every great action bears its recompense with it, the brave exploit of d'Artagnan resulted in the restoration of the tranquility he had lost. In fact, d'Artagnan believed that he might be tranquil, as one of his two enemies was killed and the other devoted to his interests.

This tranquillity proved one thing–that d'Artagnan did not yet know Milady.

Chapter 42

The Anjou Wine

After the most disheartening news of the king's health, a report of his convalescence began to prevail in the camp; and as he was very anxious to be in person at the siege, it was said that as soon as he could mount a horse he would set forward.

Meantime, Monsieur, who knew that from one day to the other he might expect to be removed from his command by the Duc d'Angoulême, by Bassompierre, or by Schomberg, who were all eager for his post, did but little, lost his days in wavering, and did not dare to attempt any great enterprise to drive the English from the Isle of Re, where they still besieged the citadel St. Martin and the fort of La Prée, as on their side the French were besieging La Rochelle.

D'Artagnan, as we have said, had become more tranquil, as always happens after a past danger, particularly when the danger seems to have vanished. He only felt one uneasiness, and that was at not hearing any tidings from his friends.

But one morning at the commencement of the month of November everything was explained to him by this letter, dated from Villeroy:

M d'Artagnan,

MM Athos, Porthos, and Aramis, after having had an entertainment at my house and enjoying themselves very much, created such a disturbance that the provost of the castle, a rigid man, has ordered them to be confined for some days, but I accomplish the order they have given me by forwarding to you a dozen bottles of my Anjou wine, with which they are much pleased. They are desirous that you should drink to their health in their favourite wine. I have done this, and am, Monsieur, with great respect,

Your very humble and obedient servant,

Godeau, Purveyor of the Musketeers

"That's all well!" cried d'Artagnan. "They think of me in their pleasures, as I thought of them in my troubles. Well, I will certainly drink to their health with all my heart, but I will not drink alone."

And d'Artagnan went among those Guardsmen with whom he had formed greater intimacy than with the others, to invite them to enjoy with him this present of delicious Anjou wine which had been sent him from Villeroy.

One of the two Guardsmen was engaged that evening, and another the next, so the meeting was fixed for the day after that.

D'Artagnan, on his return, sent the twelve bottles of wine to the refreshment room of the Guards, with strict orders that great care should be taken of it; and then, on the day appointed, as the dinner was fixed for midday d'Artagnan sent Planchet at nine in the morning to assist in preparing everything for the entertainment.

Planchet, very proud of being raised to the dignity of landlord, thought he would make all ready, like an intelligent man; and with this view called in the assistance of the lackey of one of his master's guests, named Fourreau, and the false soldier who had tried to kill d'Artagnan and who, belonging to no corps, had entered into the service of d'Artagnan, or rather of Planchet, after d'Artagnan had saved his life.

The hour of the banquet being come, the two guards arrived, took their places, and the dishes were arranged on the table. Planchet waited, towel on arm; Fourreau uncorked the bottles; and Brisemont, which was the name of the convalescent, poured the wine, which was a little shaken by its journey, carefully into decanters. Of this wine, the first bottle being a little thick at the bottom, Brisemont poured the lees into a glass, and d'Artagnan desired him to drink it, for the poor devil had not yet recovered his strength.

The guests having eaten the soup, were about to lift the first glass of wine to their lips, when all at once the cannon sounded from Fort Louis and Fort Neuf. The Guardsmen, imagining this to be caused by some unexpected attack, either of the besieged or the English, sprang to their swords. D'Artagnan, not less forward than they, did likewise, and all ran out, in order to repair to their posts.

But scarcely were they out of the room before they were made aware of the cause of this noise. Cries of "Live the king! Live the cardinal!" resounded on every side, and the drums were beaten in all directions.

In short, the king, impatient, as has been said, had come by forced marches, and had that moment arrived with all his household and a reinforcement of ten thousand troops. His Musketeers proceeded and followed him. D'Artagnan, placed in line with his company, saluted with an expressive gesture his three friends, whose eyes soon discovered him, and M. de Tréville, who detected him at once.

The ceremony of reception over, the four friends were soon in one another's arms.

"Pardieu!" cried d'Artagnan, "you could not have arrived in better time; the dinner cannot have had time to get cold! Can it, gentlemen?" added the young man, turning to the two Guards, whom he introduced to his friends.

"Ah, ah!" said Porthos, "it appears we are feasting!"

"I hope," said Aramis, "there are no women at your dinner."

"Is there any drinkable wine in your tavern?" asked Athos.

"Well, pardieu! There is yours, my dear friend," replied d'Artagnan.

"Our wine!" said Athos, astonished.

"Yes, that you sent me."

"We sent you wine?"

"You know very well–the wine from the hills of Anjou."

"Yes, I know what brand you are talking about."

"The wine you prefer."

"Well, in the absence of champagne and chambertin, you must content yourselves with that."

"And so, connoisseurs in wine as we are, we have sent you some Anjou wine?" said Porthos.

"Not exactly, it is the wine that was sent by your order."

"On our account?" said the three Musketeers.

"Did you send this wine, Aramis?" said Athos.

"No; and you, Porthos?"

"No; and you, Athos?"

"No!"

"If it was not you, it was your purveyor," said d'Artagnan.

"Our purveyor!"

"Yes, your purveyor, Godeau–the purveyor of the Musketeers."

"My faith! never mind where it comes from," said Porthos, "let us taste it, and if it is good, let us drink it."

"No," said Athos, "don't let us drink wine which comes from an unknown source."

"You are right, Athos," said d'Artagnan. "Did none of you charge your purveyor, Godeau, to send me some wine?"

"No! And yet you say he has sent you some as from us?"

"Here is his letter," said d'Artagnan, and he presented the note to his comrades.

"This is not his writing!" said Athos. "I am acquainted with it; before we left Villeroy I settled the accounts of the regiment."

"A false letter altogether," said Porthos, "we have not been disciplined."

"D'Artagnan," said Aramis, in a reproachful tone, "how could you believe that we had made a disturbance?"

D'Artagnan grew pale, and a convulsive trembling shook all his limbs.

"Thou alarmest me!" said Athos, who never used thee and thou but upon very particular occasions, "what has happened?"

"Look you, my friends!" cried d'Artagnan, "a horrible suspicion crosses my mind! Can this be another vengeance of that woman?"

It was now Athos who turned pale.

D'Artagnan rushed toward the refreshment room, the three Musketeers and the two Guards following him.

The first object that met the eyes of d'Artagnan on entering the room was Brisemont, stretched upon the ground and rolling in horrible convulsions.

Planchet and Fourreau, as pale as death, were trying to give him succor, but it was plain that all assistance was useless–all the features of the dying man were distorted with agony.

"Ah!" cried he, on perceiving d'Artagnan, "Ah! This is frightful! You pretend to pardon me, and you poison me!"

"I!" cried d'Artagnan. "I, wretch? What do you say?"

"I say that it was you who gave me the wine; I say that it was you who desired me to drink it. I say you wished to avenge yourself on me, and I say that it is horrible!"

"Do not think so, Brisemont," said d'Artagnan, "do not think so. I swear to you, I protest–"

"Oh, but God is above! God will punish you! My God, grant that he may one day suffer what I suffer!"

"Upon the Gospel," said d'Artagnan, throwing himself down by the dying man, "I swear to you that the wine was poisoned and that I was going to drink of it as you did."

"I do not believe you," cried the soldier, and he expired amid horrible tortures.

"Frightful! Frightful!" murmured Athos, while Porthos broke the bottles and Aramis gave orders, a little too late, that a confessor should be sent for.

"Oh, my friends," said d'Artagnan, "you come once more to save my life, not only mine but that of these gentlemen. Gentlemen," continued he, addressing the Guardsmen, "I request you will be silent with regard to this adventure. Great personages may have had a hand in what you have seen, and if talked about, the evil would only recoil upon us."

"Ah, Monsieur!" stammered Planchet, more dead than alive, "ah, Monsieur, what an escape I have had!"

"How, Sirrah! You were going to drink my wine?"

"To the health of the king, Monsieur; I was going to drink a small glass of it if Fourreau had not told me I was called."

"Alas!" said Fourreau, whose teeth chattered with terror, "I wanted to get him out of the way that I might drink myself."

"Gentlemen," said d'Artagnan, addressing the Guardsmen, "you may easily comprehend that such a feast can only be very dull after what has taken place; so accept my excuses, and put off the party till another day, I beg of you."

The two Guardsmen courteously accepted d'Artagnan's excuses, and perceiving that the four friends desired to be alone, retired.

When the young Guardsman and the three Musketeers were without witnesses, they looked at one another with an air which plainly expressed that each of them perceived the gravity of their situation.

"In the first place," said Athos, "let us leave this chamber; the dead are not agreeable company, particularly when they have died a violent death."

"Planchet," said d'Artagnan, "I commit the corpse of this poor devil to your care. Let him be interred in holy ground. He committed a crime, it is true, but he repented of it."

And the four friends quit the room, leaving to Planchet and Fourreau the duty of paying mortuary honours to Brisemont.

The host gave them another chamber, and served them with fresh eggs and some water, which Athos went himself to draw at the fountain. In a few words, Porthos and Aramis were posted as to the situation.

"Well," said d'Artagnan to Athos, "you see, my dear friend, that this is war to the death."

Athos shook his head.

"Yes, yes," replied he, "I perceive that plainly, but do you really believe it is she?"

"I am sure of it."

"Nevertheless, I confess I still doubt."

"But the fleur-de-lis on her shoulder?"

"She is some Englishwoman who has committed a crime in France, and has been branded in consequence."

"Athos, she is your wife, I tell you," repeated d'Artagnan, "only reflect how much the two descriptions resemble each other."

"Yes, but I should think the other must be dead, I hanged her so effectually."

It was d'Artagnan who now shook his head in his turn.

"But in either case, what is to be done?" said the young man.

"The fact is, one cannot remain thus, with a sword hanging eternally over his head," said Athos. "We must extricate ourselves from this position."

"But how?"

"Listen! You must try to see her, and have an explanation with her. Say to her: 'Peace or war! My word as a gentleman never to say anything of you, never to do anything against you; on your side, a solemn oath to remain neutral with respect to me. If not, I will apply to the chancellor, I will apply to the king, I will apply to the hangman, I will move the courts against you, I will denounce you as branded, I will bring you to trial; and if you are acquitted, well, by the faith of a gentleman, I will kill you at the corner of some wall, as I would a mad dog.'"

"I like the means well enough," said d'Artagnan, "but where and how to meet with her?"

"Time, dear friend, time brings round opportunity; opportunity is the martingale of man. The more we have ventured the more we gain, when we know how to wait."

"Yes, but to wait surrounded by assassins and poisoners."

"Bah!" said Athos. "God has preserved us hitherto, God will preserve us still."

"Yes, we. Besides, we are men; and everything considered, it is our lot to risk our lives, but she," asked he, in an undertone.

"What she?" asked Athos.

"Constance."

"Madame Bonacieux! Ah, that's true!" said Athos. "My poor friend, I had forgotten you were in love."

"Well, but," said Aramis, "have you not learned by the letter you found on the wretched corpse that she is in a convent? One may be very comfortable in a convent; and as soon as the siege of La Rochelle is terminated, I promise you on my part–"

"Good," cried Athos, "good! Yes, my dear Aramis, we all know that your views have a religious tendency."

"I am only temporarily a Musketeer," said Aramis, humbly.

"It is some time since we heard from his mistress," said Athos, in a low voice. "But take no notice; we know all about that."

"Well," said Porthos, "it appears to me that the means are very simple."

"What?" asked d'Artagnan.

"You say she is in a convent?" replied Porthos.

"Yes."

"Very well. As soon as the siege is over, we'll carry her off from that convent."

"But we must first learn what convent she is in."

"That's true," said Porthos.

"But I think I have it," said Athos. "Don't you say, dear d'Artagnan, that it is the queen who has made choice of the convent for her?"

"I believe so, at least."

"In that case Porthos will assist us."

"And how so, if you please?"

"Why, by your marchioness, your duchess, your princess. She must have a long arm."

"Hush!" said Porthos, placing a finger on his lips. "I believe her to be a cardinalist; she must know nothing of the matter."

"Then," said Aramis, "I take upon myself to obtain intelligence of her."

"You, Aramis?" cried the three friends. "You! And how?"

"By the queen's almoner, to whom I am very intimately allied," said Aramis, colouring.

And on this assurance, the four friends, who had finished their modest repast, separated, with the promise of meeting again that evening. D'Artagnan returned to less important affairs, and the three Musketeers repaired to the king's quarters, where they had to prepare their lodging.

Chapter 43

The Sign Of The Red Dovecot

Meanwhile the king, who, with more reason than the cardinal, showed his hatred for Buckingham, although scarcely arrived was in such a haste to meet the enemy that he commanded every disposition to be made to drive the English from the Isle of Re, and afterward to press the siege of La Rochelle, but notwithstanding his earnest wish, he was delayed by the dissensions which broke out between MM Bassompierre and Schomberg, against the Duc d'Angoulême.

MM Bassompierre and Schomberg were marshals of France, and claimed their right of commanding the army under the orders of the king, but the cardinal, who feared that Bassompierre, a Huguenot at heart, might press but feebly the English and Rochellais, his brothers in religion, supported the Duc d'Angoulême, whom the king, at his instigation, had named lieutenant general. The result was that to prevent MM Bassompierre and Schomberg from deserting the army, a separate command had to be given to each. Bassompierre took up his quarters on the north of the city, between Leu and Dompierre; the Duc d'Angoulême on the east, from Dompierre to Perigny; and M. de Schomberg on the south, from Perigny to Angoutin.

The quarters of Monsieur were at Dompierre; the quarters of the king were sometimes at Estree, sometimes at Jarrie; the cardinal's quarters were upon the downs, at the bridge of La Pierre, in a simple house without any entrenchment. So that Monsieur watched Bassompierre; the king, the Duc d'Angoulême; and the cardinal, M. de Schomberg.

As soon as this organization was established, they set about driving the English from the Isle.

The juncture was favourable. The English, who require, above everything, good living in order to be good soldiers, only eating salt meat and bad biscuit, had many invalids in their camp. Still further, the sea, very rough at this period of the year all along the sea coast, destroyed every day some little vessel; and the shore, from the point of l'Aiguillon to the trenches, was at every tide literally covered with the wrecks of pinnacles, roberges, and feluccas. The result was that even if the king's troops remained quietly in their camp, it was evident that some day or other, Buckingham, who only continued in the Isle from obstinacy, would be obliged to raise the siege.

But as M. de Toiras gave information that everything was preparing in the enemy's camp for a fresh assault, the king judged that it would be best to put an end to the affair, and gave the necessary orders for a decisive action.

As it is not our intention to give a journal of the siege, but on the contrary only to describe such of the events of it as are connected with the story we are relating, we will content ourselves with saying in two words that the expedition succeeded, to the great astonishment of the king and the great glory of the cardinal. The English, repulsed foot by foot, beaten in all encounters, and defeated in the passage of the Isle of Loie, were obliged to re-embark, leaving on the field of battle two thousand men, among whom were five colonels, three lieutenant colonels, two hundred and fifty captains, twenty gentlemen of rank, four pieces of cannon, and sixty flags, which were taken to Paris by Claude de St. Simon, and suspended with great pomp in the arches of Notre Dame.

Te Deums were chanted in camp, and afterward throughout France.

The cardinal was left free to carry on the siege, without having, at least at the present, anything to fear on the part of the English.

But it must be acknowledged, this response was but momentary. An envoy of the Duke of Buckingham, named Montague, was taken, and proof was obtained of a league between the German Empire, Spain, England, and Lorraine. This league was directed against France.

Still further, in Buckingham's lodging, which he had been forced to abandon more precipitately than he expected, papers were found which confirmed this alliance and which, as the cardinal asserts in his memoirs, strongly compromised Mme. de Chevreuse and consequently the queen.

It was upon the cardinal that all the responsibility fell, for one is not a despotic minister without responsibility. All, therefore, of the vast resources of his genius were at work night and day, engaged in listening to the least report heard in any of the great kingdoms of Europe.

The cardinal was acquainted with the activity, and more particularly the hatred, of Buckingham. If the league which threatened France triumphed, all his influence would be lost. Spanish policy and Austrian policy would have their representatives in the cabinet of the Louvre, where they had as yet but partisans; and he, Richelieu–the French minister, the national minister–would be ruined. The king, even while obeying him like a child, hated him as a child hates his master, and would abandon him to the personal vengeance of Monsieur and the queen. He would then be lost, and France, perhaps, with him. All this must be prepared against.

Courtiers, becoming every instant more numerous, succeeded one another, day and night, in the little house of the bridge of La Pierre, in which the cardinal had established his residence.

There were monks who wore the frock with such an ill grace that it was easy to perceive they belonged to the church militant; women a little inconvenienced by their costume as pages and whose large trousers could not entirely conceal their rounded forms; and peasants with blackened hands but with fine limbs, savoring of the man of quality a league off.

There were also less agreeable visits–for two or three times reports were spread that the cardinal had nearly been assassinated.

It is true that the enemies of the cardinal said that it was he himself who set these bungling assassins to work, in order to have, if wanted, the right of using reprisals, but we must not believe everything ministers say, nor everything their enemies say.

These attempts did not prevent the cardinal, to whom his most inveterate detractors have never denied personal bravery, from making nocturnal excursions, sometimes to communicate to the Duc d'Angoulême important orders, sometimes to confer with the king, and sometimes to have an interview with a messenger whom he did not wish to see at home.

On their part the Musketeers, who had not much to do with the siege, were not under very strict orders and led a joyous life. This was the more easy for our three companions in particular; for being friends of M. de Tréville, they obtained from him special permission to be absent after the closing of the camp.

Now, one evening when d'Artagnan, who was in the trenches, was not able to accompany them, Athos, Porthos, and Aramis, mounted on their battle steeds, enveloped in their war cloaks, with their hands upon their pistol butts, were returning from a drinking place called the Red Dovecot, which Athos had discovered two days before upon the route to Jarrie, following the road which led to the camp and quite on their guard, as we have stated, for fear of an ambuscade, when, about a quarter of a league from the village of Boisnau, they fancied they heard the sound of horses approaching them. They immediately all three halted, closed in, and waited, occupying the middle of the road. In an instant, and as the moon broke from behind a cloud, they saw at a turning of the road two horsemen who, on perceiving them, stopped in their turn, appearing to deliberate whether they should continue their route or go back. The hesitation created some suspicion in the three friends, and Athos, advancing a few paces in front of the others, cried in a firm voice, "Who goes there?"

"Who goes there, yourselves?" replied one of the horsemen.

"That is not an answer," replied Athos. "Who goes there? Answer, or we charge."

"Beware of what you are about, gentlemen!" said a clear voice which seemed accustomed to command.

"It is some superior officer making his night rounds," said Athos. "What do you wish, gentlemen?"

"Who are you?" said the same voice, in the same commanding tone. "Answer in your turn, or you may repent of your disobedience."

"King's Musketeers," said Athos, more and more convinced that he who interrogated them had the right to do so.

"What company?"

"Company of Tréville."

"Advance, and give an account of what you are doing here at this hour."

The three companions advanced rather humbly–for all were now convinced that they had to do with someone more powerful than themselves–leaving Athos the post of speaker.

One of the two riders, he who had spoken second, was ten paces in front of his companion. Athos made a sign to Porthos and Aramis also to remain in the rear, and advanced alone.

"Your pardon, my officer," said Athos, "but we were ignorant with whom we had to do, and you may see that we were keeping good guard."

"Your name?" said the officer, who covered a part of his face with his cloak.

"But yourself, Monsieur," said Athos, who began to be annoyed by this inquisition, "give me, I beg you, the proof that you have the right to question me."

"Your name?" repeated the cavalier a second time, letting his cloak fall, and leaving his face uncovered.

"Monsieur the Cardinal!" cried the stupefied Musketeer.

"Your name?" cried his Eminence, for the third time.

"Athos," said the Musketeer.

The cardinal made a sign to his attendant, who drew near. "These three Musketeers shall follow us," said he, in an undertone. "I am not willing it should be known I have left the camp; and if they follow us we shall be certain they will tell nobody."

"We are gentlemen, Monseigneur," said Athos, "require our parole, and give yourself no uneasiness. Thank God, we can keep a secret."

The cardinal fixed his piercing eyes on this courageous speaker.

"You have a quick ear, Monsieur Athos," said the cardinal, "but now listen to this. It is not from mistrust that I request you to follow me, but for my security. Your companions are no doubt Messieurs Porthos and Aramis."

"Yes, your Eminence," said Athos, while the two Musketeers who had remained behind advanced hat in hand.

"I know you, gentlemen," said the cardinal, "I know you. I know you are not quite my friends, and I am sorry you are not so, but I know you are brave and loyal gentlemen, and that confidence may be placed in you. Monsieur Athos, do me, then, the honour to accompany me; you and your two friends, and then I shall have an escort to excite envy in his Majesty, if we should meet him."

The three Musketeers bowed to the necks of their horses.

"Well, upon my honour," said Athos, "your Eminence is right in taking us with you; we have seen several ill-looking faces on the road, and we have even had a quarrel at the Red Dovecot with four of those faces."

"A quarrel, and what for, gentlemen?" said the cardinal, "you know I don't like quarrelers."

"And that is the reason why I have the honour to inform your Eminence of what has happened; for you might learn it from others, and upon a false account believe us to be in fault."

"What have been the results of your quarrel?" said the cardinal, knitting his brow.

"My friend, Aramis, here, has received a slight sword wound in the arm, but not enough to prevent him, as your Eminence may see, from mounting to the assault tomorrow, if your Eminence orders an escalade."

"But you are not the men to allow sword wounds to be inflicted upon you thus," said the cardinal. "Come, be frank, gentlemen, you have settled accounts with somebody! Confess; you know I have the right of giving absolution."

"I, Monseigneur?" said Athos. "I did not even draw my sword, but I took him who offended me round the body, and threw him out of the window. It appears that in falling," continued Athos, with some hesitation, "he broke his thigh."

"Ah, ah!" said the cardinal, "and you, Monsieur Porthos?"

"I, Monseigneur, knowing that dueling is prohibited–I seized a bench, and gave one of those brigands such a blow that I believe his shoulder is broken."

"Very well," said the cardinal, "and you, Monsieur Aramis?"

"Monseigneur, being of a very mild disposition, and being, likewise, of which Monseigneur perhaps is not aware, about to enter into orders, I endeavoured to appease my comrades, when one of these wretches gave me a wound with a sword, treacherously, across my left arm. Then I admit my patience failed me; I drew my sword in my turn, and as he came back to the charge, I fancied I felt that in throwing himself upon me, he let it pass through his body. I only know for a certainty that he fell; and it seemed to me that he was borne away with his two companions."

"The devil, gentlemen!" said the cardinal, "three men placed hors de combat in a cabaret squabble! You don't do your work by halves. And pray what was this quarrel about?"

"These fellows were drunk," said Athos, "and knowing there was a lady who had arrived at the cabaret this evening, they wanted to force her door."

"Force her door!" said the cardinal, "and for what purpose?"

"To do her violence, without doubt," said Athos. "I have had the honour of informing your Eminence that these men were drunk."

"And was this lady young and handsome?" asked the cardinal, with a certain degree of anxiety.

"We did not see her, Monseigneur," said Athos.

"You did not see her? Ah, very well," replied the cardinal, quickly. "You did well to defend the honour of a woman; and as I am going to the Red Dovecot myself, I shall know if you have told me the truth."

"Monseigneur," said Athos, haughtily, "we are gentlemen, and to save our heads we would not be guilty of a falsehood."

"Therefore I do not doubt what you say, Monsieur Athos, I do not doubt it for a single instant; but," added he, "to change the conversation, was this lady alone?"

"The lady had a cavalier shut up with her," said Athos, "but as notwithstanding the noise, this cavalier did not show himself, it is to be presumed that he is a coward."

"'Judge not rashly', says the Gospel," replied the cardinal.

Athos bowed.

"And now, gentlemen, that's well," continued the cardinal. "I know what I wish to know; follow me."

The three Musketeers passed behind his Eminence, who again enveloped his face in his cloak, and put his horse in motion, keeping from eight to ten paces in advance of his four companions.

They soon arrived at the silent, solitary inn. No doubt the host knew what illustrious visitor was expected, and had consequently sent intruders out of the way.

Ten paces from the door the cardinal made a sign to his esquire and the three Musketeers to halt. A saddled horse was fastened to the window shutter. The cardinal knocked three times, and in a peculiar manner.

A man, enveloped in a cloak, came out immediately, and exchanged some rapid words with the cardinal; after which he mounted his horse, and set off in the direction of Surgères, which was likewise the way to Paris.

"Advance, gentlemen," said the cardinal.

"You have told me the truth, my gentlemen," said he, addressing the Musketeers, "and it will not be my fault if our encounter this evening be not advantageous to you. In the meantime, follow me."

The cardinal alighted; the three Musketeers did likewise. The cardinal threw the bridle of his horse to his esquire; the three Musketeers fastened the horses to the shutters.

The host stood at the door. For him, the cardinal was only an officer coming to visit a lady.

"Have you any chamber on the ground floor where these gentlemen can wait near a good fire?" said the cardinal.

The host opened the door of a large room, in which an old stove had just been replaced by a large and excellent chimney.

"I have this," said he.

"That will do," replied the cardinal. "Enter, gentlemen, and be kind enough to wait for me; I shall not be more than half an hour."

And while the three Musketeers entered the ground floor room, the cardinal, without asking further information, ascended the staircase like a man who has no need of having his road pointed out to him.

Chapter 44

The Utility Of Stovepipes

It was evident that without suspecting it, and actuated solely by their chivalrous and adventurous character, our three friends had just rendered a service to someone the cardinal honoured with his special protection.

Now, who was that someone? That was the question the three Musketeers put to one another. Then, seeing that none of their replies could throw any light on the subject, Porthos called the host and asked for dice.

Porthos and Aramis placed themselves at the table and began to play. Athos walked about in a contemplative mood.

While thinking and walking, Athos passed and repassed before the pipe of the stove, broken in halves, the other extremity passing into the chamber above; and every time he passed and repassed he heard a murmur of words, which at length fixed his attention. Athos went close to it, and distinguished some words that appeared to merit so great an interest that he made a sign to his friends to be silent, remaining himself bent with his ear directed to the opening of the lower orifice.

"Listen, Milady," said the cardinal, "the affair is important. Sit down, and let us talk it over."

"Milady!" murmured Athos.

"I listen to your Eminence with greatest attention," replied a female voice which made the Musketeer start.

"A small vessel with an English crew, whose captain is on my side, awaits you at the mouth of Charente, at Fort La Pointe. He will set sail tomorrow morning."

"I must go thither tonight?"

"Instantly! That is to say, when you have received my instructions. Two men, whom you will find at the door on going out, will serve you as escort. You will allow me to leave first; then, after half an hour, you can go away in your turn."

"Yes, Monseigneur. Now let us return to the mission with which you wish to charge me; and as I desire to continue to merit the confidence of your Eminence, deign to unfold it to me in terms clear and precise, that I may not commit an error."

There was an instant of profound silence between the two interlocutors. It was evident that the cardinal was weighing beforehand the terms in which he was about to speak, and that Milady was collecting all her intellectual faculties to comprehend the things he was about to say, and to engrave them in her memory when they should be spoken.

Athos took advantage of this moment to tell his two companions to fasten the door inside, and to make them a sign to come and listen with him.

The two Musketeers, who loved their ease, brought a chair for each of themselves and one for Athos. All three then sat down with their heads together and their ears on the alert.

"You will go to London," continued the cardinal. "Arrived in London, you will seek Buckingham."

"I must beg your Eminence to observe," said Milady, "that since the affair of the diamond studs, about which the duke always suspected me, his Grace distrusts me."

"Well, this time," said the cardinal, "it is not necessary to steal his confidence, but to present yourself frankly and loyally as a negotiator."

"Frankly and loyally," repeated Milady, with an unspeakable expression of duplicity.

"Yes, frankly and loyally," replied the cardinal, in the same tone. "All this negotiation must be carried on openly."

"I will follow your Eminence's instructions to the letter. I only wait till you give them."

"You will go to Buckingham in my behalf, and you will tell him I am acquainted with all the preparations he has made, but that they give me no uneasiness, since at the first step he takes I will ruin the queen."

"Will he believe that your Eminence is in a position to accomplish the threat thus made?"

"Yes; for I have the proofs."

"I must be able to present these proofs for his appreciation."

"Without doubt. And you will tell him I will publish the report of Bois-Robert and the Marquis de Beautru, upon the interview which the duke had at the residence of Madame the Constable with the queen on the evening Madame the Constable gave a masquerade. You will tell him, in order that he may not doubt, that he came there in the costume of the Great Mogul, which the Chevalier de Guise was to have worn, and that he purchased this exchange for the sum of three thousand pistoles."

"Well, Monseigneur?"

"All the details of his coming into and going out of the palace–on the night when he introduced himself in the character of an Italian fortune teller–you will tell him, that he may not doubt the correctness of my information; that he had under his cloak a large white robe dotted with black tears, death's heads, and crossbones–for in case of a surprise, he was to pass for the phantom of the White Lady who, as all the world knows, appears at the Louvre every time any great event is impending."

"Is that all, Monseigneur?"

"Tell him also that I am acquainted with all the details of the adventure at Amiens; that I will have a little romance made of it, wittily turned, with a plan of the garden and portraits of the principal actors in that nocturnal romance."

"I will tell him that."

"Tell him further that I hold Montague in my power; that Montague is in the Bastille; that no letters were found upon him, it is true, but that torture may make him tell much of what he knows, and even what he does not know."

"Exactly."

"Then add that his Grace has, in the precipitation with which he quit the Isle of Re, forgotten and left behind him in his lodging a certain letter from Madame de Chevreuse which singularly compromises the queen, inasmuch as it proves not only that her Majesty can love the enemies of the king but that she can conspire with the enemies of France. You recollect perfectly all I have told you, do you not?"

"Your Eminence will judge: the ball of Madame the Constable; the night at the Louvre; the evening at Amiens; the arrest of Montague; the letter of Madame de Chevreuse."

"That's it," said the cardinal, "that's it. You have an excellent memory, Milady."

"But," resumed she to whom the cardinal addressed this flattering compliment, "if, in spite of all these reasons, the duke does not give way and continues to menace France?"

"The duke is in love to madness, or rather to folly," replied Richelieu, with great bitterness. "Like the ancient paladins, he has only undertaken this war to obtain a look from his lady love. If he becomes certain that this war will cost the honour, and perhaps the liberty, of the lady of his thoughts, as he says, I will answer for it he will look twice."

"And yet," said Milady, with a persistence that proved she wished to see clearly to the end of the mission with which she was about to be charged, "if he persists?"

"If he persists?" said the cardinal. "That is not probable."

"It is possible," said Milady.

"If he persists–" His Eminence made a pause, and resumed: "If he persists–well, then I shall hope for one of those events which change the destinies of states."

"If your Eminence would quote to me some one of these events in history," said Milady, "perhaps I should partake of your confidence as to the future."

"Well, here, for example," said Richelieu: "when, in 1610, for a cause similar to that which moves the duke, King Henry IV, of glorious memory, was about, at the same time, to invade Flanders and Italy, in order to attack Austria on both sides. Well, did there not happen an event which saved Austria? Why should not the king of France have the same chance as the emperor?"

"Your Eminence means, I presume, the knife stab in the Rue de la Feronnerie?"

"Precisely," said the cardinal.

"Does not your Eminence fear that the punishment inflicted upon Ravaillac may deter anyone who might entertain the idea of imitating him?"

"There will be, in all times and in all countries, particularly if religious divisions exist in those countries, fanatics who ask nothing better than to become martyrs. Ay, and observe–it just occurs to me that the Puritans are furious against Buckingham, and their preachers designate him as the Antichrist."

"Well?" said Milady.

"Well," continued the cardinal, in an indifferent tone, "the only thing to be sought for at this moment is some woman, handsome, young, and clever, who has cause of quarrel with the duke. The duke has had many affairs of gallantry; and if he has fostered his amours by promises of eternal constancy, he must likewise have sown the seeds of hatred by his eternal infidelities."

"No doubt," said Milady, coolly, "such a woman may be found."

"Well, such a woman, who would place the knife of Jacques Clement or of Ravaillac in the hands of a fanatic, would save France."

"Yes, but she would then be the accomplice of an assassination."

"Were the accomplices of Ravaillac or of Jacques Clement ever known?"

"No; for perhaps they were too high-placed for anyone to dare look for them where they were. The Palace of Justice would not be burned down for everybody, Monseigneur."

"You think, then, that the fire at the Palace of Justice was not caused by chance?" asked Richelieu, in the tone with which he would have put a question of no importance.

"I, Monseigneur?" replied Milady. "I think nothing; I quote a fact, that is all. Only I say that if I were named Madame de Montpensier, or the Queen Marie de Medicis, I should use less precautions than I take, being simply called Milady Clarik."

"That is just," said Richelieu. "What do you require, then?"

"I require an order which would ratify beforehand all that I should think proper to do for the greatest good of France."

"But in the first place, this woman I have described must be found who is desirous of avenging herself upon the duke."

"She is found," said Milady.

"Then the miserable fanatic must be found who will serve as an instrument of God's justice."

"He will be found."

"Well," said the cardinal, "then it will be time to claim the order which you just now required."

"Your Eminence is right," replied Milady, "and I have been wrong in seeing in the mission with which you honour me anything but that which it really is–that is, to announce to his Grace, on the part of your Eminence, that you are acquainted with the different disguises by means of which he succeeded in approaching the queen during the fête given by Madame the Constable; that you have proofs of the interview granted at the Louvre by the queen to a certain Italian astrologer who was no other than the Duke of Buckingham; that you have ordered a little romance of a satirical nature to be written upon the adventures of Amiens, with a plan of the gardens in which those adventures took place, and portraits of the actors who figured in them; that Montague is in the Bastille, and that the torture may make him say things he remembers, and even things he has forgotten; that you possess a certain letter from Madame de Chevreuse, found in his Grace's lodging, which singularly compromises not only her who wrote it, but her in whose name it was written. Then, if he persists, notwithstanding all this–as that is, as I have said, the limit of my mission–I shall have nothing to do but to pray God to work a miracle for the salvation of France. That is it, is it not, Monseigneur, and I shall have nothing else to do?"

"That is it," replied the cardinal, dryly.

"And now," said Milady, without appearing to remark the change of the duke's tone toward her–"now that I have received the instructions of your Eminence as concerns your enemies, Monseigneur will permit me to say a few words to him of mine?"

"Have you enemies, then?" asked Richelieu.

"Yes, Monseigneur, enemies against whom you owe me all your support, for I made them by serving your Eminence."

"Who are they?" replied the duke.

"In the first place, there is a little intrigante named Bonacieux."

"She is in the prison of Nantes."

"That is to say, she was there," replied Milady, "but the queen has obtained an order from the king by means of which she has been conveyed to a convent."

"To a convent?" said the duke.

"Yes, to a convent."

"And to which?"

"I don't know; the secret has been well kept."

"But I will know!"

"And your Eminence will tell me in what convent that woman is?"

"I can see nothing inconvenient in that," said the cardinal.

"Well, now I have an enemy much more to be dreaded by me than this little Madame Bonacieux."

"Who is that?"

"Her lover."

"What is his name?"

"Oh, your Eminence knows him well," cried Milady, carried away by her anger. "He is the evil genius of both of us. It is he who in an encounter with your Eminence's Guards decided the victory in favour of the king's Musketeers; it is he who gave three desperate wounds to de Wardes, your emissary, and who caused the affair of the diamond studs to fail; it is he who, knowing it was I who had Madame Bonacieux carried off, has sworn my death."

"Ah, ah!" said the cardinal, "I know of whom you speak."

"I mean that miserable d'Artagnan."

"He is a bold fellow," said the cardinal.

"And it is exactly because he is a bold fellow that he is the more to be feared."

"I must have," said the duke, "a proof of his connection with Buckingham."

"A proof?" cried Milady, "I will have ten."

"Well, then, it becomes the simplest thing in the world; get me that proof, and I will send him to the Bastille."

"So far good, Monseigneur, but afterwards?"

"When once in the Bastille, there is no afterward!" said the cardinal, in a low voice. "Ah, pardieu!" continued he, "if it were as easy for me to get rid of my enemy as it is easy to get rid of yours, and if it were against such people you require impunity–"

"Monseigneur," replied Milady, "a fair exchange. Life for life, man for man; give me one, I will give you the other."

"I don't know what you mean, nor do I even desire to know what you mean," replied the cardinal, "but I wish to please you, and see nothing out of the way in giving you what you demand with respect to so infamous a creature–the more so as you tell me this d'Artagnan is a libertine, a duelist, and a traitor."

"An infamous scoundrel, Monseigneur, a scoundrel!"

"Give me paper, a quill, and some ink, then," said the cardinal.

"Here they are, Monseigneur."

There was a moment of silence, which proved that the cardinal was employed in seeking the terms in which he should write the note, or else in writing it. Athos, who had not lost a word of the conversation, took his two companions by the hand, and led them to the other end of the room.

"Well," said Porthos, "what do you want, and why do you not let us listen to the end of the conversation?"

"Hush!" said Athos, speaking in a low voice. "We have heard all it was necessary we should hear; besides, I don't prevent you from listening, but I must be gone."

"You must be gone!" said Porthos, "and if the cardinal asks for you, what answer can we make?"

"You will not wait till he asks; you will speak first, and tell him that I am gone on the lookout, because certain expressions of our host have given me reason to think the road is not safe. I will say two words about it to the cardinal's esquire likewise. The rest concerns myself; don't be uneasy about that."

"Be prudent, Athos," said Aramis.

"Be easy on that head," replied Athos, "you know I am cool enough."

Porthos and Aramis resumed their places by the stovepipe.

As to Athos, he went out without any mystery, took his horse, which was tied with those of his friends to the fastenings of the shutters, in four words convinced the attendant of the necessity of a vanguard for their return, carefully examined the priming of his pistols, drew his sword, and took, like a forlorn hope, the road to the camp.

Chapter 45

A Conjugal Scene

As Athos had foreseen, it was not long before the cardinal came down. He opened the door of the room in which the Musketeers were, and found Porthos playing an earnest game of dice with Aramis. He cast a rapid glance around the room, and perceived that one of his men was missing.

"What has become of Monseigneur Athos?" asked he.

"Monseigneur," replied Porthos, "he has gone as a scout, on account of some words of our host, which made him believe the road was not safe."

"And you, what have you done, Monsieur Porthos?"

"I have won five pistoles of Aramis."

"Well; now will you return with me?"

"We are at your Eminence's orders."

"To horse, then, gentlemen; for it is getting late."

The attendant was at the door, holding the cardinal's horse by the bridle. At a short distance a group of two men and three horses appeared in the shade. These were the two men who were to conduct Milady to Fort La Pointe, and superintend her embarkation.

The attendant confirmed to the cardinal what the two Musketeers had already said with respect to Athos. The cardinal made an approving gesture, and retraced his route with the same precautions he had used incoming.

Let us leave him to follow the road to the camp protected by his esquire and the two Musketeers, and return to Athos.

For a hundred paces he maintained the speed at which he started, but when out of sight he turned his horse to the right, made a circuit, and came back within twenty paces of a high hedge to watch the passage of the little troop. Having recognised the laced hats of his companions and the golden fringe of the cardinal's cloak, he waited till the horsemen had turned the angle of the road, and having lost sight of them, he returned at a gallop to the inn, which was opened to him without hesitation.

The host recognised him.

"My officer," said Athos, "has forgotten to give a piece of very important information to the lady, and has sent me back to repair his forgetfulness."

"Go up," said the host, "she is still in her chamber."

Athos availed himself of the permission, ascended the stairs with his lightest step, gained the landing, and through the open door perceived Milady putting on her hat.

He entered the chamber and closed the door behind him. At the noise he made in pushing the bolt, Milady turned round.

Athos was standing before the door, enveloped in his cloak, with his hat pulled down over his eyes. On seeing this figure, mute and immovable as a statue, Milady was frightened.

"Who are you, and what do you want?" cried she.

"Humph," murmured Athos, "it is certainly she!"

And letting fall his cloak and raising his hat, he advanced toward Milady.

"Do you know me, Madame?" said he.

Milady made one step forward, and then drew back as if she had seen a serpent.

"So far, well," said Athos, "I perceive you know me."

"The Comte de la Fere!" murmured Milady, becoming exceedingly pale, and drawing back till the wall prevented her from going any farther.

"Yes, Milady," replied Athos, "the Comte de la Fère in person, who comes expressly from the other world to have the pleasure of paying you a visit. Sit down, Madame, and let us talk, as the cardinal said."

Milady, under the influence of inexpressible terror, sat down without uttering a word.

"You certainly are a demon sent upon the earth!" said Athos. "Your power is great, I know, but you also know that with the help of God men have often conquered the most terrible demons. You have once before thrown yourself in my path. I thought I had crushed you, Madame, but either I was deceived or hell has resuscitated you!"

Milady at these words, which recalled frightful remembrances, hung down her head with a suppressed groan.

"Yes, hell has resuscitated you," continued Athos. "Hell has made you rich, hell has given you another name, hell has almost made you another face, but it has neither effaced the stains from your soul nor the brand from your body."

Milady arose as if moved by a powerful spring, and her eyes flashed lightning. Athos remained sitting.

"You believed me to be dead, did you not, as I believed you to be? And the name of Athos as well concealed the Comte de la Fère, as the name Milady Clarik concealed Anne de Breuil. Was it not so you were called when your honoured brother married us? Our position is truly a strange one," continued Athos, laughing. "We have only lived up to the present time because we believed each other dead, and because a remembrance is less oppressive than a living creature, though a remembrance is sometimes devouring."

"But," said Milady, in a hollow, faint voice, "what brings you back to me, and what do you want with me?"

"I wish to tell you that though remaining invisible to your eyes, I have not lost sight of you."

"You know what I have done?"

"I can relate to you, day by day, your actions from your entrance to the service of the cardinal to this evening."

A smile of incredulity passed over the pale lips of Milady.

"Listen! It was you who cut off the two diamond studs from the shoulder of the Duke of Buckingham; it was you had the Madame Bonacieux carried off; it was you who, in love with de Wardes and thinking to pass the night with him, opened the door to Monsieur d'Artagnan; it was you who, believing that de Wardes had deceived you, wished to have him killed by his rival; it was you who, when this rival had discovered your infamous secret, wished to have him killed in his turn by two assassins, whom you sent in pursuit of him; it was you who, finding the balls had missed their mark, sent poisoned wine with a forged letter, to make your victim believe that the wine came from his friends. In short, it was you who have but now in this chamber, seated in this chair I now fill, made an engagement with Cardinal Richelieu to cause the Duke of Buckingham to be assassinated, in exchange for the promise he has made you to allow you to assassinate d'Artagnan."

Milady was livid.

"You must be Satan!" cried she.

"Perhaps," said Athos, "But at all events listen well to this. Assassinate the Duke of Buckingham, or cause him to be assassinated–I care very little about that! I don't know him. Besides, he is an Englishman. But do not touch with the tip of your finger a single hair of d'Artagnan, who is a faithful friend whom I love and defend, or I swear to you by the head of my father the crime which you shall have endeavoured to commit, or shall have committed, shall be the last."

"Monsieur d'Artagnan has cruelly insulted me," said Milady, in a hollow tone, "Monsieur d'Artagnan shall die!"

"Indeed! Is it possible to insult you, Madame?" said Athos, laughing, "he has insulted you, and he shall die!"

"He shall die!" replied Milady, "she first, and he afterward."

Athos was seized with a kind of vertigo. The sight of this creature, who had nothing of the woman about her, recalled awful remembrances. He thought how one day, in a less dangerous situation than the one in which he was now placed, he had already endeavoured to sacrifice her to his honour. His desire for blood returned, burning his brain and pervading his frame like a raging fever; he arose in his turn, reached his hand to his belt, drew forth a pistol, and cocked it.

Milady, pale as a corpse, endeavoured to cry out, but her swollen tongue could utter no more than a hoarse sound which had nothing human in it and resembled the rattle of a wild beast. Motionless against the dark tapestry, with her hair in disorder, she appeared like a horrid image of terror.

Athos slowly raised his pistol, stretched out his arm so that the weapon almost touched Milady's forehead, and then, in a voice the more terrible from having the supreme calmness of a fixed resolution, "Madame," said he, "you will this instant deliver to me the paper the cardinal signed; or upon my soul, I will blow your brains out."

With another man, Milady might have preserved some doubt, but she knew Athos. Nevertheless, she remained motionless.

"You have one second to decide," said he.

Milady saw by the contraction of his countenance that the trigger was about to be pulled; she reached her hand quickly to her bosom, drew out a paper, and held it toward Athos.

"Take it," said she, "and be accursed!"

Athos took the paper, returned the pistol to his belt, approached the lamp to be assured that it was the paper, unfolded it, and read:

"Dec. 3, 1627

It is by my order and for the good of the state that the bearer of this has done what he has done.

RICHELIEU

"And now," said Athos, resuming his cloak and putting on his hat, "now that I have drawn your teeth, viper, bite if you can."

And he left the chamber without once looking behind him.

At the door he found the two men and the spare horse which they held.

"Gentlemen," said he, "Monseigneur's order is, you know, to conduct that woman, without losing time, to Fort La Pointe, and never to leave her till she is on board."

As these words agreed wholly with the order they had received, they bowed their heads in sign of assent.

With regard to Athos, he leaped lightly into the saddle and set out at full gallop; only instead of following the road, he went across the fields, urging his horse to the utmost and stopping occasionally to listen.

In one of those halts he heard the steps of several horses on the road. He had no doubt it was the cardinal and his escort. He immediately made a new point in advance, rubbed his horse down with some heath and leaves of trees, and placed himself across the road, about two hundred paces from the camp.

"Who goes there?" cried he, as soon as he perceived the horsemen.

"That is our brave Musketeer, I think," said the cardinal.

"Yes, Monseigneur," said Porthos, "it is he."

"Monsieur Athos," said Richelieu, "receive my thanks for the good guard you have kept. Gentlemen, we are arrived; take the gate on the left. The watchword is, 'King and Re.'"

Saying these words, the cardinal saluted the three friends with an inclination of his head, and took the right hand, followed by his attendant–for that night he himself slept in the camp.

"Well!" said Porthos and Aramis together, as soon as the cardinal was out of hearing, "well, he signed the paper she required!"

"I know it," said Athos, coolly, "since here it is."

And the three friends did not exchange another word till they reached their quarters, except to give the watchword to the sentinels. Only they sent Mousqueton to tell Planchet that his master was requested, the instant that he left the trenches, to come to the quarters of the Musketeers.

Milady, as Athos had foreseen, on finding the two men that awaited her, made no difficulty in following them. She had had for an instant an inclination to be reconducted to the cardinal, and relate everything to him, but a revelation on her part would bring about a revelation on the part of Athos. She might say that Athos had hanged her, but then Athos would tell that she was branded. She thought it was best to preserve silence, to discreetly set off to accomplish her difficult mission with her usual skill; and then, all things being accomplished to the satisfaction of the cardinal, to come to him and claim her vengeance.

In consequence, after having traveled all night, at seven o'clock she was at the fort of the Point; at eight o'clock she had embarked; and at nine, the vessel, which with letters of marque from the cardinal was supposed to be sailing for Bayonne, raised anchor, and steered its course toward England.

Chapter 46

The Bastion Saint-Gervais

On arriving at the lodgings of his three friends, d'Artagnan found them assembled in the same chamber. Athos was meditating; Porthos was twisting his moustache; Aramis was saying his prayers in a charming little Book of Hours, bound in blue velvet.

"Pardieu, gentlemen," said he. "I hope what you have to tell me is worth the trouble, or else, I warn you, I will not pardon you for making me come here instead of getting a little rest after a night spent in taking and dismantling a bastion. Ah, why were you not there, gentlemen? It was warm work."

"We were in a place where it was not very cold," replied Porthos, giving his moustache a twist which was peculiar to him.

"Hush!" said Athos.

"Oh, oh!" said d'Artagnan, comprehending the slight frown of the Musketeer. "It appears there is something fresh aboard."

"Aramis," said Athos, "you went to breakfast the day before yesterday at the inn of the Parpaillot, I believe?"

"Yes."

"How did you fare?"

"For my part, I ate but little. The day before yesterday was a fish day, and they had nothing but meat."

"What," said Athos, "no fish at a seaport?"

"They say," said Aramis, resuming his pious reading, "that the dyke which the cardinal is making drives them all out into the open sea."

"But that is not quite what I mean to ask you, Aramis," replied Athos. "I want to know if you were left alone, and nobody interrupted you."

"Why, I think there were not many intruders. Yes, Athos, I know what you mean: we shall do very well at the Parpaillot."

"Let us go to the Parpaillot, then, for here the walls are like sheets of paper."

D'Artagnan, who was accustomed to his friend's manner of acting, and who perceived immediately, by a word, a gesture, or a sign from him, that the circumstances were serious, took Athos's arm, and went out without saying anything. Porthos followed, chatting with Aramis.

On their way they met Grimaud. Athos made him a sign to come with them. Grimaud, according to custom, obeyed in silence; the poor lad had nearly come to the pass of forgetting how to speak.

They arrived at the drinking room of the Parpaillot. It was seven o'clock in the morning, and daylight began to appear. The three friends ordered breakfast, and went into a room in which the host said they would not be disturbed.

Unfortunately, the hour was badly chosen for a private conference. The morning drum had just been beaten; everyone shook off the drowsiness of night, and to dispel the humid morning air, came to take a drop at the inn. Dragoons, Swiss, Guardsmen, Musketeers, light-horsemen, succeeded one another with a rapidity which might answer the purpose of the host very well, but agreed badly with the views of the four friends. Thus they applied very curtly to the salutations, healths, and jokes of their companions.

"I see how it will be," said Athos: "we shall get into some pretty quarrel or other, and we have no need of one just now. D'Artagnan, tell us what sort of a night you have had, and we will describe ours afterward."

"Ah, yes," said a light-horseman, with a glass of brandy in his hand, which he sipped slowly. "I hear you gentlemen of the Guards have been in the trenches tonight, and that you did not get much the best of the Rochellais."

D'Artagnan looked at Athos to know if he ought to reply to this intruder who thus mixed unasked in their conversation.

"Well," said Athos, "don't you hear Monsieur de Busigny, who does you the honour to ask you a question? Relate what has passed during the night, since these gentlemen desire to know it."

"Have you not taken a bastion?" said a Swiss, who was drinking rum out of a beer glass.

"Yes, Monsieur," said d'Artagnan, bowing, "we have had that honour. We even have, as you may have heard, introduced a barrel of powder under one of the angles, which in blowing up made a very pretty breach. Without reckoning that as the bastion was not built yesterday all the rest of the building was badly shaken."

"And what bastion is it?" asked a dragoon, with his saber run through a goose which he was taking to be cooked.

"The bastion St. Gervais," replied d'Artagnan, "from behind which the Rochellais annoyed our workmen."

"Was that affair hot?"

"Yes, moderately so. We lost five men, and the Rochellais eight or ten."

"Balzempleu!" said the Swiss, who, notwithstanding the admirable collection of oaths possessed by the German language, had acquired a habit of swearing in French.

"But it is probable," said the light-horseman, "that they will send pioneers this morning to repair the bastion."

"Yes, that's probable," said d'Artagnan.

"Gentlemen," said Athos, "a wager!"

"Ah, wooi, a vager!" cried the Swiss.

"What is it?" said the light-horseman.

"Stop a bit," said the dragoon, placing his saber like a spit upon the two large iron dogs which held the firebrands in the chimney, "stop a bit, I am in it. You cursed host! a dripping pan immediately, that I may not lose a drop of the fat of this estimable bird."

"You was right," said the Swiss, "goose grease is kood with basdry."

"There!" said the dragoon. "Now for the wager! We listen, Monsieur Athos."

"Yes, the wager!" said the light-horseman.

"Well, Monsieur de Busigny, I will bet you," said Athos, "that my three companions, Messieurs Porthos, Aramis, and d'Artagnan, and myself, will go and breakfast in the bastion St. Gervais, and we will remain there an hour, by the watch, whatever the enemy may do to dislodge us."

Porthos and Aramis looked at each other; they began to comprehend.

"But," said d'Artagnan, in the ear of Athos, "you are going to get us all killed without mercy."

"We are much more likely to be killed," said Athos, "if we do not go."

"My faith, gentlemen," said Porthos, turning round upon his chair and twisting his moustache, "that's a fair bet, I hope."

"I take it," said M. de Busigny, "so let us fix the stake."

"You are four gentlemen," said Athos, "and we are four; an unlimited dinner for eight. Will that do?"

"Capitally," replied M. de Busigny.

"Perfectly," said the dragoon.

"That shoots me," said the Swiss.

The fourth auditor, who during all this conversation had played a mute part, made a sign of the head in proof that he acquiesced in the proposition.

"The breakfast for these gentlemen is ready," said the host.

"Well, bring it," said Athos.

The host obeyed. Athos called Grimaud, pointed to a large basket which lay in a corner, and made a sign to him to wrap the viands up in the napkins.

Grimaud understood that it was to be a breakfast on the grass, took the basket, packed up the viands, added the bottles, and then took the basket on his arm.

"But where are you going to eat my breakfast?" asked the host.

"What matter, if you are paid for it?" said Athos, and he threw two pistoles majestically on the table.

"Shall I give you the change, my officer?" said the host.

"No, only add two bottles of champagne, and the difference will be for the napkins."

The host had not quite so good a bargain as he at first hoped for, but he made amends by slipping in two bottles of Anjou wine instead of two bottles of champagne.

"Monsieur de Busigny," said Athos, "will you be so kind as to set your watch with mine, or permit me to regulate mine by yours?"

"Which you please, Monsieur!" said the light-horseman, drawing from his fob a very handsome watch, studded with diamonds, "half past seven."

"Thirty-five minutes after seven," said Athos, "by which you perceive I am five minutes faster than you."

And bowing to all the astonished persons present, the young men took the road to the bastion St. Gervais, followed by Grimaud, who carried the basket, ignorant of where he was going but in the passive obedience which Athos had taught him not even thinking of asking.

As long as they were within the circle of the camp, the four friends did not exchange one word; besides, they were followed by the curious, who, hearing of the wager, were anxious to know how they would come out of it. But when once they passed the line of circumvallation and found themselves in the open plain, d'Artagnan, who was completely ignorant of what was going forward, thought it was time to demand an explanation.

"And now, my dear Athos," said he, "do me the kindness to tell me where we are going?"

"Why, you see plainly enough we are going to the bastion."

"But what are we going to do there?"

"You know well that we go to breakfast there."

"But why did we not breakfast at the Parpaillot?"

"Because we have very important matters to communicate to one another, and it was impossible to talk five minutes in that inn without being annoyed by all those importunate fellows, who keep coming in, saluting you, and addressing you. Here at least," said Athos, pointing to the bastion, "they will not come and disturb us."

"It appears to me," said d'Artagnan, with that prudence which allied itself in him so naturally with excessive bravery, "that we could have found some retired place on the downs or the seashore."

"Where we should have been seen all four conferring together, so that at the end of a quarter of an hour the cardinal would have been informed by his spies that we were holding a council."

"Yes," said Aramis, "Athos is right: ANIMADVERTUNTUR IN DESERTIS."

"A desert would not have been amiss," said Porthos, "but it behooved us to find it."

"There is no desert where a bird cannot pass over one's head, where a fish cannot leap out of the water, where a rabbit cannot come out of its burrow, and I believe that bird, fish, and rabbit each becomes a spy of the cardinal. Better, then, pursue our enterprise; from which, besides, we cannot retreat without shame. We have made a wager–a wager which could not have been foreseen, and of which I defy anyone to divine the true cause. We are going, in order to win it, to remain an hour in the bastion. Either we shall be attacked, or not. If we are not, we shall have all the time to talk, and nobody will hear us–for I guarantee the walls of the bastion have no ears; if we are, we will talk of our affairs just the same. Moreover, in defending ourselves, we shall cover ourselves with glory. You see that everything is to our advantage."

"Yes," said d'Artagnan, "but we shall indubitably attract a ball."

"Well, my dear," replied Athos, "you know well that the balls most to be dreaded are not from the enemy."

"But for such an expedition we surely ought to have brought our muskets."

"You are stupid, friend Porthos. Why should we load ourselves with a useless burden?"

"I don't find a good musket, twelve cartridges, and a powder flask very useless in the face of an enemy."

"Well," replied Athos, "have you not heard what d'Artagnan said?"

"What did he say?" demanded Porthos.

"D'Artagnan said that in the attack of last night eight or ten Frenchmen were killed, and as many Rochellais."

"What then?"

"The bodies were not plundered, were they? It appears the conquerors had something else to do."

"Well?"

"Well, we shall find their muskets, their cartridges, and their flasks; and instead of four musketoons and twelve balls, we shall have fifteen guns and a hundred charges to fire."

"Oh, Athos!" said Aramis, "truly you are a great man."

Porthos nodded in sign of agreement. D'Artagnan alone did not seem convinced.

Grimaud no doubt shared the misgivings of the young man, for seeing that they continued to advance toward the bastion–something he had till then doubted–he pulled his master by the skirt of his coat.

"Where are we going?" asked he, by a gesture.

Athos pointed to the bastion.

"But," said Grimaud, in the same silent dialect, "we shall leave our skins there."

Athos raised his eyes and his finger toward heaven.

Grimaud put his basket on the ground and sat down with a shake of the head.

Athos took a pistol from his belt, looked to see if it was properly primed, cocked it, and placed the muzzle close to Grimaud's ear.

Grimaud was on his legs again as if by a spring. Athos then made him a sign to take up his basket and to walk on first. Grimaud obeyed. All that Grimaud gained by this momentary pantomime was to pass from the rear guard to the vanguard.

Arrived at the bastion, the four friends turned round.

More than three hundred soldiers of all kinds were assembled at the gate of the camp; and in a separate group might be distinguished M. de Busigny, the dragoon, the Swiss, and the fourth bettor.

Athos took off his hat, placed it on the end of his sword, and waved it in the air.

All the spectators returned him his salute, accompanying this courtesy with a loud hurrah which was audible to the four; after which all four disappeared in the bastion, whither Grimaud had preceded them.

Chapter 47

The Council Of The Musketeers

As Athos had foreseen, the bastion was only occupied by a dozen corpses, French and Rochellais.

"Gentlemen," said Athos, who had assumed the command of the expedition, "while Grimaud spreads the table, let us begin by collecting the guns and cartridges together. We can talk while performing that necessary task. These gentlemen," added he, pointing to the bodies, "cannot hear us."

"But we could throw them into the ditch," said Porthos, "after having assured ourselves they have nothing in their pockets."

"Yes," said Athos, "that's Grimaud's business."

"Well, then," cried d'Artagnan, "pray let Grimaud search them and throw them over the walls."

"Heaven forfend!" said Athos, "they may serve us."

"These bodies serve us?" said Porthos. "You are mad, dear friend."

"Judge not rashly, say the gospel and the cardinal," replied Athos. "How many guns, gentlemen?"

"Twelve," replied Aramis.

"How many shots?"

"A hundred."

"That's quite as many as we shall want. Let us load the guns."

The four Musketeers went to work; and as they were loading the last musket Grimaud announced that the breakfast was ready.

Athos replied, always by gestures, that that was well, and indicated to Grimaud, by pointing to a turret that resembled a pepper caster, that he was to stand as sentinel. Only, to alleviate the tediousness of the duty, Athos allowed him to take a loaf, two cutlets, and a bottle of wine.

"And now to table," said Athos.

The four friends seated themselves on the ground with their legs crossed like Turks, or even tailors.

"And now," said d'Artagnan, "as there is no longer any fear of being overheard, I hope you are going to let me into your secret."

"I hope at the same time to procure you amusement and glory, gentlemen," said Athos. "I have induced you to take a charming promenade; here is a delicious breakfast; and yonder are five hundred persons, as you may see through the loopholes, taking us for heroes or madmen–two classes of imbeciles greatly resembling each other."

"But the secret!" said d'Artagnan.

"The secret is," said Athos, "that I saw Milady last night."

D'Artagnan was lifting a glass to his lips, but at the name of Milady, his hand trembled so, that he was obliged to put the glass on the ground again for fear of spilling the contents."

"You saw your wi–"

"Hush!" interrupted Athos. "You forget, my dear, you forget that these gentlemen are not initiated into my family affairs like yourself. I have seen Milady."

"Where?" demanded d'Artagnan.

"Within two leagues of this place, at the inn of the Red Dovecot."

"In that case I am lost," said d'Artagnan.

"Not so bad yet," replied Athos, "for by this time she must have quit the shores of France."

D'Artagnan breathed again.

"But after all," asked Porthos, "who is Milady?"

"A charming woman!" said Athos, sipping a glass of sparkling wine. "Villainous host!" cried he, "he has given us Anjou wine instead of champagne, and fancies we know no better! Yes," continued he, "a charming woman, who entertained kind views toward our friend d'Artagnan, who, on his part, has given her some offense for which she tried to revenge herself a month ago by having him killed by two musket shots, a week ago by trying to poison him, and yesterday by demanding his head of the cardinal."

"What! By demanding my head of the cardinal?" cried d'Artagnan, pale with terror.

"Yes, that is true as the Gospel," said Porthos, "I heard her with my own ears."

"I also," said Aramis.

"Then," said d'Artagnan, letting his arm fall with discouragement, "it is useless to struggle longer. I may as well blow my brains out, and all will be over."

"That's the last folly to be committed," said Athos, "seeing it is the only one for which there is no remedy."

"But I can never escape," said d'Artagnan, "with such enemies. First, my stranger of Meung; then de Wardes, to whom I have given three sword wounds; next Milady, whose secret I have discovered; finally, the cardinal, whose vengeance I have balked."

"Well," said Athos, "that only makes four; and we are four–one for one. Pardieu! If we may believe the signs Grimaud is making, we are about to have to do with a very different number of people. What is it, Grimaud? Considering the gravity of the occasion, I permit you to speak, my friend, but be laconic, I beg. What do you see?"

"A troop."

"Of how many persons?"

"Twenty men."

"What sort of men?"

"Sixteen pioneers, four soldiers."

"How far distant?"

"Five hundred paces."

"Good! We have just time to finish this fowl and to drink one glass of wine to your health, d'Artagnan."

"To your health!" repeated Porthos and Aramis.

"Well, then, to my health! Although I am very much afraid that your good wishes will not be of great service to me."

"Bah!" said Athos, "God is great, as say the followers of Mohammed, and the future is in his hands."

Then, swallowing the contents of his glass, which he put down close to him, Athos arose carelessly, took the musket next to him, and drew near to one of the loopholes.

Porthos, Aramis and d'Artagnan followed his example. As to Grimaud, he received orders to place himself behind the four friends in order to reload their weapons.

"Pardieu!" said Athos, "it was hardly worth while to distribute ourselves for twenty fellows armed with pickaxes, mattocks, and shovels. Grimaud had only to make them a sign to go away, and I am convinced they would have left us in peace."

"I doubt that," replied d'Artagnan, "for they are advancing very resolutely. Besides, in addition to the pioneers, there are four soldiers and a brigadier, armed with muskets."

"That's because they don't see us," said Athos.

"My faith," said Aramis, "I must confess I feel a great repugnance to fire on these poor devils of civilians."

"He is a bad priest," said Porthos, "who has pity for heretics."

"In truth," said Athos, "Aramis is right. I will warn them."

"What the devil are you going to do?" cried d'Artagnan, "you will be shot."

But Athos heeded not his advice. Mounting on the breach, with his musket in one hand and his hat in the other, he said, bowing courteously and addressing the soldiers and the pioneers, who, astonished at this apparition, stopped fifty paces from the bastion: "Gentlemen, a few friends and myself are about to breakfast in this bastion. Now, you know nothing is more disagreeable than being disturbed when one is at breakfast. We request you, then, if you really have business here, to wait till we have finished our repast, or to come again a short time hence; unless, which would be far better, you form the salutary resolution to quit the side of the rebels, and come and drink with us to the health of the King of France."

"Take care, Athos!" cried d'Artagnan, "don't you see they are aiming?"

"Yes, yes," said Athos, "but they are only civilians–very bad marksmen, who will be sure not to hit me."

In fact, at the same instant four shots were fired, and the balls were flattened against the wall around Athos, but not one touched him.

Four shots replied to them almost instantaneously, but much better aimed than those of the aggressors; three soldiers fell dead, and one of the pioneers was wounded.

"Grimaud," said Athos, still on the breach, "another musket!"

Grimaud immediately obeyed. On their part, the three friends had reloaded their arms; a second discharge followed the first. The brigadier and two pioneers fell dead; the rest of the troop took to flight.

"Now, gentlemen, a sortie!" cried Athos.

And the four friends rushed out of the fort, gained the field of battle, picked up the four muskets of the privates and the half-pike of the brigadier, and convinced that the fugitives would not stop till they reached the city, turned again toward the bastion, bearing with them the trophies of their victory.

"Reload the muskets, Grimaud," said Athos, "and we, gentlemen, will go on with our breakfast, and resume our conversation. Where were we?"

"I recollect you were saying," said d'Artagnan, "that after having demanded my head of the cardinal, Milady had quit the shores of France. Whither goes she?" added he, strongly interested in the route Milady followed.

"She goes into England," said Athos.

"With what view?"

"With the view of assassinating, or causing to be assassinated, the Duke of Buckingham."

D'Artagnan uttered an exclamation of surprise and indignation.

"But this is infamous!" cried he.

"As to that," said Athos, "I beg you to believe that I care very little about it. Now you have done, Grimaud, take our brigadier's half-pike, tie a napkin to it, and plant it on top of our bastion, that these rebels of Rochellais may see that they have to deal with brave and loyal soldiers of the king."

Grimaud obeyed without replying. An instant afterward, the white flag was floating over the heads of the four friends. A thunder of applause saluted its appearance; half the camp was at the barrier.

"How?" replied d'Artagnan, "you care little if she kills Buckingham or causes him to be killed? But the duke is our friend."

"The duke is English; the duke fights against us. Let her do what she likes with the duke; I care no more about him than an empty bottle." And Athos threw fifteen paces from him an empty bottle from which he had poured the last drop into his glass.

"A moment," said d'Artagnan. "I will not abandon Buckingham thus. He gave us some very fine horses."

"And moreover, very handsome saddles," said Porthos, who at the moment wore on his cloak the lace of his own.

"Besides," said Aramis, "God desires the conversion and not the death of a sinner."

"Amen!" said Athos, "and we will return to that subject later, if such be your pleasure, but what for the moment engaged my attention most earnestly, and I am sure you will understand me, d'Artagnan, was the getting from this woman a kind of carte blanche which she had extorted from the cardinal, and by means of which she could with impunity get rid of you and perhaps of us."

"But this creature must be a demon!" said Porthos, holding out his plate to Aramis, who was cutting up a fowl.

"And this carte blanche," said d'Artagnan, "this carte blanche, does it remain in her hands?"

"No, it passed into mine; I will not say without trouble, for if I did I should tell a lie."

"My dear Athos, I shall no longer count the number of times I am indebted to you for my life."

"Then it was to go to her that you left us?" said Aramis.

"Exactly."

"And you have that letter of the cardinal?" said d'Artagnan.

"Here it is," said Athos; and he took the invaluable paper from the pocket of his uniform. D'Artagnan unfolded it with one hand, whose trembling he did not even attempt to conceal, to read:

Dec. 3, 1627

It is by my order and for the good of the state that the bearer of this has done what he has done.

RICHELIEU

"In fact," said Aramis, "it is an absolution according to rule."

"That paper must be torn to pieces," said d'Artagnan, who fancied he read in it his sentence of death.

"On the contrary," said Athos, "it must be preserved carefully. I would not give up this paper if covered with as many gold pieces."

"And what will she do now?" asked the young man.

"Why," replied Athos, carelessly, "she is probably going to write to the cardinal that a damned Musketeer, named Athos, has taken her safe-conduct from her by force; she will advise him in the same letter to get rid of his two friends, Aramis and Porthos, at the same time. The cardinal will remember that these are the same men who have often crossed his path; and then some fine morning he will arrest d'Artagnan, and for fear he should feel lonely, he will send us to keep him company in the Bastille."

"Go to! It appears to me you make dull jokes, my dear," said Porthos.

"I do not jest," said Athos.

"Do you know," said Porthos, "that to twist that damned Milady's neck would be a smaller sin than to twist those of these poor devils of Huguenots, who have committed no other crime than singing in French the psalms we sing in Latin?"

"What says the abbé?" asked Athos, quietly.

"I say I am entirely of Porthos's opinion," replied Aramis.

"And I, too," said d'Artagnan.

"Fortunately, she is far off," said Porthos, "for I confess she would worry me if she were here."

"She worries me in England as well as in France," said Athos.

"She worries me everywhere," said d'Artagnan.

"But when you held her in your power, why did you not drown her, strangle her, hang her?" said Porthos. "It is only the dead who do not return."

"You think so, Porthos?" replied the Musketeer, with a sad smile which d'Artagnan alone understood.

"I have an idea," said d'Artagnan.

"What is it?" said the Musketeers.

"To arms!" cried Grimaud.

The young men sprang up, and seized their muskets.

This time a small troop advanced, consisting of from twenty to twenty-five men, but they were not pioneers, they were soldiers of the garrison.

"Shall we return to the camp?" said Porthos. "I don't think the sides are equal."

"Impossible, for three reasons," replied Athos. "The first, that we have not finished breakfast; the second, that we still have some very important things to say; and the third, that it yet wants ten minutes before the lapse of the hour."

"Well, then," said Aramis, "we must form a plan of battle."

"That's very simple," replied Athos. "As soon as the enemy are within musket shot, we must fire upon them. If they continue to advance, we must fire again. We must fire as long as we have loaded guns. If those who remain of the troop persist in coming to the assault, we will allow the besiegers to get as far as the ditch, and then we will push down upon their heads that strip of wall which keeps its perpendicular by a miracle."

"Bravo!" cried Porthos. "Decidedly, Athos, you were born to be a general, and the cardinal, who fancies himself a great soldier, is nothing beside you."

"Gentlemen," said Athos, "no divided attention, I beg; let each one pick out his man."

"I cover mine," said d'Artagnan.

"And I mine," said Porthos.

"And I mine," said Aramis.

"Fire, then," said Athos.

The four muskets made but one report, but four men fell.

The drum immediately beat, and the little troop advanced at charging pace.

Then the shots were repeated without regularity, but always aimed with the same accuracy. Nevertheless, as if they had been aware of the numerical weakness of the friends, the Rochellais continued to advance in quick time.

With every three shots at least two men fell, but the march of those who remained was not slackened.

Arrived at the foot of the bastion, there were still more than a dozen of the enemy. A last discharge welcomed them, but did not stop them; they jumped into the ditch, and prepared to scale the breach.

"Now, my friends," said Athos, "finish them at a blow. To the wall; to the wall!"

And the four friends, seconded by Grimaud, pushed with the barrels of their muskets an enormous sheet of the wall, which bent as if pushed by the wind, and detaching itself from its base, fell with a horrible crash into the ditch. Then a fearful crash was heard; a cloud of dust mounted toward the sky–and all was over!

"Can we have destroyed them all, from the first to the last?" said Athos.

"My faith, it appears so!" said d'Artagnan.

"No," cried Porthos, "there go three or four, limping away."

In fact, three or four of these unfortunate men, covered with dirt and blood, fled along the hollow way, and at length regained the city. These were all who were left of the little troop.

Athos looked at his watch.

"Gentlemen," said he, "we have been here an hour, and our wager is won, but we will be fair players. Besides, d'Artagnan has not told us his idea yet."

And the Musketeer, with his usual coolness, reseated himself before the remains of the breakfast.

"My idea?" said d'Artagnan.

"Yes; you said you had an idea," said Athos.

"Oh, I remember," said d'Artagnan. "Well, I will go to England a second time; I will go and find Buckingham."

"You shall not do that, d'Artagnan," said Athos, coolly.

"And why not? Have I not been there once?"

"Yes, but at that period we were not at war. At that period Buckingham was an ally, and not an enemy. What you would now do amounts to treason."

D'Artagnan perceived the force of this reasoning, and was silent.

"But," said Porthos, "I think I have an idea, in my turn."

"Silence for Monsieur Porthos's idea!" said Aramis.

"I will ask leave of absence of Monsieur de Tréville, on some pretext or other which you must invent; I am not very clever at pretexts. Milady does not know me; I will get access to her without her suspecting me, and when I catch my beauty, I will strangle her."

"Well," replied Athos, "I am not far from approving the idea of Monsieur Porthos."

"For shame!" said Aramis. "Kill a woman? No, listen to me; I have the true idea."

"Let us see your idea, Aramis," said Athos, who felt much deference for the young Musketeer.

"We must inform the queen."

"Ah, my faith, yes!" said Porthos and d'Artagnan, at the same time, "we are coming nearer to it now."

"Inform the queen!" said Athos, "and how? Have we relations with the court? Could we send anyone to Paris without its being known in the camp? From here to Paris it is a hundred and forty leagues; before our letter was at Angers we should be in a dungeon."

"As to remitting a letter with safety to her Majesty," said Aramis, colouring, "I will take that upon myself. I know a clever person at Tours–"

Aramis stopped on seeing Athos smile.

"Well, do you not adopt this means, Athos?" said d'Artagnan.

"I do not reject it altogether," said Athos, "but I wish to remind Aramis that he cannot quit the camp, and that nobody but one of ourselves is trustworthy; that two hours after the messenger has set out, all the Capuchins, all the police, all the black caps of the cardinal, will know your letter by heart, and you and your clever person will be arrested."

"Without reckoning," objected Porthos, "that the queen would save Monsieur de Buckingham, but would take no heed of us."

"Gentlemen," said d'Artagnan, "what Porthos says is full of sense."

"Ah, ah! but what's going on in the city yonder?" said Athos.

"They are beating the general alarm."

The four friends listened, and the sound of the drum plainly reached them.

"You see, they are going to send a whole regiment against us," said Athos.

"You don't think of holding out against a whole regiment, do you?" said Porthos.

"Why not?" said the Musketeer. "I feel myself quite in a humor for it; and I would hold out before an army if we had taken the precaution to bring a dozen more bottles of wine."

"Upon my word, the drum draws near," said d'Artagnan.

"Let it come," said Athos. "It is a quarter of an hour's journey from here to the city, consequently a quarter of an hour's journey from the city to hither. That is more than time enough for us to devise a plan. If we go from this place we shall never find another so suitable. Ah, stop! I have it, gentlemen; the right idea has just occurred to me."

"Tell us."

"Allow me to give Grimaud some indispensable orders."

Athos made a sign for his lackey to approach.

"Grimaud," said Athos, pointing to the bodies which lay under the wall of the bastion, "take those gentlemen, set them up against the wall, put their hats upon their heads, and their guns in their hands."

"Oh, the great man!" cried d'Artagnan. "I comprehend now."

"You comprehend?" said Porthos.

"And do you comprehend, Grimaud?" said Aramis.

Grimaud made a sign in the affirmative.

"That's all that is necessary," said Athos, "now for my idea."

"I should like, however, to comprehend," said Porthos.

"That is useless."

"Yes, yes! Athos's idea!" cried Aramis and d'Artagnan, at the same time.

"This Milady, this woman, this creature, this demon, has a brother-in-law, as I think you told me, d'Artagnan?"

"Yes, I know him very well; and I also believe that he has not a very warm affection for his sister-in-law."

"There is no harm in that. If he detested her, it would be all the better," replied Athos.

"In that case we are as well off as we wish."

"And yet," said Porthos, "I would like to know what Grimaud is about."

"Silence, Porthos!" said Aramis.

"What is her brother-in-law's name?"

"Lord de Winter."

"Where is he now?"

"He returned to London at the first sound of war."

"Well, there's just the man we want," said Athos. "It is he whom we must warn. We will have him informed that his sister-in-law is on the point of having someone assassinated, and beg him not to lose sight of her. There is in London, I hope, some establishment like that of the Magdalens, or of the Repentant Daughters. He must place his sister in one of these, and we shall be in peace."

"Yes," said d'Artagnan, "till she comes out."

"Ah, my faith!" said Athos, "you require too much, d'Artagnan. I have given you all I have, and I beg leave to tell you that this is the bottom of my sack."

"But I think it would be still better," said Aramis, "to inform the queen and Lord de Winter at the same time."

"Yes, but who is to carry the letter to Tours, and who to London?"

"I answer for Bazin," said Aramis.

"And I for Planchet," said d'Artagnan.

"Ay," said Porthos, "if we cannot leave the camp, our lackeys may."

"To be sure they may; and this very day we will write the letters," said Aramis. "Give the lackeys money, and they will start."

"We will give them money?" replied Athos. "Have you any money?"

The four friends looked at one another, and a cloud came over the brows which but lately had been so cheerful.

"Look out!" cried d'Artagnan, "I see black points and red points moving yonder. Why did you talk of a regiment, Athos? It is a veritable army!"

"My faith, yes," said Athos, "there they are. See the sneaks come, without drum or trumpet. Ah, ah! Have you finished, Grimaud?"

Grimaud made a sign in the affirmative, and pointed to a dozen bodies which he had set up in the most picturesque attitudes. Some carried arms, others seemed to be taking aim, and the remainder appeared merely to be sword in hand.

"Bravo!" said Athos, "that does honour to your imagination."

"All very well," said Porthos, "but I should like to understand."

"Let us decamp first, and you will understand afterward."

"A moment, gentlemen, a moment; give Grimaud time to clear away the breakfast."

"Ah, ah!" said Aramis, "the black points and the red points are visibly enlarging. I am of d'Artagnan's opinion; we have no time to lose in regaining our camp."

"My faith," said Athos, "I have nothing to say against a retreat. We bet upon one hour, and we have stayed an hour and a half. Nothing can be said; let us be off, gentlemen, let us be off!"

Grimaud was already ahead, with the basket and the dessert. The four friends followed, ten paces behind him.

"What the devil shall we do now, gentlemen?" cried Athos.

"Have you forgotten anything?" said Aramis.

"The white flag, morbleu! We must not leave a flag in the hands of the enemy, even if that flag be but a napkin."

And Athos ran back to the bastion, mounted the platform, and bore off the flag, but as the Rochellais had arrived within musket range, they opened a terrible fire upon this man, who appeared to expose himself for pleasure's sake.

But Athos might be said to bear a charmed life. The balls passed and whistled all around him; not one struck him.

Athos waved his flag, turning his back on the guards of the city, and saluting those of the camp. On both sides loud cries arose–on the one side cries of anger, on the other cries of enthusiasm.

A second discharge followed the first, and three balls, by passing through it, made the napkin really a flag. Cries were heard from the camp, "Come down! Come down!"

Athos came down; his friends, who anxiously awaited him, saw him returned with joy.

"Come along, Athos, come along!" cried d'Artagnan, "now we have found everything except money, it would be stupid to be killed."

But Athos continued to march majestically, whatever remarks his companions made; and they, finding their remarks useless, regulated their pace by his.

Grimaud and his basket were far in advance, out of the range of the balls.

At the end of an instant they heard a furious fusillade.

"What's that?" asked Porthos, "what are they firing at now? I hear no balls whistle, and I see nobody!"

"They are firing at the corpses," replied Athos.

"But the dead cannot return their fire."

"Certainly not! They will then fancy it is an ambuscade, they will deliberate; and by the time they have found out the pleasantry, we shall be out of the range of their balls. That renders it useless to get a pleurisy by too much haste."

"Oh, I comprehend now," said the astonished Porthos.

"That's lucky," said Athos, shrugging his shoulders.

On their part, the French, on seeing the four friends return at such a step, uttered cries of enthusiasm.

At length a fresh discharge was heard, and this time the balls came rattling among the stones around the four friends, and whistling sharply in their ears. The Rochellais had at last taken possession of the bastion.

"These Rochellais are bungling fellows," said Athos, "how many have we killed of them–a dozen?"

"Or fifteen."

"How many did we crush under the wall?"

"Eight or ten."

"And in exchange for all that not even a scratch! Ah, but what is the matter with your hand, d'Artagnan? It bleeds, seemingly."

"Oh, it's nothing," said d'Artagnan.

"A spent ball?"

"Not even that."

"What is it, then?"

We have said that Athos loved d'Artagnan like a child, and this somber and inflexible personage felt the anxiety of a parent for the young man.

"Only grazed a little," replied d'Artagnan, "my fingers were caught between two stones–that of the wall and that of my ring–and the skin was broken."

"That comes of wearing diamonds, my master," said Athos, disdainfully.

"Ah, to be sure," cried Porthos, "there is a diamond. Why the devil, then, do we plague ourselves about money, when there is a diamond?"

"Stop a bit!" said Aramis.

"Well thought of, Porthos; this time you have an idea."

"Undoubtedly," said Porthos, drawing himself up at Athos's compliment, "as there is a diamond, let us sell it."

"But," said d'Artagnan, "it is the queen's diamond."

"The stronger reason why it should be sold," replied Athos. "The queen saving Monsieur de Buckingham, her lover; nothing more just. The queen saving us, her friends; nothing more moral. Let us sell the diamond. What says Monsieur the Abbé? I don't ask Porthos; his opinion has been given."

"Why, I think," said Aramis, blushing as usual, "that his ring not coming from a mistress, and consequently not being a love token, d'Artagnan may sell it."

"My dear Aramis, you speak like theology personified. Your advice, then, is–"

"To sell the diamond," replied Aramis.

"Well, then," said d'Artagnan, gaily, "let us sell the diamond, and say no more about it."

The fusillade continued, but the four friends were out of reach, and the Rochellais only fired to appease their consciences.

"My faith, it was time that idea came into Porthos's head. Here we are at the camp; therefore, gentlemen, not a word more of this affair. We are observed; they are coming to meet us. We shall be carried in triumph."

In fact, as we have said, the whole camp was in motion. More than two thousand persons had assisted, as at a spectacle, in this fortunate but wild undertaking of the four friends–an undertaking of which they were far from suspecting the real motive. Nothing was heard but cries of "Live the Musketeers! Live the Guards!" M. de Busigny was the first to come and shake Athos by the hand, and acknowledge that the wager was lost. The dragoon and the Swiss followed him, and all their comrades followed the dragoon and the Swiss. There was nothing but felicitations, pressures of the hand, and embraces; there was no end to the inextinguishable laughter at the Rochellais. The tumult at length became so great that the cardinal fancied there must be some riot, and sent La Houdinière, his captain of the Guards, to inquire what was going on.

The affair was described to the messenger with all the effervescence of enthusiasm.

"Well?" asked the cardinal, on seeing La Houdinière return.

"Well, Monseigneur," replied the latter, "three Musketeers and a Guardsman laid a wager with Monsieur de Busigny that they would go and breakfast in the bastion St. Gervais; and while breakfasting they held it for two hours against the enemy, and have killed I don't know how many Rochellais."

"Did you inquire the names of those three Musketeers?"

"Yes, Monseigneur."

"What are their names?"

"Messieurs Athos, Porthos, and Aramis."

"Still my three brave fellows!" murmured the cardinal. "And the Guardsman?"

"d'Artagnan."

"Still my young scapegrace. Positively, these four men must be on my side."

The same evening the cardinal spoke to M. de Tréville of the exploit of the morning, which was the talk of the whole camp. M. de Tréville, who had received the account of the adventure from the mouths of the heroes of it, related it in all its details to his Eminence, not forgetting the episode of the napkin.

"That's well, Monsieur de Tréville," said the cardinal, "pray let that napkin be sent to me. I will have three fleur-de-lis embroidered on it in gold, and will give it to your company as a standard."

"Monseigneur," said M. de Tréville, "that will be unjust to the Guardsmen. Monsieur d'Artagnan is not with me; he serves under Monsieur Dessessart."

"Well, then, take him," said the cardinal, "when four men are so much attached to one another, it is only fair that they should serve in the same company."

That same evening M. de Tréville announced this good news to the three Musketeers and d'Artagnan, inviting all four to breakfast with him next morning.

D'Artagnan was beside himself with joy. We know that the dream of his life had been to become a Musketeer. The three friends were likewise greatly delighted.

"My faith," said d'Artagnan to Athos, "you had a triumphant idea! As you said, we have acquired glory, and were enabled to carry on a conversation of the highest importance."

"Which we can resume now without anybody suspecting us, for, with the help of God, we shall henceforth pass for cardinalists."

That evening d'Artagnan went to present his respects to M. Dessessart, and inform him of his promotion.

M Dessessart, who esteemed d'Artagnan, made him offers of help, as this change would entail expenses for equipment.

D'Artagnan refused, but thinking the opportunity a good one, he begged him to have the diamond he put into his hand valued, as he wished to turn it into money.

The next day, M. Dessessart's valet came to d'Artagnan's lodging, and gave him a bag containing seven thousand livres.

This was the price of the queen's diamond.

Chapter 48

A Family Affair

Athos had invented the phrase, family affair. A family affair was not subject to the investigation of the cardinal; a family affair concerned nobody. People might employ themselves in a family affair before all the world. Therefore Athos had invented the phrase, family affair.

Aramis had discovered the idea, the lackeys.

Porthos had discovered the means, the diamond.

D'Artagnan alone had discovered nothing–he, ordinarily the most inventive of the four, but it must be also said that the very name of Milady paralyzed him.

Ah! no, we were mistaken; he had discovered a purchaser for his diamond.

The breakfast at M. de Tréville's was as gay and cheerful as possible. D'Artagnan already wore his uniform–for being nearly of the same size as Aramis, and as Aramis was so liberally paid by the publisher who purchased his poem as to allow him to buy everything double, he sold his friend a complete outfit.

D'Artagnan would have been at the height of his wishes if he had not constantly seen Milady like a dark cloud hovering in the horizon.

After breakfast, it was agreed that they should meet again in the evening at Athos's lodging, and there finish their plans.

D'Artagnan passed the day in exhibiting his Musketeer's uniform in every street of the camp.

In the evening, at the appointed hour, the four friends met. There only remained three things to decide–what they should write to Milady's brother; what they should write to the clever person at Tours; and which should be the lackeys to carry the letters.

Everyone offered his own. Athos talked of the discretion of Grimaud, who never spoke a word but when his master unlocked his mouth. Porthos boasted of the strength of Mousqueton, who was big enough to thrash four men of ordinary size. Aramis, confiding in the address of Bazin, made a pompous eulogium on his candidate. Finally, d'Artagnan had entire faith in the bravery of Planchet, and reminded them of the manner in which he had conducted himself in the ticklish affair of Boulogne.

These four virtues disputed the prize for a length of time, and gave birth to magnificent speeches which we do not repeat here for fear they should be deemed too long.

"Unfortunately," said Athos, "he whom we send must possess in himself alone the four qualities united."

"But where is such a lackey to be found?"

"Not to be found!" cried Athos. "I know it well, so take Grimaud."

"Take Mousqueton."

"Take Bazin."

"Take Planchet. Planchet is brave and shrewd; they are two qualities out of the four."

"Gentlemen," said Aramis, "the principal question is not to know which of our four lackeys is the most discreet, the most strong, the most clever, or the most brave; the principal thing is to know which loves money the best."

"What Aramis says is very sensible," replied Athos, "we must speculate upon the faults of people, and not upon their virtues. Monsieur Abbé, you are a great moralist."

"Doubtless," said Aramis, "for we not only require to be well served in order to succeed, but moreover, not to fail; for in case of failure, heads are in question, not for our lackeys–"

"Speak lower, Aramis," said Athos.

"That's wise–not for the lackeys," resumed Aramis, "but for the master–for the masters, we may say. Are our lackeys sufficiently devoted to us to risk their lives for us? No."

"My faith," said d'Artagnan. "I would almost answer for Planchet."

"Well, my dear friend, add to his natural devotedness a good sum of money, and then, instead of answering for him once, answer for him twice."

"Why, good God! You will be deceived just the same," said Athos, who was an optimist when things were concerned, and a pessimist when men were in question. "They will promise everything for the sake of the money, and on the road fear will prevent them from acting. Once taken, they will be pressed; when pressed, they will confess everything. What the devil! We are not children. To reach England"–Athos lowered his voice–"all France, covered with spies and creatures of the cardinal, must be crossed. A passport for embarkation must be obtained; and the party must be acquainted with English in order to ask the way to London. Really, I think the thing very difficult."

"Not at all," cried d'Artagnan, who was anxious the matter should be accomplished, "on the contrary, I think it very easy. It would be, no doubt, parbleu, if we write to Lord de Winter about affairs of vast importance, of the horrors of the cardinal–"

"Speak lower!" said Athos.

"–of intrigues and secrets of state," continued d'Artagnan, complying with the recommendation. "There can be no doubt we would all be broken on the wheel, but for God's sake, do not forget, as you yourself said, Athos, that we only write to him concerning a family affair; that we only write to him to entreat that as soon as Milady arrives in London he will put it out of her power to injure us. I will write to him, then, nearly in these terms."

"Let us see," said Athos, assuming in advance a critical look.

"Monsieur and dear friend–"

"Ah, yes! Dear friend to an Englishman," interrupted Athos, "well commenced! Bravo, d'Artagnan! Only with that word you would be quartered instead of being broken on the wheel."

"Well, perhaps. I will say, then, Monsieur, quite short."

"You may even say, My Lord," replied Athos, who stickled for propriety.

"My Lord, do you remember the little goat pasture of the Luxembourg?"

"Good, the Luxembourg! One might believe this is an allusion to the queen-mother! That's ingenious," said Athos.

"Well, then, we will put simply, My Lord, do you remember a certain little enclosure where your life was spared?"

"My dear d'Artagnan, you will never make anything but a very bad secretary. Where your life was spared! For shame! That's unworthy. A man of spirit is not to be reminded of such services. A benefit reproached is an offense committed."

"The devil!" said d'Artagnan, "you are insupportable. If the letter must be written under your censure, my faith, I renounce the task."

"And you will do right. Handle the musket and the sword, my dear fellow. You will come off splendidly at those two exercises, but pass the pen over to Monsieur Abbé. That's his province."

"Ay, ay!" said Porthos, "pass the pen to Aramis, who writes theses in Latin."

"Well, so be it," said d'Artagnan. "Draw up this note for us, Aramis, but by our Holy Father the Pope, cut it short, for I shall prune you in my turn, I warn you."

"I ask no better," said Aramis, with that ingenious air of confidence which every poet has in himself, "but let me be properly acquainted with the subject. I have heard here and there that this sister-in-law was a hussy. I have obtained proof of it by listening to her conversation with the cardinal."

"Lower! SACRÉ BLEU!" said Athos.

"But," continued Aramis, "the details escape me."

"And me also," said Porthos.

D'Artagnan and Athos looked at each other for some time in silence. At length Athos, after serious reflection and becoming more pale than usual, made a sign of assent to d'Artagnan, who by it understood he was at liberty to speak.

"Well, this is what you have to say," said d'Artagnan: "My Lord, your sister-in-law is an infamous woman, who wished to have you killed that she might inherit your wealth, but she could not marry your brother, being already married in France, and having been–" d'Artagnan stopped, as if seeking for the word, and looked at Athos.

"Repudiated by her husband," said Athos.

"Because she had been branded," continued d'Artagnan.

"Bah!" cried Porthos. "Impossible! What do you say–that she wanted to have her brother-in-law killed?"

"Yes."

"She was married?" asked Aramis.

"Yes."

"And her husband found out that she had a fleur-de-lis on her shoulder?" cried Porthos.

"Yes."

These three yeses had been pronounced by Athos, each with a sadder intonation.

"And who has seen this fleur-de-lis?" inquired Aramis.

"d'Artagnan and I. Or rather, to observe the chronological order, I and d'Artagnan," replied Athos.

"And does the husband of this frightful creature still live?" said Aramis.

"He still lives."

"Are you quite sure of it?"

"I am he."

There was a moment of cold silence, during which everyone was affected according to his nature.

"This time," said Athos, first breaking the silence, "d'Artagnan has given us an excellent program, and the letter must be written at once."

"The devil! You are right, Athos," said Aramis, "and it is a rather difficult matter. The chancellor himself would be puzzled how to write such a letter, and yet the chancellor draws up an official report very readily. Never mind! Be silent, I will write."

Aramis accordingly took the quill, reflected for a few moments, wrote eight or ten lines in a charming little female hand, and then with a voice soft and slow, as if each word had been scrupulously weighed, he read the following:

"My Lord, The person who writes these few lines had the honour of crossing swords with you in the little enclosure of the Rue d'Enfer. As you have several times since declared yourself the friend of that person, he thinks it his duty to respond to that friendship by sending you important information. Twice you have nearly been the victim of a near relative, whom you believe to be your heir because you are ignorant that before she contracted a marriage in England she was already married in France. But the third time, which is the present, you may succumb. Your relative left La Rochelle for England during the night. Watch her arrival, for she has great and terrible projects. If you require to know positively what she is capable of, read her past history on her left shoulder."

"Well, now that will do wonderfully well," said Athos. "My dear Aramis, you have the pen of a secretary of state. Lord de Winter will now be upon his guard if the letter should reach him; and even if it should fall into the hands of the cardinal, we shall not be compromised. But as the lackey who goes may make us believe he has been to London and may stop at Chatellerault, let us give him only half the sum promised him, with the letter, with an agreement that he shall have the other half in exchange for the reply. Have you the diamond?" continued Athos.

"I have what is still better. I have the price;" and d'Artagnan threw the bag upon the table. At the sound of the gold Aramis raised his eyes and Porthos started. As to Athos, he remained unmoved.

"How much in that little bag?"

"Seven thousand livres, in louis of twelve francs."

"Seven thousand livres!" cried Porthos. "That poor little diamond was worth seven thousand livres?"

"It appears so," said Athos, "since here they are. I don't suppose that our friend d'Artagnan has added any of his own to the amount."

"But, gentlemen, in all this," said d'Artagnan, "we do not think of the queen. Let us take some heed of the welfare of her dear Buckingham. That is the least we owe her."

"That's true," said Athos, "but that concerns Aramis."

"Well," replied the latter, blushing, "what must I say?"

"Oh, that's simple enough!" replied Athos. "Write a second letter for that clever personage who lives at Tours."

Aramis resumed his pen, reflected a little, and wrote the following lines, which he immediately submitted to the approbation of his friends.

"My dear cousin."

"Ah, ah!" said Athos. "This clever person is your relative, then?"

"Cousin-german."

"Go on, to your cousin, then!"

Aramis continued:

"My dear Cousin, His Eminence, the cardinal, whom God preserve for the happiness of France and the confusion of the enemies of the kingdom, is on the point of putting an end to the hectic rebellion of La Rochelle. It is probable that the succor of the English fleet will never even arrive in sight of the place. I will even venture to say that I am certain M. de Buckingham will be prevented from setting out by some great event. His Eminence is the most illustrious politician of times past, of times present, and probably of times to come. He would extinguish the sun if the sun incommoded him. Give these happy tidings to your sister, my dear cousin. I have dreamed that the unlucky Englishman was dead. I cannot recollect whether it was by steel or by poison; only of this I am sure, I have dreamed he was dead, and you know my dreams never deceive me. Be assured, then, of seeing me soon return."

"Capital!" cried Athos, "you are the king of poets, my dear Aramis. You speak like the Apocalypse, and you are as true as the Gospel. There is nothing now to do but to put the address to this letter."

"That is easily done," said Aramis.

He folded the letter fancifully, and took up his pen and wrote:

"To Mlle. Michon, seamstress, Tours."

The three friends looked at one another and laughed; they were caught.

"Now," said Aramis, "you will please to understand, gentlemen, that Bazin alone can carry this letter to Tours. My cousin knows nobody but Bazin, and places confidence in nobody but him; any other person would fail. Besides, Bazin is ambitious and learned; Bazin has read history, gentlemen, he knows that Sixtus the Fifth became Pope after having kept pigs. Well, as he means to enter the Church at the same time as myself, he does not despair of becoming Pope in his turn, or at least a cardinal. You can understand that a man who has such views will never allow himself to be taken, or if taken, will undergo martyrdom rather than speak."

"Very well," said d'Artagnan, "I consent to Bazin with all my heart, but grant me Planchet. Milady had him one day turned out of doors, with sundry blows of a good stick to accelerate his motions. Now, Planchet has an excellent memory; and I will be bound that sooner than relinquish any possible means of vengeance, he will allow himself to be beaten to death. If your arrangements at Tours are your arrangements, Aramis, those of London are mine. I request, then, that Planchet may be chosen, more particularly as he has already been to London with me, and knows how to speak correctly: London, Sir, if you please, and my master, Lord d'Artagnan. With that you may be satisfied he can make his way, both going and returning."

"In that case," said Athos, "Planchet must receive seven hundred livres for going, and seven hundred livres for coming back; and Bazin, three hundred livres for going, and three hundred livres for returning–that will reduce the sum to five thousand livres. We will each take a thousand livres to be employed as seems good, and we will leave a fund of a thousand livres under the guardianship of Monsieur Abbé here, for extraordinary occasions or common wants. Will that do?"

"My dear Athos," said Aramis, "you speak like Nestor, who was, as everyone knows, the wisest among the Greeks."

"Well, then," said Athos, "it is agreed. Planchet and Bazin shall go. Everything considered, I am not sorry to retain Grimaud; he is accustomed to my ways, and I am particular. Yesterday's affair must have shaken him a little; his voyage would upset him quite."

Planchet was sent for, and instructions were given him. The matter had been named to him by d'Artagnan, who in the first place pointed out the money to him, then the glory, and then the danger.

"I will carry the letter in the lining of my coat," said Planchet, "and if I am taken I will swallow it."

"Well, but then you will not be able to fulfill your commission," said d'Artagnan.

"You will give me a copy this evening, which I shall know by heart tomorrow."

D'Artagnan looked at his friends, as if to say, "Well, what did I tell you?"

"Now," continued he, addressing Planchet, "you have eight days to get an interview with Lord de Winter; you have eight days to return–in all sixteen days. If, on the sixteenth day after your departure, at eight o'clock in the evening you are not here, no money–even if it be but five minutes past eight."

"Then, Monsieur," said Planchet, "you must buy me a watch."

"Take this," said Athos, with his usual careless generosity, giving him his own, "and be a good lad. Remember, if you talk, if you babble, if you get drunk, you risk your master's head, who has so much confidence in your fidelity, and who answers for you. But remember, also, that if by your fault any evil happens to d'Artagnan, I will find you, wherever you may be, for the purpose of ripping up your belly."

"Oh, Monsieur!" said Planchet, humiliated by the suspicion, and moreover, terrified at the calm air of the Musketeer.

"And I," said Porthos, rolling his large eyes, "remember, I will skin you alive."

"Ah, Monsieur!"

"And I," said Aramis, with his soft, melodious voice, "remember that I will roast you at a slow fire, like a savage."

"Ah, Monsieur!"

Planchet began to weep. We will not venture to say whether it was from terror created by the threats or from tenderness at seeing four friends so closely united.

D'Artagnan took his hand. "See, Planchet," said he, "these gentlemen only say this out of affection for me, but at bottom they all like you."

"Ah, Monsieur," said Planchet, "I will succeed or I will consent to be cut in quarters; and if they do cut me in quarters, be assured that not a morsel of me will speak."

It was decided that Planchet should set out the next day, at eight o'clock in the morning, in order, as he had said, that he might during the night learn the letter by heart. He gained just twelve hours by this engagement; he was to be back on the sixteenth day, by eight o'clock in the evening.

In the morning, as he was mounting his horse, d'Artagnan, who felt at the bottom of his heart a partiality for the duke, took Planchet aside.

"Listen," said he to him. "When you have given the letter to Lord de Winter and he has read it, you will further say to him: Watch over his Grace Lord Buckingham, for they wish to assassinate him. But this, Planchet, is so serious and important that I have not informed my friends that I would entrust this secret to you; and for a captain's commission I would not write it."

"Be satisfied, Monsieur," said Planchet, "you shall see if confidence can be placed in me."

Mounted on an excellent horse, which he was to leave at the end of twenty leagues in order to take the post, Planchet set off at a gallop, his spirits a little depressed by the triple promise made him by the Musketeers, but otherwise as light-hearted as possible.

Bazin set out the next day for Tours, and was allowed eight days for performing his commission.

The four friends, during the period of these two absences, had, as may well be supposed, the eye on the watch, the nose to the wind, and the ear on the hark. Their days were passed in endeavouring to catch all that was said, in observing the proceeding of the cardinal, and in looking out for all the couriers who arrived. More than once an involuntary trembling seized them when called upon for some unexpected service. They had, besides, to look constantly to their own proper safety; Milady was a phantom which, when it had once appeared to people, did not allow them to sleep very quietly.

On the morning of the eighth day, Bazin, fresh as ever, and smiling, according to custom, entered the cabaret of the Parpaillot as the four friends were sitting down to breakfast, saying, as had been agreed upon: "Monsieur Aramis, the answer from your cousin."

The four friends exchanged a joyful glance; half of the work was done. It is true, however, that it was the shorter and easier part.

Aramis, blushing in spite of himself, took the letter, which was in a large, coarse hand and not particular for its orthography.

"Good God!" cried he, laughing, "I quite despair of my poor Michon; she will never write like Monsieur de Voiture."

"What does you mean by boor Michon?" said the Swiss, who was chatting with the four friends when the letter came.

"Oh, pardieu, less than nothing," said Aramis, "a charming little seamstress, whom I love dearly and from whose hand I requested a few lines as a sort of keepsake."

"The duvil!" said the Swiss, "if she is as great a lady as her writing is large, you are a lucky fellow, gomrade!"

Aramis read the letter, and passed it to Athos.

"See what she writes to me, Athos," said he.

Athos cast a glance over the epistle, and to disperse all the suspicions that might have been created, read aloud:

"My cousin,

"My sister and I are skillful in interpreting dreams, and even entertain great fear of them, but of yours it may be said, I hope, every dream is an illusion. Adieu! Take care of yourself, and act so that we may from time to time hear you spoken of.

"MARIE MICHON"

"And what dream does she mean?" asked the dragoon, who had approached during the reading.

"Yez; what's the dream?" said the Swiss.

"Well, pardieu!" said Aramis, "it was only this: I had a dream, and I related it to her."

"Yez, yez," said the Swiss, "it's simple enough to dell a dream, but I neffer dream."

"You are very fortunate," said Athos, rising, "I wish I could say as much!"

"Neffer," replied the Swiss, enchanted that a man like Athos could envy him anything. "Neffer, neffer!"

D'Artagnan, seeing Athos rise, did likewise, took his arm, and went out.

Porthos and Aramis remained behind to encounter the jokes of the dragoon and the Swiss.

As to Bazin, he went and lay down on a truss of straw; and as he had more imagination than the Swiss, he dreamed that Aramis, having become pope, adorned his head with a cardinal's hat.

But, as we have said, Bazin had not, by his fortunate return, removed more than a part of the uneasiness which weighed upon the four friends. The days of expectation are long, and d'Artagnan, in particular, would have wagered that the days were forty-four hours. He forgot the necessary slowness of navigation; he exaggerated to himself the power of Milady. He credited this woman, who appeared to him the equal of a demon, with agents as supernatural as herself; at the least noise, he imagined himself about to be arrested, and that Planchet was being brought back to be confronted with himself and his friends. Still further, his confidence in the worthy Picard, at one time so great, diminished day by day. This anxiety became so great that it even extended to Aramis and Porthos. Athos alone remained unmoved, as if no danger hovered over him, and as if he breathed his customary atmosphere.

On the sixteenth day, in particular, these signs were so strong in d'Artagnan and his two friends that they could not remain quiet in one place, and wandered about like ghosts on the road by which Planchet was expected.

"Really," said Athos to them, "you are not men but children, to let a woman terrify you so! And what does it amount to, after all? To be imprisoned. Well, but we should be taken out of prison; Madame Bonacieux was released. To be decapitated? Why, every day in the trenches we go cheerfully to expose ourselves to worse than that–for a bullet may break a leg, and I am convinced a surgeon would give us more pain in cutting off a thigh than an executioner in cutting off a head. Wait quietly, then; in two hours, in four, in six hours at latest, Planchet will be here. He promised to be here, and I have very great faith in Planchet, who appears to me to be a very good lad."

"But if he does not come?" said d'Artagnan.

"Well, if he does not come, it will be because he has been delayed, that's all. He may have fallen from his horse, he may have cut a caper from the deck; he may have traveled so fast against the wind as to have brought on a violent catarrh. Eh, gentlemen, let us reckon upon accidents! Life is a chaplet of little miseries which the philosopher counts with a smile. Be philosophers, as I am, gentlemen; sit down at the table and let us drink. Nothing makes the future look so bright as surveying it through a glass of chambertin."

"That's all very well," replied d'Artagnan, "but I am tired of fearing when I open a fresh bottle that the wine may come from the cellar of Milady."

"You are very fastidious," said Athos, "such a beautiful woman!"

"A woman of mark!" said Porthos, with his loud laugh.

Athos started, passed his hand over his brow to remove the drops of perspiration that burst forth, and rose in his turn with a nervous movement he could not repress.

The day, however, passed away; and the evening came on slowly, but finally it came. The bars were filled with drinkers. Athos, who had pocketed his share of the diamond, seldom quit the Parpaillot. He had found in M. de Busigny, who, by the by, had given them a magnificent dinner, a partner worthy of his company. They were playing together, as usual, when seven o'clock sounded; the patrol was heard passing to double the posts. At half past seven the retreat was sounded.

"We are lost," said d'Artagnan, in the ear of Athos.

"You mean to say we have lost," said Athos, quietly, drawing four pistoles from his pocket and throwing them upon the table. "Come, gentlemen," said he, "they are beating the tattoo. Let us to bed!"

And Athos went out of the Parpaillot, followed by d'Artagnan. Aramis came behind, giving his arm to Porthos. Aramis mumbled verses to himself, and Porthos from time to time pulled a hair or two from his moustache, in sign of despair.

But all at once a shadow appeared in the darkness the outline of which was familiar to d'Artagnan, and a well-known voice said, "Monsieur, I have brought your cloak; it is chilly this evening."

"Planchet!" cried d'Artagnan, beside himself with joy.

"Planchet!" repeated Aramis and Porthos.

"Well, yes, Planchet, to be sure," said Athos, "what is there so astonishing in that? He promised to be back by eight o'clock, and eight is striking. Bravo, Planchet, you are a lad of your word, and if ever you leave your master, I will promise you a place in my service."

"Oh, no, never," said Planchet, "I will never leave Monsieur d'Artagnan."

At the same time d'Artagnan felt that Planchet slipped a note into his hand.

D'Artagnan felt a strong inclination to embrace Planchet as he had embraced him on his departure, but he feared lest this mark of affection, bestowed upon his lackey in the open street, might appear extraordinary to passers-by, and he restrained himself.

"I have the note," said he to Athos and to his friends.

"That's well," said Athos, "let us go home and read it."

The note burned the hand of d'Artagnan. He wished to hasten their steps, but Athos took his arm and passed it under his own, and the young man was forced to regulate his pace by that of his friend.

At length they reached the tent, lit a lamp, and while Planchet stood at the entrance that the four friends might not be surprised, d'Artagnan, with a trembling hand, broke the seal and opened the so anxiously expected letter.

It contained half a line, in a hand perfectly British, and with a conciseness as perfectly Spartan:

Thank you; be easy.

d'Artagnan translated this for the others.

Athos took the letter from the hands of d'Artagnan, approached the lamp, set fire to the paper, and did not let go till it was reduced to a cinder.

Then, calling Planchet, he said, "Now, my lad, you may claim your seven hundred livres, but you did not run much risk with such a note as that."

"I am not to blame for having tried every means to compress it," said Planchet.

"Well!" cried d'Artagnan, "tell us all about it."

"Dame, that's a long job, Monsieur."

"You are right, Planchet," said Athos, "besides, the tattoo has been sounded, and we should be observed if we kept a light burning much longer than the others."

"So be it," said d'Artagnan. "Go to bed, Planchet, and sleep soundly."

"My faith, Monsieur! that will be the first time I have done so for sixteen days."

"And me, too!" said d'Artagnan.

"And me, too!" said Porthos.

"And me, too!" said Aramis.

"Well, if you will have the truth, and me, too!" said Athos.

Chapter 49

Fatality

Meantime Milady, drunk with passion, roaring on the deck like a lioness that has been embarked, had been tempted to throw herself into the sea that she might regain the coast, for she could not get rid of the thought that she had been insulted by d'Artagnan, threatened by Athos, and that she had quit France without being revenged on them. This idea soon became so insupportable to her that at the risk of whatever terrible consequences might result to herself from it, she implored the captain to put her on shore, but the captain, eager to escape from his false position–placed between French and English cruisers, like the bat between the mice and the birds–was in great haste to regain England, and positively refused to obey what he took for a woman's caprice, promising his passenger, who had been particularly recommended to him by the cardinal, to land her, if the sea and the French permitted him, at one of the ports of Brittany, either at Lorient or Brest. But the wind was contrary, the sea bad; they tacked and kept offshore. Nine days after leaving the Charente, pale with fatigue and vexation, Milady saw only the blue coasts of Finisterre appear.

She calculated that to cross this corner of France and return to the cardinal it would take her at least three days. Add another day for landing, and that would make four. Add these four to the nine others, that would be thirteen days lost–thirteen days, during which so many important events might pass in London. She reflected likewise that the cardinal would be furious at her return, and consequently would be more disposed to listen to the complaints brought against her than to the accusations she brought against others.

She allowed the vessel to pass Lorient and Brest without repeating her request to the captain, who, on his part, took care not to remind her of it. Milady therefore continued her voyage, and on the very day that Planchet embarked at Portsmouth for France, the messenger of his Eminence entered the port in triumph.

All the city was agitated by an extraordinary movement. Four large vessels, recently built, had just been launched. At the end of the jetty, his clothes richly laced with gold, glittering, as was customary with him, with diamonds and precious stones, his hat ornamented with a white feather which drooped upon his shoulder, Buckingham was seen surrounded by a staff almost as brilliant as himself.

It was one of those rare and beautiful days in winter when England remembers that there is a sun. The star of day, pale but nevertheless still splendid, was setting in the horizon, glorifying at once the heavens and the sea with bands of fire, and casting upon the towers and the old houses of the city a last ray of gold which made the windows sparkle like the reflection of a conflagration. Breathing that sea breeze, so much more invigorating and balsamic as the land is approached, contemplating all the power of those preparations she was commissioned to destroy, all the power of that army which she was to combat alone–she, a woman with a few bags of gold–Milady compared herself mentally to Judith, the terrible Jewess, when she penetrated the camp of the Assyrians and beheld the enormous mass of chariots, horses, men, and arms, which a gesture of her hand was to dissipate like a cloud of smoke.

They entered the roadstead, but as they drew near in order to cast anchor, a little cutter, looking like a coastguard formidably armed, approached the merchant vessel and dropped into the sea a boat which directed its course to the ladder. This boat contained an officer, a mate, and eight rowers. The officer alone went on board, where he was received with all the deference inspired by the uniform.

The officer conversed a few instants with the captain, gave him several papers, of which he was the bearer, to read, and upon the order of the merchant captain the whole crew of the vessel, both passengers and sailors, were called upon deck.

When this species of summons was made the officer inquired aloud the point of the brig's departure, its route, its landings; and to all these questions the captain replied without difficulty and without hesitation. Then the officer began to pass in review all the people, one after the other, and stopping when he came to Milady, surveyed her very closely, but without addressing a single word to her.

He then returned to the captain, said a few words to him, and as if from that moment the vessel was under his command, he ordered a maneuver which the crew executed immediately. Then the vessel resumed its course, still escorted by the little cutter, which sailed side by side with it, menacing it with the mouths of its six cannon. The boat followed in the wake of the ship, a speck near the enormous mass.

During the examination of Milady by the officer, as may well be imagined, Milady on her part was not less scrutinising in her glances. But however great was the power of this woman with eyes of flame in reading the hearts of those whose secrets she wished to divine, she met this time with a countenance of such impassivity that no discovery followed her investigation. The officer who had stopped in front of her and studied her with so much care might have been twenty-five or twenty-six years of age. He was of pale complexion, with clear blue eyes, rather deeply set; his mouth, fine and well cut, remained motionless in its correct lines; his chin, strongly marked, denoted that strength of will which in the ordinary Britannic type denotes mostly nothing but obstinacy; a brow a little receding, as is proper for poets, enthusiasts, and soldiers, was scarcely shaded by short thin hair which, like the beard which covered the lower part of his face, was of a beautiful deep chestnut colour.

When they entered the port, it was already night. The fog increased the darkness, and formed round the sternlights and lanterns of the jetty a circle like that which surrounds the moon when the weather threatens to become rainy. The air they breathed was heavy, damp, and cold.

Milady, that woman so courageous and firm, shivered in spite of herself.

The officer desired to have Milady's packages pointed out to him, and ordered them to be placed in the boat. When this operation was complete, he invited her to descend by offering her his hand.

Milady looked at this man, and hesitated. "Who are you, Sir," asked she, "who has the kindness to trouble yourself so particularly on my account?"

"You may perceive, Madame, by my uniform, that I am an officer in the English navy," replied the young man.

"But is it the custom for the officers in the English navy to place themselves at the service of their female compatriots when they land in a port of Great Britain, and carry their gallantry so far as to conduct them ashore?"

"Yes, Madame, it is the custom, not from gallantry but prudence, that in time of war foreigners should be conducted to particular hotels, in order that they may remain under the eye of the government until full information can be obtained about them."

These words were pronounced with the most exact politeness and the most perfect calmness. Nevertheless, they had not the power of convincing Milady.

"But I am not a foreigner, Sir," said she, with an accent as pure as ever was heard between Portsmouth and Manchester, "my name is Lady Clarik, and this measure–"

"This measure is general, Madame; and you will seek in vain to evade it."

"I will follow you, then, Sir."

Accepting the hand of the officer, she began the descent of the ladder, at the foot of which the boat waited. The officer followed her. A large cloak was spread at the stern; the officer requested her to sit down upon this cloak, and placed himself beside her.

"Row!" said he to the sailors.

The eight oars fell at once into the sea, making but a single sound, giving but a single stroke, and the boat seemed to fly over the surface of the water.

In five minutes they gained the land.

The officer leaped to the pier, and offered his hand to Milady. A carriage was in waiting.

"Is this carriage for us?" asked Milady.

"Yes, Madame," replied the officer.

"The hotel, then, is far away?"

"At the other end of the town."

"Very well," said Milady; and she resolutely entered the carriage.

The officer saw that the baggage was fastened carefully behind the carriage; and this operation ended, he took his place beside Milady, and shut the door.

Immediately, without any order being given or his place of destination indicated, the coachman set off at a rapid pace, and plunged into the streets of the city.

So strange a reception naturally gave Milady ample matter for reflection; so seeing that the young officer did not seem at all disposed for conversation, she reclined in her corner of the carriage, and one after the other passed in review all the surmises which presented themselves to her mind.

At the end of a quarter of an hour, however, surprised at the length of the journey, she leaned forward toward the door to see whither she was being conducted. Houses were no longer to be seen; trees appeared in the darkness like great black phantoms chasing one another. Milady shuddered.

"But we are no longer in the city, Sir," said she.

The young officer preserved silence.

"I beg you to understand, Sir, I will go no farther unless you tell me whither you are taking me."

This threat brought no reply.

"Oh, this is too much," cried Milady. "Help! Help!"

No voice replied to hers; the carriage continued to roll on with rapidity; the officer seemed a statue.

Milady looked at the officer with one of those terrible expressions peculiar to her countenance, and which so rarely failed of their effect; anger made her eyes flash in the darkness.

The young man remained immovable.

Milady tried to open the door in order to throw herself out.

"Take care, Madame," said the young man, coolly, "you will kill yourself in jumping."

Milady reseated herself, foaming. The officer leaned forward, looked at her in his turn, and appeared surprised to see that face, just before so beautiful, distorted with passion and almost hideous. The artful creature at once comprehended that she was injuring herself by allowing him thus to read her soul; she collected her features, and in a complaining voice said: "In the name of heaven, Sir, tell me if it is to you, if it is to your government, if it is to an enemy I am to attribute the violence that is done me?"

"No violence will be offered to you, Madame, and what happens to you is the result of a very simple measure which we are obliged to adopt with all who land in England."

"Then you don't know me, Sir?"

"It is the first time I have had the honour of seeing you."

"And on your honour, you have no cause of hatred against me?"

"None, I swear to you."

There was so much serenity, coolness, mildness even, in the voice of the young man, that Milady felt reassured.

At length after a journey of nearly an hour, the carriage stopped before an iron gate, which closed an avenue leading to a castle severe in form, massive, and isolated. Then, as the wheels rolled over a fine gravel, Milady could hear a vast roaring, which she at once recognised as the noise of the sea dashing against some steep cliff.

The carriage passed under two arched gateways, and at length stopped in a court large, dark, and square. Almost immediately the door of the carriage was opened, the young man sprang lightly out and presented his hand to Milady, who leaned upon it, and in her turn alighted with tolerable calmness.

"Still, then, I am a prisoner," said Milady, looking around her, and bringing back her eyes with a most gracious smile to the young officer, "but I feel assured it will not be for long," added she.. "My own conscience and your politeness, Sir, are the guarantees of that."

However flattering this compliment, the officer made no reply, but drawing from his belt a little silver whistle, such as boatswains use in ships of war, he whistled three times, with three different modulations. Immediately several men appeared, who unharnessed the smoking horses, and put the carriage into a coach house.

Then the officer, with the same calm politeness, invited his prisoner to enter the house. She, with a still-smiling countenance, took his arm, and passed with him under a low arched door, which by a vaulted passage, lighted only at the farther end, led to a stone staircase around an angle of stone. They then came to a massive door, which after the introduction into the lock of a key which the young man carried with him, turned heavily upon its hinges, and disclosed the chamber destined for Milady.

With a single glance the prisoner took in the apartment in its minutest details. It was a chamber whose furniture was at once appropriate for a prisoner or a free man; and yet bars at the windows and outside bolts at the door decided the question in favour of the prison.

In an instant all the strength of mind of this creature, though drawn from the most vigorous sources, abandoned her; she sank into a large easy chair, with her arms crossed, her head lowered, and expecting every instant to see a judge enter to interrogate her.

But no one entered except two or three marines, who brought her trunks and packages, deposited them in a corner, and retired without speaking.

The officer superintended all these details with the same calmness Milady had constantly seen in him, never pronouncing a word himself, and making himself obeyed by a gesture of his hand or a sound of his whistle.

It might have been said that between this man and his inferiors spoken language did not exist, or had become useless.

At length Milady could hold out no longer; she broke the silence. "In the name of heaven, Sir," cried she, "what means all that is passing? Put an end to my doubts; I have courage enough for any danger I can foresee, for every misfortune which I understand. Where am I, and why am I here? If I am free, why these bars and these doors? If I am a prisoner, what crime have I committed?"

"You are here in the apartment destined for you, Madame. I received orders to go and take charge of you on the sea, and to conduct you to this castle. This order I believe I have accomplished with all the exactness of a soldier, but also with the courtesy of a gentleman. There terminates, at least to the present moment, the duty I had to fulfill toward you; the rest concerns another person."

"And who is that other person?" asked Milady, warmly. "Can you not tell me his name?"

At the moment a great jingling of spurs was heard on the stairs. Some voices passed and faded away, and the sound of a single footstep approached the door.

"That person is here, Madame," said the officer, leaving the entrance open, and drawing himself up in an attitude of respect.

At the same time the door opened; a man appeared on the threshold. He was without a hat, carried a sword, and flourished a handkerchief in his hand.

Milady thought she recognised this shadow in the gloom; she supported herself with one hand upon the arm of the chair, and advanced her head as if to meet a certainty.

The stranger advanced slowly, and as he advanced, after entering into the circle of light projected by the lamp, Milady involuntarily drew back.

Then when she had no longer any doubt, she cried, in a state of stupor, "What, my brother, is it you?"

"Yes, fair lady!" replied Lord de Winter, making a bow, half courteous, half ironical, "it is I, myself."

"But this castle, then?"

"Is mine."

"This chamber?"

"Is yours."

"I am, then, your prisoner?"

"Nearly so."

"But this is a frightful abuse of power!"

"No high-sounding words! Let us sit down and chat quietly, as brother and sister ought to do."

Then, turning toward the door, and seeing that the young officer was waiting for his last orders, he said. "All is well, I thank you; now leave us alone, Mr. Felton."

Chapter 50

Chat Between Brother And Sister

During the time which Lord de Winter took to shut the door, close a shutter, and draw a chair near to his sister-in-law's fauteuil, Milady, anxiously thoughtful, plunged her glance into the depths of possibility, and discovered all the plan, of which she could not even obtain a glance as long as she was ignorant into whose hands she had fallen. She knew her brother-in-law to be a worthy gentleman, a bold hunter, an intrepid player, enterprising with women, but by no means remarkable for his skill in intrigues. How had he discovered her arrival, and caused her to be seized? Why did he detain her?

Athos had dropped some words which proved that the conversation she had with the cardinal had fallen into outside ears, but she could not suppose that he had dug a countermine so promptly and so boldly. She rather feared that her preceding operations in England might have been discovered. Buckingham might have guessed that it was she who had cut off the two studs, and avenge himself for that little treachery, but Buckingham was incapable of going to any excess against a woman, particularly if that woman was supposed to have acted from a feeling of jealousy.

This supposition appeared to her most reasonable. It seemed to her that they wanted to revenge the past, and not to anticipate the future. At all events, she congratulated herself upon having fallen into the hands of her brother-in-law, with whom she reckoned she could deal very easily, rather than into the hands of an acknowledged and intelligent enemy.

"Yes, let us chat, brother," said she, with a kind of cheerfulness, decided as she was to draw from the conversation, in spite of all the dissimulation Lord de Winter could bring, the revelations of which she stood in need to regulate her future conduct.

"You have, then, decided to come to England again," said Lord de Winter, "in spite of the resolutions you so often expressed in Paris never to set your feet on British ground?"

Milady replied to this question by another question. "To begin with, tell me," said she, "how have you watched me so closely as to be aware beforehand not only of my arrival, but even of the day, the hour, and the port at which I should arrive?"

Lord de Winter adopted the same tactics as Milady, thinking that as his sister-in-law employed them they must be the best.

"But tell me, my dear sister," replied he, "what makes you come to England?"

"I come to see you," replied Milady, without knowing how much she aggravated by this reply the suspicions to which d'Artagnan's letter had given birth in the mind of her brother-in-law, and only desiring to gain the good will of her auditor by a falsehood.

"Ah, to see me?" said de Winter, cunningly.

"To be sure, to see you. What is there astonishing in that?"

"And you had no other object in coming to England but to see me?"

"No."

"So it was for me alone you have taken the trouble to cross the Channel?"

"For you alone."

"The deuce! What tenderness, my sister!"

"But am I not your nearest relative?" demanded Milady, with a tone of the most touching ingenuousness.

"And my only heir, are you not?" said Lord de Winter in his turn, fixing his eyes on those of Milady.

Whatever command she had over herself, Milady could not help starting; and as in pronouncing the last words Lord de Winter placed his hand upon the arm of his sister, this start did not escape him.

In fact, the blow was direct and severe. The first idea that occurred to Milady's mind was that she had been betrayed by Kitty, and that she had recounted to the baron the selfish aversion toward himself of which she had imprudently allowed some marks to escape before her servant. She also recollected the furious and imprudent attack she had made upon d'Artagnan when he spared the life of her brother.

"I do not understand, my Lord," said she, in order to gain time and make her adversary speak out. "What do you mean to say? Is there any secret meaning concealed beneath your words?"

"Oh, my God, no!" said Lord de Winter, with apparent good nature. "You wish to see me, and you come to England. I learn this desire, or rather I suspect that you feel it; and in order to spare you all the annoyances of a nocturnal arrival in a port and all the fatigues of landing, I send one of my officers to meet you, I place a carriage at his orders, and he brings you hither to this castle, of which I am governor, whither I come every day, and where, in order to satisfy our mutual desire of seeing each other, I have prepared you a chamber. What is there more astonishing in all that I have said to you than in what you have told me?"

"No; what I think astonishing is that you should expect my coming."

"And yet that is the most simple thing in the world, my dear sister. Have you not observed that the captain of your little vessel, on entering the roadstead, sent forward, in order to obtain permission to enter the port, a little boat bearing his logbook and the register of his voyagers? I am commandant of the port. They brought me that book. I recognised your name in it. My heart told me what your mouth has just confirmed–that is to say, with what view you have exposed yourself to the dangers of a sea so perilous, or at least so troublesome at this moment–and I sent my cutter to meet you. You know the rest."

Milady knew that Lord de Winter lied, and she was the more alarmed.

"My brother," continued she, "was not that my Lord Buckingham whom I saw on the jetty this evening as we arrived?"

"Himself. Ah, I can understand how the sight of him struck you," replied Lord de Winter. "You came from a country where he must be very much talked of, and I know that his armaments against France greatly engage the attention of your friend the cardinal."

"My friend the cardinal!" cried Milady, seeing that on this point as on the other Lord de Winter seemed well instructed.

"Is he not your friend?" replied the baron, negligently. "Ah, pardon! I thought so, but we will return to my Lord Duke presently. Let us not depart from the sentimental turn our conversation had taken. You came, you say, to see me?"

"Yes."

"Well, I reply that you shall be served to the height of your wishes, and that we shall see each other every day."

"Am I, then, to remain here eternally?" demanded Milady, with a certain terror.

"Do you find yourself badly lodged, sister? Demand anything you want, and I will hasten to have you furnished with it."

"But I have neither my women nor my servants."

"You shall have all, Madame. Tell me on what footing your household was established by your first husband, and although I am only your brother-in-law, I will arrange one similar."

"My first husband!" cried Milady, looking at Lord de Winter with eyes almost starting from their sockets.

"Yes, your French husband. I don't speak of my brother. If you have forgotten, as he is still living, I can write to him and he will send me information on the subject."

A cold sweat burst from the brow of Milady.

"You jest!" said she, in a hollow voice.

"Do I look so?" asked the baron, rising and going a step backward.

"Or rather you insult me," continued she, pressing with her stiffened hands the two arms of her easy chair, and raising herself upon her wrists.

"I insult you!" said Lord de Winter, with contempt. "In truth, Madame, do you think that can be possible?"

"Indeed, Sir," said Milady, "you must be either drunk or mad. Leave the room, and send me a woman."

"Women are very indiscreet, my sister. Cannot I serve you as a waiting maid? By that means all our secrets will remain in the family."

"Insolent!" cried Milady; and as if acted upon by a spring, she bounded toward the baron, who awaited her attack with his arms crossed, but nevertheless with one hand on the hilt of his sword.

"Come!" said he. "I know you are accustomed to assassinate people, but I warn you I shall defend myself, even against you."

"You are right," said Milady. "You have all the appearance of being cowardly enough to lift your hand against a woman."

"Perhaps so; and I have an excuse, for mine would not be the first hand of a man that has been placed upon you, I imagine."

And the baron pointed, with a slow and accusing gesture, to the left shoulder of Milady, which he almost touched with his finger.

Milady uttered a deep, inward shriek, and retreated to a corner of the room like a panther which crouches for a spring.

"Oh, growl as much as you please," cried Lord de Winter, "but don't try to bite, for I warn you that it would be to your disadvantage. There are here no procurators who regulate successions beforehand. There is no knight-errant to come and seek a quarrel with me on account of the fair lady I detain a prisoner, but I have judges quite ready who will quickly dispose of a woman so shameless as to glide, a bigamist, into the bed of Lord de Winter, my brother. And these judges, I warn you, will soon send you to an executioner who will make both your shoulders alike."

The eyes of Milady darted such flashes that although he was a man and armed before an unarmed woman, he felt the chill of fear glide through his whole frame. However, he continued all the same, but with increasing warmth: "Yes, I can very well understand that after having inherited the fortune of my brother it would be very agreeable to you to be my heir likewise, but know beforehand, if you kill me or cause me to be killed, my precautions are taken. Not a penny of what I possess will pass into your hands. Were you not already rich enough–you who possess nearly a million? And could you not stop your fatal career, if you did not do evil for the infinite and supreme joy of doing it? Oh, be assured, if the memory of my brother were not sacred to me, you should rot in a state dungeon or satisfy the curiosity of sailors at Tyburn. I will be silent, but you must endure your captivity quietly. In fifteen or twenty days I shall set out for La Rochelle with the army, but on the eve of my departure a vessel which I shall see depart will take you hence and convey you to our colonies in the south. And be assured that you shall be accompanied by one who will blow your brains out at the first attempt you make to return to England or the Continent."

Milady listened with an attention that dilated her inflamed eyes.

"Yes, at present," continued Lord de Winter, "you will remain in this castle. The walls are thick, the doors strong, and the bars solid; besides, your window opens immediately over the sea. The men of my crew, who are devoted to me for life and death, mount guard around this apartment, and watch all the passages that lead to the courtyard. Even if you gained the yard, there would still be three iron gates for you to pass. The order is positive. A step, a gesture, a word, on your part, denoting an effort to escape, and you are to be fired upon. If they kill you, English justice will be under an obligation to me for having saved it trouble. Ah! I see your features regain their calmness, your countenance recovers its assurance. You are saying to yourself: 'Fifteen days, twenty days? Bah! I have an inventive mind; before that is expired some idea will occur to me. I have an infernal spirit. I shall meet with a victim. Before fifteen days are gone by I shall be away from here.' Ah, try it!"

Milady, finding her thoughts betrayed, dug her nails into her flesh to subdue every emotion that might give to her face any expression except agony.

Lord de Winter continued: "The officer who commands here in my absence you have already seen, and therefore know him. He knows how, as you must have observed, to obey an order–for you did not, I am sure, come from Portsmouth hither without endeavouring to make him speak. What do you say of him? Could a statue of marble have been more impassive and more mute? You have already tried the power of your seductions upon many men, and unfortunately you have always succeeded, but I give you leave to try them upon this one. PARDIEU! If you succeed with him, I pronounce you the demon himself."

He went toward the door and opened it hastily.

"Call Mr. Felton," said he. "Wait a minute longer, and I will introduce him to you."

There followed between these two personages a strange silence, during which the sound of a slow and regular step was heard approaching. Shortly a human form appeared in the shade of the corridor, and the young lieutenant, with whom we are already acquainted, stopped at the threshold to receive the orders of the baron.

"Come in, my dear John," said Lord de Winter, "come in, and shut the door."

The young officer entered.

"Now," said the baron, "look at this woman. She is young; she is beautiful; she possesses all earthly seductions. Well, she is a monster, who, at twenty-five years of age, has been guilty of as many crimes as you could read of in a year in the archives of our tribunals. Her voice prejudices her hearers in her favour; her beauty serves as a bait to her victims; her body even pays what she promises–I must do her that justice. She will try to seduce you, perhaps she will try to kill you. I have extricated you from misery, Felton; I have caused you to be named lieutenant; I once saved your life, you know on what occasion. I am for you not only a protector, but a friend; not only a benefactor, but a father. This woman has come back again into England for the purpose of conspiring against my life. I hold this serpent in my hands. Well, I call you, and say to you: Friend Felton, John, my child, guard me, and more particularly guard yourself, against this woman. Swear, by your hopes of salvation, to keep her safely for the chastisement she has merited. John Felton, I trust your word! John Felton, I put faith in your loyalty!"

"My Lord," said the young officer, summoning to his mild countenance all the hatred he could find in his heart, "my Lord, I swear all shall be done as you desire."

Milady received this look like a resigned victim; it was impossible to imagine a more submissive or a more mild expression than that which prevailed on her beautiful countenance. Lord de

Winter himself could scarcely recognise the tigress who, a minute before, prepared apparently for a fight.

"She is not to leave this chamber, understand, John," continued the baron. "She is to correspond with nobody; she is to speak to no one but you–if you will do her the honour to address a word to her."

"That is sufficient, my Lord! I have sworn."

"And now, Madame, try to make your peace with God, for you are judged by men!"

Milady let her head sink, as if crushed by this sentence. Lord de Winter went out, making a sign to Felton, who followed him, shutting the door after him.

One instant after, the heavy step of a marine who served as sentinel was heard in the corridor–his ax in his girdle and his musket on his shoulder.

Milady remained for some minutes in the same position, for she thought they might perhaps be examining her through the keyhole; she then slowly raised her head, which had resumed its formidable expression of menace and defiance, ran to the door to listen, looked out of her window, and returning to bury herself again in her large armchair, she reflected.

Chapter 51

Officer

Meanwhile, the cardinal looked anxiously for news from England, but no news arrived that was not annoying and threatening.

Although La Rochelle was invested, however certain success might appear–thanks to the precautions taken, and above all to the dyke, which prevented the entrance of any vessel into the besieged city–the blockade might last a long time yet. This was a great affront to the king's army, and a great inconvenience to the cardinal, who had no longer, it is true, to embroil Louis XIII with Anne of Austria–for that affair was over–but he had to adjust matters for M. de Bassompierre, who was embroiled with the Duc d'Angoulême.

As to Monsieur, who had begun the siege, he left to the cardinal the task of finishing it.

The city, notwithstanding the incredible perseverance of its mayor, had attempted a sort of mutiny for a surrender; the mayor had hanged the mutineers. This execution quieted the ill-disposed, who resolved to allow themselves to die of hunger–this death always appearing to them more slow and less sure than strangulation.

On their side, from time to time, the besiegers took the messengers which the Rochellais sent to Buckingham, or the spies which Buckingham sent to the Rochellais. In one case or the other, the trial was soon over. The cardinal pronounced the single word, "Hanged!" The king was invited to come and see the hanging. He came languidly, placing himself in a good situation to see all the details. This amused him sometimes a little, and made him endure the siege with patience, but it did not prevent his getting very tired, or from talking at every moment of returning to Paris–so that if the messengers and the spies had failed, his Eminence, notwithstanding all his inventiveness, would have found himself much embarrassed.

Nevertheless, time passed on, and the Rochellais did not surrender. The last spy that was taken was the bearer of a letter. This letter told Buckingham that the city was at an extremity, but instead of adding, "If your succor does not arrive within fifteen days, we will surrender," it added, quite simply, "If your succor comes not within fifteen days, we shall all be dead with hunger when it comes."

The Rochellais, then, had no hope but in Buckingham. Buckingham was their Messiah. It was evident that if they one day learned positively that they must not count on Buckingham, their courage would fail with their hope.

The cardinal looked, then, with great impatience for the news from England which would announce to him that Buckingham would not come.

The question of carrying the city by assault, though often debated in the council of the king, had been always rejected. In the first place, La Rochelle appeared impregnable. Then the cardinal, whatever he said, very well knew that the horror of bloodshed in this encounter, in which Frenchman would combat against Frenchman, was a retrograde movement of sixty years impressed upon his policy; and the cardinal was at that period what we now call a man of progress. In fact, the sack of La Rochelle, and the assassination of three of four thousand Huguenots who allowed themselves to be killed, would resemble too closely, in 1628, the massacre of St. Bartholomew in 1572; and then, above all this, this extreme measure, which was not at all repugnant to the king, good Catholic as he was, always fell before this argument of the besieging generals–La Rochelle is impregnable except to famine.

The cardinal could not drive from his mind the fear he entertained of his terrible emissary–for he comprehended the strange qualities of this woman, sometimes a serpent, sometimes a lion. Had she betrayed him? Was she dead? He knew her well enough in all cases to know that, whether acting for or against him, as a friend or an enemy, she would not remain motionless without great impediments, but whence did these impediments arise? That was what he could not know.

And yet he reckoned, and with reason, on Milady. He had divined in the past of this woman terrible things which his red mantle alone could cover; and he felt, from one cause or another, that this woman was his own, as she could look to no other but himself for a support superior to the danger which threatened her.

He resolved, then, to carry on the war alone, and to look for no success foreign to himself, but as we look for a fortunate chance. He continued to press the raising of the famous dyke which was to starve La Rochelle. Meanwhile, he cast his eyes over that unfortunate city, which contained so much deep misery and so many heroic virtues, and recalling the saying of Louis XI, his political predecessor, as he himself was the predecessor of Robespierre, he repeated this maxim of Tristan's gossip: "Divide in order to reign."

Henry IV, when besieging Paris, had loaves and provisions thrown over the walls. The cardinal had little notes thrown over in which he represented to the Rochellais how unjust, selfish, and barbarous was the conduct of their leaders. These leaders had corn in abundance, and would not let them partake of it; they adopted as a maxim–for they, too, had maxims–that it was of very little consequence that women, children, and old men should die, so long as the men who were to defend the walls remained strong and healthy. Up to that time, whether from devotedness or from want of power to act against it, this maxim, without being generally adopted, nevertheless passed from theory into practice, but the notes did it injury. The notes reminded the men that the children, women, and old men whom they allowed to die were their sons, their wives, and their fathers, and that it would be more just for everyone to be reduced to the common misery, in order that equal conditions should give birth to unanimous resolutions.

These notes had all the effect that he who wrote them could expect, in that they induced a great number of the inhabitants to open private negotiations with the royal army.

But at the moment when the cardinal saw his means already bearing fruit, and applauded himself for having put it in action, an inhabitant of La Rochelle who had contrived to pass the royal lines–God knows how, such was the watchfulness of Bassompierre, Schomberg, and the Duc d'Angoulême, themselves watched over by the cardinal–an inhabitant of La Rochelle, we say, entered the city, coming from Portsmouth, and saying that he had seen a magnificent fleet ready to sail within eight days. Still further, Buckingham announced to the mayor that at length the great league was about to declare itself against France, and that the kingdom would be at once invaded by the English, Imperial, and Spanish armies. This letter was read publicly in all parts of the city. Copies were put up at the corners of the streets; and even they who had begun to open negotiations interrupted them, being resolved to await the succor so pompously announced.

This unexpected circumstance brought back Richelieu's former anxiety, and forced him in spite of himself once more to turn his eyes to the other side of the sea.

During this time, exempt from the anxiety of its only and true chief, the royal army led a joyous life, neither provisions nor money being wanting in the camp. All the corps rivaled one another in audacity and gaiety. To take spies and hang them, to make hazardous expeditions upon the dyke or the sea, to imagine wild plans, and to execute them coolly–such were the pastimes which made the army find these days short which were not only so long to the Rochellais, a prey to famine and anxiety, but even to the cardinal, who blockaded them so closely.

Sometimes when the cardinal, always on horseback, like the lowest GENDARME of the army, cast a pensive glance over those works, so slowly keeping pace with his wishes, which the engineers, brought from all the corners of France, were executing under his orders, if he met a Musketeer of the company of Tréville, he drew near and looked at him in a peculiar manner, and not recognising in him one of our four companions, he turned his penetrating look and profound thoughts in another direction.

One day when oppressed with a mortal weariness of mind, without hope in the negotiations with the city, without news from England, the cardinal went out, without any other aim than to be out of doors, and accompanied only by Cahusac and La Houdinière, strolled along the beach. Mingling the immensity of his dreams with the immensity of the ocean, he came, his horse going at a foot's pace, to a hill from the top of which he perceived behind a hedge, reclining on the sand and catching in its passage one of those rays of the sun so rare at this period of the year, seven men surrounded by empty bottles. Four of these men were our Musketeers, preparing to listen to a letter one of them had just received. This letter was so important that it made them forsake their cards and their dice on the drumhead.

The other three were occupied in opening an enormous flagon of Collicure wine; these were the lackeys of these gentlemen.

The cardinal was, as we have said, in very low spirits; and nothing when he was in that state of mind increased his depression so much as gaiety in others. Besides, he had another strange fancy, which was always to believe that the causes of his sadness created the gaiety of others. Making a sign to La Houdinière and Cahusac to stop, he alighted from his horse, and went toward these suspected merry companions, hoping, by means of the sand which deadened the sound of his steps and of the hedge which concealed his approach, to catch some words of this conversation which appeared so interesting. At ten paces from the hedge he recognised the talkative Gascon; and as he had already perceived that these men were Musketeers, he did not doubt that the three others were those called the Inseparables; that is to say, Athos, Porthos, and Aramis.

It may be supposed that his desire to hear the conversation was augmented by this discovery. His eyes took a strange expression, and with the step of a tiger-cat he advanced toward the hedge, but he had not been able to catch more than a few vague syllables without any positive sense, when a sonorous and short cry made him start, and attracted the attention of the Musketeers.

"Officer!" cried Grimaud.

"You are speaking, you scoundrel!" said Athos, rising upon his elbow, and transfixing Grimaud with his flaming look.

Grimaud therefore added nothing to his speech, but contented himself with pointing his index finger in the direction of the hedge, announcing by this gesture the cardinal and his escort.

With a single bound the Musketeers were on their feet, and saluted with respect.

The cardinal seemed furious.

"It appears that Messieurs the Musketeers keep guard," said he. "Are the English expected by land, or do the Musketeers consider themselves superior officers?"

"Monseigneur," replied Athos, for amid the general fright he alone had preserved the noble calmness and coolness that never forsook him, "Monseigneur, the Musketeers, when they are not on duty, or when their duty is over, drink and play at dice, and they are certainly superior officers to their lackeys."

"Lackeys?" grumbled the cardinal. "Lackeys who have the order to warn their masters when anyone passes are not lackeys, they are sentinels."

"Your Eminence may perceive that if we had not taken this precaution, we should have been exposed to allowing you to pass without presenting you our respects or offering you our thanks for the favour you have done us in uniting us. D'Artagnan," continued Athos, "you, who but lately were so anxious for such an opportunity for expressing your gratitude to Monseigneur, here it is; avail yourself of it."

These words were pronounced with that imperturbable phlegm which distinguished Athos in the hour of danger, and with that excessive politeness which made of him at certain moments a king more majestic than kings by birth.

D'Artagnan came forward and stammered out a few words of gratitude which soon expired under the gloomy looks of the cardinal.

"It does not signify, gentlemen," continued the cardinal, without appearing to be in the least swerved from his first intention by the diversion which Athos had started, "it does not signify, gentlemen. I do not like to have simple soldiers, because they have the advantage of serving in a privileged corps, thus to play the great lords; discipline is the same for them as for everybody else."

Athos allowed the cardinal to finish his sentence completely, and bowed in sign of assent. Then he resumed in his turn: "Discipline, Monseigneur, has, I hope, in no way been forgotten by us. We are not on duty, and we believed that not being on duty we were at liberty to dispose of our time as we pleased. If we are so fortunate as to have some particular duty to perform for your Eminence, we are ready to obey you. Your Eminence may perceive," continued Athos, knitting his brow, for this sort of investigation began to annoy him, "that we have not come out without our arms."

And he showed the cardinal, with his finger, the four muskets piled near the drum, on which were the cards and dice.

"Your Eminence may believe," added d'Artagnan, "that we would have come to meet you, if we could have supposed it was Monseigneur coming toward us with so few attendants."

The cardinal bit his moustache, and even his lips a little.

"Do you know what you look like, all together, as you are armed and guarded by your lackeys?" said the cardinal. "You look like four conspirators."

"Oh, as to that, Monseigneur, it is true," said Athos, "we do conspire, as your Eminence might have seen the other morning. Only we conspire against the Rochellais."

"Ah, you gentlemen of policy!" replied the cardinal, knitting his brow in his turn, "the secret of many unknown things might perhaps be found in your brains, if we could read them as you read that letter which you concealed as soon as you saw me coming."

The colour mounted to the face of Athos, and he made a step toward his Eminence.

"One might think you really suspected us, Monseigneur, and we were undergoing a real interrogatory. If it be so, we trust your Eminence will deign to explain yourself, and we should then at least be acquainted with our real position."

"And if it were an interrogatory!" replied the cardinal. "Others besides you have undergone such, Monsieur Athos, and have replied thereto."

"Thus I have told your Eminence that you had but to question us, and we are ready to reply."

"What was that letter you were about to read, Monsieur Aramis, and which you so promptly concealed?"

"A woman's letter, Monseigneur."

"Ah, yes, I see," said the cardinal, "we must be discreet with this sort of letters, but nevertheless, we may show them to a confessor, and you know I have taken orders."

"Monseigneur," said Athos, with a calmness the more terrible because he risked his head in making this reply, "the letter is a woman's letter, but it is neither signed Marion de Lorme, nor Madame d'Aiguillon."

The cardinal became as pale as death; lightning darted from his eyes. He turned round as if to give an order to Cahusac and Houdinière. Athos saw the movement; he made a step toward the muskets, upon which the other three friends had fixed their eyes, like men ill-disposed to allow themselves to be taken. The cardinalists were three; the Musketeers, lackeys included, were seven. He judged that the match would be so much the less equal, if Athos and his companions were really plotting; and by one of those rapid turns which he always had at command, all his anger faded away into a smile.

"Well, well!" said he, "you are brave young men, proud in daylight, faithful in darkness. We can find no fault with you for watching over yourselves, when you watch so carefully over others. Gentlemen, I have not forgotten the night in which you served me as an escort to the Red Dovecot. If there were any danger to be apprehended on the road I am going, I would request you to accompany me, but as there is none, remain where you are, finish your bottles, your game, and your letter. Adieu, gentlemen!"

And remounting his horse, which Cahusac led to him, he saluted them with his hand, and rode away.

The four young men, standing and motionless, followed him with their eyes without speaking a single word until he had disappeared. Then they looked at one another.

The countenances of all gave evidence of terror, for notwithstanding the friendly adieu of his Eminence, they plainly perceived that the cardinal went away with rage in his heart.

Athos alone smiled, with a self-possessed, disdainful smile.

When the cardinal was out of hearing and sight, "That Grimaud kept bad watch!" cried Porthos, who had a great inclination to vent his ill-humor on somebody.

Grimaud was about to reply to excuse himself. Athos lifted his finger, and Grimaud was silent.

"Would you have given up the letter, Aramis?" said d'Artagnan.

"I," said Aramis, in his most flute-like tone, "I had made up my mind. If he had insisted upon the letter being given up to him, I would have presented the letter to him with one hand, and with the other I would have run my sword through his body."

"I expected as much," said Athos, "and that was why I threw myself between you and him. Indeed, this man is very much to blame for talking thus to other men; one would say he had never had to do with any but women and children."

"My dear Athos, I admire you, but nevertheless we were in the wrong, after all."

"How, in the wrong?" said Athos. "Whose, then, is the air we breathe? Whose is the ocean upon which we look? Whose is the sand upon which we were reclining? Whose is that letter of your mistress? Do these belong to the cardinal? Upon my honour, this man fancies the world belongs to him. There you stood, stammering, stupefied, annihilated. One might have supposed the Bastille appeared before you, and that the gigantic Medusa had converted you into stone. Is being in love conspiring? You are in love with a woman whom the cardinal has caused to be shut up, and you wish to get her out of the hands of the cardinal. That's a match you are playing with his Eminence; this letter is your game. Why should you expose your game to your adversary? That is never done. Let him find it out if he can! We can find out his!"

"Well, that's all very sensible, Athos," said d'Artagnan.

"In that case, let there be no more question of what's past, and let Aramis resume the letter from his cousin where the cardinal interrupted him."

Aramis drew the letter from his pocket; the three friends surrounded him, and the three lackeys grouped themselves again near the wine jar.

"You had only read a line or two," said d'Artagnan, "read the letter again from the commencement."

"Willingly," said Aramis.

"My dear Cousin,

"I think I shall make up my mind to set out for Bethune, where my sister has placed our little servant in the convent of the

Carmelites; this poor child is quite resigned, as she knows she cannot live elsewhere without the salvation of her soul being in danger. Nevertheless, if the affairs of our family are arranged, as we hope they will be, I believe she will run the risk of being damned, and will return to those she regrets, particularly as she knows they are always thinking of her. Meanwhile, she is not very wretched; what she most desires is a letter from her intended. I know that such viands pass with difficulty through convent gratings, but after all, as I have given you proofs, my dear cousin, I am not unskilled in such affairs, and I will take charge of the commission. My sister thanks you for your good and eternal remembrance. She has experienced much anxiety, but she is now at length a little reassured, having sent her secretary away in order that nothing may happen unexpectedly.

"Adieu, my dear cousin. Tell us news of yourself as often as you can; that is to say, as often as you can with safety. I embrace you.

"MARIE MICHON"

"Oh, what do I not owe you, Aramis?" said d'Artagnan. "Dear Constance! I have at length, then, intelligence of you. She lives; she is in safety in a convent; she is at Bethune! Where is Bethune, Athos?"

"Why, upon the frontiers of Artois and of Flanders. The siege once over, we shall be able to make a tour in that direction."

"And that will not be long, it is to be hoped," said Porthos, "for they have this morning hanged a spy who confessed that the Rochellais were reduced to the leather of their shoes. Supposing that after having eaten the leather they eat the soles, I cannot see much that is left unless they eat one another."

"Poor fools!" said Athos, emptying a glass of excellent Bordeaux wine which, without having at that period the reputation it now enjoys, merited it no less, "poor fools! As if the Catholic religion was not the most advantageous and the most agreeable of all religions! All the same," resumed he, after having clicked his tongue against his palate, "they are brave fellows! But what the devil are you about, Aramis?" continued Athos. "Why, you are squeezing that letter into your pocket!"

"Yes," said d'Artagnan, "Athos is right, it must be burned. And yet if we burn it, who knows whether Monsieur Cardinal has not a secret to interrogate ashes?"

"He must have one," said Athos.

"What will you do with the letter, then?" asked Porthos.

"Come here, Grimaud," said Athos. Grimaud rose and obeyed. "As a punishment for having spoken without permission, my friend, you will please to eat this piece of paper; then to recompense you for the service you will have rendered us, you shall afterward drink this glass of wine. First, here is the letter. Eat heartily."

Grimaud smiled; and with his eyes fixed upon the glass which Athos held in his hand, he ground the paper well between his teeth and then swallowed it.

"Bravo, Monsieur Grimaud!" said Athos, "and now take this. That's well. We dispense with your saying grace."

Grimaud silently swallowed the glass of Bordeaux wine, but his eyes, raised toward heaven during this delicious occupation, spoke a language which, though mute, was not the less expressive.

"And now," said Athos, "unless Monsieur Cardinal should form the ingenious idea of ripping up Grimaud, I think we may be pretty much at our ease respecting the letter."

Meantime, his Eminence continued his melancholy ride, murmuring between his moustaches, "These four men must positively be mine."

Chapter 52

Captivity: The First Day

Let us return to Milady, whom a glance thrown upon the coast of France has made us lose sight of for an instant.

We shall find her still in the despairing attitude in which we left her, plunged in an abyss of dismal reflection–a dark hell at the gate of which she has almost left hope behind, because for the first time she doubts, for the first time she fears.

On two occasions her fortune has failed her, on two occasions she has found herself discovered and betrayed; and on these two occasions it was to one fatal genius, sent doubtlessly by the Lord to combat her, that she has succumbed. D'Artagnan has conquered her–her, that invincible power of evil.

He has deceived her in her love, humbled her in her pride, thwarted her in her ambition; and now he ruins her fortune, deprives her of liberty, and even threatens her life. Still more, he has lifted the corner of her mask–that shield with which she covered herself and which rendered her so strong.

D'Artagnan has turned aside from Buckingham, whom she hates as she hates everyone she has loved, the tempest with which Richelieu threatened him in the person of the queen. D'Artagnan had passed himself upon her as de Wardes, for whom she had conceived one of those tigerlike fancies common to women of her character. D'Artagnan knows that terrible secret which she has sworn no one shall know without dying. In short, at the moment in which she has just obtained from Richelieu a carte blanche by the means of which she is about to take vengeance on her enemy, this precious paper is torn from her hands, and it is d'Artagnan who holds her prisoner and is about to send her to some filthy Botany Bay, some infamous Tyburn of the Indian Ocean.

All this she owes to d'Artagnan, without doubt. From whom can come so many disgraces heaped upon her head, if not from him? He alone could have transmitted to Lord de Winter all these frightful secrets which he has discovered, one after another, by a train of fatalities. He knows her brother-in-law. He must have written to him.

What hatred she distills! Motionless, with her burning and fixed glances, in her solitary apartment, how well the outbursts of passion which at times escape from the depths of her chest with her respiration, accompany the sound of the surf which rises, growls, roars, and breaks itself like an eternal and powerless despair against the rocks on which is built this dark and lofty castle! How many magnificent projects of vengeance she conceives by the light of the flashes which her tempestuous passion casts over her mind against Mme. Bonacieux, against Buckingham, but above all against d'Artagnan–projects lost in the distance of the future.

Yes, but in order to avenge herself she must be free. And to be free, a prisoner has to pierce a wall, detach bars, cut through a floor–all undertakings which a patient and strong man may accomplish, but before which the feverish irritations of a woman must give way.

Besides, to do all this, time is necessary–months, years; and she has ten or twelve days, as Lord de Winter, her fraternal and terrible jailer, has told her.

And yet, if she were a man she would attempt all this, and perhaps might succeed; why, then, did heaven make the mistake of placing that manlike soul in that frail and delicate body?

The first moments of her captivity were terrible; a few convulsions of rage which she could not suppress paid her debt of feminine weakness to nature. But by degrees she overcame the outbursts of her mad passion; and nervous tremblings which agitated her frame disappeared, and she remained folded within herself like a fatigued serpent in repose.

"Go to, go to! I must have been mad to allow myself to be carried away so," says she, gazing into the glass, which reflects back to her eyes the burning glance by which she appears to interrogate herself. "No violence; violence is the proof of weakness. In the first place, I have never succeeded by that means. Perhaps if I employed my strength against women I might perchance find them weaker than myself, and consequently conquer them, but it is with men that I struggle, and I am but a woman to them. Let me fight like a woman, then; my strength is in my weakness."

Then, as if to render an account to herself of the changes she could place upon her countenance, so mobile and so expressive, she made it take all expressions from that of passionate anger, which convulsed her features, to that of the most sweet, most affectionate, and most seducing smile. Then her hair assumed successively, under her skillful hands, all the undulations she thought might assist the charms of her face. At length she murmured, satisfied with herself, "Come, nothing is lost; I am still beautiful."

It was then nearly eight o'clock in the evening. Milady perceived a bed; she calculated that the repose of a few hours would not only refresh her head and her ideas, but still further, her complexion. A better idea, however, came into her mind before going to bed. She had heard something said about supper. She had already been an hour in this apartment; they could not long delay bringing her a repast. The prisoner did not wish to lose time; and she resolved to make that very evening some attempts to ascertain the nature of the ground she had to work upon, by studying the characters of the men to whose guardianship she was committed.

A light appeared under the door; this light announced the reappearance of her jailers. Milady, who had arisen, threw herself quickly into the armchair, her head thrown back, her beautiful hair unbound and disheveled, her bosom half bare beneath her crumpled lace, one hand on her heart, and the other hanging down.

The bolts were drawn; the door groaned upon its hinges. Steps sounded in the chamber, and drew near.

"Place that table there," said a voice which the prisoner recognised as that of Felton.

The order was executed.

"You will bring lights, and relieve the sentinel," continued Felton.

And this double order which the young lieutenant gave to the same individuals proved to Milady that her servants were the same men as her guards; that is to say, soldiers.

Felton's orders were, for the rest, executed with a silent rapidity that gave a good idea of the way in which he maintained discipline.

At length Felton, who had not yet looked at Milady, turned toward her.

"Ah, ah!" said he, "she is asleep; that's well. When she wakes she can sup." And he made some steps toward the door.

"But, my lieutenant," said a soldier, less stoical than his chief, and who had approached Milady, "this woman is not asleep."

"What, not asleep!" said Felton, "what is she doing, then?"

"She has fainted. Her face is very pale, and I have listened in vain; I do not hear her breathe."

"You are right," said Felton, after having looked at Milady from the spot on which he stood without moving a step toward her. "Go and tell Lord de Winter that his prisoner has fainted–for this event not having been foreseen, I don't know what to do."

The soldier went out to obey the orders of his officer. Felton sat down upon an armchair which happened to be near the door, and waited without speaking a word, without making a gesture. Milady possessed that great art, so much studied by women, of looking through her long eyelashes without appearing to open the lids. She perceived Felton, who sat with his back toward her. She continued to look at him for nearly ten minutes, and in these ten minutes the immovable guardian never turned round once.

She then thought that Lord de Winter would come, and by his presence give fresh strength to her jailer. Her first trial was lost; she acted like a woman who reckons up her resources. As a result she raised her head, opened her eyes, and sighed deeply.

At this sigh Felton turned round.

"Ah, you are awake, Madame," he said, "then I have nothing more to do here. If you want anything you can ring."

"Oh, my God, my God! How I have suffered!" said Milady, in that harmonious voice which, like that of the ancient enchantresses, charmed all whom she wished to destroy.

And she assumed, upon sitting up in the armchair, a still more graceful and abandoned position than when she reclined.

Felton arose.

"You will be served, thus, Madame, three times a day," said he. "In the morning at nine o'clock, in the day at one o'clock, and in the evening at eight. If that does not suit you, you can point out what other hours you prefer, and in this respect your wishes will be complied with."

"But am I to remain always alone in this vast and dismal chamber?" asked Milady.

"A woman of the neighbourhood has been sent for, who will be tomorrow at the castle, and will return as often as you desire her presence."

"I thank you, Sir," replied the prisoner, humbly.

Felton made a slight bow, and directed his steps toward the door. At the moment he was about to go out, Lord de Winter appeared in the corridor, followed by the soldier who had been sent to inform him of the swoon of Milady. He held a vial of salts in his hand.

"Well, what is it–what is going on here?" said he, in a jeering voice, on seeing the prisoner sitting up and Felton about to go out. "Is this corpse come to life already? Felton, my lad, did you not perceive that you were taken for a novice, and that the first act was being performed of a comedy of which we shall doubtless have the pleasure of following out all the developments?"

"I thought so, my lord," said Felton, "but as the prisoner is a woman, after all, I wish to pay her the attention that every man of gentle birth owes to a woman, if not on her account, at least on my own."

Milady shuddered through her whole system. These words of Felton's passed like ice through her veins.

"So," replied de Winter, laughing, "that beautiful hair so skillfully disheveled, that white skin, and that languishing look, have not yet seduced you, you heart of stone?"

"No, my Lord," replied the impassive young man, "your Lordship may be assured that it requires more than the tricks and coquetry of a woman to corrupt me."

"In that case, my brave lieutenant, let us leave Milady to find out something else, and go to supper, but be easy! She has a fruitful imagination, and the second act of the comedy will not delay its steps after the first."

And at these words Lord de Winter passed his arm through that of Felton, and led him out, laughing.

"Oh, I will be a match for you!" murmured Milady, between her teeth, "be assured of that, you poor spoiled monk, you poor converted soldier, who has cut his uniform out of a monk's frock!"

"By the way," resumed de Winter, stopping at the threshold of the door, "you must not, Milady, let this check take away your appetite. Taste that fowl and those fish. On my honour, they are not poisoned. I have a very good cook, and he is not to be my heir; I have full and perfect confidence in him. Do as I do. Adieu, dear sister, till your next swoon!"

This was all that Milady could endure. Her hands clutched her armchair; she ground her teeth inwardly; her eyes followed the motion of the door as it closed behind Lord de Winter and Felton, and the moment she was alone a fresh fit of despair seized her. She cast her eyes upon the table, saw the glittering of a knife, rushed toward it and clutched it, but her disappointment was cruel. The blade was round, and of flexible silver.

A burst of laughter resounded from the other side of the ill-closed door, and the door reopened.

"Ha, ha!" cried Lord de Winter, "Ha, ha! Don't you see, my brave Felton; don't you see what I told you? That knife was for you, my lad; she would have killed you. Observe, this is one of her peculiarities, to get rid thus, after one fashion or another, of all the people who bother her. If I had listened to you, the knife would have been pointed and of steel. Then no more of Felton; she would have cut your throat, and after that everybody else's. See, John, see how well she knows how to handle a knife."

In fact, Milady still held the harmless weapon in her clenched hand, but these last words, this supreme insult, relaxed her hands, her strength, and even her will. The knife fell to the ground.

"You were right, my Lord," said Felton, with a tone of profound disgust which sounded to the very bottom of the heart of Milady, "you were right, my Lord, and I was wrong."

And both again left the room.

But this time Milady lent a more attentive ear than the first, and she heard their steps die away in the distance of the corridor.

"I am lost," murmured she, "I am lost! I am in the power of men upon whom I can have no more influence than upon statues of bronze or granite; they know me by heart, and are steeled against all my weapons. It is, however, impossible that this should end as they have decreed!"

In fact, as this last reflection indicated–this instinctive return to hope–sentiments of weakness or fear did not dwell long in her ardent spirit. Milady sat down to table, ate from several dishes, drank a little Spanish wine, and felt all her resolution return.

Before she went to bed she had pondered, analyzed, turned on all sides, examined on all points, the words, the steps, the gestures, the signs, and even the silence of her interlocutors; and of this profound, skillful, and anxious study the result was that Felton, everything considered, appeared the more vulnerable of her two persecutors.

One expression above all recurred to the mind of the prisoner: "If I had listened to you," Lord de Winter had said to Felton.

Felton, then, had spoken in her favour, since Lord de Winter had not been willing to listen to him.

"Weak or strong," repeated Milady, "that man has, then, a spark of pity in his soul; of that spark I will make a flame that shall devour him. As to the other, he knows me, he fears me, and knows what he has to expect of me if ever I escape from his hands. It is useless, then, to attempt anything with him. But Felton–that's another thing. He is a young, ingenuous, pure man who seems virtuous; him there are means of destroying."

And Milady went to bed and fell asleep with a smile upon her lips. Anyone who had seen her sleeping might have said she was a young girl dreaming of the crown of flowers she was to wear on her brow at the next festival.

Chapter 53

Captivity: The Second Day

Milady dreamed that she at length had d'Artagnan in her power, that she was present at his execution; and it was the sight of his odious blood, flowing beneath the ax of the headsman, which spread that charming smile upon her lips.

She slept as a prisoner sleeps, rocked by his first hope.

In the morning, when they entered her chamber she was still in bed. Felton remained in the corridor. He brought with him the woman of whom he had spoken the evening before, and who had just arrived; this woman entered, and approaching Milady's bed, offered her services.

Milady was habitually pale; her complexion might therefore deceive a person who saw her for the first time.

"I am in a fever," said she, "I have not slept a single instant during all this long night. I suffer horribly. Are you likely to be more humane to me than others were yesterday? All I ask is permission to remain abed."

"Would you like to have a physician called?" said the woman.

Felton listened to this dialogue without speaking a word.

Milady reflected that the more people she had around her the more she would have to work upon, and Lord de Winter would redouble his watch. Besides, the physician might declare the ailment feigned; and Milady, after having lost the first trick, was not willing to lose the second.

"Go and fetch a physician?" said she. "What could be the good of that? These gentlemen declared yesterday that my illness was a comedy; it would be just the same today, no doubt–for since yesterday evening they have had plenty of time to send for a doctor."

"Then," said Felton, who became impatient, "say yourself, Madame, what treatment you wish followed."

"Eh, how can I tell? My God! I know that I suffer, that's all. Give me anything you like, it is of little consequence."

"Go and fetch Lord de Winter," said Felton, tired of these eternal complaints.

"Oh, no, no!" cried Milady, "no, Sir, do not call him, I conjure you. I am well, I want nothing; do not call him."

She gave so much vehemence, such magnetic eloquence to this exclamation, that Felton in spite of himself advanced some steps into the room.

"He has come!" thought Milady.

"Meanwhile, Madame, if you really suffer," said Felton, "a physician shall be sent for; and if you deceive us–well, it will be the worse for you. But at least we shall not have to reproach ourselves with anything."

Milady made no reply, but turning her beautiful head round upon her pillow, she burst into tears, and uttered heartbreaking sobs.

Felton surveyed her for an instant with his usual impassiveness; then, seeing that the crisis threatened to be prolonged, he went out. The woman followed him, and Lord de Winter did not appear.

"I fancy I begin to see my way," murmured Milady, with a savage joy, burying herself under the clothes to conceal from anybody who might be watching her this burst of inward satisfaction.

Two hours passed away.

"Now it is time that the malady should be over," said she, "let me rise, and obtain some success this very day. I have but ten days, and this evening two of them will be gone."

In the morning, when they entered Milady's chamber they had brought her breakfast. Now, she thought, they could not long delay coming to clear the table, and that Felton would then reappear.

Milady was not deceived. Felton reappeared, and without observing whether Milady had or had not touched her repast, made a sign that the table should be carried out of the room, it having been brought in ready spread.

Felton remained behind; he held a book in his hand.

Milady, reclining in an armchair near the chimney, beautiful, pale, and resigned, looked like a holy virgin awaiting martyrdom.

Felton approached her, and said, "Lord de Winter, who is a Catholic, like yourself, Madame, thinking that the deprivation of the rites and ceremonies of your church might be painful to you, has consented that you should read every day the ordinary of your Mass; and here is a book which contains the ritual."

At the manner in which Felton laid the book upon the little table near which Milady was sitting, at the tone in which he pronounced the two words, YOUR MASS, at the disdainful smile with which he accompanied them, Milady raised her head, and looked more attentively at the officer.

By that plain arrangement of the hair, by that costume of extreme simplicity, by the brow polished like marble and as hard and impenetrable, she recognised one of those gloomy Puritans she had so often met, not only in the court of King James, but in that of the King of France, where, in spite of the remembrance of the St. Bartholomew, they sometimes came to seek refuge.

She then had one of those sudden inspirations which only people of genius receive in great crises, in supreme moments which are to decide their fortunes or their lives.

Those two words, YOUR MASS, and a simple glance cast upon Felton, revealed to her all the importance of the reply she was about to make, but with that rapidity of intelligence which was peculiar to her, this reply, ready arranged, presented itself to her lips:

"I?" said she, with an accent of disdain in unison with that which she had remarked in the voice of the young officer, "I, Sir? MY MASS? Lord de Winter, the corrupted Catholic, knows very well that I am not of his religion, and this is a snare he wishes to lay for me!"

"And of what religion are you, then, Madame?" asked Felton, with an astonishment which in spite of the empire he held over himself he could not entirely conceal.

"I will tell it," cried Milady, with a feigned exultation, "on the day when I shall have suffered sufficiently for my faith."

The look of Felton revealed to Milady the full extent of the space she had opened for herself by this single word.

The young officer, however, remained mute and motionless; his look alone had spoken.

"I am in the hands of my enemies," continued she, with that tone of enthusiasm which she knew was familiar to the Puritans. "Well, let my God save me, or let me perish for my God! That is the reply I beg you to make to Lord de Winter. And as to this book," added she, pointing to the manual with her finger but without touching it, as if she must be contaminated by it, "you may carry it back and make use of it yourself, for doubtless you are doubly the accomplice of Lord de Winter–the accomplice in his persecutions, the accomplice in his heresies."

Felton made no reply, took the book with the same appearance of repugnance which he had before manifested, and retired pensively.

Lord de Winter came toward five o'clock in the evening. Milady had had time, during the whole day, to trace her plan of conduct. She received him like a woman who had already recovered all her advantages.

"It appears," said the baron, seating himself in the armchair opposite that occupied by Milady, and stretching out his legs carelessly upon the hearth, "it appears we have made a little apostasy!"

"What do you mean, Sir!"

"I mean to say that since we last met you have changed your religion. You have not by chance married a Protestant for a third husband, have you?"

"Explain yourself, my Lord," replied the prisoner, with majesty, "for though I hear your words, I declare I do not understand them."

"Then you have no religion at all; I like that best," replied Lord de Winter, laughing.

"Certainly that is most in accord with your own principles," replied Milady, frigidly.

"Oh, I confess it is all the same to me."

"Oh, you need not avow this religious indifference, my Lord; your debaucheries and crimes would vouch for it."

"What, you talk of debaucheries, Madame Messalina, Lady Macbeth! Either I misunderstand you or you are very shameless!"

"You only speak thus because you are overheard," coolly replied Milady, "and you wish to interest your jailers and your hangmen against me."

"My jailers and my hangmen! Heyday, Madame! You are taking a poetical tone, and the comedy of yesterday turns to a tragedy this evening. As to the rest, in eight days you will be where you ought to be, and my task will be completed."

"Infamous task! Impious task!" cried Milady, with the exultation of a victim who provokes his judge.

"My word," said de Winter, rising, "I think the hussy is going mad! Come, come, calm yourself, Madame Puritan, or I'll remove you to a dungeon. It's my Spanish wine that has got into your head, is it not? But never mind; that sort of intoxication is not dangerous, and will have no bad effects."

And Lord de Winter retired swearing, which at that period was a very knightly habit.

Felton was indeed behind the door, and had not lost one word of this scene. Milady had guessed aright.

"Yes, go, go!" said she to her brother, "the effects ARE drawing near, on the contrary, but you, weak fool, will not see them until it is too late to shun them."

Silence was re-established. Two hours passed away. Milady's supper was brought in, and she was found deeply engaged in saying her prayers aloud–prayers which she had learned of an old servant of her second husband, a most austere Puritan. She appeared to be in ecstasy, and did not pay the least attention to what was going on around her. Felton made a sign that she should not be disturbed; and when all was arranged, he went out quietly with the soldiers.

Milady knew she might be watched, so she continued her prayers to the end; and it appeared to her that the soldier who was on duty at her door did not march with the same step, and seemed to listen. For the moment she wished nothing better. She arose, came to the table, ate but little, and drank only water.

An hour after, her table was cleared, but Milady remarked that this time Felton did not accompany the soldiers. He feared, then, to see her too often.

She turned toward the wall to smile–for there was in this smile such an expression of triumph that this smile alone would have betrayed her.

She allowed, therefore, half an hour to pass away; and as at that moment all was silence in the old castle, as nothing was heard but the eternal murmur of the waves–that immense breaking of the ocean–with her pure, harmonious, and powerful voice, she began the first couplet of the psalm then in great favour with the Puritans:

"Thou leavest thy servants, Lord, To see if they be strong, but soon thou dost afford Thy hand to lead them on."

These verses were not excellent–very far from it, but as it is well known, the Puritans did not pique themselves upon their poetry.

While singing, Milady listened. The soldier on guard at her door stopped, as if he had been changed into stone. Milady was then able to judge of the effect she had produced.

Then she continued her singing with inexpressible fervor and feeling. It appeared to her that the sounds spread to a distance beneath the vaulted roofs, and carried with them a magic charm to soften the hearts of her jailers. It however likewise appeared that the soldier on duty–a zealous Catholic, no doubt–shook off the charm, for through the door he called: "Hold your tongue, Madame! Your song is as dismal as a 'De Profundis'; and if besides the pleasure of being in garrison here, we must hear such things as these, no mortal can hold out."

"Silence!" then exclaimed another stern voice which Milady recognised as that of Felton. "What are you meddling with, stupid? Did anybody order you to prevent that woman from singing? No. You were told to guard her–to fire at her if she attempted to fly. Guard her! If she flies, kill her, but don't exceed your orders."

An expression of unspeakable joy lightened the countenance of Milady, but this expression was fleeting as the reflection of lightning. Without appearing to have heard the dialogue, of which she had not lost a word, she began again, giving to her voice all the charm, all the power, all the seduction the demon had bestowed upon it:

"For all my tears, my cares, My exile, and my chains, I have my youth, my prayers, And God, who counts my pains."

Her voice, of immense power and sublime expression, gave to the rude, unpolished poetry of these psalms a magic and an effect which the most exalted Puritans rarely found in the songs of their brethren, and which they were forced to ornament with all the resources of their imagination. Felton believed he heard the singing of the angel who consoled the three Hebrews in the furnace.

Milady continued:

"One day our doors will ope, With God come our desire; And if betrays that hope, To death we can aspire."

This verse, into which the terrible enchantress threw her whole soul, completed the trouble which had seized the heart of the young officer. He opened the door quickly; and Milady saw him appear, pale as usual, but with his eye inflamed and almost wild.

"Why do you sing thus, and with such a voice?" said he.

"Your pardon, Sir," said Milady, with mildness. "I forgot that my songs are out of place in this castle. I have perhaps offended you in your creed, but it was without wishing to do so, I swear. Pardon me, then, a fault which is perhaps great, but which certainly was involuntary."

Milady was so beautiful at this moment, the religious ecstasy in which she appeared to be plunged gave such an expression to her countenance, that Felton was so dazzled that he fancied he beheld the angel whom he had only just before heard.

"Yes, yes," said he, "you disturb, you agitate the people who live in the castle."

The poor, senseless young man was not aware of the incoherence of his words, while Milady was reading with her lynx's eyes the very depths of his heart.

"I will be silent, then," said Milady, casting down her eyes with all the sweetness she could give to her voice, with all the resignation she could impress upon her manner.

"No, no, Madame," said Felton, "only do not sing so loud, particularly at night."

And at these words Felton, feeling that he could not long maintain his severity toward his prisoner, rushed out of the room.

"You have done right, Lieutenant," said the soldier. "Such songs disturb the mind; and yet we become accustomed to them, her voice is so beautiful."

Chapter 54

Captivity: The Third Day

Felton had fallen, but there was still another step to be taken. He must be retained, or rather he must be left quite alone; and Milady but obscurely perceived the means which could lead to this result.

Still more must be done. He must be made to speak, in order that he might be spoken to–for Milady very well knew that her greatest seduction was in her voice, which so skillfully ran over the whole gamut of tones from human speech to language celestial.

Yet in spite of all this seduction Milady might fail–for Felton was forewarned, and that against the least chance. From that moment she watched all his actions, all his words, from the simplest glance of his eyes to his gestures–even to a breath that could be interpreted as a sigh. In short, she studied everything, as a skillful comedian does to whom a new part has been assigned in a line to which he is not accustomed.

Face to face with Lord de Winter her plan of conduct was more easy. She had laid that down the preceding evening. To remain silent and dignified in his presence; from time to time to irritate him by affected disdain, by a contemptuous word; to provoke him to threats and violence which would produce a contrast with her own resignation–such was her plan. Felton would see all; perhaps he would say nothing, but he would see.

In the morning, Felton came as usual, but Milady allowed him to preside over all the preparations for breakfast without addressing a word to him. At the moment when he was about to retire, she was cheered with a ray of hope, for she thought he was about to speak, but his lips moved without any sound leaving his mouth, and making a powerful effort to control himself, he sent back to his heart the words that were about to escape from his lips, and went out. Toward midday, Lord de Winter entered.

It was a tolerably fine winter's day, and a ray of that pale English sun which lights but does not warm came through the bars of her prison.

Milady was looking out at the window, and pretended not to hear the door as it opened.

"Ah, ah!" said Lord de Winter, "after having played comedy, after having played tragedy, we are now playing melancholy?"

The prisoner made no reply.

"Yes, yes," continued Lord de Winter, "I understand. You would like very well to be at liberty on that beach! You would like very well to be in a good ship dancing upon the waves of that emerald-green sea; you would like very well, either on land or on the ocean, to lay for me one of those nice little ambuscades you are so skillful in planning. Patience, patience! In four days' time the shore will be beneath your feet, the sea will be open to you–

more open than will perhaps be agreeable to you, for in four days England will be relieved of you."

Milady folded her hands, and raising her fine eyes toward heaven, "Lord, Lord," said she, with an angelic meekness of gesture and tone, "pardon this man, as I myself pardon him."

"Yes, pray, accursed woman!" cried the baron, "your prayer is so much the more generous from your being, I swear to you, in the power of a man who will never pardon you!" and he went out.

At the moment he went out a piercing glance darted through the opening of the nearly closed door, and she perceived Felton, who drew quickly to one side to prevent being seen by her.

Then she threw herself upon her knees, and began to pray.

"My God, my God!" said she, "thou knowest in what holy cause I suffer; give me, then, strength to suffer."

The door opened gently; the beautiful supplicant pretended not to hear the noise, and in a voice broken by tears, she continued:

"God of vengeance! God of goodness! wilt thou allow the frightful projects of this man to be accomplished?"

Then only she pretended to hear the sound of Felton's steps, and rising quick as thought, she blushed, as if ashamed of being surprised on her knees.

"I do not like to disturb those who pray, Madame," said Felton, seriously, "do not disturb yourself on my account, I beseech you."

"How do you know I was praying, Sir?" said Milady, in a voice broken by sobs. "You were deceived, Sir; I was not praying."

"Do you think, then, Madame," replied Felton, in the same serious voice, but with a milder tone, "do you think I assume the right of preventing a creature from prostrating herself before her Creator? God forbid! Besides, repentance becomes the guilty; whatever crimes they may have committed, for me the guilty are sacred at the feet of God!"

"Guilty? I?" said Milady, with a smile which might have disarmed the angel of the last judgement. "Guilty? Oh, my God, thou knowest whether I am guilty! Say I am condemned, Sir, if you please, but you know that God, who loves martyrs, sometimes permits the innocent to be condemned."

"Were you condemned, were you innocent, were you a martyr," replied Felton, "the greater would be the necessity for prayer; and I myself would aid you with my prayers."

"Oh, you are a just man!" cried Milady, throwing herself at his feet. "I can hold out no longer, for I fear I shall be wanting in strength at the moment when I shall be forced to undergo the struggle, and confess my faith. Listen, then, to the supplication of a despairing woman. You are abused, Sir, but that is not the question. I only ask you one favour; and if you grant it me, I will bless you in this world and in the next."

"Speak to the master, Madame," said Felton, "happily I am neither charged with the power of pardoning nor punishing. It is upon one higher placed than I am that God has laid this responsibility."

"To you–no, to you alone! Listen to me, rather than add to my destruction, rather than add to my ignominy!"

"If you have merited this shame, Madame, if you have incurred this ignominy, you must submit to it as an offering to God."

"What do you say? Oh, you do not understand me! When I speak of ignominy, you think I speak of some chastisement, of imprisonment or death. Would to heaven! Of what consequence to me is imprisonment or death?"

"It is I who no longer understand you, Madame," said Felton.

"Or, rather, who pretend not to understand me, Sir!" replied the prisoner, with a smile of incredulity.

"No, Madame, on the honour of a soldier, on the faith of a Christian."

"What, you are ignorant of Lord de Winter's designs upon me?"

"I am."

"Impossible; you are his confidant!"

"I never lie, Madame."

"Oh, he conceals them too little for you not to divine them."

"I seek to divine nothing, Madame; I wait till I am confided in, and apart from that which Lord de Winter has said to me before you, he has confided nothing to me."

"Why, then," cried Milady, with an incredible tone of truthfulness, "you are not his accomplice; you do not know that he destines me to a disgrace which all the punishments of the world cannot equal in horror?"

"You are deceived, Madame," said Felton, blushing, "Lord de Winter is not capable of such a crime."

"Good," said Milady to herself, "without thinking what it is, he calls it a crime!" Then aloud, "The friend of THAT WRETCH is capable of everything."

"Whom do you call 'that wretch'?" asked Felton.

"Are there, then, in England two men to whom such an epithet can be applied?"

"You mean George Villiers?" asked Felton, whose looks became excited.

"Whom Pagans and unbelieving Gentiles call Duke of Buckingham," replied Milady. "I could not have thought that there was an Englishman in all England who would have required so long an explanation to make him understand of whom I was speaking."

"The hand of the Lord is stretched over him," said Felton, "he will not escape the chastisement he deserves."

Felton only expressed, with regard to the duke, the feeling of execration which all the English had declared toward him whom the Catholics themselves called the extortioner, the pillager, the debauchee, and whom the Puritans styled simply Satan.

"Oh, my God, my God!" cried Milady, "when I supplicate thee to pour upon this man the chastisement which is his due, thou knowest it is not my own vengeance I pursue, but the deliverance of a whole nation that I implore!"

"Do you know him, then?" asked Felton.

"At length he interrogates me!" said Milady to herself, at the height of joy at having obtained so quickly such a great result. "Oh, know him? Yes, yes! to my misfortune, to my eternal misfortune!" and Milady twisted her arms as if in a paroxysm of grief.

Felton no doubt felt within himself that his strength was abandoning him, and he made several steps toward the door, but the prisoner, whose eye never left him, sprang in pursuit of him and stopped him.

"Sir," cried she, "be kind, be clement, listen to my prayer! That knife, which the fatal prudence of the baron deprived me of, because he knows the use I would make of it! Oh, hear me to the end! That knife, give it to me for a minute only, for mercy's, for pity's sake! I will embrace your knees! You shall shut the door that you may be certain I contemplate no injury to you! My God! to you–the only just, good, and compassionate being I have met with! To you–my preserver, perhaps! One minute that knife, one minute, a single minute, and I will restore it to you through the grating of the door. Only one minute, Mr. Felton, and you will have saved my honour!"

"To kill yourself?" cried Felton, with terror, forgetting to withdraw his hands from the hands of the prisoner, "to kill yourself?"

"I have told, Sir," murmured Milady, lowering her voice, and allowing herself to sink overpowered to the ground, "I have told my secret! He knows all! My God, I am lost!"

Felton remained standing, motionless and undecided.

"He still doubts," thought Milady, "I have not been earnest enough."

Someone was heard in the corridor; Milady recognised the step of Lord de Winter.

Felton recognised it also, and made a step toward the door.

Milady sprang toward him. "Oh, not a word," said she in a concentrated voice, "not a word of all that I have said to you to this man, or I am lost, and it would be you–you–"

Then as the steps drew near, she became silent for fear of being heard, applying, with a gesture of infinite terror, her beautiful hand to Felton's mouth.

Felton gently repulsed Milady, and she sank into a chair.

Lord de Winter passed before the door without stopping, and they heard the noise of his footsteps soon die away.

Felton, as pale as death, remained some instants with his ear bent and listening; then, when the sound was quite extinct, he breathed like a man awaking from a dream, and rushed out of the apartment.

"Ah!" said Milady, listening in her turn to the noise of Felton's steps, which withdrew in a direction opposite to those of Lord de Winter, "at length you are mine!"

Then her brow darkened. "If he tells the baron," said she, "I am lost–for the baron, who knows very well that I shall not kill myself, will place me before him with a knife in my hand, and he will discover that all this despair is but acted."

She placed herself before the glass, and regarded herself attentively; never had she appeared more beautiful.

"Oh, yes," said she, smiling, "but we won't tell him!"

In the evening Lord de Winter accompanied the supper.

"Sir," said Milady, "is your presence an indispensable accessory of my captivity? Could you not spare me the increase of torture which your visits cause me?"

"How, dear sister!" said Lord de Winter. "Did not you sentimentally inform me with that pretty mouth of yours, so cruel to me today, that you came to England solely for the pleasure of seeing me at your ease, an enjoyment of which you told me you so sensibly felt the deprivation that you had risked everything for it–seasickness, tempest, captivity? Well, here I am; be satisfied. Besides, this time, my visit has a motive."

Milady trembled; she thought Felton had told all. Perhaps never in her life had this woman, who had experienced so many opposite and powerful emotions, felt her heart beat so violently.

She was seated. Lord de Winter took a chair, drew it toward her, and sat down close beside her. Then taking a paper out of his pocket, he unfolded it slowly.

"Here," said he, "I want to show you the kind of passport which I have drawn up, and which will serve you henceforward as the rule of order in the life I consent to leave you."

Then turning his eyes from Milady to the paper, he read: "'Order to conduct–' The name is blank," interrupted Lord de Winter. "If you have any preference you can point it out to me; and if it be not within a thousand leagues of London, attention will be paid to your wishes. I will begin again, then:

"'Order to conduct to–the person named Charlotte Backson, branded by the justice of the kingdom of France, but liberated after chastisement. She is to dwell in this place without ever going more than three leagues from it. In case of any attempt to escape, the penalty of death is to be applied. She will receive five shillings per day for lodging and food'".

"That order does not concern me," replied Milady, coldly, "since it bears another name than mine."

"A name? Have you a name, then?"

"I bear that of your brother."

"Ay, but you are mistaken. My brother is only your second husband; and your first is still living. Tell me his name, and I will put it in the place of the name of Charlotte Backson. No? You will not? You are silent? Well, then you must be registered as Charlotte Backson."

Milady remained silent; only this time it was no longer from affectation, but from terror. She believed the order ready for execution. She thought that Lord de Winter had hastened her departure; she thought she was condemned to set off that very evening. Everything in her mind was lost for an instant; when all at once she perceived that no signature was attached to the order. The joy she felt at this discovery was so great she could not conceal it.

"Yes, yes," said Lord de Winter, who perceived what was passing in her mind, "yes, you look for the signature, and you say to yourself: 'All is not lost, for that order is not signed. It is only shown to me to terrify me, that's all.' You are mistaken. Tomorrow this order will be sent to the Duke of Buckingham. The day after tomorrow it will return signed by his hand and marked with his seal; and four-and-twenty hours afterward I will answer for its being carried into execution. Adieu, Madame. That is all I had to say to you."

"And I reply to you, Sir, that this abuse of power, this exile under a fictitious name, are infamous!"

"Would you like better to be hanged in your true name, Milady? You know that the English laws are inexorable on the abuse of marriage. Speak freely. Although my name, or rather that of my brother, would be mixed up with the affair, I will risk the scandal of a public trial to make myself certain of getting rid of you."

Milady made no reply, but became as pale as a corpse.

"Oh, I see you prefer peregrination. That's well Madame; and there is an old proverb that says, 'Travelling trains youth.' My faith! You are not wrong after all, and life is sweet. That's the reason why I take such care you shall not deprive me of mine. There only remains, then, the question of the five shillings to be settled. You think me rather parsimonious, don't you? That's because I don't care to leave you the means of corrupting your jailers. Besides, you will always have your charms left to seduce them with. Employ them, if your check with regard to Felton has not disgusted you with attempts of that kind."

"Felton has not told him," said Milady to herself. "Nothing is lost, then."

"And now, Madame, till I see you again! Tomorrow I will come and announce to you the departure of my messenger."

Lord de Winter rose, saluted her ironically, and went out.

Milady breathed again. She had still four days before her. Four days would quite suffice to complete the seduction of Felton.

A terrible idea, however, rushed into her mind. She thought that Lord de Winter would perhaps send Felton himself to get the order signed by the Duke of Buckingham. In that case Felton would escape her–for in order to secure success, the magic of a continuous seduction was necessary. Nevertheless, as we have said, one circumstance reassured her. Felton had not spoken.

As she would not appear to be agitated by the threats of Lord de Winter, she placed herself at the table and ate.

Then, as she had done the evening before, she fell on her knees and repeated her prayers aloud. As on the evening before, the soldier stopped his march to listen to her.

Soon after she heard lighter steps than those of the sentinel, which came from the end of the corridor and stopped before her door.

"It is he," said she. And she began the same religious chant which had so strongly excited Felton the evening before.

But although her voice–sweet, full, and sonorous–vibrated as harmoniously and as affectingly as ever, the door remained shut. It appeared however to Milady that in one of the furtive glances she darted from time to time at the grating of the door she thought she saw the ardent eyes of the young man through the narrow opening. But whether this was reality or vision, he had this time sufficient self-command not to enter.

However, a few instants after she had finished her religious song, Milady thought she heard a profound sigh. Then the same steps she had heard approach slowly withdrew, as if with regret.

Chapter 55

Captivity: The Fourth Day

The next day, when Felton entered Milady's apartment he found her standing, mounted upon a chair, holding in her hands a cord made by means of torn cambric handkerchiefs, twisted into a kind of rope one with another, and tied at the ends. At the noise Felton made in entering, Milady leaped lightly to the ground, and tried to conceal behind her the improvised cord she held in her hand.

The young man was more pale than usual, and his eyes, reddened by want of sleep, denoted that he had passed a feverish night. Nevertheless, his brow was armed with a severity more austere than ever.

He advanced slowly toward Milady, who had seated herself, and taking an end of the murderous rope which by neglect, or perhaps by design, she allowed to be seen, "What is this, Madame?" he asked coldly.

"That? Nothing," said Milady, smiling with that painful expression which she knew so well how to give to her smile. "Ennui is the mortal enemy of prisoners; I had ennui, and I amused myself with twisting that rope."

Felton turned his eyes toward the part of the wall of the apartment before which he had found Milady standing in the armchair in which she was now seated, and over her head he perceived a gilt-headed screw, fixed in the wall for the purpose of hanging up clothes or weapons.

He started, and the prisoner saw that start–for though her eyes were cast down, nothing escaped her.

"What were you doing on that armchair?" asked he.

"Of what consequence?" replied Milady.

"But," replied Felton, "I wish to know."

"Do not question me," said the prisoner, "you know that we who are true Christians are forbidden to lie."

"Well, then," said Felton, "I will tell you what you were doing, or rather what you meant to do; you were going to complete the fatal project you cherish in your mind. Remember, Madame, if our God forbids falsehood, he much more severely condemns suicide."

"When God sees one of his creatures persecuted unjustly, placed between suicide and dishonour, believe me, Sir," replied Milady, in a tone of deep conviction, "God pardons suicide, for then suicide becomes martyrdom."

"You say either too much or too little; speak, Madame. In the name of heaven, explain yourself."

"That I may relate my misfortunes for you to treat them as fables; that I may tell you my projects for you to go and betray them to my persecutor? No, Sir. Besides, of what importance to you is the life or death of a condemned wretch? You are only responsible for my body, is it not so? And provided you produce a carcass that may be recognised as mine, they will require no more of you; nay, perhaps you will even have a double reward."

"I, Madame, I?" cried Felton. "You suppose that I would ever accept the price of your life? Oh, you cannot believe what you say!"

"Let me act as I please, Felton, let me act as I please," said Milady, elated. "Every soldier must be ambitious, must he not? You are a lieutenant? Well, you will follow me to the grave with the rank of captain."

"What have I, then, done to you," said Felton, much agitated, "that you should load me with such a responsibility before God and before men? In a few days you will be away from this place; your life, Madame, will then no longer be under my care, and," added he, with a sigh, "then you can do what you will with it."

"So," cried Milady, as if she could not resist giving utterance to a holy indignation, "you, a pious man, you who are called a just man, you ask but one thing–and that is that you may not be inculpated, annoyed, by my death!"

"It is my duty to watch over your life, Madame, and I will watch."

"But do you understand the mission you are fulfilling? Cruel enough, if I am guilty, but what name can you give it, what name will the Lord give it, if I am innocent?"

"I am a soldier, Madame, and fulfill the orders I have received."

"Do you believe, then, that at the day of the Last Judgement God will separate blind executioners from iniquitous judges? You are not willing that I should kill my body, and you make yourself the agent of him who would kill my soul."

"But I repeat it again to you," replied Felton, in great emotion, "no danger threatens you; I will answer for Lord de Winter as for myself."

"Dunce," cried Milady, "dunce! Who dares to answer for another man, when the wisest, when those most after God's own heart, hesitate to answer for themselves, and who ranges himself on the side of the strongest and the most fortunate, to crush the weakest and the most unfortunate."

"Impossible, Madame, impossible," murmured Felton, who felt to the bottom of his heart the justness of this argument. "A prisoner, you will not recover your liberty through me; living, you will not lose your life through me."

"Yes," cried Milady, "but I shall lose that which is much dearer to me than life, I shall lose my honour, Felton; and it is you, you whom I make responsible, before God and before men, for my shame and my infamy."

This time Felton, immovable as he was, or appeared to be, could not resist the secret influence which had already taken possession of him. To see this woman, so beautiful, fair as the brightest vision, to see her by turns overcome with grief and threatening; to resist at once the ascendancy of grief and beauty–it was too much for a visionary; it was too much for a brain weakened by the ardent dreams of an ecstatic faith; it was too much for a heart furrowed by the love of heaven that burns, by the hatred of men that devours.

Milady saw the trouble. She felt by intuition the flame of the opposing passions which burned with the blood in the veins of the young fanatic. As a skillful general, seeing the enemy ready to surrender, marches toward him with a cry of victory, she rose, beautiful as an antique priestess, inspired like a Christian virgin, her arms extended, her throat uncovered, her hair disheveled, holding with one hand her robe modestly drawn over her breast, her look illumined by that fire which had already created such disorder in the veins of the young Puritan, and went toward him, crying out with a vehement air, and in her melodious voice, to which on this occasion she communicated a terrible energy:

"Let this victim to Baal be sent, To the lions the martyr be thrown! Thy God shall teach thee to repent! From th' abyss he'll give ear to my moan."

Felton stood before this strange apparition like one petrified.

"Who art thou? Who art thou?" cried he, clasping his hands. "Art thou a messenger from God; art thou a minister from hell; art thou an angel or a demon; callest thou thyself Eloa or Astarte?"

"Do you not know me, Felton? I am neither an angel nor a demon; I am a daughter of earth, I am a sister of thy faith, that is all."

"Yes, yes!" said Felton, "I doubted, but now I believe."

"You believe, and still you are an accomplice of that child of Belial who is called Lord de Winter! You believe, and yet you leave me in the hands of mine enemies, of the enemy of England, of the enemy of God! You believe, and yet you deliver me up to him who fills and defiles the world with his heresies and debaucheries–to that infamous Sardanapalus whom the blind call the Duke of Buckingham, and whom believers name Antichrist!"

"I deliver you up to Buckingham? I? what mean you by that?"

"They have eyes," cried Milady, "but they see not; ears have they, but they hear not."

"Yes, yes!" said Felton, passing his hands over his brow, covered with sweat, as if to remove his last doubt. "Yes, I recognise the voice which speaks to me in my dreams; yes, I recognise the features of the angel who appears to me every night, crying to my soul, which cannot sleep: 'Strike, save England, save thyself–for thou wilt die without having appeased God!' Speak, speak!" cried Felton, "I can understand you now."

A flash of terrible joy, but rapid as thought, gleamed from the eyes of Milady.

However fugitive this homicide flash, Felton saw it, and started as if its light had revealed the abysses of this woman's heart. He recalled, all at once, the warnings of Lord de Winter, the seductions of Milady, her first attempts after her arrival. He drew back a step, and hung down his head, without, however, ceasing to look at her, as if, fascinated by this strange creature, he could not detach his eyes from her eyes.

Milady was not a woman to misunderstand the meaning of this hesitation. Under her apparent emotions her icy coolness never abandoned her. Before Felton replied, and before she should be forced to resume this conversation, so difficult to be sustained in the same exalted tone, she let her hands fall; and as if the weakness of the woman overpowered the enthusiasm of the inspired fanatic, she said: "But no, it is not for me to be the Judith to deliver Bethulia from this Holofernes. The sword of the eternal is too heavy for my arm. Allow me, then, to avoid dishonour by death; let me take refuge in martyrdom. I do not ask you for liberty, as a guilty one would, nor for vengeance, as would a pagan. Let me die; that is all. I supplicate you, I implore you on my knees–let me die, and my last sigh shall be a blessing for my preserver."

Hearing that voice, so sweet and suppliant, seeing that look, so timid and downcast, Felton reproached himself. By degrees the enchantress had clothed herself with that magic adornment which she assumed and threw aside at will; that is to say, beauty, meekness, and tears–and above all, the irresistible attraction of mystical voluptuousness, the most devouring of all voluptuousness.

"Alas!" said Felton, "I can do but one thing, which is to pity you if you prove to me you are a victim! But Lord de Winter makes cruel accusations against you. You are a Christian; you are my sister in religion. I feel myself drawn toward you–I, who have never loved anyone but my benefactor–I who have met with nothing but traitors and impious men. But you, Madame, so beautiful in reality, you, so pure in appearance, must have committed great iniquities for Lord de Winter to pursue you thus."

"They have eyes," repeated Milady, with an accent of indescribable grief, "but they see not; ears have they, but they hear not."

"But," cried the young officer, "speak, then, speak!"

"Confide my shame to you," cried Milady, with the blush of modesty upon her countenance, "for often the crime of one becomes the shame of another–confide my shame to you, a man, and I a woman? Oh," continued she, placing her hand modestly over her beautiful eyes, "never! Never!–I could not!"

"To me, to a brother?" said Felton.

Milady looked at him for some time with an expression which the young man took for doubt, but which, however, was nothing but observation, or rather the wish to fascinate.

Felton, in his turn a suppliant, clasped his hands.

"Well, then," said Milady, "I confide in my brother; I will dare to–"

At this moment the steps of Lord de Winter were heard, but this time the terrible brother-in-law of Milady did not content himself, as on the preceding day, with passing before the door and going away again. He paused, exchanged two words with the sentinel; then the door opened, and he appeared.

During the exchange of these two words Felton drew back quickly, and when Lord de Winter entered, he was several paces from the prisoner.

The baron entered slowly, sending a scrutinising glance from Milady to the young officer.

"You have been here a very long time, John," said he. "Has this woman been relating her crimes to you? In that case I can comprehend the length of the conversation."

Felton started; and Milady felt she was lost if she did not come to the assistance of the disconcerted Puritan.

"Ah, you fear your prisoner should escape!" said she. "Well, ask your worthy jailer what favour I this instant solicited of him."

"You demanded a favour?" said the baron, suspiciously.

"Yes, my Lord," replied the young man, confused.

"And what favour, pray?" asked Lord de Winter.

"A knife, which she would return to me through the grating of the door a minute after she had received it," replied Felton.

"There is someone, then, concealed here whose throat this amiable lady is desirous of cutting," said de Winter, in an ironical, contemptuous tone.

"There is myself," replied Milady.

"I have given you the choice between America and Tyburn," replied Lord de Winter. "Choose Tyburn, Madame. Believe me, the cord is more certain than the knife."

Felton grew pale, and made a step forward, remembering that at the moment he entered Milady had a rope in her hand.

"You are right," said she, "I have often thought of it." Then she added in a low voice, "And I will think of it again."

Felton felt a shudder run to the marrow of his bones; probably Lord de Winter perceived this emotion.

"Mistrust yourself, John," said he. "I have placed reliance upon you, my friend. Beware! I have warned you! But be of good courage, my lad; in three days we shall be delivered from this creature, and where I shall send her she can harm nobody."

"You hear him!" cried Milady, with vehemence, so that the baron might believe she was addressing heaven, and that Felton might understand she was addressing him.

Felton lowered his head and reflected.

The baron took the young officer by the arm, and turned his head over his shoulder, so as not to lose sight of Milady till he was gone out.

"Well," said the prisoner, when the door was shut, "I am not so far advanced as I believed. De Winter has changed his usual stupidity into a strange prudence. It is the desire of vengeance, and how desire molds a man! As to Felton, he hesitates. Ah, he is not a man like that cursed d'Artagnan. A Puritan only adores virgins, and he adores them by clasping his hands. A Musketeer loves women, and he loves them by clasping his arms round them."

Milady waited, then, with much impatience, for she feared the day would pass away without her seeing Felton again. At last, in an hour after the scene we have just described, she heard someone speaking in a low voice at the door. Presently the door opened, and she perceived Felton.

The young man advanced rapidly into the chamber, leaving the door open behind him, and making a sign to Milady to be silent; his face was much agitated.

"What do you want with me?" said she.

"Listen," replied Felton, in a low voice. "I have just sent away the sentinel that I might remain here without anybody knowing it, in order to speak to you without being overheard. The baron has just related a frightful story to me."

Milady assumed her smile of a resigned victim, and shook her head.

"Either you are a demon," continued Felton, "or the baron–my benefactor, my father–is a monster. I have known you four days; I have loved him four years. I therefore may hesitate between you. Be not alarmed at what I say; I want to be convinced. Tonight, after twelve, I will come and see you, and you shall convince me."

"No, Felton, no, my brother," said she, "the sacrifice is too great, and I feel what it must cost you. No, I am lost; do not be lost with me. My death will be much more eloquent than my life, and the silence of the corpse will convince you much better than the words of the prisoner."

"Be silent, Madame," cried Felton, "and do not speak to me thus; I came to entreat you to promise me upon your honour, to swear to me by what you hold most sacred, that you will make no attempt upon your life."

"I will not promise," said Milady, "for no one has more respect for a promise or an oath than I have; and if I make a promise I must keep it."

"Well," said Felton, "only promise till you have seen me again. If, when you have seen me again, you still persist–well, then you shall be free, and I myself will give you the weapon you desire."

"Well," said Milady, "for you I will wait."

"Swear."

"I swear it, by our God. Are you satisfied?"

"Well," said Felton, "till tonight."

And he darted out of the room, shut the door, and waited in the corridor, the soldier's half-pike in his hand, and as if he had mounted guard in his place.

The soldier returned, and Felton gave him back his weapon.

Then, through the grating to which she had drawn near, Milady saw the young man make a sign with delirious fervor, and depart in an apparent transport of joy.

As for her, she returned to her place with a smile of savage contempt upon her lips, and repeated, blaspheming, that terrible name of God, by whom she had just sworn without ever having learned to know Him.

"My God," said she, "what a senseless fanatic! My God, it is I–I–and this fellow who will help me to avenge myself."

Chapter 56

Captivity: The Fifth Day

Milady had however achieved a half-triumph, and success doubled her forces.

It was not difficult to conquer, as she had hitherto done, men prompt to let themselves be seduced, and whom the gallant education of a court led quickly into her net. Milady was handsome enough not to find much resistance on the part of the flesh, and she was sufficiently skillful to prevail over all the obstacles of the mind.

But this time she had to contend with an unpolished nature, concentrated and insensible by force of austerity. Religion and its observances had made Felton a man inaccessible to ordinary seductions. There fermented in that sublimated brain plans so vast, projects so tumultuous, that there remained no room for any capricious or material love–that sentiment which is fed by leisure and grows with corruption. Milady had, then, made a breach by her false virtue in the opinion of a man horribly prejudiced against her, and by her beauty in the heart of a man hitherto chaste and pure. In short, she had taken the measure of motives hitherto unknown to herself, through this experiment, made upon the most rebellious subject that nature and religion could submit to her study.

Many a time, nevertheless, during the evening she despaired of fate and of herself. She did not invoke God, we very well know, but she had faith in the genius of evil–that immense sovereignty which reigns in all the details of human life, and by which, as in the Arabian fable, a single pomegranate seed is sufficient to reconstruct a ruined world.

Milady, being well prepared for the reception of Felton, was able to erect her batteries for the next day. She knew she had only two days left; that when once the order was signed by Buckingham–and Buckingham would sign it the more readily from its bearing a false name, and he could not, therefore, recognise the woman in question–once this order was signed, we say, the baron would make her embark immediately, and she knew very well that women condemned to exile employ arms much less powerful in their seductions than the pretendedly virtuous woman whose beauty is lighted by the sun of the world, whose style the voice of fashion lauds, and whom a halo of aristocracy gilds with enchanting splendors. To be a woman condemned to a painful and disgraceful punishment is no impediment to beauty, but it is an obstacle to the recovery of power. Like all persons of real genius, Milady knew what suited her nature and her means. Poverty was repugnant to her; degradation took away two-thirds of her greatness. Milady was only a queen while among queens. The pleasure of satisfied pride was necessary to her domination. To command inferior beings was rather a humiliation than a pleasure for her.

She should certainly return from her exile–she did not doubt that a single instant, but how long might this exile last? For an active, ambitious nature, like that of Milady, days not spent in climbing are inauspicious days. What word, then, can be found to describe the days which they occupy in descending? To lose a year, two years, three years, is to talk of an eternity; to return after the death or disgrace of the cardinal, perhaps; to return when d'Artagnan and his friends, happy and triumphant, should have received from the queen the reward they had well acquired by the services they had rendered her–these were devouring ideas that a woman like Milady could not endure. For the rest, the storm which raged within her doubled her strength, and she would have burst the walls of her prison if her body had been able to take for a single instant the proportions of her mind.

Then that which spurred her on additionally in the midst of all this was the remembrance of the cardinal. What must the mistrustful, restless, suspicious cardinal think of her silence–the cardinal, not merely her only support, her only prop, her only protector at present, but still further, the principal instrument of her future fortune and vengeance? She knew him; she knew that at her return from a fruitless journey it would be in vain to tell him of her imprisonment, in vain to enlarge upon the sufferings she had undergone. The cardinal would reply, with the sarcastic calmness of the skeptic, strong at once by power and genius, "You should not have allowed yourself to be taken."

Then Milady collected all her energies, murmuring in the depths of her soul the name of Felton–the only beam of light that penetrated to her in the hell into which she had fallen; and like a serpent which folds and unfolds its rings to ascertain its strength, she enveloped Felton beforehand in the thousand meshes of her inventive imagination.

Time, however, passed away; the hours, one after another, seemed to awaken the clock as they passed, and every blow of the brass hammer resounded upon the heart of the prisoner. At nine o'clock, Lord de Winter made his customary visit, examined the window and the bars, sounded the floor and the walls, looked to the chimney and the doors, without, during this long and minute examination, he or Milady pronouncing a single word.

Doubtless both of them understood that the situation had become too serious to lose time in useless words and aimless wrath.

"Well," said the baron, on leaving her "you will not escape tonight!"

At ten o'clock Felton came and placed the sentinel. Milady recognised his step. She was as well acquainted with it now as a mistress is with that of the lover of her heart; and yet Milady at the same time detested and despised this weak fanatic.

That was not the appointed hour. Felton did not enter.

Two hours after, as midnight sounded, the sentinel was relieved. This time it WAS the hour, and from this moment Milady waited with impatience. The new sentinel commenced his walk in the corridor. At the expiration of ten minutes Felton came.

Milady was all attention.

"Listen," said the young man to the sentinel. "On no pretense leave the door, for you know that last night my Lord punished a soldier for having quit his post for an instant, although I, during his absence, watched in his place."

"Yes, I know it," said the soldier.

"I recommend you therefore to keep the strictest watch. For my part I am going to pay a second visit to this woman, who I fear entertains sinister intentions upon her own life, and I have received orders to watch her."

"Good!" murmured Milady, "the austere Puritan lies."

As to the soldier, he only smiled.

"Zounds, Lieutenant!" said he, "you are not unlucky in being charged with such commissions, particularly if my Lord has authorised you to look into her bed."

Felton blushed. Under any other circumstances he would have reprimanded the soldier for indulging in such pleasantry, but his conscience murmured too loud for his mouth to dare speak.

"If I call, come," said he. "If anyone comes, call me."

"I will, Lieutenant," said the soldier.

Felton entered Milady's apartment. Milady arose.

"You are here!" said she.

"I promised to come," said Felton, "and I have come."

"You promised me something else."

"What, my God!" said the young man, who in spite of his self-command felt his knees tremble and the sweat start from his brow.

"You promised to bring a knife, and to leave it with me after our interview."

"Say no more of that, Madame," said Felton. "There is no situation, however terrible it may be, which can authorise a creature of God to inflict death upon himself. I have reflected, and I cannot, must not be guilty of such a sin."

"Ah, you have reflected!" said the prisoner, sitting down in her armchair, with a smile of disdain, "and I also have reflected."

"Upon what?"

"That I can have nothing to say to a man who does not keep his word."

"Oh, my God!" murmured Felton.

"You may retire," said Milady. "I will not talk."

"Here is the knife," said Felton, drawing from his pocket the weapon which he had brought, according to his promise, but which he hesitated to give to his prisoner.

"Let me see it," said Milady.

"For what purpose?"

"Upon my honour, I will instantly return it to you. You shall place it on that table, and you may remain between it and me."

Felton offered the weapon to Milady, who examined the temper of it attentively, and who tried the point on the tip of her finger.

"Well," said she, returning the knife to the young officer, "this is fine and good steel. You are a faithful friend, Felton."

Felton took back the weapon, and laid it upon the table, as he had agreed with the prisoner.

Milady followed him with her eyes, and made a gesture of satisfaction.

"Now," said she, "listen to me."

The request was needless. The young officer stood upright before her, awaiting her words as if to devour them.

"Felton," said Milady, with a solemnity full of melancholy, "imagine that your sister, the daughter of your father, speaks to you. While yet young, unfortunately handsome, I was dragged into a snare. I resisted. Ambushes and violences multiplied around me, but I resisted. The religion I serve, the God I adore, were blasphemed because I called upon that religion and that God, but still I resisted. Then outrages were heaped upon me, and as my soul was not subdued they wished to defile my body forever. Finally–"

Milady stopped, and a bitter smile passed over her lips.

"Finally," said Felton, "finally, what did they do?"

"At length, one evening my enemy resolved to paralyze the resistance he could not conquer. One evening he mixed a powerful narcotic with my water. Scarcely had I finished my repast, when I felt myself sink by degrees into a strange torpor. Although I was without mistrust, a vague fear seized me, and I tried to struggle against sleepiness. I arose. I wished to run to the window and call for help, but my legs refused their office. It appeared as if the ceiling sank upon my head and crushed me with its weight. I stretched out my arms. I tried to speak. I could only utter inarticulate sounds, and irresistible faintness came over me. I supported myself by a chair, feeling that I was about to fall, but this support was soon insufficient on account of my weak arms. I fell upon one knee, then upon both. I tried to pray, but my tongue was frozen. God doubtless neither heard nor saw me, and I sank upon the floor a prey to a slumber which resembled death.

"Of all that passed in that sleep, or the time which glided away while it lasted, I have no remembrance. The only thing I recollect is that I awoke in bed in a round chamber, the furniture of which was sumptuous, and into which light only penetrated by an opening in the ceiling. No door gave entrance to the room. It might be called a magnificent prison.

"It was a long time before I was able to make out what place I was in, or to take account of the details I describe. My mind appeared to strive in vain to shake off the heavy darkness of the sleep from which I could not rouse myself. I had vague perceptions of space traversed, of the rolling of a carriage, of a horrible dream in which my strength had become exhausted, but all this was so dark and so indistinct in my mind that these events seemed to belong to another life than mine, and yet mixed with mine in fantastic duality.

"At times the state into which I had fallen appeared so strange that I believed myself dreaming. I arose trembling. My clothes were near me on a chair; I neither remembered having undressed myself nor going to bed. Then by degrees the reality broke upon me, full of chaste terrors. I was no longer in the house where I had dwelt. As well as I could judge by the light of the sun, the day was already two-thirds gone. It was the evening before when I had fallen asleep; my sleep, then, must have lasted twenty-four hours! What had taken place during this long sleep?

"I dressed myself as quickly as possible; my slow and stiff motions all attested that the effects of the narcotic were not yet entirely dissipated. The chamber was evidently furnished for the reception of a woman; and the most finished coquette could not have formed a wish, but on casting her eyes about the apartment, she would have found that wish accomplished.

"Certainly I was not the first captive that had been shut up in this splendid prison, but you may easily comprehend, Felton, that the more superb the prison, the greater was my terror.

"Yes, it was a prison, for I tried in vain to get out of it. I sounded all the walls, in the hopes of discovering a door, but everywhere the walls returned a full and flat sound.

"I made the tour of the room at least twenty times, in search of an outlet of some kind, but there was none. I sank exhausted with fatigue and terror into an armchair.

"Meantime, night came on rapidly, and with night my terrors increased. I did not know but I had better remain where I was seated. It appeared that I was surrounded with unknown dangers into which I was about to fall at every instant. Although I had eaten nothing since the evening before, my fears prevented my feeling hunger.

"No noise from without by which I could measure the time reached me; I only supposed it must be seven or eight o'clock in the evening, for it was in the month of October and it was quite dark.

"All at once the noise of a door, turning on its hinges, made me start. A globe of fire appeared above the glazed opening of the ceiling, casting a strong light into my chamber; and I perceived with terror that a man was standing within a few paces of me.

"A table, with two covers, bearing a supper ready prepared, stood, as if by magic, in the middle of the apartment.

"That man was he who had pursued me during a whole year, who had vowed my dishonour, and who, by the first words that issued from his mouth, gave me to understand he had accomplished it the preceding night."

"Scoundrel!" murmured Felton.

"Oh, yes, scoundrel!" cried Milady, seeing the interest which the young officer, whose soul seemed to hang on her lips, took in this strange recital. "Oh, yes, scoundrel! He believed, having triumphed over me in my sleep, that all was completed. He came, hoping that I would accept my shame, as my shame was consummated; he came to offer his fortune in exchange for my love.

"All that the heart of a woman could contain of haughty contempt and disdainful words, I poured out upon this man. Doubtless he was accustomed to such reproaches, for he listened to me calm and smiling, with his arms crossed over his breast. Then, when he thought I had said all, he advanced toward me; I sprang toward the table, I seized a knife, I placed it to my breast.

"Take one step more," said I, "and in addition to my dishonour, you shall have my death to reproach yourself with."

"There was, no doubt, in my look, my voice, my whole person, that sincerity of gesture, of attitude, of accent, which carries conviction to the most perverse minds, for he paused.

"'Your death?' said he; 'oh, no, you are too charming a mistress to allow me to consent to lose you thus, after I have had the happiness to possess you only a single time. Adieu, my charmer; I will wait to pay you my next visit till you are in a better humor.'

"At these words he blew a whistle; the globe of fire which lighted the room reascended and disappeared. I found myself again in complete darkness. The same noise of a door opening and shutting was repeated the instant afterward; the flaming globe descended afresh, and I was completely alone.

"This moment was frightful; if I had any doubts as to my misfortune, these doubts had vanished in an overwhelming reality. I was in the power of a man whom I not only detested, but despised–of a man capable of anything, and who had already given me a fatal proof of what he was able to do."

"But who, then was this man?" asked Felton.

"I passed the night on a chair, starting at the least noise, for toward midnight the lamp went out, and I was again in darkness. But the night passed away without any fresh attempt on the part of my persecutor. Day came; the table had disappeared, only I had still the knife in my hand.

"This knife was my only hope.

"I was worn out with fatigue. Sleeplessness inflamed my eyes; I had not dared to sleep a single instant. The light of day reassured me; I went and threw myself on the bed, without parting with the emancipating knife, which I concealed under my pillow.

"When I awoke, a fresh meal was served.

"This time, in spite of my terrors, in spite of my agony, I began to feel a devouring hunger. It was forty-eight hours since I had taken any nourishment. I ate some bread and some fruit; then, remembering the narcotic mixed with the water I had drunk, I would not touch that which was placed on the table, but filled my glass at a marble fountain fixed in the wall over my dressing table.

"And yet, notwithstanding these precautions, I remained for some time in a terrible agitation of mind. But my fears were this time ill-founded; I passed the day without experiencing anything of the kind I dreaded.

"I took the precaution to half empty the carafe, in order that my suspicions might not be noticed.

"The evening came on, and with it darkness, but however profound was this darkness, my eyes began to accustom themselves to it. I saw, amid the shadows, the table sink through the floor; a quarter of an hour later it reappeared, bearing my supper. In an instant, thanks to the lamp, my chamber was once more lighted.

"I was determined to eat only such things as could not possibly have anything soporific introduced into them. Two eggs and some fruit composed my repast; then I drew another glass of water from my protecting fountain, and drank it.

"At the first swallow, it appeared to me not to have the same taste as in the morning. Suspicion instantly seized me. I paused, but I had already drunk half a glass.

"I threw the rest away with horror, and waited, with the dew of fear upon my brow.

"No doubt some invisible witness had seen me draw the water from that fountain, and had taken advantage of my confidence in it, the better to assure my ruin, so coolly resolved upon, so cruelly pursued.

"Half an hour had not passed when the same symptoms began to appear, but as I had only drunk half a glass of the water, I contended longer, and instead of falling entirely asleep, I sank into a state of drowsiness which left me a perception of what was passing around me, while depriving me of the strength either to defend myself or to fly.

"I dragged myself toward the bed, to seek the only defense I had left–my saving knife, but I could not reach the bolster. I sank on my knees, my hands clasped round one of the bedposts; then I felt that I was lost."

Felton became frightfully pale, and a convulsive tremor crept through his whole body.

"And what was most frightful," continued Milady, her voice altered, as if she still experienced the same agony as at that awful minute, "was that at this time I retained a consciousness of the danger that threatened me; was that my soul, if I may say so, waked in my sleeping body; was that I saw, that I heard. It is true that all was like a dream, but it was not the less frightful.

"I saw the lamp ascend, and leave me in darkness; then I heard the well-known creaking of the door although I had heard that door open but twice.

"I felt instinctively that someone approached me; it is said that the doomed wretch in the deserts of America thus feels the approach of the serpent.

"I wished to make an effort; I attempted to cry out. By an incredible effort of will I even raised myself up, but only to sink down again immediately, and to fall into the arms of my persecutor."

"Tell me who this man was!" cried the young officer.

Milady saw at a single glance all the painful feelings she inspired in Felton by dwelling on every detail of her recital, but she would not spare him a single pang. The more profoundly she wounded his heart, the more certainly he would avenge her. She continued, then, as if she had not heard his exclamation, or as if she thought the moment was not yet come to reply to it.

"Only this time it was no longer an inert body, without feeling, that the villain had to deal with. I have told you that without being able to regain the complete exercise of my faculties, I retained the sense of my danger. I struggled, then, with all my strength, and doubtless opposed, weak as I was, a long resistance, for I heard him cry out, 'These miserable Puritans! I knew very well that they tired out their executioners, but I did not believe them so strong against their lovers!'

"Alas! This desperate resistance could not last long. I felt my strength fail, and this time it was not my sleep that enabled the coward to prevail, but my swoon."

Felton listened without uttering any word or sound, except an inward expression of agony. The sweat streamed down his marble forehead, and his hand, under his coat, tore his breast.

"My first impulse, on coming to myself, was to feel under my pillow for the knife I had not been able to reach; if it had not been useful for defense, it might at least serve for expiation.

"But on taking this knife, Felton, a terrible idea occurred to me. I have sworn to tell you all, and I will tell you all. I have promised you the truth; I will tell it, were it to destroy me."

"The idea came into your mind to avenge yourself on this man, did it not?" cried Felton.

"Yes," said Milady. "The idea was not that of a Christian, I knew, but without doubt, that eternal enemy of our souls, that lion roaring constantly around us, breathed it into my mind. In short, what shall I say to you, Felton?" continued Milady, in the tone of a woman accusing herself of a crime. "This idea occurred to me, and did not leave me; it is of this homicidal thought that I now bear the punishment."

"Continue, continue!" said Felton, "I am eager to see you attain your vengeance!"

"Oh, I resolved that it should take place as soon as possible. I had no doubt he would return the following night. During the day I had nothing to fear.

"When the hour of breakfast came, therefore, I did not hesitate to eat and drink. I had determined to make believe sup, but to eat nothing. I was forced, then, to combat the fast of the evening with the nourishment of the morning.

"Only I concealed a glass of water, which remained after my breakfast, thirst having been the chief of my sufferings when I remained forty-eight hours without eating or drinking.

"The day passed away without having any other influence on me than to strengthen the resolution I had formed; only I took care that my face should not betray the thoughts of my heart, for I had no doubt I was watched. Several times, even, I felt a smile on my lips. Felton, I dare not tell you at what idea I smiled; you would hold me in horror–"

"Go on! Go on!" said Felton, "you see plainly that I listen, and that I am anxious to know the end."

"Evening came; the ordinary events took place. During the darkness, as before, my supper was brought. Then the lamp was lighted, and I sat down to table. I only ate some fruit. I pretended to pour out water from the jug, but I only drank that which I had saved in my glass. The substitution was made so carefully that my spies, if I had any, could have no suspicion of it.

"After supper I exhibited the same marks of languor as on the preceding evening, but this time, as I yielded to fatigue, or as if I had become familiarised with danger, I dragged myself toward my bed, let my robe fall, and lay down.

"I found my knife where I had placed it, under my pillow, and while feigning to sleep, my hand grasped the handle of it convulsively.

"Two hours passed away without anything fresh happening. Oh, my God! who could have said so the evening before? I began to fear that he would not come.

"At length I saw the lamp rise softly, and disappear in the depths of the ceiling; my chamber was filled with darkness and obscurity, but I made a strong effort to penetrate this darkness and obscurity.

"Nearly ten minutes passed; I heard no other noise but the beating of my own heart. I implored heaven that he might come.

"At length I heard the well-known noise of the door, which opened and shut; I heard, notwithstanding the thickness of the carpet, a step which made the floor creak; I saw, notwithstanding the darkness, a shadow which approached my bed."

"Haste! Haste!" said Felton, "do you not see that each of your words burns me like molten lead?"

"Then," continued Milady, "then I collected all my strength; I recalled to my mind that the moment of vengeance, or rather, of justice, had struck. I looked upon myself as another Judith; I gathered myself up, my knife in my hand, and when I saw him near me, stretching out his arms to find his victim, then, with the last cry of agony and despair, I struck him in the middle of his breast.

"The miserable villain! He had foreseen all. His breast was covered with a coat-of-mail; the knife was bent against it.

"'Ah, ah!' cried he, seizing my arm, and wresting from me the weapon that had so badly served me, 'you want to take my life, do you, my pretty Puritan? But that's more than dislike, that's ingratitude! Come, come, calm yourself, my sweet girl! I thought you had softened. I am not one of those tyrants who detain women by force. You don't love me. With my usual fatuity I doubted it; now I am convinced. Tomorrow you shall be free.'

"I had but one wish; that was that he should kill me.

"'Beware!' said I, 'for my liberty is your dishonour.'

"'Explain yourself, my pretty sibyl!'

"'Yes; for as soon as I leave this place I will tell everything. I will proclaim the violence you have used toward me. I will describe my captivity. I will denounce this place of infamy. You are placed on high, my Lord, but tremble! Above you there is the king; above the king there is God!'

"However perfect master he was over himself, my persecutor allowed a movement of anger to escape him. I could not see the expression of his countenance, but I felt the arm tremble upon which my hand was placed.

"'Then you shall not leave this place,' said he.

"'Very well,' cried I, 'then the place of my punishment will be that of my tomb. I will die here, and you will see if a phantom that accuses is not more terrible than a living being that threatens!'

"'You shall have no weapon left in your power.'

"'There is a weapon which despair has placed within the reach of every creature who has the courage to use it. I will allow myself to die with hunger.'

"'Come,' said the wretch, 'is not peace much better than such a war as that? I will restore you to liberty this moment; I will proclaim you a piece of immaculate virtue; I will name you the Lucretia of England.'

"'And I will say that you are the Sextus. I will denounce you before men, as I have denounced you before God; and if it be necessary that, like Lucretia, I should sign my accusation with my blood, I will sign it.'

"'Ah!' said my enemy, in a jeering tone, 'that's quite another thing. My faith! Everything considered, you are very well off here. You shall want for nothing, and if you let yourself die of hunger that will be your own fault.'

"At these words he retired. I heard the door open and shut, and I remained overwhelmed, less, I confess it, by my grief than by the mortification of not having avenged myself.

"He kept his word. All the day, all the next night passed away without my seeing him again. But I also kept my word with him, and I neither ate nor drank. I was, as I told him, resolved to die of hunger.

"I passed the day and the night in prayer, for I hoped that God would pardon me my suicide.

"The second night the door opened; I was lying on the floor, for my strength began to abandon me.

"At the noise I raised myself up on one hand.

"'Well,' said a voice which vibrated in too terrible a manner in my ear not to be recognised, 'well! Are we softened a little? Will we not pay for our liberty with a single promise of silence? Come, I am a good sort of a prince,' added he, 'and although I like not Puritans I do them justice; and it is the same with Puritanesses, when they are pretty. Come, take a little oath for me on the cross; I won't ask anything more of you.'

"'On the cross,' cried I, rising, for at that abhorred voice I had recovered all my strength, 'on the cross I swear that no promise, no menace, no force, no torture, shall close my mouth! On the cross I swear to denounce you everywhere as a murderer, as a thief of honour, as a base coward! On the cross I swear, if I ever leave this place, to call down vengeance upon you from the whole human race!'

"'Beware!' said the voice, in a threatening accent that I had never yet heard. 'I have an extraordinary means which I will not employ but in the last extremity to close your mouth, or at least to prevent anyone from believing a word you may utter.'

"I mustered all my strength to reply to him with a burst of laughter.

"He saw that it was a merciless war between us–a war to the death.

"'Listen!' said he. 'I give you the rest of tonight and all day tomorrow. Reflect: promise to be silent, and riches, consideration, even honour, shall surround you; threaten to speak, and I will condemn you to infamy.'

"'You?' cried I. 'You?'

"'To interminable, ineffaceable infamy!'

"'You?' repeated I. Oh, I declare to you, Felton, I thought him mad!

"'Yes, yes, I!' replied he.

"'Oh, leave me!' said I. 'Begone, if you do not desire to see me dash my head against that wall before your eyes!'

"'Very well, it is your own doing. Till tomorrow evening, then!'

"'Till tomorrow evening, then!' replied I, allowing myself to fall, and biting the carpet with rage."

Felton leaned for support upon a piece of furniture; and Milady saw, with the joy of a demon, that his strength would fail him perhaps before the end of her recital.

Chapter 57

Means For Classical Tragedy

After a moment of silence employed by Milady in observing the young man who listened to her, Milady continued her recital.

"It was nearly three days since I had eaten or drunk anything. I suffered frightful torments. At times there passed before me clouds which pressed my brow, which veiled my eyes; this was delirium.

"When the evening came I was so weak that every time I fainted I thanked God, for I thought I was about to die.

"In the midst of one of these swoons I heard the door open. Terror recalled me to myself.

"He entered the apartment followed by a man in a mask. He was masked likewise, but I knew his step, I knew his voice, I knew him by that imposing bearing which hell has bestowed upon his person for the curse of humanity.

"'Well,' said he to me, 'have you made your mind up to take the oath I requested of you?'

"'You have said Puritans have but one word. Mine you have heard, and that is to pursue you–on earth to the tribunal of men, in heaven to the tribunal of God.'

"'You persist, then?'

"'I swear it before the God who hears me. I will take the whole world as a witness of your crime, and that until I have found an avenger.'

"'You are a prostitute,' said he, in a voice of thunder, 'and you shall undergo the punishment of prostitutes! Branded in the eyes of the world you invoke, try to prove to that world that you are neither guilty nor mad!'

"Then, addressing the man who accompanied him, 'Executioner,' said he, 'do your duty.'"

"Oh, his name, his name!" cried Felton. "His name, tell it me!"

"Then in spite of my cries, in spite of my resistance–for I began to comprehend that there was a question of something worse than death–the executioner seized me, threw me on the floor, fastened me with his bonds, and suffocated by sobs, almost without sense, invoking God, who did not listen to me, I uttered all at once a frightful cry of pain and shame. A burning fire, a red-hot iron, the iron of the executioner, was imprinted on my shoulder."

Felton uttered a groan.

"Here," said Milady, rising with the majesty of a queen, "here, Felton, behold the new martyrdom invented for a pure young girl, the victim of the brutality of a villain. Learn to know the heart of men, and henceforth make yourself less easily the instrument of their unjust vengeance."

Milady, with a rapid gesture, opened her robe, tore the cambric that covered her bosom, and red with feigned anger and simulated shame, showed the young man the ineffaceable impression which dishonoured that beautiful shoulder.

"But," cried Felton, "that is a FLEUR-DE-LIS which I see there."

"And therein consisted the infamy," replied Milady. "The brand of England!–It would be necessary to prove what tribunal had imposed it on me, and I could have made a public appeal to all the tribunals of the kingdom, but the brand of France!–Oh, by that, by THAT I was branded indeed!"

This was too much for Felton.

Pale, motionless, overwhelmed by this frightful revelation, dazzled by the superhuman beauty of this woman who unveiled herself before him with an immodesty which appeared to him sublime, he ended by falling on his knees before her as the early Christians did before those pure and holy martyrs whom the persecution of the emperors gave up in the circus to the sanguinary sensuality of the populace. The brand disappeared; the beauty alone remained.

"Pardon! Pardon!" cried Felton, "oh, pardon!"

Milady read in his eyes LOVE! LOVE!

"Pardon for what?" asked she.

"Pardon me for having joined with your persecutors."

Milady held out her hand to him.

"So beautiful! So young!" cried Felton, covering that hand with his kisses.

Milady let one of those looks fall upon him which make a slave of a king.

Felton was a Puritan; he abandoned the hand of this woman to kiss her feet.

He no longer loved her; he adored her.

When this crisis was past, when Milady appeared to have resumed her self-possession, which she had never lost; when Felton had seen her recover with the veil of chastity those treasures of love which were only concealed from him to make him desire them the more ardently, he said, "Ah, now! I have only one thing to ask of you; that is, the name of your true executioner. For to me there is but one; the other was an instrument, that was all."

"What, brother!" cried Milady, "must I name him again? Have you not yet divined who he is?"

"What?" cried Felton, "he–again he–always he? What–the truly guilty?"

"The truly guilty," said Milady, "is the ravager of England, the persecutor of true believers, the base ravisher of the honour of so many women–he who, to satisfy a caprice of his corrupt heart, is about to make England shed so much blood, who protects the Protestants today and will betray them tomorrow–"

"Buckingham! It is, then, Buckingham!" cried Felton, in a high state of excitement.

Milady concealed her face in her hands, as if she could not endure the shame which this name recalled to her.

"Buckingham, the executioner of this angelic creature!" cried Felton. "And thou hast not hurled thy thunder at him, my God! And thou hast left him noble, honoured, powerful, for the ruin of us all!"

"God abandons him who abandons himself," said Milady.

"But he will draw upon his head the punishment reserved for the damned!" said Felton, with increasing exultation. "He wills that human vengeance should precede celestial justice."

"Men fear him and spare him."

"I," said Felton, "I do not fear him, nor will I spare him."

The soul of Milady was bathed in an infernal joy.

"But how can Lord de Winter, my protector, my father," asked Felton, "possibly be mixed up with all this?"

"Listen, Felton," resumed Milady, "for by the side of base and contemptible men there are often found great and generous natures. I had an affianced husband, a man whom I loved, and who loved me–a heart like yours, Felton, a man like you. I went to him and told him all; he knew me, that man did, and did not doubt an instant. He was a nobleman, a man equal to Buckingham in every respect. He said nothing; he only girded on his sword, wrapped himself in his cloak, and went straight to Buckingham Palace.

"Yes, yes," said Felton, "I understand how he would act. But with such men it is not the sword that should be employed; it is the poniard."

"Buckingham had left England the day before, sent as ambassador to Spain, to demand the hand of the Infanta for King Charles I, who was then only Prince of Wales. My affianced husband returned.

"'Hear me,' said he; 'this man has gone, and for the moment has consequently escaped my vengeance, but let us be united, as we were to have been, and then leave it to Lord de Winter to maintain his own honour and that of his wife.'"

"Lord de Winter!" cried Felton.

"Yes," said Milady, "Lord de Winter; and now you can understand it all, can you not? Buckingham remained nearly a year absent. A week before his return Lord de Winter died, leaving me his sole heir. Whence came the blow? God who knows all, knows without doubt, but as for me, I accuse nobody."

"Oh, what an abyss; what an abyss!" cried Felton.

"Lord de Winter died without revealing anything to his brother. The terrible secret was to be concealed till it burst, like a clap of thunder, over the head of the guilty. Your protector had seen with pain this marriage of his elder brother with a portionless girl. I was sensible that I could look for no support from a man disappointed in his hopes of an inheritance. I went to France, with a determination to remain there for the rest of my life. But all my fortune is in England. Communication being closed by the war,

I was in want of everything. I was then obliged to come back again. Six days ago, I landed at Portsmouth."

"Well?" said Felton.

"Well; Buckingham heard by some means, no doubt, of my return. He spoke of me to Lord de Winter, already prejudiced against me, and told him that his sister-in-law was a prostitute, a branded woman. The noble and pure voice of my husband was no longer here to defend me. Lord de Winter believed all that was told him with so much the more ease that it was his interest to believe it. He caused me to be arrested, had me conducted hither, and placed me under your guard. You know the rest. The day after tomorrow he banishes me, he transports me; the day after tomorrow he exiles me among the infamous. Oh, the train is well laid; the plot is clever. My honour will not survive it! You see, then, Felton, I can do nothing but die. Felton, give me that knife!"

And at these words, as if all her strength was exhausted, Milady sank, weak and languishing, into the arms of the young officer, who, intoxicated with love, anger, and voluptuous sensations hitherto unknown, received her with transport, pressed her against his heart, all trembling at the breath from that charming mouth, bewildered by the contact with that palpitating bosom.

"No, no," said he. "No, you shall live honoured and pure; you shall live to triumph over your enemies."

Milady put him from her slowly with her hand, while drawing him nearer with her look, but Felton, in his turn, embraced her more closely, imploring her like a divinity.

"Oh, death, death!" said she, lowering her voice and her eyelids, "oh, death, rather than shame! Felton, my brother, my friend, I conjure you!"

"No," cried Felton, "no; you shall live and you shall be avenged."

"Felton, I bring misfortune to all who surround me! Felton, abandon me! Felton, let me die!"

"Well, then, we will live and die together!" cried he, pressing his lips to those of the prisoner.

Several strokes resounded on the door; this time Milady really pushed him away from her.

"Hark," said she, "we have been overheard! Someone is coming! All is over! We are lost!"

"No," said Felton; it is only the sentinel warning me that they are about to change the guard."

"Then run to the door, and open it yourself."

Felton obeyed; this woman was now his whole thought, his whole soul.

He found himself face to face with a sergeant commanding a watch-patrol.

"Well, what is the matter?" asked the young lieutenant.

"You told me to open the door if I heard anyone cry out," said the soldier, "but you forgot to leave me the key. I heard you cry out, without understanding what you said. I tried to open the door, but it was locked inside; then I called the sergeant."

"And here I am," said the sergeant.

Felton, quite bewildered, almost mad, stood speechless.

Milady plainly perceived that it was now her turn to take part in the scene. She ran to the table, and seizing the knife which Felton had laid down, exclaimed, "And by what right will you prevent me from dying?"

"Great God!" exclaimed Felton, on seeing the knife glitter in her hand.

At that moment a burst of ironical laughter resounded through the corridor. The baron, attracted by the noise, in his chamber gown, his sword under his arm, stood in the doorway.

"Ah," said he, "here we are, at the last act of the tragedy. You see, Felton, the drama has gone through all the phases I named, but be easy, no blood will flow."

Milady perceived that all was lost unless she gave Felton an immediate and terrible proof of her courage.

"You are mistaken, my Lord, blood will flow; and may that blood fall back on those who cause it to flow!"

Felton uttered a cry, and rushed toward her. He was too late; Milady had stabbed herself.

But the knife had fortunately, we ought to say skillfully, come in contact with the steel busk, which at that period, like a cuirass, defended the chests of women. It had glided down it, tearing the robe, and had penetrated slantingly between the flesh and the ribs. Milady's robe was not the less stained with blood in a second.

Milady fell down, and seemed to be in a swoon.

Felton snatched away the knife.

"See, my Lord," said he, in a deep, gloomy tone, "here is a woman who was under my guard, and who has killed herself!"

"Be at ease, Felton," said Lord de Winter. "She is not dead; demons do not die so easily. Be tranquil, and go wait for me in my chamber."

"But, my Lord–"

"Go, Sir, I command you!"

At this injunction from his superior, Felton obeyed, but in going out, he put the knife into his bosom.

As to Lord de Winter, he contented himself with calling the woman who waited on Milady, and when she was come, he recommended the prisoner, who was still fainting, to her care, and left them alone.

Meanwhile, all things considered and notwithstanding his suspicions, as the wound might be serious, he immediately sent off a mounted man to find a physician.

Chapter 58

Escape

As Lord de Winter had thought, Milady's wound was not dangerous. So soon as she was left alone with the woman whom the baron had summoned to her assistance she opened her eyes.

It was, however, necessary to affect weakness and pain–not a very difficult task for so finished an actress as Milady. Thus the poor woman was completely the dupe of the prisoner, whom, notwithstanding her hints, she persisted in watching all night.

But the presence of this woman did not prevent Milady from thinking.

There was no longer a doubt that Felton was convinced; Felton was hers. If an angel appeared to that young man as an accuser of Milady, he would take him, in the mental disposition in which he now found himself, for a messenger sent by the devil.

Milady smiled at this thought, for Felton was now her only hope–her only means of safety.

But Lord de Winter might suspect him; Felton himself might now be watched!

Toward four o'clock in the morning the doctor arrived, but since the time Milady stabbed herself, however short, the wound had closed. The doctor could therefore measure neither the direction nor the depth of it; he only satisfied himself by Milady's pulse that the case was not serious.

In the morning Milady, under the pretext that she had not slept well in the night and wanted rest, sent away the woman who attended her.

She had one hope, which was that Felton would appear at the breakfast hour, but Felton did not come.

Were her fears realised? Was Felton, suspected by the baron, about to fail her at the decisive moment? She had only one day left. Lord de Winter had announced her embarkation for the twenty-third, and it was now the morning of the twenty-second.

Nevertheless she still waited patiently till the hour for dinner.

Although she had eaten nothing in the morning, the dinner was brought in at its usual time. Milady then perceived, with terror, that the uniform of the soldiers who guarded her was changed.

Then she ventured to ask what had become of Felton.

She was told that he had left the castle an hour before on horseback. She inquired if the baron was still at the castle. The soldier replied that he was, and that he had given orders to be informed if the prisoner wished to speak to him.

Milady replied that she was too weak at present, and that her only desire was to be left alone.

The soldier went out, leaving the dinner served.

Felton was sent away. The marines were removed. Felton was then mistrusted.

This was the last blow to the prisoner.

Left alone, she arose. The bed, which she had kept from prudence and that they might believe her seriously wounded, burned her like a bed of fire. She cast a glance at the door; the baron had had a plank nailed over the grating. He no doubt feared that by this opening she might still by some diabolical means corrupt her guards.

Milady smiled with joy. She was free now to give way to her transports without being observed. She traversed her chamber with the excitement of a furious maniac or of a tigress shut up in an iron cage. CERTES, if the knife had been left in her power, she would now have thought, not of killing herself, but of killing the baron.

At six o'clock Lord de Winter came in. He was armed at all points. This man, in whom Milady till that time had only seen a very simple gentleman, had become an admirable jailer. He appeared to foresee all, to divine all, to anticipate all.

A single look at Milady apprised him of all that was passing in her mind.

"Ay!" said he, "I see, but you shall not kill me today. You have no longer a weapon; and besides, I am on my guard. You had begun to pervert my poor Felton. He was yielding to your infernal influence, but I will save him. He will never see you again; all is over. Get your clothes together. Tomorrow you will go. I had fixed the embarkation for the twenty-fourth, but I have reflected that the more promptly the affair takes place the more sure it will be. Tomorrow, by twelve o'clock, I shall have the order for your exile, signed, BUCKINGHAM. If you speak a single word to anyone before going aboard ship, my sergeant will blow your brains out. He has orders to do so. If when on the ship you speak a single word to anyone before the captain permits you, the captain will have you thrown into the sea. That is agreed upon.

"AU REVOIR; then; that is all I have to say today. Tomorrow I will see you again, to take my leave." With these words the baron went out. Milady had listened to all this menacing tirade with a smile of disdain on her lips, but rage in her heart.

Supper was served. Milady felt that she stood in need of all her strength. She did not know what might take place during this night which approached so menacingly–for large masses of cloud rolled over the face of the sky, and distant lightning announced a storm.

The storm broke about ten o'clock. Milady felt a consolation in seeing nature partake of the disorder of her heart. The thunder growled in the air like the passion and anger in her thoughts. It appeared to her that the blast as it swept along disheveled her brow, as it bowed the branches of the trees and bore away their leaves. She howled as the hurricane howled; and her voice was lost in the great voice of nature, which also seemed to groan with despair.

All at once she heard a tap at her window, and by the help of a flash of lightning she saw the face of a man appear behind the bars.

She ran to the window and opened it.

"Felton!" cried she. "I am saved."

"Yes," said Felton, "but silence, silence! I must have time to file through these bars. Only take care that I am not seen through the wicket."

"Oh, it is a proof that the Lord is on our side, Felton," replied Milady. "They have closed up the grating with a board."

"That is well; God has made them senseless," said Felton.

"But what must I do?" asked Milady.

"Nothing, nothing, only shut the window. Go to bed, or at least lie down in your clothes. As soon as I have done I will knock on one of the panes of glass. But will you be able to follow me?"

"Oh, yes!"

"Your wound?"

"Gives me pain, but will not prevent my walking."

"Be ready, then, at the first signal."

Milady shut the window, extinguished the lamp, and went, as Felton had desired her, to lie down on the bed. Amid the moaning of the storm she heard the grinding of the file upon the bars, and by the light of every flash she perceived the shadow of Felton through the panes.

She passed an hour without breathing, panting, with a cold sweat upon her brow, and her heart oppressed by frightful agony at every movement she heard in the corridor.

There are hours which last a year.

At the expiration of an hour, Felton tapped again.

Milady sprang out of bed and opened the window. Two bars removed formed an opening for a man to pass through.

"Are you ready?" asked Felton.

"Yes. Must I take anything with me?"

"Money, if you have any."

"Yes; fortunately they have left me all I had."

"So much the better, for I have expended all mine in chartering a vessel."

"Here!" said Milady, placing a bag full of louis in Felton's hands.

Felton took the bag and threw it to the foot of the wall.

"Now," said he, "will you come?"

"I am ready."

Milady mounted upon a chair and passed the upper part of her body through the window. She saw the young officer suspended over the abyss by a ladder of ropes. For the first time an emotion of terror reminded her that she was a woman.

The dark space frightened her.

"I expected this," said Felton.

"It's nothing, it's nothing!" said Milady. "I will descend with my eyes shut."

"Have you confidence in me?" said Felton.

"You ask that?"

"Put your two hands together. Cross them; that's right!"

Felton tied her two wrists together with his handkerchief, and then with a cord over the handkerchief.

"What are you doing?" asked Milady, with surprise.

"Pass your arms around my neck, and fear nothing."

"But I shall make you lose your balance, and we shall both be dashed to pieces."

"Don't be afraid. I am a sailor."

Not a second was to be lost. Milady passed her two arms round Felton's neck, and let herself slip out of the window. Felton began to descend the ladder slowly, step by step. Despite the weight of two bodies, the blast of the hurricane shook them in the air.

All at once Felton stopped.

"What is the matter?" asked Milady.

"Silence," said Felton, "I hear footsteps."

"We are discovered!"

There was a silence of several seconds.

"No," said Felton, "it is nothing."

"But what, then, is the noise?"

"That of the patrol going their rounds."

"Where is their road?"

"Just under us."

"They will discover us!"

"No, if it does not lighten."

"But they will run against the bottom of the ladder."

"Fortunately it is too short by six feet."

"Here they are! My God!"

"Silence!"

Both remained suspended, motionless and breathless, within twenty paces of the ground, while the patrol passed beneath them laughing and talking. This was a terrible moment for the fugitives.

The patrol passed. The noise of their retreating footsteps and the murmur of their voices soon died away.

"Now," said Felton, "we are safe."

Milady breathed a deep sigh and fainted.

Felton continued to descend. Near the bottom of the ladder, when he found no more support for his feet, he clung with his hands; at length, arrived at the last step, he let himself hang by the strength of his wrists, and touched the ground. He stooped down, picked up the bag of money, and placed it between his teeth. Then he took Milady in his arms, and set off briskly in the direction opposite to that which the patrol had taken. He soon left the pathway of the patrol, descended across the rocks, and when arrived on the edge of the sea, whistled.

A similar signal replied to him; and five minutes after, a boat appeared, rowed by four men.

The boat approached as near as it could to the shore, but there was not depth enough of water for it to touch land. Felton walked into the sea up to his middle, being unwilling to trust his precious burden to anybody.

Fortunately the storm began to subside, but still the sea was disturbed. The little boat bounded over the waves like a nut-shell.

"To the sloop," said Felton, "and row quickly."

The four men bent to their oars, but the sea was too high to let them get much hold of it.

However, they left the castle behind; that was the principal thing. The night was extremely dark. It was almost impossible to see the shore from the boat; they would therefore be less likely to see the boat from the shore.

A black point floated on the sea. That was the sloop. While the boat was advancing with all the speed its four rowers could give it, Felton untied the cord and then the handkerchief which bound Milady's hands together. When her hands were loosed he took some sea water and sprinkled it over her face.

Milady breathed a sigh, and opened her eyes.

"Where am I?" said she.

"Saved!" replied the young officer.

"Oh, saved, saved!" cried she. "Yes, there is the sky; here is the sea! The air I breathe is the air of liberty! Ah, thanks, Felton, thanks!"

The young man pressed her to his heart.

"But what is the matter with my hands!" asked Milady, "it seems as if my wrists had been crushed in a vice."

Milady held out her arms; her wrists were bruised.

"Alas!" said Felton, looking at those beautiful hands, and shaking his head sorrowfully.

"Oh, it's nothing, nothing!" cried Milady. "I remember now."

Milady looked around her, as if in search of something.

"It is there," said Felton, touching the bag of money with his foot.

They drew near to the sloop. A sailor on watch hailed the boat; the boat replied.

"What vessel is that?" asked Milady.

"The one I have hired for you."

"Where will it take me?"

"Where you please, after you have put me on shore at Portsmouth."

"What are you going to do at Portsmouth?" asked Milady.

"Accomplish the orders of Lord de Winter," said Felton, with a gloomy smile.

"What orders?" asked Milady.

"You do not understand?" asked Felton.

"No; explain yourself, I beg."

"As he mistrusted me, he determined to guard you himself, and sent me in his place to get Buckingham to sign the order for your transportation."

"But if he mistrusted you, how could he confide such an order to you?"

"How could I know what I was the bearer of?"

"That's true! And you are going to Portsmouth?"

"I have no time to lose. Tomorrow is the twenty-third, and Buckingham sets sail tomorrow with his fleet."

"He sets sail tomorrow! Where for?"

"For La Rochelle."

"He need not sail!" cried Milady, forgetting her usual presence of mind.

"Be satisfied," replied Felton, "he will not sail."

Milady started with joy. She could read to the depths of the heart of this young man; the death of Buckingham was written there at full length.

"Felton," cried she, "you are as great as Judas Maccabeus! If you die, I will die with you; that is all I can say to you."

"Silence!" cried Felton, "we are here."

In fact, they touched the sloop.

Felton mounted the ladder first, and gave his hand to Milady, while the sailors supported her, for the sea was still much agitated.

An instant after they were on the deck.

"Captain," said Felton, "this is the person of whom I spoke to you, and whom you must convey safe and sound to France."

"For a thousand pistoles," said the captain.

"I have paid you five hundred of them."

"That's correct," said the captain.

"And here are the other five hundred," replied Milady, placing her hand upon the bag of gold.

"No," said the captain, "I make but one bargain; and I have agreed with this young man that the other five hundred shall not be due to me till we arrive at Boulogne."

"And shall we arrive there?"

"Safe and sound, as true as my name's Jack Butler."

"Well," said Milady, "if you keep your word, instead of five hundred, I will give you a thousand pistoles."

"Hurrah for you, then, my beautiful lady," cried the captain, "and may God often send me such passengers as your Ladyship!"

"Meanwhile," said Felton, "convey me to the little bay of–; you know it was agreed you should put in there."

The captain replied by ordering the necessary maneuvers, and toward seven o'clock in the morning the little vessel cast anchor in the bay that had been named.

During this passage, Felton related everything to Milady–how, instead of going to London, he had chartered the little vessel; how he had returned; how he had scaled the wall by fastening cramps in the interstices of the stones, as he ascended, to give him foothold; and how, when he had reached the bars, he fastened his ladder. Milady knew the rest.

On her side, Milady tried to encourage Felton in his project, but at the first words which issued from her mouth, she plainly saw that the young fanatic stood more in need of being moderated than urged.

It was agreed that Milady should wait for Felton till ten o'clock; if he did not return by ten o'clock she was to sail.

In that case, and supposing he was at liberty, he was to rejoin her in France, at the convent of the Carmelites at Bethune.

Chapter 59

What Took Place At Portsmouth August 23, 1628

Felton took leave of Milady as a brother about to go for a mere walk takes leave of his sister, kissing her hand.

His whole body appeared in its ordinary state of calmness, only an unusual fire beamed from his eyes, like the effects of a fever; his brow was more pale than it generally was; his teeth were clenched, and his speech had a short dry accent which indicated that something dark was at work within him.

As long as he remained in the boat which conveyed him to land, he kept his face toward Milady, who, standing on the deck, followed him with her eyes. Both were free from the fear of pursuit; nobody ever came into Milady's apartment before nine o'clock, and it would require three hours to go from the castle to London.

Felton jumped onshore, climbed the little ascent which led to the top of the cliff, saluted Milady a last time, and took his course toward the city.

At the end of a hundred paces, the ground began to decline, and he could only see the mast of the sloop.

He immediately ran in the direction of Portsmouth, which he saw at nearly half a league before him, standing out in the haze of the morning, with its houses and towers.

Beyond Portsmouth the sea was covered with vessels whose masts, like a forest of poplars despoiled by the winter, bent with each breath of the wind.

Felton, in his rapid walk, reviewed in his mind all the accusations against the favourite of James I and Charles I, furnished by two years of premature meditation and a long sojourn among the Puritans.

When he compared the public crimes of this minister–startling crimes, European crimes, if so we may say–with the private and unknown crimes with which Milady had charged him, Felton found that the more culpable of the two men which formed the character of Buckingham was the one of whom the public knew not the life. This was because his love, so strange, so new, and so ardent, made him view the infamous and imaginary accusations of Milady de Winter as, through a magnifying glass, one views as frightful monsters atoms in reality imperceptible by the side of an ant.

The rapidity of his walk heated his blood still more; the idea that he left behind him, exposed to a frightful vengeance, the woman he loved, or rather whom he adored as a saint, the emotion he had experienced, present fatigue–all together exalted his mind above human feeling.

He entered Portsmouth about eight o'clock in the morning. The whole population was on foot; drums were beating in the streets and in the port; the troops about to embark were marching toward the sea.

Felton arrived at the palace of the Admiralty, covered with dust, and streaming with perspiration. His countenance, usually so pale, was purple with heat and passion. The sentinel wanted to repulse him, but Felton called to the officer of the post, and drawing from his pocket the letter of which he was the bearer, he said, "A pressing message from Lord de Winter."

At the name of Lord de Winter, who was known to be one of his Grace's most intimate friends, the officer of the post gave orders to let Felton pass, who, besides, wore the uniform of a naval officer.

Felton darted into the palace.

At the moment he entered the vestibule, another man was entering likewise, dusty, out of breath, leaving at the gate a post horse, which, on reaching the palace, tumbled on his fore knees.

Felton and he addressed Patrick, the duke's confidential lackey, at the same moment. Felton named Lord de Winter; the unknown would not name anybody, and pretended that it was to the duke alone he would make himself known. Each was anxious to gain admission before the other.

Patrick, who knew Lord de Winter was in affairs of the service, and in relations of friendship with the duke, gave the preference to the one who came in his name. The other was forced to wait, and it was easily to be seen how he cursed the delay.

The valet led Felton through a large hall in which waited the deputies from La Rochelle, headed by the Prince de Soubise, and introduced him into a closet where Buckingham, just out of the bath, was finishing his toilet, upon which, as at all times, he bestowed extraordinary attention.

"Lieutenant Felton, from Lord de Winter," said Patrick.

"From Lord de Winter!" repeated Buckingham, "let him come in."

Felton entered. At that moment Buckingham was throwing upon a couch a rich toilet robe, worked with gold, in order to put on a blue velvet doublet embroidered with pearls.

"Why didn't the baron come himself?" demanded Buckingham. "I expected him this morning."

"He desired me to tell your Grace," replied Felton, "that he very much regretted not having that honour, but that he was prevented by the guard he is obliged to keep at the castle."

"Yes, I know that," said Buckingham, "he has a prisoner."

"It is of that prisoner that I wish to speak to your Grace," replied Felton.

"Well, then, speak!"

"That which I have to say of her can only be heard by yourself, my Lord!"

"Leave us, Patrick," said Buckingham, "but remain within sound of the bell. I shall call you presently."

Patrick went out.

"We are alone, Sir," said Buckingham, "speak!"

"My Lord," said Felton, "the Baron de Winter wrote to you the other day to request you to sign an order of embarkation relative to a young woman named Charlotte Backson."

"Yes, Sir; and I answered him, to bring or send me that order and I would sign it."

"Here it is, my Lord."

"Give it to me," said the duke.

And taking it from Felton, he cast a rapid glance over the paper, and perceiving that it was the one that had been mentioned to him, he placed it on the table, took a pen, and prepared to sign it.

"Pardon, my Lord," said Felton, stopping the duke, "but does your Grace know that the name of Charlotte Backson is not the true name of this young woman?"

"Yes, Sir, I know it," replied the duke, dipping the quill in the ink.

"Then your Grace knows her real name?" asked Felton, in a sharp tone.

"I know it"; and the duke put the quill to the paper. Felton grew pale.

"And knowing that real name, my Lord," replied Felton, "will you sign it all the same?"

"Doubtless," said Buckingham, "and rather twice than once."

"I cannot believe," continued Felton, in a voice that became more sharp and rough, "that your Grace knows that it is to Milady de Winter this relates."

"I know it perfectly, although I am astonished that you know it."

"And will your Grace sign that order without remorse?"

Buckingham looked at the young man haughtily.

"Do you know, Sir, that you are asking me very strange questions, and that I am very foolish to answer them?"

"Reply to them, my Lord," said Felton, "the circumstances are more serious than you perhaps believe."

Buckingham reflected that the young man, coming from Lord de Winter, undoubtedly spoke in his name, and softened.

"Without remorse," said he. "The baron knows, as well as myself, that Milady de Winter is a very guilty woman, and it is treating her very favourably to commute her punishment to transportation." The duke put his pen to the paper.

"You will not sign that order, my Lord!" said Felton, making a step toward the duke.

"I will not sign this order! And why not?"

"Because you will look into yourself, and you will do justice to the lady."

"I should do her justice by sending her to Tyburn," said Buckingham. "This lady is infamous."

"My Lord, Milady de Winter is an angel; you know that she is, and I demand her liberty of you."

"Bah! Are you mad, to talk to me thus?" said Buckingham.

"My Lord, excuse me! I speak as I can; I restrain myself. But, my Lord, think of what you're about to do, and beware of going too far!"

"What do you say? God pardon me!" cried Buckingham, "I really think he threatens me!"

"No, my Lord, I still plead. And I say to you: one drop of water suffices to make the full vase overflow; one slight fault may draw down punishment upon the head spared, despite many crimes."

"Mr. Felton," said Buckingham, "you will withdraw, and place yourself at once under arrest."

"You will hear me to the end, my Lord. You have seduced this young girl; you have outraged, defiled her. Repair your crimes toward her; let her go free, and I will exact nothing else from you."

"You will exact!" said Buckingham, looking at Felton with astonishment, and dwelling upon each syllable of the three words as he pronounced them.

"My Lord," continued Felton, becoming more excited as he spoke, "my Lord, beware! All England is tired of your iniquities; my Lord, you have abused the royal power, which you have almost usurped; my Lord, you are held in horror by God and men. God will punish you hereafter, but I will punish you here!"

"Ah, this is too much!" cried Buckingham, making a step toward the door.

Felton barred his passage.

"I ask it humbly of you, my Lord," said he, "sign the order for the liberation of Milady de Winter. Remember that she is a woman whom you have dishonoured."

"Withdraw, Sir," said Buckingham, "or I will call my attendant, and have you placed in irons."

"You shall not call," said Felton, throwing himself between the duke and the bell placed on a stand encrusted with silver. "Beware, my Lord, you are in the hands of God!"

"In the hands of the devil, you mean!" cried Buckingham, raising his voice so as to attract the notice of his people, without absolutely shouting.

"Sign, my Lord; sign the liberation of Milady de Winter," said Felton, holding out a paper to the duke.

"By force? You are joking! Holloa, Patrick!"

"Sign, my Lord!"

"Never."

"Never?"

"Help!" shouted the duke; and at the same time he sprang toward his sword.

But Felton did not give him time to draw it. He held the knife with which Milady had stabbed herself, open in his bosom; at one bound he was upon the duke.

At that moment Patrick entered the room, crying, "A letter from France, my Lord."

"From France!" cried Buckingham, forgetting everything in thinking from whom that letter came.

Felton took advantage of this moment, and plunged the knife into his side up to the handle.

"Ah, traitor," cried Buckingham, "you have killed me!"

"Murder!" screamed Patrick.

Felton cast his eyes round for means of escape, and seeing the door free, he rushed into the next chamber, in which, as we have said, the deputies from La Rochelle were waiting, crossed it as quickly as possible, and rushed toward the staircase, but upon the first step he met Lord de Winter, who, seeing him pale, confused, livid, and stained with blood both on his hands and face, seized him by the throat, crying, "I knew it! I guessed it! But too late by a minute, unfortunate, unfortunate that I am!"

Felton made no resistance. Lord de Winter placed him in the hands of the guards, who led him, while awaiting further orders, to a little terrace commanding the sea; and then the baron hastened to the duke's chamber.

At the cry uttered by the duke and the scream of Patrick, the man whom Felton had met in the antechamber rushed into the chamber.

He found the duke reclining upon a sofa, with his hand pressed upon the wound.

"Laporte," said the duke, in a dying voice, "Laporte, do you come from her?"

"Yes, Monseigneur," replied the faithful cloak bearer of Anne of Austria, "but too late, perhaps."

"Silence, Laporte, you may be overheard. Patrick, let no one enter. Oh, I cannot tell what she says to me! My God, I am dying!"

And the duke swooned.

Meanwhile, Lord de Winter, the deputies, the leaders of the expedition, the officers of Buckingham's household, had all made their way into the chamber. Cries of despair resounded on all sides. The news, which filled the palace with tears and groans, soon became known, and spread itself throughout the city.

The report of a cannon announced that something new and unexpected had taken place.

Lord de Winter tore his hair.

"Too late by a minute!" cried he, "too late by a minute! Oh, my God, my God! What a misfortune!"

He had been informed at seven o'clock in the morning that a rope ladder floated from one of the windows of the castle; he had hastened to Milady's chamber, had found it empty, the window open, and the bars filed, had remembered the verbal caution d'Artagnan had transmitted to him by his messenger, had trembled for the duke, and running to the stable without taking time to have a horse saddled, had jumped upon the first he found, had galloped off like the wind, had alighted below in the courtyard, had ascended the stairs precipitately, and on the top step, as we have said, had encountered Felton.

The duke, however, was not dead. He recovered a little, reopened his eyes, and hope revived in all hearts.

"Gentlemen," said he, "leave me alone with Patrick and Laporte–ah, is that you, de Winter? You sent me a strange madman this morning! See the state in which he has put me."

"Oh, my Lord!" cried the baron, "I shall never console myself."

"And you would be quite wrong, my dear de Winter," said Buckingham, holding out his hand to him. "I do not know the man who deserves being regretted during the whole life of another man, but leave us, I pray you."

The baron went out sobbing.

There only remained in the closet of the wounded duke Laporte and Patrick. A physician was sought for, but none was yet found.

"You will live, my Lord, you will live!" repeated the faithful servant of Anne of Austria, on his knees before the duke's sofa.

"What has she written to me?" said Buckingham, feebly, streaming with blood, and suppressing his agony to speak of her he loved, "what has she written to me? Read me her letter."

"Oh, my Lord!" said Laporte.

"Obey, Laporte, do you not see I have no time to lose?"

Laporte broke the seal, and placed the paper before the eyes of the duke, but Buckingham in vain tried to make out the writing.

"Read!" said he, "read! I cannot see. Read, then! For soon, perhaps, I shall not hear, and I shall die without knowing what she has written to me."

Laporte made no further objection, and read:

"My Lord, By that which, since I have known you, have suffered by you and for you, I conjure you, if you have any care for my repose, to countermand those great armaments which you are preparing against France, to put an end to a war of which it is publicly said religion is the ostensible cause, and of which, it is generally whispered, your love for me is the concealed cause. This war may not only bring great catastrophes upon England and France, but misfortune upon you, my Lord, for which I should never console myself.

"Be careful of your life, which is menaced, and which will be dear to me from the moment I am not obliged to see an enemy in you.

"Your affectionate

"ANNE"

Buckingham collected all his remaining strength to listen to the reading of the letter; then, when it was ended, as if he had met with a bitter disappointment, he asked, "Have you nothing else to say to me by the living voice, Laporte?"

"The queen charged me to tell you to watch over yourself, for she had advice that your assassination would be attempted."

"And is that all–is that all?" replied Buckingham, impatiently.

"She likewise charged me to tell you that she still loved you."

"Ah," said Buckingham, "God be praised! My death, then, will not be to her as the death of a stranger!"

Laporte burst into tears.

"Patrick," said the duke, "bring me the casket in which the diamond studs were kept."

Patrick brought the object desired, which Laporte recognised as having belonged to the queen.

"Now the scent bag of white satin, on which her cipher is embroidered in pearls."

Patrick again obeyed.

"Here, Laporte," said Buckingham, "these are the only tokens I ever received from her–this silver casket and these two letters. You will restore them to her Majesty; and as a last memorial"–he looked round for some valuable object–"you will add–"

He still sought, but his eyes, darkened by death, encountered only the knife which had fallen from the hand of Felton, still smoking with the blood spread over its blade.

"And you will add to them this knife," said the duke, pressing the hand of Laporte. He had just strength enough to place the scent bag at the bottom of the silver casket, and to let the knife fall into it, making a sign to Laporte that he was no longer able to speak; then, in a last convulsion, which this time he had not the power to combat, he slipped from the sofa to the floor.

Patrick uttered a loud cry.

Buckingham tried to smile a last time, but death checked his thought, which remained engraved on his brow like a last kiss of love.

At this moment the duke's surgeon arrived, quite terrified; he was already on board the admiral's ship, where they had been obliged to seek him.

He approached the duke, took his hand, held it for an instant in his own, and letting it fall, "All is useless," said he, "he is dead."

"Dead, dead!" cried Patrick.

At this cry all the crowd re-entered the apartment, and throughout the palace and town there was nothing but consternation and tumult.

As soon as Lord de Winter saw Buckingham was dead, he ran to Felton, whom the soldiers still guarded on the terrace of the palace.

"Wretch!" said he to the young man, who since the death of Buckingham had regained that coolness and self-possession which never after abandoned him, "wretch! What have you done?"

"I have avenged myself!" said he.

"Avenged yourself," said the baron. "Rather say that you have served as an instrument to that accursed woman, but I swear to you that this crime shall be her last."

"I don't know what you mean," replied Felton, quietly, "and I am ignorant of whom you are speaking, my Lord. I killed the Duke of Buckingham because he twice refused you yourself to appoint me captain; I have punished him for his injustice, that is all."

De Winter, stupefied, looked on while the soldiers bound Felton, and could not tell what to think of such insensibility.

One thing alone, however, threw a shade over the pallid brow of Felton. At every noise he heard, the simple Puritan fancied he recognised the step and voice of Milady coming to throw herself into his arms, to accuse herself, and die with him.

All at once he started. His eyes became fixed upon a point of the sea, commanded by the terrace where he was. With the eagle glance of a sailor he had recognised there, where another would have seen only a gull hovering over the waves, the sail of a sloop which was directed toward the coast of France.

He grew deadly pale, placed his hand upon his heart, which was breaking, and at once perceived all the treachery.

"One last favour, my Lord!" said he to the baron.

"What?" asked his Lordship.

"What o'clock is it?"

The baron drew out his watch. "It wants ten minutes to nine," said he.

Milady had hastened her departure by an hour and a half. As soon as she heard the cannon which announced the fatal event, she had ordered the anchor to be weighed. The vessel was making way under a blue sky, at great distance from the coast.

"God has so willed it!" said he, with the resignation of a fanatic, but without, however, being able to take his eyes from that ship, on board of which he doubtless fancied he could distinguish the white outline of her to whom he had sacrificed his life.

De Winter followed his look, observed his feelings, and guessed all.

"Be punished ALONE, for the first, miserable man!" said Lord de Winter to Felton, who was being dragged away with his eyes turned toward the sea, "but I swear to you by the memory of my brother whom I have loved so much that your accomplice is not saved."

Felton lowered his head without pronouncing a syllable.

As to Lord de Winter, he descended the stairs rapidly, and went straight to the port.

Chapter 60

In France

The first fear of the King of England, Charles I, on learning of the death of the duke, was that such terrible news might discourage the Rochellais; he tried, says Richelieu in his Memoirs, to conceal it from them as long as possible, closing all the ports of his kingdom, and carefully keeping watch that no vessel should sail until the army which Buckingham was getting together had gone, taking upon himself, in default of Buckingham, to superintend the departure.

He carried the strictness of this order so far as to detain in England the ambassadors of Denmark, who had taken their leave, and the regular ambassador of Holland, who was to take back to the port of Flushing the Indian merchantmen of which Charles I had made restitution to the United Provinces.

But as he did not think of giving this order till five hours after the event–that is to say, till two o'clock in the afternoon–two vessels had already left the port, the one bearing, as we know, Milady, who, already anticipating the event, was further confirmed in that belief by seeing the black flag flying at the masthead of the admiral's ship.

As to the second vessel, we will tell hereafter whom it carried, and how it set sail.

During this time nothing new occurred in the camp at La Rochelle; only the king, who was bored, as always, but perhaps a little more so in camp than elsewhere, resolved to go incognito and spend the festival of St. Louis at St. Germain, and asked the cardinal to order him an escort of only twenty Musketeers. The cardinal, who sometimes became weary of the king, granted this leave of absence with great pleasure to his royal lieutenant, who promised to return about the fifteenth of September.

M. de Tréville, being informed of this by his Eminence, packed his portmanteau; and as without knowing the cause he knew the great desire and even imperative need which his friends had of returning to Paris, it goes without saying that he fixed upon them to form part of the escort.

The four young men heard the news a quarter of an hour after M. de Tréville, for they were the first to whom he communicated it. It was then that d'Artagnan appreciated the favour the cardinal had conferred upon him in making him at last enter the Musketeers–for without that circumstance he would have been forced to remain in the camp while his companions left it.

It goes without saying that this impatience to return toward Paris had for a cause the danger which Mme. Bonacieux would run of meeting at the convent of Bethune with Milady, her mortal enemy. Aramis therefore had written immediately to Marie Michon, the seamstress at Tours who had such fine acquaintances, to obtain from the queen authority for Mme. Bonacieux to leave the convent, and to retire either into Lorraine or Belgium. They had not long to wait for an answer. Eight or ten days afterward Aramis received the following letter:

"My Dear Cousin,

"Here is the authorisation from my sister to withdraw our little servant from the convent of Bethune, the air of which you think is bad for her. My sister sends you this authorisation with great pleasure, for she is very partial to the little girl, to whom she intends to be more serviceable hereafter.

"I salute you,

"MARIE MICHON"

To this letter was added an order, conceived in these terms:

"At the Louvre, August 10, 1628

"The superior of the convent of Bethune will place in the hands of the person who shall present this note to her the novice who entered the convent upon my recommendation and under my patronage.

"ANNE"

It may be easily imagined how the relationship between Aramis and a seamstress who called the queen her sister amused the young men, but Aramis, after having blushed two or three times up to the whites of his eyes at the gross pleasantry of Porthos, begged his friends not to revert to the subject again, declaring that if a single word more was said to him about it, he would never again implore his cousins to interfere in such affairs.

There was no further question, therefore, about Marie Michon among the four Musketeers, who besides had what they wanted: that was, the order to withdraw Mme. Bonacieux from the convent of the Carmelites of Bethune. It was true that this order would not be of great use to them while they were in camp at La Rochelle; that is to say, at the other end of France. Therefore d'Artagnan was going to ask leave of absence of M. de Tréville, confiding to him candidly the importance of his departure, when the news was transmitted to him as well as to his three friends that the king was about to set out for Paris with an escort of twenty Musketeers, and that they formed part of the escort.

Their joy was great. The lackeys were sent on before with the baggage, and they set out on the morning of the sixteenth.

The cardinal accompanied his Majesty from Surgères to Mauzes; and there the king and his minister took leave of each other with great demonstrations of friendship.

The king, however, who sought distraction, while travelling as fast as possible–for he was anxious to be in Paris by the twenty-third–stopped from time to time to fly the magpie, a pastime for which the taste had been formerly inspired in him by de Luynes, and for which he had always preserved a great predilection. Out of the twenty Musketeers sixteen, when this took place, rejoiced greatly at this relaxation, but the other four cursed it heartily. D'Artagnan, in particular, had a perpetual buzzing in his ears, which Porthos explained thus: "A very great lady has told me that this means that somebody is talking of you somewhere."

At length the escort passed through Paris on the twenty-third, in the night. The king thanked M. de Tréville, and permitted him to distribute furloughs for four days, on condition that the favoured parties should not appear in any public place, under penalty of the Bastille.

The first four furloughs granted, as may be imagined, were to our four friends. Still further, Athos obtained of M. de Tréville six days instead of four, and introduced into these six days two more nights–for they set out on the twenty-fourth at five o'clock in the evening, and as a further kindness M. de Tréville post-dated the leave to the morning of the twenty-fifth.

"Good Lord!" said d'Artagnan, who, as we have often said, never stumbled at anything. "It appears to me that we are making a great trouble of a very simple thing. In two days, and by using up two or three horses (that's nothing; I have plenty of money), I am at Bethune. I present my letter from the queen to the superior, and I bring back the dear treasure I go to seek–not into Lorraine, not into Belgium, but to Paris, where she will be much better concealed, particularly while the cardinal is at La Rochelle. Well, once returned from the country, half by the protection of her cousin, half through what we have personally done for her, we shall obtain from the queen what we desire. Remain, then, where you are, and do not exhaust yourselves with useless fatigue. Myself and Planchet are all that such a simple expedition requires."

To this Athos replied quietly: "We also have money left–for I have not yet drunk all my share of the diamond, and Porthos and Aramis have not eaten all theirs. We can therefore use up four horses as well as one. But consider, d'Artagnan," added he, in a tone so solemn that it made the young man shudder, "consider that Bethune is a city where the cardinal has given rendezvous to a woman who, wherever she goes, brings misery with her. If you had only to deal with four men, d'Artagnan, I would allow you to go alone. You have to do with that woman! We four will go; and I hope to God that with our four lackeys we may be in sufficient number."

"You terrify me, Athos!" cried d'Artagnan. "My God! What do you fear?"

"Everything!" replied Athos.

D'Artagnan examined the countenances of his companions, which, like that of Athos, wore an impression of deep anxiety; and they continued their route as fast as their horses could carry them, but without adding another word.

On the evening of the twenty-fifth, as they were entering Arras, and as d'Artagnan was dismounting at the inn of the Golden Harrow to drink a glass of wine, a horseman came out of the post yard, where he had just had a relay, started off at a gallop, and with a fresh horse took the road to Paris. At the moment he passed through the gateway into the street, the wind blew open the cloak in which he was wrapped, although it was in the month of August, and lifted his hat, which the traveller seized with his hand the moment it had left his head, pulling it eagerly over his eyes.

D'Artagnan, who had his eyes fixed upon this man, became very pale, and let his glass fall.

"What is the matter, Monsieur?" said Planchet. "Oh, come, gentlemen, my master is ill!"

The three friends hastened toward d'Artagnan, who, instead of being ill, ran toward his horse. They stopped him at the door.

"Well, where the devil are you going now?" cried Athos.

"It is he!" cried d'Artagnan, pale with anger, and with the sweat on his brow, "it is he! Let me overtake him!"

"He? What he?" asked Athos.

"He, that man!"

"What man?"

"That cursed man, my evil genius, whom I have always met with when threatened by some misfortune, he who accompanied that horrible woman when I met her for the first time, he whom I was seeking when I offended our Athos, he whom I saw on the very morning Madame Bonacieux was abducted. I have seen him; that is he! I recognised him when the wind blew upon his cloak."

"The devil!" said Athos, musingly.

"To saddle, gentlemen! To saddle! Let us pursue him, and we shall overtake him!"

"My dear friend," said Aramis, "remember that he goes in an opposite direction from that in which we are going, that he has a fresh horse, and ours are fatigued, so that we shall disable our own horses without even a chance of overtaking him. Let the man go, d'Artagnan; let us save the woman."

"Monsieur, Monsieur!" cried a hostler, running out and looking after the stranger, "monsieur, here is a paper which dropped out of your hat! Eh, Monsieur, eh!"

"Friend," said d'Artagnan, "a half-pistole for that paper!"

"My faith, Monsieur, with great pleasure! Here it is!"

The hostler, enchanted with the good day's work he had done, returned to the yard. D'Artagnan unfolded the paper.

"Well?" eagerly demanded all his three friends.

"Nothing but one word!" said d'Artagnan.

"Yes," said Aramis, "but that one word is the name of some town or village."

"Armentières," read Porthos, "Armentières? I don't know such a place."

"And that name of a town or village is written in her hand!" cried Athos.

"Come on, come on!" said d'Artagnan, "let us keep that paper carefully, perhaps I have not thrown away my half-pistole. To horse, my friends, to horse!"

And the four friends flew at a gallop along the road to Bethune.

Chapter 61

The Carmelite Convent At Bethune

Great criminals bear about them a kind of predestination which makes them surmount all obstacles, which makes them escape all dangers, up to the moment which a wearied Providence has marked as the rock of their impious fortunes.

It was thus with Milady. She escaped the cruisers of both nations, and arrived at Boulogne without accident.

When landing at Portsmouth, Milady was an Englishwoman whom the persecutions of the French drove from La Rochelle; when landing at Boulogne, after a two days' passage, she passed for a Frenchwoman whom the English persecuted at Portsmouth out of their hatred for France.

Milady had, likewise, the best of passports–her beauty, her noble appearance, and the liberality with which she distributed her pistoles. Freed from the usual formalities by the affable smile and gallant manners of an old governor of the port, who kissed her hand, she only remained long enough at Boulogne to put into the post a letter, conceived in the following terms:

To his Eminence Monseigneur the Cardinal Richelieu, in his camp before La Rochelle.

Monseigneur,

Let your Eminence be reassured. His Grace the Duke of Buckingham WILL NOT SET OUT for France.

MILADY DE —

BOULOGNE, evening of the twenty-fifth.

P.S.–According to the desire of your Eminence, I report to the convent of the Carmelites at Bethune, where I will await your orders.

Accordingly, that same evening Milady commenced her journey. Night overtook her; she stopped, and slept at an inn. At five o'clock the next morning she again proceeded, and in three hours after entered Bethune. She inquired for the convent of the Carmelites, and went thither immediately.

The superior met her; Milady showed her the cardinal's order. The abbess assigned her a chamber, and had breakfast served.

All the past was effaced from the eyes of this woman; and her looks, fixed on the future, beheld nothing but the high fortunes reserved for her by the cardinal, whom she had so successfully served without his name being in any way mixed up with the sanguinary affair. The ever-new passions which consumed her gave to her life the appearance of those clouds which float in the heavens, reflecting sometimes azure, sometimes fire, sometimes the opaque blackness of the tempest, and which leave no traces upon the earth behind them but devastation and death.

After breakfast, the abbess came to pay her a visit. There is very little amusement in the cloister, and the good superior was eager to make the acquaintance of her new boarder.

Milady wished to please the abbess. This was a very easy matter for a woman so really superior as she was. She tried to be agreeable, and she was charming, winning the good superior by her varied conversation and by the graces of her whole personality.

The abbess, who was the daughter of a noble house, took particular delight in stories of the court, which so seldom travel to the extremities of the kingdom, and which, above all, have so much difficulty in penetrating the walls of convents, at whose threshold the noise of the world dies away.

Milady, on the contrary, was quite conversant with all aristocratic intrigues, amid which she had constantly lived for five or six years. She made it her business, therefore, to amuse the good abbess with the worldly practices of the court of France, mixed with the eccentric pursuits of the king; she made for her the scandalous chronicle of the lords and ladies of the court, whom the abbess knew perfectly by name, touched lightly on the amours of the queen and the Duke of Buckingham, talking a great deal to induce her auditor to talk a little.

But the abbess contented herself with listening and smiling without replying a word. Milady, however, saw that this sort of narrative amused her very much, and kept at it; only she now let her conversation drift toward the cardinal.

But she was greatly embarrassed. She did not know whether the abbess was a royalist or a cardinalist; she therefore confined herself to a prudent middle course. But the abbess, on her part, maintained a reserve still more prudent, contenting herself with making a profound inclination of the head every time the fair traveller pronounced the name of his Eminence.

Milady began to think she should soon grow weary of a convent life; she resolved, then, to risk something in order that she might know how to act afterward. Desirous of seeing how far the discretion of the good abbess would go, she began to tell a story, obscure at first, but very circumstantial afterward, about the cardinal, relating the amours of the minister with Mme. d'Aiguillon, Marion de Lorme, and several other gay women.

The abbess listened more attentively, grew animated by degrees, and smiled.

"Good," thought Milady, "she takes a pleasure in my conversation. If she is a cardinalist, she has no fanaticism, at least."

She then went on to describe the persecutions exercised by the cardinal upon his enemies. The abbess only crossed herself, without approving or disapproving.

This confirmed Milady in her opinion that the abbess was rather royalist than cardinalist. Milady therefore continued, colouring her narrations more and more.

"I am very ignorant of these matters," said the abbess, at length, "but however distant from the court we may be, however remote from the interests of the world we may be placed, we have very sad examples of what you have related. And one of our boarders has suffered much from the vengeance and persecution of the cardinal!"

"One of your boarders?" said Milady, "oh, my God! Poor woman! I pity her, then."

"And you have reason, for she is much to be pitied. Imprisonment, menaces, ill treatment-she has suffered everything. But after all," resumed the abbess, "Monsieur Cardinal has perhaps plausible motives for acting thus; and though she has the look of an angel, we must not always judge people by the appearance."

"Good!" said Milady to herself, "who knows! I am about, perhaps, to discover something here; I am in the vein."

She tried to give her countenance an appearance of perfect candor.

"Alas," said Milady, "I know it is so. It is said that we must not trust to the face, but in what, then, shall we place confidence, if not in the most beautiful work of the Lord? As for me, I shall be deceived all my life perhaps, but I shall always have faith in a person whose countenance inspires me with sympathy."

"You would, then, be tempted to believe," said the abbess, "that this young person is innocent?"

"The cardinal pursues not only crimes," said she: "there are certain virtues which he pursues more severely than certain offenses."

"Permit me, Madame, to express my surprise," said the abbess.

"At what?" said Milady, with the utmost ingenuousness.

"At the language you use."

"What do you find so astonishing in that language?" said Milady, smiling.

"You are the friend of the cardinal, for he sends you hither, and yet–"

"And yet I speak ill of him," replied Milady, finishing the thought of the superior.

"At least you don't speak well of him."

"That is because I am not his friend," said she, sighing, "but his victim!"

"But this letter in which he recommends you to me?"

"Is an order for me to confine myself to a sort of prison, from which he will release me by one of his satellites."

"But why have you not fled?"

"Whither should I go? Do you believe there is a spot on the earth which the cardinal cannot reach if he takes the trouble to stretch forth his hand? If I were a man, that would barely be possible, but what can a woman do? This young boarder of yours, has she tried to fly?"

"No, that is true, but she–that is another thing; I believe she is detained in France by some love affair."

"Ah," said Milady, with a sigh, "if she loves she is not altogether wretched."

"Then," said the abbess, looking at Milady with increasing interest, "I behold another poor victim?"

"Alas, yes," said Milady.

The abbess looked at her for an instant with uneasiness, as if a fresh thought suggested itself to her mind.

"You are not an enemy of our holy faith?" said she, hesitatingly.

"Who–I?" cried Milady, "I a Protestant? Oh, no! I call to witness the God who hears us, that on the contrary I am a fervent Catholic!"

"Then, Madame," said the abbess, smiling, "be reassured; the house in which you are shall not be a very hard prison, and we will do all in our power to make you cherish your captivity. You will find here, moreover, the young woman of whom I spoke, who is persecuted, no doubt, in consequence of some court intrigue. She is amiable and well-behaved."

"What is her name?"

"She was sent to me by someone of high rank, under the name of Kitty. I have not tried to discover her other name."

"Kitty!" cried Milady. "What? Are you sure?"

"That she is called so? Yes, Madame. Do you know her?"

Milady smiled to herself at the idea which had occurred to her that this might be her old chambermaid. There was connected with the remembrance of this girl a remembrance of anger; and a desire of vengeance disordered the features of Milady, which, however, immediately recovered the calm and benevolent expression which this woman of a hundred faces had for a moment allowed them to lose.

"And when can I see this young lady, for whom I already feel so great a sympathy?" asked Milady.

"Why, this evening," said the abbess, "today even. But you have been travelling these four days, as you told me yourself. This morning you rose at five o'clock; you must stand in need of repose. Go to bed and sleep; at dinnertime we will rouse you."

Although Milady would very willingly have gone without sleep, sustained as she was by all the excitements which a new adventure awakened in her heart, ever thirsting for intrigues, she nevertheless accepted the offer of the superior. During the last fifteen days she had experienced so many and such various emotions that if her frame of iron was still capable of supporting fatigue, her mind required repose.

She therefore took leave of the abbess, and went to bed, softly rocked by the ideas of vengeance which the name of Kitty had naturally brought to her thoughts. She remembered that almost unlimited promise which the cardinal had given her if she succeeded in her enterprise. She had succeeded; d'Artagnan was then in her power!

One thing alone frightened her; that was the remembrance of her husband, the Comte de la Fere, whom she had believed dead, or at least expatriated, and whom she found again in Athos-the best friend of d'Artagnan.

But alas, if he was the friend of d'Artagnan, he must have lent him his assistance in all the proceedings by whose aid the queen had defeated the project of his Eminence; if he was the friend of d'Artagnan, he was the enemy of the cardinal; and she doubtless would succeed in involving him in the vengeance by which she hoped to destroy the young Musketeer.

All these hopes were so many sweet thoughts for Milady; so, rocked by them, she soon fell asleep.

She was awakened by a soft voice which sounded at the foot of her bed. She opened her eyes, and saw the abbess, accompanied by a young woman with light hair and delicate complexion, who fixed upon her a look full of benevolent curiosity.

The face of the young woman was entirely unknown to her. Each examined the other with great attention, while exchanging the customary compliments; both were very handsome, but of quite different styles of beauty. Milady, however, smiled in observing that she excelled the young woman by far in her high air and aristocratic bearing. It is true that the habit of a novice, which the young woman wore, was not very advantageous in a contest of this kind.

The abbess introduced them to each other. When this formality was ended, as her duties called her to chapel, she left the two young women alone.

The novice, seeing Milady in bed, was about to follow the example of the superior, but Milady stopped her.

"How, Madame," said she, "I have scarcely seen you, and you already wish to deprive me of your company, upon which I had counted a little, I must confess, for the time I have to pass here?"

"No, Madame," replied the novice, "only I thought I had chosen my time ill; you were asleep, you are fatigued."

"Well," said Milady, "what can those who sleep wish for–a happy awakening? This awakening you have given me; allow me, then, to enjoy it at my ease," and taking her hand, she drew her toward the armchair by the bedside.

The novice sat down.

"How unfortunate I am!" said she, "I have been here six months without the shadow of recreation. You arrive, and your presence was likely to afford me delightful company; yet I expect, in all probability, to quit the convent at any moment."

"How, you are going soon?" asked Milady.

"At least I hope so," said the novice, with an expression of joy which she made no effort to disguise.

"I think I learned you had suffered persecutions from the cardinal," continued Milady, "that would have been another motive for sympathy between us."

"What I have heard, then, from our good mother is true; you have likewise been a victim of that wicked priest."

"Hush!" said Milady, "let us not, even here, speak thus of him. All my misfortunes arise from my having said nearly what you have said before a woman whom I thought my friend, and who betrayed me. Are you also the victim of a treachery?"

"No," said the novice, "but of my devotion–of a devotion to a woman I loved, for whom I would have laid down my life, for whom I would give it still."

"And who has abandoned you–is that it?"

"I have been sufficiently unjust to believe so, but during the last two or three days I have obtained proof to the contrary, for which I thank God–for it would have cost me very dear to think she had forgotten me. But you, Madame, you appear to be free," continued the novice, "and if you were inclined to fly it only rests with yourself to do so."

"Whither would you have me go, without friends, without money, in a part of France with which I am unacquainted, and where I have never been before?"

"Oh," cried the novice, "as to friends, you would have them wherever you want, you appear so good and are so beautiful!"

"That does not prevent," replied Milady, softening her smile so as to give it an angelic expression, "my being alone or being persecuted."

"Hear me," said the novice, "we must trust in heaven. There always comes a moment when the good you have done pleads your cause before God; and see, perhaps it is a happiness for you, humble and powerless as I am, that you have met with me, for if I leave this place, well-I have powerful friends, who, after having exerted themselves on my account, may also exert themselves for you."

"Oh, when I said I was alone," said Milady, hoping to make the novice talk by talking of herself, "it is not for want of friends in high places, but these friends themselves tremble before the cardinal. The queen herself does not dare to oppose the terrible minister. I have proof that her Majesty, notwithstanding her excellent heart, has more than once been obliged to abandon to the anger of his Eminence persons who had served her."

"Trust me, Madame; the queen may appear to have abandoned those persons, but we must not put faith in appearances. The more they are persecuted, the more she thinks of them; and often, when they least expect it, they have proof of a kind remembrance."

"Alas!" said Milady, "I believe so; the queen is so good!"

"Oh, you know her, then, that lovely and noble queen, that you speak of her thus!" cried the novice, with enthusiasm.

"That is to say," replied Milady, driven into her entrenchment, "that I have not the honour of knowing her personally, but I know a great number of her most intimate friends. I am acquainted with Monsieur de Putange; I met Monsieur Dujart in England; I know Monsieur de Tréville."

"Monsieur de Tréville!" exclaimed the novice, "do you know Monsieur de Tréville?"

"Yes, perfectly well–intimately even."

"The captain of the king's Musketeers?"

"The captain of the king's Musketeers."

"Why, then, only see!" cried the novice, "we shall soon be well acquainted, almost friends. If you know Monsieur de Tréville, you must have visited him?"

"Often!" said Milady, who, having entered this track, and perceiving that falsehood succeeded, was determined to follow it to the end.

"With him, then, you must have seen some of his Musketeers?"

"All those he is in the habit of receiving!" replied Milady, for whom this conversation began to have a real interest.

"Name a few of those whom you know, and you will see if they are my friends."

"Well!" said Milady, embarrassed, "I know Monsieur de Louvigny, Monsieur de Courtivron, Monsieur de Ferussac."

The novice let her speak, then seeing that she paused, she said, "Don't you know a gentleman named Athos?"

Milady became as pale as the sheets in which she was lying, and mistress as she was of herself, could not help uttering a cry, seizing the hand of the novice, and devouring her with looks.

"What is the matter? Good God!" asked the poor woman, "have I said anything that has wounded you?"

"No, but the name struck me, because I also have known that gentleman, and it appeared strange to me to meet with a person who appears to know him well."

"Oh, yes, very well; not only him, but some of his friends, Messieurs Porthos and Aramis!"

"Indeed! You know them likewise? I know them," cried Milady, who began to feel a chill penetrate her heart.

"Well, if you know them, you know that they are good and free companions. Why do you not apply to them, if you stand in need of help?"

"That is to say," stammered Milady, "I am not really very intimate with any of them. I know them from having heard one of their friends, Monsieur d'Artagnan, say a great deal about them."

"You know Monsieur d'Artagnan!" cried the novice, in her turn seizing the hands of Milady and devouring her with her eyes.

Then remarking the strange expression of Milady's countenance, she said, "Pardon me, Madame; you know him by what title?"

"Why," replied Milady, embarrassed, "why, by the title of friend."

"You deceive me, Madame," said the novice, "you have been his mistress!"

"It is you who have been his mistress, Madame!" cried Milady, in her turn.

"I?" said the novice.

"Yes, you! I know you now. You are Madame Bonacieux!"

The young woman drew back, filled with surprise and terror.

"Oh, do not deny it! Answer!" continued Milady.

"Well, yes, Madame," said the novice, "Are we rivals?"

The countenance of Milady was illumined by so savage a joy that under any other circumstances Mme. Bonacieux would have fled in terror, but she was absorbed by jealousy.

"Speak, Madame!" resumed Mme. Bonacieux, with an energy of which she might not have been believed capable. "Have you been, or are you, his mistress?"

"Oh, no!" cried Milady, with an accent that admitted no doubt of her truth. "Never, never!"

"I believe you," said Mme. Bonacieux, "but why, then, did you cry out so?"

"Do you not understand?" said Milady, who had already overcome her agitation and recovered all her presence of mind.

"How can I understand? I know nothing."

"Can you not understand that Monsieur d'Artagnan, being my friend, might take me into his confidence?"

"Truly?"

"Do you not perceive that I know all–your abduction from the little house at St. Germain, his despair, that of his friends, and their useless inquiries up to this moment? How could I help being astonished when, without having the least expectation of such a thing, I meet you face to face–you, of whom we have so often spoken together, you whom he loves with all his soul, you whom he had taught me to love before I had seen you! Ah, dear Constance, I have found you, then; I see you at last!"

And Milady stretched out her arms to Mme. Bonacieux, who, convinced by what she had just said, saw nothing in this woman whom an instant before she had believed her rival but a sincere and devoted friend.

"Oh, pardon me, pardon me!" cried she, sinking upon the shoulders of Milady. "Pardon me, I love him so much!"

These two women held each other for an instant in a close embrace. Certainly, if Milady's strength had been equal to her hatred, Mme. Bonacieux would never have left that embrace alive. But not being able to stifle her, she smiled upon her.

"Oh, you beautiful, good little creature!" said Milady. "How delighted I am to have found you! Let me look at you!" And while saying these words, she absolutely devoured her by her looks. "Oh, yes it is you indeed! From what he has told me, I know you now. I recognise you perfectly."

The poor young woman could not possibly suspect what frightful cruelty was behind the rampart of that pure brow, behind those brilliant eyes in which she read nothing but interest and compassion.

"Then you know what I have suffered," said Mme. Bonacieux, "since he has told you what he has suffered, but to suffer for him is happiness."

Milady replied mechanically, "Yes, that is happiness." She was thinking of something else.

"And then," continued Mme. Bonacieux, "my punishment is drawing to a close. Tomorrow, this evening, perhaps, I shall see him again; and then the past will no longer exist."

"This evening?" asked Milady, roused from her reverie by these words. "What do you mean? Do you expect news from him?"

"I expect himself."

"Himself? D'Artagnan here?"

"Himself!"

"But that's impossible! He is at the siege of La Rochelle with the cardinal. He will not return till after the taking of the city."

"Ah, you fancy so! But is there anything impossible for my d'Artagnan, the noble and loyal gentleman?"

"Oh, I cannot believe you!"

"Well, read, then!" said the unhappy young woman, in the excess of her pride and joy, presenting a letter to Milady.

"The writing of Madame de Chevreuse!" said Milady to herself. "Ah, I always thought there was some secret understanding in that quarter!" And she greedily read the following few lines:

My Dear Child, Hold yourself ready. OUR FRIEND will see you soon, and he will only see you to release you from that imprisonment in which your safety required you should be concealed. Prepare, then, for your departure, and never despair of us.

Our charming Gascon has just proved himself as brave and faithful as ever. Tell him that certain parties are grateful for the warning he has given.

"Yes, yes," said Milady, "the letter is precise. Do you know what that warning was?"

"No, I only suspect he has warned the queen against some fresh machinations of the cardinal."

"Yes, that's it, no doubt!" said Milady, returning the letter to Mme. Bonacieux, and letting her head sink pensively upon her bosom.

At that moment they heard the gallop of a horse.

"Oh!" cried Mme. Bonacieux, darting to the window, "can it be he?"

Milady remained still in bed, petrified by surprise; so many unexpected things happened to her all at once that for the first time she was at a loss.

"He, he!" murmured she, "can it be he?" And she remained in bed with her eyes fixed.

"Alas, no!" said Mme. Bonacieux, "it is a man I don't know, although he seems to be coming here. Yes, he checks his pace; he stops at the gate; he rings."

Milady sprang out of bed.

"You are sure it is not he?" said she.

"Yes, yes, very sure!"

"Perhaps you did not see well."

"Oh, if I were to see the plume of his hat, the end of his cloak, I should know HIM!"

Milady was dressing herself all the time.

"Yes, he has entered."

"It is for you or me!"

"My God, how agitated you seem!"

"Yes, I admit it. I have not your confidence; I fear the cardinal."

"Hush!" said Mme. Bonacieux, "somebody is coming."

Immediately the door opened, and the superior entered.

"Did you come from Boulogne?" demanded she of Milady.

"Yes," replied she, trying to recover her self-possession. "Who wants me?"

"A man who will not tell his name, but who comes from the cardinal."

"And who wishes to speak with me?"

"Who wishes to speak to a lady recently come from Boulogne."

"Then let him come in, if you please."

"Oh, my God, my God!" cried Mme. Bonacieux. "Can it be bad news?"

"I fear it."

"I will leave you with this stranger, but as soon as he is gone, if you will permit me, I will return."

"PERMIT you? I BESEECH you."

The superior and Mme. Bonacieux retired.

Milady remained alone, with her eyes fixed upon the door. An instant later, the jingling of spurs was heard upon the stairs, steps drew near, the door opened, and a man appeared.

Milady uttered a cry of joy; this man was the Comte de Rochefort–the demoniacal tool of his Eminence.

Chapter 62

Two Varieties Of Demons

"Ah," cried Milady and Rochefort together, "it is you!"

"Yes, it is I."

"And you come?" asked Milady.

"From La Rochelle; and you?"

"From England."

"Buckingham?"

"Dead or desperately wounded, as I left without having been able to hear anything of him. A fanatic has just assassinated him."

"Ah," said Rochefort, with a smile, "this is a fortunate chance–one that will delight his Eminence! Have you informed him of it?"

"I wrote to him from Boulogne. But what brings you here?"

"His Eminence was uneasy, and sent me to find you."

"I only arrived yesterday."

"And what have you been doing since yesterday?"

"I have not lost my time."

"Oh, I don't doubt that."

"Do you know whom I have encountered here?"

"No."

"Guess."

"How can I?"

"That young woman whom the queen took out of prison."

"The mistress of that fellow d'Artagnan?"

"Yes; Madame Bonacieux, with whose retreat the cardinal was unacquainted."

"Well, well," said Rochefort, "here is a chance which may pair off with the other! Monsieur Cardinal is indeed a privileged man!"

"Imagine my astonishment," continued Milady, "when I found myself face to face with this woman!"

"Does she know you?"

"No."

"Then she looks upon you as a stranger?"

Milady smiled. "I am her best friend."

"Upon my honour," said Rochefort, "it takes you, my dear countess, to perform such miracles!"

"And it is well I can, Chevalier," said Milady, "for do you know what is going on here?"

"No."

"They will come for her tomorrow or the day after, with an order from the queen."

"Indeed! And who?"

"D'Artagnan and his friends."

"Indeed, they will go so far that we shall be obliged to send them to the Bastille."

"Why is it not done already?"

"What would you? The cardinal has a weakness for these men which I cannot comprehend."

"Indeed!"

"Yes."

"Well, then, tell him this, Rochefort. Tell him that our conversation at the inn of the Red Dovecot was overheard by these four men; tell him that after his departure one of them came up to me and took from me by violence the safe-conduct which he had given me; tell him they warned Lord de Winter of my journey to England; that this time they nearly foiled my mission as they foiled the affair of the studs; tell him that among these four men two only are to be feared–d'Artagnan and Athos; tell him that the third, Aramis, is the lover of Madame de Chevreuse–he may be left alone, we know his secret, and it may be useful; as to the fourth, Porthos, he is a fool, a simpleton, a blustering booby, not worth troubling himself about."

"But these four men must be now at the siege of La Rochelle?"

"I thought so, too, but a letter which Madame Bonacieux has received from Madame the Constable, and which she has had the imprudence to show me, leads me to believe that these four men, on the contrary, are on the road hither to take her away."

"The devil! What's to be done?"

"What did the cardinal say about me?"

"I was to take your dispatches, written or verbal, and return by post; and when he shall know what you have done, he will advise what you have to do."

"I must, then, remain here?"

"Here, or in the neighbourhood."

"You cannot take me with you?"

"No, the order is imperative. Near the camp you might be recognised; and your presence, you must be aware, would compromise the cardinal."

"Then I must wait here, or in the neighbourhood?"

"Only tell me beforehand where you will wait for intelligence from the cardinal; let me know always where to find you."

"Observe, it is probable that I may not be able to remain here."

"Why?"

"You forget that my enemies may arrive at any minute."

"That's true, but is this little woman, then, to escape his Eminence?"

"Bah!" said Milady, with a smile that belonged only to herself, "you forget that I am her best friend."

"Ah, that's true! I may then tell the cardinal, with respect to this little woman–"

"That he may be at ease."

"Is that all?"

"He will know what that means."

"He will guess, at least. Now, then, what had I better do?"

"Return instantly. It appears to me that the news you bear is worth the trouble of a little diligence."

"My chaise broke down coming into Lilliers."

"Capital!"

"What, CAPITAL?"

"Yes, I want your chaise."

"And how shall I travel, then?"

"On horseback."

"You talk very comfortably,–a hundred and eighty leagues!"

"What's that?"

"One can do it! Afterward?"

"Afterward? Why, in passing through Lilliers you will send me your chaise, with an order to your servant to place himself at my disposal."

"Well."

"You have, no doubt, some order from the cardinal about you?"

"I have my FULL POWER."

"Show it to the abbess, and tell her that someone will come and fetch me, either today or tomorrow, and that I am to follow the person who presents himself in your name."

"Very well."

"Don't forget to treat me harshly in speaking of me to the abbess."

"To what purpose?"

"I am a victim of the cardinal. It is necessary to inspire confidence in that poor little Madame Bonacieux."

"That's true. Now, will you make me a report of all that has happened?"

"Why, I have related the events to you. You have a good memory; repeat what I have told you. A paper may be lost."

"You are right; only let me know where to find you that I may not run needlessly about the neighbourhood."

"That's correct; wait!"

"Do you want a map?"

"Oh, I know this country marvellously!"

"You? When were you here?"

"I was brought up here."

"Truly?"

"It is worth something, you see, to have been brought up somewhere."

"You will wait for me, then?"

"Let me reflect a little! Ay, that will do–at Armentières."

"Where is that Armentières?"

"A little town on the Lys; I shall only have to cross the river, and I shall be in a foreign country."

"Capital! But it is understood you will only cross the river in case of danger."

"That is well understood."

"And in that case, how shall I know where you are?"

"You do not want your lackey?"

"Is he a sure man?"

"To the proof."

"Give him to me. Nobody knows him. I will leave him at the place I quit, and he will conduct you to me."

"And you say you will wait for me at Armentières?"

"At Armentières."

"Write that name on a bit of paper, lest I should forget it. There is nothing compromising in the name of a town. Is it not so?"

"Eh, who knows? Never mind," said Milady, writing the name on half a sheet of paper, "I will compromise myself."

"Well," said Rochefort, taking the paper from Milady, folding it, and placing it in the lining of his hat, "you may be easy. I will do as children do, for fear of losing the paper–repeat the name along the route. Now, is that all?"

"I believe so."

"Let us see: Buckingham dead or grievously wounded; your conversation with the cardinal overheard by the four Musketeers; Lord de Winter warned of your arrival at Portsmouth; d'Artagnan and Athos to the Bastille; Aramis the lover of Madame de Chevreuse; Porthos an ass; Madame Bonacieux found again; to send you the chaise as soon as possible; to place my lackey at your disposal; to make you out a victim of the cardinal in order that the abbess may entertain no suspicion; Armentières, on the banks of the Lys. Is that all, then?"

"In truth, my dear Chevalier, you are a miracle of memory. A PROPOS, add one thing–"

"What?"

"I saw some very pretty woods which almost touch the convent garden. Say that I am permitted to walk in those woods. Who knows? Perhaps I shall stand in need of a back door for retreat."

"You think of everything."

"And you forget one thing."

"What?"

"To ask me if I want money."

"That's true. How much do you want?"

"All you have in gold."

"I have five hundred pistoles, or thereabouts."

"I have as much. With a thousand pistoles one may face everything. Empty your pockets."

"There."

"Right. And you go–"

"In an hour–time to eat a morsel, during which I shall send for a post horse."

"Capital! Adieu, Chevalier."

"Adieu, Countess."

"Commend me to the cardinal."

"Commend me to Satan."

Milady and Rochefort exchanged a smile and separated. An hour afterward Rochefort set out at a grand gallop; five hours after that he passed through Arras.

Our readers already know how he was recognised by d'Artagnan, and how that recognition by inspiring fear in the four Musketeers had given fresh activity to their journey.

Chapter 63

The Drop Of Water

Rochefort had scarcely departed when Mme. Bonacieux reentered. She found Milady with a smiling countenance.

"Well," said the young woman, "what you dreaded has happened. This evening, or tomorrow, the cardinal will send someone to take you away."

"Who told you that, my dear?" asked Milady.

"I heard it from the mouth of the messenger himself."

"Come and sit down close to me," said Milady.

"Here I am."

"Wait till I assure myself that nobody hears us."

"Why all these precautions?"

"You shall know."

Milady arose, went to the door, opened it, looked in the corridor, and then returned and seated herself close to Mme. Bonacieux.

"Then," said she, "he has well played his part."

"Who has?"

"He who just now presented himself to the abbess as a messenger from the cardinal."

"It was, then, a part he was playing?"

"Yes, my child."

"That man, then, was not–"

"That man," said Milady, lowering her voice, "is my brother."

"Your brother!" cried Mme. Bonacieux.

"No one must know this secret, my dear, but yourself. If you reveal it to anyone in the world, I shall be lost, and perhaps yourself likewise."

"Oh, my God!"

"Listen. This is what has happened: My brother, who was coming to my assistance to take me away by force if it were necessary, met with the emissary of the cardinal, who was coming in search of me. He followed him. At a solitary and retired part of the road he drew his sword, and required the messenger to deliver up to him the papers of which he was the bearer. The messenger resisted; my brother killed him."

"Oh!" said Mme. Bonacieux, shuddering.

"Remember, that was the only means. Then my brother determined to substitute cunning for force. He took the papers, and presented himself here as the emissary of the cardinal, and in an hour or two a carriage will come to take me away by the orders of his Eminence."

"I understand. It is your brother who sends this carriage."

"Exactly, but that is not all. That letter you have received, and which you believe to be from Madame de Chevreuse–"

"Well?"

"It is a forgery."

"How can that be?"

"Yes, a forgery; it is a snare to prevent your making any resistance when they come to fetch you."

"But it is d'Artagnan that will come."

"Do not deceive yourself. D'Artagnan and his friends are detained at the siege of La Rochelle."

"How do you know that?"

"My brother met some emissaries of the cardinal in the uniform of Musketeers. You would have been summoned to the gate; you would have believed yourself about to meet friends; you would have been abducted, and conducted back to Paris."

"Oh, my God! My senses fail me amid such a chaos of iniquities. I feel, if this continues," said Mme. Bonacieux, raising her hands to her forehead, "I shall go mad!"

"Stop–"

"What?"

"I hear a horse's steps; it is my brother setting off again. I should like to offer him a last salute. Come!"

Milady opened the window, and made a sign to Mme. Bonacieux to join her. The young woman complied.

Rochefort passed at a gallop.

"Adieu, brother!" cried Milady.

The chevalier raised his head, saw the two young women, and without stopping, waved his hand in a friendly way to Milady.

"The good George!" said she, closing the window with an expression of countenance full of affection and melancholy. And she resumed her seat, as if plunged in reflections entirely personal.

"Dear lady," said Mme. Bonacieux, "pardon me for interrupting you, but what do you advise me to do? Good heaven! You have more experience than I have. Speak; I will listen."

"In the first place," said Milady, "it is possible I may be deceived, and that d'Artagnan and his friends may really come to your assistance."

"Oh, that would be too much!" cried Mme. Bonacieux, "so much happiness is not in store for me!"

"Then you comprehend it would be only a question of time, a sort of race, which should arrive first. If your friends are the more speedy, you are to be saved; if the satellites of the cardinal, you are lost."

"Oh, yes, yes, lost beyond redemption! What, then, to do? What to do?"

"There would be a very simple means, very natural–"

"Tell me what!"

"To wait, concealed in the neighbourhood, and assure yourself who are the men who come to ask for you."

"But where can I wait?"

"Oh, there is no difficulty in that. I shall stop and conceal myself a few leagues hence until my brother can rejoin me. Well, I take you with me; we conceal ourselves, and wait together."

"But I shall not be allowed to go; I am almost a prisoner."

"As they believe that I go in consequence of an order from the cardinal, no one will believe you anxious to follow me."

"Well?"

"Well! The carriage is at the door; you bid me adieu; you mount the step to embrace me a last time; my brother's servant, who comes to fetch me, is told how to proceed; he makes a sign to the postillion, and we set off at a gallop."

"But d'Artagnan! D'Artagnan! if he comes?"

"Shall we not know it?"

"How?"

"Nothing easier. We will send my brother's servant back to Bethune, whom, as I told you, we can trust. He shall assume a disguise, and place himself in front of the convent. If the emissaries of the cardinal arrive, he will take no notice; if it is Monsieur d'Artagnan and his friends, he will bring them to us."

"He knows them, then?"

"Doubtless. Has he not seen Monsieur d'Artagnan at my house?"

"Oh, yes, yes, you are right. Thus all may go well–all may be for the best, but we do not go far from this place?"

"Seven or eight leagues at the most. We will keep on the frontiers, for instance; and at the first alarm we can leave France."

"And what can we do there?"

"Wait."

"But if they come?"

"My brother's carriage will be here first."

"If I should happen to be any distance from you when the carriage comes for you–at dinner or supper, for instance?"

"Do one thing."

"What is that?"

"Tell your good superior that in order that we may be as much together as possible, you ask her permission to share my repast."

"Will she permit it?"

"What inconvenience can it be?"

"Oh, delightful! In this way we shall not be separated for an instant."

"Well, go down to her, then, to make your request. I feel my head a little confused; I will take a turn in the garden."

"Go; and where shall I find you?"

"Here, in an hour."

"Here, in an hour. Oh, you are so kind, and I am so grateful!"

"How can I avoid interesting myself for one who is so beautiful and so amiable? Are you not the beloved of one of my best friends?"

"Dear d'Artagnan! Oh, how he will thank you!"

"I hope so. Now, then, all is agreed; let us go down."

"You are going into the garden?"

"Yes."

"Go along this corridor, down a little staircase, and you are in it."

"Excellent; thank you!"

And the two women parted, exchanging charming smiles.

Milady had told the truth–her head was confused, for her ill-arranged plans clashed one another like chaos. She required to be alone that she might put her thoughts a little into order. She saw vaguely the future, but she stood in need of a little silence and quiet to give all her ideas, as yet confused, a distinct form and a regular plan.

What was most pressing was to get Mme. Bonacieux away, and convey her to a place of safety, and there, if matters required, make her a hostage. Milady began to have doubts of the issue of this terrible duel, in which her enemies showed as much perseverance as she did animosity.

Besides, she felt as we feel when a storm is coming on–that this issue was near, and could not fail to be terrible.

The principal thing for her, then, was, as we have said, to keep Mme. Bonacieux in her power. Mme. Bonacieux was the very life of d'Artagnan. This was more than his life, the life of the woman he loved; this was, in case of ill fortune, a means of temporising and obtaining good conditions.

Now, this point was settled; Mme. Bonacieux, without any suspicion, accompanied her. Once concealed with her at Armentières, it would be easy to make her believe that d'Artagnan had not come to Bethune. In fifteen days at most, Rochefort would be back; besides, during that fifteen days she would have time to think how she could best avenge herself on the four friends. She would not be weary, thank God! For she should enjoy the sweetest pastime such events could accord a woman of her character–perfecting a beautiful vengeance.

Revolving all this in her mind, she cast her eyes around her, and arranged the topography of the garden in her head. Milady was like a good general who contemplates at the same time victory and defeat, and who is quite prepared, according to the chances of the battle, to march forward or to beat a retreat.

At the end of an hour she heard a soft voice calling her; it was Mme. Bonacieux's. The good abbess had naturally consented to her request; and as a commencement, they were to sup together.

On reaching the courtyard, they heard the noise of a carriage which stopped at the gate.

Milady listened.

"Do you hear anything?" said she.

"Yes, the rolling of a carriage."

"It is the one my brother sends for us."

"Oh, my God!"

"Come, come! Courage!"

The bell of the convent gate was sounded; Milady was not mistaken.

"Go to your chamber," said she to Mme. Bonacieux, "you have perhaps some jewels you would like to take."

"I have his letters," said she.

"Well, go and fetch them, and come to my apartment. We will snatch some supper; we shall perhaps travel part of the night, and must keep our strength up."

"Great God!" said Mme. Bonacieux, placing her hand upon her bosom, "my heart beats so I cannot walk."

"Courage, courage! Remember that in a quarter of an hour you will be safe; and think that what you are about to do is for HIS sake."

"Yes, yes, everything for him. You have restored my courage by a single word; go, I will rejoin you."

Milady ran up to her apartment quickly; she there found Rochefort's lackey, and gave him his instructions.

He was to wait at the gate; if by chance the Musketeers should appear, the carriage was to set off as fast as possible, pass around the convent, and go and wait for Milady at a little village which was situated at the other side of the wood. In this case Milady would cross the garden and gain the village on foot. As we have already said, Milady was admirably acquainted with this part of France.

If the Musketeers did not appear, things were to go on as had been agreed; Mme. Bonacieux was to get into the carriage as if to bid her adieu, and she was to take away Mme. Bonacieux.

Mme. Bonacieux came in; and to remove all suspicion, if she had any, Milady repeated to the lackey, before her, the latter part of her instructions.

Milady asked some questions about the carriage. It was a chaise drawn by three horses, driven by a postillion; Rochefort's lackey would precede it, as courier.

Milady was wrong in fearing that Mme. Bonacieux would have any suspicion. The poor young woman was too pure to suppose that any female could be guilty of such perfidy; besides, the name of the Comtesse de Winter, which she had heard the abbess pronounce, was wholly unknown to her, and she was even ignorant that a woman had had so great and so fatal a share in the misfortune of her life.

"You see," said she, when the lackey had gone out, "everything is ready. The abbess suspects nothing, and believes that I am taken by order of the cardinal. This man goes to give his last orders; take the least thing, drink a finger of wine, and let us be gone."

"Yes," said Mme. Bonacieux, mechanically, "yes, let us be gone."

Milady made her a sign to sit down opposite, poured her a small glass of Spanish wine, and helped her to the wing of a chicken.

"See," said she, "if everything does not second us! Here is night coming on; by daybreak we shall have reached our retreat, and nobody can guess where we are. Come, courage! Take something."

Mme. Bonacieux ate a few mouthfuls mechanically, and just touched the glass with her lips.

"Come, come!" said Milady, lifting hers to her mouth, "do as I do."

But at the moment the glass touched her lips, her hand remained suspended; she heard something on the road which sounded like the rattling of a distant gallop. Then it grew nearer, and it seemed to her, almost at the same time, that she heard the neighing of horses.

This noise acted upon her joy like the storm which awakens the sleeper in the midst of a happy dream; she grew pale and ran to the window, while Mme. Bonacieux, rising all in a tremble, supported herself upon her chair to avoid falling. Nothing was yet to be seen, only they heard the galloping draw nearer.

"Oh, my God!" said Mme. Bonacieux, "what is that noise?"

"That of either our friends or our enemies," said Milady, with her terrible coolness. "Stay where you are, I will tell you."

Mme. Bonacieux remained standing, mute, motionless, and pale as a statue.

The noise became louder; the horses could not be more than a hundred and fifty paces distant. If they were not yet to be seen, it was because the road made an elbow. The noise became so distinct that the horses might be counted by the rattle of their hoofs.

Milady gazed with all the power of her attention; it was just light enough for her to see who was coming.

All at once, at the turning of the road she saw the glitter of laced hats and the waving of feathers; she counted two, then five, then eight horsemen. One of them preceded the rest by double the length of his horse.

Milady uttered a stifled groan. In the first horseman she recognised d'Artagnan.

"Oh, my God, my God," cried Mme. Bonacieux, "what is it?"

"It is the uniform of the cardinal's Guards. Not an instant to be lost! Fly, fly!"

"Yes, yes, let us fly!" repeated Mme. Bonacieux, but without being able to make a step, glued as she was to the spot by terror.

They heard the horsemen pass under the windows.

"Come, then, come, then!" cried Milady, trying to drag the young woman along by the arm. "Thanks to the garden, we yet can flee; I have the key, but make haste! In five minutes it will be too late!"

Mme. Bonacieux tried to walk, made two steps, and sank upon her knees. Milady tried to raise and carry her, but could not do it.

At this moment they heard the rolling of the carriage, which at the approach of the Musketeers set off at a gallop. Then three or four shots were fired.

"For the last time, will you come?" cried Milady.

"Oh, my God, my God! You see my strength fails me; you see plainly I cannot walk. Flee alone!"

"Flee alone, and leave you here? No, no, never!" cried Milady.

All at once she paused, a livid flash darted from her eyes; she ran to the table, emptied into Mme. Bonacieux's glass the contents of a ring which she opened with singular quickness. It was a grain of a reddish colour, which dissolved immediately.

Then, taking the glass with a firm hand, she said, "Drink. This wine will give you strength, drink!" And she put the glass to the lips of the young woman, who drank mechanically.

"This is not the way that I wished to avenge myself," said Milady, replacing the glass upon the table, with an infernal smile, "but, my faith! We do what we can!" And she rushed out of the room.

Mme. Bonacieux saw her go without being able to follow her; she was like people who dream they are pursued, and who in vain try to walk.

A few moments passed; a great noise was heard at the gate. Every instant Mme. Bonacieux expected to see Milady, but she did not return. Several times, with terror, no doubt, the cold sweat burst from her burning brow.

At length she heard the grating of the hinges of the opening gates; the noise of boots and spurs resounded on the stairs. There was a great murmur of voices which continued to draw near, amid which she seemed to hear her own name pronounced.

All at once she uttered a loud cry of joy, and darted toward the door; she had recognised the voice of d'Artagnan.

"d'Artagnan! D'Artagnan!" cried she, "is it you? This way! This way!"

"Constance? Constance?" replied the young man, "where are you? Where are you? My God!"

At the same moment the door of the cell yielded to a shock, rather than opened; several men rushed into the chamber. Mme. Bonacieux had sunk into an armchair, without the power of moving.

D'Artagnan threw down a yet-smoking pistol which he held in his hand, and fell on his knees before his mistress. Athos replaced his in his belt; Porthos and Aramis, who held their drawn swords in their hands, returned them to their scabbards.

"Oh, d'Artagnan, my beloved d'Artagnan! You have come, then, at last! You have not deceived me! It is indeed thee!"

"Yes, yes, Constance. Reunited!"

"Oh, it was in vain she told me you would not come! I hoped in silence. I was not willing to fly. Oh, I have done well! How happy I am!"

At this word SHE, Athos, who had seated himself quietly, started up.

"SHE! What she?" asked d'Artagnan.

"Why, my companion. She who out of friendship for me wished to take me from my persecutors. She who, mistaking you for the cardinal's Guards, has just fled away."

"Your companion!" cried d'Artagnan, becoming more pale than the white veil of his mistress. "Of what companion are you speaking, dear Constance?"

"Of her whose carriage was at the gate; of a woman who calls herself your friend; of a woman to whom you have told everything."

"Her name, her name!" cried d'Artagnan. "My God, can you not remember her name?"

"Yes, it was pronounced in my hearing once. Stop–but–it is very strange–oh, my God, my head swims! I cannot see!"

"Help, help, my friends! Her hands are icy cold," cried d'Artagnan. "She is ill! Great God, she is losing her senses!"

While Porthos was calling for help with all the power of his strong voice, Aramis ran to the table to get a glass of water, but he stopped at seeing the horrible alteration that had taken place in the countenance of Athos, who, standing before the table, his hair rising from his head, his eyes fixed in stupor, was looking at one of the glasses, and appeared a prey to the most horrible doubt.

"Oh!" said Athos, "oh, no, it is impossible! God would not permit such a crime!"

"Water, water!" cried d'Artagnan. "Water!"

"Oh, poor woman, poor woman!" murmured Athos, in a broken voice.

Mme. Bonacieux opened her eyes under the kisses of d'Artagnan.

"She revives!" cried the young man. "Oh, my God, my God, I thank thee!"

"Madame!" said Athos, "Madame, in the name of heaven, whose empty glass is this?"

"Mine, Monsieur," said the young woman, in a dying voice.

"But who poured the wine for you that was in this glass?"

"She."

"But who is SHE?"

"Oh, I remember!" said Mme. Bonacieux, "the Comtesse de Winter."

The four friends uttered one and the same cry, but that of Athos dominated all the rest.

At that moment the countenance of Mme. Bonacieux became livid; a fearful agony pervaded her frame, and she sank panting into the arms of Porthos and Aramis.

D'Artagnan seized the hands of Athos with an anguish difficult to be described.

"And what do you believe?' His voice was stifled by sobs.

"I believe everything," said Athos, biting his lips till the blood sprang to avoid sighing.

"D'Artagnan, d'Artagnan!" cried Mme. Bonacieux, "where art thou? Do not leave me! You see I am dying!"

D'Artagnan released the hands of Athos which he still held clasped in both his own, and hastened to her. Her beautiful face was distorted with agony; her glassy eyes had no longer their sight; a convulsive shuddering shook her whole body; the sweat rolled from her brow.

"In the name of heaven, run, call! Aramis! Porthos! Call for help!"

"Useless!" said Athos, "useless! For the poison which SHE pours there is no antidote."

"Yes, yes! Help, help!" murmured Mme. Bonacieux, "help!"

Then, collecting all her strength, she took the head of the young man between her hands, looked at him for an instant as if her whole soul passed into that look, and with a sobbing cry pressed her lips to his.

"Constance, Constance!" cried d'Artagnan.

A sigh escaped from the mouth of Mme. Bonacieux, and dwelt for an instant on the lips of d'Artagnan. That sigh was the soul, so chaste and so loving, which reascended to heaven.

D'Artagnan pressed nothing but a corpse in his arms. The young man uttered a cry, and fell by the side of his mistress as pale and as icy as herself.

Porthos wept; Aramis pointed toward heaven; Athos made the sign of the cross.

At that moment a man appeared in the doorway, almost as pale as those in the chamber. He looked around him and saw Mme. Bonacieux dead, and d'Artagnan in a swoon. He appeared just at that moment of stupor which follows great catastrophes.

"I was not deceived," said he, "here is Monsieur d'Artagnan; and you are his friends, Messieurs Athos, Porthos, and Aramis."

The persons whose names were thus pronounced looked at the stranger with astonishment. It seemed to all three that they knew him.

"Gentlemen," resumed the newcomer, "you are, as I am, in search of a woman who," added he, with a terrible smile, "must have passed this way, for I see a corpse."

The three friends remained mute–for although the voice as well as the countenance reminded them of someone they had seen, they could not remember under what circumstances.

"Gentlemen," continued the stranger, "since you do not recognise a man who probably owes his life to you twice, I must name myself. I am Lord de Winter, brother-in-law of THAT WOMAN."

The three friends uttered a cry of surprise.

Athos rose, and offering him his hand, "Be welcome, my Lord," said he, "you are one of us."

"I set out five hours after her from Portsmouth," said Lord de Winter. "I arrived three hours after her at Boulogne. I missed her by twenty minutes at St. Omer. Finally, at Lilliers I lost all trace of her. I was going about at random, inquiring of everybody, when I saw you gallop past. I recognised Monsieur d'Artagnan. I called to you, but you did not answer me; I wished to follow you, but my horse was too much fatigued to go at the same pace with yours. And yet it appears, in spite of all your diligence, you have arrived too late."

"You see!" said Athos, pointing to Mme. Bonacieux dead, and to d'Artagnan, whom Porthos and Aramis were trying to recall to life.

"Are they both dead?" asked Lord de Winter, sternly.

"No," replied Athos, "fortunately Monsieur d'Artagnan has only fainted."

"Ah, indeed, so much the better!" said Lord de Winter.

At that moment d'Artagnan opened his eyes. He tore himself from the arms of Porthos and Aramis, and threw himself like a madman on the corpse of his mistress.

Athos rose, walked toward his friend with a slow and solemn step, embraced him tenderly, and as he burst into violent sobs, he said to him with his noble and persuasive voice, "Friend, be a man! Women weep for the dead; men avenge them!"

"Oh, yes!" cried d'Artagnan, "yes! If it be to avenge her, I am ready to follow you."

Athos profited by this moment of strength which the hope of vengeance restored to his unfortunate friend to make a sign to Porthos and Aramis to go and fetch the superior.

The two friends met her in the corridor, greatly troubled and much upset by such strange events; she called some of the nuns, who against all monastic custom found themselves in the presence of five men.

"Madame," said Athos, passing his arm under that of d'Artagnan, "we abandon to your pious care the body of that unfortunate woman. She was an angel on earth before being an angel in heaven. Treat her as one of your sisters. We will return someday to pray over her grave."

D'Artagnan concealed his face in the bosom of Athos, and sobbed aloud.

"Weep," said Athos, "weep, heart full of love, youth, and life! Alas, would I could weep like you!"

And he drew away his friend, as affectionate as a father, as consoling as a priest, noble as a man who has suffered much.

All five, followed by their lackeys leading their horses, took their way to the town of Bethune, whose outskirts they perceived, and stopped before the first inn they came to.

"But," said d'Artagnan, "shall we not pursue that woman?"

"Later," said Athos. "I have measures to take."

"She will escape us," replied the young man, "she will escape us, and it will be your fault, Athos."

"I will be accountable for her," said Athos.

D'Artagnan had so much confidence in the word of his friend that he lowered his head, and entered the inn without reply.

Porthos and Aramis regarded each other, not understanding this assurance of Athos.

Lord de Winter believed he spoke in this manner to soothe the grief of d'Artagnan.

"Now, gentlemen," said Athos, when he had ascertained there were five chambers free in the hotel, "let everyone retire to his own apartment. d'Artagnan needs to be alone, to weep and to sleep. I take charge of everything; be easy."

"It appears, however," said Lord de Winter, "if there are any measures to take against the countess, it concerns me; she is my sister-in-law."

"And me," said Athos, "–she is my wife!"

D'Artagnan smiled–for he understood that Athos was sure of his vengeance when he revealed such a secret. Porthos and Aramis looked at each other, and grew pale. Lord de Winter thought Athos was mad.

"Now, retire to your chambers," said Athos, "and leave me to act. You must perceive that in my quality of a husband this concerns me. Only, d'Artagnan, if you have not lost it, give me the paper which fell from that man's hat, upon which is written the name of the village of–"

"Ah," said d'Artagnan, "I comprehend! That name written in her hand."

"You see, then," said Athos, "there is a god in heaven still!"

Chapter 64

The Man In The Red Cloak

The despair of Athos had given place to a concentrated grief which only rendered more lucid the brilliant mental faculties of that extraordinary man.

Possessed by one single thought–that of the promise he had made, and of the responsibility he had taken–he retired last to his chamber, begged the host to procure him a map of the province, bent over it, examined every line traced upon it, perceived that there were four different roads from Bethune to Armentières, and summoned the lackeys.

Planchet, Grimaud, Bazin, and Mousqueton presented themselves, and received clear, positive, and serious orders from Athos.

They must set out the next morning at daybreak, and go to Armentières–each by a different route. Planchet, the most intelligent of the four, was to follow that by which the carriage had gone upon which the four friends had fired, and which was accompanied, as may be remembered, by Rochefort's servant.

Athos set the lackeys to work first because, since these men had been in the service of himself and his friends he had discovered in each of them different and essential qualities. Then, lackeys who ask questions inspire less mistrust than masters, and meet with more sympathy among those to whom they address themselves. Besides, Milady knew the masters, and did not know the lackeys; on the contrary, the lackeys knew Milady perfectly.

All four were to meet the next day at eleven o'clock. If they had discovered Milady's retreat, three were to remain on guard; the fourth was to return to Bethune in order to inform Athos and serve as a guide to the four friends. These arrangements made, the lackeys retired.

Athos then arose from his chair, girded on his sword, enveloped himself in his cloak, and left the hotel. It was nearly ten o'clock. At ten o'clock in the evening, it is well known, the streets in provincial towns are very little frequented. Athos nevertheless was visibly anxious to find someone of whom he could ask a question. At length he met a belated passenger, went up to him, and spoke a few words to him. The man he addressed recoiled with terror, and only answered the few words of the Musketeer by pointing. Athos offered the man half a pistole to accompany him, but the man refused.

Athos then plunged into the street the man had indicated with his finger, but arriving at four crossroads, he stopped again, visibly embarrassed. Nevertheless, as the crossroads offered him a better chance than any other place of meeting somebody, he stood still. In a few minutes a night watch passed. Athos repeated to him the same question he had asked the first person he met. The night watch evinced the same terror, refused, in his turn, to accompany Athos, and only pointed with his hand to the road he was to take.

Athos walked in the direction indicated, and reached the suburb situated at the opposite extremity of the city from that by which he and his friends had entered it. There he again appeared uneasy and embarrassed, and stopped for the third time.

Fortunately, a mendicant passed, who, coming up to Athos to ask charity, Athos offered him half a crown to accompany him where he was going. The mendicant hesitated at first, but at the sight of the piece of silver which shone in the darkness he consented, and walked on before Athos.

Arrived at the angle of a street, he pointed to a small house, isolated, solitary, and dismal. Athos went toward the house, while the mendicant, who had received his reward, left as fast as his legs could carry him.

Athos went round the house before he could distinguish the door, amid the red colour in which the house was painted. No light appeared through the chinks of the shutters; no noise gave reason to believe that it was inhabited. It was dark and silent as the tomb.

Three times Athos knocked without receiving an answer. At the third knock, however, steps were heard inside. The door at length was opened, and a man appeared, of high stature, pale complexion, and black hair and beard.

Athos and he exchanged some words in a low voice, then the tall man made a sign to the Musketeer that he might come in. Athos immediately profited by the permission, and the door was closed behind him.

The man whom Athos had come so far to seek, and whom he had found with so much trouble, introduced him into his laboratory, where he was engaged in fastening together with iron wire the dry bones of a skeleton. All the frame was adjusted except the head, which lay on the table.

All the rest of the furniture indicated that the dweller in this house occupied himself with the study of natural science. There were large bottles filled with serpents, ticketed according to their species; dried lizards shone like emeralds set in great squares of black wood, and bunches of wild odoriferous herbs, doubtless possessed of virtues unknown to common men, were fastened to the ceiling and hung down in the corners of the apartment. There was no family, no servant; the tall man alone inhabited this house.

Athos cast a cold and indifferent glance upon the objects we have described, and at the invitation of him whom he came to seek sat down near him.

Then he explained to him the cause of his visit, and the service he required of him. But scarcely had he expressed his request when the unknown, who remained standing before the Musketeer, drew back with signs of terror, and refused. Then Athos took from his pocket a small paper, on which two lines were written, accompanied by a signature and a seal, and presented them to him who had made too prematurely these signs of repugnance. The tall man had scarcely read these lines, seen the signature, and recognised the seal, when he bowed to denote that he had no longer any objection to make, and that he was ready to obey.

Athos required no more. He arose, bowed, went out, returned by the same way he came, re-entered the hotel, and went to his apartment.

At daybreak d'Artagnan entered the chamber, and demanded what was to be done.

"To wait," replied Athos.

Some minutes after, the superior of the convent sent to inform the Musketeers that the burial would take place at midday. As to the poisoner, they had heard no tidings of her whatever, only that she must have made her escape through the garden, on the sand of which her footsteps could be traced, and the door of which had been found shut. As to the key, it had disappeared.

At the hour appointed, Lord de Winter and the four friends repaired to the convent; the bells tolled, the chapel was open, the grating of the choir was closed. In the middle of the choir the body of the victim, clothed in her novitiate dress, was exposed. On each side of the choir and behind the gratings opening into the convent was assembled the whole community of the Carmelites, who listened to the divine service, and mingled their chant with the chant of the priests, without seeing the profane, or being seen by them.

At the door of the chapel d'Artagnan felt his courage fall anew, and returned to look for Athos, but Athos had disappeared.

Faithful to his mission of vengeance, Athos had requested to be conducted to the garden; and there upon the sand following the light steps of this woman, who left sharp tracks wherever she went, he advanced toward the gate which led into the wood, and causing it to be opened, he went out into the forest.

Then all his suspicions were confirmed; the road by which the carriage had disappeared encircled the forest. Athos followed the road for some time, his eyes fixed upon the ground; slight stains of blood, which came from the wound inflicted upon the man who accompanied the carriage as a courier, or from one of the horses, dotted the road. At the end of three-quarters of a league, within fifty paces of Festubert, a larger bloodstain appeared; the ground was trampled by horses. Between the forest and this accursed spot, a little behind the trampled ground, was the same track of small feet as in the garden; the carriage had stopped here. At this spot Milady had come out of the wood, and entered the carriage.

Satisfied with this discovery which confirmed all his suspicions, Athos returned to the hotel, and found Planchet impatiently waiting for him.

Everything was as Athos had foreseen.

Planchet had followed the road; like Athos, he had discovered the stains of blood; like Athos, he had noted the spot where the horses had halted. But he had gone farther than Athos–for at the village of Festubert, while drinking at an inn, he had learned without needing to ask a question that the evening before, at half-past eight, a wounded man who accompanied a lady travelling in a post-chaise had been obliged to stop, unable to go further. The accident was set down to the account of robbers, who had stopped the chaise in the wood. The man remained in the village; the woman had had a relay of horses, and continued her journey.

Planchet went in search of the postillion who had driven her, and found him. He had taken the lady as far as Fromelles; and from Fromelles she had set out for Armentières. Planchet took the crossroad, and by seven o'clock in the morning he was at Armentières.

There was but one tavern, the Post. Planchet went and presented himself as a lackey out of a place, who was in search of a situation. He had not chatted ten minutes with the people of the tavern before he learned that a woman had come there alone about eleven o'clock the night before, had engaged a chamber, had sent for the master of the hotel, and told him she desired to remain some time in the neighbourhood.

Planchet had no need to learn more. He hastened to the rendezvous, found the lackeys at their posts, placed them as sentinels at all the outlets of the hotel, and came to find Athos, who had just received this information when his friends returned.

All their countenances were melancholy and gloomy, even the mild countenance of Aramis.

"What is to be done?" asked d'Artagnan.

"To wait!" replied Athos.

Each retired to his own apartment.

At eight o'clock in the evening Athos ordered the horses to be saddled, and Lord de Winter and his friends notified that they must prepare for the expedition.

In an instant all five were ready. Each examined his arms, and put them in order. Athos came down last, and found d'Artagnan already on horseback, and growing impatient.

"Patience!" cried Athos, "one of our party is still wanting."

The four horsemen looked round them with astonishment, for they sought vainly in their minds to know who this other person could be.

At this moment Planchet brought out Athos's horse; the Musketeer leaped lightly into the saddle.

"Wait for me," cried he, "I will soon be back," and he set off at a gallop.

In a quarter of an hour he returned, accompanied by a tall man, masked, and wrapped in a large red cloak.

Lord de Winter and the three Musketeers looked at one another inquiringly. Neither could give the others any information, for all were ignorant who this man could be; nevertheless, they felt convinced that all was as it should be, as it was done by the order of Athos.

At nine o'clock, guided by Planchet, the little cavalcade set out, taking the route the carriage had taken.

It was a melancholy sight–that of these six men, travelling in silence, each plunged in his own thoughts, sad as despair, gloomy as chastisement.

Chapter 65

Trial

It was a stormy and dark night; vast clouds covered the heavens, concealing the stars; the moon would not rise till midnight.

Occasionally, by the light of a flash of lightning which gleamed along the horizon, the road stretched itself before them, white and solitary; the flash extinct, all remained in darkness.

Every minute Athos was forced to restrain d'Artagnan, constantly in advance of the little troop, and to beg him to keep in the line, which in an instant he again departed from. He had but one thought–to go forward; and he went.

They passed in silence through the little village of Festubert, where the wounded servant was, and then skirted the wood of Richebourg. At Herlier, Planchet, who led the column, turned to the left.

Several times Lord de Winter, Porthos, or Aramis tried to talk with the man in the red cloak, but to every interrogation which they put to him he bowed, without response. The travellers then comprehended that there must be some reason why the unknown preserved such a silence, and ceased to address themselves to him.

The storm increased, the flashes succeeded one another more rapidly, the thunder began to growl, and the wind, the precursor of a hurricane, whistled in the plumes and the hair of the horsemen.

The cavalcade trotted on more sharply.

A little before they came to Fromelles the storm burst. They spread their cloaks. There remained three leagues to travel, and they did it amid torrents of rain.

D'Artagnan took off his hat, and could not be persuaded to make use of his cloak. He found pleasure in feeling the water trickle over his burning brow and over his body, agitated by feverish shudders.

The moment the little troop passed Goskal and were approaching the Post, a man sheltered beneath a tree detached himself from the trunk with which he had been confounded in the darkness, and advanced into the middle of the road, putting his finger on his lips.

Athos recognised Grimaud.

"What's the manner?" cried Athos. "Has she left Armentières?"

Grimaud made a sign in the affirmative. D'Artagnan ground his teeth.

"Silence, d'Artagnan!" said Athos. "I have charged myself with this affair. It is for me, then, to interrogate Grimaud."

"Where is she?" asked Athos.

Grimaud extended his hands in the direction of the Lys. "Far from here?" asked Athos.

Grimaud showed his master his forefinger bent.

"Alone?" asked Athos.

Grimaud made the sign yes.

"Gentlemen," said Athos, "she is alone within half a league of us, in the direction of the river."

"That's well," said d'Artagnan. "Lead us, Grimaud."

Grimaud took his course across the country, and acted as guide to the cavalcade.

At the end of five hundred paces, more or less, they came to a rivulet, which they forded.

By the aid of the lightning they perceived the village of Erquinheim.

"Is she there, Grimaud?" asked Athos.

Grimaud shook his head negatively.

"Silence, then!" cried Athos.

And the troop continued their route.

Another flash illuminated all around them. Grimaud extended his arm, and by the bluish splendor of the fiery serpent they distinguished a little isolated house on the banks of the river, within a hundred paces of a ferry.

One window was lighted.

"Here we are!" said Athos.

At this moment a man who had been crouching in a ditch jumped up and came towards them. It was Mousqueton. He pointed his finger to the lighted window.

"She is there," said he.

"And Bazin?" asked Athos.

"While I watched the window, he guarded the door."

"Good!" said Athos. "You are good and faithful servants."

Athos sprang from his horse, gave the bridle to Grimaud, and advanced toward the window, after having made a sign to the rest of the troop to go toward the door.

The little house was surrounded by a low, quick-set hedge, two or three feet high. Athos sprang over the hedge and went up to the window, which was without shutters, but had the half-curtains closely drawn.

He mounted the skirting stone that his eyes might look over the curtain.

By the light of a lamp he saw a woman, wrapped in a dark mantle, seated upon a stool near a dying fire. Her elbows were placed upon a mean table, and she leaned her head upon her two hands, which were white as ivory.

He could not distinguish her countenance, but a sinister smile passed over the lips of Athos. He was not deceived; it was she whom he sought.

At this moment a horse neighed. Milady raised her head, saw close to the panes the pale face of Athos, and screamed.

Athos, perceiving that she knew him, pushed the window with his knee and hand. The window yielded. The squares were broken to shivers; and Athos, like the spectre of vengeance, leaped into the room.

Milady rushed to the door and opened it. More pale and menacing than Athos, d'Artagnan stood on the threshold.

Milady recoiled, uttering a cry. D'Artagnan, believing she might have means of flight and fearing she should escape, drew a pistol from his belt, but Athos raised his hand.

"Put back that weapon, d'Artagnan!" said he, "this woman must be tried, not assassinated. Wait an instant, my friend, and you shall be satisfied. Come in, gentlemen."

D'Artagnan obeyed; for Athos had the solemn voice and the powerful gesture of a judge sent by the Lord himself. Behind d'Artagnan entered Porthos, Aramis, Lord de Winter, and the man in the red cloak.

The four lackeys guarded the door and the window.

Milady had sunk into a chair, with her hands extended, as if to conjure this terrible apparition. Perceiving her brother-in-law, she uttered a terrible cry.

"What do you want?" screamed Milady.

"We want," said Athos, "Charlotte Backson, who first was called Comtesse de la Fere, and afterwards Milady de Winter, Baroness of Sheffield."

"That is I! That is I!" murmured Milady, in extreme terror, "what do you want?"

"We wish to judge you according to your crime," said Athos, "you shall be free to defend yourself. Justify yourself if you can. M. d'Artagnan, it is for you to accuse her first."

D'Artagnan advanced.

"Before God and before men," said he, "I accuse this woman of having poisoned Constance Bonacieux, who died yesterday evening."

He turned towards Porthos and Aramis.

"We bear witness to this," said the two Musketeers, with one voice.

D'Artagnan continued: "Before God and before men, I accuse this woman of having attempted to poison me, in wine which she sent me from Villeroy, with a forged letter, as if that wine came from my friends. God preserved me, but a man named Brisemont died in my place."

"We bear witness to this," said Porthos and Aramis, in the same manner as before.

"Before God and before men, I accuse this woman of having urged me to the murder of the Baron de Wardes, but as no one else can attest the truth of this accusation, I attest it myself. I have done." And d'Artagnan passed to the other side of the room with Porthos and Aramis.

"Your turn, my Lord," said Athos.

The baron came forward.

"Before God and before men," said he, "I accuse this woman of having caused the assassination of the Duke of Buckingham."

"The Duke of Buckingham assassinated!" cried all present, with one voice.

"Yes," said the baron, "assassinated. On receiving the warning letter you wrote to me, I had this woman arrested, and gave her in charge to a loyal servant. She corrupted this man; she placed the poniard in his hand; she made him kill the duke. And at this moment, perhaps, Felton is paying with his head for the crime of this fury!"

A shudder crept through the judges at the revelation of these unknown crimes.

"That is not all," resumed Lord de Winter. "My brother, who made you his heir, died in three hours of a strange disorder which left livid traces all over the body. My sister, how did your husband die?"

"Horror!" cried Porthos and Aramis.

"Assassin of Buckingham, assassin of Felton, assassin of my brother, I demand justice upon you, and I swear that if it be not granted to me, I will execute it myself."

And Lord de Winter ranged himself by the side of d'Artagnan, leaving the place free for another accuser.

Milady let her head sink between her two hands, and tried to recall her ideas, whirling in a mortal vertigo.

"My turn," said Athos, himself trembling as the lion trembles at the sight of the serpent–"my turn. I married that woman when she was a young girl; I married her in opposition to the wishes of all my family; I gave her my wealth, I gave her my name; and one day I discovered that this woman was branded–this woman was marked with a FLEUR-DE-LIS on her left shoulder."

"Oh," said Milady, raising herself, "I defy you to find any tribunal which pronounced that infamous sentence against me. I defy you to find him who executed it."

"Silence!" said a hollow voice. "It is for me to reply to that!" And the man in the red cloak came forward in his turn.

"What man is that? What man is that?" cried Milady, suffocated by terror, her hair loosening itself, and rising above her livid countenance as if alive.

All eyes were turned towards this man–for to all except Athos he was unknown.

Even Athos looked at him with as much stupefaction as the others, for he knew not how he could in any way find himself mixed up with the horrible drama then unfolded.

After approaching Milady with a slow and solemn step, so that the table alone separated them, the unknown took off his mask.

Milady for some time examined with increasing terror that pale face, framed with black hair and whiskers, the only expression of which was icy impassibility. Then she suddenly cried, "Oh, no, no!" rising and retreating to the very wall. "No, no! it is an infernal apparition! It is not he! Help, help!" screamed she, turning towards the wall, as if she would tear an opening with her hands.

"Who are you, then?" cried all the witnesses of this scene.

"Ask that woman," said the man in the red cloak, "for you may plainly see she knows me!"

"The executioner of Lille, the executioner of Lille!" cried Milady, a prey to insensate terror, and clinging with her hands to the wall to avoid falling.

Every one drew back, and the man in the red cloak remained standing alone in the middle of the room.

"Oh, grace, grace, pardon!" cried the wretch, falling on her knees.

The unknown waited for silence, and then resumed, "I told you well that she would know me. Yes, I am the executioner of Lille, and this is my history."

All eyes were fixed upon this man, whose words were listened to with anxious attention.

"That woman was once a young girl, as beautiful as she is today. She was a nun in the convent of the Benedictines of Templemar. A young priest, with a simple and trustful heart, performed the duties of the church of that convent. She undertook his seduction, and succeeded; she would have seduced a saint.

"Their vows were sacred and irrevocable. Their connection could not last long without ruining both. She prevailed upon him to leave the country, but to leave the country, to fly together, to reach another part of France, where they might live at ease because unknown, money was necessary. Neither had any. The priest stole the sacred vases, and sold them, but as they were preparing to escape together, they were both arrested.

"Eight days later she had seduced the son of the jailer, and escaped. The young priest was condemned to ten years of imprisonment, and to be branded. I was executioner of the city of Lille, as this woman has said. I was obliged to brand the guilty one; and he, gentlemen, was my brother!

"I then swore that this woman who had ruined him, who was more than his accomplice, since she had urged him to the crime, should at least share his punishment. I suspected where she was concealed. I followed her, I caught her, I bound her; and I imprinted the same disgraceful mark upon her that I had imprinted upon my poor brother.

"The day after my return to Lille, my brother in his turn succeeded in making his escape; I was accused of complicity, and was condemned to remain in his place till he should be again a prisoner. My poor brother was ignorant of this sentence. He rejoined this woman; they fled together into Berry, and there he obtained a little curacy. This woman passed for his sister.

"The Lord of the estate on which the chapel of the curacy was situated saw this pretend sister, and became enamoured of her–amorous to such a degree that he proposed to marry her. Then she quitted him she had ruined for him she was destined to ruin, and became the Comtesse de la Fere–"

All eyes were turned towards Athos, whose real name that was, and who made a sign with his head that all was true which the executioner had said.

"Then," resumed he, "mad, desperate, determined to get rid of an existence from which she had stolen everything, honour and happiness, my poor brother returned to Lille, and learning the sentence which had condemned me in his place, surrendered himself, and hanged himself that same night from the iron bar of the loophole of his prison.

"To do justice to them who had condemned me, they kept their word. As soon as the identity of my brother was proved, I was set at liberty.

"That is the crime of which I accuse her; that is the cause for which she was branded."

"Monsieur d'Artagnan," said Athos, "what is the penalty you demand against this woman?"

"The punishment of death," replied d'Artagnan.

"My Lord de Winter," continued Athos, "what is the penalty you demand against this woman?"

"The punishment of death," replied Lord de Winter.

"Messieurs Porthos and Aramis," repeated Athos, "you who are her judges, what is the sentence you pronounce upon this woman?"

"The punishment of death," replied the Musketeers, in a hollow voice.

Milady uttered a frightful shriek, and dragged herself along several paces upon her knees toward her judges.

Athos stretched out his hand toward her.

"Charlotte Backson, Comtesse de la Fere, Milady de Winter," said he, "your crimes have wearied men on earth and God in heaven. If you know a prayer, say it–for you are condemned, and you shall die."

At these words, which left no hope, Milady raised herself in all her pride, and wished to speak, but her strength failed her. She felt that a powerful and implacable hand seized her by the hair, and dragged her away as irrevocably as fatality drags humanity. She did not, therefore, even attempt the least resistance, and went out of the cottage.

Lord de Winter, d'Artagnan, Athos, Porthos, and Aramis, went out close behind her. The lackeys followed their masters, and the chamber was left solitary, with its broken window, its open door, and its smoky lamp burning sadly on the table.

Chapter 66

Execution

It was near midnight; the moon, lessened by its decline, and reddened by the last traces of the storm, arose behind the little town of Armentières, which showed against its pale light the dark outline of its houses, and the skeleton of its high belfry. In front of them the Lys rolled its waters like a river of molten tin; while on the other side was a black mass of trees, profiled on a stormy sky, invaded by large coppery clouds which created a sort of twilight amid the night. On the left was an old abandoned mill, with its motionless wings, from the ruins of which an owl threw out its shrill, periodical, and monotonous cry. On the right and on the left of the road, which the dismal procession pursued, appeared a few low, stunted trees, which looked like deformed dwarfs crouching down to watch men travelling at this sinister hour.

From time to time a broad sheet of lightning opened the horizon in its whole width, darted like a serpent over the black mass of trees, and like a terrible scimitar divided the heavens and the waters into two parts. Not a breath of wind now disturbed the heavy atmosphere. A deathlike silence oppressed all nature. The soil was humid and glittering with the rain which had recently fallen, and the refreshed herbs sent forth their perfume with additional energy.

Two lackeys dragged Milady, whom each held by one arm. The executioner walked behind them, and Lord de Winter, d'Artagnan, Porthos, and Aramis walked behind the executioner. Planchet and Bazin came last.

The two lackeys conducted Milady to the bank of the river. Her mouth was mute, but her eyes spoke with their inexpressible eloquence, supplicating by turns each of those on whom she looked.

Being a few paces in advance she whispered to the lackeys, "A thousand pistoles to each of you, if you will assist my escape, but if you deliver me up to your masters, I have near at hand avengers who will make you pay dearly for my death."

Grimaud hesitated. Mousqueton trembled in all his members.

Athos, who heard Milady's voice, came sharply up. Lord de Winter did the same.

"Change these lackeys," said he, "she has spoken to them. They are no longer sure."

Planchet and Bazin were called, and took the places of Grimaud and Mousqueton.

On the bank of the river the executioner approached Milady, and bound her hands and feet.

Then she broke the silence to cry out, "You are cowards, miserable assassins–ten men combined to murder one woman. Beware! If I am not saved I shall be avenged."

"You are not a woman," said Athos, coldly and sternly. "You do not belong to the human species; you are a demon escaped from hell, whither we send you back again."

"Ah, you virtuous men!" said Milady, "please to remember that he who shall touch a hair of my head is himself an assassin."

"The executioner may kill, without being on that account an assassin," said the man in the red cloak, rapping upon his immense sword. "This is the last judge; that is all. NACHRICHTER, as say our neighbours, the Germans."

And as he bound her while saying these words, Milady uttered two or three savage cries, which produced a strange and melancholy effect in flying away into the night, and losing themselves in the depths of the woods.

"If I am guilty, if I have committed the crimes you accuse me of," shrieked Milady, "take me before a tribunal. You are not judges! You cannot condemn me!"

"I offered you Tyburn," said Lord de Winter. "Why did you not accept it?"

"Because I am not willing to die!" cried Milady, struggling. "Because I am too young to die!"

"The woman you poisoned at Bethune was still younger than you, Madame, and yet she is dead," said d'Artagnan.

"I will enter a cloister; I will become a nun," said Milady.

"You were in a cloister," said the executioner, "and you left it to ruin my brother."

Milady uttered a cry of terror and sank upon her knees. The executioner took her up in his arms and was carrying her toward the boat.

"Oh, my God!" cried she, "my God! Are you going to drown me?"

These cries had something so heartrending in them that M. d'Artagnan, who had been at first the most eager in pursuit of Milady, sat down on the stump of a tree and hung his head, covering his ears with the palms of his hands; and yet, notwithstanding, he could still hear her cry and threaten.

D'Artagnan was the youngest of all these men. His heart failed him.

"Oh, I cannot behold this frightful spectacle!" said he. "I cannot consent that this woman should die thus!"

Milady heard these few words and caught at a shadow of hope.

"D'Artagnan, d'Artagnan!" cried she, "remember that I loved you!"

The young man rose and took a step toward her.

But Athos rose likewise, drew his sword, and placed himself in the way.

"If you take one step farther, d'Artagnan," said he, "we shall cross swords together."

D'Artagnan sank on his knees and prayed.

"Come," continued Athos, "executioner, do your duty."

"Willingly, Monseigneur," said the executioner, "for as I am a good Catholic, I firmly believe I am acting justly in performing my functions on this woman."

"That's well."

Athos made a step toward Milady.

"I pardon you," said he, "the ill you have done me. I pardon you for my blasted future, my lost honour, my defiled love, and my salvation forever compromised by the despair into which you have cast me. Die in peace!"

Lord de Winter advanced in his turn.

"I pardon you," said he, "for the poisoning of my brother, and the assassination of his Grace, Lord Buckingham. I pardon you for the death of poor Felton; I pardon you for the attempts upon my own person. Die in peace!"

"And I," said M. d'Artagnan. "Pardon me, Madame, for having by a trick unworthy of a gentleman provoked your anger; and I, in exchange, pardon you the murder of my poor love and your cruel vengeance against me. I pardon you, and I weep for you. Die in peace!"

"I am lost!" murmured Milady in English. "I must die!"

Then she arose of herself, and cast around her one of those piercing looks which seemed to dart from an eye of flame.

She saw nothing; she listened, and she heard nothing.

"Where am I to die?" said she.

"On the other bank," replied the executioner.

Then he placed her in the boat, and as he was going to set foot in it himself, Athos handed him a sum of silver.

"Here," said he, "is the price of the execution, that it may be plain we act as judges."

"That is correct," said the executioner, "and now in her turn, let this woman see that I am not fulfilling my trade, but my debt."

And he threw the money into the river.

The boat moved off toward the left-hand shore of the Lys, bearing the guilty woman and the executioner; all the others remained on the right-hand bank, where they fell on their knees.

The boat glided along the ferry rope under the shadow of a pale cloud which hung over the water at that moment.

The troop of friends saw it gain the opposite bank; the figures were defined like black shadows on the red-tinted horizon.

Milady, during the passage had contrived to untie the cord which fastened her feet. On coming near the bank, she jumped lightly on shore and took to flight. But the soil was moist; on reaching the top of the bank, she slipped and fell upon her knees.

She was struck, no doubt, with a superstitious idea; she conceived that heaven denied its aid, and she remained in the attitude in which she had fallen, her head drooping and her hands clasped.

Then they saw from the other bank the executioner raise both his arms slowly; a moonbeam fell upon the blade of the large sword. The two arms fell with a sudden force; they heard the hissing of the scimitar and the cry of the victim, then a truncated mass sank beneath the blow.

The executioner then took off his red cloak, spread it upon the ground, laid the body in it, threw in the head, tied all up by the four corners, lifted it on his back, and entered the boat again.

In the middle of the stream he stopped the boat, and suspending his burden over the water cried in a loud voice, "Let the justice of God be done!" and he let the corpse drop into the depths of the waters, which closed over it.

Three days afterward the four Musketeers were in Paris; they had not exceeded their leave of absence, and that same evening they went to pay their customary visit to M. de Tréville.

"Well, gentlemen," said the brave captain, "I hope you have been well amused during your excursion."

"Prodigiously," replied Athos in the name of himself and his comrades.

Chapter 67

Conclusion

On the sixth of the following month the king, in compliance with the promise he had made the cardinal to return to La Rochelle, left his capital still in amazement at the news which began to spread itself of Buckingham's assassination.

Although warned that the man she had loved so much was in great danger, the queen, when his death was announced to her, would not believe the fact, and even imprudently exclaimed, "it is false; he has just written to me!"

But the next day she was obliged to believe this fatal intelligence; Laporte, detained in England, as everyone else had been, by the orders of Charles I, arrived, and was the bearer of the duke's dying gift to the queen.

The joy of the king was lively. He did not even give himself the trouble to dissemble, and displayed it with affectation before the queen. Louis XIII, like every weak mind, was wanting in generosity.

But the king soon again became dull and indisposed; his brow was not one of those that long remain clear. He felt that in returning to camp he should re-enter slavery; nevertheless, he did return.

The cardinal was for him the fascinating serpent, and himself the bird which flies from branch to branch without power to escape.

The return to La Rochelle, therefore, was profoundly dull. Our four friends, in particular, astonished their comrades; they traveled together, side by side, with sad eyes and heads lowered. Athos alone from time to time raised his expansive brow; a flash kindled in his eyes, and a bitter smile passed over his lips, then, like his comrades, he sank again into reverie.

As soon as the escort arrived in a city, when they had conducted the king to his quarters the four friends either retired to their own or to some secluded cabaret, where they neither drank nor played; they only conversed in a low voice, looking around attentively to see that no one overheard them.

One day, when the king had halted to fly the magpie, and the four friends, according to their custom, instead of following the sport had stopped at a cabaret on the high road, a man coming from la Rochelle on horseback pulled up at the door to drink a glass of wine, and darted a searching glance into the room where the four Musketeers were sitting.

"Holloa, Monsieur d'Artagnan!" said he, "is not that you whom I see yonder?"

D'Artagnan raised his head and uttered a cry of joy. It was the man he called his phantom; it was his stranger of Meung, of the Rue des Fossoyeurs and of Arras.

D'Artagnan drew his sword, and sprang toward the door.

But this time, instead of avoiding him the stranger jumped from his horse, and advanced to meet d'Artagnan.

"Ah, Monsieur!" said the young man, "I meet you, then, at last! This time you shall not escape me!"

"Neither is it my intention, Monsieur, for this time I was seeking you; in the name of the king, I arrest you."

"How! What do you say?" cried d'Artagnan.

"I say that you must surrender your sword to me, Monsieur, and that without resistance. This concerns your head, I warn you."

"Who are you, then?" demanded d'Artagnan, lowering the point of his sword, but without yet surrendering it.

"I am the Chevalier de Rochefort," answered the other, "the equerry of Monsieur le Cardinal Richelieu, and I have orders to conduct you to his Eminence."

"We are returning to his Eminence, Monsieur the Chevalier," said Athos, advancing, "and you will please to accept the word of Monsieur d'Artagnan that he will go straight to La Rochelle."

"I must place him in the hands of guards who will take him into camp."

"We will be his guards, Monsieur, upon our word as gentlemen, but likewise, upon our word as gentlemen," added Athos, knitting his brow, "Monsieur d'Artagnan shall not leave us."

The Chevalier de Rochefort cast a glance backward, and saw that Porthos and Aramis had placed themselves between him and the gate; he understood that he was completely at the mercy of these four men.

"Gentlemen," said he, "if Monsieur d'Artagnan will surrender his sword to me and join his word to yours, I shall be satisfied with your promise to convey Monsieur d'Artagnan to the quarters of Monseigneur the Cardinal."

"You have my word, Monsieur, and here is my sword."

"This suits me the better," said Rochefort, "as I wish to continue my journey."

"If it is for the purpose of rejoining Milady," said Athos, coolly, "it is useless; you will not find her."

"What has become of her, then?" asked Rochefort, eagerly.

"Return to camp and you shall know."

Rochefort remained for a moment in thought; then, as they were only a day's journey from Surgères, whither the cardinal was to come to meet the king, he resolved to follow the advice of Athos and go with them. Besides, this return offered him the advantage of watching his prisoner.

They resumed their route.

On the morrow, at three o'clock in the afternoon, they arrived at Surgères. The cardinal there awaited Louis XIII. The minister and the king exchanged numerous caresses, felicitating each other upon the fortunate chance which had freed France from the inveterate enemy who set all Europe against her. After which, the cardinal, who had been informed that d'Artagnan was arrested and who was anxious to see him, took leave of the king, inviting him to come the next day to view the work already done upon the dyke.

On returning in the evening to his quarters at the bridge of La Pierre, the cardinal found, standing before the house he occupied, d'Artagnan, without his sword, and the three Musketeers armed.

This time, as he was well attended, he looked at them sternly, and made a sign with his eye and hand for d'Artagnan to follow him.

D'Artagnan obeyed.

"We shall wait for you, d'Artagnan," said Athos, loud enough for the cardinal to hear him.

His Eminence bent his brow, stopped for an instant, and then kept on his way without uttering a single word.

D'Artagnan entered after the cardinal, and behind d'Artagnan the door was guarded.

His Eminence entered the chamber which served him as a study, and made a sign to Rochefort to bring in the young Musketeer.

Rochefort obeyed and retired.

D'Artagnan remained alone in front of the cardinal; this was his second interview with Richelieu, and he afterward confessed that he felt well assured it would be his last.

Richelieu remained standing, leaning against the mantelpiece; a table was between him and d'Artagnan.

"Monsieur," said the cardinal, "you have been arrested by my orders."

"So they tell me, Monseigneur."

"Do you know why?"

"No, Monseigneur, for the only thing for which I could be arrested is still unknown to your Eminence."

Richelieu looked steadfastly at the young man.

"Holloa!" said he, "what does that mean?"

"If Monseigneur will have the goodness to tell me, in the first place, what crimes are imputed to me, I will then tell him the deeds I have really done."

"Crimes are imputed to you which had brought down far loftier heads than yours, Monsieur," said the cardinal.

"What, Monseigneur?" said d'Artagnan, with a calmness which astonished the cardinal himself.

"You are charged with having corresponded with the enemies of the kingdom; you are charged with having surprised state secrets; you are charged with having tried to thwart the plans of your general."

"And who charges me with this, Monseigneur?" said d'Artagnan, who had no doubt the accusation came from Milady, "a woman branded by the justice of the country; a woman who has espoused one man in France and another in England; a woman who poisoned her second husband and who attempted both to poison and assassinate me!"

"What do you say, Monsieur?" cried the cardinal, astonished, "and of what woman are you speaking thus?"

"Of Milady de Winter," replied d'Artagnan, "yes, of Milady de Winter, of whose crimes your Eminence is doubtless ignorant, since you have honoured her with your confidence."

"Monsieur," said the cardinal, "if Milady de Winter has committed the crimes you lay to her charge, she shall be punished."

"She has been punished, Monseigneur."

"And who has punished her?"

"We."

"She is in prison?"

"She is dead."

"Dead!" repeated the cardinal, who could not believe what he heard, "dead! Did you not say she was dead?"

"Three times she attempted to kill me, and I pardoned her, but she murdered the woman I loved. Then my friends and I took her, tried her, and condemned her."

D'Artagnan then related the poisoning of Mme. Bonacieux in the convent of the Carmelites at Bethune, the trial in the isolated house, and the execution on the banks of the Lys.

A shudder crept through the body of the cardinal, who did not shudder readily.

But all at once, as if undergoing the influence of an unspoken thought, the countenance of the cardinal, till then gloomy, cleared up by degrees, and recovered perfect serenity.

"So," said the cardinal, in a tone that contrasted strongly with the severity of his words, "you have constituted yourselves judges, without remembering that they who punish without license to punish are assassins?"

"Monseigneur, I swear to you that I never for an instant had the intention of defending my head against you. I willingly submit to any punishment your Eminence may please to inflict upon me. I do not hold life dear enough to be afraid of death."

"Yes, I know you are a man of a stout heart, Monsieur," said the cardinal, with a voice almost affectionate, "I can therefore tell you beforehand you shall be tried, and even condemned."

"Another might reply to your Eminence that he had his pardon in his pocket. I content myself with saying: Command, Monseigneur; I am ready."

"Your pardon?" said Richelieu, surprised.

"Yes, Monseigneur," said d'Artagnan.

"And signed by whom–by the king?" And the cardinal pronounced these words with a singular expression of contempt.

"No, by your Eminence."

"By me? You are insane, Monsieur."

"Monseigneur will doubtless recognise his own handwriting."

And d'Artagnan presented to the cardinal the precious piece of paper which Athos had forced from Milady, and which he had given to d'Artagnan to serve him as a safeguard.

His Eminence took the paper, and read in a slow voice, dwelling upon every syllable:

Dec. 3, 1627

It is by my order and for the good of the state that the bearer of this has done what he has done.

RICHELIEU

The cardinal, after having read these two lines, sank into a profound reverie, but he did not return the paper to d'Artagnan.

"He is meditating by what sort of punishment he shall cause me to die," said the Gascon to himself. "Well, my faith! He shall see how a gentleman can die."

The young Musketeer was in excellent disposition to die heroically.

Richelieu still continued thinking, rolling and unrolling the paper in his hands.

At length he raised his head, fixed his eagle look upon that loyal, open, and intelligent countenance, read upon that face, furrowed with tears, all the sufferings its possessor had endured in the course of a month, and reflected for the third or fourth time how much there was in that youth of twenty-one years before him, and what resources his activity, his courage, and his shrewdness might offer to a good master. On the other side, the crimes, the power, and the infernal genius of Milady had more than once terrified him. He felt something like a secret joy at being forever relieved of this dangerous accomplice.

Richelieu slowly tore the paper which d'Artagnan had generously relinquished.

"I am lost!" said d'Artagnan to himself. And he bowed profoundly before the cardinal, like a man who says, "Lord, Thy will be done!"

The cardinal approached the table, and without sitting down, wrote a few lines upon a parchment of which two-thirds were already filled, and affixed his seal.

"That is my condemnation," thought d'Artagnan, "he will spare me the ENNUI of the Bastille, or the tediousness of a trial. That's very kind of him."

"Here, Monsieur," said the cardinal to the young man. "I have taken from you one CARTE BLANCHE to give you another. The name is wanting in this commission; you can write it yourself."

D'Artagnan took the paper hesitatingly and cast his eyes over it; it was a lieutenant's commission in the Musketeers.

D'Artagnan fell at the feet of the cardinal.

"Monseigneur," said he, "my life is yours; henceforth dispose of it. But this favour which you bestow upon me I do not merit. I have three friends who are more meritorious and more worthy–"

"You are a brave youth, d'Artagnan," interrupted the cardinal, tapping him familiarly on the shoulder, charmed at having vanquished this rebellious nature. "Do with this commission what you will; only remember, though the name be blank, it is to you I give it."

"I shall never forget it," replied d'Artagnan. "Your Eminence may be certain of that."

The cardinal turned and said in a loud voice, "Rochefort!" The chevalier, who no doubt was near the door, entered immediately.

"Rochefort," said the cardinal, "you see Monsieur d'Artagnan. I receive him among the number of my friends. Greet each other, then; and be wise if you wish to preserve your heads."

Rochefort and d'Artagnan coolly greeted each other with their lips, but the cardinal was there, observing them with his vigilant eye.

They left the chamber at the same time.

"We shall meet again, shall we not, Monsieur?"

"When you please," said d'Artagnan.

"An opportunity will come," replied Rochefort.

"Hey?" said the cardinal, opening the door.

The two men smiled at each other, shook hands, and saluted his Eminence.

"We were beginning to grow impatient," said Athos.

"Here I am, my friends," replied d'Artagnan, "not only free, but in favour."

"Tell us about it."

"This evening, but for the moment, let us separate."

Accordingly, that same evening d'Artagnan repaired to the quarters of Athos, whom he found in a fair way to empty a bottle of Spanish wine–an occupation which he religiously accomplished every night.

D'Artagnan related what had taken place between the cardinal and himself, and drawing the commission from his pocket, said, "Here, my dear Athos, this naturally belongs to you."

Athos smiled with one of his sweet and expressive smiles.

"Friend," said he, "for Athos this is too much; for the Comte de la Fère it is too little. Keep the commission; it is yours. Alas! you have purchased it dearly enough."

D'Artagnan left Athos's chamber and went to that of Porthos. He found him clothed in a magnificent dress covered with splendid embroidery, admiring himself before a glass.

"Ah, ah! Is that you, dear friend?" exclaimed Porthos. "How do you think these garments fit me?"

"Wonderfully," said d'Artagnan, "but I come to offer you a dress which will become you still better."

"What?" asked Porthos.

"That of a lieutenant of Musketeers."

D'Artagnan related to Porthos the substance of his interview with the cardinal, and said, taking the commission from his pocket, "Here, my friend, write your name upon it and become my chief."

Porthos cast his eyes over the commission and returned it to d'Artagnan, to the great astonishment of the young man.

"Yes," said he, "yes, that would flatter me very much, but I should not have time enough to enjoy the distinction. During our expedition to Bethune the husband of my duchess died; so, my dear, the coffer of the defunct holding out its arms to me, I shall marry the widow. Look here! I was trying on my wedding suit. Keep the lieutenancy, my dear, keep it."

The young man then entered the apartment of Aramis. He found him kneeling before a PRIEDIEU with his head leaning on an open prayer book.

He described to him his interview with the cardinal, and said, for the third time drawing his commission from his pocket, "You, our friend, our intelligence, our invisible protector, accept this commission. You have merited it more than any of us by your wisdom and your counsels, always followed by such happy results."

"Alas, dear friend!" said Aramis, "our late adventures have disgusted me with military life. This time my determination is irrevocably taken. After the siege I shall enter the house of the Lazarists. Keep the commission, d'Artagnan; the profession of arms suits you. You will be a brave and adventurous captain."

D'Artagnan, his eye moist with gratitude though beaming with joy, went back to Athos, whom he found still at table contemplating the charms of his last glass of Malaga by the light of his lamp.

"Well," said he, "they likewise have refused me."

"That, dear friend, is because nobody is more worthy than yourself."

He took a quill, wrote the name of d'Artagnan in the commission, and returned it to him.

"I shall then have no more friends," said the young man. "Alas! Nothing but bitter recollections."

And he let his head sink upon his hands, while two large tears rolled down his cheeks.

"You are young," replied Athos, "and your bitter recollections have time to change themselves into sweet remembrances."

Epilogue

La Rochelle, deprived of the assistance of the English fleet and of the diversion promised by Buckingham, surrendered after a siege of a year. On the twenty-eighth of October, 1628, the capitulation was signed.

The king made his entrance into Paris on the twenty-third of December of the same year. He was received in triumph, as if he came from conquering an enemy and not Frenchmen. He entered by the Faubourg St. Jacques, under verdant arches.

D'Artagnan took possession of his command. Porthos left the service, and in the course of the following year married Mme. Coquenard; the coffer so much coveted contained eight hundred thousand livres.

Mousqueton had a magnificent livery, and enjoyed the satisfaction of which he had been ambitious all his life–that of standing behind a gilded carriage.

Aramis, after a journey into Lorraine, disappeared all at once, and ceased to write to his friends; they learned at a later period through Mme. de Chevreuse, who told it to two or three of her intimates, that, yielding to his vocation, he had retired into a convent–only into which, nobody knew.

Bazin became a lay brother.

Athos remained a Musketeer under the command of d'Artagnan till the year 1633, at which period, after a journey he made to Touraine, he also quit the service, under the pretext of having inherited a small property in Roussillon.

Grimaud followed Athos.

D'Artagnan fought three times with Rochefort, and wounded him three times.

"I shall probably kill you the fourth," said he to him, holding out his hand to assist him to rise.

"It is much better both for you and for me to stop where we are," answered the wounded man. "CORBLEU–I am more your friend than you think–for after our very first encounter, I could by saying a word to the cardinal have had your throat cut!"

They this time embraced heartily, and without retaining any malice.

Planchet obtained from Rochefort the rank of sergeant in the Piedmont regiment.

M Bonacieux lived on very quietly, wholly ignorant of what had become of his wife, and caring very little about it. One day he had the imprudence to recall himself to the memory of the cardinal. The cardinal had him informed that he would provide for him so that he should never want for anything in future. In fact, M. Bonacieux, having left his house at seven o'clock in the evening to go to the Louvre, never appeared again in the Rue des Fossoyeurs; the opinion of those who seemed to be best informed was that he was fed and lodged in some royal castle, at the expense of his generous Eminence.